Praise for boo

"I loved it :) Historically correct ᵕ
and they're small town as the civ
outstanding debut! You must
disappointed."

"I totally enjoyed the writing of this first time author. It was clear, concise and factually accurate to the era. I would not hesitate to read another of her works!!"

"I love historical fiction and I felt that this book was well written and factual. I can't wait for the sequels to come out. Nice job for a first time author."

"I had trouble putting the book down. Couldn't wait to find out what was going to happen next. I look forward to reading more about the other characters."

"Well written and factual. Couldn't put it down. Looking forward to the next book."

"This is an awesome book to read. It got me so involved it was hard to put down. I can't wait to read the next one. I highly recommend this book."

"I just finished the book and thoroughly enjoyed it. You included so many elements in your book that are often overlooked with the "strategy" of war. Through the relationship of 4 amazing women (and one antagonist), you were able to discuss the personal relationships of friends, husbands, and families. You presented the struggles of these women and the prejudice that existed besides that of color. And you added the struggle of faith as well."

"Read your book. It was AWESOME! And I really mean it. Interesting characters, great plot, even had tears in my eyes a couple of times!"

Other Books by Marie LaPres

The Turner Daughters Series
Though War Shall Rise Against Me: A Gettysburg Story
Be Strong and Steadfast: A Fredericksburg Story

Sammy's Struggle
Beyond The Fort (Coming in Fall 2018)

Plans for a Future of Hope: A Vicksburg Story

The Turner Daughters: Book 3

Marie LaPres

This novel is dedicated to all historic reenactors, for keeping history alive, especially the Michigan Cavalry Brigade.

Reenactors at the Gettysburg Reenactment, 2018
155th Anniversary of the Battle

To the reader…

This is a fictional novel based in Vicksburg, Mississippi during the American Civil War. Throughout the novel, the main characters have flashbacks to their past experiences. Flashback sections are written in italics. This novel also contains letters written by the characters to each other. Letters are written in bolded italics.

Since this is a historic fiction novel, some characters are individuals that I have created. Others are based on actual historic figures that lived in Vicksburg or were at Vicksburg at some point during the war. Be sure to read my Author's Note at the end of the book to learn more about these individuals. I have also included images in the back of the book of some of the individuals and places that are noted in this book and existed in real life.

Vicksburg-The town and surrounding areas

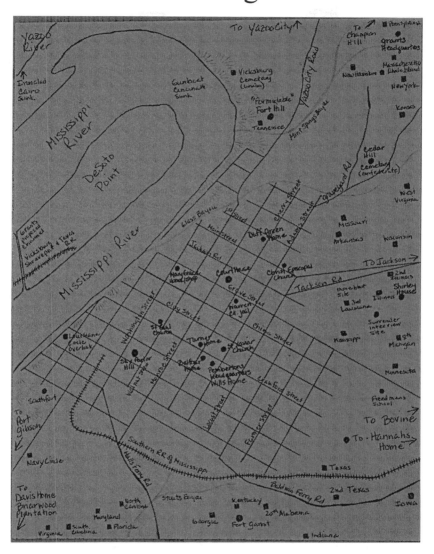

Family Trees

Turner Family

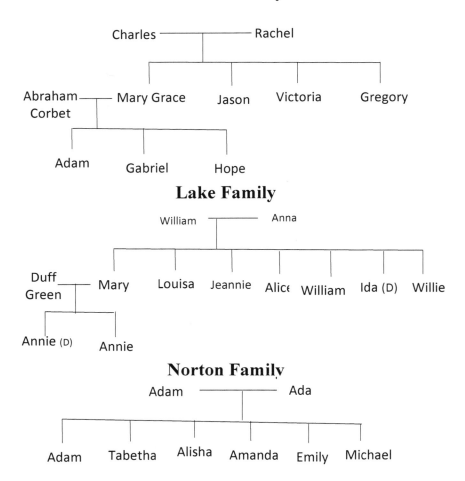

Charles — Rachel

Abraham Corbet — Mary Grace   Jason   Victoria   Gregory

Adam   Gabriel   Hope

Lake Family

William — Anna

Duff Green — Mary   Louisa   Jeannie   Alice   William   Ida (D)   Willie

Annie (D)   Annie

Norton Family

Adam — Ada

Adam   Tabetha   Alisha   Amanda   Emily   Michael

Wheeler Family

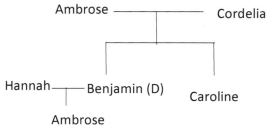

Ambrose — Cordelia

Hannah — Benjamin (D)   Caroline

Ambrose

For I know the plans I have for you," declares the Lord, "plans to prosper you and not to harm you, plans to give you hope and a future.

-Jeremiah 29:11

Part 1:
1861

Wednesday, January 9, 1861
Vicksburg, Mississippi

Victoria Turner made her way up the steep hill towards the Warren County Courthouse. She was used to walking up and down the hills of the town she had lived in all twenty-four years of her life, yet this path never failed to make her breathe just a little harder. The courthouse sat atop one of the highest bluffs in the city of Vicksburg. Victoria pushed a lock of blonde hair that had fallen from her chignon back into her low crown straw hat and took a brief rest before she began walking up the steps to the entrance of the building.

"Good morning, Miss Turner." Duff Green swept his chocolate colored Cahill hat off his head and gave a short bow. Duff was a local cotton broker and businessman, as well as the husband of Victoria's dearest friend, Mary.

"Good morning, Mr. Green. I have plans to meet with your lovely wife later today for dinner. Did she share that information with you?"

"She did indeed." Duff settled his hat back on his head. "She is very excited about it. What brings you to the courthouse today?" Duff was a handsome man, with brown hair and eyes, a kind smile and pleasant manner. Victoria knew he was a wonderful husband to Mary and a doting father to their one-year-old daughter, Annie.

"I am meeting Mr. Thompson for a picnic lunch," she replied. Mr. Jeremy Thompson, a young lawyer-turned-politician, was courting Victoria. His office was in the courthouse.

"I see." Duff frowned. "He may be a bit preoccupied today, especially with the latest news."

"What latest news?" Victoria asked. She was usually very knowledgeable about current affairs.

"It's so new that I wouldn't know it myself but for the fact that I just came from the courthouse. It is official." He shook his head in disappointment. "In spite of how Vicksburg representatives voted, Mississippi is no longer a part of the Union."

"We seceded! My goodness." Victoria gasped and her stomach fell. Three weeks ago, on December 20, South Carolina withdrew from the

United States, and many Southern states were expected to follow. "Have any other states officially done so?"

"Not yet but it is only a matter of time." Duff sighed heavily. "Absolute madness, I tell you. They'll be dragging all of us into a war, mark my words."

"Perhaps the new president will just leave us alone," Victoria said, not really believing the statement.

"Miss Turner, I know you to be a smart woman, smarter than to think that."

"I can still hope and pray," she replied.

"A good idea for us all." Duff gave her a tight smile. "Well, I shall let you go and see your young man. He should know more about our current situation. I heard he may have a new position in this government."

"New job? He didn't tell me that." Victoria frowned.

"I understand it became official after our secession. I wouldn't worry." Duff assured her.

"Thank you, Mr. Green." She smiled gratefully. He tipped his hat and continued down the courthouse steps as Victoria made her way to Jeremy's office.

"Good day, Mr. Thompson." She smiled.

"Miss Turner," Jeremy smiled back and stood, then took her hand in his and gave it a kiss. His brown eyes sparkled as he gave his impeccably trimmed hair a pat. As with everything about him, his hair was at the height of perfection, parted on the side, and combed back into smooth style. He had also started to grow the neat sideburns and chin whiskers that many men were sporting. "I thought we could walk over to Sky Parlor Hill for our picnic lunch. We have much to discuss."

"That sounds delightful, Mr. Thompson." Victoria took his offered arm as he picked up the basket he had brought for the picnic. The couple strolled the six blocks to the local park.

Sky Parlor Hill was one of Victoria's favorite places in town. It wasn't very big, and was located on a grassy hilltop near the middle of town. Victoria and Jeremy reached the top by walking up a wooden stairway that meandered up from street level. The stairway allowed Victoria to climb in a ladylike fashion, which she appreciated, as she had a tendency to be clumsy.

The hilltop itself was a small plot of grass that was kept neat and mowed. Wrought-iron chairs and tables were available for sitting, eating and visiting. On many evenings the tables would be swathed in white cloth and wine glasses would be brimming with drink. Chinese lanterns would surround the visitors. She had been to many an event here that went on long past midnight. She remembered one party in particular that lasted so late the lanterns had guttered and the lights of the town below were out.

The sky became a beautiful drapery of starlight. She would spend every evening here if she could.

To the north and east of Sky Parlor was a landscape of wilderness: thickly forested hills, valleys, swamps and ravines. To the south and southeast, the land was flatter with low hills, wide meadows and cotton plantations. To the west, across the Mississippi, one could see the swampland of Louisiana. From Sky Parlor you could see the mighty Mississippi River flowing toward town.

Victoria smiled as she looked from the view of the river to the view of the man beside her. She found it hard to believe that this handsome, successful, intelligent politician was courting her.

"I am sure you have heard the fantastic news that Mississippi has seceded." Jeremy was clearly excited about what had happened and what would be happening in the near future.

"Yes, I ran into Mr. Duff Green on the courthouse steps. He told me that you would know many more details."

"Indeed I do." Jeremy escorted her to one of the tables provided for picnickers and drew out some ham sandwiches for them to eat. "Within months, maybe even weeks, most, if not all of the states south of the Mason-Dixon line will secede. We will all join together, form an army and elect leaders. I plan on being in the thick of it."

"You plan on working for the Southern government?"

"I don't just plan on it. I already am. Mr. Henry Cousins Chambers has already approached me about working for him."

"Mr. Chambers? He isn't a representative yet, is he?" Victoria took a bite of her sandwich.

"No, but he will be and I will be very well-placed. I will have the opportunity to quickly move my way up in the government." He gave her a smile and slid his hand over the table to cover hers. "Along with whomever I need by my side."

Victoria's heart fluttered. Was he insinuating that he needed her? "You have surely earned this opportunity. You certainly work hard. When you worked for my father, he had nothing but good things to say about your legal mind and ambition."

"I appreciate the compliment." Jeremy pulled his hand back. Victoria's father, Charles, was also a lawyer, and Jeremy had worked for him as a junior partner before the young man had taken a job at the courthouse.

"So I assume you'll be moving," Victoria stated.

"Yes, to Montgomery, Alabama, most likely. Alabama will secede within days. I will be leaving in the next few weeks."

"So soon?" Victoria asked.

"This new government will wait for no one," Jeremy said. "If I want to make the best impression, I must get there as soon as possible. Make all of the connections before others do."

"Mr. Thompson, you are most charming, I am sure you will do just fine."

"You are always so complementary, Miss Turner." Jeremy stood and held his hand out, inviting Victoria to join him. "Would you care for a short stroll around the hilltop?"

"You know that I adore it up here," Victoria replied.

"Before I return to my work, I did want to speak with you of something specific. Something permanent. The future." He smiled charmingly.

"I see. Isn't that something you should speak with my father about first?"

"Perhaps, and I will, but I wanted to talk to you first to see if you would welcome an offer for a future with me."

Victoria held her breath. This was it. Her proposal. She was excited, yet also conflicted. She would hate leaving her family to live in Montgomery, where she knew no one, and she wasn't even sure that she was in love with Mr. Thompson. However, she also wasn't sure if she would ever get another offer of marriage from such a fine catch. She certainly liked Jeremy, and enjoyed spending time with him. "Mr. Thompson, of course I would consider such a thing." Victoria would speak with Mary Green and her own mother about this. They were always ready to give their opinion.

Mr. Thompson pulled Victoria to a stop. "Splendid. My plan is to speak with your father, then go to Alabama and get established. After a time, I can come back here and we can be married."

"Father will give his approval." She smiled with certainty. Perhaps by then, she would know her own mind for sure. Oh, why was she so indecisive?

"Of course he will." He smiled back, then glanced around at the other visitors in the park. He smoothly moved to hide them both behind a tree, then bent to kiss her.

Her heart fluttered. Her first real kiss from Mr. Thompson. The second time a man had ever kissed her. She smiled up at him, mind made up. He would be her future husband.

"When do you plan on speaking with Father?" She asked, anxious.

"As soon as possible." He replied.

That evening, Victoria sat in the parlor and looked at the mail she had picked up during her earlier errands.

"Anything good in the post today?"

Victoria looked up and smiled at her younger brother, Gregory, as he entered the room. "Nothing for you. Uncle Matthew wrote to Father and there were some other missives for him, but not much else."

"Not much else," he said. "Which means there was something else."

"Perhaps, but for me, not you." She fingered the letter in question.

He smiled and sat down. "I heard you had an interesting conversation with Mr. Jeremy Thompson atop Sky Parlor Hill."

"That I did," She replied. "Did you hear that from Father? Jeremy was going to speak with him as soon as possible."

"No, Jason told me." Gregory replied. Jason was Gregory and Victoria's older brother. "He said you two were seen together at the Hill, quite close, so he went and spoke directly with Mr. Thompson."

Victoria's head shot up. "He didn't!" She loved her oldest brother dearly, but he could be ridiculously overprotective at times.

"Of course he did. You do realize that Jason doesn't really care for Mr. Thompson, correct?"

"He never mentioned that to me," Victoria said, then bit her lip. She usually appreciated Jason's opinion on many matters, and he was an excellent judge of character.

"I have never had an issue with the man, personally. Jason just wants to make sure that the man you marry is right for you."

"Well, thank you both for that. I just hope my dear brother didn't scare him away."

"If my conversation with Jeremy Thompson scared him away, then good riddance." Jason Turner strode into the parlor. "If he wants to be a member of this family, he should be able to take my jesting."

"Your intimidation, you mean." Victoria gave her brother a hard look. "So help me, Jason Matthew, if you have ruined this for me…"

Jason sat on the settee and kicked his feet up, lounging comfortably. "I haven't. Worry not. He said he'll do right by you. I'm not sure I like the idea of you living in the Confederate capital, though."

"What's that, now?" Gregory sat up, a lock of brown hair falling in his face. "Why would you move? Where does Thompson plan on taking you?"

"He's going to be a member of our new Southern government. Moving to Alabama with the rest of the politicians." Jason answered for Victoria.

"Government? The yellow dog won't even fight?" Gregory shook his head. Victoria bristled at the insinuation that Jeremy was a coward.

"Gregory Turner, how dare you say that?" Her stomach churned. "Wait. Does that mean you…?"

"Plan on enlisting?" Gregory smiled. "Absolutely."

"What about school?" She asked. Gregory was getting his education, studying to be a lawyer alongside their father.

5

"I'll simply take a leave of absence from school. They say the war, once it starts, won't last but a few months."

"Yes, but…" Victoria was at a loss for words. She couldn't believe her baby brother, just nineteen years old, was going to enlist. She turned to Jason. "And what about you? Are you going to leave us as well?"

"Not exactly." Jason put his hands behind his head. "I'll stay in Warren County. The militia will be quite busy keeping the Yankees away from Vicksburg. It will be high priority, what with our position on the Mississippi. I plan on staying right here."

Victoria was quiet for a moment contemplating. "Have either of you heard what Father plans on doing?" She couldn't see her father donning a uniform and fighting, although it was hard to imagine Gregory in that role as well. "What about Abraham? Will he leave Mary Grace to fight, do you think?" Mary Grace was their sister, born between Victoria and Gregory. She and her husband, Abraham ran the local haberdashery, selling men's hats and other accessories. They had three children already, two-year-old twins Gabriel and Adam, and three-month-old Hope.

"I don't know about Father, but Abraham will enlist with me," Gregory said. "He's not one to stay behind if most of the other men are signing up."

"I believe you're right about Abraham, unfortunately for Mary Grace," Jason replied. "In regards to Father, I don't know what his plans are either. He likely wants to confer with Mother first, as he does with all major decisions."

"They do at that," Victoria murmured.

Finally, deciding that his sister was distracted enough, Gregory made his move and lunged at Victoria, quickly plucking the letter from her hand.

"Ha!" He called out victoriously. "Now we'll see who you have been corresponding with." He looked at the postmark. "Fredericksburg." He looked puzzled. "Why would you be so secretive about a letter from one of our cousins?"

"Unless it's not…" Jason took the letter from Gregory.

"You oafs! Give me that back!" Victoria didn't care that she was acting juvenile, as her brothers were acting the same way.

"Not quite yet, this is masculine handwriting, if I am not mistaken." Jason opened the envelope. "Aha!"

"Jason!" Victoria stood and tried to take the letter back. Jason swung his legs off the settee and stood, holding the letter away from Victoria and reading it.

"Mr. Nathaniel Prentiss. Of course, I recall him. Good man, he seemed." He read the letter further. "And a brave one, it appears. He says he plans on enlisting once Virginia leaves the Union. Wants you to know he thinks of you often and that he wishes he could see you again. He loves receiving letters from you and hopes they will continue even when the war, that is sure to come, actually begins." Jason finally relented and handed her the letter. "I always liked that man. Better than Jeremy Thompson, that's for sure. Why did you never court him?"

"Because he never asked." She said quickly. "It has long been my belief that he has feelings for our ever-so-perfect cousin, Belle." She smiled brightly, trying to hide the fact that she would have said yes immediately to a courtship with Nathaniel. "Besides, I have Mr. Thompson now. Nathaniel and I will remain just friends."

Jason was about to say something more when they were interrupted by their parents entering the parlor. Charles and Rachel Turner were opposite in looks, but were very similar in disposition. Charles was tall, dark-haired and well-built, while Rachel was petite with a fair complexion and golden hair. They were both quiet and kind and made sure that everyone who came into their lives felt welcomed. Following the couple were Brianne and Kendall Larson, daughters of Rachel's deceased sister. The girls had been living with the Turner family for the past eight years, ever since their mother had died in a wagon accident. Their father was a soldier with the Union Army, and could not properly care for his daughters on his own.

"How fortuitous that you three are in here already," Charles said, leading his wife to the settee that Jason had been lounging on. Instead of sitting back down in another seat, Jason strode to the fireplace and casually propped an elbow on the mantle. Victoria sat in the chair she had vacated, and Brianne and Kendall also found seats.

"Everyone is here but Mary Grace and the slaves." Gregory leaned forward and clasped his hands together loosely.

"I plan on visiting Mary Grace and Abraham tomorrow to speak with them, though I suppose there is no rush. We may have seceded today, but I doubt any armies will be mobilizing for another couple of months." Rachel clung to her husband's arm. "I believe we all need to discuss this turn of events and what it means for our family." He looked at each of his sons. "You are both old enough to make your own decisions. What are your thoughts?"

Jason spoke up first. "I am going to remain with the militia here, Father. We all know the Federals will attempt to control the Mississippi River and Vicksburg will be key to that goal. I mean to protect our home."

Charles nodded, then focused on Gregory. "And you, son?"

"I'm planning to enlist. I haven't thought much about specifics, I'm not even sure what part of the army I would do best in, but I want to do my part."

Charles gave him the flicker of a smile. Rachel's eyes welled with tears. "I did some looking into that myself as well today. As I alluded to you before, it will be a while, maybe even half a year, before any armies are formed, but I have decided I will enlist. We can do so together, Gregory."

Victoria jumped out of her seat. "Father, are you serious? You cannot be!" How could she handle both her father and her brothers fighting? She could understand Jason and Gregory's desires; they were both young men with a need for adventure, but her father...what had he to prove? "Why, Father? Why are you going?"

"I feel the need to do so," He replied. Gregory's face was difficult to read, but Jason looked as though he was quite proud of his father.

"But you disagree with secession, and even though Esther, Dinah and Caesar are our slaves, I know you don't like slavery enough to go off and die just to keep the institution." Her voice raised, shocking even herself. She never spoke like this to anyone.

"There are many reasons men will enlist, Victoria," Charles spoke softly to his daughter. "I feel as though I must defend my family. Besides, I have military experience. As you know, I went to the Virginia Military Institute and was with the Virginia Militia..."

"You were only with the militia for one year because of your injured leg, Father, and you said that military life wasn't for you. How has all of that suddenly changed?" Victoria insisted.

"My career still isn't with the military, Victoria." Charles ran a hand through his dark hair. "We all know that your Uncle Samuel is the true soldier of the family, but I have more experience and knowledge than most, and I will do what I can to help our new government."

"Victoria, please, be seated and just listen to your father," Rachel softly requested. Her eyes were filled with tears. Victoria couldn't imagine what her mother was feeling. Both of her sons and her husband...it had to be too much.

"How can you leave us?" Victoria sank to her seat, her voice now softer.

"Victoria, you must know how difficult this is for me. It is not something I have decided on lightly."

"Especially since Uncle Samuel will be on the other side of the battlefield," Jason said somberly. "And Uncle Nicholas." He looked at Brianne and Kendall. Nicholas was their father, but they seldom saw him and despite loving him, they considered their Uncle Charles to be more of a father figure.

"Yes, there is that," Charles said. Victoria looked at Jason, curious. Her Uncle Samuel and most likely her cousin Jonah would be fighting for the Union. Jason and Jonah were very close to one another, as close as they could be while living as far apart as they did, Jason in Mississippi and Jonah in Virginia. She wondered if perhaps that was one of the reasons

Jason wanted to stay in Warren County; he wouldn't have to inadvertently meet Jonah on the battlefield. Victoria sighed and rubbed her head.

"Father, I am so sorry I overreacted. I just...much has happened today."

"I understand." Charles stood and opened his arms. Victoria quickly went to him, embracing her father tightly.

"I'm just going to miss you so much, Father."

"I won't be leaving for quite some time and there is the slim possibility that no war will even come of this secession. But rest assured, I will make sure that you and your mother are taken care of." Charles released his daughter and looked at his wife. "And I must say, Jason, I am glad you will be remaining in the Warren County area. I trust you'll be able to keep an eye on your family."

"Of course, sir, and I suppose it is a good thing that you'll be able to keep an eye on Gregory." Jason reached over and gave his little brother a short punch on the arm.

"Hey!" Gregory rubbed the spot, then looked at Victoria and his cousins. "And I'm glad all of you will be able to watch over Jason."

"He'll need it most of all." Brianne laughed.

"And that is why we'll get through this conflict," Rachel said. "Because we will watch out for one another and rely on God for strength."

"Like the Bible verse you always recite, Uncle Charles," Kendall said. "For I know the plans I have for you."

"Plans to prosper you and not to harm you." Charles smiled and placed a comforting arm around his wife. "Plans to give you a future of hope. You are correct, Kendall. That is what we all must remember."

Saturday, January 12, 1861
Green Home

"Good day, Mary!"

Mary Lake Green turned and smiled when she saw her younger sister, Louisa enter the parlor. The young woman took off her hat and set it on the end table.

"Louisa, welcome! Please sit." Mary dearly appreciated her family, and enjoyed the closeness they shared. She was overjoyed when her husband Duff had built their home so close to Lakemont, the home of her family. Louisa was only two years younger than Mary, at age 25, and they were more friends than just sisters. The next oldest sibling was Jeannie, age 15, then came Alice, age 14, William, age 12 and the youngest was Willie, age 8. It was strange to Mary that her brother Willie was closer in age to her daughter, Annie, than he was to her.

Mary took a deep breath. Tragically, both Mary and her mother Anne, had lost a child three years ago. Mary's nine-year-old sister Ida, and her own three-year-old daughter, Annie had died of Scarlet Fever. Her precious Annie. Months later, Mary had given birth to a second daughter. She and Duff had decided to name that child Annie as well, something many families did when a beloved child passed away.

Mary brushed the sad thoughts away and focused on her sister. "How are Mother and Father?"

"They are well," Louisa said. "At least as far as I know. Father wants to be part of the new Southern government, which continues to grow bigger. I am sure you have heard that Florida seceded on Thursday, and Alabama made their secession official yesterday." Louisa shook her head and patted her brown hair. "We surely are heading for a war. The question is, what men will be leaving to defend our new nation?"

"Will Peter enlist?" Mary asked. Peter Slaughter was Louisa's husband. Mary was unsure of what her own husband Duff would decide. She kept meaning to discuss it with him, but hadn't been able to find the right time. There was a part of her that wasn't sure she wanted to know the answer.

"He wants to," Louisa said. "Along with many of our citizens. Our Vicksburg men may have more of a reason to fight, since they will be protecting their homes and families. The papers are full of stories that the Yankees will want to control Vicksburg. One rumor in particular is about the steamship, *The Silver Wave*, which is expected in Vicksburg any day."

"Why is that a rumor? We've seen that particular ship in port many times. It's never been a problem before."

"I am not sure of all the details," Louisa admitted. "Peter tries to shield me from the more harsh stories. I know that Duff treats you the same way. At any rate, the reports are that Northern abolitionists plan on sending steamboats, perhaps even the *Silver Wave*, loaded with volunteers to attack Southern ports up and down the Mississippi River."

"My goodness! Is this why the bells were ringing and the militia rushed over to Fort Hill yesterday?"

"Yes, indeed." Louisa answered. Fort Hill was one of the many hills in town that had a commanding view of the river. It had an especially good view of the river north of the city. "The men put four cannons in place and other troops from nearby cities have joined them."

"Listen to us." Mary shook her head. "Speaking of war and troops instead of who's courting who and what is going on in society."

"Well, we can still do that. In fact, that was one of the reasons I stopped by. Word around town is that Mr. Jeremy Thompson just left for Jackson, but not before speaking with Victoria Turner about the future." Louisa leaned forward in her seat, knowing that Mary would have more gossip.

"That is true. I spoke with Victoria on Wednesday and Mr. Thompson did make promises to her."

"Oooh, they will make a wonderful couple," Louisa gushed. "He is so handsome."

"He is handsome, I'll grant you that. As for them being a wonderful couple, I am not so sure," Mary replied. "The unfortunate thing is that Mr. Thompson told her that he would speak with her father before he left and when I saw Victoria yesterday, she was quite upset because she learned he never did. Mr. Thompson also left so abruptly that he didn't even bother to say goodbye to her in person. He just left a letter. Victoria was trying to act unaffected, but I know her better than that."

"My goodness. I believed him to be more of a gentleman." Louisa almost looked as if her own heart was broken.

"Indeed." Mary was upset on behalf of her friend but truly believed that Victoria could find a better man for a husband.

Before either sister could say anything more, the sound of gunfire broke out in the distance. Mary and Louisa both jumped to their feet and hastened to the front veranda. The winter evening air was cool, and Mary wished she would have grabbed a shawl. The commotion seemed to be coming from the bend at DeSoto point, across the river from Vicksburg. Though it was half a mile away, Mary could hear shells being shot and even splashing into the frigid, muddy Mississippi.

"Dear Lord, what is happening?" Louisa said to herself. Mary pulled her sister close and Louisa placed her head on Mary's shoulder. The sounds subsided and about twenty minutes later, they saw Duff walking up the hill in front of the house and up the driveway to their home.

"Mary! Louisa! What are you doing out here?" He seemed flustered. Mary couldn't remember the last time she had seen him like this.

"We heard shots fired," Mary replied. "We had to come out and see what was going on. It's not dangerous, is it?"

"I wouldn't say it's perfectly safe, but we're far enough away that we shouldn't be in any real danger. For now, at least." Duff turned to Louisa. "I should escort you home, though."

Louisa nodded, disappointed that the visit had been cut short. "I'll go and get my things. I must also say goodbye to Annie." She went inside.

Once she was out of sight, Duff pulled Mary into his arms and gave her a brief kiss. She turned and faced the river. His arms remained around her and she leaned back against him.

"So, do you know what happened down there?" She asked. "What were they shooting at?"

"A vessel, the *A.O. Tyler*. Our men weren't quite sure what the ship was here for, what with all the rumors around town, so they fired some warning shots. The captain, a man named John Collins, was undoubtedly wondering what all the fuss was about. Our soldiers boarded the boat to search for weapons, but they didn't find anything."

"That's a good thing, isn't it?"

"I think so. Our Republic of Mississippi, not only a week old, has shown some military might. That will help us greatly in the future. It will prevent the enemy from believing we will be an easy target."

"Everyone is saying that war is inevitable, Duff. What do you think?"

"I'd like to say the idea of war is an exaggeration in our minds, but if there is one, it shouldn't last long. I believe Vicksburg will organize troops and call for volunteers. Many men are prepared to enlist their services already."

"Will you leave?" Mary's voice was soft.

"I don't know. I am not a soldier, I am a businessman. I feel I can help our new nation in ways other than fighting, staying here where I can protect my family. I don't want to leave you."

"I don't want that either. Not at all, not even for the few weeks the war is supposed to last."

"We shall see. Perhaps it will not even be an issue. Perhaps the war will be over by the time I have to make that decision." He kissed her head.

"Let us hope and pray that is the case."

Monday, February 18, 1861
Green Home

"Mrs. Davis! What brings you into Vicksburg?" Victoria smiled as she sat down in the parlor. She thoroughly enjoyed talking with the woman seated next to Mary. Varina Davis and her husband, Jefferson, had a home just south of Vicksburg, Brierfield Plantation. "Shouldn't you be in Alabama today? Your husband is being inaugurated as the first president of the Confederacy, is he not?"

"Yes he is, but, I didn't travel with him. I will join him eventually with the children, once things have settled down." Jefferson and Varina Davis had three children, Margaret, age six, Jefferson Jr, age five, and two-year-old Joseph. They had lost their oldest son, Samuel, seven years ago to a sickness. He was only two years old at the time.

Varina shook her head. "This whole new government smells of a bad idea to me. Mr. Davis never wanted to lead the Confederacy. He's my husband, and I love him dearly, but I'm not sure he's the best choice for the position."

"Mr. Green says that Mr. Davis was the only good choice they had, in his opinion," Mary said.

Varina shook her head. "I detest the idea of war, and secession was a foolish idea. If I had the right to vote for the United States president back in November...well, John Bell would have had my vote." John Bell had run for president against Abraham Lincoln, John C. Breckinridge, and Stephen A. Douglas in the Election of 1860. He was both pro-Union and pro-slavery.

"The people of Vicksburg didn't want secession," Victoria said. "But the state of Mississippi voted for it."

"More's the pity," Mrs. Davis said. "This whole fiasco is bound to be a failure, but I will follow my husband wherever he goes and will support his decisions, as a good wife should."

Victoria knew from previous conversations that Mrs. Davis sometimes felt as though she had to work extra hard to earn her husband's love since she was his second wife. His first wife, Sarah Taylor, had died of malaria after three months of marriage back in 1835. It was well known that Sarah was his true love and he still mourned her. In fact, Varina had confided to Victoria that Jefferson had brought her for a visit to Sarah's grave on their honeymoon.

"You don't have faith that the Confederate army can win a war, if it comes to that?" Victoria asked.

"I don't believe so, no. We don't have the resources. However, as I said before, I must do my duty and support my husband. When this is all inevitably over, I will probably have to run away from the Federals along with the rest of the Confederate government."

"You'll do well to hold those opinions to yourself while you're staying in the Confederate capitol." Victoria knew the woman would not do so. Varina Davis never hesitated to speak her mind.

"As if I even could." Varina shook her head. "You know me better than that. I have my opinions and never hesitate to share them. If only Mr. Davis had just been commissioned a general as we expected."

"I have no doubt he will make Warren County proud," Victoria said.

"Thank you for saying so, Miss Turner," Mrs. Davis replied, then changed the topic. "How is everything with you and your family?"

"Quite well," Victoria replied. "Father continues his law practice, and Gregory continues his studies, looking to join my father's practice someday soon. Jason keeps busy with his job factoring cotton and he has been quite busy with the local militia, training to keep us all safe. "

"That's all very good. Your father is undoubtedly happy that Gregory is going to follow in his footsteps." Varina smiled. "Most of the town believed Jason would join your father as well."

"He may have considered it for a few moments, but it would be too stifling for him. He prefers the outdoors, and factoring allows him to work on the docks when he wants, loading and unloading the cotton. It may not be dignified, but he enjoys it." As a factor, Jason performed many different services for his planter clients in the area. He sold cotton on their behalf, gave advice concerning the condition of the cotton market and bought his clients a large portion of their supplies. He also traveled a fair amount to visit more rural planters who could not easily move their cotton.

"I suppose it is important to enjoy your work," Varina said.

"Indeed," Victoria replied. "Father, Gregory and Abraham, my sister Mary Grace's husband, plan on volunteering their services to the government once they are officially asked for."

"Your poor mother," Mary said. "She must be quite distressed to know all the men in her family may leave her."

"Yes, she is trying to stay strong." Victoria put on a smile as Varina changed the subject again.

"I should have brought my son, Joseph," Varina said, "he could play with your nephews. I brought my Margaret to play with Annie Green."

"That would have been nice, Mrs. Davis. I know my sister would consider it an honor. Perhaps next time," Victoria replied.

"Perhaps," Varina said. "I only hope we don't go to war, though as I said before, I doubt that and I doubt we will have a Southern victory in the end."

"I suppose hope and prayers for peace will be a main part of our lives," Mary said.

"And we must remember to support each other as well," Victoria added. "However we can."

Tuesday, March 12, 1861
Turner Home

"Mary Grace, I am so glad you could visit today." Victoria smiled and cuddled her niece, Hope, against her shoulder.

"You're only glad to see the children." Mary Grace smiled jokingly.

"No, they are just an added delight," Victoria replied. "I believe Mary Green and Hannah are going to join us today as well."

"Wonderful. It will be nice to speak with someone other than my customers."

"Is the business doing well?" Victoria asked.

"Yes, even though I don't look at the books much, we have been very busy, although," she looked out the window towards the haberdashery, "I will have to learn how to manage the finances, and quickly. Once Abraham leaves, the entire business will fall on me to run."

"Well, I'm no expert with numbers, as you well know, but if you need any help, please come to me."

"I will," Mary Grace said. The sisters stood as one of the Turner's slaves, Dinah, announced Mrs. Hannah Wheeler and Mrs. Mary Green.

The women entered, and all greeted one another, then settled into their seats.

"Hannah, I must say, it has been ever so long since we have been able to simply sit and visit," Victoria said.   Hannah Wheeler was one of Victoria's best friends. She was a widow; her husband Benjamin had died a few years back in a farming accident. He left not only Hannah and their son, Ambrose, who was now six years old, but also a young sister, Caroline and widowed mother, Mrs. Cordelia Wheeler. Ambrose and the women lived on a small family farm, watched over by an elderly neighbor, Mr. Wagner, and often checked on by Jason Turner.

"It has been too long." Hannah brushed her dark-blonde braid over her shoulder. Though she always looked clean and proper, she rarely cared about the latest fashion styles, even when out visiting, but it didn't detract from her natural beauty. "What is the latest news? I seldom get into town and when I do, it's usually Sunday for church."

"Most of the talk is about the inauguration of Lincoln." Victoria felt quite up to date with the news, especially with Jason knowing so much. He had a knack for getting information. She was so glad she and her mother wouldn't lose him, at least not for terribly long periods of time. Victoria continued. "It was just over a week ago, but many people are still not happy with the man. Lincoln makes it sound as though he wants peace in the country and to appease the seceded states, but then he pledges to hold all property and places that belong to our government. He argues that the Union is indissolvable yet promises that he will never be the first to attack." She sighed. "He denounced secession as anarchy, which many Vicksburgians agreed with months ago. It is all quite a mess."

"Yes, it is," Mary Grace said. "Oh, and another interesting tidbit I just heard at the shop is that Armistead Burwell has fled to the North."

Victoria scoffed. "Yes, ran away to where he belongs."

Armistead Burwell was an attorney in town who was very vocal about his support of the Union. He had abandoned his newly purchased home, which had the appearance of a castle. The stately house stood on a hill overlooking the river, and boasted of high towers, turrets and even a moat.

"Our soldiers will surely fortify that hill." Victoria added. "It is a key position."

Mary Grace spoke up. "Abraham told me our first military company, the Vicksburg Sharpshooters, has already met their quota and were mustered into service today. They'll remain in Vicksburg for the time being."

Victoria shook her head. "It is so hard to believe it's come to this. Men enlisting and leaving their homes and families for the probability of a war. I heard people in town say another company will be mustered up due to the number of men interested in defending our rights. I dread the day Gregory, Abraham and Father leave."

"I try not to even think about that day," Mary Grace said.

"What does Duff plan on doing?" Victoria turned to Mary Green.

"He hasn't decided yet," Mary admitted. "We have been talking, and praying about it. He wants to help in the best way that he can while protecting his family. He's just not sure what that will be."

Victoria nodded. "I suppose there will be a need for many different roles, not just soldiering."

"Yes, such as the politicians." Mary Grace appeared to have been waiting to bring up Jeremy Thompson. "Have you heard from your intended, Victoria?"

"You mean the man that never spoke to Father, even after he told me he would? My understanding with Jeremy Thompson now isn't official in any capacity because of that. However, I did receive a letter from him last week. He's in Montgomery, doing very well for himself."

"Yes, he is working for my father's political opposition," Mary Green said. Mary's father, William Lake was a member of the Mississippi State House of Representatives and running for Confederate Congress.

"That is unfortunate, I hadn't noticed," Victoria replied. "Even though we are banding together to fight the Federals, I suppose we will still have some divisions among us."

"Indeed." Mary Grace spoke up again, speaking to Victoria. "Has Father heard anything from our uncles?"

"No. We are quite sure that Uncle Samuel and Uncle Nicholas will stay loyal to the Union." Victoria thought back to Brianne and Kendall and the look on their faces every time the mail came and nothing was for them. A look of utter abandonment. "Brianne and Kendall haven't heard from their father in almost a year."

"That is just so heartbreaking." Mary Green said. "Those poor girls."

"Yes, but at least they have us," Victoria said. "Mother has always been the perfect person to care for them."

"Very true," Mary Grace said, "and we have been lucky to have them with us. They are so delightful. I sometimes wonder if Uncle Nicholas chooses to avoid them because they remind him of their mother. I don't think he intentionally wants to hurt the girls. Speaking of those two dears, I was hoping to see them today. Where are they?"

"Kendall is out and about, and Brianne is visiting with Alice Shirley," Victoria explained. Alice Shirley was Brianne's dearest confidante.

"I know that the four of us will remain the best of friends, but my biggest hope is, no matter what happens as a result of secession, all the families and friends will find ways to remain close," Hannah said.

"I hope that cool heads prevail and pray that God will keep all our families safe," Victoria added.

Tuesday, March 27, 1861
Sky Parlor Hill

Victoria glanced around as she stood at the edge of her favorite place in town. Chinese lanterns hung from the metal poles that surrounded the park and gave a warm glow to the night sky. The Hill City Cadets, also known as the 10th Mississippi, Gregory and her father's newly formed unit, was leaving early next morning. They were heading for a place called Pensacola, Florida, to protect Confederate military interests there. Victoria wished her family could have spent a nice, intimate evening together, but the townspeople had wanted to throw a dinner and dance for the departing soldiers. The tables around the park were draped with white cloths and wine glasses were brimming with a bubbly drink. It was quite the party.

"Why are you not dancing, my dear sister?" Gregory came up behind her. "I know how much you enjoy it."

"Well, I suppose it's because I have yet to be asked, Gregory." She took his offered arm and he led her out to the dance floor.

"Those men not asking you to dance don't know what they're missing. You've always been one of the best dancers in town, at least as far as I'm concerned."

"Well, thank you, kind sir," she replied. "I was of the opinion that no one was asking me because they are aware of my agreement with Mr. Thompson."

"Perhaps." Gregory spun her around, then pulled her back in. "I still say it's their loss."

"What am I going to do without you, Gregory? I don't think I'll be able to survive. You are the best brother a girl could ask for. I am so lucky for both you and Jason...I have been so blessed to have you in my life. Please, please take care of yourself out there. Promise me, you won't take any unnecessary risks."

"Don't fret, Victoria. I will be just fine. Even if something does happen to me, remember the faith I have in Jesus. You must know that I am confident in the fact that I will be heading for a better place."

Victoria could feel tears forming in her eyes. "Oh, Gregory. I will miss you dearly."

The song ended and he pulled her off the dance floor and into his arms. When had he gotten so tall? She couldn't believe he was going to be leaving in a few short hours. When had her baby brother become a strong, confident young man?

"Victoria...are you sure you want to see us off in the morning? I wouldn't want you to become upset."

"Wild horses couldn't keep me away," Victoria said. She reached up and adjusted his collar. "Now, you go and ask that pretty Mary Shannon to dance. She's been making eyes at you all evening."

"Thank you, Victoria." He kissed her on the cheek. "I believe I will."

Victoria smiled as her younger brother approached the daughter of their family friend and local newspaperman, Marmaduke Shannon. Gregory looked so fine in his new Confederate uniform, it would be difficult for any young lady to ignore him.

"It's hard to believe how much he has matured." Mary Grace came and stood next to Victoria.

"He's barely younger than you, Mary Grace," Victoria reminded her.

"I realize that, but he's always seemed so much younger. Perhaps I'm just that much more mature, being an old married woman." She smiled.

"That must be it," Victoria agreed. "I see your husband approaching. He must want to dance and hold you in his arms yet again." She nodded at Abraham.

"Actually, Miss Victoria, I was coming over to see if you would honor me with a dance." Abraham offered his arm. Locks of long brown hair fell in his face. He looked slightly unkempt, as always, but Victoria thought it made him look roguishly handsome.

"Well, thank you, Mr. Corbel, it would be my honor." Victoria took his arm, thankful once again for her wonderful family and friends.

Wednesday, April 13, 1861
Green Home

"Well, it is official and Lincoln got his wish." Victoria dropped the newspaper on the end table. "We are now at war." She sat down in Mary Green's parlor and thought back to the morning Gregory, her father and Abraham had left. It had been such a festive occasion, just as it was every time the men marched off to war these past few weeks. The women gave extra food and clothing to the men, then gave their loved ones final hugs and kisses before the soldiers boarded their train and waved goodbye.

"We can only hope this conflict will end quickly." Mary Green took the paper and glanced over the article about how the Confederate army bombarded Fort Sumter, a Federal stronghold in Charleston, South Carolina."

"Just a week ago, our own mayor told us that he believed the Confederacy would take its place among the independent nations with peace, prosperity and happiness. So much for that speech."

"At least no one has been killed yet," Mary commented.

"I don't think that statistic will hold for very long," Victoria said. "As I walked over here, I saw another group of men preparing to leave. Proud fathers, tearful wives and mothers, envious boys. Everyone walking around with rosettes that have President Davis's likeness in them. So much patriotism when not even five months ago, we didn't want to break away from the Union. I am finding it difficult to believe we have traded loyalties so quickly."

"Our loyalty is to Mississippi." Mary pointed out. "I still think it unlikely we will be having an all-out war. Even if there is, I feel as though it will remain far from us."

"I'm not so sure about that, but I hope you're right." Victoria sighed. "Anyways, I came to see if you wanted to accompany me to the Episcopal Church. Some women are getting together to sew uniforms, knit socks and put together some housewives."

"Housewives?" Mary looked puzzled at the term.

"Small sewing kits for the soldiers to take with them," Victoria explained.

"I see." Mary stood and spoke to the slave standing at the doorway and asked her to get her walking hat and her own sewing kit. "I believe this will be a fine way to support our boys."

"Wonderful." Victoria didn't want to press Mary, but she felt the need to know. "And Duff? Has he decided how he will help the war effort?"

"He'll do what he can from home." Mary didn't meet Victoria's eyes.

"So he's not going to enlist? At all?"

"No, he decided not to." Mary defended him. "Not all men are cut out for military or political life." She quickly changed the subject. "Speaking of politicians, have you heard from Mr. Thompson lately?" The slave returned with the requested items, and Mary put her hat on.

"It's been about three weeks since my last letter," Victoria said. "I write him about twice a week, but..." She shook her head and sighed. "I know he's busy, getting established in the government, looking towards the future. I just...I just wish he would take the time to let me know how things were coming along."

Mary was unsure of what to say to her friend. She had feared that distance would harm the relationship between Victoria and Mr. Jeremy Thompson. Perhaps it was a good thing he hadn't spoken with Mr. Turner.

"I am so sorry, Victoria," She finally said as they walked out the door. "This must be terribly upsetting for you."

"Sometimes...sometimes I wonder if I'll ever be married. I thought for sure by now, Jeremy would have sent for me or come home so we could be married." She paused. "Or even spoken with Father." She placed a hand to her temple. "I fear that once Virginia secedes, the capital will move to Richmond and then he'll be even farther away."

"Why would they move to Richmond?" Mary asked. "Why would they want the capital to be so close to Washington City?"

"I've heard a few reasons," Victoria said as they made their way to the church. "It is the South's second largest city and there is so much history there, people believe it will associate our fight with that of the Patriots during the Revolution. Virginia also has nearly as many factories as the rest of the Confederacy combined. There are likely additional reasons."

"The climate must be a sight better as well," Mary said. "The summers not so stifling."

"That is true," Victoria said. "I just hope putting the capital that far north will not end up being our downfall."

Sunday, May 19, 1861
Turner Home

"I am so glad that you could all join us today." Rachel Turner smiled at the women gathered around their parlor. "We'll have refreshments in a while, but until then, let's continue to work on our projects for the troops." She joined a circle of older women, including Cordelia Wheeler, mother-in-law of Hannah, Emma Balfour, a neighbor of the Turners and good friend of the family, and Mary Green's mother, Anna Lake.

Victoria turned to her friends who had created their own circle to work and discuss current events and other gossip. Brianne, Kendall, and some of the younger women had also created their own sewing circle.

"The 10th Mississippi is now headed out," Mary Grace said. "It was organized over at Corinth. Ohh, I miss my Abraham dreadfully."

"The Confederacy is preparing for a full-blown battle." Victoria picked up her sewing. "Our government is even selling war bonds to help finance the fighting."

"I heard that US postage stamps will no longer be honored when mailing a letter." Mary Green's sister, Louisa spoke up.

"I just hope and pray that everything will be resolved without further violence." Mary Green added.

"Indeed." Victoria wanted to say more to her friend, as she was still upset that Duff was not fighting, but she valued Mary too much as a friend, and this was not the time or place. She feared the citizens in the town would be cruel enough to her and her family. Instead, Victoria turned to Hannah. "How is life out at the farm?"

"To be honest, for us, it doesn't feel as though anything has changed. Mr. Wagner continues to help us, and Jason stops over every few days to assist with what he can. It's nice to know we have men who will watch out for us."

"Hopefully, we women will soon be able to protect ourselves. I heard that classes will be offered to teach ladies how to handle a gun, and I plan on attending." Victoria smiled.

"That is not ladylike at all, Victoria," Mary Grace repremanded.

"How is it that you have not already learned how to handle a gun?" Mary Green asked at the same time.

"I've always wanted to learn, and now is my chance." Victoria insisted.

Hannah spoke up. "Mr. Wagner has been telling Mother Cordelia for years that he thinks it a good idea for all three of us to learn how to handle firearms. Jason has offered to teach me as well."

"You see, Mary Grace, it's just practical, what with all of the menfolk leaving us," Victoria said. "We must know how to protect ourselves."

"I'm sure, with the importance of Vicksburg to both the Confederacy and the Union, that the Southern Army will have the city well-protected." Mary Green pointed out.

"That may be true, and it may keep us safe while we are in town, but I don't plan on spending this whole war holed up in town, even if it will be over in one big battle. I have friends to see and visit." Victoria smiled at Hannah. "Besides, learning something new is always a good thing."

"That is very true," Louisa piped in.

"I feel we will be learning quite a bit in the next few months, whether we want to or not." Mary Green observed.

"I certainly agree," Hannah said, thoughtfully. "Perhaps I will allow Jason to teach me how to use our firearms. It would surely make him feel better."

"I must make the observation that you and Mr. Jason Turner spend much time together," Louisa said. "Will there ever be a courtship between the two of you?"

Victoria peeked at Hannah. She had often wondered about the answer to that question as well, but both Hannah and Jason avoided answering it.

"I doubt it," Hannah replied. "We have been friends for so long, even before I married Benjamin. Jason and my husband were always so close, just as Victoria and I have been. Jason is a wonderful man, and a perfect man for Ambrose to emulate, but I'm afraid friends is all we will ever be."

"Sometimes the best marriages start as the greatest of friends," Mary Grace said. "Look at Cousin Elizabeth over in Fredericksburg. She and her husband started out as close acquaintances, then became friends and finally fell in love and got married. They have a wonderful relationship, even though they were from two different levels of society."

It was a true statement. Their cousin Elizabeth had married her brother's best friend, Joshua, a local blacksmith.

"I understand that," Hannah admitted. "But I don't know what the future holds for any of us. However, I am content to have Jason Turner's friendship and protection for now." She turned to Victoria. "Have you heard anything more from Mr. Thompson? How is he settling in?"

"As far as I know, things are going quite well for him." Victoria shrugged. "The few letters that I receive are short and to the point. It seems as though he is quite busy, but well. He makes it sound as though the connections he is making will help him much in the future. He even made reference to me as possibly one day being the First Lady of the Confederacy."

"My goodness, he has a high opinion of himself, but wouldn't that be grand?" Mary Grace quipped. "My sister, who just expressed interest in wanting to learn how to shoot a gun, as a First Lady."

"Well, Varina Davis is the First Lady now, and I guarantee that she is far from what many people thought would be the ideal First Lady." Victoria pointed out.

"That is true," Mary Green said, "but I think you would make a fine first lady, Victoria if that is what you want."

"I suppose I had never really thought of it." Victoria replied. "We shall just see what the future holds."

Monday, July 22, 1861
Turner Home

"Hello, wonderful family!" Jason walked into the Turner dining room, an extra spring in his step. He grabbed a plate and went to the serving table to fill it. He then sat down and smiled broadly at his mother, sisters and cousins.

"What are you so jovial for?" Victoria asked.

"I am surprised that you haven't heard." He smiled. "There was finally a real battle just south of Washington City near a town called Manassas Junction."

"How did our Southern troops fare?" Rachel asked.

"We did very well," Jason said. "When things looked bad, the Confederate boys stepped up. We ended up chasing the Federals from the field all the way back to Washington." He spooned some soup into his mouth. "That's not all. There were scores of civilians watching the battle who got chased home as well."

"Why ever would they think watching a battle would be a good idea?" Rachel was horrified.

"They were so sure-fired confident that they would win and 'quell the rebellion' as they put it. The spectators didn't want to miss anything." Jason replied.

"Were any of them killed?" Kendall asked, wide-eyed. Victoria could imagine that her adventurous young cousin would enjoy observing a battle.

"None of the spectators, no, I don't think so," Jason answered. "There was one elderly woman whose home was right in the middle of the battlefield. She was bedridden, so couldn't leave. She was dead by the end of the battle, probably from the stress of it all."

"How tragic," Rachel said. "I suppose that is something we never really considered, at least I hadn't. Soldiers will not be the only ones harmed in this war."

"That is true, Mother. We did lose many men, but not nearly as many as the Union," Jason replied.

"So is the war over, just like everyone expected?" Brianne asked.

"Not quite yet," Jason replied. "We may be in for a few more engagements before it's all over."

"Do we know...dare I even ask...were there any Mississippi Regiments in the fight?" Rachel asked, concern apparent in her face.

"Not sure about all the Mississippi troops, but the 10th was definitely not there. You've no worries about that, Mama. Gregory, Abraham and Father are all safe."

"For now," Brianne said. "It does make one wonder, though. When the men are killed, how on earth will the army let the families know? For all we know, our father could be dead, we haven't heard from him in years."

"The newspapers will print casualty lists." Jason explained after swallowing a bite of sandwich.

"That seems impersonal," Kendall replied. "And what if they miss someone?"

"Unfortunately, I believe there will be some men who die and their identities will remain unknown," Jason said. "The only other way to report a death would be the comrades or friends of those who are killed writing letters home. That may still happen, I'm not sure." He shook his head. "I know if something happened to my fellow militia men, I would write their family."

"Hopefully, you won't have to worry about that, Jason," Rachel said, "and girls, I am sure if your father had been killed, the army would have let us know by now."

"We can pray, at least." Jason ran a hand through his dark blonde hair.

"We will all be doing that," Victoria said. "There are days when I feel as though that is all we can do."

Sunday, August 25, 1861
Wheeler Farm

"Jason Turner! I didn't expect you today." Hannah smiled and put her hands on her hips.

"I wasn't aware I needed a reason to come out here to see you, Mrs. Wheeler." Jason dismounted and took off his hat. "However, if you would like a reason, I suppose I will tell you that this is an added bonus to my weekly check-in on you."

"I see." She smiled. Jason stopped by more often than once a week. In fact, since the war broke out, his visits occurred every couple of days. "I was at church this morning. You could have checked on me then." She bent to hoe at the row she had been working. He took the tool and began doing her work.

"I wish that could have been the case, but I was out riding patrol."

"I suppose that's a reasonable excuse." Hannah placed her hands back on her hips. "Mother Cordelia is making fried chicken for dinner. I know she'll have extra. Would you care to stay?"

"I would love to." He stopped working and propped his elbow on the hoe. "Have you considered my proposition? I would feel much more comfortable leaving you out here if you knew how to shoot a gun."

"We have been out here for years since Benjamin died and we have been just fine. Besides, Mr. Wagner…"

"We are now at war, Hannah, and Old Man Wagner is a good man, but you and I both know he wouldn't be able to defend you against trained soldiers. If this war doesn't end within a month or two, you'd best believe me, there will be Yankees trying to take the town. They'll likely try by river first, but they'll quickly realize that's nigh impossible, so they'll overrun farms just like yours to take Vicksburg by land."

Hannah didn't meet Jason's eyes as she took the hoe from him and worked it into the soil. He shook his head, frustrated.

"I have told you before, Jason, God will take care of us."

"I know that, but I have always believed that God helps those who help themselves." His chocolate brown eyes were warm and pleading. He was such a kind, caring man. It looked like he hadn't been able to shave this morning, but the scruffy look made him appear quite dashing. It made him look older, more mature. Not at all like the boy she had grown up with.

Jason grabbed the hoe, stopping her work, making her look up to him. "Hannah. I am sure you realize this, but I swore to Benjamin that I would look out for you and your family. Your husband may have been five years older than me, but he was one of my closest friends, a mentor, someone I wanted to emulate. I must do all I can to protect you and I honestly believe that making sure you can shoot a gun…well, I know he would approve of it."

Hannah's eyes watered at the thought of her husband. Benjamin had been such a good man. Though their marriage had been more of an arrangement, she had cared for him and respected him deeply. Jason was right. Benjamin would have wanted her to learn to defend herself.

"All right, you've talked me into it." She pulled her pocket watch out and checked the time. "You've got about an hour before we need to get washed up for supper. Let's get started."

Jason smiled. "Very well. Let's do just that."

The two made their way to the small but comfortable Wheeler farmhouse. She quickly found her mother-in-law and son on the back porch and told them what the plan was.

"Mama, I want to learn to fight!" Ambrose exclaimed, poking his white-blonde head up from the corn he was shucking. The boy abandoned his chore and ran up to Jason. "Can't you teach me, Mr. Jason?" He begged, his big blue eyes reminding Hannah of a puppy.

"Of course, I'll teach you, Ambrose," Jason replied. "But all in good time, my little man." Jason sank down on one knee and pulled Ambrose close, as if telling him a secret. "You see, the rule is, you have to be taller than the shotgun to shoot. But I promise you, son, once you're tall enough, I will teach you!"

"All right, I suppose that makes sense." Ambrose sighed loudly.

"Besides, I think it would be best if you stayed here and watched over your grandmother and Aunt Caroline. Your mama and I will likely work up quite an appetite." He winked and ruffled the boy's hair, then turned to Hannah. "You ready, Miss Hannah?"

"Yes, sir." She held up the aged shotgun that had been little more than a decoration above the door since Benjamin died.

Jason chuckled. "It wouldn't hurt you ladies to invest in a newer model." He took the gun and ammunition from her and followed her down the porch steps.

"Perhaps we will," Hannah replied. The two made their way back to the open clearing of the farm, where the foundation of the old barn could still be seen. Jason smiled as he pulled some empty tin cans from his haversack.

"You were that confident I would finally allow this?" Hannah laughed at his certainty.

"Let's just say that I like to be prepared. I packed them just before leaving." Jason began placing the cans on the waist high foundation that was a stone wall now.

"I see." She smiled. Jason turned back to her.

"How is it that you have been living all alone out here without knowing how to shoot? You have never had the need to even go hunting?"

"And kill poor animals?" Hannah looked horrified, but Jason could immediately tell she was joking. "I think not. We'll get our meat from town or Mr. Wagner."

"Well, when Ambrose is old enough, you best believe I'll teach him not only to shoot, but also the finer points of hunting, including how to dress a deer." He shook his head. "I don't know how we've been such good friends for so long and this has only recently come up." He muttered.

She took the shotgun. "I don't know either." She looked up at him. "I did want to say thank you yet again...for being so kind to Ambrose. You don't have to do that. I really appreciate it."

"Ah, Hannah, he's a wonderful boy. You've done a good job raising him. It is no hardship to spend time with him, trust me. I..." He was going to say something more, but then reconsidered. "Now, let's teach you to protect that boy."

Tuesday, September 17, 1861
Turner Home

My dearest Cousin Victoria   *September 1, 1861*

Life is so dull here in Fredericksburg since the war has begun. And to think, I believed it would be more exciting once we joined this rebellion. With Father and James gone, the running of the plantation has fallen to Mother, and the rest of us children. I fear things may get worse before they get better. I do hope this letter reaches you. I hear the mail service is dreadful, but writing is a good way to pass the time.

I dearly miss all of the men who are off fighting, especially our James. My siblings, niece and nephew continue to grow ever so fast. Elizabeth and her children come out to Turner's Glenn often.

I also write to Cousins Charlotte and Bekah, though again, I am not sure if they ever receive my missives. I have written Cousin Charlotte up in Gettysburg, but I am almost positive she will not receive the letters, with her being in the North and all. It seems unreal how our family has been torn apart by this war, especially our cousins in Petersburg. Uncle Samuel and Cousin Jonah remain on the Union side, while Cousin Jacob fights for the Confederacy. I do hope they can make amends when this is all over.

As I mentioned before, the monotony of my day-to-day life is only broken up with the thought of what happens after the war is over, which will be my marriage to the most wonderful of men. I know you are well-acquainted with this soldier, so I know you will wish me well..."

Victoria dropped the letter onto her lap. She couldn't read any more. Brianne looked up from her needlepoint.

"What's wrong?" She asked. "Has something happened to my father, Uncle Charles or Gregory?"

"No, no, nothing that serious." Victoria's voice was rough and she was trying not to sound emotional. *She's marrying Nathaniel. It has to be him she is writing about. Nathaniel is engaged to Belle.*

"Then what is wrong?"

Victoria shook her head. "This letter is from Cousin Belle. Apparently, she's engaged."

"Well, it's about time. Does she say to whom?"

"She doesn't come right out and say it; apparently there was an earlier letter that I never received, but the words she uses...I believe Nathaniel Prentiss is her future husband."

"Your Nathaniel Prentiss?" Brianne gave her cousin a doubting look. "Come now, Victoria, Belle Turner would never marry a common farmer, especially after all her cutting words to her sister, Elizabeth for marrying beneath her. Besides, you have no reason to be upset either way. You always insist that you and Mr. Prentiss are just friends. Furthermore, you are all but engaged to Jeremy Thompson. You have no claim to Mr. Prentiss."

"Oh, I know all that, Brianne. It's just a shock." *Then why does my stomach feel as though it's all tied in knots?*

Brianne gave Victoria a thoughtful look. "Is that really the truth? Your face tells me something else. You have deeper feelings for Mr. Prentiss than you let on, don't you?"

Victoria was going to deny the claim, then thought better of it. She had to tell someone of her feelings and Brianne would be a good person to talk with. The girl may appear to only enjoy parties, flirting and socializing, but Victoria knew that she was a wonderful listener.

"Oh, fiddlesticks, Brianne, I wish it wasn't true, but I admit, I do have feelings for him. I always have, to be honest. I thought, once upon a time, that he cared for me, or at least I thought he could, maybe in the future. When we were in Fredericksburg years ago for Elizabeth's wedding and I first met him, we connected in a way I never have with any other person. He was such a kind and interesting man. We wrote often after I returned home." Victoria thought about all of the letters that she still had and kept in her special drawer upstairs. "The last time we saw each other was two years ago. We attended a festive ball at Chatham Manor for his sister. We talked, we danced." Victoria warily looked toward the door. "We kissed."

"My goodness, do tell." A conspiratorial smile crept up Brianne's face. "How many people know that juicy tidbit?"

"You and Hannah are the only people that I have told, though I believe Jason suspects something and you'd better not tell anyone. We had such an enjoyable evening, but," she shook her head, "but the next day,

Nathaniel acted as though it never happened. I never understood why, but I feel as though it has something to do with his feelings for Belle."

"I wouldn't be so sure about that, and why is it that you keep going back to Belle?"

"Because why would anyone choose me over Belle?" Victoria knew she was being a bit too dramatic, but it felt good to speak her feelings aloud, even if they were unreasonable.

"Goodness gracious, Victoria Turner, if I said something like that, you would give me a slap right across the face." Brianne shook her head. "You know very well why someone would want to marry you. You have one of the most eligible men in Vicksburg wanting to propose to you for Heaven's sake."

Victoria couldn't stop the tears from welling up in her eyes. "Yes, and he hasn't written me in over a month." She admitted. Brianne stood and crossed the room and sat next to Victoria, putting a comforting arm around her.

"Is that what is really distressing you? The fact that your intended hasn't written you?"

"That is part of the problem, I must admit," Victoria said, "but there are so many issues I am dealing with, I just want to cry. I feel like those dramatic women who get the vapors and vex me so. Sometimes I wonder if I am making the right choice in regards to Mr. Thompson. Marriage is such an important decision, but...oh, Brianne, I just keep thinking about Father and Gregory and Jason and Abraham and all of our uncles and cousins, all of the men out there fighting. They are in so much danger. They could be wounded or killed. Sometimes, I fear the worst will happen. It is a lot to manage."

"Do you pray?" Brianne asked.

"I do," Victoria said with a short laugh. "I pray for our men every day and in regards to Mr. Thompson, I have asked God for a sign. I suppose this letter from Belle is just that. I can stop thinking that I may have any possibility of marrying Nathaniel Prentiss; he is with my cousin. I can put him out of my head and accept Mr. Thompson. This information is a sign."

"Well, I'm not convinced Belle's referring to Nathaniel Prentiss," Brianne said. "You're being silly, in my opinion, and I am still trying to decipher why you courted and all but accepted an offer of marriage from one man that you don't love while still holding a candle for another. To be honest, there could even be another man out there for you. Perhaps one you haven't even met yet." Brianne gave her an encouraging smile. "The comforting thing is that God knows, Victoria. He has His plans for you. We may not know the future, but He does and it will be better than we can imagine."

"My goodness, Brianne Marie Larson, when did you become so wise?" Victoria smiled.

"I've had good teachers," she replied with a smile. "Besides, it is a statement that I must remind myself of often."

Victoria felt a change of conversation was needed. "I assume you still haven't heard from your father?"

"No. And why should we? He hasn't cared about us in years, maybe ever. The man wants nothing to do with us; he never has. Poor Kendall still believes he cares, still holds up hope that he will come back for us." She scoffed and shook her head. "It must be nice to have the faith of a child in that respect. I gave up on him a long time ago."

"And yet, the fact that it still bothers you tells me that you do still care," Victoria said.

"Yes, well, Father could be dead for all we know," Brianne responded. "And we would never know the difference."

"Brianne..." Victoria started to speak. The young woman held up a hand.

"No, I've come to terms in regards to him. I really have. Kendall and I have been blessed to have the opportunity to live here with your family all these years. I would wager we've had a much better life living here in Vicksburg than my father could ever give us."

"Well, you do know that the two of you have become more like sisters to all of us, and you're right, our lives have been ever so much better with the two of you living here."

Tuesday, October 15, 1861
Turner Home

My dearest Cousin Victoria

I write you with the news that, if you haven't already heard, may be quite distressing to you. I recall you writing in a letter to me earlier this year that you were all but engaged to Mr. Jeremy Thompson. We just read an announcement in a paper from Richmond that Mr. Jeremy Thompson of Mississippi is engaged to Miss Genevieve Stephens, a distant cousin of our own Confederate Vice President Alexander Stephens. From what I understand, he has not hidden the fact that the match is very advantageous to his future political aspirations...

Victoria let the letter drop to her lap and looked at Mary Green, who had entered the parlor just as Victoria received the letter and had insisted that Victoria read it.

"Bad news?"

"That...that absolutely dastardly, deceptive lout! How could he..." Victoria didn't know whether to cry or be angry. She stood and threw the letter to Mary, who caught it on her lap and read it. Victoria stormed over to the window and glared out, arms crossed over her chest. How could Jeremy do this to her?

"Oh, Victoria, I am so sorry," Mary said.

"I just don't understand...Mary..." She turned back around. Her own feelings confused her. She felt more angry and deceived than anything. She did not feel as though she had just lost the love of her life, but that's how she should have felt.

Mary sipped her tea, then gently placed her cup back on the saucer and looked at Victoria. "If you ask me, this is a fortunate event. I must say, I never trusted that man," Mary said.

"Really, Mary? I...I wish you would have said something to me about it." Victoria wiped her tearful eyes with her handkerchief, angry with herself for even shedding one of them for the cad. "I am a flurry of feelings right now, but the one at the front of my mind...I can't believe I let him deceive me. I really believed that Mr. Thompson was the one, or maybe I just wanted to believe that he was interested in me."

"I did mention some of my opinions on him to you, Victoria. Unfortunately, you were so charmed by him and you wanted to be married and have a family so badly that you were blind to his flaws." Mary stood and crossed the room to stand next to Victoria. "Jeremy Thompson doesn't deserve a wife like you. If he'd rather marry some girl because she has more political connections, then good riddance to him. As I said, he wouldn't have been a good match for you."

"I suppose you're right." Victoria straightened up. "I should be grateful. He wasn't the one for me. I must remember that."

"Yes, you must."

"I suppose before making any further decision in my life, I should consult with you first and listen to your advice. You always know what to say and you're right, I wasn't listening."

"I have lived longer than you." Mary referred to the three-year difference between her and Victoria.

"Older and wiser, yes that must be it." Victoria quipped.

Mary glanced at the seat where her friend had been sitting when the conversation first began, before Dinah had interrupted with the mail. "By the way, who were you writing to when I came in?"

"Nathaniel Prentiss." Victoria sighed, trying to snap herself out of the doldrums. "I don't know if he even gets my letters, but writing to him always makes me feel better."

"Do you ever hear from him?" Mary asked.

"Rarely. The last news I heard was that he was going to enlist in the Army of Northern Virginia. I do hope he is safe. Virginia seems to be in the thick of the fighting much of the time, at least so far. Then, of course, there is the fact that I believe Nathaniel to be engaged to my cousin, Belle." Victoria quickly explained Belle's last letter. "I suppose I always knew that Nathaniel didn't like me as I liked him."

"You need to stop whining, my friend, or you will not even realize what God has planned for you. I have faith that all will work out for the best."

"That's what Brianne said as well. Thank you, Mary. I am lucky to have you as a friend."

"I am blessed to have you as well." Mary looked out the window, reflecting on her own worries. "You know, Victoria, there are many who don't approve of Duff because he refuses to fight for the Confederacy and has shown support for Union sympathizers. As his wife, I must support him, so they don't approve of me either."

"Mary, you know that I am one of those who take issue with Duff not fighting, however, I would never let that affect our friendship," Victoria replied. "Besides, your father is running for Confederate Congress. I know your family, including Duff, is loyal to Mississippi." She changed the subject. "How is your father's campaign going?"

"Fairly well, though Mr. Chambers is doing his very best to discredit my father." Mary shook her head. Henry Cousins Chambers was Mr. Lake's opposition in the Congressional race, and a politician that Jeremy Thompson had been working for. "Just because Father voted against secession back in January doesn't mean he won't support the Confederacy now."

"Well, if I had the ability, I would vote for him," Victoria said with a smile.

"I'll let him know that when he returns home."

"I hadn't heard he was out of town. Where is he?"

"He went to Arkansas, just across the river from Memphis," Mary responded. "Something to do with his campaign."

"Well, I wish him the best success," Victoria replied. "We need qualified men in the government as well as on the battlefield." *Like my Father and brothers.*

Before Victoria could say anything more, there was a knock and the door to the sitting room opened as Dinah entered.

"'Scuse me, Miss Turner, Missus Green. Mista Duff Green's here to see ya, Missus Green."

Right behind the slave was Mary's husband, Duff. He clasped his hat in one hand and ran the other through his brown hair.

"Duff, what on earth are you doing here?" Mary stood, concerned by the look she saw on her husband's face. For whatever reason he was here, it couldn't be good news. Victoria stood as well. Duff set his hat on a side table, then moved to embrace Mary.

"It's your father, my dear. I am afraid there is no easy way to tell you this, but...it seems the reason he went to Arkansas was not for political reasons. It was to defend his honor." He pulled back to look at her. "He challenged that hothead Mr. Chambers to a duel and I...I am sorry, Mary, but he was killed."

"Father...dead?" Mary's heart pounded and tears welled in her eyes. How could that be? She had dinner with him just last night. He was going to win the election and serve the Confederate States as a Representative in Richmond. "He cannot be dead, Duff, no." She pushed back from her husband and looked away.

"I am so sorry, my dear. I wish that I didn't have to give you this news." Duff pulled her back into his arms tightly. Victoria moved behind Mary and placed a comforting hand on her shoulder. She didn't know what to say to her friend. Words seemed inadequate for the news she was just given.

"Mother." Mary lifted her head from Duff's shoulder, her eyes red with tears. "I must go to her. Oh, Duff, how will Mother ever get through this?"

"With help from her family and the Lord." Duff replied, wiping a tear from his wife's cheek.

"I don't know what to say, Mary." Victoria was rarely at a loss for words. "Please, you must let me know if there is anything I can do for you."

"Of course. Thank you, Victoria." Mary nodded, and Duff escorted her out.

Victoria sat down, still shaken by her friend's tragedy. She knew men would die in the war, had tried to prepare herself for the possibility that her father or brothers may not come home, as difficult as that was. Many men had already died, especially during the Battle of Manassas back in July. However, Victoria had never expected Mary's father to be a casualty. A tear slipped down her own cheek, and she sent up a quick prayer for Mary's family, as well as her own. "Please, Lord, keep everyone in my family safe. Keep all those involved in this war safe." Then, almost as an afterthought. "Including Nathaniel, and yes, even that rake, Jeremy Thompson."

Sunday, December 15, 1861
Wheeler Farm

"I am delighted you all came for a visit." Cordelia Wheeler smiled as she continued to knead bread dough for biscuits. "I only wish we had more room." The Wheeler farmhouse was quite basic, and it was a tight squeeze for the two families.

"It is such a beautiful day. It almost feels like spring," Rachel replied. "It is so nice and warm, we could eat outside if we really wanted to."

"Can we, Gramma? That'd be fun!" Gabriel, Mary Grace's son, older than his brother Adam by minutes, pulled on Rachel's dress.

"Perhaps we could," Rachel replied.

"It is difficult to believe we will be celebrating our first Christmas as a Confederate nation," Victoria said. While Cordelia and Caroline prepared dinner, the others sat wherever there was room and worked on various sewing projects. Victoria looked at the socks she was knitting. She had hoped to finish them in time to send them out to her father for a Christmas gift, but had already found it necessary to unwind and restart the project multiple times. If only she were more patient.

"Our first Christmas without Uncle Charles, Abraham and Gregory," Kendall remarked. "At least Jason should be able to come and spend the holiday with us."

"Yes," Brianne said. "And even though many of our local men are gone, at least there will be other eligible young soldiers here to dance with at the annual Balfour Christmas Ball." The Confederacy had sent soldiers to garrison Vicksburg, knowing how important the city was in keeping control of the Mississippi River.

"That is true," Hannah said, pulling a needle and thread through a pair of Ambrose's torn pants.

"You really should attend the ball this year, Hannah." Rachel encouraged the young woman. "It is always a wonderful time."

"Perhaps," Hannah said.

"I personally cannot wait." Brianne exclaimed. This year would be her first opportunity to attend.

"Better you than me." Kendall rolled her eyes. Though the sisters were very good friends, the Larson girls were very different in many ways. Brianne loved the parties and socializing, Kendall preferred being outdoors and had an unquenchable thirst for adventure.

"Good afternoon everyone!" Jason walked through the front door, which had been left open to let a breeze in. "What are we discussing today?"

"Mr. Jason!" Ambrose ran to him.

"Uncle Jason!" Gabriel clumsily scampered right behind.

"I'm so glad you're here!" Ambrose exclaimed.

"We were discussing the Balfour ball and how Hannah should attend this year," Victoria said.

"I believe you should." Jason smiled at Hannah, then moved to hug his mother. "I always have a good time, and it would be even better with you in attendance."

"As I just said, perhaps I will." Hannah smiled.

"Jason, I didn't know you would be coming today," Rachel said.

"Your son is a tremendous help to us," Cordelia explained. "He knows he is always welcome. He comes to dinner most any Sunday that his patrols and duties permit."

"And any other day." Caroline smiled.

"Why don't you come and visit us that often?" Kendall asked.

"I visit all of you whenever I can, but you have Caesar to watch out for you in town." Jason replied.

"I suppose that's true," Kendall replied.

There was a knock on the doorframe and everyone looked up. Rachel shot to her feet when she saw who was there, and Mary Grace shrieked in happiness as three Confederate soldiers entered.

"Papa!" Gabriel ran to Abraham at the same time Gregory pulled his mother into his arms and Victoria hugged her father tightly.

"What are you all doing here?" Rachel turned to her husband and pulled him close.

"We are on furlough," Abraham explained. "We have two weeks at home before we have to head back."

"So you will be home for Christmas!" Kendall smiled.

"Indeed we will." Charles Turner kissed his wife's head. "And a Merry Christmas it will be." He nodded to Cordelia. "Mrs. Wheeler, we would like to apologize for intruding. We returned to town and learned from Esther that everyone was out here for the day."

"Mr. Turner, it is no intrusion at all. It is our honor to host three more Confederate soldiers." She smiled, then turned to speak quietly to Caroline, who nodded and headed out towards the barn.

"Are you sure you will have enough food to feed us too?" Gregory asked.

"Food will not be an issue, Mr. Turner. Space, on the other hand..."

"We really need to eat outside now. Gabriel will get his wish." Rachel laughed.

"A picnic in December." Charles smiled. "That sounds just splendid."

Part 2:
1862

Wednesday, February 19, 1862
Green Home

"It sounds as though the war is moving at a snail's pace in the east." Victoria moved her needle in and out of the dress she was mending. The war had made it necessary for the Turner women to live a bit more frugally. The fact that her father wasn't bringing in an income with his law practice affected the family, as well as the threat of a Union blockade, which had caused the price of goods in the shops to rise. Many people believed the economy would get worse before the war was over. Women all over the South were wearing out-of-date clothing and doing what they could to support the war effort.

"I would rather have the war go on slowly than to hear of battle casualties every other day." Mary Grace was mending one of Gabriel's shirts. The boy had torn off most of the sleeve while trying to climb a tree. He loved being outdoors, even at the young age of three, which was the direct opposite of his twin, Adam. Poor Adam had been sickly since birth and spent most of his time resting indoors.

"It's nice to know that many people in Vicksburg are doing their part to raise funds to support our boys in gray," Mary Green said.

"Yes, I had heard that Duff wants to donate much of the iron railing from your porch to the cause," Victoria said.

"That is true," Mary replied. "In spite of what many think, he does want to support our Confederate soldiers."

"Oh, Mary, everyone who matters knows that," Mary Grace said, "but did anyone hear the latest news from the western front?"

"Do you mean the news about that bulldog Union General Grant, capturing some of our forts over in Tennessee?" Victoria shook her head. "It will be disastrous for the Confederacy if he continues to win battles as he has done so."

"Oh, our militia and guards here won't let anything befall us," Mary Grace said. "We'll be just fine."

"I know it's a sore subject, Victoria, but I must ask how you've been fairing." Mary Green asked. "In regards to Mr. Thompson, that is. We haven't really been able to speak of the situation since the day you received the letter about his nuptials. There always seems to be other people around, and I know you'll only be honest with Mary Grace and myself, and Hannah, of course."

"I have come to the conclusion that, as painful as it is, it worked out for the best. As you said, it's better that I discovered the man's true character before marrying him," Victoria replied. "I suppose I didn't bring it up because the day I realized Mr. Thompson's true character is the same day your father died. I didn't want to dredge up those memories."

"That is considerate of you." Mary took a deep breath. "Christmas was difficult without Father. The younger children imagined that he was just gone for the holiday as were many other fathers, yet we all knew deep down that he will never come home. I must admit, even all these months later, it still seems so senseless. I do not understand why father felt the need to duel with that man."

"Oh, Mary, you shouldn't try to figure that out. We will never understand." Mary Grace sighed. "Why is it that some men feel the only way to restore or protect their honor is by dueling?"

"Heaven forbid honor and prestige are what's most important to men," Victoria muttered. "I suppose that...well, looking back on the many interactions I had with Mr. Thompson, I should have foreseen the type of man he was. Or at least recognized what he was looking for in a woman." She shook her head. "I'm sorry, Mary, I didn't mean to divert the conversation back to my issues."

"Don't worry about it, Victoria. I understand. I am the one that brought the subject up in the first place, after all. We all have our worries and we must talk about them."

"That is why we must continue to meet as we are now," Mary Grace said.

"Yes," Victoria agreed. "We can get through anything together."

Tuesday, April 8, 1862
Turner Home

Victoria and Kendall sat on the front porch in the warm spring air. Kendall was reading Daniel Defoe's *Robinson Crusoe* while Victoria read the Vicksburg *Daily Citizen*. Rachel had gone to help Mary Grace at the haberdashery and Brianne was visiting friends.

"Is there anything pressing in the news today?" Kendall asked, looking up from her book.

"Unfortunately, there is a bloody battle going on right now," Victoria replied. "Not even 200 miles away in Tennessee. The Yankee General Grant against our Johnston and Beauregard. It started Sunday and may even continue today, I am not sure."

"Where exactly in Tennessee?" Kendall asked.

"Hardin County, a place called Pittsburg Landing, near Shiloh."

"That's not far away at all," Kendall said. "Do you think the Yankees will head here next?"

"They will surely try." Victoria sighed, then stood when a familiar rider approached.

"Here comes Jason. He may know more about the battle."

"Victoria, Kendall!" He pulled up and tethered his horse. "Where is everyone else?"

Victoria quickly told him. "What is the news from Tennessee? I was just reading about the battle over at Pittsburg Landing. Is it over?"

"The battle is, yes," Jason replied. "So much blood shed, so many lives destroyed, all for nothing. We lost the battle in the end. This General Grant they have is quite the fighter." He rubbed his chin. "However, the work here in Vicksburg will just be starting."

"What do you mean?" Kendall asked.

"Trains full of wounded are arriving as we speak. The hospitals will soon be filled with soldiers."

"Here? In Vicksburg?" Victoria asked. "Why here?"

"We're relatively close to the battlefield and our train system is still running. We have the necessary quarters, and we've yet to be terribly affected by the war." He sighed. "I heard there are over 8,000 wounded men from each side."

"How can we do this to each other?" Kendall asked quietly. Jason pulled her into a comforting hug.

"I'm not sure, Kendall, but we'll get through it."

"You say that the trains with wounded are here?" Victoria glanced down toward the train station. She had heard one pull in earlier, the clacking of the wheels on the track, the vibration of the earth and the whistle of the train. She loved the sound of the train whistle, like a forlorn call in the night. She hadn't realized what this train was bringing into town, though.

"Yes, they are bringing the wounded to the hospital now. Trains will bring more soldiers, I am sure, soon the hospital will be filled to overflowing. We may have to find other lodging for the wounded," Jason replied.

"And they will need help with the wounded as well," Victoria replied. "I'll head down and offer my services."

"I'll come with you," Kendall said.

"Hold on, young lady. I don't think so." Jason shook his head. "Nor do I think it's a good idea for you either, Victoria. Some of the men, well, it will be quite gruesome and they are in a lot of pain. I don't want either of you exposed to that. You are young and innocent. At least wait until the administrators of the hospital can get things established." He gave Victoria a pleading look. "Please, trust me, Victoria. Just wait."

Victoria took a deep breath. "All right, Jason, but I mean to help where I can. I am quite capable of handling much more than you know."

"I am sure you can, but again, just trust me for now." He sighed. "I am sure you will get plenty of opportunities to help." He rubbed his chin again. "Kendall, would you mind going to Mary Grace's, tell Mother the news and that I'm here? I would really appreciate it."

"Of course, Jason," Kendall quickly left.

Victoria looked at her brother, recognizing the fact that Jason had sent Kendall away so she wouldn't hear their conversation. He strode to one of the chairs and sat.

"What is wrong, Jason?" Victoria sat next to him.

"General Johnston was badly wounded and is not expected to live. It is a huge loss for us, even if he survives." He leaned forward and clasped his hands together.

"That may be true, but that cannot be all that's upset you," Victoria insisted.

"You know me too well," He said with a sigh. "I have been in the militia for...quite some time now. I have done my part and have had to shoot before. But so far, I have been able to stay clear of the actual fighting. Today...this was the first time I have seen the result of a battle. The blood. The cries of pain. The mangled bodies. Victoria, its...it was almost too much for me. I'm not sure...I know you are a strong woman, but I wouldn't want anyone to see that horror." He stared ahead. "Fighting for States' Rights sounded so noble, so idealistic a year ago. Now I'm not so sure."

"You're not thinking of leaving the militia, are you?" Victoria asked.

"No, no, not at all. I gave my word, and my primary intent has always been to protect my family here in Vicksburg. I will continue to do so."

"That is what I thought you would say," Victoria said. "You're much too honorable to just up and quit."

"Thank you for saying that. I am grateful for your faith in me." Jason took another deep breath and stood when he saw his mother approach. "And always remember how much I love and appreciate you."

Saturday, April 26, 1862
St. Xavier Hospital

"Miss Turner!"

Victoria turned and saw her friend Mahala Roach walking toward her. She looked back and smiled at the patient she had been feeding broth to. She had been helping at the hospital for the past week but had been kept away from many of the more seriously injured patients. Many large buildings in the city had been taken over, along with a few private residences to be used as hospitals now. Mahala's mother, Elizabeth Eggleston had organized the Ladies Hospital Association to coordinate help with the wounded.

"Yes, Mahala, how may I help you?"

"When you have a moment, a young soldier has requested some help writing a letter home. The poor man has been wounded in the arm and hand and cannot hold a pencil at present."

"I am finished here, show me the way." Victoria stood and followed the woman into another crowded room.

"It is such a sad sight to see, all of the wounded filling our hospitals to overflowing," Mahala said. "It makes one realize that the war is indeed near us."

Shaking her head, Victoria agreed. "Many of the men in town have been preparing lots in the Cedar Hill Cemetery for burial of our deceased soldiers. It is only fitting."

"The men who made the ultimate sacrifice for us deserve no less," Mahala said.

"I agree wholeheartedly," Victoria replied. The two women approached the young soldier who needed the letter written.

"Lieutenant Young, this is Miss Turner. She is more than happy to write that letter for you."

"Yes, sir." Victoria smiled, picking up the paper, pencil and book sitting next to the bed to write on. "So, Lieutenant Young, how are you feeling today? Who will you be writing to?"

"I'm fairly well, ma'am, and I'd like to write to my sister. I need to let her know I'm all right, but I really need to tell her about the Angel's Glow. She needs to hear about it."

"Angel's Glow?" Victoria had heard murmurings of the strange phenomenon, but had yet to meet anyone who had actually witnessed it.

"Yes, ma'am. The fighting was quite furious at Shiloh, and those of us who were wounded and those dying on the first day were left out there on the battlefield. There was no break in the fighting, no time for us to get help. Many of us were left for days, on account of the lack of medical services and the fact that they just weren't prepared to help so many wounded. It was even raining at times, so we were lying in mud and foul water part of the time."

"My goodness, that sounds positively miserable." Victoria's stomach sank at the thought. How could any man survive that? "Is that where the Angel's Glow occurred?"

"Yes, ma'am. It was the strangest yet most magnificent thing I have ever seen. As we lay there that night, trying to imagine happier times instead of the pain we were in, I looked down at my arm, which I knew had a wide-gaping wound, and I find the darn gash glowing. A spooky, greenish-blue glow. I wouldn't have believed it if I hadn't seen it myself."

"Incredible." Victoria wished she could have seen it.

"Even more incredible, ma'am, is that one of the doctors told me here in the hospital that those of us that had the glowing wounds, strange as it sounds, are faring much better than the soldiers that didn't have the glow."

"Well now, that is quite curious." Victoria's inquiring mind desperately wanted to know everything about this marvel. What caused the glow? Was there a correlation between the glowing wounds and lack of infection, or was it just a coincidence? "Hopefully the doctors will discover what happened to cause the glowing and perhaps will use that information to help future patients."

"Wouldn't that be grand?" The Lieutenant smiled.

"That is such a fascinating story. I appreciate you telling me all the details."

"Of course, Ma'am, and I am glad you took time from your busy schedule to talk with me."

"That is no inconvenience at all." Victoria smiled. "Now, let's get a letter to your sister."

Duff entered the parlor of his home and smiled when he saw Mary, dozing in one of the chairs with Annie napping in her arms. He crossed the room and sat in the settee next to them. Mary sleepily opened her eyes and smiled at her husband.

"How were things down at the docks today?" She asked quietly.

"As good as they can be," He gave her a quick kiss on the forehead. "Unfortunately, this war is moving quite close to Vicksburg."

"Closer than Pittsburg Landing?" Mary asked.

"I would say so. That Union Admiral David Farragut's fleet has made a move to take forts in Jackson and St. Philip. They defeated our Southern forces there. That was all several days ago and I just heard word that New Orleans has fallen."

"Oh my goodness." Mary shifted underneath the weight of Annie. "Is that why the soldiers here seem to be preparing for something important these past few days?"

"Yes. Captain Harris, the Chief Engineer stationed here, along with Colonel Autry, our military commander here in town, are building more fortifications, mostly on the bluffs north of town."

Mary was quiet a moment, thinking. "New Orleans...that's not such a long ways away, is it?"

"About five days by river." Duff's reply was quiet. "Not only that, but there is very little along the way from New Orleans to Vicksburg to stop the Federals or even slow them down."

Mary sighed. "What are people in town going to do?"

"This turn of events is making many people nervous. Some are talking of leaving the city to stay with family or friends. Some say they will simply camp out in the woods, far from the danger on the riverfront. Merchants are closing up shop and packing their goods away." Duff sighed and rubbed his chin. "The most unfortunate thing, in my opinion, is the rumor that the Confederate government may order the farmers and planters to burn their cotton stores."

"Heavens! That's their livelihood! Why would our own government do such a thing?"

"So our goods don't fall into the hands of the Federals. I know it may seem wasteful, but sometimes we have to do what needs to be done."

"What will the planters do for money if they can't sell their cotton?"

"I am certain all will work out for the best, my dear," Duff replied. "We'll just have to help the folks as best we can."

Mary glanced at one of their servants, Bernice, and beckoned her over. "Would you take Annie to her room, please?"

The woman nodded and took Annie into her arms. "Yes, ma'am."

As soon as they were out of the room, Mary stood and moved to sit close to her husband. She took his hand in hers.

"Duff, my dear, I know you keep much of the news you hear to yourself, but I must say, I am so thankful when you share the details with me, like you did today."

"I only wish I didn't have any bad news to share with you at all." Duff squeezed her hand. "I wish I could guarantee your safety and security for the rest of our days and guarantee that for our children as well."

"I know that. You are a wonderful father and husband and you are a fine protector and provider." She cupped his cheek and met his kind, brown eyes. "Annie and I are so lucky to have you." Tears formed in her eyes at the memory of their first child, her other Annie. The delightful child who had died of scarlet fever back in '59. One of the tears slipped down Mary's cheek. Duff reached up and brushed it away with his thumb.

"It wasn't your fault, Mary." Duff spoke softly. He knew her all too well, had realized what she was thinking. Though it had been three years, Mary still felt partly responsible. Annie had been her daughter, placed in her care. It had been her job to keep the child safe and she had failed.

Mary shook her head. "I thank you for saying that, Duff. However, as you well know, I don't believe that most days. There had to have been more that I could have done..."

"No. Mary, as hard as it is to accept at times, children do die, people die. There isn't always an explanation. I know you realize that."

"I do. Truly. We have spoken on this matter many times. It's just...I still miss her so. Not a day goes by that I don't wonder what she would be like if she had lived."

"I do as well." Duff confessed. "Every day. But we were blessed to have her in our lives for those three years, and we have her sister, and God willing, we will have more children. I know it will never stop the hurt completely, but we will continue on. As we have been."

"Yes. As long as we're together, with the help of the Lord."

Sunday, May 18, 1862
Turner Home

"'*For I know the plans I have for you.' says the Lord. 'Plans to give you hope and a future.'*" Victoria read the pages of the family's well-worn Bible. It had been too long since she had simply sat and read Scripture. She sighed, then turned to look out over the Mississippi River. She was sitting in one of her favorite spots, the back porch of her family home. It had a wonderful view of the moving waters. "I need to remember this verse. Every day I need to remember these words." She stood and went inside to locate her journal that she knew she left in the parlor.

"When will your plans for me come through, Lord? I am waiting." She sighed again and sat down.

"Talkin' to yo' self agin, Miss Victoria?" Esther, who spent most of her time in the Turner's kitchen, came into the room. "One o deese days, yo gonna start ans'ring yo'self an I'm really go'n start worryin' 'bout you." As always, Victoria, appreciated Esther. Though Esther was only a slave, Victoria considered her a friend and confidant.

"No, Esther, never worry about me. I'll never marry and I will live here in my parents' home until the day I die." Victoria quipped.

"Ah, Miss Victoria, you know 'dat ain' true." Esther said. "Yo will fin' someone. Da Lord has plans for ya, honey chile. I neva did think to find me a good man, an' den I find my Caesar."

Caesar, another slave in the Turner household was obviously devoted to Esther.

"Thank you, Esther. I was just reading those same words." Victoria closed the Bible and smiled. "What can I help you with?"

"Mrs. Green, Mrs. Wheeler and each o' dere yung'uns are all here to see you. Can I bring dem in to ya?"

Victoria nodded, sat down and closed her eyes.

"Victoria, are you awake?"

Victoria quickly stood and smiled as her friends entered the room. "Mary! Hannah! It's so nice to see you. Where are the children?"

"Your mother took them." Hannah flipped her braid over her shoulder. "The children just adore her, and she appears to enjoy spending time with them."

"She is another grandmother to them," Mary added.

"I can believe that." Victoria knew how much her mother loved children. "How are you ladies?"

"Despite all of the excitement in town, I am doing quite well." Mary took the seat that was offered. For weeks, there had been an increased Confederate presence, more men guarding the city of Vicksburg in light of rumors that the Union Navy was moving to take the city.

"Since the beginning of the war, we have known that Vicksburg would be a Yankee target," Victoria reminded them.

"As long as our Confederate soldiers are stationed here, I have no fears," Mary replied.

"I have every confidence they will protect us as well," Hannah said. "The militia is protecting us out in the countryside. It is nice to have Jason keeping an eye on things."

Victoria opened her mouth to make a teasing comment about Jason to Hannah when the door swung open and Victoria's cousin, Brianne hastened in.

"Oh, hello, Mrs. Green, Mrs. Wheeler" The young woman pushed a light brown strand of hair from her cheek. "My apologies, Victoria, I didn't know you had company."

"What has you so excited, Brianne?" Victoria asked.

"There are Union Naval ships coming up the river," Brianne couldn't contain her excitement as she sat on the chaise lounge with confidence and leaned forward. "They say a Yankee commander by the name of Lee, who just happens to be the cousin of our own dear General Robert Lee, has dropped anchor right in front of the city. He sent a message to the leaders demanding our surrender." As usual, Brianne had a flair for the dramatics.

"Good heavens." Mary put a hand to her throat.

"What was Mayor Lindsey's reply?" Victoria asked, hoping the leader of the city would make a prudent decision.

"I don't think he has responded yet, but I am quite sure he will deny their request." Brianne replied. "I doubt Lieutenant Colonel Autry or General Smith will give in either. They both received messages as well."

Lieutenant Colonel James Autry was the Confederate military governor of Vicksburg, while General Martin Smith was the commander of the Confederate forces defending the city.

"I agree with you, Brianne, and three negative responses should be enough to send those Yankees back to New Orleans," Victoria said.

"I do hope they leave peacefully and don't decide to fight for the city," Hannah replied.

"I don't know, Mrs. Wheeler," Brianne replied. "We may finally see some action here."

"Vicksburg will be too difficult for the Union to take over due to its strategic location. You know as well as I do that many generals and leaders on both sides have called our town the key to the Confederacy." Victoria almost sounded like a book. "It's been that way since the beginning of the war."

"But why is that?" Brianne asked.

"Well, control of the Mississippi River is imperative to the Union's success of their so-called 'Anaconda Plan'." Victoria's love of history and current affairs was apparent when talk turned to war. "When you think about that, it makes sense. If we, the Confederates, have control of the river, we can block Union navigation while allowing Confederate navigation, as well as communication with states to the West. We really depend on those states for horses, cattle and reinforcements, not to mention every day supplies. Vicksburg's natural defenses are ideal. In fact, they are calling us the 'Gibraltar of the Confederacy'."

"What on earth is a Gibraltar?" Mary knew that Victoria would have the answer.

"The term comes from the Greek tale of Hercules. The Gibraltar is a towering rock formation at the entrance to the Mediterranean Sea. It protected the sea."

"Only you would know that information, Victoria." Brianne jested.

"I can't help that I enjoy reading and learning," Victoria smiled. "The legend of Hercules is one of my favorites."

"How many favorites do you have?" Hannah smiled.

"Too many," Brianne laughed.

"There is no such a thing as too many favorite characters or books or stories or any of the sort," Victoria retorted.

"Well, I for one, hope our stories will not include a great and terrible battle," Mary stated.

"I hope you're right, Mary," Hannah said. "I do hope you're right."

Wednesday, May 21, 1862
Turner Home
Victoria sat down to write a long overdue letter to her cousin Elizabeth. Of all her cousins, Victoria admired Elizabeth the most. She was kind, had an unwavering devotion to God, and had a wonderful husband with adorable children.

My Dear Elizabeth,

I hope everything is well for you and your family. We heard that Fredericksburg is under Yankee control at this time, so I am not sure you will even receive this letter. I haven't heard from you since the beginning of the war and continue to worry about all of you. I received a letter from Belle, but that was months ago. By now, I expect your sister is Mrs. Nathaniel Prentiss, or at least getting quite close, based on what she said in the letter I received. You must give her my congratulations. Such happy news, and I know they will be a wonderful couple.

Vicksburg has changed so much since the last time I wrote, as I am sure Fredericksburg has. My goodness, I can't imagine how much you have had to endure! You may have heard that the Yankees are trying to get control of Vicksburg; perhaps you have only heard about it from their perspective. I think it would be interesting to know the Union's outlook of the battles. They say that General Grant has surrounded our city, but so far, little has changed in our day-to-day living. I am confident our boys will hold them off and we will be victorious...

BOOM! An explosion erupted from the direction of the river. It startled Victoria, who smudged the ink on the letter. She immediately stood and hastened to the front of the house. Kendall met Victoria on the porch. Excitement danced in her bright brown eyes.

"What in the world is going on?" Victoria looked down toward the river.

"Victoria, I think we're being attacked!" Kendall could not contain her enthusiasm. "The Yankees are trying to take the city by way of the river."

"They'll never be able to get control of the town." Victoria watched as people ran toward the waterfront and Sky Parlor Hill. It held the perfect vantage point to see what was going on in the river below and was often where people congregated. Both soldiers and civilians raced to see what was happening. There was another explosion from the river. Kendall, always ready for adventure, rushed toward the steps.

"Where do you think you are going, young lady?" Victoria grabbed her younger cousin's arm.

"With everyone else. You know Sky Parlor Hill has the best view of the river. Whatever there is to see, we'll see from there. Come, let's go." Kendall gently pulled her arm away.

"It may not be that safe, Kendall," Victoria said, though she secretly wanted to go and investigate as well.

"Oh, come now, Victoria. We'll be fine. Don't you someday want to be able to tell your children that you watched the Yankees try and fail to take Vicksburg?" Kendall placed a hand on Victoria's arm and gave her a tug.

"I must remain alive to mother children first," Victoria countered. "I cannot do that if I'm killed trying to watch the event."

"Well, I'm going to watch and, not to be disrespectful, there is not much you can do to stop me." Kendall turned. "However, if you're that concerned about my safety, just come with me."

Victoria sighed and followed the girl. As they hurried toward the hill, Victoria could hear bits of conversation.

"Grant's surrounding the city…"

"…move to the outskirts…"

"…trying to take the city for the Yankees."

Victoria groaned as they continued toward the hill. It did not look good for the city of Vicksburg.

"Mr. Shannon!" As they reached the top of the hill, Victoria spotted her father's good friend and newspaperman, Marmaduke Shannon.

"Miss Turner! Young Miss Larson, what are you two doing up here?"

"We wanted to see the fighting!" Kendall exclaimed as a shell hit the ground way below the hill. The Yankees' cannon shot weren't even close to the town from so far below. The hills of Vicksburg stood strong. Shots were now fired from the Confederate batteries towards the Federal boats.

"I see." Mr. Shannon nodded. "Well, you should be safe all the way up here."

"Do you know what is going on, Mr. Shannon?" Victoria asked.

"The Yankee Admiral Farragut is heading upriver after his capture of New Orleans. He is clearly trying to control the entire Mississippi, and his ships are putting up a good fight, but it will all be in vain here. The hills of Vicksburg are just too high and we are well-defended." He gestured to the boats down below. "As you can see."

"Indeed." Kendall said. "They'll never take our city."

"I believe you're right, Miss Larson." Mr. Shannon said.

It was only late afternoon when Victoria and Kendall returned to the Turner home. The attack hadn't lasted long.

"Where have you two been? I have been worried sick." Rachel asked in a concerned tone. Mary Grace entered the foyer with Hope in her arms.

"Mary Grace!" Victoria said. "What brings you here?"

"Aunt Victoria!" Gabriel ran in and hugged Victoria's legs.

"Gabriel, I am so happy to see you." Victoria bent down and picked up her nephew in a big hug. "Where is your brother?"

"He's upstairs resting, but Victoria Grace Turner, you stop trying to avoid my questions." Rachel put her hands on her hips. "You two owe me an explanation right now."

"We went to Sky Parlor to see the Union ships," Kendall told her. "It was quite a sight, Aunt Rachel."

"And quite dangerous. Dangerous and foolish." Mary Grace spoke up. "Victoria, how could you take such a risk, much less allow Kendall to accompany you?"

"I'm sorry, truly I am, but everyone was just so full of excitement. I just got carried away." Victoria held her hands up in surrender.

"It's my fault, Aunt Rachel," Kendall explained. "Victoria didn't want either of us to go, but I didn't give her much of a choice. I'm sorry to have worried you."

"I suppose there was no harm done, but the two of you must be more careful, "Rachel said. "The rumors persist that the Yankees are all around us and will likely be present for a while. I spoke with Jason, who told me it may be best for us all to get out of town."

"Jason was here? I missed him?" Victoria was disappointed at the news of missing her brother.

"If you had been here and not on the hill, you wouldn't have missed him." Mary Grace pointed out.

"Where did he go? When will he be back? Where did he suggest we go?" Victoria asked.

"One question at a time," Mary Grace stated. "He rode out to the Wheelers to speak with Hannah and Cordelia. He believes their home will be a safe place for us to stay. Their house isn't very big, though, so he wanted to check with them."

"If that's what Jason thinks is best, then that is what we will do," Victoria said. "The farm house will be crowded, but at least we have someone we can stay with. Are other families moving out of town?"

"According to Jason, yes," Rachel replied. "The Yankees want the town, and they want it badly, but they are ignoring the farms surrounding the city, at least for now. Our army will defend Vicksburg to the end."

"And I know they will be successful," Victoria replied.

Monday, June 9, 1862
Wheeler Farm

"I do wish we could have gone into town yesterday, if for no other reason than to attend church." Hannah said, placing a basket of laundry next to Victoria's seat and pushing a strand of brown hair from her face. It had been almost two weeks since the Turners had moved out to the Wheeler farm.

"Yes, that would have been a nice change of pace. I wonder if they're even holding services during the artillery bombardment." Victoria pulled a damp shirt of Ambrose's out of the basket and hung it on the clothesline.

Helping the Wheelers with chores was the least the Turners could do, even if they weren't good at it. The two families were quite crowded in the four-bedroom farmhouse. Ambrose, had eagerly welcomed the twins into his room. Cordelia Wheeler and Rachel shared the master bedroom. Hope, Victoria and Mary Grace stayed with Hannah in her room, and in the last bedroom, Cordelia's daughter, Caroline, had welcomed Brianne and Kendall. Esther, Caesar and Dinah, the Turner slaves, stayed in town to watch over the house.

"I'm sure Jason will let us know when it is safe to travel again." Victoria added.

"Yes, I must say, he is quite diligent when it comes to checking up on us." Hannah smiled. "Between your brother and Old Man Wagner, I feel quite protected." She straightened as a familiar militia man rode up. "And speaking of protectors…"

"Jason!" Victoria smiled and waved to her brother, who waved back. He pulled his horse up next to them and dismounted.

"Ladies, your beauty is a sight for sore eyes." He hugged Victoria and took Hannah's hand in a brief squeeze.

"Are the Yankees gone? Can we return home?" As much as Victoria loved spending time with the Wheelers, she really wanted to go back home. "Do you have news from town? How are Mary and little Annie?"

"My goodness, Victoria, one question at a time." Jason pulled a log over and sat down. "I believe I remember them all, however. The Yanks aren't quite gone yet. Hopefully within the next few weeks, so you shouldn't move back home quite yet." He pretended to think. "There's not much news from town. We are in much the same situation as we were when you came out here, but, I did visit with the Green family yesterday and they are doing as well as can be expected, all things considered. Duff still refuses to leave town, but I suppose that is his choice." He shrugged.

"Is there any other news about the war?" Hannah asked.

"A few things," Jason replied. "Our army evacuated a place called Fort Pillow in Northern Tennessee. That is a harsh loss, and now the Yankees occupy Memphis after a big battle there. However, back east, Virginia's Robert E. Lee replaced Joe Johnston as the commander of the Army of Northern Virginia."

"Is that a good thing?" Victoria asked.

"Lee is the very best of soldiers," Jason replied. "In fact, Lincoln offered Lee command of the Union Army, which thankfully the man turned down. Lee said he couldn't fight against his home state of Virginia, so when they seceded, he became loyal to the Confederacy."

"Many Mississippians had the same dilemma," Victoria said. "Such as present company."

"Yes. I still don't agree with secession, but the Yankees are down here, threatening our homes, our families and our friends." Jason glanced at Hannah. "All people that I would give my life to protect. Father and Gregory felt the same way."

"I wonder what Benjamin would have chosen to do," Hannah commented. "He was against slavery and was against secession as well. However, he was quite fierce when it came to protecting his family."

"Yes, most protective," Jason agreed. Benjamin Wheeler was a principled man who was devoted to his family. Jason felt lucky to call him a friend, and still felt the loss every day.

Rachel and Cordelia Wheeler exited the house, followed by Ambrose.

"Mr. Jason!" Ambrose ran to the soldier, who picked him up, smiled and greeted him.

"Ambrose! How is my favorite seven-year-old?"

"I'm doing good. Gabe and Adam are sharing a room with me, so it's a bit crowded, but we're havin' fun."

"It's very good of you to let them stay," Jason said. "I appreciate the welcome you have given to my family."

"I know, but it's like Mama and Gramma say. Jesus told us to welcome the stranger, so we are, even though your family is not really strangers, but I still think it's a good thing. We have room, and they need a place to stay. It's the right thing to do."

"Yes, it is. Your Mama is teaching you well." Jason's affection for Ambrose was obvious.

"Yeah, and Gramma and Caroline too."

"It takes many people to raise a child." Hannah smiled and placed a hand on her son's blonde head.

"Jason, how are things in town?" Rachel asked.

As Jason repeated his update to the older women, Victoria and Hannah excused themselves and went inside.

"I know we're crowded in here and it's terribly inconvenient for you, but it is rather nice having all of you around." Hannah said.

"We can't express enough how much we appreciate your hospitality," Victoria replied. "I know we're not very adept at it, but helping with chores is even kind of fun."

"Yes, doing chores is much nicer with someone to talk to."

"I agree wholeheartedly," Victoria smiled. "I must say though, I am looking forward to getting home. There is nothing quite like sleeping in your own bed."

"That is true." Hannah smiled. "But as long as it is safer here, then this is where you will stay."

"I do wish that Duff Green wouldn't be so stubborn. Lord knows it is safer outside the city. Jason says many people are simply camped out in the woods."

"I'm sure he has his reasons, Victoria," Hannah said.

"Yes, just as he has his reasons for not enlisting." Victoria scoffed.

"Yes, just as he has his reasons for not enlisting." Hannah replied. "Just as your father and brothers had their reason for fighting. Don't be so judgmental, Victoria, many men have their own reasons for not fighting."

"Oh, I realize that." Victoria sighed. "I don't know why it bothers me so, I know it shouldn't, but it does. I just wish this vexing war would be over and things could go back to normal."

"I know what you mean," Hannah said. "We are slightly inconvenienced, but really, little has changed for us, yet the threat of battle and real hardship looms large."

"Indeed. It's like a subdued tension, always waiting for something to happen."

"Yes, that is a good way to describe my feelings." Hannah nodded.

Sunday, June 14, 1862
Norton Farm
Muskegon County, Michigan

Tabetha Norton walked up the porch steps of her family's two-story farmhouse. It was midday, but breezy, and she had to re-braid her dark-red hair that had become askew.

"Do you know what Mother and Father want?" She asked when she saw her younger brother, Michael, come around the side of the house. "Father waved me in from the pasture."

"I dunno," Michael replied. "I was down by the creek and saw Mr. Obenauf ride up. I figured there was a letter from Adam."

"I hadn't considered that," Tabetha replied. Her brother Adam, older than her by only ten months, had enlisted in the Third Michigan Regiment out of nearby Grand Rapids. Her brother hadn't wanted to join the army at first, but she had talked him into it. Hopefully, Mr. Obenauf did carry a letter from Adam, detailing his heroics on the battlefield. She was so sure her brother would become a great soldier.

Tabetha entered the family sitting room to see that her entire family had gathered. Her mother, father, three sisters and now Michael and herself. She immediately noticed her father's stoic expression and her mother's red-rimmed eyes.

"What's wrong?" Tabetha asked, nervous as to what the answer would be.

"Have a seat, Tabetha," Her father responded. Not wanting to disobey, she quickly complied.

"We received a letter today," Her father began to speak.

"Was it from Adam?" Amanda, Tabetha's sister asked.

"No," Tabetha could tell that her father was trying not to show his emotions, which really worried her. "It is from a young soldier who knew your brother at the Michigan Agricultural College. A Mr. James Spencer."

"I recall Adam speaking of a James Spencer. He was a year above Adam," Tabetha said. Her brother had told her that the man would be a good match for her. She had shrugged his suggestion off, not interested at the time.

"Mr. Spencer wrote to tell us that...tragically...Adam was struck in the chest with shrapnel, at a Battle near Seven Pines in Virginia. He died instantly."

"What?"

"NO!"

"That cannot be!"

"Not Adam, no!"

The sound of cries from her siblings was great and deafening. Pain shot through Tabetha's own chest. Adam couldn't be dead. He wasn't dead. He was her brother, her best friend. "It's all my fault," she cried. "He didn't want to enlist, he wasn't even going to, but I made him."

"Tabetha, dear, you didn't make Adam do anything," Her mother tried to assure her. "He made the decision himself. This is in no way your fault."

Tabetha shook her head. Her mother would say that to her, would try and make her feel better, but what her mother said just wasn't true. If Tabetha hadn't pressured Adam, he wouldn't have gone, wouldn't have died. She knew that much. Her brother was dead and it was all her fault.

"Excuse me." She stood and fled to the barn.

Usually, the barn was Tabetha's place of solace, where she could go, spend time with her horse, Ranger, and read. The smell of fresh hay always calmed her down. She had so many meaningful conversations with her brother out here as well, including the conversation where she had convinced him to go off to his death. When news came that the United States was now at war, Adam had told her that he didn't intend to fight. If she hadn't pressured him, he would be here now, safe and secure. It didn't matter what anyone in her family said, she knew that she was responsible for his death. Nothing could convince her otherwise.

"How will I ever make up for this?" Tabetha stroked Ranger's neck, wishing the horse could respond in more than just a soft whinny. "What would Adam want me to do?" She sighed. "I never should have encouraged him to enlist. What was I thinking? It would have been better for me to join up instead of him."

Ranger whinnied again. "Oh, are you telling me that you agree?" She asked, then actually considered the idea. Could she fight? Could she possibly enlist in the army and redeem herself? She had been so concerned about what the townspeople would think of Adam and her family if he didn't enlist, she hadn't even considered that he could be wounded, much less be killed. She had been purely selfish in her motivation.

"I have to make amends," She said to herself. The idea, once in her head, wouldn't leave, despite the fact that it really made no sense at all. She would have to masquerade as a man to make it work. She could cut her hair short and sign up in another state, where it would be less likely for her to be recognized. She had been mistaken for Adam before, while wearing a hat and sitting on a horse, so she felt confident she could pass as a man. She would join a cavalry unit, as folks said she was the best rider in the county and could hold her own with all of the young men in the area. "I can do this," She nodded, giving herself courage. She knew that she would have to leave tonight. She couldn't tell anyone, as she knew her family would not allow this in any way, but her mind was made up. Fighting for the Union in the cavalry would be her atonement.

Tabetha patted Ranger on the neck one more time, her decision made. She returned to the solemn house and slipped into Michael and Adam's room. She packed a bundle of Adam's clothes, then crept back to her own room to pack a few more things, then slid them under her bed. She laid on top of her covers, intending to rest until it was dark, then leave her home to make up for her mistakes.

Sunday, July 27, 1862
Christ Episcopal Church
Vicksburg, Mississippi

"It feels so good to be in church again," Hannah said. "I was so glad when Jason told us that it's safe enough to come into the city."

Mary Green smiled. "And I insist that both of your families come to our home for Sunday dinner."

"That is so kind, but we wouldn't want to inconvenience you, Mary," Victoria said. "I know my mother wanted to stop and visit with your mother at Lakemont, but we don't need to stay for dinner."

"It is no inconvenience at all. I imagine you want to check on your home while you're here," Mary added. "Some homes have been drastically disturbed with the men trying to fortify the city, but yours has been unharmed, unlike poor Mahala Roach. She had a battery placed right in her flower garden. The shrubbery, the fences, the walkways, everything was destroyed."

"How horrible!" Victoria shook her head. "I should stop and see her. I would also like to stop and see Mrs. Balfour and how the rest of the town has fared. As much as we appreciate the Wheelers' hospitality, we would like to get back home as soon as possible," Victoria said.

"Completely understandable," Mary nodded. The women began walking towards the Green home. Duff carried Annie as they walked.

When they rounded the corner towards Mary's home, they heard a commotion, almost like a cheer, coming from the riverfront.

"What on earth is going on now?" Victoria thought aloud.

"Let's go see," Mary replied, and they changed course to head down towards the river.

The city had been prepared for attack over the past year. The defenses had been constructed for nine miles east of the city's streets, and watch towers twenty feet thick overlooked the gullies and ravines. Nothing could happen without the Confederate armies knowing about it.

When they were almost to the crowd, Kendall ran up to them.

"They're gone! The last of the Yankees are gone!" She exclaimed. "I overheard some soldiers talking. The Mississippi River is getting so low that the Federal boats have to leave or they will risk being stranded on the sandbars."

"I hadn't considered that would play a factor," Victoria said. "Although I should have. How fortuitous for us."

"I have been trying to find Jason." Kendall continued. "I want to ask if we can finally move back home. I would hate to wear out our welcome at the Wheelers, and Brianne really wants to be in town."

"You mean she wants to get back to her socializing," Victoria said. "After all, it is her favorite pastime."

"Especially with all of the handsome soldiers guarding our town." Kendall added with a look of slight irritation.

"Well, if the town is truly safe again, perhaps Duff and I should hold a celebratory dinner. We can invite some of those handsome soldiers as well." She smiled and gently nudged Victoria.

"Mmm, perhaps," Victoria appreciated Mary's efforts to introduce her to new people, especially eligible men, however lately, it was simply a reminder that she was still an unmarried spinster.

"Victoria!" She turned and smiled when she saw Jason hurrying towards them. He was smiling broadly and when he reached her side, he gave her a big hug, then turned to Kendall and hugged her, picking her up and swinging her around.

"My goodness, Jason, you are acting as though we just won the war." Victoria laughed. Her brother's enthusiasm was infectious. "Did we?"

"Not quite yet, but I feel as though this was a very important victory for us."

"Well, we did have help from the river," Kendall pointed out.

"That is true," Jason said. "But I believe this also sends a strong message to the Union. We will not be defeated, even the Lord is on our side, helping us with the weather."

"That's quite a bold statement, Mr. Turner." Hannah spoke up. "What makes you think that God has chosen a side? Surely, there are Christians fighting for the Union, with family and friends, praying for Federal soldiers and a Union victory."

Jason looked chastised at Hannah's words. "I suppose I hadn't quite thought about that, Mrs. Wheeler. I stand corrected. God loves us all, even the blasted Yankees." Slight sarcasm dripped from his voice.

"So Jason, does this mean we can move back home?" Kendall interrupted.

"Yes. That's one of the reasons I was looking for you. I was able to get access to a freighter wagon. We can take it out to the Wheelers and pick up everything you brought out in one trip."

"Wonderful!" Victoria said, then turned to Mary. "I'm dreadfully sorry, Mary, but we will have to postpone dinner."

"I completely understand. I believe I will speak to Duff about that celebratory gathering." She smiled and headed towards the group of men gathered near Duff.

"If Duff even wants to celebrate a Confederate victory. That man should have a uniform on. People may start to think he's a Union sympathizer." Jason sounded upset that Duff was not fighting.

"Have you already forgotten that he donated much of the metal railing from his home to the Confederacy for bullets?" Hannah, usually quiet and soft-spoken, seemed quite comfortable challenging Jason. Victoria smiled to herself. Jason needed someone like Hannah in his life.

"Once again, Mrs. Wheeler, you are correct. I had forgotten that. I am listening to the gossip of the citizens. Forgive me." Jason gave a smile to Hannah. "Were you as hard on your husband as you are on me?'

"When it was warranted, yes," Hannah smiled back.

He turned back to Victoria. "I'll bring you all to the wagon, and we can go get Mother and the others. We should have you moved back home by this evening."

"Splendid," Victoria, Hannah and Kendall followed Jason to the wagon.

"I'll miss living with Caroline, but it will be nice to sleep in my own bed again," Kendall said.

"Yes, but remember you are always welcome," Hannah said. "I hope there is never a need, but we will always have room for you."

"The same is true for us, you know. If you ever have a need to stay in town for any reason, you had best come stay with us."

"Of course," Hannah said. "However, I have a good feeling that the danger is past, God-willing."

"Amen." Victoria added.

Monday, August 4, 1862
Union Camp, 6th Illinois Cavalry

"What was I thinking?" For what felt like the hundredth time, Tabetha wondered why she had thought enlisting in the cavalry was a good idea. So far, everything had gone as planned. She had left Michigan and enlisted in Illinois under the name Peter Kent, which had been a good idea as she hadn't recognized anyone in her camp. Cutting her hair had been heartbreaking, but necessary. With short hair and a tightly-bound chest, Tabetha doubted anyone would recognize her.

At present, her commanding officer, Captain Steven Rogers had gathered the company together for some extra drills and had begun to talk.

"Now, men, I know you have all proven yourselves on a horse, but I have learned from my own experiences that there will be times in the heat of battle where you may be pulled into a different kind of fight. Hand to hand combat." The Captain said.

"Cap't, I know all about mixin' it up." Private Josiah Reagan said, crossing his arms and spitting out a stream of tobacco juice. "Don't need no extra training to learn how."

"Is that a fact, Private Reagan?" Captain Rogers looked at the stocky redhead, a glint of challenge in his eyes. "I will make you a deal. If you can best me in a one-on-one fight, you can not only skip out on this extra training exercise, you can have an extra ration of bacon tomorrow."

Private Reagan smiled and stepped forward, looking self-assured and arrogant. Tabetha could understand why. If one only judged on appearances, there was no question as to who would win. However, Captain Rogers had a fearless look about him also, and he always carried himself with confidence. He commanded respect and most men under his command willingly gave it.

The two men faced each other. Captain Rogers bent his knees and brought his hands up to his face, as if ready to protect his head. The private fisted both hands and took a swing at the captain, who ducked swiftly and grabbed the private around the waist, then somehow took Reagan to the ground with one move. While holding the big man down, the captain looked up at the rest of the company.

"Simple moves that can take down an opponent. From here, I can inflict a variety of different injuries. Such as..." Captain Rogers stood and pulled Private Reagan up with him, his hands twisted behind his back. "This. You don't always need to use brute strength to win a fight." He released the private, who grudgingly stepped back into line. Everyone partnered up and began practicing the moves. The Captain walked up and down the line of men, explaining some other moves, pulling men out to demonstrate. Tabetha was enthralled by what he was teaching. She had wondered what would happen if she was attacked by a man who was much stronger than she, but if she paid close attention and learned what Captain Rogers had to teach, she would learn to defend herself as well as any soldier.

Later that evening, Tabetha walked from her patrol station to her tent. She had two tent mates, but she kept to herself as much as she could. Becoming close to the men in her company would present too many problems.

"Private Kent." Captain Rogers approached her. "I wanted to applaud you for your work today. If all of the men paid attention and learned as quickly as you did, I would be up for another promotion quite soon."

"Thank you for saying so, sir." Tabetha deepened her voice, as she felt she had to do when she spoke as a disguised soldier. "I just figured that, well, since I'm not the biggest and strongest of men, it would be good for me to learn how to fight and defend myself."

"A very wise choice." Captain Rogers smiled at Tabatha. She tried to keep her breathing steady. On her farm back home, she had very little interaction with men who were not part of her family, and the men she did know, well...it seemed as though the loggers and farmers of Muskegon were quite a bit different from Captain Steven Rogers. In fact, she had never met a man like the captain. He was firm, but encouraging, and she had learned that he was God-fearing as well, evidenced by the rosary she had noticed he carried with him.

"Thank you, sir." She nodded.

"If you are truly interested in learning more fighting techniques, I would be glad to train with you more. Watching you spar with Private Murphey was impressive. I must tell you, I believe you have a lot of potential. You may even be able to keep me on my toes."

"I am flattered, Captain." *Would a man use that phrase?* She shook her head, then continued. "But would that be the best idea? The other men and all." Captain Rogers was smart and observant, and if anyone could discover her secret, it would be him.

"Ah, yes, because I am your commanding officer. It is true fraternizing is frowned upon in some regiments, but we don't have to let that be an issue here."

"Well, if you think it would be alright," Tabetha replied. That hadn't been her actual concern, but it was a reasonable explanation for her reluctance.

"We'll start tomorrow, Pistol," he replied. She gave him a salute and a small smile at his use of her nickname. He returned the salute and as he walked away, she sighed. What had she just gotten herself into?

Friday, August 14, 1862
Green Home

"Hannah, welcome!" Mary smiled as her friend entered the home, which was already bustling with guests. "You didn't come alone, did you?" She led Hannah to the front sitting room where everyone was gathering.

"Unfortunately, yes. Cordelia wasn't feeling well, so she stayed home with Ambrose and Caroline. I offered to stay home and help, but they insisted I come."

"I am so glad! Victoria is already here with her mother, Brianne and Mary Grace. We were able to convince one of the regimental bands to play for us. They should be here soon. We can begin the dancing once they have set up. It will be quite successful, I feel. Several officers are in attendance, along with many friends from town."

The two women immediately located Victoria talking with her brother Jason and another soldier.

"Is that Mr. Petersen? What is he doing here?" Hannah turned to Mary. "I wasn't aware he was back." Zachary Peterson was a man Victoria had been infatuated with years ago, a man who worked with her father at Mr. Turner's law practice. He was everything Victoria thought she wanted in a future husband: smart, driven, witty, and willing to hold intelligent conversations with her. Most men thought a woman wasn't smart enough to keep up with talk of current events, history, politics and business, but Zachary wasn't most men. Unfortunately, he had fallen in love with and married Magdalena Williams, a close friend of Victoria's. After Zachary enlisted in the Confederate army, Magdalena had gone to stay with the Peterson family in Tennessee.

"I didn't know he was back either until a few days ago. He's in town on guard duty for a spell. Magdalena will be joining him while he is here. She'll be in town within the week, according to Mr. Petersen." Mary knew well why Hannah was so concerned. Victoria had been deeply hurt when she discovered that Zachary had fallen in love with Magdalena. She had never shared her feelings with either Zachary or Magdalena, but Mary well-remembered the party when Victoria had introduced the two.

March 1859
Turner Home

Hannah and Mary both watched from a distance as Victoria introduced Magdalena to Zachary Petersen. Zachary held out his hand to Magdalena, who took it and smiled, then he led her out to the dance floor.

"Victoria should not have introduced the two of them. The man looks absolutely besotted with Magdalena," Mary commented, "and I'm fairly certain that Victoria herself has feelings for Zachary Petersen"

"She most certainly does," Hannah agreed. "Poor, dear, she looks crushed. At least her cousin, Belle is with her..." as Hannah was commenting, a young man approached Belle and Victoria, spoke briefly with them, then led Belle onto the dance floor.

"Oh, dear," Mary said. "Poor Victoria." The two women joined their friend, who managed to put on a smile by the time they reached her.

"Victoria! Is everything alright?" Mary asked. She always worried for her dear friend. Victoria wanted nothing more than to get married and start a family, yet every time she met a prospect, something would happen and the relationship would fall through. Although Victoria tried to appear as though it didn't bother her, Mary knew it did.

"Of course everything is alright," Victoria replied. "Why ever would it not be?"

Mary took Victoria's arm and gently pulled her outside. Hannah followed. "Because the man that you told me you were falling for is dancing with one of your best friends. You should at least talk with Magdalena about your feelings."

"No, I can't. I know Magdalena. She deserves to be happy as much as I do and you both well know that if I were to even hint at having feelings for Mr. Petersen, she would give him up. I may have feelings for him, but that doesn't mean he has feelings for me. They both look quite happy together. Who am I to interfere with that?"

"You put a lot of thought into that answer, Victoria," Hannah said. "What you say may be true, and I appreciate the fact that you are so giving and selfless, but at some point, you really need to think about your own happiness as well."

Victoria sighed and leaned against the porch railing. "I know, but I just can't help it sometimes. I don't want to marry someone that's wrong for me and I know that God has a plan for me, I just fear that I will make the wrong decision."

"Even if we do make mistakes, God has accounted for that," Hannah said. "He has an alternative plan for us. He can take any mess we create and allow good to come from it, even if it's just learning a lesson."

"Yes, but marriage is for life. If you make a mistake, there is no going back."

"I agree with you; it is a very important decision," Mary said. "However, Mr. Petersen has only asked Magdalena for one dance, not her hand in marriage. Even if the two of them do end up together, it just means that God has something else in mind for you. There is no reason that you couldn't continue being friends with the both of them. I know how much you care for Magdalena and that you value your friendship with Mr. Petersen."

"That's true, I do. Zachary is one of the only men I have ever met that will talk to me as an equal. We hold the most intelligent conversations."

"If it's meant to be, it will happen," Hannah said.

"Oh, I know, Hannah. I simply must remember that." Victoria replied.

1862

"I do wish I could join Victoria's conversation with Mr. Petersen, but I must play hostess," Mary said.

"I will join them," Hannah offered. "I have a feeling that Jason will want to talk with me anyways. He is so protective of me and my family lately. I know he will want a full report of our activities."

Mary nodded and Hannah made her way to Victoria.

"Lieutenant Petersen!" Hannah smiled. "It is so good to see you safe and in Vicksburg once again."

"Thank you for saying so, Mrs. Wheeler. It is wonderful to be back."

"I was told that our dear Magdalena will soon be joining you." Hannah quickly glanced at Victoria. She seemed genuinely happy and not at all pining after Lieutenant Petersen.

"Yes, she is. I can't wait to be reunited with her." He smiled, clearly in love with his bride. "She should be here soon and is very anxious to be reacquainted with all of her friends here."

"And we are anxious to see her again," Victoria said. Seeing Zachery had been good for her. He was still just as easy to talk to, but the romantic feelings she had once had for him had subsided.

"Miss Turner was just telling me about the changes here in Vicksburg, such as the fact that luxury items are available, but for outrageous prices."

"Salt is now over $100 a sack, and butter $1.50 a pound." Hannah shook her head.

"I fear with the army camped so near the city and officers bringing their families, the food situation won't get better." Zachary said. "Though we get our basic necessities, more people in the town will make the demand for food higher."

"Conversation seems to center around the war and food," Victoria said.

Before anyone else in the group could speak again, Mary Green approached with a handsome, friendly-looking soldier with dark brown hair and a curled moustache and goatee with all hair on the cheeks shaven. Augusta had heard the style called the 'VanDyke'.

"The regimental band is here and warming up, so we will be able to start the dancing soon." She said. "However, I first wanted to introduce you all to Captain Philip Mason from Tennessee."

The man smiled, his kind blue eyes shining.

"Captain, may I present Corporal Jason Turner, his sister, Miss Victoria Turner, Mrs. Hannah Wheeler and Lieutenant Zachary Petersen."

The Captain focused on Victoria. "It would be my honor to escort you to the dance floor, Miss Turner, once the music begins."

"That sounds delightful, Captain Mason." Victoria said. Jason turned to Hannah as the music started.

"Mrs. Wheeler, may I have this dance?" She took his outstretched hand.

"Why yes, thank you," she smiled as he led her to the floor.

"Sorry to leave you, Mr. Petersen," Victoria said. "I look forward to seeing you again soon."

"Of course, Miss Turner, as will I." He nodded, and Captain Mason offered his arm to Victoria.

"Mrs. Green knows how to host a splendid party," He commented as soon as they were on the dance floor.

"Yes, she does, and she rather enjoys it," Victoria replied. "Mary is one of my dearest friends, we spend a great deal of time socializing. She is a gracious hostess."

"You speak as well of her as she does of you." He replied. "I actually know Mr. Green from before the war; he is a good, honest businessman. I had been introduced to Mrs. Green prior to the outbreak of the war. When I arrived here, I reacquainted myself with the Greens as soon as I was able. Mrs. Green wanted me to meet you posthaste, Miss Turner. She speaks very highly of you."

"She is always so thoughtful." Victoria glanced at Mary. Her friend was making her rounds and greeting her guests, but was frequently glancing at Victoria.

"I have been very encouraged by the kindness shown by the people of Vicksburg," Captain Mason said. "Everyone is so welcoming, though I know your city voted against secession."

"We did, but we are a people loyal to Mississippi. It also doesn't hurt that your Confederate troops are protecting us from Northern invaders."

"We are doing that," he said with a smile.

The rest of the dance passed comfortably. Victoria found it very easy to talk with Captain Mason. He was kind, funny, and though he wasn't quite as clever as Zachary Petersen, he had a quick wit that Victoria appreciated. She could tell why Mary had thought he would be a good match. Victoria smiled as she silently sent up a prayer of thanksgiving for such a good friend.

Sunday, August 24, 1862
Christ Episcopal Church

Victoria and her family, along with Magdalena Peterson, exited the church after services. It was so enjoyable to have Magdalena back in town. The energetic woman also appreciated being back in Vicksburg, a place she considered her second home. She was originally from New Orleans, but had spent almost every spring and summer in Mississippi, living with her grandparents and widowed aunt.

"I still cannot comprehend how much Vicksburg has changed since I've left." Magdalena said, holding onto Victoria's arm.

"And you missed all of the excitement," Victoria reminded her. "Vicksburg is quite the desirable place for armies. Control of the Mississippi River is imperative to both sides." She looked toward the river.

"It must be a relief that the enemy departed," Magdalena said.

"It is, but the Yankees remain just upriver. If you head up to Sky Parlor Hill, you can see them, just in sight."

"And you can hear occasional firing." Magdalena said. "I have heard the shots."

"Your husband has been so busy with his duties that I haven't had much time to visit with him," Victoria commented. "How has it been for him, transitioning from lawyer to soldier?"

"He doesn't seem to care for soldiering, but really never tells me one way or the other," Magdalena replied. "However, he will excel at being a soldier, just as he excels at everything he puts his brilliant mind to."

"And becoming a war hero could help him become a legacy, just as he's always wanted to be." Victoria pointed out.

"Yes, there is that." Magdalena shook her head. "That is how my husband thinks, always looking to leave his name in the history books, although he has already left something of himself on this earth." She gave a small smile and placed a hand on her stomach, which Victoria could now see was slightly rounded.

"My goodness! Magdalena, how could I not have noticed?"

"Well, I've only been here for a week and I believe I'm only about four months along, at least that's my best estimate."

"My friend, congratulations." Victoria tried not to draw attention, as Magdalena seemed not quite ready to tell the entire town. "I would expect Zachary is ecstatic."

"He is, yet he is worried for my health."

"Of course," Victoria smiled.

"He did tell me that you have been keeping company with a Captain from Tennessee." Magdalena changed the subject.

"Yes, a Captain Mason. He is very kind and easy to talk to," Victoria smiled. She and the Captain had gotten together for tea three times in the two weeks since they had met. He had also attended church services with her last Sunday. "In fact, I am a bit surprised that the captain wasn't in church this morning. He said that he rarely misses a Sunday service. I was going to invite him to dinner when I saw him."

"He likely has been caught up with his duties," Magdalena said. "It happens often to Zachary." The two women finally arrived at the Turner home.

"Would you like to stay for refreshments?" Victoria asked.

"I do wish I could, but I promised my Aunt Anna that I would come and dine with them. The army could move Zachary at any time and I will follow him as best I can. I must make sure that I visit with all my family and friends as much as possible."

"Of course," Victoria replied. "Enjoy your day."

Magdalena hadn't been gone for more than ten minutes when Zachary arrived. Victoria was sitting on the porch, sipping tea and reading a text on Revolutionary War heroes.

"Zachary, you just missed your wife." Victoria was unsure of why else he would be at her home.

"I am not here looking for Magdalena, I know she's with her aunt. I actually came to see you." His expression was grim.

"From the conversation I had with Magdalena after church services, I understand that congratulations are in order."

"Yes, thank you. I am truly excited, though, as always, worried about her." He gave her a small smile.

"So what does bring you here?" Victoria asked. "It is clear you didn't stop by for a friendly chat."

He looked at the book in her lap. "That is a good text," He commented. "Very informative."

"And now you're changing the subject," Victoria said. "What has happened?"

Zachary sighed heavily. "I was asked to tell you that Captain Mason sends his regrets in regards to missing church today. I spoke with him last evening. He was in the hospital. Malaria."

"Malaria? My goodness. Is he well enough to receive visitors?"

"No." Zachary said. "I stopped to see him again this morning. Victoria, I'm sorry. The doctors said he passed away last night."

Victoria's hand flew to her mouth. "That's just not possible. I saw him on Wednesday, we had tea. He seemed a bit tired, now that I think about it, but other than that..."

"I am truly sorry, Victoria. The two of you may have just met, but I know he was very fond of you."

"Why is it that something happens to every man I am interested in?" Victoria slumped back in her chair. "It is as though I'm destined to never marry."

"I don't think that's true. I know you were engaged to Jeremy Thompson, but he was a scoundrel, I told you so, long ago and you are lucky to be rid of him. I know that Captain Mason was a good man, so I can understand your being upset about his death, but are there other men who have wronged you in some way?"

Victoria gave a short laugh and shook her head. "I'm sorry. I am just saddened by your news. I really enjoyed my time with Captain Mason. He was a kind man. I must admit, I entertained thoughts of a future with him. I suppose I should not have done so since I only knew him for three weeks."

"Sometimes time doesn't matter. I knew Magdalena was the right woman for me within moments of meeting her."

"Yes, I recall. I was there, remember?"

"Of course. You introduced us, and for that, I will be forever grateful." Zachary smiled. "I only wish I could be with her more often. I am thankful for the opportunity to be in the army to make something more of myself, but I must admit, war is not what I thought it would be."

"I did wonder how you were taking to a soldier's life. Magdalena said she really didn't know." Victoria tried to keep the conversation going with Zachary. She knew when he left, she would have to truly think about the loss of Captain Mason, and she didn't want to do that.

"I try to keep a lot of my hardships from her. I don't want her to worry overmuch." Zachary sighed. "There are many days that I wish this war would just end and days that I wish I had never enlisted. I have seen many things I will never forget. Men shot, lying on the ground, dying, groaning in pain, some even begging to die so they can be free from the pain. Men who have lost limbs and whose lives will never be the same. How can men, farmers, skilled laborers, how can they go back to work with arms and legs missing? These are the men who are on the battlefields, not the politicians and planters who dragged us into this conflict. It's not glory, Victoria, not at all. It is horror, plain and simple."

"I recall my uncle Samuel saying much the same thing once." She threaded her hands together in her lap. "He fought in the war with Mexico. I'm not sure why he decided to make soldiering his life's work, yet he says it's all he can imagine doing."

"To be honest, I haven't been in that many engagements, and I wouldn't mind if I never saw another battlefield again." He rubbed his chin. "I just want to focus on my career, especially with Magdalena in her condition. I want the chance to meet our child."

"I'm sure you will. Just keep the faith."

"We have lost many good men, Miss Turner. Men who had much more faith than I could ever muster. Captain Mason, for example. He was a devout Christian." He shook his head. "It didn't save him in the end."

"It depends on what you consider the end to be." Victoria said. "It may not have saved him in this life, but I have no doubt his faith has him in Heaven now. No more suffering here on earth, just eternity with the Lord."

"We've had this conversation many times before. You know I am a man of thinking and reason. I don't think there is room for both faith and knowledge." Zachary sat back in his chair.

"I would disagree with that. Many of the early Christian leaders were quite the scholars. I recently read a book from father's library, _Disputed Questions on Truth_ by a theologian named Thomas Aquinas. He wrote many commentaries on biblical books, and also about more scholarly topics. The Catholic Church later named him a saint. He was a brilliant and faithful man. I would enjoy learning more about him and his thoughts, and I believe you would as well."

"Perhaps," Zachary admitted, then checked his pocket watch. "I must be going. I'd like to spend time with my wife before heading back to my post."

"Of course," Victoria stood as he did. "Thank you for letting me know about Captain Mason. I wish you and I had more time to talk like we used to."

"As do I," he said. "As I said before, hopefully, this war will end soon and we can go back to life as it was."

She walked with him down the steps, then down the footpath to the fence at the road.

"Take care of yourself, Mr. Petersen." She held out her hand.

"You as well." He took her hand and gave it a gentlemanly kiss, then headed towards Magdalena's Aunt Anne's. Victoria watched him go, then wiped a tear from her eye and went inside the house.

Friday, September 19, 1862
Green Home

Mary sat with Magdalena Peterson on the front porch. It was a nice day, cool and comfortable, the perfect day to spend outside, working on sewing projects and conversing with friends. Magdalena had hinted at some important news, but Victoria would be arriving shortly, so she was waiting to make the announcement.

"How are you, Mary? Really?"

"We're getting along." Mary suspected the question was directed at the fact that Duff was not fighting in the war.

"I couldn't believe it when I heard about your father," Magdalena said. "I was so sorry to hear the news."

"Thank you for saying so," Mary said, then smiled when she saw Victoria walking up the hill towards the house. "Here comes Victoria now."

After greeting one another, Victoria sat down. "I am sorry for my tardiness. I was talking with Jason. There has been the most horrible battle in Maryland. Near a town called Sharpsburg on the Antietam Creek." She shook her head. "The Union's George McClellan against our Robert E. Lee."

"Who won?" Magdalena asked.

"Jason said it's being called 'inconclusive'. The Union lost many more men that we did, but Lee withdrew from the field and slipped back into Virginia." Victoria explained, trying to withhold her tears. "They are calling it the bloodiest day on American soil. Over 3,600 men were killed, almost 18,000 wounded." She brushed a tear from her cheek. She knew the regiment that her father, Gregory and Abraham were in, the 10th Mississippi, was not involved in any of those eastern battles, but she also knew that her extended family members and friends were. She had learned after the fact that the 10th regiment had fought in the Battle of Shiloh and later in a battle near Corinth, Mississippi. Jason had learned that they were all alive and well. The regiment was now up in Kentucky, trying to get support from the Border States and, according to Jason, draw the Union forces beyond the Ohio River.

"Good heavens," Magdalena replied. "That can't be possible. How can we justify that much killing?"

"I don't believe we can." Mary tried to hold her own emotions in, but the news Victoria brought was difficult to take.

"No one could have predicted this," Victoria commented. "It seems there will be no end to the killing until one side gives up and surrenders. Perhaps Varina Davis was right all along. Maybe the Confederacy was ill-fated from the beginning." She shook her head and tried to lighten the conversation. "Magdalena, tell us, what is your news?"

Magdalena averted her eyes. "Unfortunately, not what you expected, I am sure." She glanced at Mary. "The news I wanted to share. Zachary is being transferred. He hasn't told me exactly where, but he did say that I will be able to travel with him."

"You're leaving?" Victoria was stunned. "You haven't been here for long at all. This is truly upsetting news. I was just getting used to having you around again."

"I know," Magdalena replied. "But there are so many women who are without their husbands during this infernal war, and with our child on the way, I want to spend as much time as possible with Zachary."

"I can understand that," Victoria said as she thought of the many times she had longed for the war to be over, for her family all to be home and for life to be as it was before. "I wish you and Zachary all of the best and you both know you are welcome to come back as soon as possible."

"Of course we know that, but it is always good to hear," Magdalena replied. "I will try to write you both as much as I can, though in a few more months, I will be quite preoccupied."

"You most certainly will be." Mary smiled.

"Yes, but I am sure I will be able to take time to write my family and dear friends."

"And perhaps a visit will be possible in six months or so." Victoria smiled.

"That would be very nice. We would enjoy visitors." Magdalena smiled. "I will keep you updated on our location, and with any luck, this conflict will soon be just a memory."

"Lord willing," Mary said. "I do hope you're right."

Friday, October 3, 1862
Turner Home
My dearest sister, Victoria,

I hope this letter finds you in good health and spirits. I miss my home and family so much. As many have discovered, war is not all glory, although I hadn't been disillusioned about that as so many of my comrades have been. I remember when we were growing up, Uncle Samuel would tell us his stories of the Mexican-American war, and he never concealed that war was not all honor and glory.

In case you haven't received previous letters, we have been reassigned to the 12th Mississippi Infantry and were sent to Virginia. I was able to meet up with Cousins Jacob and James not too long ago.

We had quite the reunion. Father was able to catch up with Uncle Matthew as well. Jacob told us that his father and Jonah both chose to stay with the Union. We all suspected this, but now we know for sure. Aunt Susannah and Bekah remain in Petersburg, as far as he knows. The worst news, however, is that, soon after we met up, Father and I heard that James was wounded at a battle called Glendale. He was sent to a hospital in Richmond and he eventually succumbed to infection. My heart aches for Aunt Miriam and the rest of the family. I am so sorry to be the bearer of this news. Please inform our other family members if they have not yet heard.

It is always wonderful to receive letters from home. I realize the mail service is quite unreliable, but they are much appreciated when they do make it through. I find it strange that they sent us Mississippians so far east when there is fighting to be done in the West. I feel better knowing that at least Jason is near the home front, protecting you all. How I miss Vicksburg!

In other news, I am excited to say that I have finally mastered setting up not only my tent, but also a fly for the front, all on my own. It is not an easy task, and I am quite proud of my accomplishment.

Victoria stopped reading and looked across the room to Jason, who had brought Gregory's letter.

"What on earth is a fly? A type of tent?"

"Of sorts," Jason replied. "It's kind of like the porch for a tent. It's a piece of canvas with a pole in each corner, then a slightly higher pole and beam down the middle. Just a roof, no sides."

"I see," Victoria glanced at the letter again. "Gregory makes it seem as though he has learned to build some great mansion all on his own."

Jason laughed. "Gregory would be proud of himself for that. They can be difficult to set up." He gave a soft smile. "I miss that kid."

"As do I." Victoria finished reading the letter, then put it back in the envelope and slipped it into her dress pocket. "At least I have you to visit with often." She let her mind comprehend the content of the letter. "Did you know about Cousin James?" She asked quietly.

"James Turner? No." His expression turned somber. "What happened?"

"He's dead." Tears formed in Victoria's eyes, remembering kind, always-happy James. "I can't imagine what his family is going through. Belle...she and James were so close, such good friends. She must be..." Victoria thought of what it would be like to lose Jason or Gregory. She realized just how quickly she could lose her brothers or her father as Belle and Elizabeth had lost James. Abraham and her friends Zachary and Nathaniel Prentiss could also be killed. She didn't think she could bear the loss.

"Oh, Jason!" She stood and he quickly knew what she needed, taking her into his arms. "I don't want to lose you. What would I do?"

"If something were to happen to any one of us, you would go on. You're strong and Mama's always telling us that earth is only our temporary home anyways."

"I know, but I would miss talking with you and seeing Gregory's goofy smile, I would miss hearing Father read from the bible on Christmas Eve." She paused. "That was such a noticeable void in our celebration last year."

"Indeed it was, and I understand what you feel. However, I've realized and come to terms with the fact that we will lose good men in this war. We already have. I'm sure God does not want it to happen, but as you know, He gave us free will, and this is what we have done with our choices. We chose this path as a country when we stopped compromising, stopped trying to be united." He shook his head. "I'll do my best to be compassionate when I can be, fight hard to protect my loved ones and try to honor God in whatever I do."

"You are such a God-fearing man, Jason, and an even better brother." Victoria wiped her eyes. "I suppose being compassionate and honoring God is all we can do."

Jason smiled sadly. "We'll have to keep our Fredericksburg cousins in our special prayers."

A knock on the open door frame caused them both to turn. Esther stood there.

"Sorry, Masta Turner, but der be a soldier here ta see ya." She said in a soft voice.

"Show him in, please, Esther." Jason buttoned up his vest and threw his wool jacket on to look more professional.

"Turner, there's more fighting up near Corinth, near the border. We've just been placed on alert."

"Sir, Corinth is a half day's ride from here. Do they really believe we might be the next target?"

"There's no way of knowing for sure. We just need to be ready for the possibilities."

"Of course, sir." Jason said, then turned to Victoria. "I'll be back when I can. Take care, dear sister."

"Yes, sir." Victoria hugged her brother tightly. "You stay safe as well."

Wednesday, November 5, 1862
Union Cavalry Camp

Tabetha sat alone at the fire, waiting for her turn to go on guard duty. Twilight was falling when Captain Rogers approached her. She stood at attention.

"May I?" He asked, gesturing to the log across the fire from her.

"Of course," Tabetha deepened her voice and pulled her hat over her dirt-stained face. As much as it made her cringe, she had decided to keep her face grimy for more of a disguise. She also kept her short-cropped hair dirty. "Would you care for some coffee?"

"Yes, thank you," He took her cup with a grateful nod. "I wanted to let you know that I am very impressed by the ease with which you have taken to soldiering, especially your riding skills. You seem to be a natural cavalryman."

"Thank you, sir." Tabetha was pleased at his words, but tried not to show it. Her brother Adam would have just expected the praise. He was always so good at everything.

"To be completely honest, I am curious as to why you didn't enlist sooner."

"I let my Ma talk me into staying home but then we lost my brother, Adam. He was killed at Glendale so I figured I had to finish what he started." She decided that was a safe enough answer. She simply couldn't give too many details.

"I'm sorry about your brother," Captain Rogers said. "We've lost too many good men in this war." He stared into the flames, as if remembering someone himself. "I have to ask though, Pistol. How old are you? I won't say anything if you are a bit too young."

"I'm old enough. Twenty." At least she could answer that question honestly.

"Really? I meant no offense, but you just don't look any older than sixteen. Do you even shave?"

"Naw. My Ma's whole side of the family is like that." Again, that was true. "I'll likely always be smooth-faced."

"That would save you lots of time, not having to shave." Captain Rogers rubbed his own scruffy chin.

"Reckon that's true," Tabetha nodded, then took a chance at learning more about the man she found so fascinating. "Not to pry, sir, but I get the feeling that you lost someone in the war as well."

"I did," he replied. "One of my younger brothers, Caleb. He was a good boy, wanted to make our mother proud, and wanted to impress me. I told him not to enlist, called him a kid, told him that he would probably get hurt. He was killed at the Battle of Pea Ridge." The man rubbed his temple. "He was only seventeen."

"I am so sorry, Captain," Tabetha longed to comfort the man, place a consoling hand on his shoulder or even embrace him, however she knew that it was not what most men would do and it could compromise her secret.

"Yes, I am as well," He replied. "Perhaps if I had been kinder to him, more supportive of him staying at home and taking care of our mother…"

"If I may speak my mind, sir?"

Captain Rogers nodded.

"Your brother made his choice. Seventeen may not be old enough to fight by the army's standards, but he is old enough to make his own decisions. I think that when something happens to those we love, we immediately think of how we could have done something to prevent it. I did the same thing with my brother." *And I still blame myself.* She thought. "We must remember our loved ones who have passed and know they are in a better place."

"That is what my mother told me in a letter, after the shock of losing her son wore off. She said that 'It was part of God's plan." He scoffed. "I am a churchgoing man, but I struggle with the idea of a Father who allows this war to go on."

"The way I see it, Captain, God doesn't want bad things to happen. We just make bad choices. However, I also believe that God can make good things happen from anything bad."

"I suppose. Perhaps," He sighed, then checked his pocket watch. "I have enjoyed our conversation, Pete, truly I have, but I must finish my rounds." He poured the dregs of his coffee into the fire and stood. "If you need anything, let me know."

"Yes, sir." Tabetha stood, then saluted.

He nodded. "Have a good evening, Pete."

Sunday, December 14, 1862
Christ Episcopal Church

"I wish Jason could make it to Church more often." Victoria commented as her family, along with the Wheelers and Greens, exited the church.

"He comes when he is able, dear." Rachel said, then looked at Cordelia. "You're still planning on dining with us this afternoon, correct?"

"Of course." Cordelia smiled. "It will be delightful to have a meal that we did not have to prepare, much less a delicious meal like Esther can conjure up."

"She is extremely talented and we are blessed to have her. I don't know how she can continue to make such excellent dishes with the shortages of food we have." Rachel turned to Duff and Mary. "You two and Annie are more than welcome to join us as well."

"We appreciate the offer, Mrs. Turner, but we already have plans to dine with the Lake family," Duff said, referencing Mary's mother and siblings.

"Well, I am sure your mother will enjoy the visit." Rachel gave a quick wave to Mrs. Lake.

"Have a wonderful rest of the day," Mary said, and the Green family walked in the direction of Lakemont.

The Turners and Wheelers made their way to the Turner home and were immediately met with tea from Esther in the parlor.

"Esther, you are a peach!" Mrs. Turner sat on one of the chairs and immediately started pouring for the rest of the women.

"It ain't no problem, ma'am. I make sure Dinah sees to da children and den get back ta makin' dinna fos ya all."

"Thank you Esther." Mrs. Turner smiled as the rest of the women sat down. "I would be absolutely lost without Esther, Dinah and Caesar." She shook her head. "We depend on them for so much, they are more like family."

"And yet, you don't question the institution of slavery?" Hannah asked. Everyone knew that the Wheelers didn't agree with slavery, but the women kept those thoughts relatively quiet. Hannah's husband, Benjamin had been quite outspoken on his views against slavery. Some townspeople even hinted that the farming accident that killed him was not an accident, but a result of his beliefs.

"I must admit, there are times when I do," Rachel admitted. "Mr. Turner and I have spoken on the matter many times. He believes that slavery will just die out naturally, and I tend to agree with him."

"To be honest, slavery was dying off naturally in the early 1800's," Victoria said. "I read an article that reported that Eli Whitney's cotton gin made it profitable to grow cotton. It transformed our Southern economy, along with the textile mills in New England and Europe."

"So we blame him for all of this." Brianne scoffed. "An inventor like that, he must have been a Yankee."

"Yes, from Massachusetts, if I recall correctly," Victoria said. "But we all know this war is not just about slavery. There are many more reasons. In fact, we know more Southern men who are fighting for their homes and rights than just to keep slaves."

"That is true," Hannah said. "I know that to be the case with the men in your family."

"And would have been the reason Benjamin enlisted, had he lived to have the opportunity," Mrs. Wheeler said, no doubt in her mind that her son would have fought for the Confederacy.

"I believe that as well." Hannah nodded.

"Hello, ladies." Jason smiled as he entered the parlor. The women stood, and Rachel immediately went to embrace her son.

"Jason, what a pleasant surprise," she said as he hugged his sisters and cousins, then gave a polite nod to the Wheelers. "You can join us for dinner, correct?"

"That shouldn't be an issue," He replied. "However, I come bearing some distressing news. It may concern family."

"My goodness, who?" Victoria asked.

"We just received word that there has been terrible fighting in and around Fredericksburg. The Yankees crossed the Rappahannock right in front of Chatham Manor on the Stafford Heights side and invaded the town. There was some fierce fighting and many homes were damaged or destroyed."

"Good Heavens!" Mrs. Wheeler exclaimed.

"Oh, God be with them." Rachel added. "Do you know of any...have they reported any casualties?"

"I haven't heard of any casualties from the 12th Mississippi. It may be a challenge to learn of how the Fredericksburg branch of the family fared. I would suggest writing a letter to them, if you can find the time."

"I will write to Belle and Elizabeth this very evening," Victoria said. "Oh, I do hope everything is alright." Her thoughts flew, not only to her family, but also the friends she had made there, such as Nathaniel Prentiss and his sisters AJ and Liberty. How were they surviving? And the beautiful Chatham Manor and wonderful town of Fredericksburg... though she only visited a few times, she had very fond memories of the place. Her thoughts drifted to the ball for AJ that Victoria had attended at Chatham Manor. It was the evening she first got a chance to talk with Nathaniel Prentiss.

Fall 1859
Chatham Manor

Victoria stepped out onto the back veranda. She had been having an absolutely wonderful time with her cousins and the people of Fredericksburg. Victoria had been dancing almost non-stop and needed a breath of fresh air. She waved a hand in front of her face, trying to cool herself, wishing she had a glass of something cool to drink. She looked around, hoping to find a slave carrying glasses of water or even champagne.

"You look a bit parched," A male voice spoke from behind her. She turned to see Nathaniel Prentiss, AJ's brother. She had briefly met him a few days prior while visiting AJ with Charlotte, Belle and Bekah. He smiled and held out a glass of claret.

"Thank you," Victoria took it with a grateful smile. "I don't usually drink wine, but I will make an exception tonight." She took a sip. "I really appreciate your kindness, Mr. Prentiss." Nathaniel escorted her down the steps.

"Of course, Miss Victoria." He smiled and sat on the ground, then leaned back on his hands. It was rather comical, with his impeccably-trimmed hair, elegant suit and white gloves, to see him so casual.

"Come, join me," He said with a challenging smile and a pat on the ground next to him.

"I'm wearing a ball gown," Victoria protested. *"With a hoop skirt."* She loved the dress she was wearing; a burgundy embroidered silk taffeta with the bodice trimmed in lace with a ruffled collar that was trimmed with gold thread. The shoulders were accented with handmade silk fabric roses with green velvet leaves. It made her feel more beautiful than she ever had felt, and she didn't want to get it soiled. She did, however, want to talk more with this handsome young man with whom she immediately felt at ease

"I have a sister, I know the hoop will lay down flat." His eyes teased her, almost challenging her to sit next to him on the grass. She smiled and bit her lip.

"Turn your head, just in case." She insisted, and once he acquiesced, she sat down as gingerly as she could, then arranged her hoops and skirt into place. *"All right, thank you for your discretion."*

"Much more comfortable, am I correct?" Nathaniel smiled.

"It is," she agreed, leaning back as he was.

"Tell me, Miss Victoria, how are you enjoying your stay here in Fredericksburg? How does it compare to..." he thought for a moment. *"Mississippi, correct?"*

"I am quite impressed you remember," Victoria replied. *"I wasn't very talkative when we met the other day."*

"Well, I know with Belle talking, it is hard to get a word in, if she doesn't allow you."

"Very true," Victoria said. *"She is the socialite of the family."* She looked across the river. The sunlight was fading, but the town across the Rappahannock was softly lit up. She could almost see Turner's Glenn in the distance from the vantage point. *"This is such a lovely view."*

"Yes, Stafford Heights is a wonderful place to live. And farm." He added.

"Yes, I found that information quite interesting the other day. You have lived on a farm your whole life, yet you felt as though you needed to go to college to get a degree in agriculture," Victoria commented.

"'Experience is a good teacher, but education is never a waste,'" he replied. *"That's what my father has always said. I don't want to be just a farmer, I want to be the best farmer possible. I want to learn how to best care for crops and animals, and to learn the science behind agriculture. It may not seem worth it to you, but to me, it is."*

"I think it's wonderful, actually. Many people only get as much education as they need to get by. You have a farm, you have what you need to survive and care for a family, yet you are striving to be better. I can appreciate that."

"I'm glad you do. Not everyone does," Nathaniel replied. *"So, Miss Victoria Turner, what do you enjoy doing down in Vicksburg?"*

"I enjoy what most young women do. I socialize with my friends. I dearly enjoy dancing, and though I am not good at it, I enjoy singing. I like going for walks and experiencing nature. Some areas on the banks of the Mississippi River are quite beautiful."

"I would imagine." He plucked a piece of longer grass and put it in his mouth. *"I would guess that you also like to read? If you're like my sister she enjoys reading the novels of Miss Jane Austin."*

"I do enjoy novels, but I actually prefer reading about current matters and history."

"A woman who enjoys history. That's something you don't find every day." He smiled. *"What is your favorite time period to study?"*

"I love reading about the heroes of the American Revolution. Washington, Hamilton, Lafayette, Greene..." She stopped when Nathaniel tried to hide a laugh. *"What is so amusing?"*

"You would get along splendidly with my family. My parents like to show honor towards their American heroes and named their children after some of them. My full name is George Washington Nathaniel Greene Prentiss. My sister AJ's full name is America Joan and our younger sister's name is Liberty Elizabeth."

"My goodness. A very patriotic family indeed."

"Well, my father was born in Ireland and migrated here early in his life. He really wanted to embrace everything about his new country."

"I think that's wonderful." Victoria said.

Nathaniel glanced toward the house, then back at Victoria. *"Miss Turner, are you quite rested? I would love to ask you to dance."*

"I would greatly enjoy that, Mr. George Washington Nathaniel Green Prentiss."

The two of them laughed as Nathaniel helped Victoria up and they started towards the Manor.

1862

"I will let you know what I find out as soon as I can," Jason was saying as Victoria focused again on the present conversation.

"Thank you, Jason. We appreciate it," Rachel said. "I don't know what we would do without you keeping us updated." She nodded at Victoria. "And I know you will let us know if you hear from Belle or Elizabeth."

"Of course. I may even try to write AJ and Nathaniel Prentiss to see if they know anything," Victoria responded.

"That would be a fine idea," Rachel said. "And we will simply keep hoping and praying that this all ends soon and brings us together again quickly."

Wednesday, December 24, 1862
Balfour Home

"Victoria! Hello!" Mary Green wove through the guests of the annual Christmas gala at the home of Dr. and Emma Balfour and approached her friend. "Merry Christmas!"

"Merry Christmas to you as well." Victoria gave her friend a quick hug. "I am so glad that you made it! I hope you're feeling better."

"Yes, I am," Mary couldn't hide a blush. She took Victoria's arm and leaned over to speak softly. "It may be a little early to share my news. I will only tell you as my dearest friend. Little Annie will be a big sister come spring."

"Oh, Mary, congratulations!" Victoria smiled and hugged her friend again, glad that the Greens would be blessed with another child. "I must be honest, I wondered if you were with child. There were a few signs that I noticed. I am so happy for you!"

"Yes, thank you so much." Mary smiled, then looked around the room. "Now we have to simply find you a husband."

"Simply?" Victoria laughed. "My dear Mrs. Green, you and I both know that finding me a husband is anything but simple."

"We have been over this before. None of the men in your past were worthy of you." Mary continued to look around, as if looking for someone specific.

"Who are you looking for?" Victoria asked, feeling a pang of sadness as she thought of Captain Mason.

"A delightful major from Alabama. I met him just the other day and believe he could be a good match for you." Her search for the major ended. "Ah! I see him now. Come, and I'll introduce you." Mary all but dragged Victoria to the soldier. Victoria put on her best airs. He was handsome, almost too handsome, with clean-cut, well-groomed black hair and a perfectly trimmed beard and mustache. Friendly mutton chops was the name of the style. Victoria didn't care for the look.

"Major Harris, it is so good to see you," Mary said to him. He smiled at both women.

"Mrs. Green! It is an absolute pleasure to see you again." The man had a thick drawl.

"Major, may I introduce my dearest friend, Miss Victoria Turner."

"Miss Turner," The major took her gloved hand in his and kissed it. "I must say, you look ravishing."

Victoria blushed and self-consciously brushed her other hand down her dark green silk ball gown. "Thank you, Major," she replied. "It is a pleasure to meet you."

"I do hope there will be room for me on your dance card this evening," the major said.

"Of course, Major," Victoria replied. "I look forward to it."

Victoria and Mary continued to greet people from town. Most of the talk was in celebration of the Confederates defeating the Union General Grant and his forces in northern Mississippi.

"I still find it strange that we are a town who voted against secession initially, yet we are now in favor of Confederate victories." Victoria commented to Mary when it was just the two of them once again.

"It's Southern loyalty," Mary replied. "As Mr. Shannon wrote at the beginning of the war, 'Once we knew that Mississippi has chosen a position, we also take our position by its side.'" Marmaduke Shannon, the local newspaper editor was a close friend of the Turner family.

"Mr. Shannon always argued quite forcefully for staying with the Union," Victoria glanced around the room. "I do wonder if he'll show up tonight, I'm quite sure his daughters Emily and Anne will be here."

"I'm sure they're all here somewhere," Before she could locate the reporter, the band began to play and Duff approached to claim his wife for a dance.

"May I have this dance, my dear?" He asked with a smile.

"But of course," Mary replied, unable to contain her joy as he led her to the dance floor. Victoria sighed and looked around at all of the couples pairing up. Major Harris was dancing with one of the young women from town. Even Mary Grace had found a dance partner, an older, distinguished-looking officer.

"I am always befuddled as to why the prettiest unmarried woman is left unattended." A familiar voice said from behind her. Victoria smiled and turned to give her brother a hug.

"Oh, Jason!" She held him tightly. "What a wonderful Christmas surprise! I am so glad you're here."

"Yes. I just saw Mother, who was ecstatic to see me. I cannot wait to see Mary Grace's little ones tomorrow morning, and their excitement. These holidays are the best time of the year."

"If only Father, Gregory and Abraham were here, it would be absolutely perfect," She said. "I suppose that's one nice benefit for you being with the local unit."

"Indeed," he smiled. "I did mean what I said about you not dancing. I know how much you enjoy it."

"Yes, well, there are more ladies here than gentleman, so I am left without a partner." She shrugged.

"Not anymore," Jason said. "Come, let's dance."

The two made their way to the dance floor.

"Is there any news from Fredericksburg?" Victoria asked anxiously.

Jason opened his mouth to answer, but before he could, a wet, mud-covered Confederate soldier barged into the room.

"Pardon me, Commander, but I have been sent to alert you to the fact that the arrival of the Union Expeditionary force and General Sherman is imminent."

The men in the room began talking with one another and many of the women gasped.

"Jason..." Victoria's stomach felt sick. Would her family be forced to go out to the countryside again?

"It will be alright." Jason placed a comforting hand on her back and sighed. "I suppose Christmas with my family is not to be this year. That disappoints me greatly, I..."

Jason was interrupted by the commander's declaration. "I apologize, ladies and gentlemen but this ball is at an end. All non-combatants must leave the city."

Jason shook his head. "I don't think that's necessary quite yet, Victoria. Go home with Mother and the girls, I'll bring Mary Grace to her home and make sure Caesar watches out for her there. I'll see just what the situation is. We've had these threats before, but as you know, the Yanks just don't know how to take Vicksburg. They don't realize how well-positioned we are." He looked around at the crowds moving from the house and quickly located his mother and cousins. They hastened towards each other.

"My first Christmas gala ends like this," Kendall exclaimed, excitement apparent in her voice. "I had no idea it would be so exciting, or that I would enjoy it so much."

"Let's get you all home," Jason said. "I'll come and get you or send word if I think you all need to get out of town."

"Thank you, Jason," Rachel said, hugging her son tightly. Victoria saw tears in her mother's eyes. She felt like crying as well, but she knew she would have to help her mother get everyone settled. She needed to stay alert and strong, as the days ahead would likely prove to be stressful. They would have to be prepared for anything.

Saturday, December 27, 1862
Green Home

"Victoria Turner, you must be plumb crazy to be coming all the way over here with the city on alert like it is." Mary looked at her friend with disapproval in her face.

"It's only a few blocks," Victoria reminded Mary. "Besides, we haven't heard anything terribly pressing about a Yankee invasion since Christmas Eve."

"I suppose you're right." The two women sat down. "How was your Christmas celebration?"

"Mary Grace and the children stayed over. It was actually quite enjoyable. I dearly love having them around." Victoria smiled. "Having Jason home would have made it better, and Father, Gregory and Abraham, of course."

"Of course," Mary said softly. Though she tried not to, there were many times when she felt guilty for having Duff and Annie with her. Unlike so many of her friends, she didn't have to worry about his safety on a daily basis.

"They say there's been fighting down the Chickasaw Bayou way, near Walnut Hills," Victoria said. "We hope to get word from Jason any day now about the details."

"Yes, I am sure you're quite anxious to hear. Duff told me that just today, General Pemberton published a notice recommending all non-combatants, especially women and children, to leave the city."

"We heard that as well. Mary Grace is very frightened and wants to leave town with her children. She even mentioned going east to stay with our cousins or west to stay with Abraham's family in Texas."

"West would likely be safer," Mary said. "Especially after the fighting in the east earlier this month."

"I agree. I worry about Aunt Miriam and her family constantly. Fredericksburg has had so much conflict. I write often to both Elizabeth and Belle, but the Lord only knows if any of my letters actually get delivered."

"Will any of you be leaving town?"

"For now, Mother is going to take Mary Grace and the children out to the Wheeler's again. Brianne, Kendall and I will stay at the house with Esther and Caesar. I believe Mary Grace will benefit from Hannah's calming influence. I love my sister dearly, but she can be overly dramatic." Victoria shrugged. "How about your family? Does Duff want to move away?"

"No, not quite yet. He wants to stay in town, in our home. I'm glad he feels that way. I know I'm not very far along, but it would be dreadful to be in my condition and displaced. I cannot imagine giving birth anywhere but in my own home."

"I doubt as though you will have to worry about that." Victoria assured her friend.

"I do hope you're right," Mary replied, settling her hand on her slightly rounded stomach.

"Did Annie enjoy her Christmas? Where is that beautiful little girl?"

"She's currently down for a nap, and yes, she loved the celebration. She's just getting old enough to start understanding how special a day it is. She is enjoying the new doll Duff and I gave her."

"That is wonderful. Hopefully, by Christmas next year, this war will be over and our lives will have returned to normal."

"God-willing." Mary replied, then changed the subject. "It is a shame that Major Harris was called away from the gala at the Balfour's before you could really talk or dance with him."

"Yes. Pity." Victoria's voice told Mary that her friend felt just the opposite.

"Come, tell me. What was wrong with the major?"

"He was too handsome." It sounded so silly when she actually said it out loud.

"I must say, he is extremely good-looking, but for Heaven's sake, Victoria, how can a man be too handsome?"

Victoria tried to put her feelings into words. "The major gave me the impression that he well-knows just how handsome he is. He was not only flirting with me, but also every other unmarried woman at the gala, as well as some married women." Victoria looked down at her hands. "Mary, I would hate to marry a man who would stray. I feel as though Major Harris would be that kind of man, and to be honest, why would a man that good-looking even choose me to be his wife?" She gave a short laugh and placed a hand to her temple and groaned. "What is wrong with me, Mary? The moment I meet a potential suitor, I start thinking about marriage to him, and ever since Jeremy Thompson, I focus on what could go wrong. Why does my mind immediately think negative thoughts?"

"I believe it's because you want a fulfilled life. You want a good marriage and family, you don't want just a husband, you want a caring husband who will treat you the way you deserve." Mary reached across and comfortingly took Victoria's hand. "There is nothing wrong with you. You must get that idea out of your head. Jeremy Thompson was a devious rake, and he hurt you. He fooled us all. Why, I believe Mary Grace was secretly planning your wedding."

"Oh, that wasn't a secret to me," Victoria wiped a tear from her eye. "And apparently not everyone was fooled. You told me you had your doubts and Jason never liked the man." She took a deep breath. "I apologize for getting emotional, Mary. I'm not sure why I'm telling you this all of a sudden."

"Victoria, you are the dearest friend I have ever had. I don't mind in the least, you confiding your feelings. It's what friends are for. I just feel badly that we haven't talked about your feelings sooner. You can always share with me. The Lord knows that I share enough of my feelings with you."

But you also have Duff. Victoria thought.

"Now, answering a question you asked earlier," Mary continued. "A man like Major Harris would marry you for many reasons. You are beautiful inside and out. You are enjoyable to be around. You're not flighty or flirty or overly dramatic and you don't care for gossip. You are a wonderful friend and will make some lucky man a wonderful wife. You know this."

"Thank you for saying so, Mary. I appreciate it more than you can ever imagine."

"As I said earlier, that's what friends are for," Mary replied. "Now, what else is new?"

"There are many new people moving into town, in spite of the Yankee threat. In fact, I met someone on my way over here, a Mrs. Dora Miller. She arrived in Vicksburg with her husband very recently. She seems to be on the quiet side, but I did learn that she was married just under a year ago. Her husband is a lawyer, and they moved here from Arkansas. They lived in New Orleans before that. She didn't really say why they moved around so much, and she seemed to be quite lonely."

"Well, then, I suppose we should invite her to tea as soon as possible." Mary smiled, excited as always, to meet someone new.

Tuesday, December 30, 1862
Turner Home

"Is anyone home?" Jason Turner's voice called through the house. Victoria immediately came into the entryway.

"Jason! Thank goodness you're alright!" She threw her arms around her brother, then pulled him into the sitting room. "Mother is with Mary Grace and the children out at the Wheeler's."

"I was just about to head out there. Why didn't you go with them? I would have thought you would jump at the chance to go see Hannah."

"Hannah actually came into town today and we had a light lunch at the Green home. I'm glad you're going out to their farm, though. I know Ambrose will love to see you and hear stories of your daring accomplishments."

"I look forward to seeing him as well," Jason smiled.

"Tell me about the most recent battle," Victoria implored. "Am I correct in assuming we won?"

"Yes, we did. As we believed, the Yanks were trying to capture Vicksburg again. The Union General Sherman's men were on the river and landed near the Johnson Plantation. They headed through the swamps toward the town. We were waiting for them at Walnut Hills. They tried getting around us, but we had perfect position and held the land. Sherman tried a frontal attack yesterday, but we repulsed them again and he withdrew. The Yanks certainly lost more men than we did, maybe three times as many. We think they may try to regroup and try again, so we're preparing for just about anything they could throw at us."

"It's good to hear we won. Is there any other news? Have you any official word on the battle over in Fredericksburg?"

"Nothing official, no." Jason replied. "Rumors are the Confederate Army of Northern Virginia has settled in and around the town of Fredericksburg for the winter and the Yankees are camped on the other side of the river, around Chatham Manor."

"Oh, I have such fond memories of Chatham Manor and the people of Fredericksburg. I think of them often," Victoria said, reminiscing of her friends and family from the town again, and another specific memory.

1859

"Miss Victoria Turner! How are you this lovely day?" Nathaniel Prentiss smiled at Victoria when she came to the door of Turner's Glenn Plantation house.

"Mr. Prentiss. I am doing well." She smiled back, glad the young man had come over to visit, and that he had asked to see her, not any of her cousins. "What brings you over to Fredericksburg?"

"My sisters wanted to come over for a visit, so I offered to escort them. I enjoyed our conversation during the ball at Chatham very much, and wanted to talk with you more. I was hoping that I could escort you to one of our confectionaries in town and treat you to some ice cream. You do ride, don't you?"

"Ice cream?" She had read about the desert, but had yet to try it. "I would love to have some." She smiled. "Just let me tell my father where I will be. Should I ask Daniel to have a horse saddled for me?"

"If you are comfortable with it, you can ride Lafayette, AJ's horse. He is still saddled and ready to go." Nathaniel smiled back, then took her arm when she returned and led her out to the horses.

"I don't ride that often," Victoria confessed. "But I do enjoy it."

"It is one of my favorite things to do." Nathaniel admitted. "You spoke the other night about your love of reading and learning. Do you

have any interest in attending college? More and more women are doing so."

"I have some interest," Victoria replied. "The thing of it is, I enjoy reading and learning a great deal, but I like it to be on my own terms. Even in school, I would do what I was supposed to do as quickly as I could, then spend the rest of my free time learning things more to my liking. It is as if you tell me I have to read something, I do not want to do it, but if I do not have to do it, I am very interested." She shrugged. "I suppose it's just a part of my stubbornness."

Nathaniel gave a short laugh. "Stubbornness must be a family trait. I know your cousins well, and know that they can be quite stubborn as well."

"Indeed," Victoria replied. "I must tell you, I am quite excited about this ice cream. I have read about it and have always wanted to try it."

"Well, Fredericksburg may be considered a 'finished' town, but we do have many places to get delicious candies and other treats." Nathaniel said.

"I am looking forward to this very much. I hope to bring some of those candies home." Victoria and Nathaniel made good time, and they quickly reached the Noteware's Confectionary.

"This is my favorite place to get ice cream." Nathaniel dismounted and tethered his horse to the hitching post, then went to Victoria and helped her down. Butterflies fluttered in her stomach at the feel of his hands on her waist.

"I am sure it will be wonderful." She took his offered arm. "Besides, I will have nothing to compare it to."

"That is true." He replied. "Now, I will tell you that my favorite flavor is chocolate. AJ and Liberty both prefer strawberry, though."

"My goodness." Victoria hadn't realized that she would have that many choices of flavor. "I suppose I will have to try chocolate."

"Wonderful choice." He replied, and ordered the two ice creams.

Once the treat was ready, he led her to a table and they both sat down. He watched her as she took her first bite.

"Oh, my goodness, I don't know that I have ever had anything better in my life!" Victoria exclaimed as the cool, creamy chocolate flavor ran across her tongue and down her throat. She quickly took two more bites, not caring that it wasn't ladylike.

"Careful," Nathaniel cautioned her. "If you eat too quickly, you may get a headache."

"Thank you for the warning." She smiled. "Did you know that Benjamin Franklin, George Washington, and Thomas Jefferson were known to have regularly eaten and served ice cream? I read an article that detailed how records, kept by a merchant in New York, show George

Washington spent about $200 on ice cream in the summer of 1790. And First Lady Dolley Madison served ice cream at President James Madison's Inaugural Ball in 1813."

"I knew ice cream has been around for some time, but did not know those details." Nathaniel smiled in amazement of her knowledge. She was like a textbook of information. "I love learning, but I believe I could use you at school. I cannot remember facts like that as you can."

"It has always been a gift," Victoria replied. "I can read something and will remember it even years later."

"That would be a wonderful gift to have, especially at college," Nathaniel said.

"Do you receive good marks at school?" She asked.

"I do all right. I do much better at the practical classes. The classes that will help me turn my home into a very profitable farm. Perhaps even big enough and good enough to be called a plantation one day."

"I know it's improper to ask, but do you own slaves?" Victoria asked.

"We have two to help with the farm, and one of our neighbors is hiring one out to us while I am away at school, but it is mostly just me and my father. My sisters care for the household."

"I remember you said your mother died years ago. I can't imagine losing a parent." She spoke softly.

Nathaniel got a longing look in his eyes. "Very difficult. There are times when...just...I don't know. My father is a wonderful, caring man and he never hesitates to show us affection. But there are times when I wish I had the care of a mother."

"I don't think there is anything wrong with feeling like that," Victoria said.

"Thank you for saying so." Nathaniel reached out a hand toward her face, then hesitated. "You, uhh...you have some chocolate ice cream on your face." He wiped at the corner of his mouth, indicating where the cream was. She reached up, trying not to show her mortification, and wiped it away with the cloth napkin.

"Thank you for telling me," She said. The two finished their ice cream and continued their conversation. She had never enjoyed conversing with a young man more. Nathaniel treated her as an intellectual equal, not as a woman who wasn't smart enough for intelligent conversation like so many other young men she had talked to throughout the years.

Much earlier than she wanted, they were in sight of Turner's Glenn. He seemed reluctant for their time together to end as well. He brought her up to the front door.

"I do wish we could spend more time together." He took her hands in his, looking quite nervous all of a sudden.

"I do too, but we leave within the week and I know you must get back to school."

"Yes. However, as we spoke before, I would love to have your permission to write to you from Michigan." His blue eyes shone brightly, and contrasted sharply with his dark hair. It was a very attractive look, in Victoria's opinion.

"I would enjoy that very much, Mr. Prentiss." She replied.

"Wonderful. And again, you must call me Nathaniel." He took a step closer, and she could tell that he was nervous.

"Only if you call me Victoria."

"That seems a little long." He thought a moment. *"I think Tori suits you rather well."*

"All right then." She inwardly gushed at the thought that this handsome man had given her a nickname. Something only he would call her. *"I will have to come up with a nickname for you as well."*

"That sounds splendid." Nathaniel said, then nervously took a step closer to her. Victoria's heart sped up. Was he going to kiss her? *"I really want to kiss you right now."* His words were sweet, as if he were asking permission to do so.

"I'd like that too." She replied, and he gently bent and gave her a chaste, soft kiss.

"Well, then, I suppose I should go see to my sisters." He smiled, standing straight again. She gently held his arm.

"Take care of yourself, Nathaniel." She smiled as he ushered her inside.

"I will. I hope to hear from you soon, Tori." He smiled, and they parted.

1862

Victoria smiled at the memory of her first kiss. Nathaniel was such a good man. He had kept the promise of writing to her, and she always enjoyed his letters. Unfortunately, the relationship had never progressed in a romantic way past that kiss. He never brought it up in their correspondence, and she didn't feel it was appropriate for her to do so. Besides, the information from Fredericksburg told her that he had moved on.

"Victoria! You are deep in thought."

"Sorry, Jason." Victoria smiled apologetically. "I was just thinking about Fredericksburg and the Turners. The Prentiss family also."

"Ah, yes. I keep meaning to ask you about them. Do you still keep in touch with either of the older Prentiss siblings?"

"Yes, but I haven't heard from either Nathaniel or AJ since early in the war," she replied.

"The same with Belle and Elizabeth, I would wager." He said. "I recall you and Nathaniel enjoyed each other's company when we visited. I'd always hoped more would come of that relationship. I liked the man."

"We did enjoy each other's company, but it went no further than that. We're just good friends. Besides, I am fairly certain that by now, he is married to Belle."

"Our cousin, Belle?" Jason tried not to laugh. "I find it hard to believe that Belle would stoop down so low as to marry a common farmer."

"Yes, well, the last letter I received from her said she was marrying 'a young man of my acquaintance'. She must have changed her mind."

"I suppose it's possible. She always has been the flightiest member of the family." Jason stood. "I must go. I'm glad to see you're all safe here. I'll head out to the Wheeler's and see to Mother and Mary Grace's family."

Victoria stood as well and embraced her brother. "I'll see you when you return," she told him. "Take care of yourself, Jason."

Part 3:
1863

Saturday, January 3, 1863

My Dearest Cousin Bekah
I hope this letter reaches you and finds you well. There is such fierce fighting in Virginia. Between your family staying outside Petersburg and the Fredericksburg Turners under occupation so often there, it is difficult to imagine what will become of all of us. I am thankful every day we are safe here in Vicksburg, though we have had some excitement and close calls. Jason tells me that General Grant will stop at nothing to take our city and get control of the Mississippi River. That will be quite hard to do, however. The Federals have even attempted to dig a canal so that they can bypass Vicksburg. I must say, I am torn whether or not I want them to succeed in that endeavor. If they are able to dig it, they will be able to take control of the Mississippi and split the Confederacy in two, and that would not be good. However, if they are successful, then we here in Vicksburg will be in less danger as our city will be unimportant.
I hope things are going well for you and your mother. I simply cannot imagine the pain you are going through with your family split in two. I know that you were usually quite neutral when it came to the arguments between the North and the South, and tried to look at things from both sides. I wonder if that is still the case. And your mother, I dearly miss her. I truly believe we all need to come together after the war and have a reunion of sorts, so that we can see each other and catch up in person instead of simply through letters.
I hope to hear from you soon!
Cousin Victoria

Victoria looked at the letter. She did want to visit with all of her cousins once the war was over and it was safe, but she was unsure about meeting up with the married Nathaniel and Belle. She tried to get him out of her head, but could not. She wasn't sure why. Jeremy Thompson was little more than a distant memory, and that fact alone bothered her. She had been ready to marry the man. How could it be that she could forget him like it was nothing. She shook her head and pulled out her journal so she could copy the letter for herself, as she always did with her letters. She liked having copies of what she wrote others. It was almost like a diary. Just as she put her pen to the paper, the door burst open and, before she could fully turn around, a three-year-old boy threw himself into her lap.

"Gabriel!" She exclaimed, a smile on her face. She gave him a tight hug and kissed his smooth, blonde hair. "I didn't know you all were coming over today."

"Mama closed up the store early. Not a lot of people are coming in." He pushed off her lap and stood, then pulled at her hand. "Come on! Can we go play a game?"

"But of course." Victoria couldn't help but smile as the boy pulled her down the stairs to the parlor. "There are card games, checkers, Goose, and I bet we could even play your Uncle Jason's *Checkered Game of Life* or *Mansion of Happiness*." Her brother loved games of all kinds and collected them whenever he could. *The Checkered Game of Life* was his newest game, created by a Yankee named Milton Bradly, who was famous for creating a lithograph of Federal President Abraham Lincoln.

"Not checkers," Gabriel said. "If we do that, we can only have two people play and I want Adam to be able to play." Victoria was touched by the energetic boy who would slow down to play quiet games with his sickly brother.

"That is a very good point." Victoria said. "What is Adam's favorite game to play?"

"I dunno. We can ask him." Gabriel said.

"All right." Victoria looked up and saw her mother hugging Mary Grace in her father's study. "You go ask Adam and get things set up while I say 'Hello' to your mother."

"Yes, Ma'am." Gabriel said, then bounced away.

"Mama, Mary Grace, is everything all right?"

Mary Grace pulled away from her mother and wiped a tear from her cheek. "Yes, it is. I just miss Abraham so much sometimes it makes me overly emotional. Mama understands."

Victoria nodded, slightly hurt from the assumption that just because she wasn't married, she didn't miss the soldiers or ever get emotional. However, she couldn't imagine how much her sister missed Abraham.

"Of course," Victoria said. "Did you hear any news as you came through town?"

"General John Pemberton is stationed down the street, next door to the Balfours, and he is reinforcing our ranks. When the Federal General Sherman heard this, he loaded his men and headed back upriver. Everyone in town is saying that it is a Confederate victory."

"Well, that is a good way to begin the year," Victoria said. "I hope that will be a sign of things to come." She gave her sister a hug. "You do know that you can come to me if you ever need to talk, correct?"

"I know, Victoria. You are a wonderful sister and friend." Mary Grace smiled. "And a wonderful aunt. Gabriel and Adam were very excited to come and see you today."

"I am so glad they did." Victoria smiled back. "I should get into the parlor. Gabriel was going to choose a game for us to play."

"Wonderful," Mary Grace said. "We can all go in there and spend time together before dinner." She took Victoria's arm and they walked into the parlor.

February 18, 1863
Turner Home
Dear Gregory

It has been strange not hearing from you in such a long time. You may have heard that we had an exciting Christmas, and that is true. I was not happy about the Yankees ruining my most favorite of holidays. There we were, having a gay old time at the Balfour's annual party, when we heard that the Yankees were coming and the party was ended. Then, we spent the entire holiday worried that the Yankees would attack. We were able to spend the day together, singing Christmas carols around the piano, and we made gingerbread cookies. Fear not, we remembered to sing your favorite carol, **Silent Night,** *and Father's favorite,* **God Rest Ye Merry Gentlemen.** *It was as enjoyable as we could make it.*

As I wrote you before, Vicksburg is much changed. Ever since the attacks last year, our defenders have worked hard to make the defenses here even stronger. We feel much protected by the troops and militia who keep the city from falling into enemy hands.

We miss you dearly. You and Father will not even believe your eyes when you see the children. Adam and Gabriel grow more and more unique every day. Adam is quiet and studious, even at his age of three. He is always watching and observing, and loves looking through books and being read to. He is much like Father in this way. Gabriel loves to explore and would go off towards the river or woods every day on his own if Mary Grace allowed it. I am sure he will do so more as he grows up. Our little Hope grows more and more every day, too. She is already such a proper young lady. I know I sound a bit like their mother and not their aunt, the way I talk about them, but I dearly enjoy watching them grow.

As always, I must ask that you take care of yourself, and Father. It is my constant prayer that you all return home safe and sound soon.

Your loving sister,
Victoria

"I am starting to appreciate a quiet town, as we had before this war," Mary Green said. "If only we could go back to a time when we only needed a small militia to protect us."

"That will not be the case until the confounded war is over," Victoria said. "And hopefully that will be soon. We have defeated the Yankees in just about every major battle, especially over in the East."

"It was quite alarming, though, to hear the Federals won at Corinth," Mary said, thinking back. "It brings the war closer than I would like it to be." She placed a hand on her stomach. Well into the sixth month of her pregnancy, Mary couldn't hide her condition any more. As best as she could figure she would have the child in early May, and thankfully would not be heavy with child in the suffering heat of a Mississippi summer. "And those Yankees did defeat us back in September, in Maryland...what was the city?"

"Sharpsburg. Antietam Creek. It was a hollow victory for them. They lost so many men." Victoria pointed out. "Jason said it was a Union victory in name only, but it gave Lincoln the opportunity for that ridiculous Emancipation Proclamation."

"I still cannot believe he thinks he can free our slaves," Mary said. "Does he not realize how lost they would be without us to guide them?"

"To be honest, I would be lost without our slaves." Victoria admitted. "Esther is a miracle-worker with any and all foods and she is such a good listener. Having Caesar around makes me feel much safer, especially with Father, Gregory, and Jason gone, and Dinah is just wonderful in so many things. I'm not sure what we would do without them. They're like part of the family."

"I agree," Mary said. "Duff told me that we shouldn't have to worry about Lincoln's proclamation anyways, as we are not under his command any more. He no longer has the right to tell us what to do."

"And yet, Mr. Green doesn't want to fight to protect his rights." Victoria couldn't help but mention.

"Victoria, I wish you would stop bringing that up. Duff is a businessman, not a soldier." Mary felt the need to defend her husband. "He needs to stay here to protect us and our future. He's not the only man of fighting age who chose not to fight. Besides, he helps the cause in his own way. I know you heard we donated all of the iron from our side porch banister to the Confederacy." Mary knew Victoria took issue with Duff not fighting, as did many people in town, but Duff was the type of man who needed to be home with his family. Mary had to admit that she was quite glad he wasn't a soldier, especially in her condition. She had already suffered through losing one child and her own father. She couldn't bear losing someone else she dearly loved.

"If those thoughts are what make you feel better, Mary. My father is a lawyer, not a soldier, and Gregory was also studying the law, not military strategies. Jason has some background in the military, but he is not a career soldier either. Mary Grace's husband is a businessman as well." Victoria felt bad about what she was saying, but her frustration grew with every week her family was away.

"I know all that, Victoria," Mary argued back. "But there are many men who stayed behind. Nobody forced your father and brothers to go and enlist, they chose to do it. You simply cannot blame Duff for not enlisting. You cannot blame him for making a choice that is different from what your family members did."

"But you can keep giving me your weak excuses about Duff when the men in my life are fighting for their beliefs. They want to be home with their families as well, but they enlisted because they knew it was their duty. They stood up and did what they had to do to protect their family."

"That is what Duff is trying to do!" Tears fell from Mary's eyes. "He is protecting his family the best way that he knows how."

"But it's not right! All able-bodied men should join the fight." Victoria realized she was standing and she and Mary were actually yelling at one another. That had never happened before. She sank down in her seat, then sighed and rubbed her temple. "I hate this war and what it is doing. Causing you and me to fight. We never fight."

"No, we don't." Mary sighed. "I am sorry, Victoria. I wish I knew what I could say to you. I am sorry that so many people in your life have left. I wish they could be here with you."

"Yes, I do as well." Victoria picked up the needlepoint she had been working on as Mary returned to knitting a pair of booties for her new child. "I suppose we should just...avoid the topic. I don't know if we'll ever be able to discuss it without getting upset with each other."

"You're right. I suppose there is nothing more for us to do now except to change the subject."

Victoria nodded and Mary continued. "I might be prying, but I must ask, have you heard from Major Harris at all?" Mary asked. "I saw him from a distance last week, but didn't have the chance to speak with him."

"We have gotten together for tea a time or two," Victoria admitted. "He is very polite and charming. I'm just not sure he's the right man for me."

"Well, I suppose one never quite knows what will happen. Perhaps he will be, eventually."

"Perhaps. I suppose I'll just continue to pray for guidance." Victoria added, then looked toward the doorway as her mother hastened through. "Mother, what's wrong?" Victoria stood and approached Rachel.

"Nothing for you to worry about, my dear. I just wanted to let you know that Mary Grace wanted me to come over and help with the children. Adam is sick again, the poor dear. Mary Grace feels I can be just the cure he needs. At the very least, I can help with Gabriel and Hope."

"They do so enjoy your company, Mama." Victoria's smile could not completely mask her concern. "Please let me know if I can be of any assistance."

"Yes. I will send Joyce to let you know if we need extra help or to let you know if I won't be home tonight." Joyce was Mary Grace's slave.

"All right. Give them my love." Victoria nodded and returned to her seat. Mary could tell that the news about Adam worried her friend.

"I'm sure he'll be just fine," She tried to reassure Victoria.

"I hope so," Victoria's voice cracked. "I just worry about him so much. You know he's always been sickly, ever since the boys were born. Gabriel's always been the stronger of the two. Adam sometimes has trouble breathing just playing and trying to keep up with Gabriel. I just...I just don't know, Mary, he's such a smart, sweet, funny little boy. I sometimes fear he will get so sick we'll lose him. I don't know how I would handle that. I love him so."

"It is never easy," Mary said, feeling emotional herself. No matter how much time passed, she still missed the first child she and Duff had. A year later, Mary had given birth to her second daughter and, as many families did, they named the little girl after her sister.

"Oh, Mary, please forgive me, I'm so sorry." Victoria wiped at her tear-stained eyes. "I forgot just for a moment."

"You're concerned for your nephew. I can understand that." Mary smiled through her own tears. There were many times that she wished she could forget. She never wanted to forget her older daughter, Annie, rather, she wanted to forget the pain she felt. The girl would be turning seven this year. What would she have been like? "I'm just thankful that little Annie is healthy and that this pregnancy has been relatively easy so far."

"I am sure that he or she will be healthy as well," Victoria assured her friend. "I must tell you, I do pray for you every day."

"Thank you. I pray for you as well, your family, your brothers and Father. I pray that they'll return home safely."

"I suppose we all need prayers, no matter what our situation is."

"That is very true," Mary said. "So very true."

Friday, March 20, 1863
Turner Home

Mary Green, Hannah, and Victoria sat in the Turner's parlor, all working on small sewing projects.

"Is there any news from the Eastern states?" Hannah asked, knowing that Victoria would be the best person to ask, as interested in the current news as she was.

"A bit," Victoria replied. "There have been some minor battles, with us being the victors, of course, but from what I hear, the political news is a bit more interesting. The heavy-handed Lincoln signed another law, this one requiring each state to fill a quota of draftees. However, the law also says that any man who is drafted may buy their way out of service if they can pay $300."

"That hardly seems fair to the poor or even middling farmers and factory workers," Hannah pointed out.

"I agree with you, but it also seems to me that a draft...well, they're taking on men who didn't volunteer. Is a man who is being forced to fight really going to make a good soldier? I know the Confederacy drafted men last April, but...I just don't know if I agree with this."

"It is a difficult situation," Hannah said. "Mary, have you heard of any current events?"

"Duff mentioned a tragedy in Richmond," Mary added. "There was a horrific explosion in the James River, on Brown's Island. It was at the Confederate Ordnance Laboratory. Almost 70 workers were killed." She shook her head.

"I heard that as well," Victoria said. "Something they call a friction primer exploded. Sixty-two of those killed were women and girls."

"How terribly sad! Those poor souls." Hannah shook her head. "I assume they were workers in the factory."

"Yes," Victoria replied. "I understand many women have been stepping in to men's roles throughout the South." She thought of her cousin, Charlotte, from Pennsylvania, who had likely taken over her father's farm. "All throughout the North too, I'd presume."

"Indeed, but women taking over the family business is not unheard of." Hannah reminded her. "For example, Cordelia, Caroline and I have been running the family farm since Benjamin passed. We never even had slaves to help, but even if we did, with this war, I don't know if we would have been able to keep them. I am continually hearing about how other plantations and farms are losing them constantly. So many runaways." She shook her head, then changed the subject. "What is the news closer to home? I assume the Federals still want control of Vicksburg?"

"They'll always want Vicksburg," Victoria said. "It's their General Grant's main objective. Some Admiral named Farragut was recently stopped at Port Hudson. I also heard a rumor that two Federal ships slipped into the garrison here at Vicksburg. I'm not sure exactly what that means, but they are not in our area anymore."

"It means we can expect more military operations against the city," Jason entered the room. "Pardon me, ladies." He tipped his hat to them. Victoria stood and embraced her brother. "I don't mean to interrupt, but I had to let you know the news myself."

"What news? Is it bad?" Victoria asked.

"Pemberton and his staff have given orders that all non-combatants should leave town again or prepare accordingly." Jason replied.

"What do you think we should do? Leave again?" Victoria asked.

"I'm not sure anymore." Jason pulled his hat off and ran a hand through his hair, which was in desperate need of a trim. "My impulse is to have you all move back out of the city to the Wheelers farm, if they would allow you."

"Of course you're welcome there," Hannah said.

"What else is on your mind?" Victoria knew Jason wanted to say something more.

"I'm not so sure that would be for the best anymore." Jason admitted. "I don't believe the country will be any less dangerous than the city. We moved you all out there last year and there was no real danger. Some bombardment of course, but no one was injured. My instinct tells me that you will all be okay if you just stay aware of the daily situations."

"Well, we'll do whatever you suggest," Victoria said. "I will defer to you and mother, of course."

"I appreciate your confidence in my decisions," Jason smiled, then turned to Mary. "I spoke with Mr. Green on my way over, and he will be here shortly to bring you home." She nodded and Jason turned to Hannah. "I saw your horse tethered up outside. I can escort you to your farm, then come back and speak with my mother."

"You don't need to escort me, Jason," she said. "I'll be just fine."

"I am well aware that you can take care of yourself, Mrs. Wheeler, however, the crowds are quite excited right now. I wouldn't be a Southern gentleman if I allowed you to travel unescorted." He gave her a smile that Victoria knew was his most playful.

"Well, we can't have anyone believing that you're not a proper Southern gentleman," She smiled back. "All right, I will accept your kind offer." She stood to gather her things in her basket, and Jason took it from her arm.

After they had left, Mary turned to Victoria. "Those two make a fine couple, don't you think?"

"I agree, and I have thought that for a while," Victoria said. "I believe Jason has feelings for Hannah, and always has, but I believe she is hesitant to give her heart away again. She cared for Benjamin, and Jason and he were such good friends as well. I think Hannah and Jason would do well together, if and when Hannah is ever ready."

Mary nodded, then stood when she heard a knock on the parlor door. Caesar introduced Duff, who walked in and greeted Victoria, then spoke to Mary.

"My dear, I am here to escort you home. Things are getting exciting in town again with the arrival of some Federal ships down by the river."

"Yes, Jason Turner was just here and told us." She gathered her things. "Thank you for your company, Victoria. I'm sure we'll see each other soon."

"Yes, I'm still planning on attending church Sunday." Victoria said.

"Wonderful. I will see you the day after tomorrow."

Thursday, April 16, 1863
Streets of Vicksburg

"My dear daughter, may I present to you Mrs. Mary Loughborough?" Mary Green's mother approached her daughter with a smile. Mary smiled back and greeted the two women.

"Welcome to Vicksburg, Mrs. Loughborough. I do hope you enjoy your stay here. Where are you visiting us from?"

"Oh, I have been all over this magnificent country in my twenty-five years." The bubbly young woman smiled. "I was born in New York, but my husband James, is from Kentucky. We lived in St. Louis for a time; that's where I developed my strong sympathy for your Southern cause. James is now a Major with your Confederate army. My daughter and I follow him wherever he is stationed. We are in Jackson for now, but I knew so many wonderful people from Vicksburg, we decided to come for a visit."

"We are glad to have you. How old is your daughter?" Mary asked.

"My dear Jean is two. She is with one of my servants right now."

"You should bring her over to play with my daughter, Annie. She is three. They would get along splendidly, I am sure. As you can probably see, she will soon be an older sister."

"I would have guessed that, but didn't want to be rude and ask." Mrs. Loughborough replied.

"Mary!" All three women turned as Victoria approached them. Mary Green smiled. "You may have to be more specific when calling me, Victoria. This is Mrs. Mary Loughborough. Mrs. Loughborough, may I present my dearest friend, Miss Victoria Turner." Mary turned to Mrs. Loughborough. "Miss Turner has a sister named Mary as well, Mrs. Mary Grace Corbet ."

"My goodness. That is likely quite confusing." Mrs. Loughborough laughed.

"It can be, but we are able to keep things sorted for the most part," Victoria smiled. "I would love to stay and get to know you better, Mrs. Loughborough, but I was on my way to my sister's home. I do hope to see you again soon. Perhaps we could have tea sometime."

"I would enjoy that," Mary Loughborough said. The women turned to continue walking, but before she took her first step, Victoria froze. Mary Green looked to where her friend's attention was and cringed when she saw Captain Harris escorting Miss Winifred Craig, a distant cousin on her mother's side. The two looked quite cozy, and as they arrived at Winifred's home, he bent and kissed her hand, then turned and headed toward the outskirts of town. Mary looked back at Victoria, who looked a bit stunned, then cleared her throat.

"Well, I suppose I should have known that would happen. Perhaps not with Winifred, but with someone." She shook her head. "At least things worked out well for Nettie Green. I heard she and her Captain James Burem were married yesterday." She shrugged her shoulders. "My apologies, ladies, but I do need to get to my sister's." Then, with a last look at Mary Green, almost as if silently saying 'I told you this would happen,' she left.

Mary sighed. "Victoria has been unlucky in love in the past, Mrs. Loughborough, and that Captain we just saw had been paying her special attention, but it is now apparent that he is paying special attention to at least one other young woman in town. She told me when I first introduced them that she suspected he wasn't sincere."

"I see. That's too bad."

"She is quite a wonderful friend, however. You really should join us for tea sometime while you are here in town."

"I would really enjoy that very much, Mrs. Green. I must ask, is that Nettie Green she spoke of any relation?"

"Not directly, no. Hers and Captain Burem's story is a romantic one, though."

"Do tell."

"Music won the heart of her soldier. The captain was returning to camp from picket duty back in March when he heard music and briefly called at Nettie's home. She was playing the piano, 'Annie Laurie', I believe. He fell in love with her immediately and they were married yesterday. I heard the wedding was a sensation, and the captain made a wonderful speech about his happiness."

"That is a wonderful story." Mary Loughborough checked her pocket watch. "Oh, botheration, it is much later than I thought. I should be catching up with the rest of my party, but do find me when you set up a time to visit."

"I will do that," Mary Green replied, and the women all went their separate ways.

Thursday, April 16, 1863
Turner Home

Victoria lit a candle and pulled some letters out of her box of mementos. It was late, possibly after midnight, but she couldn't fall asleep. Seeing Captain Harris with Miss Craig had affected her more than it should have. She didn't have anything against Winifred; she was a nice enough young woman, but she had so wished that she could have been special to a man like Captain Harris, or anyone really. She unfolded one of the first letters that Nathaniel Prentiss had sent her so long ago.

Miss Turner,   *1859*

I have made it safely back to Michigan and can once again focus on my studies. I must say that, while I love my family and enjoy being home, there are many distractions there. However, meeting you wasn't a distraction, but a breath of fresh air. I thoroughly enjoyed making your acquaintance and the conversations that we had were most invigorating. I hope we can continue that through our letters to one another. I don't mean to presume too much, but I truly felt the start of a wonderful friendship between us.

BOOM! Victoria jumped at the sound of the explosive cannon fire and dropped the letter on the desk. She quickly grabbed her robe and slippers and scurried downstairs to the veranda as the cannonading continued. Kendall was right behind her.

"My goodness!" Kendall said, staring out towards the river in horror.

"Oh, Lord, be with us," Victoria said. The river was illuminated with flames on the banks of the Mississippi River. They could see huge, black masses floating down the river with the currents. Another shell exploded, this time coming from the upper part of town. Kendall clutched Victoria's arm as Rachel joined them on the porch. The night was pitch black, but with the fires on the riverbank, the women could clearly see gunboats.

"Oh, dear," Rachel exclaimed. "I do hope Brianne and the other guests at the ball are safe. She went with Anne Marmaduke and her family, they'll certainly take care of her."

Brianne was at a ball at the home of a popular Confederate officer, along with many other young women and soldiers.

"It's almost as if we lit the fires so that we could see their boats." Kendall appeared entranced by the sight.

"You may be right," Victoria said. She could hear sounds of galloping horses on the paved streets and the voices of the soldiers on the riverside. The Yankee boats fired back at the Confederate batteries, and it sounded as if shells boomed all around the entire city.

"I am not comfortable with how close those shells are coming to us," Rachel said.

"I know there are caves in some places around town," Kendall said. "We could find one and stay there for protection."

"A cave? Underground?" Victoria's heart pounded at the thought. "Absolutely not. No. There is no possible way I could do that. You all can go, but I am staying right here."

"They're more like dugouts than caves, Victoria," Kendall explained.

"We should all stay together," Rachel said. "I'm sure it's not necessary to leave the house, at least not yet. This shelling will hopefully be over soon."

The three women continued to look out over the city. Victoria tried to remain calm and collected, but she found herself slightly anxious. Shell after shell crashed, and the sound was deafening. Just when it appeared as though the danger had passed, there was another explosion and, one of the Union transports burst into flames. As it continued to burn, it slowly began to sink into the river.

"That's almost a beautiful sight." Kendall was transfixed.

"Unfortunately, all of the other Yankee boats appear to have passed by successfully," Victoria pointed out. "I'm sure that's not good."

"Miss Turner! Ladies." Duff Green approached and strode up the porch. "I told Mary I would check on all of the Turners. I am so glad to see that you are all well. I'll head down to Mrs. Corbet's home and check on her."

"Thank you so much, Mr. Green," Rachel said. "I will go with you to Mary Grace's, if that's all right."

"Mr. Green, what is the news? What did you hear as you passed through town?" Victoria asked.

"Most of the citizens are quite astounded that the majority of the Union ships passed through safely. Apparently, very few Confederate guns were even discharged. They say some were defective, others had questionable fuses."

"That is unfortunate. I am assuming Mary and Annie are safe?"

"Shaken and scared, but safe," Duff replied, then turned to Rachel. "Now that I have seen to you all, shall we go and check on the haberdashery?"

"Yes," Rachel said, then turned to Victoria. "I will be back shortly."

Kendall and Victoria continued to look out over the river. The glare from the burning boat lit the white magnolias, paled the pink crape myrtles, and brightened the veranda.

"I can't help but think of all the people on the boat," Kendall said quietly. "I know they are Yankees, but they are still human beings." Her voice was soft and she sounded like a five-year-old girl. Victoria put an arm around her cousin's shoulder and pulled her close. "I know they have wives and mothers who are praying for their safety too," Kendall continued. "I wonder, do they have children who are now fatherless?"

Victoria pulled Kendall into a full embrace. She knew what the girl was thinking. Would the war leave either of them fatherless?

Sunday, April 19, 1863
Christ Episcopal Church

"I am so glad we were able to have services today," Hannah told Victoria as they walked out of church. "Especially after all of the excitement we've had this week. I desperately needed the reflection time."

"Yes, Thursday night was particularly exciting," Victoria said.

"Some people had more excitement than others" Kendall grinned saucily at her sister. "Some young ladies, Brianne included, were at a party with Confederate officers. Dear sister, you should share your experience with Mrs. Wheeler."

Brianne tried not to seem too exasperated. "If I must." She turned to Hannah. "We were attending a party at Major Watts home, as Kendall alluded. Victoria was going to come, but last minute she said she wasn't up to it." Hannah quickly glanced at Victoria in question, then refocused on Brianne. "Anyways, three of the guests, young ladies, when they first heard the commotion, asked where they should go. A brigadier-general who had been dancing with one of the girls, jokingly told them that the safest place was in the countryside. The ninny actually thought he was serious so she and two of her nitwit friends set off alone. Luckily, one of the gentlemen noticed their absence and managed to catch up with them. Whenever a shell would come near them they would all drop in the dust, dresses and all. Eventually, a carriage was sent out to retrieve them."

"My goodness. Were they all safe?" Hannah asked.

"Yes, just dirty and feeling a bit foolish, I would wager." Brianne said. "I had met the young ladies earlier, but they were from Jackson and have already departed for home."

"I see," Hannah said, then pulled Victoria close to have a more private conversation. "Why did you not go to the Major's party?"

Victoria sighed. "Earlier in the day, I saw Captain Harris with Winnifred Craig. They looked as though they were courting. Even though

I should have expected I wouldn't be the only woman in town that a man who is that handsome and sure of himself would be interested in. It shouldn't have affected me the way it did, but I couldn't help but be slightly upset."

"I suppose I can understand that, but really, Victoria, I don't know why you have such a low opinion of yourself. We have been through this millions of times, it seems." Hannah then changed the subject. "I missed Mary today. Is she feeling poorly again?"

"Yes, and I'm sure she will explain the reason for that soon." Victoria tried to be cryptic, but Hannah smiled in understanding.

"I will have to make sure I go and visit her the next time I am in town," Hannah replied.

"Yes, you should," Victoria said. "And speaking of visiting, I understand that my brother has visited you a few times."

"Yes, he is so kind, and very protective of my family. I sometimes wonder if he feels a responsibility to us because of how close he was with Benjamin."

"Perhaps," Victoria said, though she suspected something more. "It does make me feel better, knowing that Jason and Old Man Wagner are watching out for you."

"Indeed," Hannah said. "I must confess, it makes me feel better as well."

Monday, April 27, 1863
Union Cavalry Camp

Tabetha halted her horse and surveyed the area. For the past ten days, she and the rest of her regiment had been riding around in hostile territory, tearing up railroads and burning crossties, freeing slaves, burning Confederate storehouses, ripping up bridges and generally causing as much damage as they possibly could in enemy territory. She did not approve of all the destruction, it was such a waste. What they were doing wasn't just defeating the enemy, it was as if they were attacking the army and the civilians. Tabetha rubbed at the dirt on her face, wishing desperately that she could bathe, but she knew the grime lent an added layer of protection to her disguise.

"Pistol Pete!" Captain Steven Rogers rode up beside her. "I need you to come with me to scout ahead. Grierson said Grant wants to cross the river at Port Gibson. We won't go that far South, but he wants a report on Confederate movements."

"Yes, sir." Tabetha nodded, then followed her commanding officer. "Gladly." She tried to say the last word quietly.

"What makes you so glad to ride with me?" Rogers asked. She should have known he would hear her.

"I just suppose raiding is not much to my taste," she replied. "With all due respect, sir, I don't know why we have to destroy so much property."

"Grant was tired of the Rebel cavalry riding circles around us and I can't blame him. Those Reb leaders Forrest, Morgan and Stuart have embarrassed our armies. We must burn any and all of their supplies and destroy their resources so the cavalry is unable to use them. Unfortunately, the civilians suffer as well. It cannot be helped."

"It doesn't mean we shouldn't try harder to make it easier on the poor families," Tabetha muttered.

"Perhaps," The Captain said. "However, I believe luck is on our side. It appears as though Forrest is distracted, off chasing our Colonel Streight over in Alabama. Also their Lieutenant General Pemberton over in Vicksburg, doesn't appear to have a lot of cavalry to defend his position. That's one of the main pieces of information we're trying to confirm. The Union army needs control of the Mississippi River and that means control of Vicksburg."

Tabetha nodded. She didn't have much knowledge about the geography of the area, but had heard of the importance of Vicksburg many times.

The two crossed a railroad track, then looked around, making sure there were no enemy soldiers about.

"How far are we expected to scout?" Tabetha asked once they had continued toward the west.

"Grierson wants us to ride as far as we can until nightfall, then rest up and head back to find him in the morning."

"All right," Tabetha tried to sound unflustered, but her insides churned. She already felt uncomfortable at how improper it was for her to be in such close contact with the men of her regiment, but it was going to be highly improper for her to be alone with a man. Even if he didn't realize she was a woman and it was an improper situation. Why did he have to be so handsome? And kind, and...

A shot rang out; her thoughts interrupted.

"Ride! Get to the tree line!" Captain Rogers shouted as Tabetha spurred on Ranger.

Tabetha glanced back as another shot rang out. She saw at least three Confederate soldiers riding hard behind them. Gripping the reins with one hand and trusting her horse, she spun around, almost sitting sidesaddle and fired her pistol at them. She wanted to feel a sense of pride when she saw one of the men fall off his horse, but couldn't. She cocked and aimed again, then pulled the trigger. This time she missed, but it seemed to be enough of a threat that the Confederates stopped chasing them. She continued riding hard, but heard another shot ring out. She felt a sharp sting at her side, but kept on for the tree line.

"Are you alright?" Captain Rogers yelled. He must have noticed her flinch.

"Yes, sir!" She called back. "I can keep going!"

He pointed. "It looks like there's a stream over there." She nodded and tried not to show the pain she was feeling on her side. She squeezed her eyes shut.

Please, Lord, don't let me faint. Please don't let him discover my secret. She prayed.

Tabetha and Captain Rogers pulled up their horses at the stream and dismounted. Ranger and the captain's horse, Duke, immediately drank from the stream. Captain Rogers looked at Tabetha, concern on his face.

"I heard you cry out. Were you hit?"

"Just grazed, I think," she replied, trying to act unaffected, but her side burned. "I'll be fine." She grinned and tried to change the subject. "At least we found the Confederates we were looking for."

"Are you sure you don't want me to take a look?" He insisted.

"No!" She tried not to sound alarmed at his suggestion as she pulled off her jacket. "Like I said, I'll be fine."

"All right," He nodded and then knelt next to the creek to splash water on his face. She followed suit, pulling her bandana off her neck and soaking it so she could wipe both her face and then her side. Fortunately, the wound was on her left side, and the captain was on her right. She pulled up her shirt and glanced at the wound, immediately grateful when she saw it truly was just a graze. She adjusted her binding slightly so that it was also covering the wound, then put her shirt back in place.

"How does it look?" Captain Rogers asked, standing.

"Like I thought, just a nick. It burns a bit, but it's hardly even bleeding."

"You're something else," He placed his hands on his hip. "You saved our lives back there. That was some of the most impressive riding and shooting I have ever seen. I wouldn't have believed it if I hadn't seen it myself. I see where you get your nickname."

She smiled softly. "My brother taught me. We would always fun around and practice when we were growing up. It was something we both enjoyed and were always trying to best each other."

"It's wonderful to have that kind of connection with another person. My brother, Caleb was like that for me. We have another younger brother, Ezekiel, but there was always something between Caleb and me. He was my best friend." The captain grabbed his canteen and thrust it into the cool stream water. "Let's head back to the regiment. We may not have found out as much information as I would have preferred, but it will have to suffice."

"That sounds like a plan to me," Tabetha nodded. "Let's go."

Saturday, May 2, 1863
Union Cavalry Camp

Tabetha adjusted her bindings before she walked outside to break down her A-frame tent. Captain Rogers saw her and motioned her over.

"General Grant has crossed the Mississippi River below Fort Gibson, as he planned. He wants to move quickly and decisively so the Rebs won't be able to unite their forces. I'm sending you, Privates Reagan and Robinson out to scout near Vicksburg. See if you can get us information about how many Confederates are at the garrison there."

"Yes, sir," Tabetha nodded, then packed the rest of her gear. Once Reagan and Robinson were ready, the three rode out. Tabetha didn't mind riding with either man. Josiah Reagan liked to talk, which meant that she didn't have to, and Hugh Robinson was a recruit who was always very friendly.

They had been riding for a few hours when they came upon some Confederate scouts.

"Get down!" Josiah yelled as a shot was fired at them. Another shot rang out and Josiah fell to the ground, clearly hit in the chest.

"Josiah!" She yelled, throwing herself off Ranger and checking on her fallen comrade. It took only a few seconds for her to realize that he was dead. Choking back tears, she remounted her horse and looked around. Sergeant Robinson was already riding away, leaving both her and Josiah behind. Tabetha glanced back towards the Confederates and her heart sped up at the sight of a Rebel on a horse charging her. Before she could turn and ride away, he had drawn his saber and was almost in range. She was just about to draw her pistol, but realized that she wasn't in position to shoot the man. Instead, she pulled her horse around and dug her heels into Ranger's flanks.

With a bloodcurdling yell, the Rebel swung at her, catching her shoulder with his saber and sending a sharp pain through her whole body. She threw her arm at him, pushing him away, then kicked her leg out, hoping that she could throw him off balance. She was successful, and she turned Ranger sharply into the horse of the Rebel soldier. The Reb fell completely off his mount. She groaned, pain still shooting through her, and clutched her shoulder, knowing that this wound was far worse than her wound just days before.

"Come on, girl," She said to Ranger, hunching over the horse's neck. She wasn't sure how far they had gone before she just couldn't hold on

103

anymore. She slid off her horse and as she hit the ground, everything went black.

Monday, May 4, 1863
Turner Home

"Miss Victoria!" Esther entered the parlor and gestured to Victoria, who was reading her Bible. "Miss Hannah, Miss Caroline and Miss Kendall need yo' help up in yo room." Esther replied. "De asked me to get you and tell yo mama when she get home too."

"Is everything alright?" Victoria asked, standing.

"Oh, I think you should go see fo' yo'self," Esther said, piquing Victoria's interest. She tucked her Bible under her arm and climbed the stairs. Caroline and Kendall stood in front of the door.

"Oh, good, Victoria, you're here." Caroline spoke. "Hannah is inside with the soldier right now. We brought him here because it was closer than our farm, and Kendall pointed out that you had more room anyhow."

"A soldier? Here?" Victoria was shocked.

"Yes. Hannah made us leave on account that, well..." Kendall's voice got quiet. "She needed to clean him and didn't want us to see a man without his clothes."

"My goodness." Victoria quickly went into the room.

"Victoria." Hannah turned, a strange look on her face that Victoria was unable read.

"How can I help?" Victoria looked at the bed. The soldier had a bloody, dirty Union uniform on, with an awful-looking gash across his shoulder. His face was pale and his eyes were closed. His thick light-red hair was long enough that it would brush his collar when standing. "A Yankee? Is he alive?"

"Well...yes...I didn't realize this at the time..." Hannah shook her head. "I can hardly believe it, although I suppose I should..."

Victoria moved and got a better look at the wounded man. Across his chest was a bandage, which at first glance, Victoria had assumed was Hannah's doing. Upon closer inspection, however, she saw that the bandage was cut, as if it had already been in place when the soldier was injured.

"It looks like he was slashed by a saber, but why was he already bandaged?" Victoria asked.

There was a knock on the door and Esther entered, carrying a pile of fresh bandages. Hannah worked at the cut below the bandage, washing it clean. She turned to Esther.

"What do you make of this?" Hannah asked. Esther's eyes widened.

"What are you being so secretive about?" Victoria asked, looking from Hannah to Esther.

"Hab you looked under dem bandages yet?" Esther asked cautiously.

"No, not yet."

"Why ever not?" Victoria was confused and slightly frustrated with her friend and her servant. "He was probably just wounded before." Victoria approached the soldier and began to cut the bandage as carefully as she could. Luckily, the man was of slight build and looked to be quite young. It didn't take her long to undo the bandages, but as she got a closer look at the soldier's chest, she made a startling revelation.

"My goodness," Hannah said. "I wondered…"

"This soldier is a woman!" Victoria tried to keep her voice down, but her shock made it difficult. "How…why…" Her mind raced. They not only had an enemy soldier in their house, the soldier was a woman posing as a man. Victoria wasn't sure if that was legal or not, but she did know they were harboring an enemy soldier, which was grounds for arrest.

"Women ha' been dressin' as soldiers an' fightin' proly as long as wars ha' been fought," Esther said. "I not su'prized a'tall. Jus' neber thought I'd see one here."

"We must keep this a secret," Hannah said. "She needs to recover and we need to keep her protected. I am no expert, but I would bet that this binding saved her life. It appears as though the deepest cut was taken at the chest, but the binding protected her. Had it not, I believe she may have bled out before we had even found her."

"I just couldn't imagine…" Victoria looked down at the young woman. She knew it was possible; she had read stories of women like Molly Pitcher and Deborah Sampson of the American Revolution, and Joan of Arc in France fighting in wars, but she never expected she would find one in Mississippi. She had not even considered that a woman would fight in the War Between the States. What compelled this young woman to do so? "Will she live?"

"I believe so," Hannah said. "I'll feel better once she wakes up, or once your mother gets here."

"Mother will insist that she stays here for as long as necessary, perhaps longer," Victoria said. "Even if the soldier was a man, she would insist upon it, but with him being a her…well, Mother will most likely treat her like another daughter, you know she will."

"Indeed," Hannah said. "You may have to make up some sort of backstory for her, in case she wishes to stay in Vicksburg. I can't imagine she will be able to mount a horse and ride in the cavalry again anytime soon." She finished cleaning the young woman's wound and then began winding fresh bandages around her with the help of Esther and Victoria. Esther left to get some clothes as Victoria and Hannah fluffed the pillows under the soldier's head, stripped away the rest of the clothes, and gave her a good washing. The poor girl was filthy.

"I wonder why she did this," Victoria said.

"There are likely countless reasons why," Hannah answered. "Just as there are countless reasons why a man would fight in the war."

"I suppose," Victoria said. "I just know that I could never do that."

"I doubt as though you could keep a secret that important," Hannah smiled at her friend. "However, we don't know her motivation. With some luck, she will wake up and tell us her whole story."

Esther came back into the room. "I took one o' Miss Brianne's old nighties. Dis young woman shoul' fit just fine."

"Yes, she should," Hannah shook her head. "I wonder how long she was wandering around before we found her." They quickly put the nightgown on her and pulled some sheets over her. She rolled her head from one side to the other and muttered something inaudible.

"How did you find her?" Victoria asked.

"Caroline, Kendall and I were coming back from Bovine. It's quite a drive, but Mother Wheeler still likes to get certain supplies from there, as she and her husband did business with a family there for years." Bovine, Mississippi was a town about ten miles away. "The young soldier stumbled into our path, quite literally, and fell right in front of us." Hannah shook her head. "I was lucky to stop the horses in time. We made some room in the wagon and the three of us easily managed to get him...rather her...in the back."

"Union cavalry led by a colonel named Grierson have been raiding in the area," Victoria replied. "I didn't think they were quite this close, but as you said before, we have no idea how long or far the young soldier wandered."

"I'm just glad we found her. No telling what may have happened had someone else found her."

"No..." the young soldier mumbled, still unconscious. "Not Adam, no..."

"She must be having a nightmare," Victoria said. "It's good that she's strong enough to speak." She picked up the soiled clothes. "I do wonder who Adam is." She shook her head. "I hope we have a chance to find out." She held out the clothes. "Do you think I should just burn the lot of this? I don't want anyone finding a Union cavalry uniform here."

"I would agree with you," Hannah said. "She may not like it when she wakes up, but you all have to protect yourselves as well."

"I burn dem, Miss Victoria," Esther took them from Victoria, then went out of the room. Victoria bit her lip nervously.

"What are you thinking, my friend?" Hannah asked.

"I just don't know. She's a Yankee, Hannah. I'm not sure if I'm comfortable with a Yankee staying in our home."

"She is a young woman in trouble, Victoria. We cannot just...abandon her."

"Hannah is right, my dear."

"Mother!" Victoria turned as Rachel enter the room.

"Esther just told me what happened. This young woman will be staying here until she is healthy and voluntarily leaves. I will not have it any other way."

"I suspected you would say that," Victoria said, "but, she is a Yankee, Mother. What if she's a spy?"

"We'll cross that bridge when we come to it," Rachel replied. "However, I don't believe that will be an issue."

"I do hope you're right," Victoria replied, knowing she was outnumbered. She could only hope and pray their Christian compassion would not backfire and cause more harm.

Sunday, May 5, 1863
Turner Home

Tabetha felt as though she were ten years old again. The one time she had fallen into a murky spot in the Muskegon River while trying to cross where she knew she shouldn't. She hadn't been able to see well, and her wet clothes pulled her back down into an undercurrent. Luckily, Adam had been there, as he always was to help, and pulled her out. But Adam would never be there again, and it was all her fault...

April 16, 1861
Norton Farm~Muskegon, Michigan

"Did you hear, Adam? President Lincoln called for 75,000 volunteers to defend the Union. Men are signing up for three month stints." Tabetha *had found her brother repairing a harness in the barn.*

"I heard, although I don't feel this war will only last three months like everyone says," he replied.

"Folks in town are talking all about who's going to enlist."

"I'm sure a lot of men will." Adam *hung up the finished harness and grabbed a bridle that needed repairs.* *"But I have no intention of enlisting."*

"What? Why not? You cannot be serious, Adam." Tabetha *was appalled at her brother's response.*

"Because I don't believe I will make a good soldier, and to be honest, I sometimes believe that if the Southern states want to form their own country, they should be given that opportunity."

Tabetha tried to hide her shock, but it was quite difficult. "So you go off to college and come back home with foolish ideas like that? I thought school was supposed to make you smarter."

"It did. It taught me a lot, even though it was just an Agricultural college and not some fancy college out East."

"They taught you nothing of loyalty though, or defending your home and country," Tabetha retorted. Adam set the bridle down with a sigh and turned to his sister.

"One of my classmates, Nathaniel Prentiss, has a better reason for fighting for the Confederacy than I do for the Union. He will be defending his home. I feel much of the fighting will likely be in Virginia, his home state."

"So you're afraid to enlist because you don't want to fight your friend?" Tabetha tried to understand her brother's perspective.

"I would never want to meet Nathaniel on the battlefield, that's true, but the main reason I don't want to go is that I don't think this war will really solve any of the current conflicts. Hence, I don't see the point."

"So you'll just stay here in a comfortable setting and avoid the fighting altogether?" She shook her head. "And to think I actually believed you would step up and do your duty. Do you have any idea what it will make our family look like?"

"What do you mean?" Adam asked.

"At least one man from almost every family in the area will be enlisting. Unless they have a physical ailment or they have no one else to work in their stead, they are going to fight for the Union. You are well aware that Father cannot enlist. His leg injury would not allow him to march with everyone else and he needs to stay here to run the farm. You only help work the farm. You have the ability to enlist and if you don't, you'll be looked at as a coward and the family will be disgraced."

Tabetha and Adam's father had broken his leg in a farming accident long ago and his leg never healed properly.

"I know many of the lumber mill hands are enlisting. I spoke with George Root, Thomas Waters, and William Ryan when I stopped by the Averill's boarding house yesterday." Adam gave Tabetha a meaningful look. "By the way, Root asked me to give you his regards. You do realize he would marry you at a moment's notice if you gave him the time of day, right?"

"I know that. If he was five years older or if I was five years younger that might be an option for me." Tabetha said. "However, you are changing the subject. Do you really want to be the only able-bodied man between the age of eighteen and forty who stays home? Honestly think about it. And imagine when the war ends and all of the men come home as heroes; you will be the only one who didn't offer his services to your country. Will you be able to live with that?"

Adam sighed, then sat on a bale of hay. "You know how to ask the difficult questions of me, don't you?"

"You're not just my brother, Adam. You are the best friend that I have ever had." Tabetha sat next to him. "It isn't as if I want you to go off and be killed in this war. If I were a man, you can bet I wouldn't hesitate to join. I really believe you will regret your decision if you don't enlist. Perhaps not right away, but as the years go by, I can see you getting bitter."

"You may be right." He rubbed at his stubble-covered chin. "I suppose...you wouldn't steer me wrong, and it would make Mother and Father proud."

"It would. Who knows, you could even come home a great war hero."

"That is possible, although I do believe that you would make a better soldier than I would," Adam said. "You will keep tormenting me until I do enlist, won't you?"

"That is quite possibly true." Tabetha answered. "I just feel it will be the best choice for you."

"Perhaps you're right," Adam replied. "I'll have to think more on it."

1863

"I'm sorry. So sorry, Adam." Tabetha tried to apologize, but Adam couldn't hear her.

"How is the patient doing?" A soft, drawling voice penetrated through Tabetha's fuzzy haze.

"She's still restless." Another voice with a similar Southern accent replied. "Talking about Adam again. Whoever he is, it is clear she believes that she wronged him." The voice paused, then asked. "Do you thing the head wound made her a bit feebleminded?"

What happened and where am I? Tabetha slowly regained consciousness. The last thing she remembered was the Confederate cavalryman on a horse, his arm raised in her direction, slicing pain, and falling from Ranger, her horse. She could tell she wasn't on the hard ground. She was actually quite comfortable. But...had one of the voices she heard called her a 'she'? Had she been found out? She groaned and struggled to open her eyes and sit up, but immediately fell back onto the pillow.

"Mama, I think she's waking up." The second voice spoke and, through hazy eyes, Tabetha saw a woman slightly older than herself, with blond hair and a kind, but worried smile. "We can finally get some answers."

"Remember not to rush her, Victoria. She will likely be a bit muddled. Imagine what she's been through."

"Yes, Mother."

Another woman, old enough to be the first woman's mother, came into Tabetha's line of view. She had the same blonde hair as the younger woman, and a caring smile.

"Hello, dear. Don't try to talk until you're ready." The older woman sat on a chair next to the bed where Tabetha was lying. Licking her dry, cracked lips, Tabetha tested her voice.

"Water, please."

"Of course. Let's help you sit up a bit, if you can." The two women gently pulled Tabetha up and adjusted her pillows, then the younger woman handed the older one a glass with water in it. She helped her sip the water, but Tabetha pushed the cup up, needing to quench her thirst.

"Not too fast, my dear. Nice and easy."

Tabetha tried to smile. "Thank you so much, ma'am."

"Don't rush talking if you're not up to it." The older woman said, placing a comforting hand on Tabetha's shoulder.

"I'll be alright," Tabetha replied. *I am a solid, strong girl from Michigan.*

"I'm sure you have many questions," The older woman said. "However, I want you to know that you are safe here with us. Only a few people know that you're here, and when you're feeling better, we'll discuss your future. You are welcome here for as long as need be, rest assured."

Tabetha nodded and placed a hand on her temple. She could now feel a sharp pain from that area. She must have hit her head when she fell from her horse. *Ranger.* A feeling of sorrow coursed through her as she realized the mount was likely gone from her forever.

"My name is Rachel Turner." The older woman continued. "This is my daughter, Victoria." She gestured to the younger woman. "We live in Vicksburg, Mississippi. You were found by two family friends and my niece, Kendall. My niece Brianne and two servants are the only other ones who know you're here." The daughter, Victoria, gave a short chuckle.

"That seems like quite a few people when you list them, Mama." She said, then spoke to Tabetha. "But you needn't worry. They are all extremely trustworthy."

Tabetha nodded again. "Tabetha Norton." She said. "I'm...I want to explain."

"We do look forward to hearing your story, but no explanations are necessary." The mother, Rachel, smiled. "Do you feel up to some broth?"

"Yes, ma'am. That sounds quite good," Tabetha nodded, and Victoria left the room. Tabetha took a deep breath, the past few months of hiding her emotions finally overcoming her. She didn't want to break down into tears, but they still threatened.

"My dear Tabetha, don't worry yourself. You're safe now. You will be just fine. Feel free to let your emotions show. I will completely understand."

A tear slipped down Tabetha's cheek. "I...it's just..."

Rachel handed Tabetha a handkerchief as tears continued to fall, then sat onto the bed next to her and pulled her into her arms.

"There, there, you're safe, Tabetha. Everything will be okay."

Wednesday, May 7, 1863
Wheeler Farm

"Her name is Tabetha and she is from the west side of Michigan. A place called Muskegon." Victoria leaned on the fence as she spoke. She had finally been able to come see Hannah for a visit and had been pleasantly surprised to see her brother had been helping and visiting the Wheelers. "Her family farms, but the area is apparently well-known for lumber."

"And Mother has no issue harboring a Yankee?" Jason shook his head. "I suppose that shouldn't surprise me. She'd probably make Abe Lincoln himself welcome at our home."

"Showing kindness to a stranger is a very compassionate thing to do." Hannah looked at Jason. "And your mother is a very merciful person. I would have taken the girl in here, but you both know how crowded we are here."

"Would have been safer." Jason grunted. "I don't know how you all got a Union soldier into our home with all of the Confederates guarding the city."

"We had a lot of supplies to carry in and are trusted in town. Not one soldier even stopped us to ask questions. Then we brought the wagon to the back of the house and Caesar and Esther helped us get her upstairs. It was all quite simple."

"Perhaps I should suggest more pickets and checkpoints." Jason shook his head.

Hannah gently slapped him on the arm. "Oh, Jason, don't be like that. You know perfectly well that Tabetha is not a threat to anyone."

"I don't know that, Hannah." He drove the ax he had been using to cut some firewood into the woodblock. "She could be. She could be a spy, she could be just lying in wait to..."

"Jason Turner, what is wrong with you?" Victoria was troubled by her brother's reaction. "Do you honestly believe Mother would do that? Risk our lives to help someone? She may risk her own life to help others, but she would not do so if her children or grandchildren would be in any danger."

Jason rubbed his face. "I'm sorry, really I am. I must admit that I am a bit tense. The Yankees are very close, as evidenced by your patient. We're trying to do what we can, but that Yankee General Grant seems determined to get Vicksburg. He's like a bulldog with a bone; he just won't let it go."

"Jason, I understand how frustrated you must be, but…"

"Hannah!" A scream sounded from the other side of the house, and the three looked to see Caroline Wheeler running towards them as fast as she could, tears running down her cheeks and fear apparent in her face. "Oh, Mr. Turner, I am so glad you're here. It's so awful." Her chest heaved as she threw herself into Hannah's arms, muttering ineligible words. Hannah could just barely make out the words: "Just lying there" and "so stiff". She thought back to where the girl might have gone, then remembered that Cordelia had sent Caroline to bring Old Man Wagner a pie.

"Caroline, what happened? Is Mr. Wagner all right?" Hannah asked.

Caroline shook her head 'no'. She looked up. "He…I think he's dead, Hannah. He didn't answer when I knocked, so I went in and he was just lying on his bed like he was sleeping, but he wouldn't wake up."

"Dear Lord, no…" Hannah looked up at Victoria and Jason.

"I'll go see him." Jason grabbed his jacket from the post he had draped it on and jogged to his horse, then rode off towards the Wagner place.

"Caroline, was there any blood or signs that he was hurt?" Hannah asked, brushing a strand of the girl's hair back from her damp face.

"No. It was like he was just sleeping. Maybe he just didn't wake up this morning, but he was fine yesterday."

Hannah nodded. Their neighbor had stopped by yesterday, bringing them some venison he had managed to obtain.

"I wonder if his heart just gave out," Victoria said quietly.

"You're probably right." Hannah sighed. "Come, Caroline. Let's get you in the house. You deserve a rest after all this excitement."

"But…I just remembered. The pie. I dropped the pie. I need to go and get it." Caroline shook her head.

"Don't you worry about that," Hannah said. "I know Jason will take care of everything.

"He is good like that." Victoria smiled in agreement as the three women went into the house.

When Jason finally returned, dusk was falling and Victoria had gone home. Caroline had gone to bed very early, and Cordelia was reading to Ambrose and getting him ready for bed.

"Everything is taken care of." Jason sat in the rocking chair next to Hannah. She put down her knitting.

"I was just about to saddle a horse and see what was taking you so long, see if you needed some help. What happened?"

"One thing led to another, unfortunately." Jason sighed. "Wagner is dead, just as Caroline said. It seems as though he died in his sleep, as I suspected."

"That is what Victoria and I concluded as well," Hannah said. Jason nodded again.

"I buried him and did my best to carve him a marker. I plan on riding into town first thing tomorrow and see if I can round up a preacher and see if he can come out and say a few words over him. I'm willing to bet Reverend Lord will be able to do it."

"I agree with that," Hannah said.

"After that, I had to clean up a little bit, so that the wild animals don't get in. Caroline must have dropped the pie she was bringing. I have the pan in my saddlebag."

"Yes, she was a bit distressed about that," Hannah commented. "That poor man. I wonder what will become of his place. He had no family, as far as I know."

"I'm fairly sure my Father did any legal work he needed. I'll get a hold of his file and see if he left a will," Jason replied.

"Are you sure you'll have time for that?" Hannah asked.

"No," Jason chuckled. "I'll ask Mother or Victoria to look. Victoria will have a better handle on that information anyway. I have never met someone, man or woman, who has the brains and memory that she does. She would have made a great lawyer herself."

"No reason she can't," Hannah said. "When this war is over, I can see things changing. Many women have shown that they can take care of the family businesses with the men away. Perhaps women will be more likely to go to college and have careers."

"Is that something you would like?" Jason asked. "I think it would be difficult for a woman to have a family and a career."

"It may be difficult, but I have been doing it, with help of course, since Benjamin died."

"That's true, I suppose." Jason thought for a moment. "If you could have a career, or just have a family; anything in the world, what would you want to do?"

"I love being a mother and I loved being the wife of a farmer. It may sound silly, but farming gives a person so much purpose. It's hard work, and I have never shied away from that. To be able to plant a seed and have something grow from it, well, it's almost spiritual to me."

"Spiritual? That is something I haven't heard in regards to farming." Jason laughed.

"To me, it's as if God is allowing us to partake in creation," Hannah explained. "And I don't think there is another job where you depend on God as much, for good weather, and the like."

"I suppose." Jason smiled as he looked over at Hannah. "You never fail to amaze me, Mrs. Wheeler. You make me look at things in a new way almost every time we talk."

"I'm glad. I know I'm not great at book learning, but if I can help people see God a little better, I feel that is just as important."

"Well, I think it may be even more important," Jason said.

"Thank you for saying so." Hannah smiled.

Jason checked his watch. "I must be heading back to camp. I will come and see you tomorrow when I round up a preacher. I figure you will want to attend any service we can have."

"Of course, thank you." Hannah smiled. Jason hesitated, as if he wanted to say something more, then shook his head and smiled. "Take care of yourself, Jason."

"Until tomorrow then, Mrs. Wheeler."

Friday, May 9, 1863
Miller Home, Vicksburg

"I must say, Mrs. Green, I have felt quite lonely since my arrival here in Virginia. Most people know where my loyalties lie and so don't wish to associate with me." Mrs. Dora Miller set her cup of berry tea on the saucer.

"I am so sorry that's been the case," Mary replied. "I would come visit more often but it is difficult to make plans these days, especially with my young one and my condition. Not too long ago, it would have been socially unacceptable for me to even step out of the house."

"Oh, Mrs. Green, I completely understand your position," Mrs. Miller said. "I was not trying to make you feel bad. I appreciate your efforts. Have you been able to keep up with the war news?"

"Yes," Mary said. "Unfortunately, my husband believes our situation here in Vicksburg will get difficult soon. They say a siege is expected. Just this past Sunday, a tugboat came down the Mississippi and Confederate batteries fired at it."

"Ah, yes. I remember the commotion. The barges were set on fire and the tugboat was hit," Dora said.

"Yes. The Confederacy captured 25 prisoners, and three reports from New York," Mary added. Mrs. Miller was about to speak again when the doorbell rang.

"Oh, botheration, please excuse me." Mrs. Miller went into the entryway and curious, Mary followed. A Confederate orderly stood there with an official-looking envelope in her hand.

"Who lives here?" The orderly asked.

"My husband, Mr. Miller, and myself," She replied. Mary was a little shocked at the harshness of Mrs. Miller's tone.

"Which Mr. Miller?" The man asked.

"Mr. Anderson Miller," She answered.

"Is he here at present?" The soldier appeared to be getting slightly irritated.

"No." Mrs. Miller said.

"Where can he be found?"

"At the office of the deputy," She replied. It seemed as though she was insistent about not sharing any more information than she needed to.

"Well, I am not going all the way down there." The soldier took a breath as if to calm himself. He held out the envelope. "This is an order from General Pemberton stating that you must move out of this house within two hours. He has selected it for his new headquarters. He will furnish you with wagons to move your belongings."

Mary shook her head. She was aware that the army could take over any home, and thought it a very unfortunate effect of the war.

"Will the General furnish us with another home?" Mrs. Miller asked.

"Of course not," The soldier replied.

"Well, we rent this home. Has the owner been consulted?"

"He has not, ma'am, and that is of no consequence to me. This home has been confiscated. It is necessary for the defense of the city." He motioned for her to take the document. "Take this order."

"I shall not take it," Mrs. Miller shook her head. "And I shall not move, as there is no place to move but the street."

The man let out a very heavy sigh. "Then I will deliver this notice to your husband. He can deal with you."

"You just go ahead and do that." As soon as he walked off, Dora locked and bolted the door. "I am so sorry, Mary. I now feel the need to bar every door and window."

"I understand. I wouldn't want to be here alone either." Mary replied. "I am more than happy to stay here until your husband arrives."

"I would appreciate that very much, Mrs. Green." Dora replied. "Thank you ever so much."

Thursday, May 14, 1863
Turner Home

"It seems a siege is inevitable," Victoria said, sitting next to Tabetha's bedside. Even though she was a Yankee, Victoria had quickly grown to like Tabetha, which was good, seeing as though they now shared a room. "I suppose that means you won't have to decide whether or not to go home. You'll soon be stranded here with us."

"Or you'll be stuck with me. Staying with your family is anything but being stranded somewhere. I have enjoyed my time with you all immensely, even though the circumstances have not been ideal."

"You know you are more than welcome here; you are no problem whatsoever. Mama already sees you as another daughter."

"I love my own mother dearly, but your mother is extremely welcoming. She makes you feel like a part of the family."

"That's my Mama," Victoria stated. "How are you feeling today? Mother believes you should be up and about as soon as tomorrow."

"I feel as though I should have been up days ago," Tabetha admitted. "Back home on the farm, I would have been."

"Well, you won't have to go back to work any time soon. As far as anyone in Vicksburg will be concerned, you are a cousin of ours, visiting from Northern Virginia. We've decided on that story just in case. We want to make sure no one discovers you are actually a Union soldier. We're not sure how folks would react to us housing an injured Yankee, much less one that is a woman."

"It makes sense," Tabetha smiled. "I've been masquerading as a man for almost a year. I believe I can manage to act as a Southern cousin of your family. In fact, it will prove to be a refreshing change."

"Very good," Victoria smiled. "And just so you know, we were able to get that letter sent to your home. I'm not sure if it will get there, as the mail service is horrid, but we did try."

"Thank you. I would like to write more." Tabetha replied.

"We'll see if we can do that." Victoria looked at her bedside table. "Can I get you anything? Another book to read, perhaps?"

Tabetha reached over and lifted the book off the table. "I did enjoy *Emma*, do you have any more written by this Miss Austin?"

"I am sure I can track down another one," Victoria took the book. "I usually don't prefer novels myself, but I like Miss Austin. She has very good storylines."

"And good characters," Tabetha added.

"That as well," Victoria stood. "I will see if I can find you another novel."

Friday, May 15, 1863
Evening, Turner Home

Bullets whirred overhead, sounding angry as they hit the trees with sharp 'pings'. Tabetha clutched her revolver and peered over a fallen log. She took aim at a Confederate who was charging toward her. She felt the kickback of the revolver as she pulled the trigger. Her target fell, a stain of crimson spreading across his chest. She jumped up and moved to check on him. When she got a good look, she crumpled to the ground. She recognized the corpse.

"Adam!" She screamed, trying to stop the blood pouring from the corpse. "No, Adam, No!"

"Tabetha!"

Tabetha woke up, covered in perspiration. Victoria stood above her, concern obvious in her face. "Are you okay? You have been tossing and turning for the past few minutes. I had to wake you up once you started calling out."

"Goodness. I am so sorry." Tabetha sat up as Victoria returned to her own bed. "What was I saying?"

"You were calling out for Adam. He is your brother, correct?"

"Yes. Not even a year older than me."

"I can't imagine your devastation." Victoria shook her head. "Was the dream about when you heard that he was killed?"

"No, it wasn't." Tabetha rubbed her head. "I dreamt that I was back in battle myself. It was always so nerve-wrecking. Being killed was at the top of my fears, of course, but I also feared injury. That would lead to my secret being discovered, and I'd likely be disgraced at home."

"That would be unfortunate." Victoria adjusted the blankets on her bed.

"Yes," Tabetha agreed.

"So how did your brother factor into your dream?"

"Well, you know how dreams go. In this particular battle, I shot an enemy soldier and killed him. For some reason, I approached the man and the unknown Confederate soldier had become my brother. I had killed Adam."

"Goodness," Victoria said. "Do you have dreams like that often? I noticed you often have restless nights."

"The dreams vary, but yes, I am often brought back to the battlefield when I fall asleep. I see the men that I have killed."

"So you know that you have killed men?" Victoria asked.

"Unfortunately, yes." Tabetha shook her head. "If I could somehow take it back, I would. I wish I hadn't..." She sighed. "I just didn't think my actions through. A common thing with me. Adam always joked that I was so unpredictable that I never even knew what I was going to do next."

Victoria smiled. "That sounds like something a brother would say."

"Yes, it had gotten the both of us into many scrapes as children. Adam could always make it better, though, but he never will fix things again and I can blame no one but myself."

"Why do you say that?" Victoria asked.

"He never would have enlisted if I hadn't badgered him into it." Tabetha confessed. "I joined the army to try and make up for what I did. I should have known that wouldn't have worked. I am still responsible and I still feel enormous guilt."

Victoria never imagined she would feel sorrow for an enemy soldier dying, but she didn't think of Adam Norton as an enemy soldier. He was the beloved brother of her new friend. She then thought of her uncles and her Cousin Jonah, who were fighting for the Union army. She could never hate them. After all, they were only fighting for what they believed in. Just as not all Confederates were fighting to keep slavery, not all Yankees were fighting to oppress or take away the rights of the Southerners.

"You know," Victoria said. "I realize you're hurting. If one of my brothers were to be killed, I am not sure how I would get through it. But I don' believe you can blame yourself for your brother's death. We all make rash decisions. Goodness, I almost married a man who I just found out was a philanderer." She referenced the letter she had received from her cousin Bekah a few days ago. The man who had such a promising political career was now looked at as a lout.

'*Folks are saying that he will never get as high in the government as he wanted.*' Bekah had said.

"Yes, but that rash decision…even if you had married that man, that's not life and death." Tabetha pointed out.

"I'm not sure about that." Victoria may not have died a physical death if she had married Jeremy, but she would have died a spiritual death. "However, I didn't mean to divert the conversation away from your issues. I only want to help you. You mentioned that you are Catholic, and I am fairly certain you believe that God has a plan and that He can bring good from the bad things that happen."

"I know that," Tabetha replied.

"I mean, how many good things came from you enlisting in the army?"

Tabetha knew Victoria was right. She had met many new people, learned much about herself, and had even been credited with saving the lives of her comrades.

"You are very right. In all honesty, I have learned so much about life and about myself. I love Muskegon, but I had never traveled anywhere before I joined the cavalry."

"Yes, and our lives have been very blessed by having you here."

"Thank you. I hope that my being here never becomes an imposition. You know what Benjamin Franklin says about guests."

"Yes, as a matter of fact, I do," Victoria replied. "'Guests, like fish, begin to smell after three days.' However, note that he said 'unwelcome'. You would never be that."

"Even though I've woken you and kept you up so late?"

"Not at all!" Victoria smiled. "It reminds me of the days when I shared a room with Mary Grace before she married. Good conversation is never a bad thing."

"I suppose. Thank you for understanding." Tabetha said.

"Of course." Victoria laid down. "Anytime."

Sunday, May 17, 1863
Christ Episcopal Church

"I must say, going to church was a good way to start what will probably be a very stressful day." Mary Grace clutched her daughter to her. Little Hope had fallen asleep on her mother's shoulder during the first hymn. Victoria held both of her nephew's hands. Rachel and Brianne had already gone to the Turner home to start dinner while Kendall, Victoria and Mary Grace moved at a slower pace with the children.

"I agree. I feel as though we are all going to need to band together in the coming days." Victoria said.

"The city seems empty." Mary Grace said, looking around. She was right, with the exception of occasional soldiers rushing by with a blanket and canteen and occasional wagons rattling down the street, there were very few people. It wasn't long, however before straggler after straggler of soldiers passed by, and by the time they were almost to the Turner home, groups of soldiers were passing by. They were worn and dusty and looked as though they had been marching all week.

"I wonder what's going on," Mary Grace said.

"I'll try and find out." Victoria said. "You all go on and bring the children in the house."

"I'll stay with you, Victoria." Kendall insisted.

Mary Grace looked as though she wanted to argue, but instead shook her head. "You two be careful."

Kendall nodded and Victoria listened closely to the men in the streets that were now filled. It was incredible how quickly things had changed. Victoria and Kendall made their way back to the main street, hoping they could hear what was going on.

"We are whipped." One of the soldiers said. "The Federals are not far behind us."

"Where are you going?" A women standing on the sidewalk called out. Victoria couldn't tell who she was. None of the soldiers looked as though they wanted to answer the woman's question. Some of the men even had embarrassed, pained looks on their faces.

"Where on earth are you boys going?" Another townsperson called out.

One of the soldiers looked up, and with an almost surly tone, replied: "We are running."

Victoria's stomach felt ill. If the soldiers were deserting the town that meant it could be taken over by the enemy.

"From where?" Another young women from town asked. Victoria didn't know this girl's name either, or the name of her friend who answered.

"The Feds, to be sure." She looked as though she didn't know whether to laugh or be embarrassed.

"Oh, shame on you!" Cried some of the ladies who had gathered, directing their anger, likely created by fear, at the soldiers.

"It's all Pemberton's fault!" Replied an awkward-looking soldier.

"I would say it's all your own fault." A woman from the crowd yelled. "Why don't you stand your ground?"

"Shame on you all!"

Victoria looked around, a little sickened at the attitude of her town's citizens. It was clear that the soldiers were simply following orders and many did not want to retreat. The people of Vicksburg should be cheering the men on, encouraging them, and thanking them for their protection. The soldiers looked ashamed and some didn't even carry firearms.

"Do you think they lost their weapons?" Kendall asked quietly. "What is going to happen to us?"

"It appears as though they did." Victoria put an arm around her cousin. "But I am sure we'll be just fine."

"We are disappointed in you!" Cried some of the ladies. "Who shall we look to now for protection?"

"Our apologies. I must say, this is the first time I have ever ran." One of the soldiers replied. "We are Georgians, and we never ran before. We saw the others all breaking and running, but we could not bear up alone."

Victoria shook her head and called out to the soldiers. "Do any of you men need water?" Some of them looked up in surprise, and then came into the yard to get the offered water. Victoria quickly went to get a pail and dipper at the water pump.

"Thank you, ma'am." One of them said. "We do appreciate your hospitality."

"It is I who should thank you." Victoria said. "In spite of what some of the townsfolk out there are saying, many here are very appreciative of the protection you have given us so far."

They nodded thanks again.

"Victoria." Rachel called to her daughter from the porch. "Please invite those men in for some supper."

Victoria turned to the men. "We would be honored if you would take supper with us. Do you have the time?"

"We have to eat sometime." One of the men said with a smile that showed several missing teeth. Victoria smiled back and gestured for them to follow her. The Yankees were coming, just not here quite yet, and she suspected they would be prevented from entry into the city.

Esther had set the table for many guests, and the men sat down. After one of the men said grace, they began eating.

"We must thank you again for your kindness." The soldier with the missing teeth said.

"Aye." A second soldier, with a black eye said.

"It's the least we can do." Rachel said. "I only wish it could be under happier circumstances."

"I hate placing blame, but it's all General Pemberton's fault." One of the soldiers said. "We're from Missouri, and our boys stood up to the Yankees during this battle. We were almost alone in that. We fought as long as possible, it felt like everyone was leaving us. We were obligated to fall back. You must know, ma'am, we Missourians always fight well, even in retreat."

"That is the truth." The soldier with the black eye said. "We could have taken them Yanks, but General Pemberton rode up to us and told us to stand our ground. He told us that he would fight with us, but the next we saw of him, he was sitting on his horse behind a house. It was then that I knew it would be no use to keep fighting, if he was just going to sit there." His anger at the situation was apparent. "We may have lost at Champion Hill, but we will prevail in this war."

Victoria couldn't help but wonder how true the story was.

"What will you be doing next?" Rachel asked.

"We'll regroup here in town and hunker down." A soldier assured them. "Once we stick our heels in, it will be almost impossible for the Yankees to win."

The men quickly finished their meal, thanked the family again, and went on their way.

"We'll protect you ladies." Missouri said, tipping his hat. "Have no fear."

Darkness had fallen and Victoria had lit a candle to read some old letters again. Rachel had gone to Mary Grace's house to stay for the night, leaving Victoria in charge of Tabetha, Brianne and Kendall, who had all already gone to bed. Tabetha was still weak and unable to do much, but Brianne, Kendall and Victoria had spent most of the evening carrying buckets of water to the soldiers passing by. The streets were jammed with wagons, caissons, horses, soldiers, mules, livestock and sheep, coming in from the countryside and settling in for what may be a long siege.

From what Victoria could understand, there had been a battle not too far from Vicksburg at the Big Black River Bridge. The Federals won decisively and the Confederates had retreated to Vicksburg, hoping to dig in and save the city.

Victoria heard shouting, a little more distinct than had been earlier. She quickly made her way to the porch. She watched as fresh troops headed toward the entrenchments to the rear of the city. Ladies lined the road again, this time waving their handkerchiefs, cheering the men on, and crying.

"These are our troops!"

"These men won't run!"

"You'll stand by us! You will protect us, won't you?"

"You boys won't retreat and bring the Federals behind you!"

These soldiers appeared fresh and lively. They swung their hats and called back.

"We will die for you! That is a promise!"

"We will never run!"

"We will not retreat!"

The other soldiers, the ones who had been retreating earlier that day, sat on the pavement, wrapped in blankets. Some were lying down or leaning against trees, anything to rest their wearied bodies. They looked on, silent and dejected. Victoria knew deep down that these men were not to blame for the defeat at the Big Black River Bridge and the retreat into town. She tried to find Jason in the crowd, but he wasn't there.

Lord, keep Jason safe. She prayed. *And watch over everyone here in Vicksburg.* Tabetha wasn't the only new civilian arrival. Many women and children from the outskirts of town had also fled to safety, fearful of the Yankees coming towards the town. Victoria watched, astounded by not only the people and soldiers coming in, but also the livestock that the army brought with them.

"At least we won't starve with all of the animals here," Victoria muttered to herself.

The sun had set, but the streets of Vicksburg had gas lamps for the people to see by. It allowed Victoria to continue to look up and down the road, hoping to see her brother Jason. Suddenly, she saw a different, yet slightly familiar face. The soldier's eyes lit up when he noticed her on the porch.

"Nathaniel!" She hastened to him as he rushed toward her, and without thinking, she threw her arms around him. "My dear friend, what are you doing here?"

"Trying to defend the lovely ladies of Vicksburg, of course." He smiled, but she could tell that he was in pain. It didn't take her long to see why that was the case.

"What happened to your arm? There is blood all over you."

"I'm not sure if it was a bullet that grazed me or a piece of shrapnel, but I was hit by something in the arm. I'll be fine."

"I'm sure you will be, but you must get the wound taken care of. Come inside and let me clean you up."

"Tori, I can't impose…"

She tried not to smile at the nickname only he used for her. "As if you could ever be an imposition. Come on. Besides, you must tell me why you are so far from your home."

He followed her inside and down the hall to the kitchen, took off his jacket, then sat in a chair. Victoria gathered some water and cloths, then sat next to him.

"It's difficult to see…" She tried to examine the wound. Her heart beat steadily at Nathaniel's nearness. He was in desperate need of a bath, a shave, and a haircut, but she still thought him the handsomest man she had ever met. "It is difficult for me to get a good look. May I tear the sleeve off of your shirt to see better? I promise, I will repair it."

"If it helps," he replied. "I must admit, it does hurt like the dickens, but if you tell anyone I said that, I'll deny it." He smiled at her as she took a knife and tore off his sleeve. The wound was quite bloody, but appeared to have clotted somewhat.

"I'm just glad you are able to walk and talk. So many men have been very badly wounded. Come, tell me why you are so far from home."

"All in good time," Nathaniel said, groaning slightly as Victoria rubbed at the blood on his arm. "I am sure you know, many men have died today as well."

"We noticed." Victoria replied. "My cousins and I were giving water to the men passing by and we also saw many ambulances passing by with both wounded and dead. Some of those wagons were actually dripping blood. I was quite impressed that Brianne didn't swoon."

Nathaniel looked at his arm, then at Victoria. "I'm impressed that you aren't queasy at the sight of blood, but I suppose I should know better than to be surprised by what you can handle."

"Indeed." Victoria replied with a smile. "You are lucky that this wound is what they call a 'flesh wound'. It isn't too bad."

"It still hurts." He replied, grinning back at her.

"Hmmm." She replied playfully. It felt good to banter with Nathaniel again. "It is so good to see you. I cannot believe you are here, in Vicksburg. How did that even happen? The last I heard from your letters, you were in a Virginia regiment."

"I am a scout for the Confederacy and have been carrying a lot of information for the Army of Northern Virginia." He replied. "I was meeting a contact with some vital information for Pemberton. My contact never showed, so I decided to come and find Pemberton myself."

"That sounds foolish to me," Victoria applied some salve to the now-clean wound. "Foolish or dedicated."

"I'll go with the latter," Nathaniel said. "I don't like the sound of being called foolish."

"If you say so." Victoria smiled, then wrapped a bandage around his upper arm. He stood and faced her.

"Are you sorry that I came in for a visit?" He asked.

"Not at all." She replied. "I just...it makes me..." She placed a hand to her brow, trying to think of how to put what she was thinking into words. "I have been worrying about you." She took a step back. Her feelings for him were too powerful and he was married to her cousin.

"I worry about you too." He reached out and touched her elbow. "Once I considered coming further west to find Pemberton myself. I thought of the possibility of seeing you. I couldn't get that vision out of my head."

Victoria took another step back. She was puzzled at the familiarity of his tone. "I must ask, have you any news of the Turners in Vicksburg? Have you been able to visit Belle?"

"I have a few times." Nathaniel said. "They are all well, as far as I know, with the exception of your cousin, James." He gave her a somber look. "You did hear about James, didn't you?"

"Yes, that was an unfortunate piece of mail that did get through the lines." Victoria took a deep breath. "Belle is lucky she had you there for support."

"I suppose." Nathaniel said. "I feel she took James's death much harder than she did Samuel's."

"Samuel?" Victoria asked. The name sounded familiar, but she couldn't exactly place where she had heard it.

"You must remember Samuel Gray. Belle's intended." Nathaniel said. "Samuel died of dysentery in camp. Belle was upset about that, but then James...it was unimaginable for her." He shook his head.

"Samuel...Belle was going to marry Samuel Gray?" Victoria had been so sure that her cousin was engaged to Nathaniel. She tried to think back to the exact wording of the letter Belle had written. '*All but engaged to a handsome young man with whom you are acquainted.'* "Samuel Gray was the handsome young man," She said, more to herself than Nathaniel. He looked at her, a bit perplexed.

"I suppose one could consider him handsome," He replied.

"No," Victoria shook her head. "My apologies. I just...toward the beginning of the war, I received a letter from Belle and what she said...her wording was a bit confusing. I was under the impression that she was marrying you." She felt foolish. A blush crept up her cheeks.

"That she was marrying...me?" Nathaniel asked. He ran a hand through his hair, a smile on his face. She turned away, completely embarrassed as he continued. "Tori, I must be honest with you. I was stationed near Fredericksburg when the fighting broke out back in December. I spoke with Belle, tried to get her to leave Turner's Glenn."

"Belle would never abandon Turner's Glenn," Victoria said.

"You are right about that," Nathaniel nodded. "Your cousin did ask me to be her protector, but when we parted, well...I realized that she and I could never be more than friends. I could never give her the lifestyle she is accustomed to. Besides..." He took Victoria's hand in his. "There is another Turner cousin that I enjoy communicating with so much more than Belle."

"Is there?" Victoria met his eyes. "Well, then. Who can that be, there are so many of us..."

"Indeed. Unfortunately, I am not sure your Uncle Matthew will let me make an offer of marriage to Lainey." He smiled.

"Cousin Lainey is a very special young woman." Victoria nodded in agreement and looked at their joined hands. "But don't you think she might be a bit young?" Nathaniel hesitated, then pulled Victoria close with his one good arm.

"I just wish the circumstances were different," He whispered. Victoria put her other arm around Nathaniel's shoulder.

"I am confident that our Confederate boys will protect us." She replied. He pulled back and looked into her eyes.

"I hope we can." He sighed, then pulled away from her and rubbed the back of his neck. "I must tell you, Victoria, the situation doesn't look good. Grant is a termagant of a general and we are badly outnumbered. We have the high ground of course, which is good, but that is the only advantage we have."

"Before you came, I was afraid to retire for the night. Not knowing whether the Federal army would advance or not frightened me," Victoria said.

"The Federals are still miles away." Nathaniel assured her.

"That is good to know." Victoria commented. "And the streets are getting quiet."

"They are." He turned to her. "Where is your mother?"

"She's staying with Mary Grace and her children tonight."

"She just left you here on your own?"

"I am not on my own. My cousins Brianne and Kendall are here, as well as Tabetha, a young woman who has been living with us." Victoria explained. "At any rate, we will be perfectly safe. You needn't worry." She smiled bravely. "Where will you be staying tonight? With what regiment?"

"Well, at this moment, I have no regiment," Nathaniel replied. "I plan on sleeping on your porch tonight."

"Nathaniel…" Victoria began to protest.

"No arguments," Nathaniel interrupted. "You and your family are far too important to me, Tori. At the risk of sounding overprotective, as long as I am in Vicksburg, I will be looking after you all."

"I appreciate that. I suppose some protection would be a good thing." Victoria was touched by his kindness. It was so like Nathaniel. "However, I will not have you sleeping on the porch. You are an old, dear friend and we have spare rooms here. Gregory's room will be the best place for you to stay." She turned to go up the stairs, but he grasped her arm to stop her.

"I don't think that would be a good idea. Not with your mother being gone. It wouldn't be proper."

"Good heavens, Nathaniel, be reasonable. I will not have you sleeping outside with all of the room we have in here. If you insist on being our protector, you must at least stay inside."

"If you're going to insist, I'll stay inside, but I will stay down here, in the kitchen," Nathaniel said.

"All right, then," Victoria shook her head. "Sometimes you are just too stubborn for your own good, Nathaniel Prentiss."

"A woman of the notoriously headstrong Turner family is calling me stubborn?" He said, teasing in his voice. "I'm not quite sure how to take that."

"We're not always stubborn," she said. "However, I will be in this case. I will not have you sleeping outside. I would prefer you stay in Gregory's room, but I will compromise for now, and you won't sleep in the kitchen, you will sleep on the sofa in the parlor. Esther will be down early in the morning to cook breakfast and you'd better not leave without eating or without saying goodbye."

"I won't," he smiled.

"I'd better let you get some rest, then." Victoria didn't really want her time with Nathaniel to end. She had forgotten how easy it was to talk with him. She reached into a closet and pulled down a blanket. "This should help keep you comfortable."

"You need your sleep as well." He appeared unwilling to part from her.

"Oh, Nathaniel, I am so glad you are here. It was good to talk with you again."

"Well, if this engagement progresses the way I think it will, you can be assured that I will be around for a bit longer." He took her hand and gave it an exaggeratedly debonair kiss. "Good evening, milady."

"Thank you, kind sir," she replied. "Please don't hesitate to ask if you need anything."

"Of course," Nathaniel laid the blanket on the settee to keep it from getting dirty and Victoria ascended the stairs. She wouldn't admit it to anyone, but she felt much safer knowing that Nathaniel was downstairs keeping watch. Before preparing for bed, she stepped onto the balcony of her room. *What will tomorrow bring?* She wondered. *Will Nathaniel and the others abandon us to the enemy?* She didn't want to think about what would happen without the Confederate soldiers protecting them. It was strange, after the fighting earlier in the day, to have the streets so calm, and just as quickly, the peace could be disturbed again.

"Lord, please keep us all safe." She looked up into the sky. "Especially my family and Nathaniel. I thank You for bringing him back into my life."

Monday, May 18, 1863
Green Home

"Victoria, I'm glad you've come by," Mary said. "There's so much going on in town and Duff tries to shield me from any and all bad news."

"As a good husband should, especially in your condition," Victoria smiled. "But I agree, there is much news, and I need to share some of my own news with you."

"Splendid! I already have Martha bringing in some tea."

"That sounds delicious. How have you been sleeping?'

"Relatively good, all things considered," Mary replied. "It was quite an exciting day yesterday."

"I agree," Victoria tried to hide her own yawn, but Mary caught it.

"The noise outside seems to have kept you up quite late." She commented.

"It wasn't the noise, I actually had a late-night visitor." Victoria smiled.

"I see. How is Jason?" Mary asked, assuming that he would be the only person that would visit Victoria that late into the evening.

"I'm not sure, I haven't seen him in a few days. I am quite concerned about him but it wasn't Jason." Victoria was anxious to tell someone of her encounter with Nathaniel and Mary was the perfect person to talk with.

"Then do tell! Who was this visitor?" Mary asked.

"You'll never guess." Victoria teased. "I can hardly believe it myself." She shook her head with a short laugh. "Nathaniel Prentiss."

"Never say so!" Mary said. "What on earth is he doing here in Vicksburg?"

Victoria relayed Nathaniel's story to her friend.

"He was gone this morning before I made it downstairs for breakfast, but he told Esther that he would return as soon as he was able. Apparently, we have more to talk about."

"I would say so!" Mary smiled. "That is such wonderful news, Victoria. I always had such high hopes for you and Nathaniel, up until we believed he was married to Belle, but now my faith has been restored. Praise Jesus."

"I know," Victoria bit her lip. "I just... it would be so nice if this all worked out. I care deeply for Nathaniel and have always cherished our friendship. I don't know, perhaps I am reading too much into his words. It's not as if that hasn't happened before."

"You need to forget the past, Victoria. You should remember the lessons learned, but then let them go." Mary reached over, awkwardly with her stomach as large as it was, and clasped her friend's hands. "And always remember that you are a fine catch and God has wonderful plans for you."

Victoria nodded and smiled.

"Now, what other news is there?" Mary asked. "I need to know absolutely everything."

"Well, the news is quite confusing," Victoria replied. "We seem to be cut off from the outside world, so information can't be validated. There is a rumor that our General Johnston has retaken the city of Jackson. If we can hold off the Yankees until Johnston comes to our aid, all shall be fine. We just need to be patient for the next few days since we will be unable to leave the city and those who are outside the city limits won't be able to come in."

"Oh dear, that must include the Wheelers," Mary said.

"Most definitely. They are still at the farm and won't be able to come in until all this madness is at an end. I also heard that there is an entire division of our soldiers, Loring's division, who were separated from Pendleton and the main army. Pendleton could unite with Johnston elsewhere, but..."

"But that will reduce our forces here." Mary finished the thought. "That is unfortunate." The conversation continued for a short while, then Victoria stood and sighed.

"Oh, Mary, I have enjoyed our visit and I do wish that I could stay longer, but I have some errands to run, and I would like to get home in case Jason does come by. It's possible he may be stuck on the outskirts of town and it worries me, not knowing if he's safe or not."

"I understand. You also wouldn't want to miss Mr. Prentiss if he were to come back for a visit." Mary smiled and stood awkwardly. Victoria blushed.

"No, I suppose not."

As Victoria made her way back home, she looked at her pocket watch. "3:00," She murmured. "I wonder…" Her next thought was interrupted by an explosion that almost knocked her to the ground. The blast came from the entrenchments east of the city.

"Artillery!" Someone yelled. Roar after roar of cannon fire followed, then the popping sounds of musket fire.

"The Federals are attacking!" Another person called out.

Victoria turned towards the the direction of the commotion, then made a quick decision to find out what was going on. She headed to the highest point in town, Sky Parlor Hill.

As she made her way up the hill, Victoria could see smoke billowing, and she couldn't help but feel concern for Nathaniel and Jason and all her loved ones who were exposed to frequent gunfire. Her heart pounded with every thunder of cannon.

Victoria finally reached the top of the hill and looked around. Groups of people stood on every available spot where they could get a view of what was going on. The hills in the distance had streams of white smoke constantly rising from among the trees. She could see people on their balconies, and the cupola of the Courthouse was full of civilians as well. She turned toward the river. The firing seemed continuous in the center of town and east of the river. Many of the people around her were speaking in fearful tones.

"Whatever will happen next?"

"I dread to see."

Victoria continued to scan the horizon beyond the city. In the far distance, she could see cultivated hills, some already yellow with grain, she could see Federal batteries, with the frequent puffing of smoke from their guns. She turned back to the river where she saw a gunboat advance closer to town. It was just out of reach of the Confederate batteries. Two more gunboats lay about half a mile above the canal that Grant and his men had started to dig the previous year in an attempt to bypass Vicksburg along the Mississippi River. As she watched, two large Confederate vessels started out from shore, with two larger boats tied to them. All of the boats were packed full of soldiers.

"What on earth?" She wondered. At the same time, she saw her father's friend, newspaperman Marmaduke Shannon.

"Hello, my dear Miss Victoria. I can't say I'm surprised to see you up here. I trust your family knows where you are?"

"I was out visiting when all of this started, so no, they do not. I have to ask, though…do you know…what is going on down there with those boats of men?"

"The soldiers on the boats are mostly Federal prisoners," He responded. "They've been held here in town, but we just paroled them. We're sending them back to their encampment."

"Why would we give the Yankees more men to fight us?" She asked, incredulous at the news.

"If we keep them here, we must care for them. We need to save our resources for our own men, especially since we may need to withstand the siege that is likely coming."

"Do you really think we are in any danger?" Victoria asked.

"That is dependent on quite a few things, Miss Victoria," He answered. "It appears we are surrounded by the Federal army. It will still be difficult for them to take the town, but I fear we won't be able to hold out very long if we cannot get any supplies in here."

"My goodness." Victoria had known they were in danger, had actually expected it, but to stand here on the hill and look at the danger and devastation…it was a difficult thing to comprehend. The cannon and musket fire continued.

"I must be on my way, so this story makes the morning edition," Mr. Shannon said. "Please tell your mother to not hesitate to come to me if your family needs anything."

"Of course, Mr. Shannon, thank you. Please give my regards to Mrs. Shannon and Annie and Emily." She turned and began walking home, suddenly wanting to be with her family.

As she hurried through town to finish her last errand, she was disheartened to see wounded men and ambulances passing through. She passed by an officer, who had his head bandaged, and his arm in a sling. His servant walked by his side, leading his horse. She could hear the continual sound of artillery fire, and wondered if it would stop any time soon.

"Victoria! Where in heaven's name have you been?" Her mother asked, worry apparent in her voice.

"I was visiting with Mary Green, then I got caught up in the excitement and lost track of time. I am so sorry for being late and causing you any distress." She gave her mother a hug. "Have we heard anything from Jason?"

"No. I fear he was caught outside the lines," Rachel replied. "I hope that's the case at least, the only other reason he wouldn't have stopped by would be that he..." She paused as if she couldn't even speak the words. "That is my prayer every night, for all my boys, that they are safe."

"Mine as well," Victoria replied. "Every night and throughout the day."

Tuesday, May 19, 1863
Turner Home

No one in the Turner household slept much that night, as the cannon fire continued into the morning. Victoria went to the front porch after breakfast on her way to visit Mary, but stopped and smiled when she saw a slightly cleaner but still unkempt Nathaniel standing there.

"Nathaniel! I am so happy you're back." She invited him into the parlor, thoughts of visiting Mary gone. "How long will you be here? Can you stay for dinner?" *Can you stay forever?* She wanted to ask.

"I can only stay for a short visit, I just wanted to check on you. I can't stay for dinner, though I do appreciate the invitation." He ran a hand through his shaggy black hair, a habit Victoria enjoyed.

"Well, come along then. Have you eaten? There are eggs and fruit left over from breakfast."

"I'm fine, thank you." He followed her into the house and sat next to her on the settee.

"What news do you have from the battle lines?" She asked.

"The Yankees are right on the other side of our entrenchments, they were that close last night."

"Yes, we could hear the gunfire. It sounded as though a great battle was being fought."

"It's well on its way to being that for sure. Firing all along the left wing and towards the center," Nathaniel explained.

"I must ask, why were there so many homes burning last night?" Victoria thought back to the grand, yet horrible spectacle of the night before. The darkness of the evening had been lit up by burning houses all along the Confederate lines.

"It was an unfortunate necessity," Nathaniel answered. "They had to be burned so that our firing would be unobstructed. It was sad for us to see as well. I know many of those homes were quite beautiful."

"Yes, they were. Do you know what happened to the occupants? Were they brought to safety?" Victoria asked.

"I'm not sure. I haven't heard." He looked toward the entryway. "Where is the rest of your family?"

"Mary Grace and the children are staying here. Mama and Mary Grace went over to the haberdashery, just in case there was any business. Tabetha, Brianne and Kendall are watching Mary Grace's children out back."

"You mentioned this Tabetha before. Who is she?" Nathaniel asked.

"A close family friend from…Virginia." Victoria hesitated. It would be hard to deceive Nathaniel about Tabetha's origins because he knew so much about her family. She met his eye and saw that he did not quite believe her, but was going to accept her explanation for now.

Nathaniel nodded and leaned forward. "Victoria, I stopped by because I wanted to see you, as I said, but I also came by to speak with you and your family about your safety."

"Do you think we may be in danger? Jason thought the city would be safer than the countryside this time." Victoria asked.

"I'm not sure where it will be safe, but it's too late to leave town now, regardless. Shells and bullets from the Yankees could reach any part of town, since they have us surrounded. Their Navy gunboats have blocked us from getting out by river route and Grant and his army have surrounded the other three sides of the town. The homes on the east side of town should be a bit safer, as the gunboats will be able to shoot over our entrenchments, while the army will have more trouble reaching the town."

"I see." Victoria did not like where the conversation was heading.

"Many residents are looking to take refuge in caves on the east side of the hill," Nathaniel paused. "At any rate, I would be more than willing to help provide one for your family. I already have space set aside and the tools needed to dig."

"A cave?" Victoria's stomach clenched at the thought of staying in a cave. Darkness everywhere, walls moving in and the ceiling crashing down on her. "You can speak with my mother and Mary Grace, but I will not be confined to a rat hole." Another round of shots fired. This one was continuous and Victoria felt the bombardment would never end. The full realization of their situation and the danger they were now exposed to set in. She shook her head, frightened for herself, her family, and her friends. What if Adam, Gabriel or Hope were caught in the crossfire? She couldn't bear to lose her nephews or niece. "I just don't believe I can stay in a cave, Mr. Prentiss. Besides, when will you find time to dig one?"

"I've been acting as a courier between the officers on the lines and here in town. I'll do my share of the work in the entrenchments, but I will also be able to help you."

Victoria nodded, happy that she would be able to spend time with the man in front of her, but she still could not get over the fact that he wanted her to take shelter in a dank, dark cavern. "That's all well and good, and I dearly love your company, but living in a cave..." She shook her head.

"It is a matter of safety, Miss Turner." Nathaniel sighed.

"How is that? How are these caves any safer than a house?"

"When the shells hit a house, the house will vibrate and could collapse. If you are in a cave, when the shell hits the ground, the dirt absorbs the vibrations," Nathaniel explained. "Could I at least start preparing one for you and your family? Then, if it becomes necessary, it will be there for you."

"And if we decide it's not? You would have spent all that time and effort for nothing."

"It won't be for nothing," Nathaniel said. "If your family decides not to use it, I can sell it or rent it out or give it to someone else in need. However, I have a feeling that your mother and sister will make use of it."

"And you would do this for my family? And ask for nothing in return?"

"When you are helping people you care about, you don't expect anything in return, Victoria," he said softly. "Perhaps I didn't make myself clear the other night. I care for you. I want you to know that if we were together under different circumstances, I would speak with your father today and ask his permission to court you."

Victoria was unsure of how to respond. Finally, gesturing towards the still loud gunfire, she joked: "Your words would be much more romantic if it wasn't for the sounds of war and destruction all around us. Shouldn't we be hearing violins?"

"And the sounds of birds chirping and frogs croaking." He smiled. "You deserve that and so much more."

"Well, we can't change the circumstances." She looked down.

"Victoria," Tabetha entered the parlor, then halted when she saw Nathaniel. "I beg your pardon. I didn't know you had company." He stood and smiled, though Victoria saw confusion on his face.

"I am so sorry, ma'am...I don't mean to stare," he said. "You look familiar. I believe...did I go to school with your brother? At the Michigan Agricultural College?"

"Yes, my brother Adam did go to school there." Tabetha admitted without thinking.

"Of course, Adam Norton, and you must be his sister."

"Yes, I am Tabetha." She walked across the room to retrieve the copy of *Jane Eyre* she had been reading.

"Of course. The mysterious Tabetha. He spoke of you often and had a picture of you and your family. You bear a remarkable resemblance to him." Nathaniel glanced at Victoria, who remained silent, then focused on

Tabetha again. "What on earth are you doing here in Vicksburg? Outside of Michigan, even?"

Tabetha looked at Victoria, unsure of what to say.

"Nathaniel, I must ask for your discretion with Tabetha's identity." Victoria placed a hand on his sleeve. "For reasons I cannot explain right now. The townsfolk believe her to be a family friend, who came from Virginia to visit us and…"

Nathaniel placed his hand over hers and smiled. "Victoria, say no more. You know you had my cooperation from the beginning. I will say nothing of this to anyone, you have my word."

"Thank you, Mr. Prentiss. It was good to finally meet you." Tabetha said, then turned to leave, book in hand.

"Miss Norton, please don't leave on my account. I would love to hear news of your family. How is Adam? Do you hear from him?"

Tears formed in Tabetha's eyes. "I am afraid he was killed earlier in the war."

Nathaniel's expression fell. "I am deeply sorry for your loss. Adam was a great friend."

"Yes, he was." Tabetha nodded, not wanting to talk of her brother. She turned to Victoria. "With all of the fighting, there are many wounded soldiers. I have heard many buildings are being used as hospitals. I would like to go out and see what I can do to help, but I don't want to put your family at risk."

"No, Tabetha, that is very admirable. I feel our story is a strong one. No one should suspect you, and honestly, I believe folks will be too busy to care much about the details of your background. However, do take care of yourself. You are still recovering from your own wound."

"Yes, I will." Tabetha turned to leave when Nathaniel stopped her again.

"Miss Norton, I was just getting ready to leave myself. Please allow me to escort you."

"Thank you, Mr. Prentiss. I would appreciate that." Tabetha responded.

"We will be off, then." He turned to Victoria. "Tori, I will see you again as soon as I can, and I will start on that project."

"Take care, Nathaniel," she replied.

Victoria and her family sat in the parlor that evening, working on sewing projects and reading. The constant cannon fire continued, but thankfully Adam, Gabriel and Hope were already sleeping. There was a knock on the parlor door, and Esther poked her head in.

"Pardon me, Mr. Prentiss to see you all." She let Nathaniel in, who smiled as he entered.

"Ladies, what a pleasure to see you all again." He nodded to each of them as Victoria stood. She introduced Nathaniel to Brianne and Kendall, as they had never met.

"Is it as bad as it sounds out there, Mr. Prentiss?" Rachel asked.

"As you all probably know, the town was attacked from the rear today and, unfortunately, judging from the movements on the Mississippi and Yazoo Rivers, the gunboats will likely attack tonight."

"Oh, Lord, be with us," Mary Grace said. "I don't know that I will sleep a wink again tonight."

"Many people are going to their caves tonight," Nathaniel said. "I'm not nearly finished with the one I'm digging for you, but there are some community caves that you may be able to stay in."

"I believe we'll just stay here tonight, thank you," Victoria said.

"The caves may become a necessity, Victoria." He sounded exasperated. "Some townsfolk have already…" he glanced at Brianne and Kendall. "I don't have any details, but some townsfolk have already been wounded on the streets by shell fragments."

"Well, we are not on the streets, Nathaniel." Victoria could tell by the tone of Nathaniel's voice that he did know more, but she let it rest. Shells continued to burst outside while the Turners tried not to let the commotion bother them. Suddenly, a loud boom sounded that shook the whole house and all three of Mary Grace's children began crying out.

"Oh, heavens," Mary Grace exclaimed. "Mama, Brianne, could you come help me?"

"Of course," Rachel said rising. Brianne followed. Nathaniel looked at Victoria, who somehow knew that he wanted to talk in private.

"Mr. Prentiss, would you mind escorting me to the porch? I'd like to get a breath of fresh air."

"Of course." He followed her out the door, leaving Kendall and Tabetha in the parlor.

"Didn't she just make a point that she was safe in the house and not on the streets?" Kendall asked Tabetha as Victoria shut the door.

Outside, it was much louder with the screams of mortar shells.

"I know it's only been a couple of nights, but it's hard to remember what a quiet evening is like after what we've been experiencing," Victoria said.

"Yes," Nathaniel answered, sitting down in a rocking chair, leaning his elbows on his knees and clasping his hands together. Victoria sat in the chair next to him, wanting to comfort him when he was so clearly distressed.

"Please, Nathaniel. Tell me what's wrong. You are obviously upset about something."

"Grant assaulted our stronghold, but he failed," he replied.

"Well, that's good, isn't it?" Victoria asked.

"It's good that he failed, but the cost was just too high." Nathaniel rubbed his temples

"Are you talking about the people who were wounded in the street that you mentioned earlier?" She said.

"Not wounded, Tori. Killed. There have been too many men lost in this war, and even some civilians. More will die and I tell you, it just doesn't get any easier to deal with."

"Nathaniel, I know something more has happened. What is really troubling you?"

"You know me better than anyone, Tori." He looked out to the sky, which continued to be steadily lit up with shells. "I don't know many people here since being trapped in the city. I told you that I have been delivering messages from the lines to Pemberton and his officers. In the short amount of time I've been here, though, I had become quite friendly with a Major James B. Anderson. He was mortally wounded this morning. He was a good man, and he was a good soldier, too. Now, he's gone."

"Oh, Nathaniel! I am so sorry. What happened; do you know?"

"He was shot by a sharpshooter while maneuvering his battery in front of the entrenchments." Nathaniel sighed and ran his hand through his hair. "I know I only knew him a short time, but we would have been good friends."

"I am so sorry for your loss." Without thinking, she reached out and placed her hand on his wrist. He looked down and took her hand in his.

"It just makes me realize how precious life can be, how short our time may be here on earth. I appreciate your concern. Having you here to talk to is so helpful."

"I am always here for you, Nathaniel." She replied. "And if we can't talk like we are right now, if distance separates us, you can always write to me."

"We both know that just because I write to you doesn't mean you will receive the letter," he said.

"That is true." She thought for a moment. "Wait here." She went inside and hastened to her room, grabbed two bound books, and quickly rejoined Nathaniel. The sky was still lit up by the shells streaking through the air. She handed him one of the books, and he flipped through the blank pages.

"A journal?" He asked, a smile on his face.

"Yes. Instead of writing letters, we can write in these journals. Then, when we meet back up we can exchange the diaries." She looked at him, suddenly unsure of how he would receive her idea. Perhaps it sounded foolish to him.

"I think it is a wonderful idea." He looked at her. "You always know what I need. This will be...this is such a nice gesture." He smiled. "Thank you so much." His voice was soft.

"I'm glad you like the idea," she replied, not looking at him.

"I really do," he answered.

Victoria finally looked at Nathaniel. He was staring off toward the Mississippi. She spoke up again. "You know, you...you can stay here whenever you need to."

"I thank you for the invitation. I'll keep that in mind, but for now, I will be staying closer to the lines." After another moment, he glanced at Victoria and gave her a small smile. "I must be getting back. I'll try and stop by tomorrow. I hope to have your cave ready soon." He stood.

"Thank you, Nathaniel," she said. "For everything."

Wednesday, May 20, 1863
Turner Home

The firing continued all through the night and into the next day again.

"Oh, will this infernal cannonading ever end?" Victoria looked out the window toward the river. She stood in the parlor with Brianne and Tabetha. Rachel and Kendall had brought Mary Grace and the children back to the haberdashery for the day.

"It can't last forever." Tabetha looked up from the book she was reading. "But you could ask that handsome Mr. Nathaniel Prentiss when he comes next time." She gave Victoria a sly smile.

"Perhaps I will." Victoria hoped she didn't blush at the mention of Nathaniel. "I must say, though, with Jason missing, it has been nice to have another soldier around to keep us informed."

"Yes, and Nathaniel is just visiting to keep us informed of what's going on in regards to the war." Brianne added, picking up Tabetha' lead. "I will add that I agree with Tabetha he is a fine-looking gentleman. I can see why you are attracted to him, Victoria."

Victoria's response was interrupted by Esther rushing into the room.

"Mistresses, come, come quick ya'll have to come and see." She exclaimed. "Dem Yankees are pourin' ober da hill past da entrenchments an' our men be a runnin'."

Victoria stood slowly, unsure of what to do. She wanted to rush outside to see what was happening, yet she also wanted to make sure everyone in her family was safe. The news startled her as she never imagined a Rebel running from a fight.

"Miss Victoria, Miss Tabetha, da rest a you, we needs to get to safety. Y'all can hear dem. De shells be fallin' all around us. Y'all be killed if yo stay her." Esther was insistent.

"We'll go, Esther." Tabetha stood. She should feel unconcerned, as she had been under fire many times before, but she was nervous, as always. "Thank you. Come, let's get some things packed up and head to the cave."

Nathaniel had told them the location of where he was digging their underground hideout the day before, so they would know where to go. Victoria shook her head as Tabetha and Brianne went upstairs to pack.

"I still don't understand why it will be safer in a cave," Victoria muttered. She had no intention of going to the community cave that her mother had arranged for their family with the help of Nathaniel. The very thought of being trapped underground made her breath catch. She went into her father's study, took the spyglass from his desk, and continued to the front porch, where she could view most of the action. She held the spyglass to her eye and saw Confederate soldiers pouring over the hill beyond the entrenchments towards town. Wagons with what she assumed held wounded men followed. The soldiers halted while the wagons continue into town. Victoria breathed a sigh of relief. The men weren't retreating, they were simply repositioning themselves.

"Victoria, come. We must find your mother and sister and get to the cave." Tabetha gripped Victoria's arm.

"I was serious the other day." Victoria insisted. "I will not go into a cave. I know I..." she shuddered at the thought. "I know I can't do it. I will risk staying here. Besides, I don't believe we will be in much danger."

"Victoria Turner..." Brianne started to say, but Victoria held her hand up.

"You two can go. Take Esther, Dinah and Caesar too, but I tell you, I cannot stay in a cave."

Brianne had tears in her eyes, and Tabetha looked flustered.

"All right then, Victoria. I will bring Brianne and the others to safety, then I will be back to talk some sense into you." Tabetha turned and stomped down the porch.

⌒⌒⌒

"Tabetha, how can we just leave Victoria there?" Brianne asked, tears running down her cheeks.

"We can't force her, but like I said, I will go back and do my best to talk some sense into her," Tabetha replied. "She may be correct. There could be no danger at the house, but I am not willing to take any chances, and I think it wise of you not to take any. We'll go to the cave and wait for the rest of your family."

"What if Aunt Rachel scolds us for Victoria not coming?"

"Your Aunt Rachel and Mary know how stubborn Victoria can be. They will understand that it's not our fault."

Gunfire continued popping and Tabetha could hear artillery fire in the distance. She and Brianne quickly made it to the Turner cave, which was just on the east side of the hill from where the Turners lived. Just as they entered, they heard an explosion quite close to the entrance. Tabetha's heart raced as the ground shook beneath her. She reached out to steady herself on the wall.

"Brianne! Tabetha! I have been so worried. Where is Victoria?" Rachel Turner asked. She sat against one of the walls, her arms around Adam and Gabriel. Sitting next to Gabriel, Mary Grace was clutching Hope to her chest. The two-year-old was wailing, which is what Tabetha wanted to do. She had been in the thick of battle before, but it never got any easier, and hearing the cries of the children made it even worse.

"Victoria refused to come." Brianne shrieked as she collapsed next to Kendall, who was now sitting on the other side of Adam. "She said she would rather die than be holed up in a dark, dank cave."

"Good heavens." Rachel stood and started for the door. "I must go get her."

"She will probably not listen to you, Mrs. Turner." Tabetha said. "She seemed quite adamant about staying as far away from the caves as she could. I will go back and try to talk to her now."

"That girl is too stubborn for her own good." Rachel walked to the entrance of the cave. "You stay here, Tabetha. I will try to talk some sense into her."

"Are you sure you don't want me to go with you, Mrs. Turner?" Tabetha asked.

"No, I would feel better if you stayed here," Rachel answered.

Tabetha took the place that Rachel had been sitting in, put her arms around the twins, and looked around. She hoped they wouldn't have to stay in the cave for long. She understood why Victoria didn't want to be here. The sense of suffocation from being underground was overwhelming. There would be no way to escape if a cannonball exploded at the entrance and caused a cave-in.

"I feel like we are caged in here, like an animal caught in a trap." Mary Grace said so softly that Tabetha could barely hear her.

"Well," Tabetha said, looking around and hoping to lighten the mood. "If we end up staying in a cave for an extended period of time, we could brighten it up a bit, once Mr. Prentiss has our own cave ready, that is. We can bring in rugs, dig holes in the wall to place candles in and perhaps even bring in some furniture."

"We could dig separate rooms as well," Kendall said. "Maybe have rooms for sleeping and rooms for living."

"That's a good idea, Kendall." Tabetha smiled at the girl. "Mary Grace, how would you make cave living better?"

"I would like to bring some photographs," She said with a small smile.

"That would be good." Tabetha smiled. "How about you boys? What would make a cave feel more like home?"

"Candy!" Adam exclaimed. Mary Grace, Brianne, Tabetha and Kendall laughed.

"How about you, Gabriel?" Kendall asked.

"Hats." He replied seriously. "Hats and buttons and needles, like at the shop."

"That would make it feel like home." Mary Grace smiled, brushing her son's hair back. "What would you bring, Brianne?"

"It would be nice to have all of my dresses and hats," she replied.

"I should have known you would say that." Kendall teased her sister.

"I do hope Aunt Rachel can get Victoria to come here," Brianne said with concern in her voice as another cannonball shook the ground outside.

"I do too, Brianne," Mary Grace said. "If anyone can convince her, it's Mother."

"Mother!" Victoria stood from the porch rocking chair as she saw Rachel make her way up the steps to the Turner home.

"Victoria Grace Turner, what are you thinking? Why did you not come with Kendall and Tabetha?" She hugged her daughter tightly, glad she was unharmed. "Why are you not safely in the cave with them?"

"I just couldn't do it, Mama. The other day, I said I would not stay in the cave and I meant it."

"We didn't think you were serious, Victoria. You cannot really be that frightened of enclosed spaces." Rachel brushed a stray hair from her daughter's face. Victoria took a deep breath, trying not to think about staying in a cave, with dirt walls all around her and above her and feeling like the ceiling would come crashing down on her at any moment.

"I just...Mama, please understand me. I just can't." She tried not to cry. She couldn't let her mother see how scared she was, how the thought of being in an enclosed space like that absolutely terrified her. "Please just let me be." She turned and walked back into the house.

"You must be out of your head if you think for one moment that I am just going to leave you here. You are my daughter. What is going on, really Victoria?"

"The very idea of living in an enclosed space like a cave...it terrifies me." She shook her head. "I would rather risk being hit by a cannonball in my own home than take shelter in a cave. I don't see how a cave is any safer than my home."

"My dear." Rachel blew out a breath as another cannonball exploded and shook the ground near the house. Rachel pulled Victoria close.

"Where is your faith in God? You know as well as I do that He will protect us and see us through, but you must let Him do His work."

"I know, Mama, I know. I just. It is difficult to explain to myself, much less someone else."

Rachel saw the determination and fear in her daughter's face, something she hadn't seen since Victoria was a child. "I will make a compromise with you. When the Yankees are bombarding heavily and people are going to the caves, will you go with them and at least just...sit outside? That way, if something comes your way, you can take cover in the doorway." She hugged her tightly again. "We need you, Victoria. Your cousins, your sister, the children. We cannot let anything happen to you. Don't let your fears take control of your life when you know deep down they are unfounded. Trust in the Lord."

Victoria looked at her. "I suppose I can do that. If it will make you all feel better."

"Fine, now let's go." The two made their way to the cave, weaving through the people that filled the streets. They were almost to the cave when Nathaniel approached them.

"Victoria! What are you thinking?" Nathaniel ran a hand through his shaggy black hair. "I went to the cave and your family told me of your refusal to join them. What is wrong with you?"

"Nathaniel! I am so very sorry. I'm not thinking straight." She looked at her mother. "However, my mother, with her determination, has talked me through it..."

"What else was I to do, Victoria?" Rachel smiled at Nathaniel as they began walking toward the cave. "Thank you for checking up on us, Mr. Prentiss. Is there any word on what's happening?"

Nathaniel shook his head. "Not that I can tell you with any certainty. I did hear some news that may ease your minds. Many of the Mississippi militia men are caught outside the lines. They'll likely be out there for as long as we are under siege here. Since Jason, hasn't stopped by lately to see you, he is likely out in the countryside."

"That is what we were hoping to hear. Will they be able to help us?" Victoria asked.

"They will be able to do some maneuvering, perhaps some small attacks and sniper shooting, but what we really need is for General Joe Johnston to come in from the east and reinforce us." He rubbed at his dirt-stained forehead as they reached the cave. "Ladies, I must be on my way. I'll come back as soon as I can to update you." He tipped his hat and vanished into the crowds.

Rachel grasped Victoria's arm as they walked into the cave. "It may not seem like it, but the cave is much safer than our home."

"You say it is so, but I still will not spend any more time in this cave than I need to. In fact, I plan on staying right outside unless I absolutely need to go in."

Rachel shook her head. "But you will come in now. I need your help. You must show your nephews, niece and cousins how to be brave."

Victoria groaned. "You know just how to get me to do something unpleasant." She blew out a breath. "All right. I will be anxious every second I am in there, but I will do it for the children."

Friday, May 22, 1863
Turner Home

"I do hope Nathaniel comes by sometime today." Brianne shook out the undergarment that Dinah had just washed before hanging it on a line. "He always has the most updated information of what's going on now that Jason can't come."

The family was able to go back to the house when the sporadic cannon fire subsided. The shelling was almost on a schedule now. It seemed the Yankees needed time off for breakfast, lunch and dinner.

"I'm sure Victoria wants him to stop by as well, but not to get an update on the news." Kendall smiled in a teasing manner.

Victoria shook her head, but Kendall was correct. Nathaniel stopping by was the highlight of her days. The more time she spent with him, the better she liked him.

"The last time he was here, he told me that many of our men and the Yanks are actually holding conversations. He said that in one instance, two brothers in the Third Regiment of Missouri discovered that their brother is in the regiment opposite them." Victoria commented. "I can't remember their names, but can you imagine being in that situation."

"It's like they say, this is truly a brother's war." Brianne said.

"That's what concerns me," Victoria responded. "Remember, our own cousins in Petersburg are divided. At the beginning of the war, a letter from Bekah said that Jonah followed Uncle Samuel and stayed in the Union army while Jacob enlisted in the Confederacy, and I'm quite sure Uncle Hiram is fighting for the Union as well. Two of Papa's own brothers, fighting against him. And your father as well." She nodded to Kendall.

"It is a tragic situation," Kendall admitted, then turned to Tabetha. "Did you have any division in your family, or is Illinois decidedly Union?"

Tabetha hesitated. She had let the Turner family assume that she was from Illinois. She wasn't sure why she didn't tell them the whole truth. Victoria knew, and it had made no difference to her.

"There are some Confederate sympathizers," Tabetha admitted. "However, most of the people I know are very pro-Union. It has little to do with emancipation, it is mostly to preserve the Union, as they feel secession is unconstitutional."

Kendall nodded and then picked up the laundry basket and went into the house.

"Why don't you just tell Brianne, Kendall and my mother? It makes no difference to them whether you're from Michigan or Illinois. Brianne probably doesn't even know the difference between Michigan and Illinois."

"Michigan is, in my opinion, the best state. Granted," She shrugged. "I haven't been to many other states, but Michigan is so beautiful, especially along the lakeshore. I love the changing seasons. Snowy winters, springs that warm to new life, hot summers perfect for swimming in a nearby river, and crisp, cool autumns. I really miss it."

"It sounds as though you can't wait to get back home," Victoria stated.

"Someday," Tabetha replied. "Unfortunately, my family may not want me back."

"You've mentioned that before, Tabetha," Victoria said. "But I find that hard to believe. I think you're wrong to feel that way."

Artillery began to hammer at the city once again. Victoria shook her head. "Nathaniel mentioned that it won't take long for Grant to realize he can't win Vicksburg in a battle. When he does realize that, he'll either retreat or lay siege to the town."

"From what I know of Grant, it will be the latter," Tabetha said. "The troops respect his tenacity, they call him a bulldog."

"Well, our general Johnston will get here soon from Jackson, and none of that will matter," Victoria stated. Before Tabetha could answer, a cannonball screamed overhead.

"Get down!" Tabetha yelled, diving behind a bale of hay that had been placed in the back as a makeshift shelter. Victoria dropped to the ground as the ball hit the ground. It was a near miss, and dirt and straw showered the two women. Tabetha lifted her head and saw Victoria lying on the ground, her arms covering her head.

"Victoria, have you been killed?" She asked, hoping that her question would end up being as absurd as it sounded to her.

"No," Victoria replied with equal concern. "Have you?" Victoria picked herself up off the ground, then looked at her friend. Tabetha shook her head and started laughing. Victoria couldn't help but laugh as well. Their fatigue and the absurd conversation made it difficult to be serious. Victoria was unable to stop and hunched over in laughter.

Brianne, Esther, Kendall and Rachel rushed out from inside the house, followed by a concerned-looking Nathaniel.

"Whatever happened here?" Rachel asked.

"A shell hit right there, can you believe it? But we were able to get out of the way." Victoria explained, still laughing. "The hay bales helped protect us, I am so glad we moved them here."

"Yes, we can see that, and the hay has covered you both." Nathaniel said, approaching Victoria. He brushed her shoulder, then reached up and pulled some pieces of straw from Victoria's blonde hair. Tabetha and Victoria's laughter was contagious as the others began to laugh as well.

"Thank you," Victoria said, still chuckling as she took a step back. "What news have you? How is it on the lines?"

"The fighting has been horrific, and the Yankee gunboats have come up and engaged our batteries on the riverfront. Mortars continue shelling us endlessly. We're now penned up in a two square mile-radius with fighting all around."

"Will Grant give up soon?" Tabetha asked, although she was sure of the answer.

"No," Nathaniel replied. "It appears they will besiege the city and try to starve us into submission. We will hold out and defeat them, though."

"I have faith that our men will be victorious." Victoria smiled. Nathaniel smiled back, then looked at the rest of her family.

"I'm going to head to the cave and do some more digging. I want to widen the entryway for you and dig another exit. I would strongly suggest you all pack up more of your belongings and head there. Grant is going to throw everything he has at Vicksburg in the next few days, and I doubt we'll get much rest or quiet time in the next week or so."

Victoria nodded, and they all went into the house to prepare for a long week.

That evening, Nathaniel and Victoria sat on the steps of the Turner's porch as he told her about the latest news from the trenches. Victoria and her family had moved many of their belongings to the cave, and Nathaniel had gone back to the lines for a brief time after he had worked on their cave. Victoria was deeply touched at his loyalty to her family. He had come back to the cave when the cannon fire had subsided and asked her to go for a walk. They ended up at the Turner home.

"Conversations still occur every night between us and the Yankees. Those three Missouri brothers are still talking. They even sent gifts across the lines, coffee for whiskey."

"I find that intriguing," Victoria said. "Yet quite sad at the same time."

"That's not the strangest part." Nathaniel reached down and took her hand in his free one. "When they parted at the end of the latest conversation, one brother told the other that he would 'blow his brother's head off' tomorrow?"

"How tragic," Victoria replied. "It is odd to hear of the stories that go on during the battles. The soldiers see so much blood and carnage, and yet there are so many incidents of kindness."

"Yes," Nathaniel agreed. "Have you heard the story of the Angel of Marye's Heights?"

"I know there is a Marye's Heights in Fredericksburg," Victoria stated.

"Yes, that is the place, awful fighting happened there." Nathaniel closed his eyes as he remembered the sights and sounds. "Richard Kirkland, that is his name. He is a soldier in the South Carolina infantry. During the battle, he and his unit inflicted heavy casualties on the Yankees who thought they could take the Heights. During one of the nights, many Yankee soldiers were unable to move on the field, suffering terribly from their wounds and lack of water."

"My goodness, that sounds horrible." Victoria shook her head. Nathaniel squeezed her hand and looked up at the sky, lost in his memory.

"Soldiers from both sides were forced to listen to the cries of the wounded for hours upon hours, but neither side was able to help for fear of being shot by the enemy. That fear didn't matter to Kirkland. The man gathered all the canteens he could carry, filled them with water, and ventured out onto the battlefield. He went back and forth several times, giving the wounded Union soldiers water and doing whatever he could do to ease their pain. Soldiers from both sides watched him and no one fired a shot. He worked for about an hour and a half, though it felt much longer for everyone there."

"It's incredible that no one shot at him. How brave, and so very compassionate." Victoria longed to rest her head on Nathaniel's shoulder, but she didn't want to be too forward.

"I wish I could act in that fashion if the situation presented itself." Nathaniel continued staring at the sky.

"I believe you would." Victoria told him. Nathaniel looked at her and smiled.

"Thank you for believing in me." They fell into a comfortable silence, watching the shells fly overheard. It was easy to see the path they were taking because of the lit fuses. Suddenly, Nathaniel cried out.

"Victoria, inside, now, run!" He pulled Victoria up and pushed her into the house. Victoria tried to get her feet underneath her, but stumbled in the front door, Nathaniel right behind her. She was just inside the door when the explosion came. Victoria was thrown the rest of the way to the floor, and Nathaniel jumped on top of her to help shield her, covering her head with his arms. Victoria could feel pieces of wood and plaster falling on her. After a moment, Nathaniel pushed up just a little bit.

"Victoria, are you alright?" He asked. She could barely hear him, but nodded.

"Just shaken," she replied. He rolled off her and knelt, helping her to sit up.

"Are you sure?" He asked, then reached over and re-lit the candle he had managed to grab. It was difficult to see, as the room had filled with smoke. The candle that Nathaniel had lit was useless in the denseness of the smoke. Victoria tried to wave the smoke away, but it was several minutes before it began to dissipate enough to where they could see.

"Oh, Nathaniel!" When she finally got a look around the house, she saw that a section of the wall in the parlor was heavily damaged.

"It will be alright, Victoria." He gave her a quick hug, then greeted a small group of soldiers who had entered the house.

"Is anyone hurt?" One of the men asked.

"No," Nathaniel replied. "But I could use your help boarding up the break in the wall. We wouldn't want looters to enter the house."

The men nodded. Nathaniel found some old planks of wood, nails and tools in the back shed and with the salvaged wood from the wall, they began the temporary repairs. It didn't take them long, and when they finished, Nathaniel turned to Victoria.

"Come. It's been an exciting day. I will bring you back to the cave. You've had two close calls already."

"Yes, you are right." She gave him a small smile, still shaken by the excitement.

"You must admit, you would have been safer at the cave tonight," Nathaniel said.

"Perhaps," Victoria replied. "At this point, however, I feel as though there is no safe place in all of Vicksburg. The shot and shell are crashing in every direction. I dare say, even the men in the hospitals are in danger."

"Agreed," Nathaniel stated. "However, if there is a safe place in Vicksburg, it will be underground."

"I suppose you're right." Victoria replied. "I am glad you were here tonight. I don't know that I would have noticed that shell coming our way." She smiled. "Perhaps the safest place in Vicksburg is next to you."

Nathaniel grinned back. "I would expect to hear a comment like that coming from your cousin, Belle."

"I can be flirtatious on occasion." Victoria replied. "Not often, but I can be, I just prefer to be direct with people."

"That's one of the things I love best about you," Nathaniel said, almost without thinking. Victoria stopped walking and looked at him.

"I beg your pardon, kind sir, did I just hear you correctly?" Her heart pounded.

He stopped and turned to face her, a sheepish grin on his reddening face.

"You did. I didn't mean to let it slip so casually, but it's true," He took her hands in his. "I love you, Victoria. I have since the day we met."

"I love you too, Nathaniel." She reached up and brushed a strand of hair from his face. "I must say, I am so relieved you feel the same way."

"It would be nice if we could have a regular courtship, but obviously that's not going to happen while our lives are constantly in danger."

"I understand what you mean," Victoria said. "However, I don't care about that, I'm just glad we found each other in the most illogical of scenarios. I have known for a long time that you are a special man."

"I've known for a while that you are the one for me. When we first met, and in the letters we wrote. I just never thought it would work out with the distance between us." Nathaniel leaned down and gently kissed her forehead. "Odd how things work, isn't it? Come. I need to get you back to that warm, cozy new home of yours."

Saturday, May 23, 1863
Communal Cave

Shells continued to explode throughout the town as Victoria made her way to the section of the cave where Mary Green was lying. Even though it was difficult to visit in the caves, Victoria had a great need to see her friend. The Greens had been staying in a communal cave about two blocks from their home for the past few days.

"Victoria! What a pleasant surprise." Mary Green sat up on the cot that Duff had brought in for her. She gestured for Victoria to sit on the bed.

"I just had to see you," Victoria said. "If I am to be holed up in a cave, I am at least going to visit with family and friends. My goodness, I don't mean to speak poorly of you, Mary, but it looks as if that baby will be with us quite soon."

"I would like to say that this baby can't come soon enough, but I most assuredly do not want to give birth in this cave, especially surrounded by the citizens of Vicksburg. I hope I can wait until we are safely back in my own home."

"Let's pray your new child cooperates with you," Victoria replied.

"I surely hope so." Mary looked over to where her mother, Anna Lake was entertaining little Annie. She noticed other women sewing by candlelight and gossiping.

"Do you get no privacy?" Victoria asked, taking in Mary's temporary home. She despised being enclosed in a cave, but this large communal cave had been dug all the way through one of the hills in the city. It was more like a network of tunnels and adjoining rooms than just one big room like the cave her family was staying in. She had entered on one of the streets, and could exit onto another. It was difficult to imagine that something like this could have been built. Victoria wouldn't have believed it possible if she hadn't seen it with her own eyes.

"It may not be much, but the blankets and screens do help somewhat," Mary answered. "We are much safer here than we would be at the house. Duff says he has a plan that may keep our house safe. I don't see how that can be guaranteed with all of this shelling, but I trust him. He is also working on getting us our own cave built in the hill beneath our home."

"That's good news," Victoria said. "Nathaniel continues to work on our cave, when he has the time, that is. He also plans on building a smaller one nearby, for the future, he says." She smiled to herself, wondering who it was for. "I know I will never be comfortable in any cave, ever. Thankfully, we have set up a fly tent just outside the entrance to shelter our cooking and eating. Isn't that funny? A few months ago, I didn't even know what a fly tent was. The tent also protects us from sun and rain, as our cave is not very deep. I really only have to be inside at night."

"That's good," Mary groaned and adjusted herself.

"Good day, Miss Turner!"

Both women turned and smiled as 11-year-old Lucy McRae poked her head into the makeshift room.

"Hello, Miss Lucy," Victoria replied. "How are you?"

"Very well, thank you," The girl replied. "Willie Lord and his family moved in here not too long ago. He may be a boy, but he's fun to be around. In fact, he likes pretending that Ali Baba's forty thieves lurk in the corners of the caves."

"My, that sounds like a good way to pass the time," Victoria laughed.

"Yes," Lucy said. "But I think he's trying to keep his mind off the fact that he's worried about his father."

"Ahh, yes, I can well understand that. How perceptive of you, Lucy," Victoria said. Dr. William Lord was the reverend at the nearby Christ Episcopal Church. He was still going to the church daily to hold services. It was a dangerous escapade, as cannon balls, or parrot shot, as they had learned to call them, continued to rain down on them. "Reverend Lord is doing a very good and brave deed."

"Yes, he is. Willie is quite proud of him."

"And well he should be…" Mary said, then gripped her stomach. "Oh, goodness, my…Lucy, be a dear, and send Willie to fetch Duff and the doctor? I believe our child is coming."

Victoria sat on a stool in the communal cave outside Mary's room later that evening. She wanted to remain close to Mary in case her friend needed her, but the physician and Mrs. Lake were in attendance in their cave room. Duff was trying to occupy himself by reading in a corner while keeping an eye on two-year-old Annie, but was clearly concerned for his wife. Victoria couldn't imagine what Mary was going through. Giving birth was difficult enough in the comfort of your own home, but to be in a dark, damp cave, surrounded by civilians, lizards, ants, mosquitoes and other insects seemed intolerable. Victoria brushed at the dry mud on her skirt, then closed her eyes and leaned against the wall behind her.

"Tori." A low voice said her name and she opened her eyes to see Nathaniel crouched down in front of her, a concerned look on his face. "I came to escort you back home, well, to your cave. Your mother was concerned when you didn't return, but Reverend Lord just told me about Mrs. Green's condition. I assume you'd like to remain here?"

"Yes, I would." Victoria replied. She looked over at a group of adults sitting and visiting in the main room. Reverend Lord sat propped in a chair, his leg and foot bandaged from an injury he'd had earlier that day. Lucy McRae wandered into the common room, looking as if she was simply trying to find something to do.

"How many people are in this cave?" Nathaniel asked, moving to sit on the floor next to her, taking her hand in his.

"I believe Mary said around twenty," Victoria replied. "That includes slaves, recuperating soldiers, poor whites and wealthy plantation owners all living together."

"Funny how class status seems to vanish in situations like this," he said, bringing his knee up and resting his arm on it.

"Very true," Victoria agreed, then watched as Reverend Lord allowed little Lucy to lie down on a plank bed near his feet.

"The poor girl probably can't sleep, what with all the commotion of a child being born in a nearby room and shells crashing down and exploding outside." Victoria leaned her head back against the wall again. "I feel like I'll never sleep soundly again, even when this bombardment ends, I fear I'll hear these sounds in my sleep for the rest of my life."

Nathaniel started to reply, but before he could say anything, a shell came down on top of the hill, burying itself, then exploding. The entire cave shook. Victoria shrieked and fell to the ground. Nathaniel quickly covered her, protecting her with his own body. A large mass of earth slid down the wall and bits of earth rained down on them.

Not again! Victoria thought. *And now I'm trapped in a cave.*

"Lucy!" Mrs. McRae let out a bloodcurdling scream. Victoria looked over to see Reverend Lord's leg, caught in a pile of dirt. Reverend Lord and Mrs. McRae were digging frantically at the dirt. By the time Nathaniel reached them, they had managed to uncover Lucy's head. Nathaniel and the other men who had rushed over quickly pulled her from the dirt. The terrified girl was obviously distraught. She screamed and choked, blood pouring from her mouth and nose. Victoria stood there, unsure of what to do, but feeling the need to do something.

"Victoria, get the doctor!" Nathaniel yelled. She nodded, then stumbled towards Mary's room.

"Doctor, we need you! Quickly, please, it's Lucy!"

The physician looked up and quickly followed Victoria. In the common area, Mrs. McRae clutched Lucy to her. Nathaniel and Reverend Lord were keeping other people from crowding them too much. Victoria stood next to Nathaniel.

"Will she be all right?" She clutched his arm, still shaking from what had just happened.

"I'm not sure," He replied, putting an arm around her shoulder and pulling her close. His presence calmed her.

"There does not appear to be any broken bones," the doctor told Mrs. McRae. "Unfortunately, I cannot tell what her internal injuries may be. I will continue to check on her. We will know more later."

A cry came from Mary's room, and the physician excused himself and quickly went back to Mary, but before he could reach her, another thunderous explosion shook the cave.

"Nathaniel!" Victoria cried out, terror coursing through her. "It's going to cave in!" She gripped his arm, then released him and rushed out of the cave into the street, trying to contain the screams she wanted to let out. Nathaniel was right behind her. As they reached the street, another shell burst just above them. Victoria threw her arms over her head, and Nathaniel grabbed her and pulled her quickly back into the cave.

"I can't take much more of this, Nathaniel." Tears fell from her eyes.

"You can, Tori, I promise. You are much stronger than you think."

She leaned back and looked into his eyes. "How can you say that? Look at me. I am falling apart." He reached up to wipe a tear from her cheek.

"Because I know you. You have already been through so much, but you still keep the faith. Like right now. You may panic initially, but just as quickly, you regain your senses and do what needs to be done. You help with your family..."

Victoria interrupted and voiced something that had been on her mind for some time. "I'm also thinking about helping out at one of the hospitals in town."

Nathaniel groaned. "I wish you wouldn't. The hospitals are so exposed, Tori, not only to the shells coming into the town, but also to disease, and the men are in such agony and pain, I would hate for you to witness that much suffering."

She shook her head. "I understand your concern, but you are in no position to tell me what I can and cannot do," Victoria pointed out.

"What if I were?" Nathaniel's voice was suddenly very serious, his eyes intense. What was Nathaniel insinuating?

"Nathaniel..."

"Miss Victoria!" Mrs. Lake, came up to the entrance of the cave. Victoria stepped away from Nathaniel.

"What is it, Mrs. Lake?" She asked.

"Mary would like to see you, please. There is someone she would like you to meet."

Victoria smiled. "Oh, that's wonderful news, Mrs. Lake." She followed Mary's mother back into the Green's room. Mary lay there, holding a small bundle in her arms. She looked exhausted, sweat covering her face and her hair all askew, yet at the same time, she looked radiant. *How is that possible?* Duff sat on a chair next to Mary, holding a sleeping Annie in his arms.

"Victoria, I am so glad you're still here. I do appreciate your support."

"I'm happy to see that you're both doing well."

"I am," Mary looked down at the tiny bundle in her arms. "I would like you to meet our son, William S. Green." Mary touched the soft hair on top of the baby's head.

"William, after your father, of course, but what does the 'S' stand for, Mary?" Victoria asked.

Duff smiled. "Well, we had to commemorate the unusual circumstances of his special birth somehow. The 'S' is for Siege."

"That is quite clever," Victoria chuckled, then tried to hide a yawn. "My apologies. It's been a long day, I'm sure you can all agree with that." She reached down again, touching Baby William's cheek. "I should be going. You must all get some rest."

"Thank you again for all of your support today," Mary said.

"Of course. You know I would rather be nowhere else. God bless you and your family, Mary."

Sunday, May 24, 1863
St. Paul Catholic Church

Tabetha exited the church, happy to know that she had enough time to stop and see Mary before volunteering at St. Xavier School and convent, one of the town's many buildings that had been turned into a hospital. Victoria had given her the news of little William's birth that morning.

Yesterday had been overcast and rainy, but today had dawned bright and clear. It would have been the perfect day, had it not been for the constant barrage of artillery fire.

Tabetha ducked into the cave and followed the tunnel to where she knew Mary was staying.

"Tabetha!" Mary smiled as her new friend entered the room. Mary looked tired, but content, wearing a nightgown with her hair in a single braid that draped over her shoulder. A small bundle of blankets was in her arms.

"Good morning, Miss Tabetha!" Annie chirped as Tabetha bent down and kissed the newborn baby's head that poked out from the blankets in Mary's arms. "I have a new baby brother."

"Yes, I've heard. I hope it's okay that I came to visit."

"Of course it is. We've had lots of visitors already," She gently patted the baby's head. "Love you, baby William."

"You are a wonderful big sister," Tabetha replied, then focused on Mary. "And how are you feeling, Mrs. Green?"

"Quite well, actually. Yesterday was more than a bit exciting. I truly did not want to give birth to my child in a cave full of people, with constant explosions that felt like the world was going to collapse."

"And yet, you managed it," Tabetha smiled. "Especially with the artillery firing constantly." The baby lay quiet. "I'm surprised that William is so content, especially with all of the noise outside, and inside for that matter."

"He hasn't been this content the whole time, trust me," Mary said with a timid smile. "He has a very healthy set of lungs."

"Yes, William cries, but it's 'cause it's so loud outside." Annie piped up. "I don't blame Baby Brother for crying."

"No, I don't either," Tabetha laughed. "There are times when I feel like crying."

"Me too," Annie said, then turned to look at her mother. "Mama, can I go play?" She looked over towards one of the Green's servants. "Sissy, can watch me."

"Yes, dear, make sure you mind her."

"Yes, Mama," The two went off to the common area of the cave. Mary gestured towards a chair next to the bed.

"Please have a seat. We haven't spoken in a while." She gently held up the bundle in her arms. "Would you like to hold him?"

"I would love to," Tabetha said, holding out her arms and taking the newborn. "Oh, Mary, he's perfect." She touched his tiny fingers and tiny nose.

"Thank you, Tabetha. I must say that I agree with you." Mary adjusted herself on the bed. "Tell me, what are you doing to keep busy these days?"

"I have been volunteering at the hospitals, mainly the one at St. Xavier," Tabetha replied. "It has been quite an experience, to be honest.

"My goodness. Are there many Federals for you to care for?" Mary asked.

"The hospitals have mostly Confederate soldiers," Tabetha admitted. "Although somehow we have some Federal patients."

"You don't have an issue helping men that you once fought against? Men who were your enemy such a short time ago?"

"No. A man in need is a man in need. In fact, the Gospel readings at Mass today reminded me of that," Tabetha said. "It was the Parable of the Sheep and the Goats."

"Ahh, yes. 'Because you did it for one of the least of my brothers, you did it to me," Mary said.

"Yes, that is the one. It also reminded me of the passage about how Jesus calls us to love our enemies and pray for those who persecute us. I had been hoping for a sign that I was doing the right thing. Today's homily was the answer to my prayers."

"I'm glad for you," Mary said. "Not many people would care for their enemy. They would say that it doesn't make sense."

"Compassion will always make sense to me." Tabetha looked down at the baby in her arms. "And obviously, it does to the Turners as well. They cared for me and took me in and I am the enemy."

"I have always wondered why you decided to enlist. You don't seem like the type of young woman who would pursue living life as a soldier, especially living a lie on a daily basis. You and I have never really spoken of your past. I don't mean to impose, and you don't have to tell me if you don't want to."

"No, it's no problem. I have shared my story with the Turner family, and I trust you." Tabetha took a deep breath and told Mary the story of Adam and her family.

"I am so sorry, Tabetha. I do hope you still aren't blaming yourself."

"No, not really." Tabetha didn't quite meet her friend's eyes. Mary sensed that Tabetha still felt responsible.

"I must say, that is definitely not the reason why I believed you enlisted," Mary admitted. "I thought it was more romantic, such as you followed the man you loved into battle or just the opposite; that you were trying to escape a bad marriage."

'No, nothing quite like that." Tabetha smiled. Mary noted the somber look on Tabetha's face and changed the subject.

"Is there any news outside of this cave?"

"The birth of your child is the talk of the town from what I hear. New life, when there are so many people dying, well, it gives people hope," Tabetha answered. "There's also talk of Lucy McRae's near death experience last night, and I heard that two people in town were killed, though I didn't get any names or specifics on how they died."

"Oh, how distressing!" Mary gasped. "I do hope that is just a false rumor."

"Yes, me too. There have been many homes hit by shells. The Balfour home had a piece of mortar shell tear through the third floor roof, and I'm sure you heard about the Turner's parlor."

"Yes. My goodness, I feel as though no building nor any person will escape unscathed."

"We'll just have to keep praying for the safety of the citizens and all soldiers and for an end to this nightmare," Tabetha looked down at William. "I tell you, Mary, when I look at this beautiful baby boy, it surely gives me hope."

Turner Cave

"Nathaniel! You're back!" Victoria was helping Esther prepare dinner. She didn't usually help in such a way, but she had wanted to do something to pass the time.

"I just came to check on you and make sure the Turner family has survived yet another day." He stepped underneath the fly tent in front of the cave.

"We're fine, though it would be nice to get some good news from the trenches." She gestured to a chair that she had recently brought from the house. Nathaniel sat and Victoria continued her work.

"Well, there continues to be…" He paused as Gabriel exited the cave.

"Good afternoon, Mr. Prentiss," The three-year-old said politely. "Didja kill any Yanks today?"

"Gabriel Corbet! That is not a polite thing to ask anyone." Victoria turned and placed a cornmeal-covered fist on her hip.

"Sorry, Aunt Victoria." Gabriel looked slightly sheepish. "Beg your pardon, Mr. Prentiss." Nathaniel tousled the boy's hair, and Gabriel brightened once again. "What's for dinner?"

"Cornbread and bacon," She replied. "Esther is going to try and find some flour so she can make biscuits later."

"Again?!" Gabriel looked dejected at what was for dinner, then shrugged and headed off.

"Probably going to hunt for some more exploded shells." Victoria shook her head. It was a pastime he and many of the other children in town were able to do during lulls in the action. "You know even if Esther can manage to find flour, she won't be able to make bread since we don't have any soda or yeast." She sighed. "Cornbread and bacon, three times a day. No wonder Gabriel looked so sad." She tossed a ball of cornmeal on the table she was working at. Trying to be optimistic, she added. "At least we don't have to make a decision about what to make for dinner."

"Well, then perhaps you don't want this." Nathaniel pulled out a package from his haversack. He pretended to hand it to her, then pulled it away when she reached for it. "I was thinking that Esther could cook this up tomorrow, but…" She reached out and grabbed it, then opened it.

"Beef! Oh, Nathaniel, you can't give this to us! It must be all of your rations."

"Not exactly, but I was lucky enough to procure it. With Esther's culinary skills, I look forward to sharing it with you all, hopefully for midday meal tomorrow."

"Nathaniel, thank you so much! I can't tell you what a treat this will be." In her excitement, she threw her arms around him. *Imagine, me being this excited about a small side of beef.* She pulled away and smiled.

"I know how frustrating it must be, not having the provisions that you are used to having." He replied. "Besides, we need to enjoy what we can while it is still available."

"Do you really believe the food shortage will get worse?" Victoria set the beef down and pulled a chair over to sit next to him.

"Tori, I don't know that Vicksburg can hold out for more than a week or two. The garrison was poorly provisioned even before I arrived. One of Pemberton's staffers told me that the city now has about fifteen-thousand soldiers. Major General Loring was supposed to come with reinforcements and provisions, but he was cut off after the Battle of Black River."

"I had heard about Loring's soldiers getting trapped outside the city." Victoria hoped they hadn't been captured by the Federals. "The women in town are adamant that we should never surrender."

"They'll likely change that opinion. We've been under siege for only a week. Just wait until it's been a fortnight or longer."

"You think this will last more than a fortnight? I can't see how they can continue this constant bombardment, and you are right, there is already a dearth of food."

"Even more so now," Nathaniel said, clasping his hands together. "We just drove hundreds of mules across the lines to the Yankees."

"Why on earth would we give the enemy our livestock?" Victoria asked.

"We don't have the provisions to feed them. There's no corn to be issued for horses, except for those of the officers in the field. The animals can only salvage for themselves." He sighed. "I believe the commander feared having to use them for food, but I fear we'll regret this rash decision."

"My goodness, it's getting bad." Victoria shook her head. "I had no idea we would find ourselves in this predicament. I feel naive that I didn't even consider it. I should have."

"Don't be so hard on yourself." Nathaniel gave her a smile. Victoria smiled back. It was good to have a casual conversation. After her behavior last night, which still puzzled her, she was more than happy with today's visit. "I don't think anyone thought it would get this bad."

"Well, thank you for saying so." She was glad that her hysterics hadn't damaged their relationship.

"Mr. Prentiss, Miss Victoria." Esther nodded at the couple as she came back to the cave from shopping

"Esther." Nathaniel nodded back.

"Will ya be stayin for suppa?" She asked him.

"No," he said, standing. "I must be off. However, I will be here for dinner tomorrow at noon."

"Yes, he was kind enough to share this beef with us." Victoria added excitedly, handing the beef to the black woman.

"Gracious, what a treat. Dat be right kind o you, Mr. Prentiss." Esther nodded.

Victoria turned to Nathaniel. "Thank you again for everything you do."

"Anything for the Turner women," he replied, then turned and left.

Monday, May 25, 1863~Evening
Turner Home

"If only this flag of truce could last forever." Rachel said as she sat on the back porch of their home with Brianne, Victoria, Tabetha and Kendall, working on some mending.

"I had forgotten how peaceful life can be." Victoria replied. The morning had been full of furious fighting but by afternoon, it had quieted down. News had quickly made its way through town that a flag of truce had been set out at around 1:00 that afternoon from Pemberton to Grant, asking for an armistice for a few hours to bury the dead. Grant had agreed, which led to the calm and quiet afternoon. "I dread the fact that we will have to return to the caves though. It is inevitable."

"Goodness Victoria." Kendall rolled her eyes. "Be thankful you're not one of those dead men or women who need to be buried. I wish you would stop complaining about the caves. You're such a killjoy when you do."

"I'm not trying to be a killjoy," Victoria argued.

"We understand that you dislike the caves, but you must stop being so whiney."

"I'm not..." Victoria started to protest, then looked up and smiled when she saw Nathaniel coming down Cherry Street. "We can finish this discussion later, if necessary," she replied in a hushed tone.

Nathaniel approached them and leaned against the porch railing. "How are you ladies this evening?"

"Quite well, thank you," Rachel said.

"We missed you at dinner." Victoria stood. "Esther is keeping some stew warm for you."

"Wonderful." He smiled.

"I'll get it!" Kendall said, still upset with Victoria's thoughtlessness and stomped into the house.

"Were you on the detail that buried our dead today?" Victoria asked.

"I helped." He took a deep breath. "It was disheartening, yet strangely, encouraging. We met some Federal officers who were burying their dead as well." He took off his kepi and patted it against his leg. "I was actually surprised; there were fewer casualties than I expected, and we were able to gather over 400 arms. That will help keep our cause greatly." The look on his face, however, told Victoria that the day had really had an effect on him.

"When will the armistice end?" Brianne asked.

"At 9:00 tonight," he replied. "So, expect the bombardment to commence at that time. I would like to take advantage of the quiet evening." He turned to Rachel. "Mrs. Turner, may I have your permission to take Victoria on a stroll? After I eat the delicious meal you have provided of course."

"Most certainly." Rachel nodded as Kendall came out with a bowl of beef soup.

"Here you are, Mr. Prentiss." Kendall looked up at Nathaniel, adoration clear in her eyes.

"Thank you so much, Miss Kendall," he said, then sat down at the offered chair and ate.

"So you would recommend staying in the cave tonight?" Rachel asked.

"I would," Nathaniel answered. "I can escort Victoria back to the cave, that is..." He focused on Victoria. "If she would like to go for a stroll."

"Of course." Victoria smiled. Nathaniel finished his dinner as the women continued talking. Nathaniel enjoyed the female banter, as it reminded him of his sisters back in Virginia. How he prayed they were faring well. When he was finished eating, Kendall offered to take care of his dish. He smiled, thanked the girl again and then offered his arm to Victoria. She took it and nodded at her family. "I will see you all back at the cave." Nathaniel escorted her down the porch steps and onto the sidewalk.

"Victoria, I am so relieved you are staying in the cave now," Nathaniel said.

"You've mentioned that a time or two," Victoria replied, then changed the subject, still feeling the pang of Kendall's words. "I know you went to college in Michigan. You must know many Northerners. Have you met up with any former classmates in the ranks of the Yankees, especially during today's armistice?"

"Thankfully, I have not," He said. "I did ask around about one of my closest friends, James Spencer, but no one knows of him, which doesn't surprise me, as I know he was in Fredericksburg last June. I would doubt his regiment would go from the eastern front to the western front within one year." He chuckled. "I believe I am the only one who does that."

"It must be difficult, knowing that your dearest friend is now your enemy."

"That is putting it mildly," he replied. "But I am certainly not the only one with a friend on the opposite side. At least I don't have a brother or father fighting with the Yankees. That happens far too often. The truce today had the makings of a spectacle. Regimental flags were displayed along both lines, the troops were chatting cordially with each other. Men with opposite opinions and views were actually discussing the issues of the war. There were a few debates and disputes over their differences, but for the most part, it was like a church social. Some of our men even accepted invitations to visit the enemy's lines and the Yanks gave them some provisions and supplies. If you want to speak of contradictions, that is simply madness." He sighed. "I am glad we were able to take care of our dead and wounded, though. It was only fitting. Yesterday, I was with the 1st Missouri on the lines. Some Yankee wounded were lying right in our sight, they died because they didn't get the attention they needed. It was quite difficult to witness, and I didn't have the courage to help them like that man in Fredericksburg."

"Don't do this to yourself, Nathaniel. No one else could help either." Victoria looked at Nathaniel. He stared straight ahead, his expression blank. She tried to lighten his mood.

"In the middle of all this carnage and destruction, it is touching to see so many works of God, don't you think?" She said. "The birds are singing and teaching their young to fly. Gardens are full of flowers in bloom with the air smelling of jasmine and honeysuckle. Fruit will be plentiful on the trees. I have never seen the apricots in such abundance." She smiled at Nathaniel. "Nature is more lovely than usual."

He smiled back. "You're talking of flowers and birds. I can tell that you are simply trying to brighten my spirits. Is my melancholy so obvious?"

"To the ordinary person, probably not. You hide it well. To me...well, I don't know that you can hide any of your moods from me."

"You know me well, then." He smiled. "Which brings up one of the subjects I wished to talk with you about tonight." He pulled her to a stop and faced her. "Victoria, I don't think I've been hiding my feelings for you. We have been good friends for quite some time. Since we met that day in Fredericksburg, I have felt as though I can talk with you about anything. You are kind, understanding, and you make me laugh as no one else does. You are beautiful, both inside and out."

Victoria held her breath.

"Victoria, I love you. I care about you more than I care about anyone on this earth. I wish more than anything that I could ask your father's permission to marry you. I will have to settle for talking with your mother. However, before I spoke with her, I wanted to be sure if...if you wanted me to ask her. Is there ..." He looked nervous and wouldn't meet her eyes. Victoria reached up and put her hands on his shoulders and smiled as he looked into her eyes.

"Yes," she replied. "Yes, I would love to marry you."

"I'm not asking you officially." He smiled back at her enthusiasm. "I want to propose the proper way. I just wanted to be sure you felt the same way."

"Nathaniel, I am nearly twenty-five years old. I think I can make this decision for myself," She replied.

"Twenty-five. I forgot that you are one year my senior." He pretended to be disconcerted. "Perhaps I should withdraw my proposal. You are quite the old maid." His smile softened the blow that his words would have had if it were anyone other than Nathaniel. He reached up and brushed her hair back. "I do love you. I would, however, like to speak with your mother first."

"Of course I understand. I do love you too," Victoria said. "It has been such a joy being with you these past few weeks, in spite of all the danger around us, but I have to ask..." She took a deep breath. "Am I the girl you really want to marry, or do you still have feelings for Belle?"

Nathaniel nodded thoughtfully. "I cannot lie to you, I do have feelings for Belle. I always will. After all, she is my sister's dearest friend but she is more like a sister to me. I am in love with you, and you are the only woman I want to marry. The one I want to spend the rest of my life with." He smiled. "I was going to tell you all of this when I actually asked for your hand, but my plans have gone awry."

"Well, then, you have my permission to speak with Mother. I doubt she will give you any argument. Truth be told, she has been teasing me about you since you came to Vicksburg."

"I'm glad to hear that." He said. "I'll speak with her next time I have the chance and we can start making plans soon after."

"Will you want a long engagement?" Victoria asked, excited to plan for the wedding she had always dreamed of.

"We'll talk about that once I have your mother's official blessing." He smiled. "But the sooner I make you my wife, the better."

Tuesday, May 26, 1863
Turner Cave

My dearest cousin Elizabeth,

I write to you knowing that it will do me no good to try and post it until this siege has been lifted. I believe the news must have reached you all the way in Fredericksburg and you must have heard what we are going through. We are caught, trapped inside the city, completely ignorant of anything that is happening outside of our community. We will occasionally have a courier who is able to slip through the lines safely and bring papers for General Pemberton or extra ammunition. That is a rare occurrence, however. Rumors of all kind are rampant throughout the town. We hear frequently that we will soon be liberated and Grant will leave in disgrace. Unfortunately, so far none of those rumors have proven true. We do get some official news from the Confederate officers. You can assure your friend Miss America Joan Prentiss that her brother Nathaniel is safe and sound here in our city. He was carrying a message to General Pemberton and was caught in the city when the siege began. He has been so kind bringing us news and watching out for us, which has been fortuitous, as Jason has been caught outside the lines. At least Jason is able to watch over my friend Hannah Wheeler and her family, whom we have also been cut off from.

We are quite inconvenienced and must withstand daily bombardments, but we are all managing to survive. Mary Grace's son, Adam, is still ever so weak, but I feel that will never change. Unfortunately, we have been reduced to living in caves, and I fear the dampness will make Adam's condition even worse. Gabriel and Hope are well, though, as is the rest of the family. I hope your children and my younger cousins are all safe. I was devastated to receive word of James. I offer you my most sincere condolences. Your entire family has been in and will continue to be in my prayers. I shared these thoughts in previous letters, but I am unsure if they made it to you, as we have had no response from anyone in your family.

I will end for now, as I am to start some work at a hospital and should be there soon. There are so many soldiers in need. I never thought I would find myself helping out at a hospital, and yet, it is what I find myself doing. Today is my first day, so I pray I am strong enough to withstand the state of affairs.

Sincerely yours,
Victoria

"Victoria! I'm glad you made it. Better late than never!" Tabetha smiled as her friend entered the St. Xavier School and convent, now a busy hospital.

"I stopped to post a letter and then made a brief visit to Mary Green's cave," Victoria explained.

"I can understand visiting Mary, but posting a letter?" Tabetha was clearly confused.

"I'm thinking in a positive manner," Victoria explained.

"I see," Tabetha replied. "How is the Green family and that adorable little William?"

"They are all well, although their house was damaged somewhat by a shell. Duff is quite upset about it. They are lucky they were in the cave at the time."

"Was anyone else harmed when the Green's home was hit?" Tabetha asked.

"No, none of the servants were in the house at the time either, thank the Lord," Victoria said as Tabetha reached one of the linen closets.

"I'm still thankful that neither you nor Nathaniel were harmed when your home was hit a few days ago." Tabetha handed Victoria an apron, then focused on the job at hand. "I spoke with the matron about your volunteering. She told me what your duties will be, and I will assist you and oversee you until you're comfortable on your own."

"All right then," Victoria took the apron and tied it around her waist, then pulled up the attached square of fabric and pinned it to her dress just below the neckline. "Where shall we begin?"

"We'll go from room to room, or wards, as they call them, and see what help and comfort we can offer the soldiers. We can read to them, pray with them, and write letters for them. If a doctor needs assistance, you may help to your ability. At this hospital, we primarily care for sick soldiers, not wounded. There are so many men ill with diseases like malaria, smallpox and dysentery. I overheard one of the doctors say that many men on the lines are ill as well, and that number is growing constantly every day, but many refuse to leave their post. It's no wonder they are getting sick. The soldiers need food to be cooked by others and then brought to them. They all remain together in those unsanitary trenches. Excuse my bluntness, Victoria."

"My goodness, I hadn't thought of that aspect. Nathaniel has expressed his gratitude for the ability to move about the city. I can't imagine sitting in this Mississippi heat for days on end in, those conditions like our men must do."

"It is horrible, to be sure." Tabetha said, then entered one of the rooms. "The more you work here, the better you'll get to know the soldiers. You have true gentlemen here in your rebel ranks."

"Of course," Victoria said. "That's how we raise our Southern boys."

Tabetha stopped at the bed of a gruff-looking soldier with dirty brown hair. "Good morning, sir, I don't believe we've met." She reached down and pulled his blanket up a bit higher. "My name is Miss Norton, and this is Miss Turner."

My name's James McCarty, Miss Norton. I just came in yesterday. Dysentery, they say." Victoria took in his appearance, weary and gaunt-looking, with pale skin and cracked lips. She made a mental note to learn more about the disease. Her father had some medical books in his library, perhaps she could read through them and study them to better help the men.

"It's good to meet you, sir. Is there anything we can get you?"

"An apple would be right nice, miss, and some water. I'm powerful thirsty." His voice was soft and polite.

"I know we can get you the water and I'll see what I can do about finding that apple." Tabetha told him, then went to a corner of the room, where there was a pail of water and a dipper. She handed the pail to Victoria. "Go back to him and assist him with drinking the water. Talk with him, visit with him. I'll check on some of the other men and then see about that apple. He may fall asleep, he looks exhausted. If that happens, simply find another man who looks a little lonely and visit with him for now."

"That seems simple enough," Victoria replied, then went back to the first soldier. "Here we are, Private McCarty."

"You came back. That was right quick," he said quietly.

"I have the water you requested, and Miss Norton is checking on that apple." She ladled some water and carefully held it for him as he drank.

"Thank you so much, miss. I appreciate your kindness."

"Anything for our Confederate boys. It is I who should thank you for defending our city."

"I just hope we don't fail you all." He replied, closing his eyes.

"I don't believe you will." She whispered, not sure if he had fallen asleep or had just closed his eyes to rest. "I will be back to check on you later."

Victoria collapsed in the bundle of blankets on the floor of the Turner cave.

"How in the world are you not exhausted every time you work at the hospital?" She asked Tabetha, who lit some candles, then sat at the dining room table that had been moved from the house.

"You must remember, I went from being a farm girl to being a soldier in the US Cavalry and now I am considered a nurse. I'm used to working hard all day."

"I suppose. This is the first time I've ever worked so hard, especially with no rest and I just waited on the men. You did so much more." She put the back of her wrist on her forehead. "Does it get any easier?"

"Yes, it does. I know you will adapt quite easily. I have every confidence in your abilities," Tabetha replied. "Other than the fatigue, what did you think of your first day?"

Victoria groaned and sat up, leaning against the dirt wall. "It wasn't quite what I expected, though I'm not sure what I did expect. I do feel a sense of accomplishment, like I did something useful, something of value. In spite of how tired I am, I feel proud."

"Capital!" Tabetha exclaimed, then looked up as Brianne came into the cave.

"Mr. Prentiss is here. He specifically asked after you, Victoria." She smiled. Victoria groaned. She didn't even want to know what she must look like after a day of work and a week of no bathing.

"I really must sneak down to the creek and wash up soon," she mumbled. Sponge baths were not cleaning her as well as she wanted.

"That does sound good." Brianne led the way out of the cave and under the fly. Even though Nathaniel had dug their cave, he insisted it wasn't proper for him to visit inside. Tabetha followed the two out.

"Victoria, Miss Norton." Nathaniel was resting on a camp chair that he had bought from a sutler and left at the cave, but stood when they exited the cave. The rest of the family had gathered around the entrance.

"Any news, Mr. Prentiss?" Tabetha asked.

"Well, those darn Yanks are still shooting at us, as I'm sure you've gathered." He gave her a small grin and looked at the sky, where shells continued to fly overhead, screaming, and then exploded in an area they couldn't see.

"That is quite obvious." Victoria smiled in spite of the danger she knew they were constantly in.

"Both sides continue to dig in," Nathaniel stated. "The enemy has determined that they cannot take our position by force, so they are now digging underground to get close. General Pemberton gave an order that prohibits expending ammunition needlessly. We're not allowed to use the artillery or return the fire of their sharpshooters. We are to simply watch the enemy approach the city as they get nearer every day. They are a mere 30 yards from our defensive breastworks."

"Oh, goodness," Rachel said.

"You don't agree with those orders?" Victoria asked.

"I do not," Nathaniel answered bluntly. "I believe we should send out a small contingent of men each day as sharpshooters. This would prevent the army from approaching so quickly and give us more time to make a better plan or get reinforcements."

"How are they managing to get close so quickly?" Kendall asked.

"They dig all day and night," Nathaniel replied. "They have relentless energy and of course more manpower, more food, more munitions, all with a bulldog determination."

"So they're almost here?" Brianne asked, sounding afraid.

"Yes, but fear not, Miss Larson, we will protect you," Nathaniel said.

"That's just what Boone told you, isn't it, Brianne?" Kendall asked in a teasing tone.

"Excuse me, just who is this Mr. Boone?" Rachel asked.

"Not Mr. Boone, Aunt Rachel. Boone Reynolds. You met him years ago at Mary Grace and Abraham's wedding. He's Timothy Reynolds's half-brother," Brianne responded.

"Abraham's cousin, Timothy?" Mary Grace asked. "I haven't seen him in years. I know he signed up with one of the Texas Brigades. Do we know if he's here too?"

"He's in the city somewhere, according to Boone," Kendall said.

"And how did you both happen to meet up with him?" Victoria asked Brianne. She vaguely remembered the young Boone Reynolds. A handsome young man, a bit on the wild side, she remembered and was half-Blackfoot Indian. Abraham's uncle was father to both Boone and Timothy, but they had different mothers.

"Boone is with the 1st Texas Infantry, Company K, the Daniel Boone Rifles," Kendall explained. "Both he and Timothy are. Boone is a messenger, like Nathaniel. He was a scout before being trapped in the city." Brianne looked annoyed with her sister, who kept talking. "Brianne and Boone recognized each other right off and struck up a conversation."

"He's a family friend, there's nothing wrong with that." Brianne defended herself.

"Is Boone even old enough to fight?" Mary Grace asked.

"He's nineteen," Brianne replied. "Besides, Kendall, you wouldn't want me to tell them about your new friendship with Private Lassiter, would you?"

"Brianne! Don't be ridiculous. We truly are just friends."

"If you say so." Brianne shrugged.

Victoria caught Nathaniel's eye. He smiled at her.

"Perhaps we should direct the conversation to a subject that Mr. Prentiss can follow."

"On the contrary, I dearly miss conversations between sisters. It reminds me of my own family in Fredericksburg, you must all remember the two sisters that I adore. As a matter of fact, I am acquainted with Captain Timothy Reynolds. I didn't realize he was familiar to you all. I've met Boone as well."

"I wonder if the captain still keeps in contact with Cousin Bekah." Mary Grace thought aloud, picking up Hope. "She and Tex, I mean, Timothy, got along quite well if I recall correctly."

"That may have been true before our beloved cousin Belle stepped in," Victoria stated. "You all know that Bekah always does what Belle tells her to do."

"Unfortunately, that is true, Bekah was always quite persuaded by whatever Belle thought," Rachel said.

"Well, don't leave me in the dark, what happened between Bekah and Tex? How did I not know something was amiss?" Mary Grace asked. "They were getting on so well before I left."

"As I said, Belle happened." Victoria replied, her thoughts drifting to the day after Mary's wedding.

March 1859
Vicksburg, Mississippi

Victoria sat in the family parlor, surrounded by her cousins. Mary Grace and Abraham had left on their wedding trip the day before, and the girls were having tea.

"Bekah, I cannot help but notice the way you and Abraham's cousin have been spending so much time together," Victoria said.

Bekah couldn't hide her blush. "Yes, I suppose we have. I enjoy his company very much. I am hoping that he will ask Father's permission to court me."

"Well, that is unfortunate." Belle took a sip of her tea.

"Why is that unfortunate?" Victoria asked warily. She loved her cousin dearly, but Belle had a tendency to judge people according to their appearance or their social status.

"Because you cannot possibly court Timothy Reynolds," Belle replied.

"And why is that?" Charlotte asked. Charlotte was Uncle Hiram's daughter, and they had both come for the wedding all the way from Gettysburg, Pennsylvania.

"Well, courting leads to marriage and my dear Bekah, you cannot possibly marry that man," Belle said.

"Pray tell, why not?" Victoria was irritated.

"He's too wild, for one thing," Belle pointed out. "Bekah, you deserve someone who can take care of you, someone who lives in a nice home in a civilized city. Mr. Reynolds is the second son of a Texas rancher. He will never inherit any land and seems content to work as a ranch hand for the rest of his days. He has no ambition and not much of a future. You deserve much better. There are plenty of eligible young men in the Richmond area who would serve your purpose better."

"Belle, you're being a bit unfair to Mr. Reynolds," Victoria said. "Just because he doesn't have the social status you feel is necessary for a good match doesn't mean he will make a poor husband. Look at your own sister's marriage. It is one of the best matches I have ever seen."

Belle shrugged. "Well, Bekah, it is your choice, of course. If you feel Mr. Reynolds will make a good husband, then by all means, encourage a courtship." The tone of Belle's voice, however, made it clear what she thought Bekah should do. Victoria shook her head.

1863

"As much as I love all of my cousins, Belle does exasperate me the most," Victoria said. "Always so focused on material things and outward appearances."

"That doesn't surprise me at all, coming from Belle," Nathaniel said. "You'd be surprised though, the last time I saw her, she had changed in many ways. A maturity that comes only from living through hard times."

"That is the best news I have heard in quite a while," Rachel said. "It has been nearly four years since we've seen Belle. I am glad to know that this war has accomplished one good thing."

Victoria looked at her folded hands. A feeling of slight jealousy crept over her. In spite of his assurances to the contrary, she wondered if Nathaniel still had feelings for Belle. Perhaps it would be wise to distance herself from Nathaniel's courtship.

"Victoria, would you like to join me for a stroll? It is our one hour window for peace while the Yankees eat." Nathaniel stood. Victoria shook her head, making a quick decision.

"I'm sorry, I must decline tonight, Mr. Prentiss. I'm very tired after my long day of work, Miss Norton can verify that. When we came home, I just collapsed on my pallet."

Nathaniel looked disappointed, and sensed there was another reason Victoria didn't want to walk with him. "All right, then. I'll stop by again when I get the chance." He put on his kepi and tipped his head. "Good night, ladies. Take care of yourselves."

When he was out of earshot, Mary Grace turned to Victoria. "If working at the hospital is going to be so exhausting, perhaps you should find another place to volunteer."

Victoria shook her head. "It was my first day. I'll be fine." She stood. "But as I said, I am tired, I believe I'll turn in. Good night, everyone." She then turned, went inside the cave and fell onto her pallet, hoping she would fall asleep easily and not allow her mind to wonder about Nathaniel's feelings for her cousin.

Wednesday, May 27, 1863
Streets of Vicksburg

Victoria and Tabetha walked towards Sky Parlor Hill after another long day of working in the hospital. Even though she was tired, Victoria wanted to get a look at the ships on the river. She noticed many citizens had gathered at the hill. It was the quiet hour of dinner for the Yankees.

"Mother says that Mrs. Balfour has only stayed in the caves for two nights. If their home is safe enough from bombardment, ours should be as well." It was strange to Victoria how the citizens of Vicksburg adjusted to the commotion, the constant shelling and the constant shake of the earth when they exploded. This morning, the firing had been heavy along the North side of town.

Victoria and Tabetha finally made it to the top of the hill and looked out around the surrounding countryside. It was a devastating sight. Victoria had not been to the hill since prior to the siege. Trenches were dug into the earth around the entire city. In some parts of town, the streets had been plowed up. Holes and caves filled the landscape and reminded Victoria of an image she had once seen in one of her father's books, depicting a prairie dog colony out West. It was disheartening to see the city in such disrepair.

"I was talking with a Lieutenant today about the conditions in the trenches," Tabetha said. "He told me that the soldiers are packed so tightly next to each other, sitting in the hot sun. If a head or even a hand appears above the breastworks, it is shot at. The Confederates don't fire in return because of the edict Pemberton wrote like Nathaniel described yesterday. The southern army seems quite discouraged by it." She paused. "Speaking of Nathaniel, that reminds me. What is the real reason you didn't go for a walk with him last night? You always look forward to spending time with him."

"I truly was tired." Victoria was not quite ready to share her feelings with Tabetha, mostly because she couldn't quite understand what she was feeling herself. "I did notice you were tossing and turning quite a bit. Were you having a nightmare again?"

"Once you've been in battle, you just never forget it," Tabetha replied. "Many a soldier has nightmares. It will be no different for folks living through this bombardment."

"I hadn't thought of that," Victoria said. "In just the two days I've worked at the hospital I have seen more pain and suffering than I have in my whole life. It has been an experience and you're right, I keep seeing visions of poor Lucy McRae, buried alive, the night of William Green's birth..." She trailed off, looking toward the river. A firefight had broken out between Yankee gunboats and Confederate artillery. Five boats from below and one terrible monster from above shot at the batteries. It wasn't long before Tabetha realized that the large boat had been hit.

"My goodness. The Confederates hit the boat!" She exclaimed as a tugboat came to assist.

"She is sinking!" Someone cried out. The hundreds of women who had gathered to watch cheered loudly and waved their handkerchiefs. The steamship sank slowly until all that could be seen were the chimneys stacks.

"Well, it appears we are victorious today!" Emma Balfour exclaimed as she approached Victoria and Tabetha. Other people began heading back to their homes after witnessing such a grand event.

"Yes. Perhaps I can convince Mother that it will be safe to stay in the house tonight," Victoria responded. "I have heard, Mrs. Balfour, that you stay in your home most of the time, not in a cave, and have not had any unfortunate incidences."

"That is a fact," Mrs. Balfour stated. "However, I can understand perfectly well why your mother has chosen to stay in the caves, especially after your house was badly damaged by that shell, as well as the yard out back. Obviously many people, including the soldiers believe it is the best option or there wouldn't be so many staying in caves."

"I suppose so." Victoria thought of Nathaniel and his support of the idea.

"I know you see Mrs. Green often, how is she fairing?" Mrs. Balfour asked. "I have not seen her since the siege started, but I have heard of the new addition to their family."

"They're all doing well," Victoria answered. "Little William is quite handsome."

"It's wonderful how you all continue to visit, despite our predicament," Mrs. Balfour said. "It has been far too long since I have had tea with your mother. How are Mary Grace and her young ones?"

"Adam is still struggling, but hasn't gotten any worse. Gabriel and Hope are adjusting very well to all of this chaos. How are your own children?"

"They are all well, as you said, adjusting. It amazes me how resilient the children are."

Victoria nodded.

"I don't believe the Federals will test the Confederate batteries again," Tabetha said. "The fight today is over."

"Mrs. Balfour, excuse me." Victoria shook her head. "I don't believe you've met our houseguest. May I introduce Miss Tabetha Norton? She is a dear friend from Virginia. Tabatha, this is Mrs. Emma Balfour, a friend of my mother's."

"From Virginia, you say? You don't sound like you're from Virginia," Mrs. Balfour stated.

"I moved to Virginia to live with my aunt several years ago." Tabetha explained with a glance at Victoria. "I was born in Michigan. It is very nice to meet you, Mrs. Balfour."

"You as well," Mrs. Balfour smiled.

"Well, if the excitement is over, I suppose we should be on our way, Tabetha," Victoria said. "It was good seeing you, Mrs. Balfour. I will give Mother your regards."

"Thank you, Victoria, Miss Norton."

Friday, May 29, 1863
Communal Cave

"Good day to you, Mary Green!" Victoria said, ducking into the Green's room in the communal cave.

"Victoria! Tabetha! How nice of you to visit," Mary Green smiled. She was sitting up in her bed, baby William in her arms and Annie sitting nearby, playing with a doll.

"I only regret that I didn't send my calling card!" Victoria laughed. "My goodness, he's growing so fast!"

"Yes, I can hardly believe he's already five days old," Mary said. "Would you like to hold him?"

"You know I never pass up an opportunity to hold a baby," she replied, taking the newborn and sitting in a nearby chair.

"We heard your home was hit by a shell," Tabetha said. "Has Duff been able to arrange for repairs?"

"Yes, and thankfully everyone is safe. Duff is devising a plan to save our home from future attacks, but first, he must finish the work on the cave he is digging in the side of our hill."

"That will be much more convenient for you!" Victoria stated, happy for her friend. "I don't know how you manage living in a communal cave. It's hard enough living in a cave with all your neighbors around, much less with a newborn. It's so dark and dreary in here."

"It hasn't been ideal, that's for sure," Mary replied. "I won't be content until we're safe in our own home and this dastardly siege is over."

"Amen," Victoria said.

"How is the weather today? I can't wait to move for many reasons, but one is that I will finally get to see the sky again," Mary said.

"It's quite clear today, though hot and humid," Tabetha said. "It has been a relatively quiet morning, as I am sure you've noticed."

"Yes, as a matter of fact, I have,"Mary said. "I am hoping that it means the Federals will soon give up, though I doubt it." She wiped a stray strand of hair off her forehead. "Do you hear much news while working at the hospital?"

"We do," Tabetha said. "I heard yesterday that a courier from outside the Union lines found his way in town with 18,000 rifle caps."

"Good Heavens," Mary said. "That is good news for our side. More ammunition can only help."

"Indeed," Victoria added. "Although I wonder how trustworthy these couriers are. They could very well be spies, you know, bringing us the munitions to gain our trust and really discovering all our secrets."

"What makes you say that, Victoria?" Mary asked.

"It's just some rumors that I have been overhearing. The Federals will try anything and everything to get control of Vicksburg. It only makes sense that they would try to learn how we are faring by sending in spies."

Mary turned to Tabetha. "I suppose we could have a spy in our midst right now."

"I'm not devious enough to be a spy." Tabetha chuckled. "I had a difficult enough time pretending to be a man. I'm fairly certain that if anyone would have asked me straight out if I was a woman, I would have admitted to it. When I look back, I feel fortuitous that I was wounded and found by the Turners before my secret was discovered."

"I was only jesting about you being a spy," Mary smiled. "If the Turners trust you, then so shall I."

"I don't know when you would find the time to supply the Yankees with information anyways," Victoria added. "You're either busy at the hospital or busy helping my family."

"Now that is the truth."

Victoria looked at little William, then reluctantly gave him to Tabetha to hold.

"He is such a dear, Mary." Tabetha smiled as the baby grasped her index finger. "And quite strong."

"Mmm, yes." Mary smiled back. "He is such a blessing."

All too soon, it was time for Tabetha and Victoria to depart.

"Hopefully, the next time we visit, you'll be situated in your new cave," Tabetha said.

"Or even better yet, in your parlor," Victoria added.

"I do hope so. That would be divine, an answer to my prayers," Mary said, waving goodbye.

Tabetha and Victoria were halfway home when Nathaniel approached them.

"Ladies, I'm glad for the opportunity to meet up with you today." He turned to Victoria. "May I take this time to have a private conversation with you?"

Victoria checked her watch. Five minutes until 5:00. "No, not really, Mr. Prentiss. We need to get home and help Esther prepare dinner." For whatever reason, she was still apprehensive about trusting Nathaniel.

"Don't be silly, Victoria, there isn't much to even make for dinner," Tabetha said. "Take your time and walk with Mr. Prentiss."

That wasn't what Victoria wanted at all. She didn't want to be alone with Nathaniel right now, but she also would never be intentionally rude. "Thank you, Tabetha."

Tabetha turned and briskly walked toward the cave. Victoria turned to walk as well, but Nathaniel gently grabbed her arm and stopped her.

"Victoria, what on earth did I do wrong? Did I offend you in some way? I feel as though you're trying to avoid me the past few days. Ever since..."

"Well, I'm truly sorry. I have been quite busy. I am doing my best to help everyone." She didn't mean to be curt.

"I know that, and I wish you wouldn't put so much pressure on yourself." Nathaniel ran a hand through his hair, agitated. "I just feel...I don't know. It's almost as if you don't want me around. Victoria, I want..." He never had a chance to finish the sentence, as a parrot shell screamed almost directly above them, then crashed into the hill behind them. Debris showered them as Nathaniel grabbed Victoria, pulling her to the ground, and shielding her with his own body. Several more shells exploded in quick succession as people ran in every direction. Nathaniel glanced around and pulled her into a small indention in the hill, as if someone had started digging a cave there, then abandoned the project. There was barely enough room for the two of them.

What are you doing to me, Lord? Here I am, trying to distance myself from this man and now you trap me with him?

The shells continued to slam into the ground shaking the earth to its core.

"It may be loud, but at least we can finally talk." Nathaniel raised his voice so that she could hear him. "Victoria, I consider you to be one of my closest friends and you have been since the day we first met. We have always been able to talk about everything and anything. What has happened? Is it because I told you I loved you? I admit, I may have been forward in admitting my feelings for you, but was I wrong to pressure you to reciprocate those feelings? Victoria, please, what have I done?"

"I'm scared, Nathaniel," she admitted after a moment.

"I believe we're safe here, Victoria, I won't let anything happen to you."

"No, you misunderstand. I'm scared of...I don't want to have my heart broken. I know that you would never hurt me on purpose, but what if this doesn't work? When you leave, what if you find somebody else and no longer want me?"

Nathaniel shook his head. "I don't understand, Tori. You have told me of your dream to be married, to have a family of your own, but when you actually have the chance to marry someone who actually loves you, you retreat." He sounded frustrated. "Wait, a moment, perhaps I do understand." He scoffed. "I didn't realize you were so much like your cousin Belle. I never thought you would reject someone who isn't in the same social class as you. I am, after all, just a simple farmer."

Tears formed in her eyes. "Nathaniel, that's not fair, you know that isn't true."

"I thought I knew, but perhaps I don't. I always wondered why you courted Jeremy Thompson, and pined after Zachary Peterson when I thought you had feelings for me, but now I understand. They are better placed in society, and will keep you in the comforts that you are used to."

"That's just not true, you know I'm not like that." Victoria protested. She wiped at her damp cheeks and softened her voice. "I don't think that about you. I don't care what your position in life is." She looked away. He gently forced her to look at him, then touched his forehead to hers. A movement that seemed awkward in the cramped hole as artillery fire continued thundering outside.

"Victoria, I love you. Only you. Why else would I ever agree to be the messenger that travels from Virginia to Mississippi?"

Victoria sighed as his arms went around her in a comforting embrace. "I love you, so much it scares me." She poked her head out to check the situation on the street. "When will you allow me to leave this cramped hole?"

"When this artillery storm ends," He replied. "There is no way I'm letting you go out there right now."

The dangerous reality of their situation hit Victoria, and a fear of what could happen to her or her family rushed over her.

"Lord, I pray that Tabetha and my family members are all safe. I worry so about Hannah and her family every day." She murmured against his shoulder.

"They should all be fine." Nathaniel reassured her. "Your family should have made it to the cave and you told me that your brother Jason is keeping an eye on the Wheelers."

"Well, that's only if he's alive and still with the militia. It's hardest not knowing, yet it's amazing, almost miraculous, how safe we have stayed with the constant bombardment," she commented. "I must admit that the Lord has been good to us in that respect."

"Yes, he has," Nathaniel agreed. "We'll have to continue to pray that God will watch over us, all of us, including Jason and the Wheelers."

The bombardment lasted just under an hour. Once Nathaniel felt it safe enough, he helped Victoria stand and led her to the street below. They noticed right away how much damage had been done. Several homes had been hit, and debris was strewn everywhere.

"Oh, Nathaniel. This looks...absolutely devastating. It's one of the worst attacks." Townspeople were starting to come out and survey the damage and Victoria could hear parts of the conversation.

"The Willis house was struck twice...two horses were killed."

"...lost their servant in the bombardment..."

Nathaniel led Victoria through the small crowd toward the family cave.

"Victoria! Mr. Prentiss, thank the Lord you're safe!" Rachel hugged her daughter tightly, then pulled Nathaniel into an embrace. "We were worried sick about you two."

"Nathaniel was there to protect me." Victoria glanced up at the man.

"I have no doubt of that." Rachel smiled.

"Is everyone here safe?" Nathaniel asked.

"Yes, Tabetha just barely made it back in time and we are all safe. The children have been asking for you, Victoria."

"All right, I'll go and see them." Victoria turned to Nathaniel. "Will you come in?"

"I should be going. There is a special project I'm working on that needs my attention." He smiled at Rachel.

"Very well." Rachel ducked back into the cave, leaving Victoria with Nathaniel.

"So, have I reassured you?" Nathaniel asked. "Do you know how much I care for you and only you?"

"You have." Victoria tucked his hair under his kepi. "I'm sorry for my indecision. It's just... I almost married the wrong man once..."

"You wouldn't have married him," Nathaniel said confidently. "I have every bit of faith that you would have realized that he wasn't the man for you."

"You're probably right. I know how much you care for me, and I know my feelings for you." She smiled at him. "I feel much better now. Thank you."

"Splendid." Nathaniel glanced into the cave, then bent towards Victoria. "Because I love you." He gently kissed her. "I'll see you soon."

"Take care, Nathaniel," She replied with a smile, then turned to go inside.

Wheeler Farm

"Mama, why can't you go hunting?" Ambrose asked, hanging on the fence as Hannah pulled the weeds in the vegetable garden.

"I don't want to risk it. There are too many soldiers from both sides in the woods. Besides, I doubt there is any game with all the commotion out there."

"I suppose." Ambrose sighed. "I don't mean to complain, but eggs and vegetables are getting boring."

"I agree, but imagine what the poor people in town have to eat," Hannah said. "No way to get any food in since the siege started."

"You're right." Ambrose admitted. "I shouldn't be so selfish."

"I wouldn't say you're selfish," Hannah replied. "Eggs and vegetables are getting boring, but we should be thankful for what we have."

"I know." Ambrose jumped off the fence. "I suppose I should help you weed too."

"You work hard, Ambrose, you deserve a break and weeding relaxes me." Hannah was touched by her son's thoughtfulness.

"I wish Mr. Jason would come by. It's been a long time since we've seen him."

"Yes, it has," Hannah agreed. Jason had visited them a few days after the siege began, so she knew he wasn't in the city, yet it had been several days since he checked on them last.

"Why don't you and Mr. Jason get married?" Ambrose asked. "I know you like each other. He would be a good pa. Don't you think he would be a good pa to me?"

Hannah wasn't quite sure how to answer. It wasn't as if she never thought of marrying Jason. He was such a dear friend, and they got along so well. She could imagine being married to him. He was kind, funny, and, though it wasn't an important thing, he was one of the handsomest men she had ever known. "I believe Mr. Turner would be a good husband, of course. However, there is more to marriage than being friends."

"But don't you love him?" Ambrose asked with all the innocence of a child. "Like you loved my pa?"

Hannah was again unsure of how to answer. She had cared for Benjamin deeply, and loved him in a special way, but theirs was more of a marriage built off of respect and, in her case, convenience.

"And what are we discussing out here?" Cordelia smiled as she approached Hannah and her son.

"Mr. Jason," Ambrose said. "I was asking Ma if she loved him like she loved my pa. I think he'd be a good man for her to marry. Don't you think so, grandmother?"

"I see. A seven-year-old matchmaker." Cordelia knelt in the garden. "Ambrose, Caroline is waiting for you. It's time for your lessons."

"Aww, do I have to?" Ambrose asked.

"Yes, sir, you do," Hannah said, grateful for the reprieve.

"Oh, all right." Ambrose pushed himself up, dusted off his hands, and plodded into the house.

"Sounds like an interesting conversation," Cordelia stated.

"Yes, it was. I should have expected it, he's a young man who wants a father, but I don't know how to answer him."

"I must confess, I have often wondered myself why you and Mr. Turner have never courted. It's been three years since Benjamin left us. I hope you're still not mourning him."

"I do miss him dreadfully, but that's not it." Hannah paused. Was it appropriate to discuss her feelings for a man with the mother of her deceased husband? Hannah loved Cordelia as much as she had loved her own mother, but Cordelia was Benjamin's mother first. "I care for Jason, and I do believe I could love him as a wife loves a husband, but he has always kept his distance from me in that way. I believe he feels he is somehow responsible for Benjamin's death, and that's why he is always here to help, not because of any feelings he may have for me."

"Benjamin's death was an accident," Cordelia said.

"I know." Hannah wasn't entirely convinced of that, but she didn't want to concern Cordelia with her theories. "I wonder if he keeps his distance from me out of his friendship and loyalty to Benjamin."

"That could be possible," Cordelia replied. "Men can be complicated in that way."

"Benjamin wasn't." Hannah smiled at the memory of her husband. "He always spoke his mind. Even when he proposed to me." She remembered the day well. She was eighteen years old, and her parents had just died in a fire that also destroyed their home. Benjamin had approached her, told her that he greatly admired her, and thought it would be beneficial for both of them to marry. He had never flowered her with romance, he was too practical for that, but she knew he cared for her in his own way. He was easy to talk to, kind, a good provider, and a wonderful father to Ambrose. It wasn't his fault that he never stirred her heart quite like Jason Turner had been doing the past two years.

"Benjamin was always blunt and honest to a fault," Cordelia replied.

"He was a good man and a great father," Hannah said.

"And a good son." Cordelia smiled. "But you must know that I want you to be happy. I think of you as a daughter, and have for many years. I can't imagine it is easy for you to speak with me about another man when you were married to my son, but it does not offend me. I would never expect you to live the rest of your life as a widow. You are still young and beautiful. You must live your life to the fullest. That is as it should be. If you ever have a need to talk, please know that I am here for you."

"Thank you," Hannah said softly. "I know that is true, but it is good to hear it."

"Of course." Cordelia stood and wiped her hands on her dress. "I believe I will head in now, it's too hot for this old lady. I will check on the two children and see about starting dinner. Remember what I said, Hannah. I love you."

"I love you too," Hannah replied with a smile.

Saturday, May 30, 1863
Communal Cave

"How are you, my dear?" Duff entered the room in the cave, gently kissed Mary and William's forehead, then scooped up Annie and cuddled her on his lap.

"Duff, I am so glad you're safe. Tell me, what is the situation in the city? I have been hearing so much bombardment." Mary sat up in her bed.

"I heard that a bomb exploded at the courthouse today." He looked at his daughter, who played quietly with her church doll. "They say that two men were killed and seven more wounded. Another house was hit with several injuries, but I have not been able to confirm this. Other than that, the hits have been futile."

"Well, that is good news. Do you know those that were injured or whose house?"

Duff shook his head negative.

Mary nodded. "I do hope they're just rumors. Aren't the Federals about ready to give up?"

"Doubtful," Duff replied. "They are trying to wear down the weakest of the city, the women and children and of course the sick. I believe General Pemberton will be impatient to surrender because of that, but I must say I think he is wrong. The spirit of our Vicksburg women has been very strong. Some of the civilians, led by Judge Barnett, signed a petition last week that asked Pemberton to grant a flag of truce to allow the women and children to travel out of the city beyond the entrenched lines."

"What was Pemberton's reply?" Mary asked.

"He said he could not do it for an individual or a small group, but if a majority of the citizens would sign the petition, he would do so."

"My goodness. Clearly that didn't happen, as we are all still here."

"You would be correct, my dear. Barnett is trying to get more signatures, but so far has not been very successful." Duff sighed. "I don't want to sign it, and I probably won't, but if I knew for sure it would get you and the children to safety, I would. I don't even know where I could send you. The farmhouses outside the siege lines are likely overrun with

Federals and who knows what those poor women must be going through. I fear every day for your friends, the Wheeler family. Three women alone with a boy is prime pickings for the Yankees." He paused and glanced at his wife. He hadn't wanted to share that much information, but it had come out before he could stop himself. "At any rate, I prefer to have you here, where I can watch over you."

"As nice as it would be to stay in a dry, clean house and not be concerned with the constant alert of cannonballs, I prefer to stay here with you also," Mary agreed.

"Know this, Mary. I will continue to do whatever it takes to protect my family, even if it means our neighbors will shun me."

"Whatever do you mean, Duff?"

Duff sighed and averted his eyes. "I have this sinking feeling that the Union will eventually take over the town. If they ask me to sign an oath of allegiance to keep my family and property safe, I will. Our fellow citizens may not support me in this decision, but mark my words, I will do whatever I must to take care of you, my children and my home."

Mary gently set William on the edge of the bed and leaned forward to place a comforting hand on his arm. "You are my husband, Duff. I know you will do what's best for us."

"I hope you're right, Mary. I do hope you're right." He looked back at his wife. Suddenly, an explosion shook the ground.

"Lord in Heaven, that was so close! I thought you said it was quieting down," Mary remarked.

"I thought it was," Duff replied.

"Well, then, I'm glad you're back here with us," Mary said. Another shell rocked the ground. "It sounds as bad as yesterday."

Duff dreaded his next statement. He had avoided the topic earlier, but knew he had to tell her the latest. "Our house was hit again, Mary. More than once. I have been thinking about ways to stop the assault on our neighborhood, and I may have a plan."

"I had a feeling you were keeping something from me. Since you don't seem to be terribly upset, the damage must be minimal again. What is this plan of yours?" Mary asked.

"No, you are correct, the damage can easily be repaired, but Mary, there are wounded and sick soldiers throughout town, and more men being brought in daily. Both Confederate and Union men need medical care. I believe our home would suffice as a hospital."

"Well, I agree that it is large enough, with plenty of room," Mary agreed. "But how would having soldiers in our home help the neighborhood or us for that matter?"

"I believe if we take in both Union and Confederate wounded and sick, we can somehow let the Union troops know their own men are being cared for in our home. We would be sure to put the Union men on the very top floor. The Federal Army would most likely direct their fire elsewhere, to avoid hitting a house that is helping their wounded."

"I suppose that could work, and you're right, it wouldn't just help us, it would help the entire neighborhood."

"Yes, that was my thought as well." Duff stood and paced the floor. "One way or the other, we will get through this."

Sunday, May 31, 1863
Vicksburg Streets

"Mrs. Miller!" Victoria called out to Mrs. Dora Miller, the woman she had met in town a few weeks back. The day was clear, but there was still no relief from the threat of the Northern Army's shadow. Thank goodness the men had to eat, which gave the townspeople some reprieve three times a day.

"Miss...Turner, correct?"

"Yes. I know you are new in town, so I was wondering if you and your husband would like to join my family in a midday meal of sorts. We don't have much to offer, but it would be nice to get to know you better." Victoria remembered that Mary Green had told her that Mrs. Miller didn't seem to have many friends in town. Victoria knew that she wouldn't like being trapped in a foreign city with no family or friends, so she took the initiative to be friendly.

"Do you have anything more than cornbread?" The woman asked. It was difficult for Victoria to ascertain whether the woman was being witty or not. "It has been difficult to get much of anything else."

"That is so true." Victoria ducked instinctually as a random Parrot shell flew overhead. It crashed against a distant hill. Mrs. Miller shook her head. The fortnight of being under siege was starting to take a toll on the provisions in town. The Turners were lucky to get a quart of milk daily from a family that lived nearby, but with the supply of meat dwindling, Victoria wasn't sure how long it would be before the cow would be killed, either by a stray shell or for the meat it could provide.

Mrs. Miller shuddered. "I thank you for the invitation, but I must apologize. I do wish I could join you today, but I must get home."

"Of course," Victoria said. "Another time, perhaps."

"Yes," Mrs. Miller answered, then was on her way. Victoria walked back to the cave.

Kendall looked up from reading the *Vicksburg Citizen*, one of the town's newspapers. "Good morning, Victoria."

"Kendall." Victoria nodded. "What's our midday meal going to be?" She sat down and took the paper from Kendall's hand.

"Mule meat, rice and milk." Brianne answered with a grimace. "At least we have a reprieve from corn bread. I declare, I hadn't liked it before the war, but having to eat it with almost every meal, well, it is most intolerable."

The sound of shelling starting back up could be heard.

"Parrot shells, mortar shells, rifle shells," Victoria muttered. "Will it never end?" She folded the paper and set it next to her. "Sometimes, I wake up at night and think that it's storming outside. The artillery is loud as thunder."

"You do tend to be jumpy when you're sleeping," Tabetha said, although she knew she had a hard time sleeping as well.

"Perhaps we should warn Mr. Prentiss about your tossing and turning all through the night." Brianne smirked.

"Don't you dare." Victoria blushed. "Besides, we haven't made any official announcement."

"Why would Mr. Prentiss care if Cousin Victoria tosses and turns all night, Brianne?" Kendall asked. Her older sister ignored the question and addressed Victoria.

"I know he will make things official soon, Victoria. I just know it."

"I hope so." Victoria tried to hide her smile, but was unsuccessful. After their conversation in the hole yesterday, she was reassured of her relationship with Nathaniel. She sighed. "But more importantly, I pray that we all stay safe, and that this siege ends soon."

Monday, June 1, 1863
Green House~Hospital

Tabetha smiled at the blonde Confederate who lay on the cot. She had decided to spend more time at the Green House with her newly acquired nursing skills, and fewer days at St. Francis Xavier.

"How are you this afternoon, Private?" She asked, pulling up the bed sheet.

"Doin' alright, Miss," He replied. "How has your day been?"

"Oh, not so bad, sir. How is your arm?" She reached down and adjusted the bandages that covered the stump just below his right elbow. The young man's left arm had been seriously injured by an artillery shell and had been amputated. The bandage was in need of changing already. She hadn't anticipated that it would get saturated so quickly. Tabatha realized she had to change the dressing, but needed more clean bandages. "Is there anything I can bring back for you?"

"Some food would be nice," The boy said with a weak smile.

"I shall see what I can round up." Tabetha replied, then briefly checked the next wounded soldier. There was always so much work to do in the many hospitals that had sprung up in Vicksburg.

"Miss Norton." Nathaniel Prentiss walked in, a smile on his face.

"Mr. Prentiss, whatever are you doing here?"

"I was helping to transport patients here," Nathaniel answered. "I wanted to let you know that, I appreciate the work that you're doing for our men, especially since I know where your loyalties are." He gave her a conspiratorial smile. "I know Victoria comes with you on occasion and she finds the work a very fulfilling endeavor."

"Yes, she is actually here somewhere. Now that would be an added benefit to your visit today."

"The thought did cross my mind," Nathaniel replied. "Do you find this work to be worthwhile as she does?"

"Oh, yes," Tabetha said. "To be completely honest, I find that it gives my life a purpose in a way that my, ahh...previous work never did."

"Do you ever think of returning to your previous position?" Nathaniel asked.

"I have thought about it," Tabetha admitted. "But it is unlikely I would do so even if I had the chance. To be able to heal the wounded instead of causing the wounds is, I find, a much greater calling."

"I am glad to hear you say that." Nathaniel nodded. "I know I have told you this before, but I am very sorry about your brother. He was a good friend. I must say, it is still canny, your resemblance to him."

Tabetha nodded as tears threatened. "I appreciate your kind words and I thank you for your discretion in regards to my former life."

"Of course." He nodded. "Now, can you point me in the general direction so I may find Miss Turner?"

"The last I saw her, she was upstairs, writing a letter for a soldier," Tabetha answered. "She is likely still there."

"Thank you, Miss Norton," Nathaniel replied, then headed toward the stairs. Tabetha smiled. She liked Nathaniel and felt Victoria and he were meant for each other.

"Lord, do you have a man out there meant for me?" She sent up a quick prayer, and her mind immediately went to Steven Rogers. She sighed. She would likely never see her former commanding officer again, which was probably a good thing, because if he recognized her, well...she wasn't quite sure what would happen if he discovered her duel identity.

It had been so difficult keeping her secret from him, once she realized she was attracted to him. Field training had been very awkward, especially when he decided to personally work with her on hand-to-hand fighting skills. Thankfully, they had only had a few opportunities to spar one-on-one, but they had spent a lot of time on patrol and other military engagements. Tabatha had been able to shield her identity from him as well as her growing desires. She sighed as she looked out the window. She did miss cavalry life, being out of doors all day and caring for and riding her beloved horse, but she also loved her new-found family and didn't want any harm to come to them. She wanted the Confederate troops to hold out against her own Federal troops, mainly because if the Union did take control of the city, her old company might come into town, and she didn't want to be recognized, but also because she didn't know how the Federals would treat the citizens.

⌒〜〜〜

"Victoria, Victoria, come quick!" Kendall burst into the cave. Victoria looked up from her needlework.

"What on earth is the matter, Kendall?" Concern was apparent in her voice.

"There is a fire! Another one, but this one is big."

"Oh, heaven help us." Victoria stepped out and looked in the direction of Crutcher's store, where she could see flames lighting up the early evening sky in an evil-looking glow. "That's the third fire in that neighborhood since the siege began," she muttered. "I should go and see if I can be of any help."

"Whatever could you do to put out a fire?" Kendall asked. It's not as if you can smother it by yourself."

"Of course not, and I may not be able to get close enough to throw buckets of water on it or whatever else they may do, but I can certainly help those who can." Victoria left her cousin in a hurry and made her way towards the fire. It had been a clear and warm day earlier, but now, it was hot and incredibly smoky.

"Lord, please don't let the fire get close to the powder magazine." She prayed, knowing that if the fire reached that building, it would explode, and that could demolish the whole city. As she quickly walked, mortars from the west and Parrott shells from the east crossed each other over the blaze of the awful fire.

Nearing the inferno, she saw Captain J. Beggs, who had been appointed Chief of the Fire Brigade. He was directing the men combating the fire. Men, both civilian and soldier stood in line passing bucket after bucket of water to each other and throwing it on the flames. She placed a hand on her stomach. It looked as if the whole neighborhood would be lost this time.

"Victoria!"

She whirled around and saw a soot-covered Nathaniel coming toward her. He had taken his hat and jacket off, and was wearing a once-white shirt with the sleeves rolled up and a gray vest.

"Nathaniel!" In spite of his filthiness, she threw her arms around him. "I'm relieved to see you're safe."

"What are you doing here?" He hugged her tightly, then pulled away and looked into her eyes. "It could be dangerous, Tori."

"I came to see if there was anything I could do to help."

"Are you sure you're up to it?" He asked.

"Of course." She followed him to one of the pumps. He spoke to the soldier who was working it, then nodded and turned to Victoria.

"Can you pump water when an empty bucket is brought to you?"

"Of course I can." She nodded and took her place.

"Thank you," Nathaniel kissed her briefly on the forehead, then headed back to fight the fire.

They worked for hours, and by the end, Victoria felt as though her arms would fall off, but finally, the fire was under control and Nathaniel came back to her.

"I am impressed you are still here, Tori. You look no worse for the wear." He smiled at her. "We all appreciate what you did here."

"Is the fire out, then?" Victoria asked.

"Almost, just some hot spots. Come, I'll escort you home. I wished to speak with you tonight anyways, but then the fire broke out."

"You already visited me once today, at the hospital." She said, taking his offered arm.

"Yes, but I didn't get to speak with you privately as I wanted to." He slid his other hand to hers and pulled her to a slower pace.

"I see." She smiled up at him. "Do they know what started the fire? Was it the shelling?"

"No one is sure yet, but there is no doubt in my mind that it was set on purpose." Nathaniel's jaw clenched.

"Oh, Nathaniel, that can't be possible, can it? Do you think it was enemy agents?" Victoria suggested. "I've heard talk that there are spies in our midst."

"I believe so, and Captain Beggs feels the same way."

"It is a frightening thought. Such a dastardly thing for any person to do." Victoria shook her head. "It puts all of the women and children in harm's way. It's more like murder, not warfare."

"I agree." Nathaniel wiped at his face with his sleeve, his shirt becoming even dirtier.

"Are you sure you are alright? You didn't get burned while fighting the fire, did you?" Victoria reached up and tried to brush some soot from his shoulder.

"No. I'm just a bit overheated and dirty. I'll head down to one of the Yazoo streams and wash up. I had planned on doing that before I saw you this evening anyway."

"I don't mind you being dirty, Nathaniel." Victoria smiled.

"Well, I wanted to talk with you about something special. I spoke with your mother regarding my intentions, then I spoke with your nearest male relatives. I wanted to ask them how they would feel about my marrying you."

"My nearest male relatives?" Victoria was puzzled. "My father and both of my brothers are unreachable."

"That may be so, but I had a special conversation with Adam and Gabriel. They take their job of watching over the family quite seriously." Nathaniel gave her a grin. "They are delightful boys."

"You asked my four-year-old nephews permission to marry me?" She was touched by his thoughtfulness. "That was really sweet of you."

"I enjoy talking with them," he said. "And now it's time for me to speak with you." They were in the middle of the sidewalk, still a few blocks from the cave. The gaslights had been lit, and the firelight made his face glow. "Victoria Turner. You know that I love you with all of my heart. Will you marry me?"

"You know my answer." She threw her arms around him. He held her tightly and kissed her forehead.

"I love you, Victoria," He said, then pulled back and looked into her eyes. "But you haven't yet answered the question."

"Oh, you dunce." She hit him gently on the chest. "Of course my answer is yes. When?"

"I don't want to wait much longer. Once the siege ends, I will have to go back to Virginia and my own regiment. I would like to spend my time here as your husband."

"I want that too." She said, reaching up to give him a brief kiss.

"Could you be ready by Sunday? That would give us six days."

"I will make sure I am ready." Victoria stated. "Pastor Lord still holds services every day at Christ Episcopal, so I am sure he will perform the ceremony, unless..." She bit her lip. "Nathaniel, are you okay with getting married in the Episcopal Church? I know you were raised Catholic."

"I am Catholic, it's not something you stop being. However, at this point, in the midst of a war, I would be fine getting married at the top of Sky Parlor Hill, much less the Episcopal Church. I hope your pastor is alright with my background."

"I'm sure he will be." She smiled. "If not, we will find someone else to perform the ceremony."

"Good. Unless something truly catastrophic happens, I will be there." He smiled. "I may not be able to see you much the rest of the week. I am heading back into the trenches. I will let you know if something arises and I cannot make it."

"Why the trenches again? You are a courier..." She wiped at his forehead, trying to brush more of the ash away.

"I know, but I just go where they need the most help."

"All right. I will plan on Sunday." She reached up and kissed him. "I cannot wait."

Wednesday, June 3, 1863
Green Cave

"Greetings, Green family!" Victoria ducked into the cave dug into the side of the hill that the Green home was situated on. Duff finally completed it. She smiled at her friend. "How is everyone doing? I am so happy to see you settled into your own home, well, if you can call a cave a home."

"We are all quite well, and so happy to be in our own cave." Mary looked down at baby William. "It is good to see you, Victoria. It has been a few days and I understand you have some news to share with me."

"I do, but I cannot stay long. The women of Vicksburg are all desperately busy working with the sick and wounded. I wanted to stop in, give you my news, and ask if you needed me to take care of anything while I'm working in your house."

"I thank you for stopping by, and I don't need anything, not today, at least. One of these days, I just may need something, though." Mary smiled.

"I will be sure to keep checking with you," Victoria sat in a chair. "Now, about my news. I am so excited, Mary. As I'm sure you've heard, Nathaniel proposed to me and of course, I have accepted. We are to be married this Sunday."

"Congratulations, Victoria. I am so happy for you. Nathaniel will make a splendid husband. I have known for quite some time that you held a candle for him."

"For quite a while, that is true." Victoria nodded. "How did you know that I had such feelings for Nathaniel?"

"You are one of my dearest friends, Victoria. I know you well. If I was not sure about it before, I had no doubt once he came into town. You were a changed woman."

"I suppose I cannot hide something like that from you. I do hope you can make the ceremony."

"I will make every effort to be there," Mary replied. "Have you heard any other news?"

"It's said that several women and children from town crossed over the Yazoo River. Their provisions ran out and they were desperate. Hopefully, the Yankees will assist them."

"I feel certain they will. They are all just refugees," Mary replied.

"I hope that means something to the Yankees," Victoria said.

"You said that the women of the town are all busy with the wounded. It is distressing to hear that there are so many."

"According to Nathaniel, the boys in the trenches are becoming careless and reckless and exposing themselves needlessly. There are few positions near the lines that are relatively safe and secure, but the ditches can only help so much."

"Oh, those poor men," Mary said.

"That's not the only problem. The soldiers are so crowded in the makeshift hospitals. We are lucky that the Sisters of Mercy returned to town just before the siege began." The Religious Sisters of Mercy were Catholic nuns who had originally come from Baltimore before the war to open a school and teach the children of the town who could not afford an education. Two years later, their school was closed when families fled into the countryside to avoid the first attack in Vicksburg. With no students to teach, the nuns had gone to Jackson, Mississippi to help nurse the wounded there. When they returned to Vicksburg, their school was filled with sick and injured soldiers, so they immediately began providing nursing care. "The sisters are very diligent workers and excellent teachers. It is good to watch and learn the ways to comfort and care for the men."

"At least the hospitals are safe from enemy fire," Mary commented.

"That is the main reason Duff offered our home. If the enemy knows it's a hospital and may have wounded Union soldiers, they will try to avoid shelling it."

"You would think so," Victoria said. "However, that may not be as helpful as we thought. Even though we have hospital flags waving over every hospital, they are still in danger of being hit. In fact, the shelling has been responsible for the death of several. Perhaps not immediately and directly, but killed just the same." She shook her head. "The wounded men are naturally nervous. This keeps them in a state of excitement and constant alarm. The poor boys are confined to their beds without the ability to escape if something does happen. They are compelled to just submit to the consequences of their helplessness. Somehow, this irritates their wounds and increases their tendency to fever. Some of the doctors say this is related to the stress which results in death. The doctors believe that peace and quiet is imperative to help an injured person during their recovery."

"I wish I were in a position to help," Mary said.

"No one faults you for being confined while in your condition, Mary. You must recover yourself," Victoria assured her. "We all continue to pray that General Johnston will arrive soon from the east and end this siege."

"I pray that more ardently than you do." Mary smiled. "I have tried to accustom myself to this cave living as much as anyone is able, but I don't want to stay here any longer than I must. I need to have fresh air and sunlight." She smiled. "Speaking of caves, where will you and Nathaniel go for your wedding night? There must be some elegant cave in Vicksburg."

"Well, obviously a wedding trip is out of the question." Victoria quipped. "We are going to try and stay at my family's house when the cannonading isn't dangerous. We will have some privacy there. I will continue to stay with my family when he is on patrol. I have finally gotten over my fear of caves, well, somewhat. I definitely never want to be in one alone. When there is shelling and he is here, we have a small, one-room cave near my family where we will stay. It is a special project that he has been working on."

"A wedding night with fireworks and imminent danger. That surely is unique." Mary smiled. "And what will your wedding feast consist of?"

Victoria laughed. "No more unique than the birth of your baby under these same circumstances. And the food will likely be whatever we can round up. Perhaps between now and then I can find a tasty recipe for pea meal bread."

"If you can find that, you will be the most appreciated woman in all of Vicksburg." Mary shook her head. As the food supplies continued to dwindle in Vicksburg, the civilians and soldiers had been using whatever food source was available. Peameal, or peas that had been dried and ground up into a flour-like substance, was still quite abundant, so those doing the cooking were making bread from the peameal. It was usually mixed with cold water and baked, but never turned out the way that a person could enjoy eating it. The longer it was cooked, the harder it became on the outside, yet stayed uncooked on the inside. Many women were trying to find a way to make it more palatable.

"I wish we could find a recipe that was both healthy and tasty," Victoria said, checking her pocket watch. "Oh, botheration, I really should be on my way." Victoria stood. "I'll try to visit before the wedding, but if I can't, I will see you Sunday."

"You will be quite busy, I understand. You take care of your plans, I'll be just fine. Please let me know if there is anything I can do for you." Mary waved, and Victoria left with a smile.

Thursday, June 4, 1863
Wheeler Farm

"But Mama…"

"No arguing, young man." Hannah poured the last bucket of hot water into the tub. "It has been a long day and you are filthy."

"But we're not going to church or doing nothing special. Grandma and Aunt Caroline don't care if I'm clean or not."

"I daresay they do," Hannah replied. Her mother-in-law and Caroline had brought some food to a sick neighbor. Hannah had stayed behind to finish dinner and oversee Ambrose taking a well-needed bath, as the boy had gotten quite dirty while playing near the marshes.

Just as Ambrose began to unbutton his shirt, they heard the rumble of many horses approaching through the open window.

"Mama, is that Mr. Jason?" Ambrose ran to the doorway. Hannah quickly joined him on the front porch. Her heart pounded when she saw that it was Union soldiers. She took a deep breath to steady her nerves. Ambrose took a step behind her, suddenly apprehensive. The leader, a handsome man with brown hair poking from beneath his kepi, pulled up his horse right at the porch.

"Good afternoon, ma'am." He greeted her. "I am Captain Steven Rogers of the 6th Illinois Cavalry, here on behalf of the quartermaster. I am sorry to have to do this, but I am here to requisition supplies. Is your husband here?"

"No, he died years ago." She said, hoping her voice was steady and strong.

"So there is no man on this farm?" The soldier looked slightly more compassionate at that news.

"That is correct, sir. I live with my late husband's mother and sister, and my son. Just women and a child." The soldier appeared to be a gentleman. Perhaps he would let them be. They didn't have much left, and their harvest in a few months wouldn't be as profitable as in past years. She had hidden some food supplies in different locations just in case this scenario happened, but not nearly enough.

"I am sorry to hear that, ma'am, but we have troops that need food. I have my orders." He told her what they needed; livestock, flour, vegetables. While it may not have sounded like much to an army, it was more than half of what they had stored up.

Hannah shook her head. "Sir…"

The Captain held up his gloved hand. "Again, I am truly sorry, as I said, ma'am, I am afraid I have no choice. My hands are tied." He turned and nodded towards some of his men, who then rode off towards the barn. One of the soldiers drove a wagon. "I assure you, we will not leave you completely destitute. I will discuss your situation with the quartermaster and ask that he avoid your farm in the future. However, we must get what we came for today."

Hannah clenched her jaw and reached down to grasp Ambrose's hand. Her son was gripping her skirt so tightly she thought he might tear the fabric. She knew there was nothing she could do to prevent this. Even if Cordelia and Caroline were here, they wouldn't be able to stop the soldiers.

"Mama, are they going to take all our food? Why are you letting them steal from us?" Ambrose's voice was quiet. "If Mr. Jason were here, he would shoot them all dead."

"Hush, Ambrose, don't say another word. If they find out about Mr. Turner, they will surely kill him and make it worse for us. We don't have a choice." She spoke firmly, trying to convince herself of that fact as well. "Sometimes, we must decide whether to fight or let things go."

"What will we eat if the Yankees take all of our food?" He asked.

"God will provide. He always does." She looked down at her son, as if realizing how much he had grown in the past year. Now eight years old, he was able to do many of the chores around the farm, but he should be attending school, preparing for his future. Hannah wanted something more for her son than just the farm. She sighed. The war was affecting everyone's life in ways they hadn't ever thought about.

"Mama, the soldiers are leaving." Ambrose tugged at her arm, pulling Hannah from her thoughts. She focused on the soldiers who were now riding away. The handsome captain nodded as he passed by. She tried to hold her emotions in as the wagon they brought rolled by, filled with vegetables, four young pigs, several chickens, and one of their two milk cows. Hannah even saw a basket full of jars; they must have found her canned preserves.

"The Lord will provide," She murmured again to herself, hoping the words would prove true.

Friday, June 5, 1863
St. Xavier Hospital

Tabetha wiped the soldier's forehead with a cool cloth. It was hard to believe that more men were dying from illness than battle wounds. Wounded soldiers were sent to certain hospitals, like the Green home, while the sick were sent to others.

At present, the soldier she was sitting with had swamp fever, better known as malaria. She was trying to get him to drink as much water as possible, but it was not an easy task.

"Is there anything more I can do for you, Private?" She asked.

"No, ma'am. You being here is enough," He replied.

"I'm glad to help. I'll be back tomorrow," Tabetha smiled, then looked at the clock on the mantle. It was almost time for her to leave for the day. She wished she could stay, but Rachel Turner had talked to her about working too hard. The motherly woman had reminded her that if she didn't care for herself, she wouldn't be able to care for any of the soldiers. Tabetha's stomach rumbled and she groaned. She usually looked forward to mealtime, but with food being so sparse lately, it wasn't even worth eating.

"Have a wonderful evening, Miss Norton." One of the nuns, Sr. Stanislaus, waved goodbye.

"You as well, Sister Stan." Tabetha waved back. She enjoyed working with the Sisters of Charity. They were wonderful women and there were times that Tabetha wondered if God wasn't calling her to join them.

Tabetha stepped into the street and smiled when she saw Mary Loughborough, a young, vibrant woman who was always kind and friendly. The woman and her Confederate-soldier husband had been trapped in the city when the siege began.

"Miss Norton!" Mrs. Loughborough smiled. "How are you this fine day?"

"Quite well, all things considered," Tabetha said. "And yourself? Are you and Mr. Loughborough keeping safe?"

"Yes, we are, thank you. I am fortunate to hear from him quite often through the couriers that come into town. I'm able to write him messages back as well." She gave a short laugh. "He is quite entertained by the fact that I have learned to bake bread and brew sweet potato coffee."

"My goodness, sweet potato coffee actually sounds tasty."

"Well, I fear we may soon have nothing if this standoff continues," Mrs. Loughborough said. "My dear husband wrote that he is living on pea meal. All our soldiers on the lines are. What they must endure is frightening."

Tabetha made a face. "I have heard that as well. I know the Turner's slave, Esther, is quite talented but there is not much one can do with pea meal."

"I heartily agree," Mrs. Loughborough said. Before Tabetha could speak again, a shell whizzed by overhead and crashed into a home behind them. Both women ducked instinctively, though it was unnecessary. "I will never get used to that, no matter how hard I try." Mrs. Loughborough shook her head. "Well, Miss Norton, I should be off. I don't wish to leave my little girl with the servants for too long. It's not that I don't trust them, mind you. I simply don't like being away from her. She is such a dear one."

"I understand completely," Tabetha said, and bid the woman good-bye.

As Tabetha neared the Turner cave, she saw Gabriel and Annie Green, playing. Tabetha found it curious how the children were still allowed to spend time outside with the constant bombardment. They had quickly become knowledgeable about the danger and had adapted well. They were still able to climb trees, and gather papaws and blackberries, as Gabriel and Annie were now doing.

"Hiya, Miss Norton," Gabriel called out. "Look at who gets to come over and play today! Aunt Victoria is gonna bring Annie back to the Greens later."

"How exciting for you both. How is the berry picking?" She would have thought the fruit would have already been picked clean off. However, if the children were able to get some…"

"It isn't easy, but we must find them. It is very important work. Miss Victoria's wedding is tomorrow and she needs a special dessert prepared." Annie said proudly holding up a pail that was about one quarter full.

"My goodness what a very kind gesture for both of you to assist Miss Victoria in the preparations. She and Mr. Prentiss will be very grateful for all of your help."

"Yep! Mama says we just have to pray that all goes well and Mr. Prentiss gets back here on time," Gabriel said.

"Indeed." Tabetha looked up as she heard a shell coming in their direction. "Gabriel, Annie, get down!" She grabbed both children and tugged them to the ground, covering them as best she could. The shell buried itself in the ground not five feet away.

"That was a close 'un." Gabriel stated. "Perhaps…I think we have enough berries for now."

"But mine spilled, Gabe. Can you pick them up?" Annie was close to tears.

"We'll both help Annie, then I'll walk with you back to the cave," Tabetha said, thanking God for a narrow escape. Would they ever be truly safe again?

Saturday, June 6, 1863
Green Home~Hospital

"I hope tomorrow is as clear a day as today." Victoria looked back at the sky as they entered the Green home. "And that our plans for the wedding continue to go smoothly."

"It really is sad that you can't enjoy a better atmosphere for your nuptials," Tabetha said. The two women made their way to the storage closet to get their aprons.

"That doesn't really matter to me. As long as I can marry Nathaniel, I will be happy," Victoria replied. Tabetha smiled sadly as she pinned the bib of her apron to her blouse. "What's wrong, Tabetha?"

"Oh, nothing. I just...I envy your relationship with Nathaniel. I'm not jealous, mind you, I just wish I had someone to share my life with too. If that makes any sense."

"It makes perfect sense to me. I have felt that way in regards to Mary Grace, Mary Green, Hannah, my friend Magdalena and countless other married women. I know what you are feeling. I wondered for years if I would ever find a husband, but my patience has paid off." Victoria placed a comforting hand on Tabetha's arm. "You'll find someone who cares for you and treats you like the wonderful woman you are."

"'For I know the plans I have for you', says the Lord," Tabetha quoted. "'Plans to prosper you and not to harm you, plans to give you hope and a future'."

"Exactly," Victoria smiled. "You and I must be kindred spirits. We have so much in common. You have no idea how much that scripture passage has helped me through the years." As the two women moved to find the hospital matron for their assigned daily tasks, Victoria looked at Tabetha: "We will finish this discussion later."

"Shall we finish our talk from earlier today?" Tabetha asked as they walked back to their cave. Her heat clenched when she saw a train of wagons pass through the streets, making their rounds as they did daily, to pick up those who had died that day. She shook her head. "It sounded as though you had more to say." She spoke loudly on account of the cannon fire that could be heard from the direction of the Big Black River.

"I wanted to ask you if you thought...well," Victoria sighed. "I am quite sure about marrying Nathaniel. I love him dearly and I want nothing more than to spend the rest of my life with him. However, I wonder if we are rushing the wedding. He only asked for my hand a week ago. If you were in my position, would you wait until the war is over? Or at least until the siege is over?"

"If I were in your position, having the love of a good man and loving him back, I would have married him the same day he asked." Tabetha smiled and reassured her friend. Suddenly, there was an explosion as fire from the enemy increased. The two women ducked into a nearby cave.

"Do you even know whose cave this is?" Victoria asked.

"No," Tabetha looked around. It was a small, one-room cave that was empty. She sat on the ground against the wall. "However, its location is convenient."

"Do you ever miss the excitement of battle?" Victoria asked.

"Sometimes," Tabetha admitted. "I felt useful. You know I joined because of the guilt I felt over the loss of my brother, but I was actually quite good at being a soldier."

"Would you go back, if given the opportunity?" Victoria asked.

"At this point, no," Tabetha replied. "I do feel nursing is a very special calling and I must add, it is so much easier to help the soldiers rather than being the reason they are here. I certainly don't miss pretending to be a man."

"I would agree with you about nursing," Victoria said. "I am glad that many of the doctors are starting to appreciate our work, and I know the soldiers do. It gives us value."

"Indeed." Tabetha went to the mouth of the cave and looked out. Shells were still incoming, making it too dangerous to leave for the Turner's cave.

"You rarely speak of your time in the Cavalry," Victoria pointed out.

"It rarely comes up," Tabetha replied, "but also, I do need to be careful talking about my past life. I'm no expert on the law, but I imagine a woman pretending to be a man and a soldier would not be looked upon favorably. It may even be illegal."

"I can't believe it would be illegal, but you are right, you would become an outcast, at least in Vicksburg you would." Victoria shook her head. "Even if you did risk your life for a cause you believed in."

"That brings up another reason I should keep my past quiet. I wasn't just a soldier, but to those here in Vicksburg, I was an enemy soldier. I am fortunate you and your family have been so kind and understanding."

"We are blessed to have you with us, Tabetha." Victoria smiled. "I may not agree with your views, but I can appreciate that you fought for your brother's name and what you believed in."

"Thank you for saying so." Tabetha looked out the mouth of the cave. "It sounds like the artillery fire has slowed enough for us to make it to the cave."

"Then let's do so." Victoria said. "I need to get a good night's sleep before my big day."

Sunday, June 7, 1863
Turner Home

"I am glad the day has dawned and is warm and clear for the wedding." Mary Grace said with a smile.

"A nice, clear, warm day," Victoria smiled back, meeting her sister's eyes in the mirror. Mary Grace had offered to style Victoria's hair, and Victoria had gladly accepted. Mary Grace was a very talented hairdresser. Victoria knew that she wouldn't have a beautiful new dress, and there would be no great feast and certainly no exciting wedding trip. She may not even get a quiet hour in the day to say her vows with all of the shelling around them, but she would have beautiful hair, family and friends surrounding her and a handsome groom waiting for her at Christ Episcopal Church.

"When we're done here, we'll head over to the church." Rachel had tears in her eyes as she looked at her daughters. "You look absolutely beautiful, my dear Victoria."

"I should hope so. I have waited long enough to be a bride," Victoria joked.

"You have had your share of disappointments when it comes to men," Mary Grace said. "However, I believe you are marrying the best of the lot."

"I heartily agree," Rachel said. "Nathaniel is a wonderful young man, and I know he will take good care of you."

"He will make a good father as well, someday," Mary Grace added. "He is so good with my children. The boys adore him."

"Yes," Victoria agreed. "I am so happy to have him in my life. I only wish this siege and the entire war would end so that we would not have to be separated. I know that once the siege ends, Nathaniel will have to leave and report back East."

"Which is why I am glad that you two are able to get married now. You should enjoy as much time together as possible." Mary Grace put the finishing touches on Victoria's hair. "Even if you have to spend your honeymoon in a war-torn city."

"It's not ideal, but it is better than not spending time with him at all." Victoria stood and hugged her sister. "It looks beautiful. You are truly an artist, Mary Grace. Thank you so much."

"Of course. Come, now. Let's get you to the church."

Christ Episcopal Church was still in use for daily services, so an afternoon wedding was easy enough to arrange with Reverend Lord. The building was riddled with holes and fragments of shell, though it had only been struck outright once during actual services. Thankfully, no one had been injured. Victoria was sad to see that, over the course of the siege, a great deal of the beautiful ivy that had covered the exterior brick for years had been scorched and killed.

"It just breaks my heart to see that every pane of glass has been broken." Mary Grace commented as they entered the church.

"But remember, not a drop of blood has stained the floor," Rachel said.

"Well, let's hope today isn't the day that will change that," Mary Grace said, then hugged her children as they ran to greet them. They had arrived earlier with Rachel, Brianne, Tabetha and Kendall.

"Ladies, it is such a delight to see you all looking so beautiful," Reverend Lord greeted them. "Your groom is here, Victoria, as well as some members of the town who wanted to witness this happy event. We can get started right away."

"We're ready," Victoria said. The women were seated and anticipation filled Victoria. She was sad that her father was unable to walk her down the aisle, but she had decided that her mother would have the honor. The moment Nathaniel came into view, Victoria's heart skipped a beat. He looked as handsome as ever, his face cleanly shaven, and his Confederate uniform as clean as he could get it under the circumstances. His smile made her feel cherished and as she neared him, she was quite sure that he had a tear in his eye. She had to take a deep breath. She was so happy that she may cry as well.

The ceremony flew by, and before Victoria knew it, the Reverend Lord pronounced them man and wife. Nathaniel bent down and kissed her gently when prompted by the Reverend, then pressed his forehead to hers.

"I love you, Victoria," he whispered.

Turner Home

"Just what every bride dreams of," Victoria joked. "Spending her wedding night in a house that has been bombarded with the threat of being shelled again at any time." The ceremony and celebration had gone as well as could be expected. The Greens and the Lords were the only guests outside of Victoria's family at the dinner. Luckily, some of Nathaniel's comrades had given their ration of bacon for the celebration as a wedding present. Esther had done her best with the meager food supplied.

"Let's just hope for a quiet night." Nathaniel replied. "I wish I could give you more,"

Victoria placed her hands on his shoulders.

"George Washington Nathaniel Greene Prentiss. It doesn't matter to me. I am married to you, and that's what is important."

He bent down to kiss her.

"I am so lucky to be the man who married you? You should have been snatched up by someone else long ago."

"I almost was, but God had better plans." She was so thankful of that.

"It would be perfect if we weren't in the midst of this infernal war, and a siege where anything could happen at any time. A hushed conversation with my bride on our wedding night would be nice."

"Nathaniel." She blushed. He gave her another quick kiss.

"I must say, once again, I am impressed with Esther. She is a miracle-worker in the kitchen."

"Yes, well, your army rations helped, as well as the generosity of your friends," Victoria said. Nathaniel sat down in a chair. Victoria bit her lip, wondering if it would be too forward for her to sit on his lap. They were man and wife after all. He gave her a smile and she made her decision. "I hope she is able to teach me more of her skills. We haven't really talked much about how we will live our lives after the siege and war are over." She sat on his lap and his arms immediately went around her. "Will I even need to cook? I know a few recipes."

"It depends on how the war ends, but I should be able to go home and take over the family farm. I never thought to ask, you won't mind living in Virginia, will you?"

"It's what I expected we would do." She lay her head on his shoulder. "I would go anywhere with you. Besides, we will be just minutes away from my cousins."

"I feel the same way, Tori." He said, kissing her gently on the cheek. "In answer to your question, though, I don't believe you should distress yourself about cooking just yet. You can learn from Esther, of course, but when we get to Virginia, my sister, AJ can help you learn. She is a darn good cook. She has been feeding us since she was just a girl. As you may remember, we were never able to afford a house slave before."

"I realize that," Victoria said. "You know I didn't marry you for your wealth." She leaned down to kiss him and chuckled. "I married you because you are so handsome and you make my heart race, and because I love you, I suppose."

Monday, June 8, 1863
Prentiss Cave

"Good evening, wife!" Nathaniel strode into the cave he had dug for the two of them. Victoria straightened from the fire she had been cooking over. A benefit of her marrying Nathaniel was that she was able to use his army rations for cooking. She gave half of it to her family, but she still felt guilty about having more than her neighbors.

"Good evening, husband." She pulled him into a tight embrace. "I am glad you're back. I didn't know if I should expect you or not."

"I'd say it's safe to assume that I'll be here almost every night. If I don't show up, though, don't worry." He reached over her shoulder and pulled a slice of bacon from the plate. "I will definitely be home if I am greeted with a meal like this." He kissed her gently. "And a beautiful wife."

"How was your day? Did you spend time in the trenches?" Victoria asked.

"I got close to the lines." He sighed, then pulled a crate next to the fire and sat down. "Conditions are not good, Victoria. Our poor men have been lying there for three weeks now with no relief. Day and night, the hail of bullets and cannon is falling on them and men are dying or getting wounded by the hundreds. I know you are aware of that because of your work in the hospitals." He leaned against the wall and held out his hand, silently asking her to join him. She sat on his knee and leaned against his shoulder. "It is difficult to even get them their rations, and the Yankees continue to plow the land with their missiles."

"This weather isn't making the conditions any better," Victoria states. "It's so dry."

"You are right about that," Nathaniel agreed. "It's so hot that it makes one dizzy to remain in the sun very long. Especially with the dust filling everyone's eyes, nose and hair, just about everything. The enemy's lines are slowly, but surely approaching our breastworks. The fighting is becoming fiercer every day." He shook his head. "I fear we will lose this fight. The darn Yankees are getting clever."

"How so?" Victoria asked.

"They obtained a railway car-frame, placed it on wheels and loaded it with cotton bales. Then, they pushed their cart along Jackson Road right in front of our soldiers. With the protection of the cotton, they were able to construct new breastworks. Our men fired as much as possible, but they could not penetrate those blasted bales of cotton. We don't have the artillery that would take them down either." Nathaniel rubbed his temple. "The Yankees are just a hundred yards away from us and we can only watch what they're doing. It is a waiting game. Soon they will be right in front of us and it will be hand-to-hand fighting. Do you know how frustrating that is? To sit under constant fire to know that soon you may die."

Victoria knew that Nathaniel just needed to talk, so she simply sat and listened.

"Death has become so familiar to our men that a fellow soldier falling is looked upon with almost...stoic indifference." He shook his head. "I sometimes feel guilty. I have the ability to move around, to come and go more or less, as I please. I can take time to do what I need to do between assignments, and now, I have a wife to come back to in a passably-comfortable home with provisions that you can make into a hot meal for me...I wish I could do something, anything...ahhh, this infernal waiting!" His fist struck the wall behind them.

"It is a difficult situation for everyone, Nathaniel," Victoria replied. "You do what you are told to do, and you will keep doing that. The army has given you a job and you need to focus on that."

"I know." He stared blankly across the room.

Victoria sighed, then tried to lighten the mood by changing the subject. "Honestly, I was just thinking about how unfortunate it is that I haven't been able to take a good bath in weeks. Just a shame."

Nathaniel smiled, knowing that she just wanted to pull him out of his melancholy. "That is a pity," he said. "Your poor husband, not able to have a wife with clean clothing and smelling of lilacs."

"He is a saint for putting up with me," She replied.

"Well, you can cook a decent meal, and you are quite adept at discerning his feelings and acting appropriately. I would actually say that you have quite a lucky husband."

"I'm the lucky one, Nathaniel," She replied, then stood and walked to the fire. "Dinner should be about ready."

"Thank you, Victoria. For everything." Nathaniel smiled again, glad that God had given him this wife.

Tuesday, June 9, 1863
Green Cave

"I wonder if we'll ever have peace and quiet again." Victoria sat down outside of the Green's Cave. Mary smiled in understanding as she passed Baby William to her. Victoria cuddled the boy close to her.

"I think the same thing every few hours." She shook her head. "I would ask how married life is treating you, but from the smile on your face, I can tell that all is well."

"You would be correct. I could say that it was perfect if not for this siege." She shrugged her shoulders. "Nathaniel is wonderful, though. I was disheartened when he left this morning because he thought he would come back each night, but it sounds as though the fight is heating up along the lines."

"Duff reported the same thing to me," Mary said, then looked up and smiled when she saw Brianne and Tabetha approach the Green's fly tent. "Miss Norton! Miss Larson! What a pleasant surprise."

"Good day, Mrs. Green." Brianne looked at Victoria. "We were hoping you would be here, Victoria. You weren't in your cave and we didn't know you had left."

"Yes, I wanted to check on Mary, Annie and Baby William."

"I knew it would be different with you being married and not living with us, and I know you are staying right next to us, but I didn't realize how much I would actually miss you," Brianne said.

"I miss you all as well," Victoria said. "Did you need me for something specific, have I missed any news? I know all the military news, obviously, but not much social news."

"We lost Major Hoadley," Brianne said sadly. "He was killed in camp. Many of the young women in town have been quite distressed by the news."

"Hoadley," Victoria tried to remember where she had heard that name before. "How do we know Major Hoadley?"

"Really, Victoria? He was one of the most handsome men in the army," Brianne exclaimed. "You must remember him. He was a prominent Arkansas political figure, but was fighting with the 1st Tennessee Heavy Artillery."

"From what I understand, he was a man of fine intelligence and unwavering zeal in his cause," Tabetha added. "They say he was kind to the men he commanded and a gentleman in every sense. I would not have minded being under his command, if he were on the right side, of course. He was quite dashing and a great favorite of the ladies."

"How tragic," Victoria said. "Nathaniel did mention the situation in the trenches is quite distressing, but he never goes into any detail."

"The hospitals are no better," Tabetha said. "They are all overcrowded. Some of the poor fellows are compelled to lay out in the open air and beg for the attention of any doctor who happens to pass their way. The sick lists are ever so long. Your soldiers are lying in the trenches for weeks with no protection." She shook her head. "The hot sun, burning and blistering them. The freshly dug earth is poisoning them with malaria, which is a major cause of death. The boys come into the hospital half-starved, shaking with ague. So many of them are afflicted with fevers and dysentery due to the unsanitary conditions."

"Nathaniel said the men in the trenches can't even stand up without having a dozen bullets whistle around their heads, and it's been difficult for them to get their rations. Just walking around is certain death." Victoria sighed. "I feel our troops are carrying on so nobly, yet I fear they cannot hold the city much longer."

"Even our streets are getting difficult to walk through," Brianne said. "The stench from the mules and horses that have been killed by the shells is becoming intolerable."

"Yes, that was an aspect of war I had never considered," Mary replied, looking over to see Duff enter the tent fly.

"Duff, I wasn't expecting you. What's happened?" Mary asked.

"I wanted to tell you an interesting story from last night." He crouched on an empty crate. "The Yankees turned a wagon of cotton bales into a movable breastwork earlier this week. They were using it to protect them as they dug trenches closer and closer to our lines."

"Nathaniel told me of that," Victoria said. "He said it was very frustrating for our troops."

"It was," Duff replied. "Our soldiers had nothing that could penetrate the cotton, but someone finally came up with a plan last night. One of our Lieutenants filled the cavity in the butt of his rifle with flammable materials that would ignite when fired from the rifle. He then took a shot at the cotton bales on the Yankee's wagon."

"That's an ingenious idea!" Brianne exclaimed.

"I thought so to, and our men sent other blazing missiles over, but nothing appeared to work." He leaned forward, smiling. "Or so they thought. Before long, smoke was seen coming from the wagons, our boys grabbed their rifles and kept up a constant and rapid fire to keep the enemy from extinguishing the flames. The Federals tried to put out the fire with dirt and water, but the glow of the fire gave our men a clear view of their target." He shook his head. "This war is surely inspiring the soldiers to think of new and different tactics to get the job done. Both the Federals and the Confederates have been quite inventive."

"I can believe that," Victoria stated.

"It's actually quite interesting from a business perspective as well," Duff said. "They say that necessity is the mother of invention. Both the Union and the Confederacy are making quite a few advancements in how wars are fought. Mostly in weaponry, but there are also advancements in boats that can completely submerge under water, and the Yankees have these contraptions called balloons. From what I can understand, they are sheets filled with some special type of air and have a basket beneath them. A man can stand in the basket and both he and the balloon will rise in the air. The Yankees have been able to get information on our troop's positions using these contraptions in the east."

"My goodness," Mary Green said. "How do they keep these balloons from flying away?"

"They keep them tethered to the ground." Duff explained.

Tabetha shook her head. "I declare, what will they think of next?"

"Whatever it takes," Duff said. "And it's all very exciting."

"Indeed." Victoria checked her watch, then stood and handed Baby William back to Mary. "I hadn't realized it was this late. I need to be on my way. I must see to a few other errands and I wanted to help Esther with dinner. After all, I must learn how to cook now." She kissed William on the forehead.

"Thank you for stopping by," Mary said. "Take care."

"Same to you!" Victoria replied, then followed Tabetha and Brianne back to their cave.

Wednesday, June 10, 1863
St. Xavier~Hospital

"I didn't think the dust in this town could get any worse, but this is absolutely unbearable," Victoria said as she saw Tabetha. "We really could use some rain to dampen it down."

"Yes, but that would create mud, and that would not be good for anyone, especially your soldiers who have no protection from the elements," Tabetha replied.

"You're right." Victoria hastened to an armoire and put on an apron. "Is there anything I should be aware of today?"

"Not that I can think of," Tabetha replied. "I was talking to Sr. Stanislaus and she told me how glad she is that your husband allows you to work."

"I must admit, he doesn't love the idea, but he knows it's important to me and to the men. He also worries that the buildings are not completely safe from the bombardment, but he spoke with Reverend Foster, who reminded him that the women are desperately needed in the hospitals."

"Ahh, yes, the Reverend. He is a fine man. I tell you, I am not comfortable with the fact that I have met so many good rebels. It causes a great conflict within me," Tabetha replied. The Reverend William Foster was the chaplain of the 35th Mississippi Infantry. He spent a good deal of time at the different hospitals, ministering to the soldiers.

"Indeed. We're not all bad, and neither are all the Yankees." Victoria smiled. "I must get to work. I'll just make my way from room to room and see what the men need."

"It's gotten busier since the last time you were here," Tabetha told her.

"I can see that. It's as you were saying yesterday, the hospitals are overflowing their rooms."

The first room that Victoria went into, she could see that Tabetha had underestimated the problem of overcrowding. Men were lying in every available spot. They were in bunked beds, and even on the floor. She took a breath and went to a young man who looked to be about Gregory's age.

"Good morning. My name is Mrs. Prentiss." She beamed inwardly at being able to use her new name. "Is there anything I can get for you?"

"Just hearing your voice, Ma'am, is like a balm to my soul." The man appeared feverish, but she was unsure of the cause. She knew many soldiers had malaria. "I have a copy of the newspaper, it was brought to me earlier, but I am having trouble reading it and I couldn't hold the paper anyhow. He held up his arm, which didn't have a hand. Another amputee. "Could you maybe spare a moment and read to me?"

"Of course," Victoria replied. "I love to read," She bent and picked up the copy of the *Vicksburg Citizen*. "Is there anything in particular that piques your interest?"

"Ma'am, you could read me just about anything, even the book of Leviticus would keep my interest right about now. Just to hear a soft, friendly voice is helpful."

Victoria smiled and scanned the paper. "So you are a Christian, then?"

"Yes, Ma'am. Especially with all this fighting, one can do nothing else but pray."

"You have a point," she replied. "There is a notice here from the Soldier's Christian Association of the 42nd Georgia Regiment. It says 'they are resolved to set apart all or a portion of the hour between sundown and dark of each day to supplicate Almighty God that He will pardon our sins, receive us graciously and deliver us from the hands of our cruel enemies, and that we solicit all Christians and soldiers throughout this beleaguered army to enter with us in prayer at that time.'" She smiled. "An hour for prayer. I think that is a splendid idea." She looked at the soldier, who appeared to be even weaker than when she first arrived.

"I think so too, Ma'am," he whispered. His breathing was rapid and shallow, as though he was fighting for every breath. She placed a hand to his forehead, only to find that he was burning with fever. She stood and looked around, but only saw patients and another volunteer like herself. Finally, she caught the eye of a Dr. Whitfield. She motioned him over.

"I've been speaking to this young man for about five minutes and just in that time, he has grown ever so weak."

The doctor examined the man, sighed and stood. He pulled Victoria aside and spoke to her quietly.

"Unfortunately, that boy has a severe infection. He is septic."

"What does that mean?" Victoria asked.

"He's dying," the doctor replied solemnly.

Victoria put a hand over her mouth and tried to hold back tears as the doctor continued.

"I doubt he'll survive the next hour. All we can do is keep him as comfortable as possible."

"Should I stay with him?" She asked quietly.

"If you have the time. Yes, it's always better to die with someone at your side." The doctor nodded. "I'm sorry I don't have better news, ma'am." He then turned and hastened away.

Victoria sank down next to the dying man. He opened his eyes just slightly.

"It's okay, ma'am. Really. I know I'm 'bout to die. But I ain't afraid. It's like the Bible verse says, I'm movin' on. God has his plan for me and I musta accomplished it. Not sure what it was, but I'm at peace with dyin'."

Victoria couldn't help the tears from rolling down her cheeks. She reached out and held the brave young man's hand in hers. "I'd like for you to tell me more about yourself, such as where you are from, and perhaps we can get a letter written for your family." She wiped one of the tears from her cheek. She asked a few more questions so she could write a letter later, then asked if he wanted to pray with her.

"I'd like that very much, ma'am."

She bent her head and prayed with him until he breathed his last breath.

⌒⌒⌒

"Oh, I wish I would have gone to Mother's cave," Victoria said to herself. The heavens had opened up and rain poured down, which fit with her mood. After the young soldier had died, she had seen to his burial, wrote a letter to his family and left, not wanting any more heartbreak. The realization that Nathaniel, Gregory, Jason or her father or any of the men she held dear in her heart, could die so easily with no loved ones around drastically affected her. As she started to prepare for dinner, she thought of the conversation she had with Tabetha earlier in the day. This rain would be good for the vegetation and animals and would keep the dust down. It would also give the occupants of Vicksburg a fresh supply of water. She had filled one cistern for just that reason, but she couldn't help but worry about the soldiers out in the elements, especially Nathaniel. She had been married for three days now, and she missed her husband terribly whenever he was away. Perhaps she could make her way out to his post if he did not return by tomorrow evening.

Many of the Confederate officers were heroes in the eyes of the young girls of Vicksburg, Brianne included. The young women knitted socks and hemmed handkerchiefs, put blossoms in the soldiers' buttonholes, and welcomed the officers into their caves where they would entertain with homemade candies, flowers, songs, flirtations and games of whist. When the officers were unable to leave their posts, the fearless girls assembled riding parties and entertainment and went out to the trenches. They would go during twilight so that they could see the fuses of any shell heading their way and have time to dodge it. Victoria could do the same.

"If I don't see him by Friday, I'll join the next riding party and find him myself." She said to herself.

"If you're talking about finding me, you had better not ever think of endangering your life like that."

Victoria spun around and smiled when she saw a rain-drenched Nathaniel. He had two days' worth of beard on his face and he was breathing heavily as if he had run to their cave. She hurried into his arms and gave him a hug. He was drenched, but she didn't care. "I have missed you so much." She murmured.

"I have missed you as well, Victoria." He sighed.

She stroked his chin. "I am glad you braved the storm to come home."

"Seeing you made all my troubles worthwhile." He gave her a kiss. "Come, let's sit in the doorway. The lighting is creating quite the spectacle. It is much better than cannon shells."

Nathaniel was right. It was as if the heat of the past few days had infused the air with electricity. The lightning struck with jagged edges that darted from the dark clouds over the city, and then thunder would follow, a deep, heavy roll.

"How are the men on the lines going to handle this, trapped in the trenches?" Victoria asked only loud enough to be heard over the rumblings.

"The men are exposed and unsheltered. The trenches are filling with rainwater, thoroughly wetting them. They will be quite miserable." He sighed. "I wish it could be different, but I have no way of helping them. They need to be where they can best protect the city." He began rubbing her arm. "What are people talking about in town?"

"Everyone is frightened about what the next day will bring, even the animals seem jittery. When I was a little girl, I used to wish that we had a dog. I love animals, but I am glad we don't have one now. Many families in town are struggling to feed their children. Feeding a pet would be almost impossible." She leaned her head on his shoulder.

"Yes, people are getting desperate for food and I fear they will eat just about anything soon. I do, however, remember you telling me that your favorite animal isn't a dog. It is a river otter, if I am not mistaken."

Victoria smiled at the knowledge that he remembered that detail of a previous conversation. "That is true, I think they are the most adorable of all animals."

"Yes. I haven't seen one in years." Nathaniel nodded, then changed the subject. "I heard a rumor of a child being killed. Is that true? Do you know of any such report?"

"Unfortunately, yes," Victoria replied. "The dear little girl's mother had taken her into their cave and put her to bed, then the mother sat near the cave entrance, as we are. A mortar shell came flying through the air and crashed into the earth above the child's bed. It actually penetrated the cave wall and the debris...well...it crushed the child." Tears fell down Victoria's face, as they had when she first heard the story and now whenever she thought of the young mother losing her child. Nathaniel wiped her tears. "What if it were Gabriel, Adam, Hope or one of Mary Green's children," she whispered.

Nathaniel voice was hoarse, as though he was trying to hold back his own tears. "I can't imagine that woman's pain."

"It makes one think, why would you even have a child right now, when our lives are constantly in danger?" Victoria wasn't quite sure where her question had come from, but felt compelled to ask. "But then I think of the joy on Mary Green's face when she is holding Baby William."

Nathaniel thought for a moment. "I believe God gives a child as a gift. He has his reasons. 'For I know the plans…'"

"Jeremiah," Victoria murmured. "One of my favorite verses. It helps me get through every difficult day."

"Me too," Nathaniel hesitated, then asked. "You do want children, do you not?"

"Of course I do," Victoria replied. "I'm surprised that you even have to ask. You know how I love my niece and nephews."

"That's what I thought your answer would be. I would have been shocked if you'd said no," He answered. "I think you'll make a wonderful mother."

"And you will be a wonderful father, Nathaniel. I see how Gabriel, Adam and Hope enjoy your company. Do...do you want children?"

"I do. As many as the good Lord sees fit to bless us with." He smiled and kissed her cheek. "I can well imagine having seven or eight children with you."

She smiled and leaned her head against his shoulder. "I am sorry I am so tearful, but I had a trying day at the hospital." She explained about the young man she had sat with. As they talked, Victoria could almost believe they were in a normal home having a typical conversation that all married couples shared. "Do you think we'll ever have a normal marriage? Will we ever live in a real house with you coming home safely every night?"

"That will happen someday. We just have to have faith."

Friday, June 12, 1863
Wheeler Farm

"I wonder how the people in town are faring." Caroline looked towards Vicksburg. "Almost a month trapped in the city."

"I hope they don't run out of food," Ambrose said, then bit into a biscuit. It had been challenging for the Wheelers after the Federal army came through and took so many supplies, but they had been able to make do. Hannah had finally felt comfortable enough to put her new skill with a rifle to work and had gone hunting successfully a few times. She, Cordelia and Caroline all knew how to dress and prepare wild game, so that had been helpful. They wanted to conserve what food they had, in case something drastic happened. They had found better hiding places for all the canned and non-perishable supplies.

Hannah took a bite of her venison stew. It was one of her latest successes, and they had been able to share some of the meat with their very grateful neighbors.

"I hope they are all safe," Hannah said. The family could hear the constant bombardment the Yankees were pouring on the city. Hannah prayed all of the civilians were surviving, yet she feared most for the Turner and Green families. "Mary Green surely has given birth to her child." She shook her head. How had her friend been able to go through childbirth with that constant danger around her?

There was a knock on the door, and Hannah stood to answer it. She smiled when she saw Jason Turner on the other side.

"Jason! Thank the Lord you're safe. It has been far too long. I hope you walked in and hid your horse well out in the woods. This area is crawling with Yankees."

He hadn't been able to stop by as much with the city under siege. The militia was busy, trying to harass the Federals in any way they could while helping protect the civilians outside of the siege lines. It was a difficult task, and she really missed his visits.

"Yes and yes, and it has been far too long."

She invited Jason in and he hesitated when he saw they had been eating. Cordelia stood to get him a bowl for some stew.

"You must stay for dinner, Mr. Turner," she said.

"You know I cannot turn good food down." Jason smiled and came into the dining area and ruffled Ambrose's hair as he passed by.

"Sit next to me, Mr. Jason." The boy called out.

"Of course, Ambrose." Jason pulled up a chair and squeezed between Ambrose and Hannah. He smiled after his first bite of stew. "Venison?" He caught Hannah's eyes. "How did you get venison?"

"Mama finally went hunting. She shot the deer for us." Ambrose said proudly.

"Very impressive, Mrs. Wheeler." He nodded.

"I had a good teacher." She returned the smile.

"Is there any news? Any updates on what is happening in the city?" Caroline spoke quickly. "How much longer can they hold out? Or will the Yankees give up first?"

"My goodness, Caroline, let Mr. Turner settle in before you bombard him with questions." Cordelia chided her daughter.

"It's alright, Ma'am, truly. Unfortunately I don't have much to tell. As you know, we spend our time harassing the Yankees and trying to help families like you as much as we can. I have no idea how long this siege will last. I do know the Yankees will not give up easily. Not only that, but I don't have confidence in our own General on the inside. Name's John Pemberton and he has Yankee relations. I can only hope he is trustworthy."

"Wouldn't he have already given the town up if he was a turncoat?" Caroline asked.

"Probably," Jason said. "I must admit, I worry that Vicksburg will fall." He glanced down at Ambrose. "And if it does, I fear the Yankees will never leave."

"I don't like those stinking Yankees," Ambrose spoke up. "They stole our food."

"What?" Jason's head shot up. He looked down at Ambrose, then met Hannah's gaze. "When did this happen?"

"A little over a week ago. Federal cavalrymen came by to 'requisition supplies', as he put it. They took about half our food stores and livestock." Hannah averted her eyes as she stood to begin clearing the table of dirty dishes.

"Hannah, why didn't you tell me?" He reached out and gently placed his hand on her wrist.

"Now when was I supposed to do that, Jason? We haven't seen you in almost a month." She looked at him. His eyes were full of concern. "I know you come when you can and you don't even need to do that. There is no reason for you to feel responsible for us."

"Hannah, I…" Jason shook his head and ran a hand through his hair.

"Hannah, take Mr. Turner to the porch. Caroline, Ambrose and I will take care of the dishes." Cordelia smiled.

"I thank you for the offer, Mother, but…"

Jason stood. "Please, Hannah." He gestured to the door. "Please."

Hannah let out a breath and nodded. Jason was too good a friend to simply ignore. She allowed him to escort her outside, then sat on the rocking chair.

"I am sorry for snapping at you earlier, Jason. As much as I try not to let these added burdens affect me, they occasionally do." Her smile wasn't quite genuine, something that Jason noticed right away. "I must remember that God is always watching out for us. He will not leave us or forsake us."

"Of course." His voice led her to believe that he didn't quite agree with her, which was worrisome. "Where have you been attending church since the siege began? You must be missing your services."

"We haven't been able to attend, unfortunately. We've been having prayer services with just the four of us. You're more than welcome to join us. We usually start around 9:00 on Sundays, but we could wait for you."

"That is quite all right, Hannah. I'll come if I can, but don't delay on my account." He leaned back against the porch railing, facing her. "Why didn't you tell me that you had been robbed? That is exactly what the Yankees did, you know."

"Was I supposed to tell you the moment you walked through the door, or ride out to find you after it happened, just to tell you? Come now, Jason, you know as well as I do, that wasn't going to happen."

"Would you have told me if Ambrose hadn't said something?"

"I don't know. Possibly, it's not like you wouldn't notice half our pigs and chickens missing and one of the cows, of course. But really, Jason, it's not your concern."

"Perhaps. It doesn't mean that I don't worry." Jason smiled. Hannah sent him a comforting look.

"Jason, you don't have to feel responsible for Benjamin's death. I know for some reason, you need to...atone for what happened to him. I don't know why you feel that way..."

"Hannah..."

She held out her hand. "And I know you won't tell me for whatever reason. Perhaps someday you will trust me enough. At any rate, I know you are a kind, gentle man and I will always consider you a very dear friend."

"Thank you. I appreciate your words." He hesitated. "Unfortunately, I must be going. This was supposed to be a short check-in with you, not a visit. I will say goodbye to your family, of course, and then be on my way."

"You'd better say goodbye. Ambrose would be quite distressed if you didn't." She smiled and stood, wishing he could stay longer.

"Thank you for dinner," He said.

"You know you are welcome anytime." She reached for his arm and he stopped. "Also know that you can come and talk to me any time about anything."

"I know that, Hannah, someday I will." He blew out a breath. "There are some things that I am just not ready to share yet. Not just you, but with anyone." He took her hand in his. "Rest assured, when I am ready to talk about it, you will be the first to know."

"Thank you, Jason." She smiled, then led him into the house.

Sunday, June 14, 1863
Christ Episcopal Church

"I could get used to the peace and quiet." Victoria said, clutching Nathaniel's arm outside the entrance to the church. The past two days had been relatively quiet, and Nathaniel was able to join the family for church service this morning. Mary Green and her family were in attendance as well. Tabetha had gone across town to attend the Catholic service at St. Paul's. She had invited Nathaniel to go with her, but he chose to stay with his wife.

"I agree. It has been nice." Mary Green smiled down at Annie, who clutched her hand. Baby William was back at the cave with one of the servants.

The streets were congested with the citizens of Vicksburg. Women and children deserted their caves with joy. Ladies were leisurely strolling down the streets, a pleasant change from hurrying back and forth as they did most days due to the bombardment.

"Such a blessing, to walk in silence." Brianne smiled. "Perhaps soon, as you say, Victoria, this will be the normal routine again."

"We had another courier reach the city with a supply of percussion caps," Nathaniel said. "It seems like such a triumph until you realize that the enemy is reinforcing their army daily." He smiled sadly as he saw the dejected faces. "My apologies, ladies, for being a thundercloud on your sunny day."

"You only speak the truth," Kendall said. "Their army grows while every man injured in the trenches causes our defenses to weaken."

"You are being a thundercloud as well, Kendall," Brianne said. "I choose to look at the happiness we have today." She smiled. "Birds singing sweetly, a gentle breeze rustling through the leaves…"

"My, aren't you poetic, Brianne." Nathaniel grinned, then waved at two familiar soldiers who approached them. The older one, Timothy Reynolds, was around the same age as Nathaniel. He walked confidently, his dark blonde hair poking from underneath his hat and days-old stubble covering his face. The younger one, Boone, had a 'devil-may-care' look to him, with a tanned, smooth face and dark hair that brushed his shoulders. It was easy to see the young man was of Indian descent.

"My goodness, its Mr. Boone Reynolds," Kendall sighed.

"Tex, it's good to see you in town," Nathaniel held out his hand for a shake. "I believe you already know the Turner family here. My new bride, Victoria, her mother, Rachel, and these lovely young ladies are Kendall and Brianne Larson, Victoria's cousins. I have been told that Mary Grace here is a cousin of yours by marriage."

"Yes, of course." Timothy spoke with a thick Texas drawl. "I had the pleasure of meeting all of you at Abraham's wedding to the lovely Mrs. Corbet. It's good to see you all looking so well. I am sorry I haven't been able to visit Mrs. Corbet, we have been busy with these Yankees."

"That is quite all right, Mr. Reynolds," Rachel said. "May I present Mrs. Duff Green and her daughter, Annie?"

"It is a pleasure, Mrs. Green," Timothy Reynolds, informally known as Tex, smiled at everyone. Victoria was struck again by the charm he held. It was no wonder her cousin, Rebekah, had fallen for him. If only Belle hadn't intervened.

"Mr. Reynolds, may I invite you and your brother to Sunday dinner?" Rachel asked.

"That's ever so nice of you, Mrs. Turner, but we were only granted a short reprieve to come into town. We can't stay long. Perhaps another time." Tex smiled apologetically.

Victoria couldn't help but notice the strained look in his face, as if he were remembering a painful memory. She had wondered if he ever thought of Bekah and how she passed him over, or if he had moved on. Clearly, it was the former.

"Of course, I understand," Rachel said.

"Before we depart, I would like to ask if you have heard anything from your husband, Abraham." Tex focused his question to Mary Grace.

Mary Grace put on a brave face, then answered. "I haven't heard from him in months, long before the siege. All was well at that time." Victoria knew how much her sister was hurting. Tex smiled down at Adam and Gabriel.

"Even if Abraham hadn't written me about his children, I'd know you two are his sons. You look just like your father did at this age."

"Thank you, sir." Gabriel said. Adam just smiled.

"And his daughter is the very image of her mother. She is beautiful, Mary Grace," Tex said. "Well, we must be off. It was nice seeing ya'll again." He then tipped his hat. Boone winked at Brianne, then followed his brother.

"It is nice to finally meet that man. I have heard you all speak well of him, but I have never been formally introduced." Mary Green looked at her pocket watch. "Oh, the time flies. I must get home, well, that hole in the ground we currently call home. William will be ready to nurse soon."

"Of course," Victoria said, and they all departed for their homes. Nathaniel glanced down at Adam, who was unsteady on his feet. He released Victoria's arm and knelt in front of the boy.

"Adam, would you like to ride the rest of the way home?"

"Ride what?" Adam asked, his voice shaky.

"My back," Nathaniel answered, swiveling around. "Grab my neck." Adam did so, and Nathaniel stood, reaching back to grab Adam's legs and secure them around his waist. Victoria smiled at the kindness shown by her husband. *He really will make a good father.* She thought.

The peacefulness of the town didn't last long. The mortar boats from the river opened fire upon the city. A cloud of white smoke rose up from across the peninsula. Shells screamed and exploded, sending pieces of earth everywhere. Panic erupted in the streets once again. Mothers searched for their children, everyone abandoned their homes and the streets and raced back to their caves.

"Hurry, we must get to safety," Rachel yelled. The family hastened back to their cave. Once the children were settled in, Nathaniel and Victoria returned to the front of the cave. The streets had cleared already and a feeling of dread and suspense came upon Victoria. She could tell that Nathaniel was subdued as well.

"I had hoped, I knew it was not likely, but I had hoped that the mortars would be silenced permanently." She said quietly.

"They were probably just out of ammunition for a while," Nathaniel said. "Now they have been restocked."

"We are back to the way we were," she said, shaking her head. He stretched his neck and rubbed it. Victoria gently pushed him down on a crate, then moved behind him and began massaging his shoulders.

"Was Tabetha supposed to be back right after Mass?" Nathaniel asked. "I probably should have gone with her, but I didn't want to pass up the opportunity to spend time with my wife and her family."

"She was going to go to St. Xavier's and help for a few hours," Victoria answered. She continued to ease the tension from Nathaniel's shoulders. He reached up and took her hand, then pulled her over to sit on his knee. "I am actually quite torn about the siege ending," She admitted quietly. "It sounds silly, I know."

"I understand completely." Nathaniel's eyes look over the city. "You want the siege to end for all the obvious reasons. No more danger, no more caves, good food to eat, and the comforts of your own home. But when the siege ends…" He trailed off.

"When the siege ends, you'll be heading back east." Victoria finished his statement, tears in her eyes. "I don't want you to go, Nathaniel, yet I know you must. You wouldn't be the man I love if you didn't."

He smiled and looked in her eyes. "I'll say it again, from the moment we held our first conversation on the grounds of Chatham Manor, my life was changed, and now, by some miracle, I am on the other side of the country in the most unusual of circumstances and I am married to you. I tell you, God surly had plans of his own."

Victoria simply smiled. "

Thursday, June 17, 1863
Green Home Hospital

"Nine transports loaded with Federal troops came down last night and landed at the old Yankee landing just above the head of the canal." Victoria read from yesterday's *Vicksburg Compiler* to a wounded soldier. "Yesterday morning the Federal sick and wounded were brought down the Yazoo from Grant's besieging army and landed in the same place. Tents for a large number of men were visible during the day."

Many Confederate wounded had died this week, but in spite of that, Victoria believed it her duty to bring comfort and hope to those who most needed it. She had overheard Chaplain Foster and a doctor discussing the state of affairs. The doctor seemed to believe that the first ten days after an injury generally decided whether the wound would prove fatal to a man or not. He also insinuated that the warm weather caused many men to die who may have recovered otherwise.

She looked at the soldier she was reading to, Confederate Captain Cropwood. She enjoyed speaking with him. He enjoyed the art of conversation, but she noticed recently that he wanted to talk more about eternal life. This made her nervous as many men who thought they were about to die wanted to talk about God and Heaven. It was difficult for Victoria to see the captain, or anyone for that matter, in so much pain. There were times it was so bad, he was unable to even collect his thoughts. Victoria often wondered what these men were like prior to the war. Who were they, really? What were their hopes and dreams?

"Thank you for your kindness, Mrs. Prentiss. If not for your care, as well as the others here, I don't believe I would have lived as long as I have."

"Just have faith, Captain," Victoria said, hoping to comfort him. "You will get through this." She reached out and felt a fluttering pulse.

"No, Mrs. Prentiss. I know that I will not. The doctor confirmed it yesterday, I fear." He had tears in his eyes, and was struggling to say the words he needed to say. He gestured to his servant, a black boy around the age of twelve. Victoria had noticed the child faithfully watching over his master's bedside day and night. The captain looked with fondness at the young slave. "I ask you, please, Mrs. Prentiss, will you take care of Cicero for me? Watch over him until he can be sent back to our home? The home I will never return to…"

"Of course, Captain. He will be well cared for." Esther, though a very motherly woman, had never been blessed with children of her own. Victoria knew both Esther and Homer would treat Cicero as their own.

Victoria saw the chaplain approached quietly, and she knew the end was near for this brave soldier. She stood at the foot of the bed and silently prayed with the chaplain. A few moments later, Captain Cropwood shut his eyes for the last time.

Victoria could not hold back her tears. This kind gentleman, like so many others, would never walk or talk or smile again. It was small comfort that he had made his peace with God at the end. She tried not to think of what would happen next. His body would be wrapped in a blanket, then placed in an inferior box, and buried in a shallow grave.

Victoria sighed, then spoke to the boy, who was quite distraught. "Come, Cicero. I'll bring you to my Esther. We'll care for you."

The Streets of Vicksburg

"Good day, Miss Norton! How are you this fine morning?"

Tabetha smiled as she saw Sr. Stanislaus, one of the Sisters of Charity. She had become acquainted with many of the nuns over the course of the siege, not just from church, but also while working in the hospitals. The nun was accompanied by a black boy.

"Sister Stanislaus! What a pleasant surprise to see you. I'm just fine. I am going to the Green home to help with the patients."

"God bless you, Miss Norton. I stopped by there the other day. Some very difficult losses of late."

"Yes, I know. I was there yesterday and we lost yet another young man. He never seemed to recover from the effects of the chloroform he had been given. The poor boy was so pale and lethargic. He just grew weaker and weaker."

"I fear hundreds of soldiers have passed away in the same manner," Sr. Stanislaus replied. The two women continued to walk, followed by the boy. As they passed a convalescing corporal, he respectfully stood and nodded at the two women, allowing them more room to pass. They acknowledged the young man with a nod of their own. As they were about to continue their journey, a small shell from the Federal artillery landed at the feet of the corporal. Its fuse slowly burned.

"Good heavens!" Tabetha froze. The soldier did the same, but just for a moment. Almost without thought, he stepped back and rolled down the sloping side of the embankment to safety. Tabetha had just decided what to do when the black boy grabbed the shell and threw it as far as he could to the other side of the embankment. Tabetha was relieved to see the shell explode mid-air before it reached the ground.

"Henry!" Sr. Stanislaus exclaimed, gripping the black boy's arm in gratitude. "That caused me quite a fright, but what wonderful, quick thinking."

"Yes, Henry, you surely saved our lives," Tabetha added.

"Twasn't nothin', ma'am," The boy responded.

"It was more than either of us did," Tabetha said. "Or that corporal. Thank you so much, young man." Young Henry smiled at the complements, and Tabetha and Sr. Stanislaus continued walking together.

"Tabetha, something has been weighing on my mind, and I have wanted to address it for a while. I suspect that you are hiding something from us," Sr. Stanislaus commented. "You rarely speak of your past, though I know you are a Northerner from your accent."

"I am not the only Northerner in town," Tabetha said. "And I really never planned to end up here, but I can't say that I am sorry that I did. In fact, it has been a blessing in disguise."

"Many things are." The nun smiled. "God works in mysterious ways. I am confident that your being here now is part of His plan, and from what I have witnessed, you have already proven to be more than capable."

"You are so kind, Sister." Tabetha smiled. "Thank you for all your support."

"I want you to know that if you ever need someone to listen to your thoughts, you can always come to me. I know you live with a good family, but I wanted you to know that I am always willing to give you counsel."

"I appreciate that, Sister Stanislaus, more than you know," Tabetha said. She did appreciate the friendships she had formed with the Turners and Mary Green, but it would be nice to talk with Sr. Stanislaus, to have a spiritual advisor of sorts. "I will keep that in mind."

"Very good," The nun said. They came to the intersection where they would have to part ways, "I will continue to keep you and your family in my prayers."

"Thank you, as I will you." Tabetha smiled, then headed to the Turner cave.

Thursday, June 18, 1863
Green Home~Hospital

"You're quite distracted today," Tabetha said, standing next to Victoria. "What's on your mind?"

"I haven't seen or heard from Nathaniel since Sunday night. Since he is a courier, and doesn't actually belong to a regiment here he hasn't had to stay out at the entrenchments, but he wants to help however he can," Victoria replied. "It's frustrating to know he's so close, yet I can't see him. I just want to check on him, make sure he's all right." She shook her head. "Then there is my worry for Jason and Hannah and her family. What are their lives like out there? And what has become of Papa and Gregory?"

"I can't answer about your brother and the Wheelers or your father and Gregory. However, in regards to Nathaniel, why can't you go see him?" Tabetha asked. "Many of the women and girls go out to the lines when the officers cannot leave their posts."

"I have thought about that, but I wouldn't want...Nathaniel made it clear he didn't want me to risk my life..." she thought for a moment. "Would you risk it?"

Tabetha lowered her voice. "I enlisted in the Union army to atone for my role in my brother's death." She choked a bit on the last word. "Of course I would take that risk if I were in your position."

"All right, then. He made mention that he likes the men in the 21st Texas. I believe I know the general location of their regiment, I will start there." Her decision made, Victoria finished her work at the hospital, then began the walk towards the entrenchments.

Victoria realized she was being careless but she also felt a rush of excitement. Before she knew it, she was close to the lines. Though it was an overcast day, it was still hot and muggy. Her heart sank when she reached her destination. She could see the soldiers lying in the trenches, the heat causing them great agony. She knew the conditions in the hospitals were terrible, but they were so much worse out here. The soldiers appeared half-starved, shaking with fever and chills. The stench was overpowering.

Victoria looked around, hoping to find someone she could get some information from.

"Miss Victoria!" A voice called out and she was quickly pulled down as rifle fire exploded over her head. She looked at the young soldier who had pulled her to safety.

"Boone Reynolds!" She exclaimed pushing a strand of blonde hair behind her ear. "My goodness, I'm so...thank you ever so much!"

"Miss Victoria, what in the world are you doing here?"

"I...I came to get some information. I know that other young women come out here to visit soldiers, I suspect my own cousin, Brianne has been a part of that group a time or two."

Boone's slightly guilty look confirmed Victoria's suspicions.

"I know where your husband is." He helped her stand. "I can bring you to him, but I don't think he'll be too pleased to see you." As the young man led her away, they both remained crouched over, avoiding the barrage of cannon fire. Dirt sprayed at them and her heart raced. The noise was so much louder this close to the guns, it was almost deafening.

"Victoria!" When she heard Nathaniel's voice, she knew right away that he was furious. "What in the name of all that is holy are you doing here?"

"I haven't seen nor heard from you in so long." Her heart continued to pound. By the haggard look in his eyes, he was in need of a good night's sleep. "I had to see that you were all right."

Nathaniel sighed and pulled her behind a mound of dirt, an earthenwork, she had heard them called. He hugged her tightly.

"Don't get me wrong, I miss you terribly and I am always happy to see you, I just...you never should have put yourself in danger just to see me. I told you that before and I thought you understood. Not to mention I don't want you to see what these men are subjected to. It isn't proper."

"Nathaniel, it may be dangerous here, but I'm not all that much safer in town. Besides, I have seen patients in the hospital with similar symptoms as what's happening here." She glanced over to the trenches. "It is difficult to see suffering anywhere."

Another cannon shell crashed overhead. Nathaniel muttered a curse under his breath. "It may not seem like it but the earthenwork here is stable. We should be all right for the time being. Is everyone in town safe? Why are you here?"

"Yes, they are. Tabetha is actually the one who persuaded me to come out here. Well, not really, but when I asked her what she would do." Victoria replied.

"Of course she would come out here, she enlisted and fought in the Union army," Nathaniel said as quietly as he could. "She isn't the best person to be asking about taking risks."

"She just said that if she was married and her husband was in the trenches and she hadn't seen him for days, she would check on him. Besides, I believe Brianne is coming down here and visiting the soldiers, specifically Boone Reynolds. And besides, the last I heard, there have been three women killed and many more wounded in town, so no matter where I go, my life is in danger."

Nathaniel sighed, then sat down on the ground and leaned back against the dirt. He patted the ground next to him.

"Well, since you're here and it would be quite dangerous for you to move at the present moment, let's talk. However, the moment the firing has subsided enough to get you to safety, you are going."

She sat down next to him. "Yes, sir."

Nathaniel put his arm around her and pulled her close. "How is the family? I do miss everyone."

"We're trying to keep our spirits up," She continued. "Some people in town have even developed a warped sense of humor about the situation we find ourselves in." She gave a short laugh as he took her hand. "One man even wrote a bill of fare for a fictitious hotel. *The Hotel de Vicksburg*, he called it. Some of his dishes include mule tail, mule bacon, and mule beef jerked a la Mexicana..."

He laughed. "I suppose when times are rough, one finds many ways to lighten up the situation."

"The situation is deplorable. Almost every building has been hit or damaged in some way. Many of them are completely demolished now. Our city is a ruined pile of rubble." She wiped a tear from her eye. "I miss my town. I miss the peaceful river walks, our gaslight lanterns glowing in the evenings, the sound of the trains passing through..." She shook her head. "I'm sorry. It is so aggravating. The price of supplies are so high that I wonder if the merchants have a scrap of mercy in their souls."

"What do you need me to do to take your melancholy away? I know my army rations aren't much, but…"

"No, no, no. I am just expressing my frustration, Nathaniel. The authorities help however they can. Pemberton even gave us corn to grind at the government mills, but, as I said, we'll keep doing whatever we can. Many of the wealthy families are helping as well. Mr. Kaiser, one of the farmers trapped within the lines handed hundreds of bushels of corn over to the appropriate committee. He did, of course, save enough for his family."

"So your spirit is damaged, but not broken." Nathaniel gave her a kiss on her temple. "All of the citizens are doing heroic works. I am proud to call you my wife, even when I am upset at you for putting your life at risk. I can be proud and angry at the same time, you know."

"Oh, I know, Nathaniel." She gave him a smile. "Now, you tell me, what has been keeping you here in the trenches for four days?"

"Nine more transports of Federal troops arrived at the old Yankee landing. You may have seen the tents visible at Grant's place."

"I read about that, but didn't see them. Boone Reynolds pulled me to the ground before I could get a really good look at the other side."

"Both sides are digging tunnels, trying to gain the advantage over the other. A couple of Confederate couriers got through the lines and brought us 200,000 caps, which is quite an acquisition. I believe we are now expected to hold out for some time."

"Nathaniel, do you think we will be successful? Will Grant retreat, or are we just prolonging the inevitable?"

"I honestly don't know. The soldier in me says we'll be forced to surrender eventually. We don't have enough food to last more than a couple of weeks, and that is eating sparingly. It may not even last that long, as our vegetables have been disappearing, stolen by our own soldiers, before the crops are ready for harvest."

"That is so sad, yet no one can really blame them," Victoria said. "They're just hungry."

"But the soldiers steal at night, and can't tell whether the food is ripe or not, so they take vegetables that are still green. That doesn't do anyone any good."

"If they could just leave them to ripen…" Victoria groaned.

"Exactly," Nathaniel sighed. "As you said, however, they're hungry. An empty belly can make men do things they wouldn't do otherwise."

"So many businesses are struggling. Did you know that even the *Citizen* no longer has paper to put the news on, so to make adjustments, they are printing on old wallpaper?"

"I heard that," Nathaniel paused as the explosions ceased. "It must be the dinnertime ceasefire." He stood and helped her up. "This will be a perfect time for you to get back to town." He took her hand and started to lead her away.

"If I must." She followed him closely. "Is there anything you need?"

"I need you to stay in town. Stay alive. Stay healthy. Wait for me to come to you. I should be able to get back soon."

"All right, sir. Anything else?"

"We do need sandbags for our earthworks. Many of the men are tearing up their tents to make them. If you can gather extra heavy material and possibly find time to sew some..."

"Consider it done. As many as I can get." She smiled. "I will put the women in town to work."

"Thank you so much." He replied. "This is where I stop, you can go the rest of the way. I will see you soon." He kissed her forehead. "I love you."

"I love you too," She responded, trying not to cry, then went on her way.

Saturday, June 20, 1863
A Stream off the Yazoo River

"I don't think this is a good idea." Victoria said, stepping into the cool river water, clothed in her oldest, dirtiest dress.

"We both agree that we need to bathe," Tabetha replied. "I'll keep a lookout for you and you can look out for me. Besides, it's not even daybreak yet."

"The better friends we become, the more I wonder if you are a poor influence on me," Victoria said, only half-joking. Tabetha just smiled and checked her pistol, making sure that it was still primed and loaded, just in case they needed the protection.

"How is the water?" She asked.

"It feels quite good, actually. Refreshing." Victoria had never bathed fully clothed, but it was better than stripping all the way down to her chemise and taking the risk that someone might see her.

Just as Victoria was about to soap up her wet hair, a tremendous cannonading began. Victoria jumped and almost fell all the way into the water.

"Hurry! Let's get back to the cave!" Tabetha grabbed a towel and thrust it at Victoria, who stumbled out of the river.

As they hastened back to town, both women noticed the confusion and bustle among the citizens. Some women and children had been sleeping in their homes and were now hurrying back to their caves. It reminded Tabetha of rabbits scurrying back to their nests when a fox was approaching.

 217

Tabetha and Victoria finally reached the Prentiss cave, both breathing heavily.

"That might be some of the heaviest firing we've had this entire siege," Tabetha commented. "I'm certain some of those shots went clear across town. They're probably falling halfway across the river."

"I swear I heard some hit the water," Victoria said, drying her hair. She was glad she hadn't had soap in her hair when the bombardment started. "Some shots sounded as if they were hitting rock." She gave a short laugh. "I don't even want to know what I looked like, scurrying through town like a drowned rat."

"I don't think anyone even noticed. They all just wanted to get to safety like we did." Tabetha moved to the front of the cave. "I can hear that rifles have joined in the fight. There must be no place in town that is safe right now."

"Our situation seems to be getting bleaker and bleaker," Victoria quickly changed into a dry dress and laid the wet dress over a chair to dry. "I only hope that the generals on both sides can come to a peaceful resolution, and soon."

"With Grant's reputation, that is likely not going to happen," Tabetha replied.

<hr />

Tabetha left when the heavy bombardment stopped, leaving Victoria to cook a small meal for herself. She promised Tabetha that she would help at St. Francis Xavier after church the next day, and she would stay with the family for the evening. Her dinner was once again pea bread and mule meat. She could now eat mule meat without choking it down. It was actually more difficult for her to eat the pea bread. She had to remind herself to be thankful for what she did have. Her clothes were fitting rather loosely now, due to lack of food, and it pained Victoria to see how thin and gaunt her family members were becoming. It wasn't just the weight loss that was affecting the citizens. Ankles were swelling and cankers were forming, making everyone feel simply miserable. Adam, who wasn't healthy to begin with, really needed some fresh fruits and vegetables with a good night of uninterrupted sleep. If only they could get him what he needed.

"Tori," Nathaniel said solemnly from the doorway. She smiled, but her joy at seeing her husband was short-lived when she saw he was hunched over, clutching his thigh. Blood covered his leg and hands.

"Nathaniel!" She hurried to him and helped him to a chair. "What happened?"

"Cannon ball. Explosion. I caught some shrapnel in my leg," He sat down and stretched his leg out.

"Why didn't you go straight to a hospital?" She tore his pant leg open and held a lantern as close as she could to the wound to examine it.

"I have faith in you. I...I didn't want to go to the hospital, they'll just want to take the leg off. I can't allow that, not if I have a chance to save it." His face was pained and Victoria felt nauseous when she saw a piece of metal poking from Nathaniel's leg "I need you to pull that piece of metal out of my thigh. I already tried but can't get a good grip on it. It's not in the bone, so I know I will be okay if you can just pull it out. I haven't lost much blood yet."

"Nathaniel, you look at me." She took his face in her hands. "I love you dearly, but you are not thinking clearly right now. You need to have a surgeon look at this."

"Victoria. I need you to do this. I know you can do it. I have faith in you." Nathaniel was fighting to remain calm.

"No. We need to do what's best for you and that does not include me. What if I bring a doctor here? You won't have to go to the hospital." Victoria was stunned at Nathaniel's fear of seeing one of the surgeons. He gripped her hand and looked into her eyes.

"I cannot lose my leg. No amputations, Tori. You know the reasons why. Too many men die, just like your cousin, James. I strongly believe your cousin James might still be alive if they hadn't amputated his arm."

Victoria touched his cheek. "We don't know that for sure, Nathaniel. He may have died regardless. I have seen men die from infection too. As much as I hate to say it, if you need an amputation, I would rather they take your leg than to become a widow. I don't think you'll need one, though. Please. I know a doctor, a good one. He doesn't just perform amputations to make his life easier, he only does them when they are truly necessary. Please, let me ask him for help."

He shook his head, his teeth clenching his lips to keep from crying out.

"Nathaniel, I may be able to get this out and stitch you up, and I will care for you, but I would feel so much better if you would let me go and get Dr. Balfour. Please."

Nathaniel clenched his jaw and nodded. "If you're sure he's just not some sawbones."

"He's not. I promise. He's been a friend of the family since before I was even born." Victoria assured him, then helped Nathaniel to their makeshift bed.

"Get some rest. I'll be back as soon as I can." She gave him a quick kiss and hastened to the hospital.

Sunday, June 21, 1863
Prentiss Cave

Nathaniel lay sleeping on the thin mattress as Victoria tore up an old skirt and rolled up the strips for bandages. Dr. Balfour had been by already to check Nathaniel's condition. Yesterday, he had come as soon as Victoria found him. He removed the long piece of shrapnel and had found two smaller ones. He cleaned Nathaniel's wounds, then stitched them up loosely. He had told them both that he didn't believe an amputation was warranted at the time, and then reminded Victoria of the signs to watch for. He stressed to Nathaniel that if he took it easy for a few days, he would make a much quicker recovery and be back to full strength sooner.

"Victoria are you in here?" Mary Green stepped into the cave.

"Mary! Please come in." Victoria said in a hushed voice as she stood.

"I missed you at church today. Your mother explained what happened. How is Nathaniel?"

"He's doing as well as can be expected, sleeping now. He is exhausted not only from the injury, but for months of not sleeping well." Victoria pulled two chairs outside of the cave, and the two women sat. "How was church? Where are your children?"

"The children are with my mother and siblings. Reverend Lord always has a good sermon, but I have a couple of interesting stories to tell," Mary replied. "The most exciting news is that a most daring man by the name of Bob Lowder, passed the gunboats on the Yazoo River, dressed as a fisherman. He was able to bring dispatches to Pemberton and some other letters from the outside."

Victoria swatted at a mosquito. "Does anyone know the content of the dispatches?" She asked. Would Johnson finally come with reinforcements so the siege could be over? Would she finally be able to hear from Jason and the Wheelers? She desperately wanted information on how they were faring.

"No," Mary replied. "We hope to hear more soon." She sighed. "I stopped by to see Mrs. Dora Miller on my way over here. Her home was hit by a shell and caught fire, but thankfully only suffered minor damage."

"My goodness! She was still staying in the house and not a cave. Was anyone harmed?"

"No, thankfully no injuries, either," Mary said. "The real talk of the town is about the dwindling food supply. As I'm sure you know, most citizens have been reduced to eating mules and even rats."

Victoria shuddered. "Of course I know. We had mule for dinner yesterday. Fruits and vegetables cannot be found at any cost, molasses is $10 a gallon. Flour is $5 a pound. The other day, I saw a man who had bought a small bag of sugar, no doubt at an enormous price. He was walking along, eating the sugar right out of the bag with his hands."

"That's gluttonous," Mary said. "I have also heard that the planters of Warren County offered General Pemberton the contents of their smokehouses and barns. All Pemberton would have to do is furnish the horses and wagons, but Pemberton turned them down. Quite rudely, if the rumors are to be believed. So all that corn and sugar and bacon is probably feeding General Grant's men now. Oh, what that food would have meant to the town."

"How can that be true, Mary? Why would Pemberton decline food? How would the wagons even get through the lines? The couriers have a hard enough time getting into the city. They must sneak through the swamps and often times are unsuccessful. How would they expect to get wagons through?"

"I wondered the same thing," Mary admitted. "That's why Duff suggested that it was only a rumor. He feels someone is trying to create negative sentiment toward Pemberton."

"I suppose there are some who want to cause strife," Victoria sighed. She never understood how some people delighted in verbally putting others down. She couldn't grasp the concept. "Enough talk about the war. How are your beautiful children?"

"They are doing well for the most part," Mary said. "William continues to grow, though I do worry that he isn't growing enough. The nursemaid I found isn't producing well, with the lack of good food. Annie has become a bit jealous of her brother. I believe she has finally realized that he will be staying with us for good and she must share all the attention."

"I'm sure she'll adjust, the poor little dear. There are many changes going on in her young life right now."

"You are right, I know. She has just been a handful lately." Mary replied. "If only our lives could get back to normal."

Victoria heard a noise from the cave, turned and looked back at Nathaniel, who was now awake, sitting up and leaning against the dirt wall. He was carving a piece of wood she had found to keep him occupied while he convalesced. He had told her it was an amusement that many soldiers did while lying in the pits to pass away the time as the men couldn't change their positions often, stand erect or rise above the breastworks for almost certain death from a Yankee sharpshooter.

"Good morning, Nathaniel." Victoria looked into the cave. "Can I get you anything?"

"No, Ma'am. I'm doing just fine. Good day, Mrs. Green. It is good to see you up and about. I hope you don't mind that I overheard your conversation."

"No, no. It is good to see that you are making a good recovery," Mary replied, standing. "However, I really must be on my way."

Victoria stood as well. "I am glad you stopped by. Thank you for all the information. We should get together more often as we used to, perhaps for coffee, well," she laughed, "if we can manage to find some."

"Yes. The women of Vicksburg are becoming very accomplished at making sweet potato coffee." Mary smiled, then turned towards Nathaniel in the cave.

"Mrs. Green, thank you for the visit. My poor wife is becoming a hermit in her own cave because of my injury. She is refusing to leave me." He smiled.

"Of course. Believe me, I know how she must feel. I am glad your wound is healing under Victoria's meticulous care, and I hope you are completely healed soon."

"Thank you," He smiled.

"Stay safe," Victoria gave her friend a quick hug.

After Mary had gone, Nathaniel beckoned her over. She obliged him, and he handed her the item he had been carving. She sat down next to him.

"This is for you. When I am not with you, it can remind you of me."

Victoria looked at the carving, tears in her eyes. It was her favorite animal.

"I remembered you told me once how much you loved river otters. How, if it were possible, you would like to have one as a pet." He smiled.

"I did say that, and it is still true." Victoria wiped her eyes. "Thank you, Nathaniel. I will always cherish this." She turned and pulled him into an embrace, touched that he remembered her comment. "I love you."

"And I love you." He kissed her forehead. "Come, help me up. I'd like to assist you in making some mule ears fricasseed a la gotch."

"Oh, we don't have anything quite so fine a fare today, Mr. Prentiss." Victoria leaned against his shoulder. "Today, we'll be dining on cooked rats." She tried not to let the thought make her nauseous. It was either eat the rat meat or not eat at all. "I remember the days when cakes and pies and fresh berries could be bought on every street corner."

"Tomorrow, I'll go to the commissary and see if I can get some rations. I'm supposed to receive two biscuits, two rashers of bacon, a few peas and a spoonful of rice each day, if they have any, that is. Maybe I'll get lucky and find some beef."

Victoria groaned. "What I wouldn't do for roast beef or prime rib. Even a nice, fat ham or fried chicken." Her mouth watered at the thought.

"Did you have to mention such fine delicacies?" Nathaniel groaned as well. "I would be in Seventh Heaven if I could take my wife out to a nice Vicksburg eating establishment for the elegant dinner she deserves." He sighed. "Unfortunately, that won't be in the near future. Did you know all the eating establishments are closed?"

"I did know that. A siege is not good for a city's economy." Victoria pulled away from Nathaniel and went to the outdoor table. She began preparations for the meal.

"No, they are not." He smiled and held out his hand. "Come back, Victoria. I need my wife's help. I am feeling the need for some fresh air. I cannot sit in this cave forever."

"All right." She went to him and helped him stand, then assisted him to the cave entrance and into the seat that Mary had occupied. "But I must insist that you sit here. You can best help me by keeping me company."

Tuesday, June 23, 1863
Green House Hospital

Tabetha wiped her face with an apron the moment she reached the hospital. It was raining again, but she needed to volunteer at the hospital. For thirty-seven days, the town of Vicksburg had been surrounded. The conditions of their situation had continued to deteriorate. At least the rain would allow fresh water to be collected in the cisterns.

"Miss Norton. How are you this dreary morning?" Chaplain Foster approached her.

"I am doing quite well, Chaplain. Is there anything in particular I should know about today?"

"The *Citizen* has reported that an uninjured Yankee was captured yesterday morning. He was immediately placed in jail. He is apparently acting crazy and refuses to say anything about himself. Claims the Yankees forced him into the army in the first place. Many believe he should be hung as a spy."

"My goodness, that seems harsh." Tabetha was nervous, as she often was when talk of spies came up. "Was he dressed as a civilian or was he in uniform? Where was he caught? Do you believe he should be hung?"

"Woah, woah, so many questions. I don't know all the details," the chaplain admitted. "And no, I don't believe he should be killed. There are still many details of his story that must be corroborated."

"Of course," Tabetha agreed. "Well, where do you need my help today?"

"We have a young man from Louisiana who has a dreadful wound in his shoulder. I don't wish to go into much detail, but nearly all the flesh from his shoulder down to the middle of his back has been removed."

"Good heavens!" Tabetha said. "How can I be of assistance?"

"The wife of the soldier's superior officer is in town. She has become a particular friend to the boy, and will be attending him. However, I'm sure it would be a great comfort if you would check on them every hour or so. Make sure she doesn't need anything and allow her some free time."

"Of course. Just show me where I can find them."

The chaplain led her to the bedside, and she met the young man and the captain's wife. They both seemed pleasant, but the soldier was in obvious distress. Tabetha knew she would do whatever she could to help the young man.

After exchanging some pleasantries, Tabetha began to move from patient to patient, helping the men in any way they needed. She gathered information as she went. It sounded as though the battle was heating up along the lines, if that were possible. One patient told her that the Yankees were so close that the Confederates could throw a Ketchum hand grenade over to the enemy trenches and the Yankees could throw it back before it even exploded. Tabetha sighed. The stormy, dark skies outside seemed a perfect complement to the dark feeling that permeated the town. She wanted this siege to end for the sake of all the people, even though it meant she would have to face her past.

Victoria stood at the entrance of the cave next to a panting Nathaniel, both watching Tex Reynolds as he packed the earth around the cave firmly and deepened the drainage ditch to the side of the cave. They had awoken that morning to rain that was causing the ground around them to flood, and was encroaching into the cave. Nathaniel had been trying to make the repairs, quite unsuccessfully due to his injury, when Tex ran by. The soldier had immediately stopped to assist his comrade and Nathaniel was doing his best, but needed a break. Victoria felt a cool mist on her face and listened to the heavy splashing of rain.

"I need to get back out there." Nathaniel muttered, and pounded a fist against his uninjured thigh in frustration. He leaned on her for support.

"Hush, now." She took his fist and curled her hand around his. "If you go back out there in your condition, you risk the chance of slipping and injuring yourself again, perhaps even worse than before and listen to you. You are so weak, you can't even catch your breath."

He sighed heavily and watched as Tex finished up and walked toward the cave. Suddenly, the earth above Victoria and Nathaniel gave way and a spout of muddy water burst through and began cascading over their feet and onto their blankets and pillows.

"Good Heavens!" Victoria sprang into action and picked up the blankets and pillows from the bed, throwing them on the furniture. Water flowed into the cave as Tex hastened outside to see what he could do to stop the deluge. Nathaniel started to dig a trench for the water to flow out of the cave while Victoria continued to move about piling trunks and furniture on top of each other and hanging the now wet blankets on whatever she could find, doing her best to save the belongings in their temporary home.

"I think the ground above the cave has stabilized. It shouldn't fall anymore," Tex said, coming into the cave. Victoria smiled at him, then looked around. The floor of the cave had already turned to mud. "I was able to put the fly tent back up too. It's not the best, but it can be adjusted later."

Nathaniel limped outside to see the damage, then sighed and came back in, shaking his head.

"The water overflowed the ditch, made a new channel and washed away the little terrace that we had." He turned to Tex. "You're right, everything looks stable now and the water is flowing from the hill as it should. I can't tell you how lucky we are that you were passing by. I don't know what we would have done without you."

"Think nothing of it." Tex shook out his hat and his grey jacket.

Victoria sat to remove her shoes. She hated the feeling of wet stockings.

"Are you sure you want to take off those shoes?" Nathaniel asked. "As endearing as you are in your bare feet, this rain may bring in snakes." Water dripped from his hat and coat, to the ground, making puddles on the floor.

Victoria jumped and quickly laced her boots back up. "What else is damaged out there? I do hope nothing happened to Mama's cave."

"There's a good size trench in front of their entrance and your family's cave is higher up the hill, so I doubt it is damaged. I built this one too fast, I'd wager. Didn't take the time to do it right." Nathaniel took his hat off his head and shook the water from both the hat and his hair.

"You must let us treat you to a late breakfast, Mr. Reynolds. We don't have much, but Nathaniel was able to bring some bacon from the commissary…"

"I thank you for the invitation, Mrs. Prentiss, but I have a previous engagement that I was heading to."

"My goodness, we didn't make you too late, did we?" Victoria asked. "Are you sure you want to go out in the rain again?"

"No, you didn't make me late, ma'am, it will be alright. My hosts will understand. I'll share a meal with you another time, if the invitation still stands."

"Of course it does. Thank you again, Tex." Nathaniel shook the man's hand and clapped him on the back. Mr. Reynolds tipped his hat to Victoria and went out into the rain again.

Nathaniel looked at the sky. "I think the storm is coming to an end."

He hobbled over to the spade he had left near the entrance and began to slowly and awkwardly dig a flat surface under the fly tent.

"Nathaniel, what are you doing?" She sloshed through the muddy water to the entrance of the cave and placed her hands on the spade, stopping his movements. "You'll hurt yourself again."

"I'm fixing the entrance so I can build you a fire so we can have a late breakfast of pea meal biscuits and that bacon."

"Put the spade down, I'll do it."

"I can do it, Victoria." His voice was slightly testy. She took a breath. She didn't want to anger him or make him feel less of a man, but she also didn't want him to overexert himself.

"What if you let me do this while you find some dry wood? Then, you can grab those camp kettles and fill them with this rainwater. Once I get this finished, we can start a fire and heat the water and have some of that sweet potato coffee you like so much."

"All right." He flashed her a grin. "However, we both know you are the one who really enjoys that sweet potato coffee."

"Don't be ridiculous, I cannot wait until the day I can actually drink real tea again," Victoria threw her weight behind the spade and began to make the ground level again, being careful not to disrupt any of the newly dug ditches. "Sometimes I wonder how much longer we can last."

"I'm afraid that we'll soon be using wood from the damaged houses and fences for firewood," Nathaniel said.

"We already are," Victoria told him. He shook his head. Working together, they soon had a fire blazing next to the cave entrance and began cooking a decent meal together.

"I hope no one else has had the trouble we had in this deluge," Victoria said. "We have a lot of damage out here, but not everyone is as good a cave builder as you are." She gave him a smile. "Even if you say it is flawed, and with the rain letting up, I can see that Mama's cave is undamaged."

"I will check on them after we eat if you'd like. I assure you, my leg is feeling just fine."

"You really should rest for a while first." Victoria frowned. "I can clean up, then I'll go. Perhaps I could check on the Greens as well. To be honest, I don't feel secure in the cave right now." She looked behind her at the mess.

"Do you ever truly feel a sense of security in the cave?" Nathaniel asked with a curious smile.

"No, I don't," Victoria said. "Which is why I would like to be the one who checks on Mama."

"All right. Once the rain stops, I'll let you head out and I'll see what I can do here. It should take the Yankees a while to dry out as well, so they won't start bombarding us for a while."

"Thank you," Victoria said, glad that she married such an reasonable man.

⤳⤳

After checking in with her family and assisting with some minor clean-up, Victoria went to check on Mary.

"Is everyone alright in here?" Victoria called out, knocking on the wood that surrounded the cave's door frame.

"Yes, Victoria, come in." Mary placed William in the cradle and turned to her friend. "Did you survive the downpour we had?"

"Barely. We suffered some damage to the outer part of the cave and the floor is a muddy mess, but I saw others had it much worse on my walk over. Mother's cave is fine, luckily."

"Oh, goodness. I hope there were no injuries," Mary stated.

"Not that I've heard, no. Not yet, at least," Victoria said. "I can see how the rain caused cave-ins all around town. The mortar shells leave deep gorges in the earth that collapsed with the rain water. The other day, I heard that a mass of dirt fell and knocked a young woman to the ground. She would have been crushed and killed, but an artilleryman broke the force of the falling earth by throwing himself at the dirt and pushing it away with his shoulder."

"My Heavens. She was lucky he was there." Mary said.

"Blessed is more like it. He must have been her guardian angel." Victoria sighed. "Also, the other day, the entrance to a cave collapsed and separated those who were inside the cave from those who were outside. They were able to excavate it and no one was injured." She shook her head. "And everyone said my fear of living underground was irrational."

"Oh, Victoria, I never thought it was irrational for you to feel that way." Mary assured her.

"Yes, well, the final tragic story, the one I heard on my way over here is the worst. A mother was watching her three-year-old son play when a sudden bombardment started. As she ran to her son to bring him to safety, her hand and arm were hit by shrapnel and shattered. The boy was uninjured, but who knows what will happen to the poor mother."

"Lord, have mercy on us. How many women and children must be harmed before this is all over? It is bad enough that our soldiers are dying by the hundreds and thousands." Mary shook her head.

"It saddens me. Even one is too many," Victoria replied. "At first, I worried about my family and friends being killed, but now, I realize that lives can be severely altered by simply being injured." She turned and smiled when Nathaniel came into the cave. He tipped his cap towards Mary.

"Good day, Mrs. Green. I am glad to see all is well here. Tori, I hate to rush you, but it turns out we will be having some visitors this evening."

"Guests? In our cave? Our flooded, muddy cave?" Victoria was a bit miffed with her husband. "Who, pray tell will these guests be? And why did you walk all the way over here on that injured leg? You are supposed to be resting it. It will never heal if you don't give it a chance."

"Don't nag me." He smiled good-naturedly. "Some men from an Arkansas brigade. I know them from delivering messages. We became friends, I think you'll like them. I also invited your family." He turned to Mary. "May I extend the invitation to you and Mr. Green? We would love to have you."

"Thank you, Nathaniel. I will speak with Duff, but I do believe we'll stay in with the children tonight."

"All right, but the invitation stands."

Nathaniel and Victoria said their goodbyes, and he escorted Victoria slowly back to their cave.

Hours later, Victoria was glad that Nathaniel had invited the soldiers to spend the evening with them. Rachel, Mary Grace, Tabetha, Brianne and Kendall had also joined the festivities. Esther and Dinah were watching the children

"Prentiss!" One of the men called out. "Your walls are looking a little bare here."

"What do you expect me to have up there, Lieutenant Lassiter? Priceless heirloom paintings?" Nathaniel smiled. It was good to see Nathaniel relaxed with his comrades.

"We have some experience with decorating, if you'd like to call it that." The friendly man smiled and looked at Kendall. "Young Miss Larson, will you do us the honors?"

"What would you have me do, sir?" Kendall asked. The men had her sit in a chair next to one of the walls. They used a candle to cast her shadow on the wall. Then, one of the men took his pocketknife and carved her silhouette into the dirt.

"Very nice!" Victoria said with a smile.

"Will you be next, Miss Brianne?" Another soldier asked.

"Of course, good sir." She happily agreed, then smiled and took a seat. Another soldier, a Lieutenant John Sullivant, turned to Victoria.

"Mrs. Prentiss, I notice you have a dearth of shelf space." He smiled. "I could remedy that quite easily."

"You really should, Mrs. Prentiss." Yet another man said. Victoria believed he had been introduced as Lieutenant John Underwood. "Sullivant here is quite talented. He can fashion some very artistic niches by cutting into the dirt wall."

"All right, then," Victoria said. "It would be nice to have a place to set my candles and some books." As Lieutenant Sullivant began working,

Victoria was encouraged to sit for her own silhouette. After all of the women had posed, the soldiers carved their own silhouettes into the walls.

"I wish I had brought the children," Mary Grace said. "They would have enjoyed the evening." Esther and Dinah were caring for the Corbel children.

"They would have. Oh, I do miss them dearly," Victoria said. "But Mary Grace, you needed this time for yourself. You have been giving your undivided attention to them ever since you shut down the store."

"I know," Mary Grace agreed. "But I do worry about them ever so much."

"I believe that's called being a mother." Victoria smiled.

"All right, ladies, it is time for some music! Let's head outside." One of the men, GW Palmer, pulled out a fiddle and they headed to the street. Nathaniel had introduced Palmer as the chief musician. Another soldier pulled out a harmonica. The women all smiled as the men began playing some favorites. First, *Then Let the Old Folks Scold if They Will*. After that, they played *Dixie*, and then, *The Bonnie Blue Flag*. Nathaniel quietly spoke to the musicians. They smiled and nodded, then began playing *Believe Me If All These Endearing Young Charms*.

Nathaniel approached Victoria and offered his hand. "We've yet to have a dance as man and wife." She took his hand and he led her to the middle of the streets and pulled her into his arms. Victoria smiled and allowed him to lead her in a waltz. One of the officers, a young Captain Trezevant had a beautiful tenor voice, and sang as they danced to the love song.

> *"Believe me, if all those endearing young charms,*
> *Which I gaze on so fondly today,*
> *Were to change by tomorrow, and fleet in my arms,*
> *Like fairy-gifts fading away,*
> *Thou wouldst still be adored, as this moment thou art,*
> *Let thy loveliness fade as it will,*
> *And around the dear ruin each wish of my heart*
> *Would entwine itself verdantly still."*

After a few more verses, the song ended and Victoria and Nathaniel thanked the musicians.

"It is our pleasure," Mr. Palmer replied. "Now, let's have some festive dancing!"

"Mrs. Prentiss, do you have anything that could take the place of a rose?" Lieutenant Lassiter asked.

Victoria looked around and grabbed a small handful of kindling sticks from the wood pile and tied them together with a ribbon from her hair, then everyone lined up for the dance. The soldiers who were not playing an instrument stood, almost shoulder to shoulder, facing the women, who also stood shoulder to shoulder. At the head of the lines, Victoria stood between Captain Trezevant and Nathaniel. The musicians began playing *The Girl I Left Behind Me*. Everyone began clapping along to the music.

The rules of the Rose Dance were simple: Victoria held the bundle of sticks, and had the option of choosing one of the men standing next to her with whom she preferred to dance. She glanced at Nathaniel, gave him a wink, and then handed him the bundle. She then turned to the young captain, took his hands, and they sashayed down the middle of the two lines. Brianne and Kendall, the next two women in line, came and stood on either side of Nathaniel. He looked back and forth between the two, gave an apologetic nod to Brianne as he handed her the bundle and then danced with Kendall. Next, two young soldiers took their positions on either side of Brianne, and it was her turn to choose. The dance continued until the song ended.

"Gentlemen, ladies, I am so glad you could all spend the evening with us," Nathaniel said, pulling Victoria to his side. I find my injury has taken much of my energy, if I want to get back to my duties anytime soon, I should rest it, but please continue with the festivities."

"Of course, Prentiss," Lassiter agreed. "Here, let me get you a chair."

The music continued and the evening was a great success, despite the periodic shelling.

All too soon, the men of the Arkansas brigade had to take their leave.

"Take care of yourself, Nathaniel. I hope you didn't overdo it," Mary Grace said as she, Tabetha, Rachel, Kendall and Brianne prepared to leave. "Make sure you visit us before you head back to the lines." She hugged both Nathaniel and Victoria. Finally, Victoria and Nathaniel were left alone.

"Tonight was simply delightful," Victoria said. "I am so glad you invited the men."

"I'm glad you enjoyed it. I knew you would like them." He sighed. "I only hope they all survive."

"It must be difficult to make friends while in the army, especially in the trenches," Victoria commented. "Never knowing when a friend may be injured or even killed."

"That is the truth," he replied, dropping a kiss on her head. "I can't believe Pemberton will allow this siege to go on much longer and when that happens, well, I don't know what will happen to any of us, Tori."

"We will persevere, darling. We will persevere."

Thursday, June 25, 1863
Green House~Hospital

Tabetha sat down on a spare chair outside the house, needing a moment to rest. She hadn't slept or eaten well in over a month, and she could feel the toll it was taking on her. Even the lightest work brought on exhaustion. Her ankles were starting to swell and her gums were starting to bleed. Tabetha had spoken to one of the doctors about it and he had told her that those were the first sign of scurvy, a disease that was brought on by malnutrition. If they didn't start eating better meals with fruits and vegetables, the people would not survive.

"Tabetha!" Victoria waved and approached her friend. "Are you feeling well?"

"I'm all right, just tired." Tabetha answered, wiping her face with the edge of her apron.

"Yes, I heard you've been staying busier than usual. Mother told me about your evening stroll last night."

Tabetha blushed. Last night, a young lieutenant from Arkansas who had been at the Prentiss cave the night of the gathering had stopped by asking to take her on a stroll. It had been a beautiful evening, and he had been very pleasant company.

"He was very kind and polite," Tabetha admitted. "However, I...well, it was difficult, having to be constantly on my guard, afraid that I might say something suggestive about my past. As a matter of fact, it was downright difficult."

"I can see how that would cause an issue," Victoria said. "It's imperative we keep your past a secret. I don't think you can be arrested by the Union army for impersonating a man, but I would be willing to bet that you would be put in a Confederate prison for suspicions of being a Federal spy. We know you're not, of course, we trust you implicitly, but life could get very difficult for you if your true identity were ever discovered, and in reality, for our whole family."

"I know," Tabetha said. "I had no idea when I joined the Cavalry that the repercussions would extend so far. In my haste to seek repentance, I didn't think much about the repercussions at all."

"Sometimes we all make rash decisions. Once this war is over, you won't have to worry about your secret so much."

"I hope you're right," Tabetha said. "Has Nathaniel brought you any new information?"

"The *Daily Citizen* was published on wallpaper again. I just think that is so silly. There is more news of General Johnston finally arriving from Nashville with reinforcements to help lift the siege, but I don't believe that any more. They are probably just rumors to give us hope."

"As they have been before," Tabetha said.

"I know. Tabetha, is hope really such a bad thing?" Victoria shook her head. "There have been more tragedies as well. The news reported that a little black girl had her arm blown off by a shell, and young Mrs. Porter had her thigh bone crushed by falling debris, and sadly, Miss Holly was killed in the suburbs of Vicksburg."

"It is tragic to hear of the injuries and death sustained by civilians," Tabetha said. "It is unfathomable for war to be fought in this manner."

"I agree with you. In the blink of an eye, one can become crippled. That would certainly altar one's life, and some may even consider being crippled being worse than death."

"Some may feel that way," Tabetha said. "I suppose in death, there is no more pain. After witnessing all I have seen, I don't know how the wounded can bear the pain."

"Do you think it a bad omen that every night, I lay down expecting death, and every morning, I rise with the same expectation?"

"I don't think so," Tabetha said. "What I mean is, death really could come for any of us at any time, siege or not. Are these thoughts consuming you overmuch?"

"No, not really." Victoria looked toward the river. "Are you ever scared of death, Tabetha?"

"I'm not afraid of dying. I am more afraid of losing my loved ones. I am far from perfect, but I know that eternal life in Heaven awaits me. Maybe you are comfortable in your beliefs of everlasting life, so you have these thoughts."

"I do look at death that way," Victoria said. "Do you ever question Heaven or God?"

"No. My faith is just a part of my life," Tabetha said. "Do you have doubts, Victoria?"

"You may be the only person I will ever admit this to, but sometimes. Especially lately, I don't feel as though God really cares. I mean, look around you, Tabetha. Why would a loving God allow any of this to happen? The suffering, the hunger, all of this death and destruction." Victoria hated that she felt this way, but she couldn't help it. The things she had witnessed…

"Remember God gives us free will. We're the ones choosing to make war with each other." Tabetha always had a difficult time explaining her faith to others.

"I know. I know all that, really I do, it's just hard to accept." Victoria sighed, then stood. "Oh, botheration, we should get back to work. The men need our help and comfort."

"I need to check on my young soldier and his captain's wife. She has been staying with him nonstop. Chaplain Foster asked me to watch over both of them."

"You will have him better in no time," Victoria said.

The two women went their separate ways once inside the hospital, going to work to ease the suffering.

Monday, June 26, 1863
Green Cave

"This is most devastating! Six more women were wounded last week." Mary said to Tabetha and Victoria. "The wounds are mostly from fragments of shells and splinters, although our dear Miss Rawlings was stuck with a minie ball. I believe they're all recovering well. "

"It's frustrating," Victoria replied. "I heard at the hospital today that Pemberton will not surrender this city so long as there is a mule or dog left."

"Some families are trying to leave." Tabetha remarked. "I spoke briefly with Mrs. Dora Miller on my way here. She and her husband thought they might be permitted to get through the lines with a passport they've had for some time. She was in the tent of one of our generals and while there, she heard a conversation between the Union and Confederacy under a flag of truce. They said General Grant will not allow any humans to pass through, and the Yankee flag of truce officer insinuated that the Yankees are confident that Vicksburg will surrender by the end of the week."

"Well, I won't believe that for an instant," Victoria said. "Our men on the lines will fight to the death, as they have been. In fact, the men are digging a countermine. Nathaniel said the laborers from both sides are so near each other they can hear each other's pick-axes, and at times, even the voices of the enemy."

"How nerve-wrecking that must be for the soldiers," Mary said. "To be that close to your enemy but unable to attack."

"And to be digging in a mine." Victoria shuddered, still hating the thought of being trapped underground.

"The situation is getting dire." Mary sighed. "We have so little food and the food we have is unpalatable. We can't afford to buy more as it is so expensive. I fear for little William's life."

Tabetha chuckled. "I'm sorry, Mary, not to trivialize your concerns for William, but I just remembered something interesting in regards to food. I was talking with a young soldier from the 1st Missouri. Their troop adopted a camel, which I now understand is one of the few remaining in the south. Apparently, President Polk had an experimental importation of the animal years back and there are some still around these parts. Unfortunately, a Federal sharpshooter killed the camel, but the Missourians were treated to camel steaks."

"I had forgotten there were still camels in the area," Victoria commented. "Oh, I hate to leave, but I should be going. Nathaniel told me he would be back to eat with me tonight, and though all I have is pea meal and rat meat, I want it to be ready when he returns."

Mary shook her head. "I still have yet to meet anyone who has successfully made pea meal bread."

"I didn't say I could make the food taste like a fancy French meal," Victoria laughed.

"I must leave as well," Tabetha said. "I wish you a wonderful evening. Mary, Victoria, of you don't mind the company, I will walk with you."

Mary's two friends hadn't been gone long when Duff came into the cave.

"Good evening, my dear," he said. "How was your day?"

"You just missed Victoria and Tabetha. I had a nice visit," Mary told him, "and Martha took Annie to visit Mother. They should be back soon. How is our home faring?"

"Still standing." He sat at the table and rubbed his temples.

"Is there something wrong, dear?" Mary sat next to him and placed a comforting hand on his arm.

"The destruction only continues." He shook his head. "Our soldiers had to pull back their cannon yesterday, because the Yankees tried digging underneath the lines to blow them up from underneath. Thankfully, it didn't work, but the town is in shambles and feels like one vast hospital. I would estimate that 6,000 men are in our makeshift hospitals, and what's even more distressing is that I heard not one-half of the men in the trenches are fit for duty. Unless Grant lifts this siege and gives up, or we somehow miraculously get supplies, we're going to have to surrender. As much as I hate to admit this, I would guess that the end is near."

"That means the Union will take control of our town." Mary said. "What will we do then?"

"We will do whatever it takes to care for our family," He replied. She reached up and touched his cheek.

"I know we will get through this together, Duff. The children and I have faith in you."

Duff leaned over and gave her a brief kiss. "At the risk of the neighbors having more to despise about us, we will continue to do what we must to survive."

Sunday, June 28, 1863
St. Paul's Catholic Church

"Thank you so much for inviting me to Mass." Lieutenant Roger Davidson from Arkansas smiled at Tabetha as he escorted her out of the building. "I do appreciate the traditional aspect of the Catholic Mass."

"I am glad you were able to attend," She answered. They had just walked down the steps when the enemy opened fire on the city with Parrot guns. Shells screamed wildly through the streets, some exploding against the church wall and some even breaking through the wall and entering the church. Men, women and children ran quickly to seek shelter.

"Blasted Yankees! How can they fire so ruthlessly at civilians who are just worshipping the Lord? Barbarians!" Lieutenant Davidson yelled, pulling Tabetha to a more secure place behind an overturned wagon. Tabetha looked around and saw a young woman fall to the ground as she tried to get to safety. A piece of rock had hit her leg. A man assisted her to the side of the church. Tabetha scrambled over to the couple.

"I saw you fall, ma'am, are you alright?" Tabetha looked at the leg. It was bleeding profusely. Tabetha pulled at her underskirt and tore a strip of cloth from it. She quickly tied the bandage around her leg. "This should help for now, but you should get to a hospital as soon as you can." She told the woman.

"Thank you so much, Miss." The woman said, tears streaming from her eyes.

The bombardment continued, and Tabetha moved from the injured woman to another wounded civilian. She continued to help the injured people however she could. Tabetha glanced back at Lieutenant Davidson, who was also helping those who had been hurt. She was on her way back to him when a shell exploded right behind him. He was knocked forward and fell hard to the ground. She ran to assist him.

"Lieutenant!" His back was blood-soaked already. She used all of her strength to roll him over. He didn't appear to be breathing. She placed her ear to his chest. She wasn't able to hear a heartbeat. She wiped at the tear in her eyes as she held his shoulders on her lap. "Oh, Lieutenant Davidson." She cried softly.

"Miss Norton!"

Tabetha looked up through blurry eyes to see Nathaniel rushing to her side.

"Are you alright? You have blood all over you. The whole city feels like its exploding." He fell to his knees beside her, immediately recognizing the young man. "Lieutenant Davidson. Is he…"

"He's not breathing, Nathaniel. A shell exploded right behind him. He was too busy helping others to see it coming. No one could have survived that kind of blow."

Nathaniel sighed and looked around. The bombardment had lessened slightly and people were starting to rush back to their homes.

"I'll take care of him, Miss Norton. You get back home. I promise, Lieutenant Davidson will be well tended to. I'll make sure he's buried with the respect he deserves."

"Thank you, Nathaniel," she whispered, slowly standing and wiping her blood-stained hands on her dress. She gave the Lieutenant one last look and turned as more tears welled up in her eyes.

⌒〜〜⌒

Victoria sat at Mary Green's table, drinking sweet potato tea and cuddling baby William.

"I hope Tabetha is all right. She went to St. Paul's this morning and there was some heavy bombing in that vicinity when we left church. I wanted to walk over there to see if she was all right or if there was anything I could do, but Nathaniel insisted I come here right away, and he would go find her and bring her home."

"Husbands can be overprotective," Mary said. "But it just shows they care."

"Indeed," Victoria replied.

"I haven't seen Brianne and Kendall in a while." Mary commented. "Are they well?"

"They're well, although Brianne has been a bit sullen lately. I'm not sure what happened, but she's not talking and Kendall insinuated that Brianne's mood has to do with a young man."

"I see." Mary smiled, remembering what it was like to be Brianne's age. "And Mary Grace and the children?"

"I fear for Adam. He is getting weaker and weaker," Victoria said softly. She didn't want to think about his condition too much. "Gabriel is just bored all the time, and Hope should be growing like a weed, but she's not getting the food she needs." She shook her head. "Mary Grace is beside herself with worry, as you must be with your children."

"Yes, I am. Annie is the same as your niece and nephew. Bored and not getting the food she needs," Mary replied.

"I tried to help Esther with her shopping yesterday, but we weren't even able to buy anything," Victoria said. "Fifty cents a pound for mule meat now. Flour was $600 a barrel, biscuits $8 a dozen, small pies are $4 apiece and the baked goods, I don't even know what they are using to make them."

"Sweet potato coffee like this is even a commodity," Mary said.

"The sad thing is, it can only get worse. Nathaniel brings home his rations, but even those have become sparse. Do you want to hear something asinine, Mary? Nathaniel told me that most of the army mules were driven out of the city to save green pasture for the army horses, like

⌒ 236 〜⌒

his. Now isn't that ridiculous? We send our mules out of the city to save them from dying, yet the people of the city are dying because the mules were sent out. The Yankees are probably feasting on our mules as we speak."

"You're right. That's meat we could have used." Mary sighed. "Did you know that Major Reed's wife had her arm blown off by a piece of shell and two other ladies were struck by shrapnel and severely wounded? They're not expected to live." A tear ran down her cheek and she brushed it away. "Duff said that the Federals placed sharpshooters on the opposite bank of the river to annoy our soldiers and the civilians as they go to the river's edge to fill their casks with water. We can't possibly hold out much longer."

Victoria sighed. "Six weeks, six very long weeks, we have been under siege. We still hear nothing definite from Johnston. No one even knows where he is. Our own government won't send us any help. I feel Vicksburg will fall because our government simply won't help us. Will all of the deaths and the blood spilled here be in vain? Will all our suffering be for naught? Oh, Mary, how much more of this can we take?"

"Come now, Victoria, we will triumph, we can withstand anything."

"Yes, yes. You always remind me of that." Victoria gave her friend a small smile. "You always put me in my place."

"I thought I was the one who put you in your place," Nathaniel said, approaching the two women.

"Nathaniel! You've made it back safely. Did you find Tabetha? Where is she, Nathaniel?"

"She should be back at the cave. I don't wish to rush you, I just wanted to let you know that she is safe." His hand brushed her arm. "But she may need some comforting. There was indeed heavy shelling near the church, and Lieutenant Davidson died in her arms today. She looked quite shaken."

"Oh, how tragic! Thank you for letting me know. We were just finishing up our conversation anyways." Victoria stood, then turned to Mary. "I must be off, Mary. Thank you for the tea."

"Of course, Victoria. Keep me updated on Tabetha's condition. The poor child has been through so much." Mary stood as well to see the couple off.

It didn't take long for Nathaniel and Victoria to reach their cave. They had stopped to see Tabetha, but the young woman had been napping after her ordeal.

"How long can you stay before leaving again?" Victoria asked. She mixed up some pea meal and water while Nathaniel stoked the fire.

"Until tomorrow," he replied, then tossed his haversack on the table. A scrap of paper fluttered down from the pack. Victoria put the pea meal bread in the Dutch oven, then picked up the paper.

"What's this?" She asked, looking it over. *"To our friends in Vicksburg: Cave in, boys, and save your lives, which are considered of no value by your officers. There is no hope of relief for you...."* She looked at Nathaniel. "Is this true?"

"No. I brought it home to burn." He took it from her and tossed it in the flames. "The Yankees are trying to break our spirits. Those notes are circulating through the lines. It's propaganda. I don't know how the Yankees got it inside the lines to our troops, but they did."

"Nathaniel, are the troops giving up? How bad is the morale?" She was worried about his answer.

"I heard someone slipped an anonymous plea into Pemberton's headquarters. It basically said that, unless the men don't get more rations soon, they won't just lie down and perish, they will retaliate. It also said that hunger may compel the men to do almost anything. Quite threatening if you ask me. I think the letter was written by a Union sympathizer in the city."

"My goodness. Any ideas who wrote it?"

"No, but somehow the Yankees got these pamphlets across the lines and other notices as well. Like I said, it wouldn't surprise me if the Yanks did it so they can put the fear of mutiny in Pemberton's mind."

Just as they were finishing their dinner, the couple heard several townspeople cry out in shock and fear. Nathaniel and Victoria looked out, and frowned at what looked like a ball filled with air floating above their heads.

"What on earth..." Victoria said, confusion apparent on her face.

"They're hydrogen balloons." Nathaniel shook his head. "Remember, I told you about them in a letter. Well, perhaps you never received it. I first heard of them back in '61. The Yankees use them for spying. Can you see that basket underneath?" Victoria nodded. "There is usually a soldier standing in there to observe. They can see quite a bit from their vantage point. If we try and shoot at the balloon, it's difficult to hit them from the ground, but it's easy for soldiers in the balloon to shoot at us."

"They are amazing." Victoria said. "That is quite ingenious. Duff actually mentioned them some time ago, but it is much more impressive to see them in action."

"Yes, when we see them go up, we have learned how to cloak our positions with camouflage and blackouts. We can build fewer fires so they underestimate our strength and by painting fake wooden cannons black so they think we have more artillery."

"Ahh, so you were clever right back," Victoria replied.

"Yes. I do wonder why they're flying them over Vicksburg. They already know our positions."

A Confederate sharpshooter from the hill by the hotel-turned-hospital took aim and fired hitting the balloon. When it burst, pieces of paper fluttered down toward the ground. Nathaniel strode forward and grabbed one out of the sky. He read it, then crumpled it in his fist. Angrily, he stomped back to Victoria and threw the leaflet into the fire.

"More Yankee propaganda. They're now trying to break the will of the people to resist."

Victoria sighed. "They'll do whatever it takes to capture the city."

Nathaniel rubbed his forehead. "I just wish that there was more we could do, but the men have no more energy, they are exhausted and starving. It's difficult to walk through town and see all the emaciated women and children. The demolished buildings, are...it's just so demoralizing."

Victoria leaned into Nathaniel and he pulled her into his arms. "It's not what anyone thought a war would be like. I know you're doing all you can. All of our men are doing their best. If we do give up the city, it will not be from lack of effort. Our brave soldiers were not beaten by the enemy, we simply ran out of resources."

Nathaniel held her tightly. "Thank you for saying that." He whispered.

Monday, June 29, 1863
Wheeler Farm

Hannah held up her hand to shield her eyes from the sunlight, then set down the hammer she was using to repair a fence post. Federal soldiers, a small company of six men, rode straight toward her. She pushed back strands of her hair as they pulled their horses up right in front of her.

"How can I help you gentlemen?" She asked, praying they wouldn't raid the storehouse again.

"We are in search of Confederates, Ma'am." The sergeant spoke, then spit a stream of tobacco juice on the ground. "Rebel raiders have been reported in the area. We're to check all the properties for them."

"We are all Confederates here, but there are no Confederate soldiers on my farm, Sergeant. If you don't believe me though, you are welcome to look." Her heart pounded. Thank goodness the men hadn't come yesterday when Jason and a comrade stopped by.

"We'll do just that." The sergeant nodded to his comrades as Hannah made her way to the house to inform the rest of her family what was happening. Cordelia met her on the porch.

"What do they want?" The woman asked.

"They're looking for our Confederate soldiers." Hannah explained. "Where are Ambrose and Caroline?"

"Inside. Caroline is finishing the soup while helping Ambrose with his reading. I told them to stay inside."

"That was wise," Hannah replied. The two women stood at the railing of the porch and watched the soldiers search their land and outbuildings. As usual, Hannah appreciated her mother-in-law's presence. Though Cordelia deferred to Hannah when it came to the farm matters, it was always nice to have her support and guidance.

Before long, the soldiers gathered in front of the house, empty-handed, of course.

"I trust you have completed your search, gentlemen," Hannah said.

"Yes, Ma'am. But you best take care, aiding the enemy can have dire consequences." The captain spit another stream of tobacco juice.

"Of course, Sergeant." Hannah nodded, though she wanted to point out the fact that the Confederates were not the enemy to her. She let out a breath as the man touched the brim of his kepi and turned to lead the men away.

"I would like to see Ambrose before I finish the fence." Hannah needed to check on her son. Cordelia nodded in understanding. Just as they reached the door to the house, gunshots rang out. Hannah spun around and watched in horror as the sergeant fell from his horse.

"Inside!" Cordelia shoved Hannah into the house, where it would be safer. Ambrose and Caroline had also fallen to the floor and crawled under the table. Hannah peeked out of the window from her knees. Confederate militia had ambushed the Yankees. The Federals fought back, and men from both sides fell to the ground, wounded or dead, she couldn't tell. Hannah glanced over at her family. Tears were streaming down Caroline's cheeks as she clung to her mother. Cordelia was holding tightly to both Caroline and Ambrose. Hannah quickly crawled over to them and pulled her son into her arms. She held him as tightly as she could, her heart pounding.

"Mama, will we get shot?" Ambrose asked, his voice small.

"No, Ambrose. We'll be just fine." She smiled, trying to put him at ease, and brushed his hair back.

The fighting went on for what felt like hours, but in reality, it was only about ten minutes. When the gunfire ceased, Hannah braved another look out the window. The men that remained on their horses were all Confederates. There were both blue and gray-clad bodies, wounded or dead, on the ground.

Hannah glanced at Cordelia. "Will you watch Ambrose? I am going to see what I can do to help." She dreaded what she might find. She was sure that she had glimpsed Jason among the Confederate ambushers. She prayed he would not be one of the wounded men, and that he had survived. She couldn't bear to find his lifeless body on her land.

Hannah hiked up her skirts as she hastened to the tree line where the skirmish had occurred. Confederate soldiers were already helping their wounded comrades to her house.

"Please, bring them right in." Hannah pointed, then went to a blue-clad man lying on the ground. Blank, dead eyes stared back at her. She stifled a cry and moved to the next man, a Confederate. Blood oozed from his thigh.

"Let's get him to the house," Cordelia said from behind her. Hannah turned and nodded, glad that her mother-in-law had followed her. The two women took the soldier's arms and helped him up, then steadied him as they made their way to the house.

"Thank you, ladies." The man groaned. Hannah continued to look at the dead and wounded men, especially the Confederates, but didn't recognize any of them. She knew she was being selfish. Those men were dear to someone. She shook her head and focused on the task at hand. Caroline had put Ambrose to work toting water.

The next hour flew by as Caroline, Hannah and Cordelia helped the wounded as best they could. Ambrose did his part as well, mostly hauling water back and forth so the wounds could be cleaned and the men could quench their thirst. The five remaining Yankees had all died, and she was told by one of the wounded Confederates that a contingent of rebel soldiers had ridden after the sixth Union soldier. Two of the Confederate soldiers had died, and another five were injured, but none too severely. While the women had cared for the wounded, a few uninjured Confederates cleaned the area of the attack and tied the dead soldiers to their horses to bury farther away from the farm. When all the wounded had been patched up, all the soldiers mounted their horses, some needing extra help.

"Ladies, we thank you for all your kindness and assistance." The Confederate captain tipped his hat at Hannah and Cordelia. "You have a good evening."

"Sir, do we need to fear another Yankee attack? What happens if your other men don't catch the soldier that escaped and he can identify our farm?" Cordelia asked.

"Probably not, Ma'am. One of the men who was chasing after that darn Yankee was Jason Turner. Believe me, every man in this company knows he would chase that man into Tennessee before he allowed him to get away. We all know how he feels about your family."

Hannah hoped her blush wasn't obvious. *Oh, Lord, please keep him out of harm's way.* She prayed silently. "Thank you for your reassurance, Captain." She went to her son and hugged him. "Let's get you to bed, young man. It's been quite an exciting day for you."

"Yes, mama." Ambrose looked exhausted.

"Hannah, I can get Ambrose ready for bed," Cordelia stated. "I will have Caroline clean the house if you want to finish the other chores."

"Are you sure?" Hannah asked. "I know you have been feeling poorly lately."

"I'll be just fine." Cordelia looked around the room. The soldiers had left quite a mess.

"All right." Hannah kissed the top of Ambrose's head. "Good night, my dear. I love you."

"Love you too, Mama." He rubbed his eyes tiredly.

Hannah went out to the barn and began her chores. As she fed the chickens, she said a silent prayer for the souls of the fallen soldiers, even the Yankees. She was so lost in her thoughts that she didn't even realize she wasn't alone until a hand covered hers and took the feed bucket from her. She jumped.

"Allow me."

Hannah looked into the sad blue eyes of Jason Turner. He was dirty, with his dark blonde hair mussed and he looked exhausted, but he wouldn't let go of the bucket. She released it, and he began feeding the chickens.

"You shouldn't be out here alone." He scolded her. She blew out a breath and decided to ignore his comment.

"And who, pray tell, is going to feed the chickens and pigs and who is going to milk the cow?" She put her hands on her hips.

"You're lucky it was me coming up behind you. It could have been anyone." He continued his lecture.

"I'm sorry, Jason, it's been a long day. Cordelia and Caroline are cleaning the house so no evidence of the attack can be found and I said I would finish all the outdoor chores." She shuddered again at the thought of the days' events.

He sighed. "I know it hasn't been easy for you, today, but I will have you know that my captain said that you would make a fine general. He said you were brave and strong and you are a no-nonsense kind of woman."

"May I be so forward as to ask what happened to that last soldier?" Hannah asked,

"He's dead, Hannah. We couldn't let him get away. He would have reported back, told his superiors what had happened, and that would have put you all in danger. I'm sorry."

She nodded. "Yes, of course. Thank you." She noticed that Jason's demeanor was more somber than she had ever witnessed. It occurred to her that the two Confederate soldiers who died could have been good friends of his.

She met his eyes. "Oh, Jason, I should have realized that you lost two of your comrades. I am sorry."

He shrugged and tried to act unaffected, but Hannah could tell he was upset. He thrust the bucket at the ground and turned to her.

"It may sound callous or insensitive, but I find that I'm not as affected by the deaths of my comrades as I would have been at the beginning of this conflict. I mourn the loss of life, but it's almost to be expected."

Hannah stepped close to Jason. She wasn't surprised that the war affected the soldiers in this way. It would be concerning if it didn't. What they went through, the horrors they were forced to endure, the acts they were forced to commit. She reached out and gently touched his arm.

"But it still must pain you." She spoke softly.

"I try so hard to not let it bother me." He avoided her eyes, "but sometimes, sometimes, I just can't. Yet I must."

Jason didn't speak further as they continued working. Hannah longed to help sooth his pain away, as she knew he needed.

"Why did you come back, by the way?" She asked as she began to fill the pig's trough with corn.

"I apologize for getting you caught in the middle of the attack. I am sorry you had to witness the skirmish." Jason shook his head. "I've been keeping an eye on your place ever since the Yankees stole your supplies. I had to make sure that you and your family were safe."

"Thank you, Jason." She was once again touched by his kindness. She thought back to the words the Confederate captain had said. 'Believe me, every man in this company knows he would chase that man into Tennessee before he allowed him to get away. We all know how he feels about your family.' Did the captain suspect something more than she did?

"I know that you are more than capable of running this farm, Hannah, but you all mean a lot to me," He replied.

"Have you eaten?" She brought her thoughts back to the present. "We don't have much left after the soldiers ate, but I am sure we can rustle something up."

"I would enjoy that," he said, though his smile seemed forced.

"All right, then. Perhaps Ambrose is still awake. He would enjoy seeing you."

"And I, him." Jason carried the buckets back to the corncrib, strolling next to Hannah. "I know I just saw him yesterday, but he always brightens my day."

Hannah desperately wanted to talk with Jason more about his losses, but she didn't want too upset him. She also wanted to know what his true feelings for her family really were. She sent up a silent prayer that all the soldiers would be free from physical pain as well as emotional pain, because with what she could tell from Jason's state of mind, a man's emotional state could affect him just as much as physical pain.

Thursday, July 2, 1863
Streets of Vicksburg

"Oh, Mama, look at Henry's horse! How he plays!" Julia, Mary Loughborough's six-year-old daughter cried out in excitement. Mary smiled at her daughter, then turned to Tabetha.

"That soldier there, Henry, has really noticed my little girl. He's brought her flowers, an apple, and even a young mockingbird. She is very attached to him."

"I can understand why." Tabetha recognized the young soldier. Henry was a kind and merry young man. At that moment, he was riding a small black horse that seemed quite wild. Henry rode the horse to the river, left it tethered, and headed further down the bank out of sight.

"I don't believe Henry has a girl back home, Miss Norton." Mary Loughborough smiled suggestively. "Perhaps you would like to become better acquainted with him."

"Oh, I'm not so sure about that," Tabatha replied. He was handsome, but he was likely five years younger than she was, still a boy.

"And why not? Have you become attached to some other fine young soldier in town?" Mrs. Loughborough asked.

"I don't have time for any of that," Tabetha replied, her mind going back to the young Lieutenant Davidson, who had died in her arms.

"Oh, we will find someone for you! Don't you worry yourself." Mary replied, then looked over to see Henry coming down the opposite side of the hill, a Confederate courier just a step behind him. Henry had something in his hands.

"That really is kind of you Mrs. Loughborough," Tabetha said. "There are days when I ..." Her words were interrupted by an explosion in the ravine, followed by an agonized cry. Tabetha and Mrs. Loughborough looked up to see the soldier who had been behind Henry roll over into the ravine, motionless. Mary screamed, and Tabetha jumped into action. She raced toward Henry, who was staggering around, holding out his mangled arms. Other Confederate soldiers joined Tabetha and hurried to the men. As she neared, she saw a dreadful-looking wound in the soldier's head, in addition to the mutilated, bloody stumps he now had for arms. Henry continued to cry out, delirious. "Where are you, boys? Oh, I am hurt! Boys, come to me! God have mercy!"

Tabetha helped Henry lie down. His body was trembling, and he was covered in dirt, sweat and blood. When she heard shrieks of horror, she looked over to the Loughborough's as little Julia clung to her mother's dress, her body shaking and sobbing. "Oh, Mamma, my poor Henry! Now he'll die, Mamma!" Mary picked her up quickly and carried her away from the morbid scene.

"We'll need litters, you!" Tabetha pointed towards a soldier. "Go to the nearest hospital, find a doctor as quickly as you can!" She knew from her hospital experience that she wouldn't be able to do much for either wounded soldier but she had to try. She glanced around to see if anyone else had been hurt, but it didn't appear so. "We need a stretcher!" Tabetha cried out again. She ripped up Henry's torn shirt to use as a tourniquet and tied the strips around both lower arms. She then used her skirt to apply pressure to the head wound. Her heart pounded as she looked up again, praying that help would come soon.

Henry was still rambling, crying out for God's mercy. Tabetha pulled out a handkerchief and wiped his face. It was all she could think to do.

"Don't you fret, Henry, help is on the way." Tabetha spoke to the young man softly, trying not to sound revolted at his appearance. His hands were almost detached from his wrists but the blood that had been pouring from his wounds was subsiding. Tabetha lifted him up and situated herself so she could hold his head and shoulders in her lap to comfort him as best she could. A quick glance at the other soldier confirmed her initial belief that he was dead. She swallowed the bile that was forming in her mouth.

"They found an unexploded shell." Another soldier approached her. "They were trying to take out the screw so they could secure the powder inside, but they must have somehow ignited the mechanism."

"What foolishness," she whispered, then looked around. "We need a stretcher!" Tabetha cried out again.

After what felt like hours, two men ran up, carrying a stretcher between them. As they quickly loaded Henry onto the stretcher, Tabetha tore another strip from her skirt and wrapped it around his head wound to keep the bleeding abated. The two soldiers lifted the young man and headed to the nearest hospital. Tabetha stood and wiped her bloody hands on her torn skirt, then followed the men up to the hospital. She saw two more orderlies coming down with another stretcher to transport the soldier that was already dead. From what she had experienced and witnessed in the hospital, Tabetha believed Henry's wounds were mortal but she still wanted to go with him to the hospital. Perhaps she could be of comfort to him in his final moments.

As Tabetha passed Mrs. Loughborough's cave on the way to the hospital, she saw the woman standing at the entrance, as if waiting for her.

"Miss Norton!" Mary cried out. "Henry...is he..." She couldn't finish her thought.

Tabetha went to the cave entrance. "It appears Henry was struck in the head by a shell fragment. His hands..." Tabetha shook her head, not wanting to tell Mary that they had been blown off. "I also saw at least one other small fragment of a shell lodged in his torso."

"Will he live?" Mrs. Loughborough asked.

"I honestly don't know," Tabetha admitted. "I haven't seen any man survive the kind of wounds he sustained, but miracles happen, so please pray for him."

"Yes, of course," Mrs. Loughborough said, tears in her eyes.

"How is Julia?" Tabetha asked.

"She is quite distressed, the poor dear cried herself to sleep." Mrs. Loughborough choked back a sob. "Those poor boys. The one who died, I know he died, didn't he, he was a courier. I know his mother, she lives over in Yazoo City. He is her only son. Whatever will she do now?"

"What a tragic loss for her..." A wave of guilt washed over Tabetha as she thought of her own family. She had lost her brother, but her parents had lost a son and without a thought for anyone else, she had taken off, impulsive as always, and now her family had no idea where Tabetha was. They had now lost a daughter as well.

Suddenly, the two women heard another, smaller explosion a few blocks away, followed by loud wailings and cries. Tabetha excused herself and hurried in the direction of the commotion. She immediately saw Mary Green and skirted through the crowd to her friend.

"Mary, what's happened?"

"A negro woman was walking through the yard there. She was struck by a parrot shell. They say she was killed instantly."

"Oh, dear Lord, what a horrible day this has been so far." Tabetha brushed a tear from her face, then ducked and pulled Mary with her as another shell came hurling in the direction of the crowd. The crowds of people cried out in fear and hastened back to their caves as debris flew through the air.

"I need to get back to the hospital and check on Henry," Tabetha said. "You need to get back to your cave, Mary. Take care of yourself."

"You as well, Tabetha." They both hastened away.

Tabetha didn't have to stay at the hospital. She immediately saw one of the stretcher-bearers who had brought the boy over. He met her eyes, then shook his head sadly. Henry had died.

Tabetha wiped her tears, but knew she had to go on. Shells were still flying by overhead, but she needed to be with the only family she had at the moment.

When Tabetha arrived at the Turner cave, she found Victoria there, along with Rachel, Mary Grace, Brianne and Kendall. Hope and Gabriel played in a corner and Adam was in the other corner, napping.

"Tabetha! I am so relieved you made it back!" Rachel stood. "I was worried."

Tabetha smiled sadly. "It has not been a good day," she replied, then quickly told the women what she had witnessed and Henry's fate.

"Everything in Vicksburg is so despondent." Mary Grace sighed. "It seems all one has to do is step out of a cave and they are certain to be wounded or killed."

"That may be a slight exaggeration, Mary Grace," Victoria said.

"You must have heard that Patience Gamble was killed on Sunday, Victoria," Rachel added. "She was trying to get her son to safety."

"I had heard that," Victoria responded sadly.

"Have you heard what will happen to the Gamble children?" Mary Grace asked. The eight children were now orphans. Their father, Andrew had been killed three years before the war broke out. He was found dead in the shallow waters near a New Orleans dock. No one ever knew what happened. His wife had been distraught, as she was pregnant with their youngest child at the time.

"Pleasant will care for the children until the siege is over. You remember her, she is the family servant," Rachel explained. "I believe they have family in St. Louis and will likely go there when everyone is able to leave this town."

"Those poor children, will this never end?" Victoria shook her head. "I will not miss the moans and anguished cries over the dead when this is all over."

"If it's ever over," Mary Grace said. "There are days when I feel this siege will never end."

"It will, Mary Grace, don't you fret." Kendall added. "I hear everyone saying that we'll likely surrender within the week."

"And yet others are insisting that we will never surrender," Brianne said.

Mary Grace looked at her children in the corner. "Yes, well those causes we are fighting for, those people who want to resist the Yankees to the death? They don't have children who are starving." She wiped her eyes. "All the dear children suffering. For what? How much more can we bear?"

Victoria reached over and placed a comforting hand on her sister's arm. "I wish I could do more for you and the children."

"You already do so much for us, I know that, you and Nathaniel both."

"Nathaniel?" Victoria was confused. "What has he been doing?"

"He is very discreet about it but he has been giving us most of his rations, for the children of course. He says he's not sacrificing much, but we know he is." Rachel smiled. "He is a true gentleman, Victoria."

"Yes, he is." Victoria smiled to herself.

Friday, July 3, 1863
Prentiss Cave

"They say the siege may end tomorrow." Mary Green sipped a cup of lukewarm water.

"I heard that as well. There has been very little bombardment today. Oh, Mary, I wish this siege would be over, for obvious reason, but there are times when I stubbornly don't want to ever give up. The stubbornness you often remind me that I have." Victoria smiled.

"Mmm, yes, I am quite familiar with that attribute of yours."

"I know it's selfishness on my part, but I'm primarily concerned about Nathaniel and what will happen to all the Confederate soldiers if we surrender. I fear they'll all be taken prisoner and I don't want Nathaniel in one of those ghastly prisons up north. I know how cold it can get up there. Nathaniel says that when he went to college in Michigan, the winters would chill him clear to the bones. They are relentless, those Michigan winters."

"I hadn't thought of that," Mary replied. "If we do surrender, General Pemberton will negotiate for good terms."

"I hope you're right." Victoria reached down and rubbed her sore, swollen ankle. Many civilians had the same pain, an effect of not eating well.

Mary stood. "Annie will be done with her nap soon and Missy needs to get something together for dinner." Missy was one of the Green's slaves. "I should get going."

Victoria stood with her friend. "You be sure to give those children a hug for me."

"I most definitely will," Mary answered, then went on her way.

After she left, Victoria puttered around the cave. It was almost dinnertime, but she had nothing to prepare other than pea meal. She was hungry as well, but her gums were starting to get tender, and she knew that if she ate it would be uncomfortable. Oh, she would never complain about eating vegetables again! What she wouldn't do for some carrots or beans.

Victoria gazed at the books she had brought from her father's library, now sitting on the shelves that Corporal John Sullivant had carved the night the Arkansas officers had joined them. Sitting on another shelf was the river otter that Nathaniel had carved for her. She smiled and picked up the figurine.

"Pemberton's going to betray us." The voice of an angry, frustrated Nathaniel sounded from the doorway.

Victoria whirled around to see her husband step into the cave. She immediately went to him and embraced him. "What do you mean, Nathaniel?"

"The word is out that yesterday, he contacted Grant about an armistice. Pemberton is going to surrender. Grant sent a message back this morning. He wants unconditional surrender of the city. We give up and the Yankees take over."

"That's why it's been so quiet today." Victoria gently brushed some dirt from his cheek. "I heard news of Pemberton and Grant speaking with each other. I just thought it was more rumors or maybe I simply didn't want to believe it was true."

"So you don't want to surrender?" Nathaniel asked.

"Well, no, after forty-seven days of living in hell, just giving up would feel like it was all for nothing."

"There has got to be something good that comes from all of this."

"Maybe not." She leaned back and took a good look at him. "You are getting so thin and gaunt. I hear that you've been giving most of your rations to my family."

"The children need food more than I do," Nathaniel said.

She gave him a quick kiss. "I love you, Nathaniel. I'm glad that I get to spend the rest of my life with you."

"And I with you," he replied. "Though I'm certain that this will be our last night in Vicksburg under the Confederate flag. Since the bombardment has subsided would you like to go for a stroll before we become an occupied city?"

"Certainly, Mr. Prentiss." She clutched his arm.

They walked outside arm in arm and meandered through the streets.

"It's eerily quiet, yet there are so many people about," Victoria commented. Other townspeople had apparently heard the rumors and with no more shelling, had emerged from the caves. "Everyone looks so somber."

"You're right. I haven't seen the streets this congested in a while," Nathaniel said, then hailed a familiar soldier. "Tex!"

Timothy Reynolds walked over to them and saluted Nathaniel.

"Nathaniel, Miss Victoria. I suppose you've heard the news that it's over. The siege that is, not the war. The Yankees will take possession of the town tomorrow."

"What does that mean for all of the soldiers?" Victoria asked.

"No one is sure yet," Timothy admitted. "But the city and its people have suffered terribly, I would hope the terms will be reasonable."

Nathaniel rubbed his bearded chin. "I hope you're right." He looked down at Victoria and squeezed her hand. "There should be no more danger tonight. We can pack up some things and leave the cave. Stay at your parents' home if you'd like."

Victoria was a mix of emotions, but his comment elated her. "Oh, could we?"

"There's no longer any reason we can't. Let's go speak with your mother, see if they'd like to move back into the house," Nathaniel said.

"That will be so good for Adam," Victoria added.

"It was good to see you, Tex," Nathaniel said, shaking Timothy's hand. "I'll catch up with you later."

"Take care, Nathaniel," Timothy replied. Nathaniel and Victoria made their way to the Turner's cave.

"Mother!" Victoria said. "We have some news that I think will please you."

"Does this news have anything to do with how strangely quiet it is?" Brianne asked. "It's actually strange. Everyone is walking around in a daze."

"Yes," Kendall added. "We've come to the conclusion that all this silence can only mean the most dreadful of situations will happen on the morrow."

"Is Grant going to attack tomorrow and fight to the death? Is that the news?" Tabetha asked.

"Ladies, let Nathaniel and Victoria tell us what the news is," Rachel said as Mary Grace came to the mouth of the cave.

"The children are finally asleep." She brushed dirt from her skirt. "Hopefully they'll sleep more soundly tonight than they have these past two months."

"We were hoping to catch you before they went to bed." She looked around at her family. "The siege will be over tomorrow. We were going to take some supplies and stay in the house tonight."

"That's a capital idea!" Brianne said. "Aunt Rachel, can we, please?"

"Of course." Rachel turned to Mary Grace. "I can stay here with the children if you'd like."

"Or we can bring them with us." Nathaniel offered.

"Thank you all," Mary Grace said. "But I think I'll stay here with them. They are sleeping so soundly, for a change. I would hate to wake them up. The knowledge that we can leave tomorrow will be comfort enough."

"I'll stay here with you," Rachel said. "Brianne, Tabetha and Kendall, you go with Nathaniel and Victoria."

"Splendid!" Brianne said, then she, Tabetha, and Kendall went inside to pack some overnight belongings.

"Have them stop by our cave when they are ready," Victoria said. "Nathaniel and I will be waiting."

"All right." Rachel hugged both Victoria and Nathaniel. "I am so thankful that we all survived this horrible ordeal."

"I am as well, Mama," Victoria said, tears in her eyes. Nathaniel gave her arm a gentle squeeze. "But I fear the worst is yet to come."

Saturday, July 4, 1863
Turner Home

Victoria woke up alone. The night before, Nathaniel had told her he intended to leave before first light. He had left his pistol with her, assuming that he would be forced to turn in all of his firearms. He had been quite proud to learn that she knew how to shoot and would be able to defend herself if the need arose.

"Victoria? Are you awake?" Kendall quietly entered the room.

Victoria sat up and nodded. "Yes, last night felt quite strange with all of the silence don't you think? It still feels odd." Victoria went to her wardrobe and looked inside. She had not unpacked last night and many of her dresses were still in the cave. "I want to change into a clean dress, but I would prefer to bathe first." She sighed. "What time is it?"

"Half-past nine." Kendall answered.

"My goodness, I can't believe I slept that late." Victoria reached up and finger combed her hair, then quickly braided it and wound it into a bun at the nape of her neck.

"I wanted to let you know that the Yankees are in town. Grant officially took control of the city at 8:00 this morning. Our men must turn in their firearms. I'm still not sure what is going to happen to them."

"If only we could have held on a bit longer, I just know Johnston would have come," Victoria said as she and Kendall went down the stairs.

"Tabetha went to St. Xavier Hospital already, and Brianne is still sleeping."

"Neither of those things surprise me." Victoria reached the breezeway of the house and checked the rooms on the main floor. The damage wasn't as bad as she thought it would be. The dining room chimney had a hole in it, but could be repaired. A piece of mortar shell had come through a front-room window and crashed through the parlor floor to the basement. The nights of rain had caused some dampness, but the house wasn't too musty. She saw some hurried repairs had been done and realized that Nathaniel must have been doing some work. Victoria sighed. She thought of what the house looked like before the siege. It seemed like years had passed, yet it had been just over six weeks.

"There's some commotion towards the center of town," Kendall called. She had moved out to the front porch and was watching the situation develop. "Can we go? Is it safe?"

"Other townspeople are out and about. I see the Lord family, the McRae family... I believe we'll be okay," Victoria responded.

"All right, let's go." Kendall and Victoria made their way to the city center.

The Confederate soldiers they saw appeared very solemn. Tears welled up in Victoria's eyes. One of the passing Confederates took off his kepi and spoke to the women.

"Ladies, we would have fought for you forever. Nothing but starvation whipped us!"

"Aye," another soldier agreed. "We never could have been whipped on the front, but old General Pemberton sold us to the enemy for a price, but we gave them Yankees 'Hail Columbia' for forty-eight days and nights."

The two women nodded their thanks. Victoria scanned the crowd trying to locate Nathaniel. Mixed among the ragged, gaunt Confederate soldiers were dapper-dressed Yankees. White flags waved from the fortifications along the entire Confederate lines. In the distance, Victoria could hear a Union band playing 'Yankee Doodle'. When that was finished, they struck up 'The Star-Spangled Banner'. It was then that Victoria realized the significance of the day. July the 4th. Independence Day. No doubt the Yankee celebration would be in full swing tonight.

The Union soldiers seemed to be heading toward a certain spot in town with a purpose. The Confederates mumbled and cursed as they were herded by the Yankees. Victoria's heart pounded in fear.

"Where are they taking them?" She asked no one in particular. Were the Yankees taking them prisoner? Moving them out already? Where was Nathaniel? Was she even going to be able to say goodbye? "Nathaniel, where are you?" She murmured, her eyes watery as she surveyed the crowd. Civilians filled the streets as well, starving men, women and children with dirty, ragged clothing. It was a pitiful sight. Many had bare feet and swollen ankles, all were gaunt, and some were even partially naked as they came in a steady stream. Many people, both citizens and soldiers, still complained about Pemberton yielding the city against their will and insisting they would never serve under him again.

"I'm going to find out where the crowd is going," Kendall said, then used her small stature to weave through the crowd.

"Victoria!" Brianne, finally awake had come down to the city center. "Where's Kendall?"

"She went to try and find out where all our men are being led to," Victoria replied.

"Where's Nathaniel? Have you seen any of our other particular friends?" Brianne asked.

"No, not yet." Victoria wiped a tear from her eye. "All of our sacrifices were for naught."

"I hate the Yankees." Brianne's face was stone cold. Victoria couldn't believe those words came from her cousin's mouth. How could her cousin say that about her own father?

"They're not all bad," Victoria said, gesturing at some enemy soldiers who had stopped and emptied their haversacks for some children, giving them hardtack and whatever they had available. The children devoured the food like starved animals. It surprised Victoria that the Yankee soldiers were showing so much respect.

Finally, Kendall returned. "I have news," she said. "The Yankees are having our soldiers stack their arms right now. I don't think the Yanks are going to send them to prison. It sounds like the Confederates will have a chance to sign some oath of allegiance and be paroled, then be allowed to go free. They've hired Mr. Swords to print the parole papers."

James M. Swords was the editor of the *Daily Citizen*. Though he and his wife, Marie Antoinette Swords were born in the north, they were ardent Confederate supporters.

Victoria shook her head. "I know Nathaniel won't sign an oath of loyalty to the Union." *Lord, what will happen to him when he refuses?*

"What else did you discover?" Brianne asked.

"Dozens of Union vessels have docked down on the wharf from both upstream and downstream, and the Yankees are already moving to raise the US flag above our courthouse."

"Our lives are going to change again, aren't they?" Brianne asked softly.

"Yes." Victoria said quietly. "Yes, I'm afraid so."

Mary Green made her way through the cluttered, crowded streets. She was still shocked by what she saw. Shell fragments and unexploded shells littered the streets and yards of private residences. The hills resembled a potato, because of the holes that formed when shells struck the ground before exploding. Buildings lay in ruins, countless houses and other structures showed signs of damage. It appeared as though all the windows in the city had been broken.

"Mary! What are you doing out here?" Duff approached her, concern on his face.

"I had to see what was going on down there. I can't believe my own eyes."

Duff took her arm as he led her towards the center of town. "I know what you mean."

As they walked, Mary continued to look around. Ill soldiers lay on the ground, dirty and ragged, along with emaciated animal carcasses that emitted a nasty, sickly, putrid smell.

"The soldiers in our house are not much better off than the ones lying around here." He gestured to the withered bodies of the soldiers on the ground, with filthy clothing and open sores. "And now we will be forced to take in more Union wounded from their field hospitals."

"Don't you think we can move back home?" Mary asked.

"I think it might be best if we stay at your mother's home," he replied.

Mary took special note of the civilians as they continued to walk. Tears could be seen in the eyes of many of the women, while others looked relieved that the siege was over. Mary herself was relieved. It was the worst thing imaginable to see the pains of hunger on her daughter's face and she struggled to see that her newborn son was fed.

"There are more Negroes in town than normal." She observed. Those individuals were just as ragged and dirty-looking as the people who had been trapped in the city for over 40 days.

"Yes," Duff answered. "Many freed blacks have rushed into town from the countryside. The Federal army is bringing in food for all noncombatants."

"Well, isn't that kind of them?" She looked toward the river where many people were congregating.

"Mary!" Victoria's voice came from behind Mary. The two women embraced one another. "We were heading down to the wharf, won't you join us?"

"What is at the wharf?" Mary asked. "And where is Nathaniel?"

"I haven't seen him since last night, but I am hoping he's down at the river. People are gathering there to get food, mainly, but also more information."

Union military bands continued to play, adding to the noise throughout the city. Union soldiers celebrated loudly and Victoria had been depressed to see that there was looting in some areas by both Union and Confederate soldiers. Union guards were attempting to keep the crowds in line, but it was proving ineffective. Victims were being urged to make claims of stolen property.

"I have to find Nathaniel," Victoria said, then quickly moved to the side as a man on horseback pushed his way through the crowd. "Good Heavens, and I promised Mary Grace that I would get some food."

"I will let you go, then, maybe we can meet up later," Mary said.

"Are you sure you wouldn't like an escort?" Duff asked. "I can take you where you need to go."

"That's quite all right, really. Kendall and Brianne are already there," Victoria said. "I appreciate the offer, but I will be just fine."

"Yes, ma'am." Duff said. "God go with you."

Duff Green House-Hospital

Tabetha looked around at all the new patients in the Duff Green house. The Union army had been busy moving their patients into the hospitals of Vicksburg. She made her way to one of the new soldiers, and frowned when she saw that he was merely a boy who couldn't have been older than 15.

"Afternoon, ma'am." The boy nodded. Tabetha sat next to him and placed a gentle hand on his bandaged leg.

"Good afternoon, soldier. My name is Miss Tabetha Norton, and I am a nurse here."

The boy gave her a smile. "Orion Perseus Howe, ma'am, out of Portage County Ohio. I'm a drummer for the 55th Illinois Volunteers. Got shot in the leg during this campaign."

"Well, I thank you for your service and your obvious bravery, Mr. Howe. Is there anything I can do for you?"

"Not at present, ma'am, though I do appreciate your offer." He nodded. "I do have to say, you don't sound like you're from Mississippi."

"No, I'm actually from Michigan. Through a series of events, I found myself here."

"Thought you seemed like a good, Northern woman." Orion spoke with confidence beyond his years. The war seemed to make men of boys very quickly.

"Yes, sir," she replied. "I'll be around for a few more hours. You let me know if you need anything."

"Will do, Ma'am." He nodded, and Tabetha stood to go help more patients.

When she had finished her shift and checked on young Orion Howe again, Tabetha emerged from the Green house, blinking at the bright sunlight. She looked around at the crowds that filled the streets. She avoided one woman who was in hysterics, raving, pulling her hair, stamping her feet and cursing the Yankees. It was a pathetic spectacle. Tabetha thought it quite interesting to see the different reaction of the people to the fall of Vicksburg. She was relieved to know that life would be much easier for the citizens and she would also be able to contact her family back home in Michigan. She hoped she wouldn't run into any of her former comrades from her regiment. She had disguised herself well enough while in the cavalry and knew she wouldn't be recognized, but there was that small, minute chance that someone would discover her past.

Tabetha was so lost in her thoughts that she didn't see the horses and rider barreling toward her, hollering and crying out, clearly intoxicated.

"Look out!" A Union soldier grabbed Tabetha's arm and pulled her out of the path of the horses as they raced by. "Are you alright, ma'am? I must apologize. That is inexcusable behavior for a soldier. He should not be acting in that manner."

"You are correct, he shouldn't be. I thank you for your quick thinking and actions." Tabetha smiled.

The soldier who rescued her smiled back, a broad smile that likely charmed many women. He swept his kepi off his head, showing dark blonde hair. "Lieutenant Noah Campbell, ma'am, of the 6th Illinois Cavalry."

Tabetha's heart pounded. She recognized Lieutenant Campbell; he was a member of her regiment. He was known as a cheerful man, kind, and rarely serious. He was a good friend of Steven Rogers. If Lieutenant Campbell was here, that meant the entire 6th Illinois would be present also. She would have to be more cautious.

"I'm Miss Tabetha Norton," she replied. "I am ever so grateful to meet you."

"And I you." He nodded. "You don't sound as though you are a native of Mississippi, Miss Norton." He remarked.

"No, I am not. I was visiting family in town when the siege began." She slipped into the story she and the Turners had been using.

"Ahh, and you were caught up in it. That is very unfortunate."

"Granted, it wasn't ideal, but we all must adjust," she responded.

"Strong, Northern women tend to do that," he said.

"I have learned that the women down here are extremely tenacious as well," she replied.

"They do appear to be that." He nodded.

"I should be on my way," Tabetha said. "Again, thank you so much for assisting me."

"It was my pleasure, Miss Norton. I hope to see you again."

She nodded and headed back home.

Turner Home

Victoria stood on the porch that evening, waiting anxiously for Nathaniel. She hadn't seen or heard from him all day, and she was worried about his condition. She and her family had moved most of their belongings back in to the house. Victoria was surprised that their home hadn't been taken over to be used as a hospital, as many of the other houses had. Rachel came out and stood beside her, placing a comforting arm around her.

"Silence and the night are once more united," Rachel said. "It was so good to have wheat bread today, along with meat and fresh fruit. So many provisions we have been without for so long."

"Yes, and the men wasted no time at all getting their whisky." Victoria hoped she didn't sound too upset by that fact. "But you're right, the healthy food, with peace and quiet should help Adam recover."

"Yes, that is my prayer," Rachel replied. "The Union soldiers have been quite respectful overall. I've seen many instances of them sharing food and water, swapping stories about the campaign, and engaging in friendly debates about the war, politics, and even society."

"Yes, along with looting and pillaging all over town." Victoria grumbled. "It sounds like Washington Street was quite the scene. Soldiers robbed private residences, absconded with furniture and displayed a particular fondness for pilfered mirrors." She sighed and looked out towards the city. The Federals were in full celebration for their victory and for their holiday. "I heard it said that the Union soldiers insist they have every right to loot the city and take all that we have. Stores cleaned out, calico and ribbons stretched out across the street, colored flannels flying in the breeze, and the officers just stand by and watch the destruction. And to make matters worse, the officers watching it all claim to oppose pillaging. No one will do a thing to stop it, yet they oppose it. How contradictory! It's purely despicable."

"There will always be good and evil, Victoria," Rachel said. "Keep in mind that it is much calmer now. Provost guards have been patrolling, and it appears the Federal officers are getting their men out of town and back to the siege lines. We'll be fine, just fine."

A tear slipped down Victoria's cheek. "I hope so, Mother."

Victoria retreated to one of the chairs and picked up a copy of the *Vicksburg Daily Citizen* that Kendall had brought home. The initial date of the newspaper read 'Thursday, July 2', but it seemed as though the editor had set the type and abandoned it to the Yankees, as there was a section at the bottom that had been clearly set by Federals that morning.

"Two days bring about great changes. The banner of the Union floats over Vicksburg. General Grant had 'caught the rabbit'; he has dined in Vicksburg and he did bring his dinner with him. The "Citizen" lives to see it. For the last time it appears on "Wall-paper". No longer will it eulogize the luxury of mule-meat and fricasseed kitten-urge Southern warriors to such diet never more. This is the last wall-paper edition, and is, excepting this note from the type as we found them. It will be valuable hereafter as a curiosity."

Victoria crumpled the corner of the paper. A curiosity. Their horrible experiences of the past 47 days whittled down to this. Occupation and mockery from their captors. She was about to go back into the house when she spotted a familiar form hurrying through the crowd. "Nathaniel!" She cried out, relief coursing through her. She tossed the newspaper to the chair and hastened down the stairs to meet him on the sidewalk. He threw his arms around her and kissed her, then held her tightly. "Nathaniel, where have you been?"

"It's been a very long day," he said. "Much too long." He led her to the porch steps. Rachel moved inside once she made sure Nathaniel was uninjured.

"I am glad to have you back home. I was so concerned for your safety. Where have you been?" She laid her head on his shoulder.

He clutched her hands. "I spent the entire day transporting the sick and wounded from the trenches to the hospitals in town."

"Please tell me, I have worried all day about what is going to happen to you and all the other Confederate soldiers?"

"They are requiring all of us to sign individual paroles." He sighed.

"What does that even mean? Please explain this to me," Victoria asked with pleading eyes.

"If I sign the parole, I will avoid going to a prison camp, but I will be obligated to not serve in the Confederate Army until I am formally exchanged for a Yankee prisoner."

"That doesn't make sense. Why would they make that kind of offer?" Victoria asked. This sounded too good to be true.

"The Yankees won't have to transport and imprison thousands of Confederate soldiers this way. They will have more of their own men free to expedite their current military maneuvers beyond Vicksburg. This will free up their soldiers who would otherwise have to guard the Rebel prisoners."

"I must say, this is good news. You won't have to leave then, will you?" Victoria still wasn't quite sure how this parole would work.

"Unfortunately, no, we all still have to leave. I'll go back to Virginia." He sighed and ran a hand through his shaggy hair. "Our wounded will sign paroles as well, but can stay until they are well enough to travel. It is said that we can take horses and wagons with us, and all the food rations we will need."

Victoria shook her head. "How do they know you just won't sign a parole and go back East to fight right away? It isn't as though they know you or have your name on any rosters here. Besides, we are your family now, shouldn't you be allowed to stay with me?"

"I thought about that. I don't know what I'm going to do yet, Tori." He admitted. "I turned my rifle in. When or if I do leave, I'll have to somehow sneak my pistol out."

"I'm not complaining, believe me, but I still don't understand why they're not putting you all in prison, even just here in town."

"For the reasons I explained earlier, and because I believe the parole that makes me sign an oath of allegiance is more demoralizing than imprisonment."

"What are you going to do?" Victoria asked, pulling back to look into his eyes.

"I want to refuse. Believe me, the parole is just as despicable as signing the oath of allegiance that the Yankees are having the civilians sign."

"Nathaniel, you must!" Victoria sat up straight. "If you don't sign it, they'll send you to prison! Prison conditions are horrible in the North. Men die there every day! You must do whatever it takes to remain free."

"I know, I know you're right." He looked out at the street. Soldiers from both sides meandered through the town and citizens continued to emerge from their hillside caves, moving back into their homes.

"There is something else, I haven't told you, Tori. Another battle in the east that may affect one of your cousins."

"Oh, no, what happened?" She felt sick to her stomach. "A cousin? Where? Which cousins?"

"While we were under siege, and not able to receive any news from the east, our General Lee marched into Union territory."

"Well, that's a good thing, isn't it?"

"You would think so, but his troops clashed with General Meade's Yankee army at Gettysburg just a few days ago."

"Gettysburg!" Victoria exclaimed. "Oh, dear, Cousin Charlotte is all alone on that farm. How will we know if she's all right? Tell me what happened. Did we win the battle?"

"No one is really sure, yet. I believe we have the battle in control, but apparently, it isn't over yet."

Victoria buried her face in her hands. "When will this all end, Nathaniel? How much longer must this go on?"

Nathaniel pulled her into his arms and held her tight. A moment later, an explosion blasted through the air. Both Nathaniel and Victoria jumped.

"Why are they shelling again? I don't understand." Victoria shook her head.

"I cannot believe it, look. Fireworks." Nathaniel sighed. "I wonder if it's in celebration of the fall of Vicksburg or in honor of Independence Day." He couldn't hide the bitterness in his voice. Victoria gave him a comforting hug. "What do you think I should do, Tori? You know I value your opinion."

"If you mean in regards to the parole, I think you should sign it, and as much as it pains me to say this, you must go back to Virginia. You'll have to leave town anyways. Report to your superiors and tell them what has happened. You can see if there's any way they can request to expedite your exchange or something along those lines. You could visit your sisters, my family and then rejoin the fight if that's what you need to do." She squeezed his hand, then brought it to her lips and kissed it. "Then, when this foolish war is over, you can come back to me and we will continue our lives together."

"The moment this war is over, I will make all haste to get back to you, you can depend on that." He leaned over and kissed her. "I don't know what the next few days will hold, but I will make sure you and your family are safe before I leave."

"And I will be here for you in whatever capacity you may need," Victoria replied. Nathaniel put an arm around her and she curled up into his embrace. They looked up at the sky. "The fireworks really are quite beautiful." She commented.

"You all managed to move everyone and everything from the caves back home?" He asked.

"Yes, though Tabetha is staying with Mary Grace and the children for now."

"Why won't Mary Grace stay here? Wouldn't it be safer?"

"She hasn't quite confided in me yet, but I believe she wants to get her life back to normal as much as she can. She and Mother talked about opening the haberdashery again."

"Well, the Yankees could use some culture," Nathaniel said with a smirk. "I bet Mary Grace is an excellent saleswoman. She'll likely convince many a Yankee to spend his paycheck at her establishment."

"Yes, she is quite good at all that," Victoria agreed. "Good saleswoman, good mother, good wife, good sister..." she sighed. "She's excels at everything."

"You do as well." Nathaniel suspected Victoria often compared herself to Mary Grace. "Why else would I have married you?"

"Oh, I love you, Nathaniel," she responded. "There's no one on earth I would rather spend my life with."

"I feel the same way, Tori," he replied.

Sunday, July 5, 1863
St. Paul's Catholic Church

"Excuse me, Miss."

Tabetha glanced up at the Union soldier who had accidentally bumped into her. She recognized the voice right away, and had thought about the man it belonged to every day since her injuries.

"Captain..." she caught herself before she said his complete name. She could get away with recognizing and addressing him by rank, but calling him by his name would only raise questions she wasn't ready to answer. "Quite all right, Captain." She looked into the clear, blue eyes of Captain Steven Rogers.

"I must apologize again. I am Captain Steven Rogers of the 6th Illinois." He smiled at her, a flicker of recognition in his eyes. She prayed that he would not recognize her, hoped that her soldier's disguise had been good enough. "And you are?"

"I'm Miss Tabetha Norton," she replied, smiling back.

"It is a pleasure to meet you, Miss Norton." He turned toward the doors of St. Paul's. "Are you attending Mass?"

"Yes, sir, I do so every Sunday that I can."

"Are you attending alone or are you in need of an escort?" He asked. She wasn't surprised at his kind attentions; she had known that he was a gentleman.

"I normally do attend alone, and I haven't had need of an escort yet," she replied.

"Miss Norton, if it wouldn't offend you to be on the arm of a Yankee officer, would you allow me to escort you into Church today?" He asked.

"I wouldn't be offended at all, Captain. I am actually from the north myself. Western Michigan," she replied.

"Ahhhh, I thought as much, once I heard you talk. You have a Midwest accent, not southern." He offered his arm to her. She took it and allowed him to escort her up the steps.

Captain Rogers turned to her once they were seated. "If you are from Michigan, what brings you to Mississippi?" He asked quietly. "It can't be easy, living among Yankee-hating secessionists."

"Family ties," she responded softly. It was a true statement, she reasoned, and the Turners had insisted she continue to masquerade as a cousin. "It may interest you to know that the city of Vicksburg voted against Mississippi seceding. There are more Union sympathizers here than you think. At least, there was before the war broke out."

"I was aware of that, actually, however, I have yet to see any support from them. I must admit, I was surprised by how many of the men signed the loyalty oath so quickly, yet we have met with quite a bit of resistance from the citizens. The women seem particularly bitter."

"You only need to look around you for the answer to that question, Captain. You and your men have been wreaking havoc on this town for well over a month. All the people were starving, no matter where their loyalties lied. We lived in constant fear under great duress. Women were killed, children wounded, homes destroyed. One of my friends had to give birth to her son in a communal cave during the bombing. Another friend got married and even though it was the happiest day of her life, there was constant shelling, and her wedding feast was celebrated in constant danger, and she spent her first married nights in a cave. Her little nephew still has a cough that he developed from the dampness of the cave he was forced to live in." Tabetha wanted to add more, but the ring of the church bells stopped her.

As Mass started, she took a deep breath. She had wondered what would happen if she met any of her former fellow soldiers, the Captain especially, but she hadn't imagined holding a conversation with any of them. She tried to clear her mind and focus on the service, but she was extremely conscious of the man sitting next to her. His deep baritone voice, the one she was so familiar with calling out commands and giving instructions, sang loudly, though slightly off-key. It made her smile to realize that he wasn't proficient in everything.

Fr. O'Reilly had once again delivered a fine sermon. When the recessional song had been sung, Captain Rogers offered her his arm.

"I must ask that you allow me to escort you home," he said.

"I wouldn't want to take up your time, Captain. Besides, I am heading to one of the hospitals in town." She was no longer worried that he would recognize her. He would have already said something, she reasoned. She was truly enjoying the attentions of Captain Steven Rogers.

"Then I shall take you there. It is no problem, Miss Norton, I have the day to myself and I would enjoy the walk."

"Well, in that case." She took his offered arm. "Where are you staying, Captain?"

"Right now, in a tent, still outside the city limits. However, the Provost Marshal will be placing us in some of the homes around town soon. We'll be staying in Vicksburg for a while. The cavalry will be instrumental in several ways. We suspect guerilla bands will try and wreak havoc now that we have the city. We'll be scouting and patrolling the area."

Tabetha nodded, acting as though she only knew the basics about the cavalry. She had always enjoyed her time with the Captain and wondered if she could perhaps, cultivate a friendship with him. The two continued to walk and converse and before she knew it, they arrived at the Duff Green Hospital.

"Thank you so much for your time, Captain." Tabetha smiled.

"You are most welcome. Perhaps I will see you about town? Or perhaps in church next week."

"Either is possible, sir." She smiled and curtsied, then went inside.

Tuesday, July 7, 1863
Lakewood Home

Victoria was ushered into the parlor of the home of Mary Green's mother. Mary soon joined her.

"Victoria, how nice to see you." Mary was delighted her friend had come for a visit.

"And you," Victoria replied. "So much has happened since we last saw one another."

"Yes," Mary agreed. "I suppose you've heard what Duff has done."

"I have," Victoria replied. Duff Green had been one of the first civilians to sign the Oath of Allegiance. He was no longer a very popular man with the loyal Confederate citizens.

"He felt it was best for the entire family." Mary defended him.

"Of course." Victoria didn't want to discuss the issue. Though she understood Duff's motivation, she didn't approve, so she changed the subject. "I'm glad to see that you still have servants. Our Caesar has already used his newfound freedom to leave us and join a Negro regiment for the Union. He feels it is his duty. If he leaves Vicksburg, Esther will surely follow him and she will take Cicero with her. It is quite distressing. I thought they would be more loyal and stay with us. I believe Esther would stay if she were the only person involved in the decision, but when Caesar has other ideas, well." She shrugged. "She is loyal to him most of all, which I do understand." She shook her head. "I'm glad Mother and I are both learning some cooking skills from her. We won't be completely helpless if she does leave."

"I don't know what we would do if that were to happen to us," Mary said. "But I don't believe our servants will leave."

"Keep in mind, there is absolutely nothing we can do if they choose to leave." Victoria sighed, then changed the subject quickly. "How is everything at your house? I have been volunteering mostly at St. Francis Xavier, as it is right down the road from our house."

"It is very busy," Mary said. "I haven't been over there yet, but Duff says it's filled with both Union and Confederate soldiers. They are keeping them on two separate floors to keep the peace, as they did during the siege." Mary wanted to ask about Nathaniel and his plans, but didn't want to upset her friend. "How are Mary Grace and the children?"

"Hope and Gabriel are both recovering quite nicely from life in the cave. Adam, on the other hand...well...he was already weak before we moved to the damp, dark cave." A tear slipped down Victoria's face. She hated seeing her nephew so pale and sick, and now he was even more so than before the siege. And his cough... "He is not doing well at all. I worry about him so much."

"I'm so sorry, Victoria." Mary placed a comforting hand on her friend's wrist.

"We just have to pray for a speedy recovery." Victoria tried to bring herself out of her doldrums. "Nathaniel keeps busy with the men. They are shoveling debris out of the way so they can repair the destroyed buildings. He has begun work on our home and it already looks much better. I was relieved that Father's library wasn't damaged."

"That is fortuitous. I know how much pride your father has in that particular room," Mary said. "Duff told me that it's been difficult to repair homes that have been converted to hospitals because of all the men crowded there."

"I can see how that would be a challenge," Victoria said. "Cleaning up the town will take months. There is so much garbage and waste, not to mention the animal carcasses and the shallow graves we had to bury the dead in. The holes from the shells have made certain streets impassable and some of them near the river still have barricades and trenches, which make them impassable as well."

"At least there are men around to help put our city back to rights," Mary said.

"Yes, but the Yanks are building additional fortifications, and Grant has ordered all of the cave entrances be filled in. I won't be surprised if the Yankees change Vicksburg into a Northern town." Victoria scoffed.

Mary had rarely seen this bitter attitude from her friend before. She didn't know how to respond to Victoria' rant, so once again, the subject was changed. "How is Tabetha faring? Will she try and go home?"

"Well, the 6th Illinois is here. That is her old unit and she already ran into her commanding officer and had a lengthy conversation with him, but he didn't recognize her as a former soldier."

"That must have been a great relief to her," Mary said.

"Yes, and she does want to go home, yet she is not sure if she should. It would be dangerous for her to travel back to Michigan without an escort, though she doesn't see that as a major obstacle. She is quite capable of caring for herself and as you know, she can be obstinate. She is conflicted though, as she has found a calling in nursing, and she is quite adept at caring for the sick and injured, I can attest to that. I believe there is some fear in regards to how she will be received at home."

"I can understand that," Mary said, "and Nathaniel?"

"He is doing as well as can be expected. He spoke of me going back to Virginia with him after he is paroled, I just don't know if I can leave now, especially with Adam so sick."

"He believes Grant would give you a pass to leave?" Mary asked.

"Yes. Apparently the man isn't as heartless as I would like to believe. I trust you heard about Mrs. Josephine Erwin?"

"I heard that her husband was killed a few days before the fall of the city. Has something else happened to her?"

"A man from her husband's Missouri regiment met up with a fellow Missourian on the Yankee side. Both soldiers went to speak with Grant about her. She wanted to go and stay with her husband's family in Lexington. Grant is not only allowing it, he is giving her and her children transportation and assigned a guard of honor to accompany them. He also gave her fifty Yankee dollars."

"Well, that was very Christian of him."

"Yes, well," Victoria said grudgingly, then checked her watch. "As much as I wish to stay longer, I really must head back home. Mother feels we'll be forced to take in soldiers as borders, so she is preparing for that and she is trying to get Mary Grace reestablished by opening up the haberdashery. There is just so much to do."

"Of course." Mary stood. "I am glad you stopped by. Now that we have access to food, we should have tea or even supper together soon."

"That would be delightful," Victoria replied. Mary smiled and walked her friend to the door, happy for even the short visit.

Thursday, July 9, 1863
Turner Home

"Well, I've done it." Nathaniel entered the library, where Victoria was taking a break from doing laundry. "I signed my parole. I'm a prisoner of war and I will remain one until officially exchanged. As long as I remain out of active military service, until that official exchange, Grant and the Union army don't care what I do."

"I suppose you will leave, then. When will you go?" She asked.

He sat down in the chair next to her.

"All paroled soldiers are to remain within the Union lines here in Vicksburg until the rest of the soldiers that agreed to accept parole have signed the papers, and that could take another few days." He took her hand in his. "So I am yours until then." He kissed her on the temple.

"What about the men who refuse to sign?" Victoria asked.

"They will be kept on Federal boats in the river, where they'll stay until they accept terms. If they still refuse, they'll be transferred north to a prison camp."

"Good heavens. And there is no way for any of you to escape the city undetected?"

"Not likely," Nathaniel said. "Yankee guards occupy a line that stretches from the river above, around the entire town, to the river below. They'll shoot anyone trying to sneak through and ask questions later."

"What about those trying to sneak in?" Victoria thought of Jason. She continued to worry about her brother. Was he all right? And what of Hannah and her family? What had life been like outside of the siege lines for them?

"Unless they have a pass, they won't be allowed in. If you're thinking of Jason, he will have to be extremely careful. Militiamen fighting against the Union can and will be taken prisoner. It would be safer if you somehow arranged a rendezvous at the Wheelers when the smoke settles here."

"That is exactly what I was thinking. Is it possible to obtain a pass out of the city?" Victoria asked.

"Like I said, I wouldn't advise it quite yet, but perhaps in a few days when things settle down." He took a deep breath. "Victoria, there is something I must talk to you about."

"Nathaniel, whatever is wrong? Has something happened?"

"You know I will be heading east in a few days. I was thinking that it might be best if you came with me. I can request a pass from General Grant. He's been allowing others to leave. Mrs. Thomas Dockery petitioned Grant to allow her to bring her wounded husband home to Arkansas. He has agreed. He must not be completely heartless. I ran into Captain Burem, who was married back in April to Nettie Green, you remember, don't you? Grant is allowing him to bring a carriage and his wife through the lines. I could do the same. You could travel with me, then stay with my sisters or your cousins, whichever you prefer. That way, I could check on you occasionally and make sure you're safe."

"Do you really believe I need to be cared for?" Victoria asked.

"No, that isn't what I meant." Nathaniel rubbed his face. "I know you are very capable of caring for yourself. It's just...perhaps I'm being selfish, wanting you to be near me always. I don't want to leave you, yet I know I must."

"I don't want that either," she said, the dilemma she faced clear in her mind. She wanted to go with Nathaniel, for obvious reasons, but she wasn't ready to leave Vicksburg. How could she, when Adam was so sick? Both Mary Grace and her mother needed her help. She bit her lip. She knew Nathaniel would never force her to do anything, and he would accept whatever her decision was. "Nathaniel. I know we agreed to live in Virginia after the war, and I still intend on doing that, but I don't feel I can leave Vicksburg yet, there is so much I must do first."

"Of course. I don't know what I was thinking. Virginia is not safe and is no place for you to be anyway." Disappointment was apparent in his voice and on his face. "I understand how important your family is to you. Honestly, I don't want to leave Adam right now either."

"I would ask you to stay longer, but I know you have your duty." Victoria nodded, thankful that he was such an understanding man. She leaned over and kissed him. "I love you." Emotions cascaded over her: fear of Nathaniel leaving, fear of losing him, and a longing to start a new life with her husband. At the same time, she felt the pull to stay home as she would dearly miss her family.

"I love you too," he replied.

"Have you heard news of the Reynolds brothers? Timothy and Boone?"

"Yes, unfortunately," Nathaniel replied. "They are on one of those Federal vessels for refusing to accept parole."

"Oh no!" Victoria was shocked. "Why won't they accept?"

"Some men don't want to risk the possibility of going to a parole camp, others are hoping to escape future military service. With the Reynolds it's a little more complicated. Pure stubbornness for one thing. Last time I saw them, Boone was resolute that he would never accept parole, and if Boone doesn't, there is no way Tex would leave him behind. They will likely both go to prison unless Tex can talk some sense into Boone."

"Tex is a loyal man," Victoria murmured.

"I understand them. I should be on that boat as well. I'm not going to lie, I wanted to refuse. I hate this pretending. Acting as though we are no longer enemies. Some Confederates are even friendly with the Yankees, talking with them, drinking with them." He shook his head, agitated. "These Yankees are so smug. I just want to..." He fisted his hand. Victoria placed her hand over his.

"You must keep your temper. Remember, you will be arrested for the smallest infractions. You won't be able to go back east if you are in a Yankee prison or the local jail. I detest the Yankee's presence as much as you, but we must all keep our tempers."

"I know." Nathaniel blew out a breath. "I wish it could all be different. I wish this blasted war was over, and that the Yankees would just leave us alone." He closed his eyes. "I want it done, finished," he said after a brief pause. "I don't want to have to kill any more." His voice was so soft that she barely heard him. He looked away, then stood slowly, and strode to the window. She followed him and placed a comforting hand on his back.

"I can't imagine what you've been through, Nathaniel. I have shared a room now with two people who have fought in this war. Both you and Tabetha suffer from nightmares."

"I didn't realize I woke you with mine, Tori. I'm sorry."

"No, my love, I'm not blaming you. I completely understand. As I said, Tabetha has bad dreams as well, as do many of the men in the hospital."

He paused. "I pray to God that I never have to fight in another battle."

"Then don't go back." She gently pulled him around so he would face her. "We can burn your parole papers and uniform. You can wear Jason's or Gregory's old clothes. Live here until the war is over. There are many men here who are ordinary citizens. You could get a job..."

"I can't do that, Tori, you know I can't. For one thing, I am a farmer. I can't live in the city." He sighed and cupped her cheek. "As much as I want to stay here, I would be without honor. I wouldn't be able to live with myself. I took a vow to serve the Confederate army, and I will not be a deserter. I take my promises seriously."

"I knew you would say that, but I had to try," Victoria replied. "To be honest, you wouldn't be the man I fell in love with if you did. I just hate to see you hurting."

He scoffed. "I don't like that you see me when I'm hurting."

Victoria smiled. "Well, I married you for better or for worse, you recall."

Friday, July 10, 1863
Streets of Vicksburg

Tabetha hastened through town, on her way to the Green's house hospital she was running late for her shift. She noticed Union soldiers and Negroes working together, cleaning the refuse left behind. Other Union soldiers patrolled the streets. The Federals were preparing to have the Confederate parolees move out. It would be a slow process. Tabetha thought of Victoria and how she was acting strangely this past week, almost distant. Tabetha knew she was worried about Nathaniel and Adam, whose health was actually declining now. Tabetha feared the young boy would not live to see the end of the month.

"Miss Norton!" Mary Green smiled and greeted her friend. "It has been far too long since I've seen you."

"Yes," Tabetha agreed. "How is your family?"

"We are all still adapting to the changes, but much better than during the siege." The two women continued walking. "The children are with my mother now. I was going to my home to see how it is fairing."

"I was on my way to your home as well," Tabetha said. "I understand Mr. Green is being credited for saving your entire neighborhood from destruction thanks to his decision to turn your house into a hospital."

"Yes. I only wish the people in town weren't so upset with him for signing the loyalty oath. There are still those who are miffed that he didn't join the Confederate Army." She sighed. "Oh dear, Tabetha, my apologies for complaining. I must remember that so many of the townspeople have lost loved ones to this ridiculous war. They only want to find a scapegoat."

"I suppose." Tabetha was just happy that she wasn't targeted as a scapegoat for being from the north. "Have you heard that the Confederates surrendered Port Hudson? Now the entire Mississippi River is in the hands of the Union and the Confederacy is cut in two, as President Lincoln had predicted." Tabetha shook her head. "Victoria is not happy about this news at all."

"From what I've observed, Victoria isn't happy about much these days."

"I would agree with you," Tabetha said. "I was just thinking about her and wondering what is upsetting her so. We all have changes to accept in our lives, but she doesn't seem as controlled and confident as usual."

"How is Adam?" Mary asked. "Victoria said she was very worried about his deteriorating condition."

"He is not doing well at all. He caught a chill living under ground in the damp conditions. I'm no expert, but I fear for his well-being. I know that's one reason Victoria is so depressed lately. She loves that little boy as if he were her own. She is also preparing for Nathaniel to leave. He asked her to go with him to stay in Virginia with his family, but she said she can't leave Adam right now."

"No, of course not, and she won't." Mary agreed. The two women were about to walk up the drive to the Green home when a commotion broke out in front of them. A Union soldier pushed into a second Union soldier, then, more pushing ensued. A punch was thrown, and one of the men tackled the other. Soldiers, both Union and Confederate, surrounded the brawlers. Finally, two Union officers intervened and pulled the two men from each other.

"What are you thinking, Campbell?" The first officer yelled at one of the fighters. Tabetha recognized both men. The officer was Captain Steven Rogers and the man he was chastising was Lieutenant Noah Campbell. Captain Rogers pulled the man aside. "You cannot go off half-cocked like that, Noah."

"Come now, Steven, you know that Lorenzo Thomas is a rude, condescending..."

"I don't care if he is. You're an officer and you're supposed to be a gentleman."

The other men had dispersed. Captain Rogers looked up and noticed the two women, tipped his hat to them, then pulled Lieutenant Campbell around to the side of the house.

"Well, that was exciting," Mary said. "I must say, both of those officers were quite handsome." She nudged Tabetha with an elbow. "Perhaps I will try to get an introduction for you. Now that Victoria is happily married, I should turn my focus to finding you a beau."

"Oh, Mary, you don't need to worry about that. Besides, I have already met both of those officers."

"Really?" Mary smiled. "Do tell."

"Well." Tabetha lowered her voice. "They're both from the 6th Illinois, my old regiment."

"You don't say?" Mary covered her mouth with her hand. "I'm so glad they didn't recognize you. Or have they?"

"No, they have not, thankfully. The captain was my commanding officer, and I met him again at church this past weekend. He had no idea

269

that we had met before, and he would be the one man that I would be most worried about."

"Well, you must be terribly relieved," Mary said.

"You have no idea."

"I still say he is a handsome man. Is he also agreeable?" Mary smiled.

"Agreeable? You sound just like a novel by Jane Austin." Tabetha shook her head, blushing. Captain Rogers was not only the handsomest man she had ever met, he was also extremely agreeable.

"Yes, agreeable. Is he?" Mary asked again.

"Yes, he is. Very charming and easy to talk to."

"Very well," Mary said with a shrewd smile. "I will see what I can do to help the both of you along in a relationship."

"You don't need to do that, Mary," Tabetha assured her friend.

"I know, but I so enjoy matchmaking," Mary said. "I'm quite happy in my own life and marriage, I just want all of my friends to be the same."

"Well, thank you. I do appreciate the thought." Tabetha truly did. "Oh, dear, the time flies by. I must get on with my daily work. I enjoyed the talk."

"Have a wonderful day, Miss Norton."

Victoria sat on Adam's bed that evening, cuddling her nephew, reading to him from Hans Christian Anderson's Fairy Tales. He was almost sleeping when Nathaniel knocked on the doorframe and gave them a small smile. Nathaniel had shaven his face clean that morning and Victoria had given him a haircut before leaving for her sister's.

Nathaniel came to the side of the bed. "How is my little man? May I join you, Adam?"

"Of course, Uncle 'Thaniel," Adam said weakly. "I'm ever so glad you're here."

Nathaniel laid on the opposite side of the bed and put an arm around the boy. "Me too." He met Victoria's eyes over Adam's head. "Unfortunately, I have to leave early tomorrow morning. I may not see you again for quite some time."

"I understand, Uncle 'Thaniel. Maybe the war will end soon and then you can come back." He looked concerned for a moment, then spoke to Victoria. "You're not leaving too, are you?" He coughed.

"No, my little love, I am staying right here. I wouldn't leave you for the world." She dropped a kiss on his head.

"I'm glad." He looked back at Nathaniel. "Did you come to say goodbye, just in case I go to Heaven before you come back?"

Tears welled up in Victoria's eyes. What would she do without this sweet boy?

"What makes you think that, Adam?" Nathaniel asked gently, his voice cracking. He brushed Adam's blonde hair back. Victoria reached behind Adam and placed a comforting hand on her husband's arm.

"Sometimes I hear everyone talking when they think I'm sleeping." Adam coughed again. "I asked Kendall once, what would happen if I died, and she said I would go to Heaven with Jesus, like her mama."

"Well, Kendall is correct, that is what happens when you die, but what makes you think that you're...that you'll die, Adam?" Nathaniel's eyes shimmered with tears.

"Just a feeling, Uncle 'Thaniel. If I do die, please don't be too sad. I want you to be a good fighter and you can't beat the Yankees if you're sad. Promise me that?"

"Yes, Adam, I promise." Nathaniel's voice was hoarse. "I want you to know that I love you. I wish with all my heart that I could stay here with you and your Aunt Victoria."

Adam coughed yet again. "I said I understand." The boy's voice weakened with every word spoken. His eyes drifted shut. "Love you too..." And he was then sleeping quietly.

Nathaniel bent over and gave Adam a kiss on the forehead, stood and strode out to the hallway. Victoria hurried after him. She found him looking out the window, arms crossed over his chest. She approached him, then pulled him around and into her arms.

"Thank you for coming to visit him."

"I only wish I could do more. I don't know how to help him." He sighed. "I don't want this to be the last time I see him, or you."

Then don't leave. She wanted to say to him, even argue with him, but she didn't want to sour their last night together, nor cause him further anguish. "It won't be. You'll come back soon. I know I will see you again. This...today? This is not where our relationship ends. We must believe that."

Nathaniel kissed her, then pulled her into an embrace. "I know, and I will carry you with me in my heart until I do see you again."

Mary Grace came up the stairs. "Nathaniel, Victoria. Is Adam all right?"

"Oh, yes. Don't fret, Mary Grace. He just fell asleep. Other than that, there is no change." Victoria assured her sister.

"Goodness, by the looks on your faces, I had feared the worst. Thank you, Nathaniel, for visiting with him. Adam thinks the world of you." Mary Grace smiled sadly, then entered Adam's room.

"We should go home," Victoria said. "It's your last night here and I fear the morning will come all too soon."

Sunday, July 12, 1863
Lakemont

"What a very special delight that you are all here. It's been far too long since we have enjoyed each other's company." Mary Green smiled at Hannah, Victoria and Tabetha. Hannah and her family had finally received passes to come into town. They had been searched and questioned at the siege line, but had been let through to attend church and visit with friends.

"Thank you for having us," Tabetha replied. "I'm glad for the excuse to take a day for myself, well, at least part of the day. I do have to stop at the hospital later."

"Oh, Tabetha, you simply should take the entire day to yourself. You work much too hard," Mary said.

"I am used to it, being raised on a farm, and besides, there are far too many men that need help." Tabetha said.

"That is true." Mary focused on Victoria, who was quietly staring out the window. "Victoria, how is Adam? I was disappointed when I didn't see Mary Grace, knowing she would be with him."

She looked at her friends, though it was clear her thoughts were elsewhere. "Not well. In fact, I'm not going to stay long. I just wanted to catch up with Hannah. Have you seen Jason at all?"

"I have, as a matter of fact, several times," Hannah replied. "The last time was only last Thursday."

"What was life like on the outside?" Mary asked. "I do hope nothing dreadful happened to you or your farm?"

"Life was definitely different," Hannah said. "Our home was often surrounded by Yankees. They set up an encampment just to the South of us for a short time. I really don't know how Jason was able to get to the house as often as he did. But worst of all, they stole many of our supplies and livestock."

"How awful for you," Mary said. "Will you be able to recover your losses?"

"Yes, we eventually will recover the losses." Hannah assured them. "It surely isn't pleasant, being under the command of the Yankees. We try to have faith, yet we are in constant fear that we may be injured or killed. Much like it is here, I would guess. After hearing what you've all been through this past month, I can say that my life wasn't comparable. At least we had food to eat and a warm, dry house to live in."

"Nothing disastrous happened?" Tabetha asked.

"We did have one close call," Hannah said, then told the story of the skirmish and the Union men dying. "We were lucky, though. A similar episode happened over near the Barlow farm. The Yankees were ambushed after Mr. Barlow told them they hadn't seen any Confederates.

The Yankee soldiers were so enraged at the family for supposedly lying that they torched the home and told Mr. Barlow that if he wasn't gone by sundown, they would hang him."

"Oh, good Heavens," Mary Green exclaimed. "I hope the family was able to safely get away."

"They were, thank the good Lord," Hannah replied.

"These situations should no longer be an issue," Victoria said.

Hannah shook her head. "It will be a long time before anyone feels completely safe. Mrs. Messenger, down on the banks of the Big Black River was held prisoner in her own home while Yankees hauled all her possessions away, and Mrs. Newman had all the cows in her dairy stolen."

"So clearly these Northern abolitionists don't care for the blacks the way they claim," Victoria scoffed. Candis Newman was a free woman of color. Victoria shook her head. "I do apologize, ladies, but I need to relieve Mary Grace and watch Adam." She gave her friends a quick nod and walked out the door.

"She certainly is not herself today." Hannah sounded worried. "I know much has happened over the past couple of months, but I expected more...life from her. Is she not happy with Nathaniel?"

"It's not that at all. She's been acting morose since the siege ended." Tabetha said. "Nathaniel leaving was difficult enough, yet with Adam so sick... she just has so much on her mind."

"I wish she would be more at peace, but at least she isn't like the other women," Mary said. "So many Vicksburgians are terribly angry. I understand why, really I do, but this occupation is not going away. The Union army will not give up what it has struggled so hard to win. We must accept it and not ostracize or further anger the conquerors and those that have surrendered."

"Are you in reference to those who have signed the Oath of Allegiance?" Tabetha asked. "Are you and Duff being ridiculed because he signed?"

"From many of the townspeople, yes." Mary admitted. "Nothing overt and nothing that has made me feel unsafe, but there have been looks and whispers and more than a few cutting remarks."

"I am so sorry you have to endure that, Mary," Hannah said in her comforting way. "I don't believe you deserve to be treated with such disrespect. Those who do are likely just afraid. No one knows what is going to happen next, and people always fear the unknown. They don't know how to deal with change."

"Yes, I believe you are right," Mary said, "but I do hope this animosity ends soon. Duff and I can handle their attitudes, but I dread Annie or William being mistreated because of it."

Tuesday, July 14, 1863
Turner Home

Victoria stood in the breezeway and rubbed her forehead. She hadn't felt well since she woke up this morning. In fact, she hadn't really felt herself this past week. Her stomach ached and her forehead felt warm to the touch. She wanted to go to Mary Grace's house and tend to Adam, but she was hesitant. If she was sick, her illness could make Adam even weaker, and she couldn't risk that. As Victoria thought about what to do, Tabetha entered the house, her eyes bloodshot and puffy.

Victoria's stomach felt worse. "Tabetha, whatever is wrong?"

"Victoria, I need a word with you." Tabetha gently pulled her friend into the parlor. "I was just by Mary Grace's. You know your mother is there with Brianne and Kendall."

Victoria shook her head assertively and continued to stare at Tabetha, who choked out her next words.

"I'm sorry, Victoria, its Adam...he...Adam is gone. He died this morning."

Tears welled in Victoria's eyes and she hunched over, feeling even more nauseated. "Oh, Lord, please, no. God, please, no." Her heart pounded and her legs gave out as she fell back onto the settee. "No, no, no..." She covered her face with her hands.

Tabetha sat down next to Victoria, tears falling again, and placed a hand on her back. "He's at peace now. Victoria, he has no more pain." She suspected her words were useless. Tabetha was overwhelmed at the loss of the little boy she had only known for a short time, but had grown to love.

Victoria wiped at her cheeks, then coughed and gasped, trying to catch her breath. "I knew this day would come, somehow I knew, but I kept hoping and praying for a miracle to happen." Her nausea became stronger and she hurried to the backdoor. She tried to make it to the back fence, but lost her breakfast before she could get that far. Tabetha came up behind her and rubbed her back gently. When Victoria stood, Tabetha felt her forehead.

"You're burning up, Victoria. How long have you been feverish? What are your other symptoms?"

Victoria groaned. "It doesn't matter. Nothing matters. I must go to Mary Grace and Mother...the children."

Tabetha directed her friend back inside the house. "You most certainly will not. Victoria. You look as though you're going to swoon. We need to get you to bed."

"I can't. Adam..."

Tabetha shook her head. Victoria was becoming delirious. "Victoria Prentiss, your family has just lost one member of the family, God rest little Adam's soul. They can't lose you too. Besides, you mustn't be so selfish as to expose everyone in the family to whatever illness you have. Don't act impulsively as you normally do."

"That's contradictory, coming from a woman who learned of her brother's death and decided to enlist in the Yankee army that very evening." Victoria's voice was weak and almost incoherent.

"Yes, well, I have learned from my mistakes. You must make better decisions than I have." She helped Victoria up the stairs and into bed. "As I said, you really don't want any of your family members to lose you as well? Think of Nathaniel."

"No, I love him so, I really love my whole family...." Victoria cried, finally hearing the wisdom of Tabetha's words. "I am so sorry. I just want to be with my family in their time of need, Tabetha."

"I know, I know, but let's get you settled into bed and as comfortable as possible, then I'll go and talk with your mother."

A tear fell from Victoria's cheeks. "Thank you, Tabetha." She mumbled. "I know I have been irritable lately, I don't know why, but I'm so, so sorry."

"Come now." Tabetha covered Victoria with a sheet and a light blanket. "You have nothing to be sorry for. It is quite evident that you have been under the weather."

After Tabetha put Victoria to bed, she tracked down Esther and explained the situation. The former slave sat down and wept for the little boy she had helped bring into the world such a short time ago. When she was through, she wiped at her tear-stained cheeks, then focused on Victoria's illness.

"What d'you think it is?" She asked.

"If I had to make a guess, I'd say dysentery. She has all the symptoms. We'll need to keep a close watch over her and make sure she drinks a lot of water. That seems to help. Can you stay with her while I go to Mary Grace's and let them all know about Victoria."

"I kin do dat, Miss Tabetha," Esther said, placing the lid over the soup she was cooking.

"Thank you," Tabetha replied, then left to go back to the haberdashery.

Thursday, July 16, 1863
Turner Home

"Is she any better today?" Mary Green asked as she entered the room. Tabetha was reading a book at Victoria's bedside.

"She's about the same." Tabetha gestured to a chair. "Please sit down. She occasionally wakes up, keeps asking about Adam and Nathaniel. It's as if she hopes when she wakes up, everything that happened these past few weeks will just have been a bad dream."

"I know the feeling," Mary said quietly, thinking of her firstborn daughter.

"How was the walk over here?" Tabetha asked.

"The streets are crowded. People of all social classes are out and about. Refugees desperate for food, shelter and security are flooding into the city. Folks who fled the city before the siege are returning home. Families from miles around who have been preyed upon by both armies, like the Wheelers, are coming in the hopes that they can get food and supplies that are affordable."

"It sounds as though Jason is making sure Hannah's family is well taken care of." Tabetha stated. "I haven't met the man yet, but I feel like I already know him from listening to all of the stories from his family. He sounds quite dashing."

"He is a very special gentleman and wonderful brother," Mary said. She was about to speak of Jason's friendship with Hannah when Kendall entered the room.

"Tabetha, are you able to come downstairs? Aunt Rachel is still at Mary Grace's and there are some Yankee soldiers at the door saying they're to be quartered here. They have papers from the provost marshal that I don't understand. Brianne went to get Aunt Rachel, but they insist on coming in."

Tabetha stood. "Can you stay with Victoria, Mary?"

"Of course," Mary replied. "Go."

Tabetha hastened downstairs with Kendall. She immediately saw three Union soldiers standing in the breezeway. Her heart beat a bit faster when she saw one of the soldiers was Captain Steven Rogers and the other as Lieutenant Noah Campbell.

"Captain Rogers, gentlemen." She greeted him politely. *Of course he would be one of the men here.* Tabetha didn't recognize the third man, another lieutenant. He bore a resemblance to Captain Rogers, just a bit younger.

"Miss Norton, what a pleasure to see you again." Captain Rogers smiled. "However, I must inform you that I am no longer Captain Rogers, I have been promoted to Major."

"Congratulations, Major Rogers," Tabetha said. "May I ask what your business is here?"

"We have been sent here by Provost Marshal General Loren Kent. I'm actually supposed to speak with a Mrs. Charles Turner. I understand that she is not here at the moment. Her niece has gone to retrieve her."

"Yes," Tabetha answered, taking the orders from Major Rogers. "Mrs. Turner is currently staying with her daughter, Mrs. Abraham Corbet. Mrs. Corbet just lost her young son, Mrs. Turner's grandson, Adam, after a lengthy illness brought on by the siege. Mrs. Turner's other daughter, Mrs. Nathaniel Prentiss, is sick with dysentery upstairs. As you can see, Mrs. Turner is understandably under a great deal of stress. May I be of service to you?"

"I am so sorry to hear of all those troubles. My condolences to the family," The major said sympathetically.

"Thank you for your concern," Tabetha said quietly. "There are several family members staying here, but this order states you are to be quartered here. How many rooms will you require, Major?"

Major Rogers gestured to the two men, the younger one first. "Lieutenant Rogers and I can share a room and Lieutenant Campbell will need one. If it will be helpful, we can all stay in one room for a few days, while you adjust the living arrangements. I am fairly certain there will be another border coming soon, and he can board with Lieutenant Campbell."

"I see," Tabetha said.

"I apologize, for not introducing my fellow comrades officially." He gestured to the sergeant. "This is Lieutenant Noah Campbell."

The officer tipped his hat and gave her a charming smile. "It's good to see you again, ma'am."

Major Rogers gestured to the younger man. "And this is my younger brother, Lieutenant Ezekiel Rogers."

Tabetha vaguely remembered Steven telling her about a younger brother, a brother that he had hoped would never enter the army.

"It is a pleasure to meet you both," Tabetha said. The door opened behind the men and Mrs. Turner walked in, followed by Brianne.

"Good day, gentlemen." Rachel Turner sounded welcoming, as usual, although her eyes were red and puffy. Tabetha was impressed by how this woman was able to hold herself together. She had lost her beloved grandson, her daughter was very ill, she had two sons and a husband away fighting and hadn't heard from them in months, and her home was heavily damaged during the shelling. Now, enemy soldiers were invading her home, yet Mrs. Turner was still solid as a rock.

"Mrs. Charles Turner, I presume." Major Rogers gave her a short gentlemanly bow and introduced himself and the others again. He then handed Rachel the papers that Tabetha had given back from the Provost Marshal General.

Rachel sighed. "We will have to do some rearranging, gentlemen, and as Miss Norton here must have told you, we have sickness in the house. We'll try to have everything ready by this evening."

"Thank you, ma'am," the Major said. "Miss Norton told us of your troubles. Please let us know if we can be of any help."

"Thank you, Major. I appreciate your offer." Mrs. Turner replied. "Dinner is at four o'clock."

"We'll be here, ma'am," Lieutenant Campbell said. "Never could resist a good home-cooked meal." He winked at Kendall, who blushed.

"Thank you, ma'am," Ezekiel Rogers added, tipping his hat.

As soon as the officers left, Rachel turned to Tabetha. "How is Victoria?"

"I believe she is slightly improved somewhat. Mary is with her now. Are the plans set for the funeral?" Tabetha hesitated to ask.

"Yes," Rachel answered, a tear slipping down her cheek. "Our dear Adam will be laid to rest at the Cedar Hill Cemetery on Saturday. Reverend Lord will perform the service." She swiped another tear from her cheek.

Tabetha placed a comforting hand on Mrs. Turner's arm. "Please let me know what I can do for you. Anything at all. I have been praying so hard for your family, and for Adam's soul. He was such a sweet boy."

"He was." Rachel started crying freely, as did Kendall and Brianne. Tabetha pulled them all into a hug. Rachel held her tightly and cried the tears she had been holding in. "We will get through this. We must. I don't know how, but we will."

Saturday, July 18, 1863
Turner Home

"You are looking much better, Victoria," Mary Green said. The rest of the family and servants had gone to the Episcopal Church for Adam's funeral service. Mary Green had volunteered to watch over Victoria, who was still too weak to attend.

"Yes, but I should be with my family, not lying abed." Victoria stated. Not wanting to talk of Adam, or think of what she was missing, she changed the subject. "I find it difficult to believe that Mother is allowing Union officers to stay here."

"She doesn't have much of a choice, Victoria," Mary said. "The town is under martial law. The Union army could actually force you out of your house if they really wanted to."

"So you're telling me I should be thanking the Yankees for simply taking over a few rooms and not my entire home?" Victoria's voice was weak, yet angry.

"No, no, I am not saying that at all," Mary replied. "I'm just telling you how it is. My, but you must be getting better, you are quite disagreeable."

"Perhaps if I had something to agree with, I wouldn't be so disagreeable," Victoria stated. Mary frowned. This wasn't like Victoria, not at all. She wasn't quite sure how to respond.

"Oh, Mary, will it ever go away?" Victoria asked, closing her eyes. "This heaviness in my heart, deep inside."

Mary sighed, closing her eyes as she pictured her own little girl, gone now for over four years.

"Unfortunately, no, Victoria. It never completely goes away. The pain, the grief is always there, you just learn to push it deeper inside. There are still days when I wake up and don't want to get out of bed because I miss my baby so, and I wonder what kind of girl she would be today. She would have turned seven this year." Mary leaned her head against the wall behind her. "No, it never goes away, but it will get better," She said again, more to herself than her friend.

"It is good to hear that Mrs. Prentiss is feeling better," Major Steven Rogers said, taking a bite of baked chicken. "And this chicken might be the tastiest meal I have ever eaten."

Tabetha glanced at Brianne, then Rachel. Kendall had elected to eat upstairs with Victoria to keep her company.

"We are quite relieved about Victoria," Rachel replied. "And our cook, Esther, is quite a blessing. We are quite lucky. She will actually be moving out of the house at the end of next week."

Brianne dropped her fork. "Esther is leaving?" She asked. "Where is she going?"

"She's going to be staying with Caesar. He is now a member of the Colored Infantry Regiment." Rachel stated for the benefit of the guests. She tried to remain poised. "She has promised to come over every day to help us prepare meals, however..."

"So this is yet another tragedy brought on by these infernal Yankees. I suppose Dinah will leave us as well." Brianne threw her napkin down and stood, tears streaming down her face. "I hate this war! I hate the Yankees!" She then fled the dining room.

Rachel set her fork down. "I apologize for my niece, gentlemen. You must forgive her outburst. She's had a difficult time with the loss of Adam, she loved him so, and with Victoria's illness, all of the changes here in town." *Not to mention the betrayal she has always felt from her Yankee father.*

"Quite understandable, Mrs. Turner," Major Rogers said. "I can imagine that our being in her home hasn't made life any easier."

"Thank you for your kindness. As a matter of fact, her father is an officer in your army." Rachel was a pleasant host as always. Tabetha didn't know how she managed to do it. "May I ask, gentlemen how have you been spending your days? I see soldiers cleaning and repairing the streets, policing the town, and yet I see many just loitering."

"Yes, ma'am. The soldiers are doing that, but we've been assigned patrol duty. It isn't my personal favorite, but we must corral the guerrillas fighting against us. The Rebels have militia units that are wreaking havoc on our perimeter. We are not only tracking down these men, but we are also arresting the civilians who are supporting these guerrillas."

"General Orders 100 was issued back in April and gives us a lot of leeway to handle circumstances as we see fit." Lieutenant Ezekiel Rogers spoke up.

"What's General Orders 100?" Tabetha couldn't resist asking.

"It identifies the goal of war for the Union to restore the peace," Lieutenant Rogers explained. "It distinguishes peaceful civilians from the violent classes who target Federal soldiers. We try to be compassionate to the former and call for severe measures toward the latter."

"I see," Tabetha said. "You still desire to win the war at all costs."

"Hard war," Lieutenant Campbell added. "It sounds harsh, but yes. If we persevere, we can all go home and get back to our peaceful lives all the sooner."

"Peacefulness. I wonder if that will ever be possible again," Rachel sighed.

Monday, July 20, 1863
Turner Home

Victoria took a sip of tea and turned to Mary Green. Her friend had stopped by to visit yet again.

"I appreciate all of your support during my illness. My recovery has been expedited with all the fine care I have received." She admitted.

"You are most welcome, though no thanks are necessary," Mary replied. "You are a dear friend. I don't know what I would do without you, Victoria."

Victoria wiped a tear from her eye. "I'm afraid there are yet more changes to come. I'm just not...oh, I just can't believe that Adam is dead. I have yet to see Mary Grace, she hasn't come by to visit, though I can't say I blame her. I wish Hannah could come in for a visit, but those blasted

Yankees make it difficult to get a pass, according to Mother, and Mother..." She shook her head. "I simply do not know how Mother has the inner strength to carry on despite all the tragedy we've had of late."

"She is an amazing woman, with such strong faith."

"I'm..." Victoria hesitated. "Lately, I don't feel..." She sighed.

"You wonder if God really cares." Mary finished the thought.

"Yes." Victoria's voice was barely audible. "I hate admitting it, but that's exactly it. First the war, then the siege, then Nathaniel leaving, then Adam, no one knows what's become of my father and brothers. So many lives lost or destroyed, and for what? Now we must contend with this Yankee occupation and their invasion into our very homes. It just seems hopeless."

"It has been difficult, and it won't get easier anytime soon," Mary added. "I have my doubts as well, but when I do, I read from the Bible for comfort. One passage in particular, a verse I know you read as often as I do."

"Jeremiah," Victoria replied. "God knows the plans He has for us, plans to help us and not to harm." She sighed again. "I know, and I know deep down that God cares about us. It's just difficult to remember with so much tragedy. The Yankees seem bent on robbing us of everything, including our souls."

"The Federals cannot be blamed for all the death and destruction. In fact, if you were to get to know some of the soldiers, you might find them to be quite enjoyable. Even you would have to admit that General Grant is a fine figure of a man."

"I don't believe I will ever find any Yankee enjoyable, especially that nasty man."

"You've befriended Tabetha. I know the two of you have become close. Have you forgotten that she is a Northerner? That she was once a Union soldier?"

"I haven't forgotten," Victoria replied. "It's different with Tabetha. I don't believe she ever really wanted to be a soldier. She just made a rash decision and was caught up in her actions before she knew what she had done."

"What makes you think these Yankee soldiers are any different?" Mary asked. "Did your father and brothers really want to fight? No. They had specific reasons. They chose to do what they thought was best. Just like Tabetha, Nathaniel and the Federal soldiers."

"Yes, I suppose there is some truth to that." Victoria admitted. "I have been out of touch with what has been happening in the city. What news have I missed?"

"It is good to hear you ask. It is a sign that you are getting back to your old self. There is talk that some missionaries are coming to Vicksburg to teach the Freedmen," Mary said.

"So more Yankees will descend on our town to give our freed slaves more of a reason to leave. For Heaven's sake, most of our white children don't have the opportunity to go to school," Victoria scoffed.

"Yes, that is true, and the blacks may leave, but it was unavoidable. You and I both know slavery would have died out eventually." Mary said. "Also, I hate to upset you with more bad news, but Judge Houghton's little daughter, Laura, has died too. I'm not sure how and I hate to be the bearer of such sad news, but I thought you ought to know."

"How many of our children must die?" Victoria cried as she tried to hold back tears. "Why must any child die?"

"Are you able to hear more news or shall we change the subject?"

"Just tell me and get it over with."

"I must talk with Duff, or even Hannah to confirm this rumor, but I heard that the Yankees are taking over abandoned plantations along the Mississippi. They are leasing them out to private individuals, many from the north. The Federals are trying to bring commerce back to the city and surrounding areas, it will just be for the wrong side."

Mary was right, Victoria wasn't glad to hear this piece of information. "Hmmm." She wondered if the Yankees had ulterior motives by bringing more of their people to the area. "I believe this will end badly."

"Possibly," Mary said. "Either way, Duff is positive Vicksburg will soon be a thriving center of trade again, for both Northerners and Southerners alike."

"Of course," Victoria replied. "Everyone wants our cotton. It is still a lucrative industry."

"Yes, it is," Mary agreed. "And I know the commerce will only help us in the future. It will bring us back to prosperity."

"But do we want prosperity at such a high cost? I don't if it means allowing the Yankees to run our cities."

"I don't like it much either," Mary said. "But, we'll just have to learn to live with the situation as best we can. We must adapt to change, Victoria, or we will never grow."

Wednesday, July 22, 1863
First Church~Oberlin, Ohio

"And if you join me, you not only will help educate the neediest of people, you will also be an active participant in the Union war effort." Reverend Samuel Cook spoke with passion and conviction. "Only the destruction of slavery can save the republic. Missionaries play an integral role in this most holy crusade for emancipation." Jessica Spencer sat in the crowd, transfixed. She was always captivated when Reverend Cook was at the pulpit. She couldn't look away from his sharp blue eyes and firm jaw. Such a handsome, passionate man.

Jessica's friend Amanda Bell leaned over. "He is such a fervent speaker, as always," she whispered.

"Yes," Jessica agreed, watching as the man continued to promote his mission. "I believe joining him may be the answer to my prayer."

"Thank you and God Bless." The reverend finished his speech, then stepped down from the pulpit as the crowd burst into applause.

"I must speak with the Reverend," Jessica said to her friend. "If I join his mission, I can do something of value and be able to pay my own way. I won't have to depend upon the goodness of my friends, and I won't have to impose upon my aunt and uncle."

"Jessica, you know you are never an imposition," Amanda said.

Jessica was grateful for her friends' kind words, but didn't agree with her. Jessica's father, a widower since Jessica was five and a professor at Oberlin College, had passed away the previous month. Jessica had been staying with her dearest friend, Amanda, and Amanda's husband Joe, who was an apothecary. While Amanda and Joe were incredibly welcoming, Jessica was now nineteen years old, and she knew that she had to move on.

The plan was for Jessica to live with her aunt and uncle on their farm in southwest Michigan. However, Reverend Cook's mission called to her. She had admired the Reverend for years. He was a very sought-after bachelor, but didn't seem to be serious with any of the young ladies who were thrown in his path. Perhaps attending this mission trip would also help the Reverend learn more about Jessica as a woman.

Jessica found the Reverend quickly, but the reception line was long and it took a while before she was able to speak with him.

"Reverend Cook. I know we have been introduced before..."

"Yes, Miss Jessica Spencer. I must apologize for not stopping by to offer my condolences after your father's untimely passing. I meant to do so, but other responsibilities kept interfering. I was very fond of him and had wonderful and inspiring conversations with him. He was a good man and a brilliant professor. Very well-respected."

"I thank you for saying so, Reverend. What I wish to speak with you about...well, actually, the loss of my father does correlate with what I wish to speak with you about. You see, I hold a teaching certificate and believe I am being called to travel south with you to Vicksburg. I find myself needing to teach those poor men, women and children who need an education so desperately."

"That is splendid," Reverend Cook replied with a kind smile. "It is very refreshing to find someone like yourself so willing to serve."

"Your passionate speech was very convincing," she stated. "I have been praying, asking God to help me find my true mission, the direction my life should go from here. I feel your plans are an answer to my prayers." While waiting to speak with him, she had thought long and hard about what she was going to say. She was very happy with herself for staying as composed as she was while speaking to the charming man.

"I believe that may be the truth, Miss Spencer." Reverend Cook said with another smile. "An answered prayer, indeed. I first must ask you one question, and I hope I don't offend you. How old are you?"

"I understand, Reverend." Jessica laughed. "And I don't believe you need to worry about my being too young. I turned nineteen just last month."

"Splendid," he replied. "I assume you can leave Oberlin at any time."

"That is correct," She replied.

"Wonderful, I will be in touch, then. We'll be leaving within a fortnight. As you prepare, make sure you pack lightly. One trunk and a carpet bag that you can carry."

"I can manage that," Jessica said. "It shall not be a problem at all. I am currently staying with Mr. and Mrs. Bell above the apothecary. You can find me there."

"Splendid," he nodded. "I am very glad that you attended my speech today and that my words made such an impact on you. I look forward to working with you."

"And I you," Jessica answered.

Sunday, August 2, 1863
Wheeler Farm

Hannah Wheeler smiled at her friends. "I am so glad you accepted my invitation for dinner. I have missed our visits." She put an arm around Victoria and gave her a side-hug. "And so glad that you have made a full recovery."

"We are grateful for the invitation," Tabetha replied. The Wheeler family: Hannah, Ambrose, Cordelia and Caroline, had invited the Turners for the afternoon: Victoria, Rachel, Mary Grace and her children, Brianne, Kendall and Tabetha had all decided to make the trek out of the city limits for the first time since before the siege. It was also Mary Grace's first time out of her home since Adam's death. She was still in deep mourning. Before the war, a mother in mourning wouldn't leave her home for six months, but times had changed. If individuals followed the traditional mourning rituals, few people would ever leave their homes.

"I'm just glad to be away from the Yankee scum all around town." Brianne scowled. "Especially the ones in our house."

Victoria, Tabetha and Hannah sat outside on the porch, shucking corn for the dinner. The Wheelers had been fortunate to not have all of their crops destroyed like many of their neighbors. Tabetha was distressed and embarrassed at what she had seen and heard lately of how and what some Federal soldiers had done around town and in the area. Burning, thieving and plundering. The soldiers were misbehaving and it shamed her to have once been a part of the Yankee Army.

Hannah glanced towards the tree line. "We may have one more guest."

"Who would that be?" Victoria asked. "There are Yankees riding all over this land. Have you befriended some of them?"

"No. We keep to ourselves and haven't had any issues with them. We are lucky for that," Hannah said.

"I hope, that continues to be the case, especially with the newest General Order we heard about yesterday," Victoria said. "While the order targets guerilla groups and other pro-Confederate forces and the civilians who aid them, Grant advises civilians to cooperate with all their emancipation policies, can you believe that? The Yankees want to encourage those who hire former slaves to give them wages, and to distribute provisions to destitute civilians."

"I can never understand how you are able to remember all the details of what you read." Hannah smiled.

"Oh, there's more," Victoria said. "This is actually good for us. The order promises severe punishment for Union soldiers who prey upon civilians and their property."

"That is splendid news," Tabetha said. "I hope that starts as soon as possible."

Victoria continued, "There is a catch. It does not protect anyone who is suspected of aiding our militia men who are harassing the Yankees in any way they can." Victoria gave Hannah a meaningful look. Her friend averted her eyes. "I worry about you, Hannah, I really do. I know you've been seeing Jason. If you're caught…"

"We won't be," Hannah interrupted. "Jason is extremely careful and he won't come in if there's even a small chance of anyone getting caught by the enemy. Besides, I don't think I could stop him if I wanted to."

Victoria shook her head. "It doesn't matter how careful you are. You are all still at risk."

"I am aware of that, Victoria." Hannah sighed and changed the subject. "Has your family taken advantage of the rations that the Federals are providing?"

"We have a couple of times," Victoria admitted. One of the surrender terms Pemberton had insisted upon was that the Union army share rationsarass1 with the Confederate soldiers and civilians. "I went just the other day. There are so many citizens applying for the rations. We were behind Mrs. Virginia Rockwood, you remember her, don't you? She was quite entertaining."

"Ah, she can be that. I assume she was her usual feisty self, then?"

"She was indeed. The man writing her order referred to her as a destitute citizen, but without a pause, she told him to change the wording to 'robbed citizen'. The man did so, and doubled her rations."

"Good for her," Hannah said.

"Yes. Then when her list was being filled by a clerk, Virginia sarcastically informed him that asking for the food did not humiliate her one bit, as she was only getting back what the Yankees stole in the first place."

"Bravo." Hannah nodded, then glanced toward the tree line and smiled as a gray-clad figure darted from the woods across the field.

"What in the world..." Tabetha shielded her eyes to look.

The soldier came closer. "Jason!" Victoria stood and ran to her brother. She threw her arms around him. "I have missed you so." She pulled back to look at him and playfully slapped him on the arm. "You should not have come. It is far too dangerous. Come, get into the house."

"I'm here for Sunday dinner," He replied with a smile, though it wasn't as carefree as Victoria remembered prior to the war. "Mrs. Wheeler is a wonderful cook." He glanced at Hannah. "Both Mrs. Wheelers, that is."

"You do realize what would happen to you if you were caught?" Victoria asked as the rest of the group picked up the corn and went into the house.

"Of course I know," Jason turned to Tabetha.

"You must be Miss Norton. It's good to finally meet you. I hope we can trust you to keep my presence here a secret."

"Jason!" Hannah was embarrassed at his implication that Tabetha would be disloyal to the family.

"You have nothing to worry about, Mr. Turner." Tabetha assured him.

He nodded, then turned to Victoria. "I just had to see you all. Not being able to check on you for almost two months has been bothering me greatly. First, I have to congratulate you on your nuptials, Mrs. Prentiss." He smiled. "I told you that I believed you and Nathaniel would make a good match, and I completely approve."

"Thank you," Victoria said.

Jason continued. "We didn't get any news out here for quite some time after the city was taken. I worried so much, but you all stayed safe until after the occupation. I tell you, Hannah almost had to lock me in the cellar to stop me from sneaking into town when I heard how sick Adam was, and then he..." His voice cracked, then moved on, "and we could have lost you too." He gave her a quick kiss on the cheek. "I'll talk more with you later. I have to see Mama, and the rest of the family." He darted into the house.

Victoria turned to Hannah. "Why does it seem as though he is here for Sunday dinner quite often?"

"Because he is. He used to come as often as possible, more so at the beginning of the war." She hesitated, not quite knowing if she should confide her fears about Jason to her friend. Hannah feared he was becoming more depressed and despondent, but Victoria didn't need any new worries in her life.

"I just need you all to be more careful."

"I know," Hannah said. "I can't promise that nothing will happen, only God knows who of us will make it through this war."

Wednesday, August 5, 1863
Turner Home

Tabetha was hungry and ready for dinner. She had just finished work at the Green Home hospital, and it had been another exhausting shift.

Major Rogers smiled when she entered the dining room. "Miss Norton, what a pleasure to see you. There is some hearty beef stew in the kettle on the side table." He gestured. "Mrs. Turner told me that if you came in, you should help yourself." The rest of the family had already eaten.

"Thank you," She nodded. "You don't mind if I join you at the table, do you?"

"Of course not. I would rather enjoy the company," he replied. "We haven't had the chance to socialize much, and I must admit, I would like to get to know you better. You remind me of someone I used to know, though I can't place who."

"I suppose it's just one of those things." She wanted to tell him where he knew her from, and knew it would be best if she told him the truth now. If only she could muster up the courage. "Where is everyone else?"

"From what I understand, Mrs. Turner and your cousins went to Mrs. Corbet's home, and Mrs. Prentiss is out visiting a friend."

"I see." She took a bite of her beef stew, glad that Esther still cooked for the family. "What have you been busy with today?"

"Riding patrol, trying to capture the Rebel guerillas who are raiding and attacking our men. They are quite a nuisance."

"I see." Her stomach twitched. Jason Turner was one of those raiders, and many could argue that she was committing treason by not telling Major Rogers about his frequent visits to the Wheeler home. "What is your opinion of the Major General?" Major General James McPherson of the Union Army was now in command of the District of Vicksburg. He was a West Point graduate, like many of the high-ranking officers on both sides of the war.

"I believe him to be a competent, compassionate commander," Major Rogers responded. "I respect both Grant and Sherman, and they are excellent officers but, between you and me, I don't always agree with their tactical methods."

"The idea of hard war?" Tabetha clarified.

Major Rogers gave a short nod.

Tabetha continued. "Yes, I saw the effects of 'hard war' recently when I visited a friend in the countryside, and I think what the Union soldiers did to this town was terribly destructive." She was surprised with her anger toward the Union Army.

Major Rogers clenched his jaw. "I understand why our commanders and even our Congress want to carry out the war in such a manner. It is supposed to expedite its end, but I agree with you. I don't approve of seeing homes burned and crops destroyed solely because a family is suspected of helping a Confederate soldier who may actually be a friend or family member."

Tabetha thought back to the work she did while in the cavalry, tearing up railways, using beautiful fences for firewood, taking livestock and destroying people's' livelihood. She thought it a crime then, and she still believed it.

Major Rogers sat back in his chair and stared at his now-empty bowl. "I didn't expect the war to be like this. It's not all honor and glory as many believe. There is far too much needless death and pain and destruction. To fight in battle is one thing, but the after effects, the looting that happens, how the women and children are affected...the looks in their eyes. I never wanted Ezekiel to be exposed to this kind of life." He shook his head. "My apologies, Miss Norton. I never meant to drone on in such a depressing way."

"It's quite alright, I don't mind your honesty. I agree with what you're saying and I can understand your frustration."

He gave her an appreciative smile. "You are incredibly easy to talk with, Miss Norton. I am glad we've had this opportunity."

"I feel the same way, Major." Tabetha smiled. She never would have imagined that a man like Steven Rogers would be interested in her as a woman. She had always assumed she would marry a logger or a farmer from Muskegon. Was it possible God had a different plan for her?

"I was wondering if you would like to go for a stroll one of these evenings when you're available, of course. I know you are quite busy working at the hospital, but I would enjoy escorting you through town."

"I would enjoy that, Major, truly I would." She smiled, grateful for the opportunity to get to know this man further.

Monday, August 10, 1863
St. Francis Xavier Hospital

"Tabetha!" Victoria called from the doorway. Tabetha gave a comforting pat to the shoulder of the soldier she had been reading to, placed the man's Bible on his pallet, and pushed herself up from the floor.

"Is everything alright?" Tabetha pushed a wayward strand of hair from her face.

"Major Rogers was just brought in. He has a very high fever."

"Do they know what is causing it?"

"They haven't said yet." Victoria led Tabetha out of the room.

"I should have known." Tabetha was concerned. "I noticed he was a bit pale this morning and I could tell that he wasn't feeling well."

"Yes, I agree. When I saw him at breakfast he didn't look well." Victoria nodded. "He apparently lost consciousness, fell off his horse and hit his head on the ground. He refused to come to the hospital prior to that. When I was helping to get him situated, he was quite groggy, but he spoke your name when he recognized me."

The two women reached the room where Victoria had left him. Tabetha paled a bit herself when she saw the usually strong and vibrant major looking weak and feeble.

"He's burning up." Tabetha could tell just by looking at him. Beads of sweat covered his face, and he appeared to be in severe pain. She quickly knelt beside him. "Has a doctor been to see him?"

"I'm not sure, I left to find you first," Victoria said. "I'll go and talk to the doctors now."

Tabetha stood and found a bucket of water and a washrag. She returned to Major Rogers and began to wipe his face. Seeing him brought down by an illness more affected her more than she could imagine. Too many men seemed to succumb to illness than actual battle wounds. She had to do whatever she could to get him through this sickness.

"Miss...Miss Norton..." Major Rogers mumbled, his eyes still closed. Tabetha's heart fluttered. Did he know that she was there or was he subconsciously thinking of her?

"I'm right here, Major," she said, then smiled as he opened his eyes slightly.

"I thought I heard your voice. What happened? Where am I?"

"You're in the hospital. You passed out while you were on duty and hit your head." Tabetha tentatively touched his forehead, which had a large gash from his fall, then wiped it gently with the cloth.

"I don't faint," he said, trying to sit up, but was unable to do more than lift his head a few inches off the thin pallet.

"With all due respect, Major, you will faint when you have a fever as high as you do and fail to take care of yourself properly."

"What day is it today?"

"Do you see what I mean? You can't even remember what day it is." She shook her head. "It's Monday. You were just brought in, I'm not sure by whom. Victoria came to find me."

"I'm glad she did. Being around you comforts me." He tried to smile, but it was weak.

"I am pleased you feel that way." Tabetha felt contentment running through her. It was good to be needed by a man she greatly admired. "We need to keep you as cool and comfortable as possible. I'll make sure you have lots of fresh water to drink, but first, let's get this wound cleaned up."

She dipped the cloth in the water and focused on cleaning the blood from his forehead. "We must get you back to good health as soon as possible."

"I appreciate your care, Miss Norton. You don't know how much." He struggled to keep his eyes open.

"You need your sleep as well," She told him. "Don't fight it. Close your eyes and rest, it will help you get better sooner."

"If you say so. You are the one with all the medical experience." His eyes closed.

"By necessity, Major. By necessity only." She finished cleaning the wound.

Victoria came to Tabetha's side. "I found Lieutenant Campbell, he helped bring the Major in. He told me the doctors believe its yellow fever." She placed a hand on Tabetha's shoulder. "How is he doing?"

"As one would expect. He woke up briefly, we were able to talk for a few minutes." Tabetha looked up at her friend with concern. "Perhaps you should stop working here, Victoria, and only help at the Green's Hospital. I would hate for you to get sick again so soon after your recovery. Yellow fever may be contagious."

"I don't think so, most people get it from the swamps. There is a medical book, Gray's Anatomy, back in Father's library. I can look through it and learn more about the illness." She shrugged and began stripping the empty bed next to Major Rogers. "The wounded at Mary's home need help and comfort as well. I suppose until I read more about Yellow Fever, it wouldn't be a bad idea to work there." She placed a hand on her forehead. "To be completely honest, I've been quite tired since my illness. I can't seem to get my energy back."

"Perhaps you should check with a doctor. You were quite close to dying, Victoria."

"I am more worried about the children. Especially now with Major Rogers getting yellow fever. They have been exposed to so much illness and sorrow lately." She finished gathering the sheets.

"That is true." Tabetha rearranged the sheets on Major Roger's cot.

"I am just about finished up here," Victoria held the sheets in a bundle. "I'll bring these down to the laundry and then head home. Shall I wait for you?"

"No, I'll see you there for dinner." Tabetha stood. "I promised a few of the men I would write letters for them." The two began to walk toward the back of the building, where the laundry was done.

"So many men to tend to," Victoria said. "It seems a never-ending process. I often wonder how the doctors feel, trying to care for all of the men injured and sick." She sighed. "Are we only getting these men healthy so they can go back and fight our Confederate boys again?" She shook her head. As usual, her mind was a river of conflicted thoughts. The Yankees were the enemy, and she shouldn't help them in any way. However, when she was actually faced with their pain and suffering, she was unable to turn away from them. Many of the Yankees she had met were kind and considerate. "All right, then." She sighed. "I'll see you at dinner. I do hope Mary Grace comes over with the children. I'd really love to see them. Don't be late, now, you hear? Mama and Esther are probably cooking up something good."

"Anything other than pea meal or mule meat sounds heavenly. I realize you're not happy that the officers are staying with us, but it is nice to have their rations available."

"You have a point," Victoria said. "We would survive without them, though. My father left us in good standings with his accounts. Now that we have access to food that doesn't cost such exorbitant prices, we would manage. We don't need the stinking Yankees." She placed the dirty sheets in a basket and wiped her forehead. "I'm sorry, Tabetha, I didn't mean you. I'll see you later. Try not to stay too long. I know you'll want to spend time with Major Rogers, but remember to take care of yourself as well."

"I will," Tabetha replied, grateful to have a friend looking out for her.

Tuesday, August 18, 1863
Turner Home

Jessica glanced at the slip of paper that Reverend Cook had given her. She would be boarding with a family named Turner at their home on the corner of Cherry and Crawford Street. She found the house and knocked on the door, then glanced down the hill toward the mighty Mississippi River. Despite the town's despondent appearance, the location was quite beautiful. The door to the home was opened by a girl around the age of fourteen.

"May I help you, Miss?" She asked, confusion on her face.

"Yes," Jessica said brightly. "I'm Miss Jessica Spencer. I believe the lady of the house is expecting me. The Provost Marshal sent me. I am your new border."

"You're the new boarder?" The girl's face went from confusion to concern. "Are you quite sure?"

"This is the Turner residence, is it not?" Jessica asked, trying to remain calm and confident. "Are you one of the Turner daughters?"

"I am Mrs. Turner's niece, Kendall Larson." The girl opened the door to let her in. "We heard we were getting another boarder, but we assumed it would be another officer."

"I see." Jessica set her bags down and removed her gloves. "I hope this misunderstanding can be resolved."

"I'm sure Aunt Rachel will make the arrangement work. I will be back directly with her. Please have a seat." Kendall replied, shutting the door and going down the hall.

Jessica looked around. She could tell that the house had once been very elegant, but the damage and neglect during the recent siege was evident. It appeared the family had done their best to make repairs, but they obviously were still in the midst of a wartime economy.

As Jessica moved to take a seat on the chair Miss Larson had offered her, the front door slammed open and hit Jessica on the arm. She muttered an 'ouch' and stepped away as a handsome Union officer stepped through. He looked at Jessica from head to toe, then smiled, his blue eyes shining.

"Begging your pardon, Miss." He swept off his hat to show light brown hair. He bowed slightly and rubbed his bristly cheek. "I didn't mean to startle you." He stepped closer to her. "My name is Lieutenant Noah Campbell. Please let me know what I can do to make up for my thoughtlessness." He gently touched her upper arm, which she believed was now bruised, thanks to his carelessness.

She stepped away. "I'll be quite all right, thank you."

The soldier continued standing there as if waiting for her to do something, but she could think of nothing witty to say. Thankfully, a beautiful, elegant-looking woman walked through the parlor door, followed by Kendall Larson. The older woman's smile immediately put Jessica at ease.

"Welcome, Miss Spencer, is it? I am sorry I was not here to greet you; I was helping our cook prepare dinner." She led Jessica into the parlor and gestured for her to sit.

"It was a pleasure to meet you, miss." Kendall said, then headed toward the back of the house. Lieutenant Noah Campbell followed them into the parlor and leaned casually against the door frame.

"I was told we would be getting a new boarder, but as my niece told you, we were anticipating another soldier who could room with Lieutenant Campbell there."

"I would be more than happy to share my room with Miss Spencer," Noah Campbell said from the doorway. Rachel Turner looked at him, half-amused, half-annoyed.

"You may enjoy those accommodations sir, but I doubt the young lady would." She chastised him as she would her own son. "Was there something you needed Lieutenant Campbell?"

"No, ma'am, I just wanted to welcome Miss Spencer to your home." Jessica glanced at him and gave him a forced smile. He winked at her, and tipped his head.

"Ladies." He then left the room.

Mrs. Turner smiled at Jessica again. "He may seem like an undignified rake, but he can be quite the gentleman once you get to know him."

"I will take your word on that," Jessica replied. "Although I must admit, I thought... the way you two treated each other, I almost believed he was your son."

"I should think not!" She exclaimed. "He is a Union officer. I do have two sons, both away fighting for the Confederacy, as well as my husband, and that is where my loyalties lie. However, having the officers living here makes me somehow feel like my boys are home." She gave a genteel shrug.

"You are a gracious hostess," Jessica stated.

"We have another young lady staying with us as well. She is here from Michigan. She has become like another daughter to me. Don't be shocked when that happens to you as well, my dear."

Jessica tried to remain unaffected by the woman's words, but a single tear fell down her cheek, and she quickly wiped it away. Her father tried his best to be a good parent and he was a wonderful father, but, there had been times when she really wished she had a mother.

"I would like to thank you for allowing me to stay here. I am so very grateful. I was unsure how I would be received by a Confederate family."

"Of course, you are welcome," Rachel said. "You'll meet the rest of my family later. My niece, Kendall, whom you've met, has an older sister, Brianne. They both live here while their father is away fighting in the army. The Union army, that is. The girls lost their mother, my sister, at a young age."

"I know how that feels," Jessica replied with a frown.

Rachel comfortingly placed a hand on Jessica's arm. "Oh, my dear Miss Spencer, I am sorry to hear that. What happened?"

"My mother died in childbirth when I was five. The baby girl died as well. I still miss her terribly."

"I am so sorry for your loss, Miss Spencer," Rachel said.

"She was a wonderful woman." Jessica held her tears in. "My father was a good man as well. He died recently, which is why I decided to become a missionary."

"I am sorry you have been through so much."

"'I can do everything through Christ, who gives me strength.'" Jessica quoted the Bible verse that had gotten her through so much.

"That is a wonderful thought to lean on," Rachel said. "Well then, let me tell you more about your new housemates. Tabetha Norton is the young woman from Michigan, she's volunteering as a nurse. My daughter, Victoria, is visiting a friend. I have another daughter, Mary Grace, who lives down the street with her children. They visit quite often. Finally, we have our three Union officers. You met Lieutenant Campbell. There is also Major Rogers, and his younger brother, Lieutenant Rogers. The major has taken sick and is at one of the local hospitals in town."

"My goodness," Jessica hoped she didn't look as overwhelmed as she felt. If she couldn't remember the names of those she was sharing a house with, how would she ever remember the names of her students?

"I hope I didn't give you too much information too quickly." Rachel sensed Jessica's reactions. "Come, I will show you to your room. Kendall should have everything ready by now."

Jessica nodded and followed the woman upstairs.

"Did you bring more than what is in that bag?" Rachel asked.

"I have a trunk that is still at the railroad station. It will be delivered later." She shrugged. "Military supplies are apparently much more important than dresses and books."

Rachel nodded. "Books. Ahh, yes. You mentioned you are a teacher, of course. My husband has quite the collection of books. Thankfully the library was not damaged during the bombardment. You may feel free to borrow any books you can use."

Jessica paused. "Ma'am, you do know...I mean, you are aware...I will be teaching at a Freedman's school."

"Yes, dear, I assumed that." Rachel opened the door to one of the bedrooms.

"And you would...you would allow me to use those books to help former slaves learn?"

"Of course." Rachel smiled. "I grew up having slaves, Miss Spencer. We still have Esther, our cook, staying here with us, though she is now free. Her husband was one of our people as well but he is now in a

Colored Regiment stationed here in town. Whether I like it or not, slavery is no more in Vicksburg and those poor souls need some education if they are to survive. I see so many of them, penniless, sick, and vulnerable. They need an education so they are not taken advantage of. They must learn how to make a living so they have hope for a future. As a Christian, I must support that. Besides, even the Confederacy's own hero, General Thomas Jackson, God rest his soul, formed a colored Sabbath School and taught his slaves to read."

"I hadn't heard that." Jessica was slightly confused. She had always believed that all Southerners were horrid to their slaves, but that wasn't the case according to Mrs. Turner.

"Here is where you will be staying." Rachel told her. Jessica looked inside. The room only had one large bed and was very nicely furnished.

"I was under the assumption I would be sharing a room." She set her carpet bag down. "Are you sure you have enough room for me to have my own..."

"Oh, here you are, Aunt Rachel," A young woman around the age of seventeen barged into the room. "Can you tell me what happened to our room? It looks as though a cyclone hit it. Blankets and quilts moved around and some of your things on Kendall's bed..."

Jessica immediately realized whose room she was in. "Oh, dear, Mrs. Turner, no. I cannot take you from your own bedroom. Please. I can share a room with someone, really, I don't mind at all."

"That wouldn't be proper." Rachel stated.

"No, no, I don't mind at all," Jessica said. "In fact, I would prefer it."

"If you're sure that is satisfactory." Rachel asked one final time.

"Yes," Jessica answered firmly.

"All right, then." She turned to the young woman. "Brianne, will you find Kendall and help her move my things back in here?"

"If I must," the girl sighed. "It appears I'll have to share a bed with Kendall no matter what."

"I heard you." Kendall walked into the room. "It's not as if I never shared a bed with you before." She turned to Jessica. "Back when our mother was alive, we lived in a small homestead. Brianne and I slept in a loft. Do not worry about putting us out."

Jessica bit her lip nervously. It hadn't occurred to her that the people she would be boarding with may be inconvenienced by her presence. She had been so caught up in her own excitement of serving with Reverend Cook and making a difference in the lives of the Negro children that she had overlooked details. In fact, if Reverend Cook hadn't spoken with the Provost Marshall and arranged for the lodging of his teachers, she may not even have a place to stay. His thoughtfulness was yet another reason that she was attracted to him. She shook her head and focused on the southern family in front of her.

"Miss Spencer, I would like to introduce my niece Brianne to you. Brianne, if you hadn't realized, is Kendall's sister."

"It is nice to meet you, Brianne," Jessica said.

"You as well, Miss Spencer." Brianne replied with a dramatic curtsey. "I am so appreciative to you all for taking me in, more than you will ever know."

"Well, we didn't really have a choice." Brianne mumbled.

"Bri-ane!" Kendall glared at her sister, then turned to Jessica apologetically. "Miss Spencer, you're a part of the family now, whether you want to be or not. You'd best get used to it."

"I believe I will enjoy that very much," Jessica replied with a smile.

Victoria poked her head into the room that Major Rogers was recuperating in and saw Tabetha talking with the weak and surly-looking captain.

"Honestly, Captain Rogers, if you really want to get back to your post before you're completely well, then just go. You'll just be required to come right back here due to a relapse of your symptoms." Her voice was firm, yet caring. Victoria smiled. Tabetha was treating the Captain just as Victoria would treat Nathaniel.

"I despise this hospital. I'm not getting any sleep, as you tell me I should, and the food here isn't nearly as hearty as Esther's. Can't I convalesce there? I know you and the Turners could care for me just as well as the staff here. Present company excepted, the care here is mediocre at best." He gave her a soft, pleading look. "Please, I promise not to report to my post, or overexert myself for another week."

Victoria saw Tabetha bite her lip nervously. She knew that the captain still didn't realize that the soldier 'Pistol Pete' was the woman who was nursing him back to health.

"I must do whatever I can to keep all soldiers healthy." She said, placing her hand on his arm.

"Good afternoon, Major Rogers." Victoria interrupted. "I have been out making plans I know will make you happy. Lieutenant Campbell and your brother have volunteered to help bring you back to our home. The doctors agree that you are well enough to travel the short distance, but you mustn't return to your duties for another two weeks. Mother is agreeable and the doctors here need your bed for others."

"Wonderful." He swung his legs around, ready to stand and leave. Tabetha placed a hand on his shoulder to stop him.

"Not quite yet. Whether you like it or not, you are still weak. You likely wouldn't get to the front door without collapsing."

"We could get a stretcher for you, if you would prefer that," Victoria teased. The major sighed and leaned back against the headboard.

"Nagging women," he muttered, but there was a light tone to his voice.

"Yes, and you might be interested to know you will have one more nagging woman in the house." Victoria told him. "The new boarder arrived today, but he is not a soldier. We have a missionary teacher staying with us now. Kendall informed me when I returned from visiting Mary Green. Her name is Miss Jessica Spencer and she is from Ohio."

He smiled at Tabetha, who tried not to blush. "Splendid."

"I'm going to head home now to be sure all is ready. Your escorts should be here at any time," Victoria said. "I just wanted to bring you the news."

"Thank you, Mrs. Prentiss," Major Rogers said.

Victoria smiled, in spite of herself. "I will see you both at home, then."

Monday, August 24, 1863
Freedman's School, Outside of Vicksburg

Jessica looked around the small, crowded room at her new pupils. When she left Ohio, she thought she knew what to expect, but after speaking with fellow teacher, Fannie J. Scott, she had been less confident about her first day with the children. Mrs. Rachel Turner and Miss Tabetha Norton, however, had encouraged her and she was grateful for their kindness.

The schoolroom was hot, humid and the windows were so small and dirty, very little light penetrated through them. There was already a stench permeating throughout the room. Perhaps she could find a cool place outside to hold classes, though there would likely be too many distractions there.

Jessica strode to the desk, which was really just a plank of wood placed over crates. She picked up her Bible that she had placed there earlier, and looked out at almost sixty faces staring at her, waiting for her to share her knowledge. The students varied in age from five to thirty. It was almost 9:00, which was starting time.

Reverend Cook leaned toward Jessica. "I will get you started with a prayer, then leave you to your students." He spoke softly in her ear. He was trying to get to as many of the schools as he could to open the sessions officially for the teachers.

"Thank you." Jessica's heart fluttered. She thought he would stay with her longer this first day of class. *You can do this. You are a certified teacher.*

The reverend checked his watch, then cleared his throat. "Brothers and sisters in Christ, I would like to welcome you all. I am so glad that you are here. Knowledge is imperative in securing a better life for oneself. We shall begin this day in prayer."

Everyone bowed their heads and Reverend Cook led them in a short prayer. He then turned to Jessica. "This is Miss Jessica Spencer. She will be your teacher. I'm sure you will all get along amicably." He put on his straw hat, gave Jessica a brief smile, and left.

Jessica took a deep breath, then faced her class once again. They stared back, silent and expressionless. She looked around and smiled at one familiar face. Cicero, a young boy that had been taken in by the Turner's former slave and cook, Esther. The boy gave her a quick smile in return. That was enough to encourage her.

"Good morning!" She said brightly. "As the Reverend Cook said, my name is Miss Jessica Spencer. I came to Vicksburg, Mississippi from a city called Oberlin in the state of Ohio. Does anyone know where that is?"

The students looked at her blankly, awkwardly silent. She looked around, trying to persuade her pupils to try and answer the question. Finally, Cicero spoke up. "North,"

"Yes!" Jessica smiled. "Yes, it is." She turned to point at the map behind her, then realized she didn't have one. "I would love to show you on a map, but I don't have one with me. I will try to locate one and bring it so we can learn about different places." She hoped the Turners had a map or a globe that she could borrow. "I would like to start out today and every day with a Bible reading. I believe that in no time at all, we will be able to take turns reading a verse." She quickly opened her bible.

"Jeremiah, Chapter 29, verse 11. *For I know well the plans I have in mind for you, oracle of the Lord, plans for your welfare and not for woe, so as to give you a future of hope.*" She closed the Bible. "This is one of my favorite scripture verses. It is meaningful in so many ways." She looked from student to student. They all simply continued to stare back at her. "Alright. I think the first thing we should do is divide you up into groups based on experience. I would like to speak with each of you and take your names down so I know where to begin and see what level you are at." She took a deep breath, picked up some paper, and worked her way through each student, asking them questions so she could best plan how to help them. It would be a difficult task, but with the help of the Lord and the support of Reverend Cook, she could accomplish anything.

Wednesday, August 26, 1863
Lakemont

Mary Green hurried into her mother's parlor, excited to speak with Victoria. She had been meaning to visit with her, but had not found the time. There were so many topics to discuss with her dear friend.

"Victoria, I am so glad you came to visit. I have already arranged for tea."

"Splendid. It is hard to believe that just over a month ago, we would be having sweet potato tea in a cave." *And Nathaniel was with me and Adam was alive.* Victoria shook her head. She had promised herself and her mother that she wouldn't be so dour. "I would have been here earlier, but the streets are horrendous. The Yankees are drilling up and down, preparing for a dress parade and with the civilians and refugees, the streets very congested. The Yankees must feel the need to demonstrate their strength to us Rebels."

"And practice their skills too, I would wager," Mary said.

"I suppose."

"How have you and your family been?" Mary asked.

"They are as well as can be expected. Mary Grace is still grieving deeply for Adam, as we all are. She seldom eats and isn't sleeping well. I am quite worried about her. Mother wants her to move into our house, but she refuses. Brianne, Kendall and I are taking turns staying with her in the shop. Tabetha too, on occasion. Mother is caring for everyone else. She is such an efficient housewife. She has been helping Esther with the cooking and cleaning and even treating our Yankee boarders as if they were her own children."

"It's possible she needs to do that," Mary suggested. "Perhaps it's how she is able to cope with the unknown whereabouts of her own sons' and husband's."

"That thought has crossed my mind, which is why I haven't told her of my disapproval." Victoria added bitterly. "We are now being forced to follow yet another Yankee order. It requires all operators of Vicksburg hotels and boarding houses, which we were forced to become when the Provost Marshall made us take in soldiers and young Miss Yankee teacher. We must provide the post headquarters with a weekly list of our lodgers. We need to do so, even though our boarders will remain the same for the foreseeable future and they are the ones that sent them." She shook her head. "It is ridiculous, yet we must follow orders. I tell you, Mary, the Yankees continue to take all of the enjoyment from our lives."

"I wouldn't say that, Victoria," Mary countered.

"You must not have heard the latest, then. General Grant ordered the Provost Marshall to take possession of all the billiard tables in the city, and place a reliable man in charge of them. Reliable man my foot."

"I did hear that. According to Duff, that order was issued to protect the civilians, not deny them access to the tables."

"They are to be kept for the amusement of the officers and soldiers of their armies." Victoria insisted.

"Yes, and not to charge a price of over ten cents for each game played. The northern speculators were practically extorting the money from hard working men on both sides."

Mary was saddened by Victoria's attitude. Her friend was harboring so much bitterness that she wasn't listening to reason, which was very strange. Prior to the siege, even if Victoria disagreed with someone, she at least listened to what they had to say. Mary could distinctly remember Victoria having scintillating conversations with men and women, including First Lady Varina Davis. Victoria hadn't always agreed with those individuals, but she let them speak their mind and tried to understand different points of view. Lately, it seemed Victoria was quick to make judgements about situations without all the facts.

Victoria shook her head. "Well, I say the Yankees are still trying to control every move we make. If you can't see that, then..." She shrugged her shoulders in indifference.

Mary sighed and sent up a quick prayer for patience and guidance in what to say, but before she could process another thought, Victoria rose. "As much as I would like to stay, I must be off."

"You just got here." *My friend, what is wrong with you?* "Can't you stay a little longer?" Mary stood. "I feel we could spend hours catching up."

"Unfortunately, not today. As much as I wish to stay longer, I have errands to run for Mother. We must feed all those Yankees, after all." She turned to leave the room. "I will see you soon."

"Of course," Mary tried to hide her disappointment. After she walked her friend to the door, she turned and went to the back porch where she had left her mother.

"Did Victoria leave already?" Mrs. Lake asked, a bit surprised.

"Yes, she did," Mary sat down. "I'm so worried about her, Mama. When she first arrived she was acting like the Victoria I used to know, but as we began our conversation, I could tell that she still harbors bitter feelings. I wish she would confide in me more or allow someone to know what is troubling her so."

"Perhaps you should speak with her mother or sister and ask if they have similar concerns."

"I have considered that, but they are both so busy and still in mourning for Adam." Mary pointed out.

"Such a tragedy. Poor Rachel, and Mary Grace, of course."

"I suppose I could speak with Brianne or even Kendall, but they're feeling the loss of Adam quite keenly as well. Not to mention the fact that they are much younger than Victoria and might not even realize Victoria's changed attitude."

"Rachel is a dear friend," Mrs. Lake added. "I confess, I haven't visited her since I attended Adam's funeral. I really should do so. Perhaps I can gain some insight on Victoria from her."

"Could you, Mother? I don't believe she confides much with anyone anymore, including Tabetha, and I get the impression that she doesn't care for any of the new boarders. She used to share her feelings with Nathaniel, in the letters she wrote him and she never would hesitate to share her feelings with me." Mary sighed. "Until the siege, it always comes back to the siege. I'm losing her friendship, Mama, and I don't know why."

"It may feel that way, dear, but you and Victoria have been friends for a very long time, and that friendship has weathered much adversity. She will get through these trying times with love and support. Please don't take any offense to what she may say or do right now. Remember, she didn't give up on you during one of the lowest point in your life."

Mary shook her head. Her mother was right. Victoria had been the one to pull Mary from the indifference she felt in life when her little girl had died. Mary's thoughts drifted back in time.

March 1859
Lakemont

Mary lay in bed, looking out the window. It had been three weeks since Annie had died...or was it four? She couldn't exactly remember. She knew the date of Annie's death, she would never forget it, however, she wasn't sure what day it was now. It didn't matter anyway.

"Miss Mary, ya have a visitor. Miss Victoria is here." Missy, one of her house slaves, peeked into the room.

"I'm not up to visitors today, Missy. Please tell her that," Mary replied.

Unexpectedly, Victoria pushed her way into the room. "You have been saying that for far too long, Mary Green." She sat down. "I know you are in mourning and I cannot imagine what you're feeling right now..."

"You're right, and I don't want to speak with anyone, Victoria." Mary insisted. "Please just leave me alone."

"All right, then you can just listen to me for a moment. You are my dearest friend, Mary, and I must say, your attitude is distressing to me. I wish I knew what I could do or say to make you feel better, but I don't. I just want to be here for you. Promise me, if you need someone to just sit and listen, if you need a shoulder to cry on or someone to pray with you, please send for me." Mary's eyes welled up as Victoria continued. "I *won't try and tell you that I understand how you feel because I don't. I won't try and tell you that everything will be okay, because I know right now, you don't feel as though it will. Just let me be your friend, your confidant. Let me be there for you. Let me help you."* Victoria leaned forward and placed a hand on Mary's shoulder. *"Annie has been gone for almost a month. I know you will never forget her, I won't either, but if you let Him, God will give you the strength to carry on. It may not seem like it now, but God does have a plan for you."*

Mary sighed. *"It's your favorite verse if I'm not mistaken, but right now, I have no hope for my future."*

"That is my favorite verse, and it has helped me to understand that what I want may not be what God has planned for me."

"Hope." Mary repeated. *"A future of hope."* She wiped the tears from her eyes. *"Right now I have no hope, but I thank you, Victoria, for trying to help me. I can't promise I won't be melancholy anymore, but...I will make more of an effort."*

"That's all I ask of you, Mary, and I will be here for you because that is what friends are for."

1863

"She is the best friend I could ask for," Mary remarked.

"Yes, she is, Mary, and she has so many worries right now. Be patient with her, my dear."

"Of course you're right, Mother. I will be patient with her, just as she was with me."

Thursday, September 3, 1863
St. Xavier Church

"Miss Norton!"

Tabetha stood on the stairs of the Hospital and turned toward the now-familiar voice. Her work day so far had been fulfilling, though her favorite patient, young Orion Howe had been discharged and was now heading home to recuperate.

"Major. It is good to see you out and about. I assume that means the doctor, and more importantly, Mrs. Turner, approved of your returning to your duties." She smiled.

"Yes. The doctor said I received impeccable care." Steven smiled back. "I would like to thank you, Miss Norton. The care you gave me helped me recover quicker than most."

"It wasn't just me, Major. You know the entire Turner family assisted in your care." Tabetha didn't want to take all of the credit. She had enjoyed the time she spent with the Major, discussing many topics from the war to farming, their families and even some of their dreams. He never once suspected her of being Pistol Pete.

"We both know that you gave me the most diligent care possible, and I thank you."

"I was glad to be of service to you." Tabetha didn't want to be forward and tell him how much she had really enjoyed caring for him.

"Miss Norton, I was hoping to ask you something later, but since you are here..."

Tabetha's heartbeat increased. He couldn't be asking...

"I have never met anyone quite like you. I know the conditions are not ideal, but I feel as though we have established a special friendship in the short time we have been acquainted. I don't know how long I will be stationed here or how long this war will last, but I would like to consider myself your beau. Would you allow me the privilege of courting you?" He smiled. "I did speak with Mrs. Turner and asked her what she thought about us courting, since we live under the same roof and because I am unable to get permission from your father for obvious reasons. Mrs. Turner was very enthusiastic about the prospect."

Tabetha smiled at Steven. "I would consider myself lucky to call you my beau, Major Rogers."

"Very good," he replied. "I would ask you to dinner tonight, but we will already be dining together. Could I possibly entice you into taking a stroll with me afterwards?"

"That would be very nice." Tabetha was already looking forward to it.

"Wonderful. Until tonight, then." He smiled and tipped his hat. Tabetha gave him a brief curtsey, then watched him walk towards the main headquarters. He was such a kind man. Tabetha felt bad for what she had just done. She wasn't being honest with Steven by not telling him her true identity, but she felt the best time to do so had passed. She wondered now if she even had to tell him, yet down deep, she knew that she would never be able to live with herself if she kept the truth from him. Unfortunately, she risked losing Steven if she did tell him. Tabetha wondered what would have happened if she had followed her instincts and told him long ago, after that first battle when their friendship had begun.

"Miss Norton! Can you assist us today? We could really use your help here!" Tabetha was pulled from her memory by Sister Stanislaus. She quickly went to the kind nun's side. The war still raged on.

Sunday, September 6, 1863
Turner Home

Dear Amanda,

I have arrived safely in Vicksburg and established my classroom. I love all my students, though there are many more than I had anticipated.

I am very glad to be with the American Missionary Association as opposed to others like the Cincinnati Contraband Relief Commission, who believe the best way to improve the overall character of teachers and missionaries is to exclude unmarried women. The nerve! I truly hope that idea never takes root. We did have an American Missionary Association representative complain that certain teachers sent by the United Presbyterian Church were not good enough to be performing the missionary work. There are petty quibbles on both sides.

So far I am finding great fulfillment in my teaching. I have even begun to improve the daily living conditions of my students, though I understand it is a slow process. My students are longing for the education we provide them and have a great capacity for learning. They are also very appreciative of our being down here. Not only that, Reverend Cook seems very pleased with my efforts, and we are able to speak once every couple of days.

Life isn't all wonderful, though. While I have splendid living conditions with a local family, we must deal with much illness, a horribly hot climate, primitive facilities for teaching, hectic and long work schedules, as well as the constant threat from nearby Confederate guerillas, which adds a level of excitement to our lives.

I am very confident that I made the right decision in coming down here, though I do miss you. I am very happy here and I am so glad that God has given me this opportunity. I will write to again you soon, and hope to hear from you as well.

All my love,
Jessica

"Mother, do you need any help in here?" Victoria asked, entering the kitchen.

"Victoria! Yes, as a matter of fact, I am a little behind in my dinner preparations. Now that Major Rogers is better, Lieutenant Campbell has asked to bring a friend for Sunday dinner, so there will be one more person at the table."

"Ah, the Yankees are feeling so settled that they are now inviting their friends over."

"Victoria, hush. You said you would make more of an effort to be optimistic about our situation."

Victoria moved to her mother, who passed a crock of lard to her for the biscuits. "I am sorry, mama, and I am. I still don't feel quite myself lately." The smell of the lard made her stomach churn. "Ugghh, and feeling queasy for no reason at all." She pushed the crock away and stepped back. "I am sorry, Mama. I thought I could help, but my stomach is saying otherwise." She turned and walked out of the kitchen. Rachel followed her, concerned.

"Victoria, stop. What is causing your pain?"

"Too much," Victoria replied. "Mama, my heart is broken from all of the losses we've suffered. I miss Adam so much, and Nathaniel. I am tired all the time. I have no motivation to do anything or eat anything. I am impatient and unpleasant around others. I don't want to be, but I just can't seem to help myself." She shook her head. "I wish I knew what was wrong with me. I have never been one to be overly dramatic."

"Hmmm." Rachel thought for a moment, then put her hand over Victoria's. "I may be able to answer that question, dear. May I ask when your last monthly was?"

Victoria frowned as she thought back. "I'm not sure exactly, but now that I think of it, I haven't had one since the siege was lifted. Since before Nathaniel left..." She trailed off, her thoughts racing. Her hand went to her stomach. Could what her mother be insinuating...could it be true?

"I have been observing you this past week and all these symptoms of yours could certainly be a sign that you are with child." Rachel smiled.

Victoria was still a bit shocked at what she now realized. "I was blaming it all on my grief and the occupation. Could it be possible? I mean, I know that it is possible. I just didn't think it would happen so quickly."

"I believe you should see a doctor within the next few days; he can verify our suspicions," Rachel said. "However, as your mother, I am quite sure that you will be having a baby come spring."

⤚⤙

Lieutenant Noah Campbell's friend, infantryman John Reese was quite pleasant. He was from Illinois, and spoke very fondly of his family back home.

"We almost lost John to illness," Lieutenant Campbell said. "A case of smallpox and time in the trenches rendered him barely able to walk."

"It was almost worse than a battle wound," Private Reese agreed. "I just wrote a letter home asking my wife to inoculate herself and our children. The sores in my mouth and the headache that lasted for weeks was awful and I don't want any of my family to suffer like that, much less die. Doc said the illness can be prevented."

"Indeed it can." Victoria didn't particularly wish to add to the discussion with the Yankees, but she couldn't help but share her knowledge. She had read the medical manual about smallpox, and was intrigued. "In fact, during the American Revolution, there was a smallpox epidemic that ravaged the American camps. General Washington had a Dr. Shippen inoculate the Continental troops that were moving through Philadelphia. It was a widespread practice in Europe, and it may have saved our cause against the British."

"My goodness, I didn't realize that," Major Rogers stated. "Very impressive." He turned to Private Reese. "Good timing, though, Reese. It's not as if you were missing much in terms of excitement. These past weeks of unending monotony and boredom have only aggravated our men's depression, loneliness, and homesickness. I don't have a wife or children to miss, but I still miss the rest of my family." He quickly glanced at Tabetha.

"Letters from home are a balm for the soul," Reese said. "It is often what gets me through the days." He took a bite of his baked chicken.

"Have you been wandering the battlegrounds in your spare time again?" Lieutenant Campbell asked. "You know how melancholy you get when you do that."

"I do, I confess it," Reese replied. "My mind often wanders as I think about our fallen comrades. These men who will never see their families again. I really need to write a letter to the wife of one soldier in particular who died. His widow continues to write him, not knowing that her husband was killed."

Victoria quickly stood. All eyes went to her. "I beg your pardon. I haven't felt well all day. Please excuse me." She then went in the direction of the stairs. Tabetha glanced at Rachel, with concern, but the woman smiled brightly and continued the conversation.

"Gentlemen, are you finding your living conditions acceptable?"

"I must admit, we have quite the life here at your home, Mrs. Turner. You are a gracious host," Major Rogers said. "Many of the soldiers stationed here in Vicksburg have difficult living situations in addition to their tedious duties. The heat, in those small tents, well, it's not pleasant for them at all."

"Is that why there is so much alcohol abuse and lapses in discipline?" Jessica thought back to some of the altercations she had witnessed on the streets of Vicksburg.

"There have been and likely will continue to be a steady stream of court martials and arrests." Major Rogers glanced at Lieutenant Campbell, who shrugged his shoulders.

"I may have gotten into a scuffle or two, but at least I don't ride into the countryside and harass locals like some of our men." He pointed out. It was unfortunately true.

"Your soldiers feel they have the right to attack any civilian at any time," Brianne muttered under her breath.

"There is room for improvement on the behavior of our soldiers, actually both sides," Major Rogers said.

"It must be at least a little exciting for you as an officer, Major Rogers, is it not?" Rachel asked.

Lieutenant Rogers spoke up to answer the question. "The life of an officer: 5AM roll call, write up the sick list, then breakfast. After eating, he must inspect his men on duty, then inspect the men's barracks until around 9." He took a quick drink of water. "Next, they are bogged down in paperwork until lunch, then more paperwork, another roll call and finally at 3:00, he must drill his men for three hours. At sundown, he has another roll call, then officer school, and one final roll call before bedtime." The Lieutenant smirked at his brother. "Truly exhilarating, to be sure."

Major Rogers shook his head. "I dislike many aspects of this so-called occupation duty, but I do enjoy being an officer. Unfortunately, even officers are not immune to lapses in discipline. We often fail to live up to the standards that we should."

"Officers generally receive leave more often and more easily than we enlisted men," Reese said.

"Unfortunately, many officers, present company excepted, undermine our confidence in their leadership," Lieutenant Rogers said.

"I must admit," Major Rogers said, "I haven't adjusted to occupation duty. I would like to be reassigned. I prefer to be more active. I realize riding patrol is essential, but I have more specific goals." He glanced again at Tabetha, who held his gaze. "There are reasons worth staying here, to be sure, but I want to contribute to our cause in a more important way, such as the battle last week, in Arkansas. We took the victory when the Confederates retreated and we captured Fort Smith gained a foothold in the Arkansas River Valley." He looked around the table. Brianne glared at him and Victoria tried to hide her disdain. "I hope to be part of a campaign like that again soon."

"I would imagine your mind needs stimulation as well," Jessica said.

"That is true ma'am," Private Reese said. "Garrison duty is looked at in a less romantic way than active campaigning."

"It is less important," Major Rogers said. "I see it as little more than manual labor."

Tabetha sensed dejection in Major Rogers's voice. He had alluded to her before how he had doubts that his current service to the war effort was lacking while stationed in Vicksburg.

"We didn't sign up for the disease-ridden camps and the horrid sanitation." Major Rogers continued. It was clear he was frustrated. "I end up in a hospital, seriously ill from God knows what, and it isn't even a war wound."

"Surely there is something good about camp life," Jessica said.

"Of course there is," Reese said. "I find the camaraderie comforting, exchanging stories around the campfires, listening to music from our bands, though sometimes they play too late into the night, and a little off-key."

"A benefit of being billeted in a home," Lieutenant Campbell said, "is that I enjoy the comfort and hospitality of the Southern women." He winked at Brianne. "It's also nice to attend the theater, have horse races, and there are many choirs and musical groups. Some men, like Lieutenant Ezekiel Rogers here, enjoy debate societies, and then there is my favorite, the athletic clubs. In fact..." he looked at Private Reese. "The next time you feel the need to wander through the killing fields, let me know. We can get some men together and play baseball someplace."

"That would be a fine thing," Reese said. "I look forward to it."

With dinner finished, the women cleared the table and washed the dishes, and the men left for their rounds. Once the chore was completed, Tabetha excused herself and made her way to the bedroom she shared with Victoria, who was sitting on the balcony in a rocker, knitting. Tabetha pulled up another chair. "May I join you?" She asked.

"Of course," Victoria replied. "I am glad you're here, to be honest. I would like to apologize. I haven't been acting myself as of late. I'm afraid I've let my circumstances take a toll on me and in the process taken it out on you, my family and my other friends. I am truly sorry."

"You have been through much, Victoria. I understand completely." She looked at what Victoria was working on. Her interest was piqued, as it looked like the beginning of a baby bootie. "I just hope you're feeling all right. It's not like you to leave in the middle of dinner."

"Sometimes I let my emotions get the best of me, and I am definitely quite emotional lately." She placed a hand on her stomach. "Though there is a good reason, I suspect."

Tabetha smiled. "What are you saying, Mrs. Prentiss?"

"Well, I am not knitting booties for William Green," Victoria replied. "Mother believes I'll be having a baby in early spring."

"How wonderful!" Tabetha exclaimed. "Congratulations!"

"Thank you," Victoria didn't seem nearly as excited as Tabetha thought she should be. "It will be good to have a baby around again, and a part of Nathaniel will be with me if the unthinkable happens." She sighed.

"Is that what's worrying you?" Tabetha asked.

"I just fear the world I am bringing our child into will not be one of joy and contentment as we knew growing up," Victoria admitted. "What will his or her life be like in a town that is crawling with nefarious people?

Men and women who are here to get rich off the losses of our own neighbors, despite it being against the law. Soldiers who do little or nothing to keep the peace." She shook her head. "You see, I am so negative. I should be thankful that I at least have my family here with me. Have you heard from your own family lately?"

"Yes, actually, I have. I didn't give them any details, just that I ran away to help the war effort, I didn't mention my need to atone for my brother's death. They are all doing well. They want me to come home, of course, but they understand my need to stay here."

"So all is forgiven, just as we told you from the beginning."

Tabetha smiled. "Yes, I suppose, from my family's perspective. Now I must learn to forgive myself. I'll go home eventually, but there is still much to be done here."

"I fear that will be a continuous issue. Always caring for your patients, helping my family, and let's not forget the soldiers." Victoria teased. "At least one officer in particular."

Tabetha blushed. "What are you saying, Victoria, are my feelings that noticeable? But you are correct in your assumption, I would like to get to know the major better. I have never felt drawn to anyone as I have to him."

"I understand, believe me, I do. That's how I was with Nathaniel. Have you spoken with him about your past?"

"Oh, Heavens no, Victoria. I know I need to do so soon, because it will become more difficult as time goes on." Tabetha rubbed her temple. "I just need to find the right moment. I'm so afraid that when I do tell him, I will lose his friendship, which is so dear to me."

"Well even so, you must tell him, and sooner rather than later," Victoria warned. "His reaction will only get worse the longer you keep the secret."

"I know," Tabetha looked out towards the river. "I know."

Thursday, September 15, 1863
Turner Home

"A dance? Here?"

Victoria entered the parlor to hear Brianne's upset voice.

"Yes, a dance," Rachel answered. "Lieutenants Campbell and Rogers are making all the arrangements."

"It will be difficult to have a dance with no women for these soldiers to dance with," Victoria muttered.

"The animosity of the women in town isn't stopping the soldiers from pursuing them, that is for sure," Kendall remarked. "Aunt Rachel, how could you agree to such a thing?"

"She probably had no choice, Kendall," Victoria said. "The Yankees will do what they please, when they please, with no regard to anyone else."

"I am sorry you feel that way." Major Steven Rogers entered the parlor. "Noah and Ezekiel rushed into this idea as young men often do. I told them it would not be such a good idea to host a dance at this time. I understand where your loyalties lie. I will talk to them about not having a dance here unless Mrs. Turner approves."

"I don't believe it has to do with loyalties, Major. Not to me at least." Tabetha added. "It just seems to be in poor taste to have a celebration such as dancing in general. There is still much death and sickness and the city is far from being rebuilt. This town and our country, for that matter, is still suffering immensely."

"It is because of all this tragedy and turmoil that we should take some time to enjoy ourselves when we can." Rachel was always the calm voice of reason. Tabetha smiled to herself. She admired Rachel's ability to calm the roughest situation. "Besides, you all know I love entertaining, perhaps a dance would start the healing process between Yankee soldiers and our townsfolk."

"You can't fix all that's wrong with the city with a dance, Mama." Victoria said, then turned to leave. Brianne followed close behind.

Rachel smiled. "My apologies, Major, for Victoria and Brianne's behavior. I fear those girls can be gloomy at times."

"It's understandable, Mrs. Turner." Major Rogers nodded.

"I'd best go and see if Esther needs help in the kitchen. Come, Kendall, you can assist me," Rachel said, and she and Kendall left, leaving Tabetha alone with Major Rogers.

"Is Mrs. Turner always so peaceful and welcoming?" Major Rogers asked. "She treats me and the others like we're her own children."

"I believe it keeps her from missing her own boys so much," Tabetha said. "She enjoys bringing people together. I believe planning this dance will help keep her mind off missing the men in her life, including little Adam."

"I hope so," Major Rogers said. "She is right about the townsfolk, though. The local citizens hate our presence here."

"Many do, but can you blame them? They are a conquered people," Tabetha reminded him. "If you do the right thing, and treat them with the dignity they deserve, then God will be with you."

"You always seem to know how to help me best." Major Rogers smiled. "I suppose a social isn't the worst thing in the world, as long as you save a dance for me."

"There's no one else I would rather dance with," She admitted with a blush. "However, I must confess that I am not a very accomplished dancer."

"Nor I," Major Rogers said. "I suppose we'll just have to practice together."

"That sounds like a plan," She answered, suddenly looking forward to this dance. Spending time together, preparing for an evening where Major Rogers would hold her in his arms sounded very nice, very nice indeed.

Saturday, September 17, 1863
Turner Home

The evening of the dance had arrived. Both civilians and soldiers were invited, and many accepted the invitation. There were, of course, many more men than women. Hannah and her family came into town for the event, and Victoria was delighted to have all of her dearest friends in one place. Hannah, Mary Green, Mary Grace, and now Tabetha. Lieutenants Campbell and Rogers had persuaded one of the regimental bands to play, and Rachel Turner, with Esther's help, had made some refreshments for the guests, including chocolate kisses, lemon biscuits and wafer cakes.

"One of the young men, that one there," Mary Green gestured toward a young, smooth-faced lieutenant. "He was searching for a woman to escort here tonight. He would approach random houses, ours included, knock at the door and ask to see the daughter of the house. When we told him there was no daughter available for courting, he claimed to have the wrong house and asked if the 'lovely lady he sought' resided next door. Apparently his technique worked, for here he is, with a nice clean shirt and a young Yankee teacher on his arm."

Victoria smiled. "I suppose there have been stranger ways for couples to meet." She looked at Tabetha and Major Rogers, who were on the dance floor once again.

"Yes, that's true." As Mary Green looked in the same direction. "If the two of them end up married, it will be quite the story to tell. Much more exciting than the story Duff and I have."

Victoria unconsciously placed a hand on her stomach. "Or Nathaniel and mine." Mary noticed the gesture and smiled.

"I wondered if you had news to share," she said quietly.

Victoria looked down, then back at Mary and smiled. "I do, actually. Come March, I will be a mother."

Mary smiled and hugged her friend. "Oh, Victoria, I am so happy for you!"

Victoria shook her head. "I still find it hard to believe. Nathaniel and I weren't married very long before he left, I mean, I knew it was possible, of course, but I just never believed it would actually happen. Not this quickly."

"Have you written to Nathaniel?" Mary asked.

"I have, but there is no way of knowing if he receives it. He may not know until we see each other again." She felt tears in her eyes and quickly wiped them away. "At least we now know why I've been so emotional as of late."

"Yes, that does explain your change in personality." Mary gave Victoria another hug. "I remember those days well. You let me know if there is anything I can do for you."

"I will." Victoria smiled and tried not to be jealous when Duff came to claim Mary's hand for a dance. She wished Nathaniel were here. Dances always made her think of him, as it had been at a dance at Chatham Manor in Fredericksburg where she had first met him.

Victoria once again placed a hand on her stomach, then glanced at her mother and Mary Grace, who were both speaking with a Yankee colonel. Tabetha, Brianne, and Kendall were all dancing with soldiers. Victoria checked her watch. It was getting late. Surely no one would miss her if she headed up to bed a bit early.

Jessica leaned on the railing of the porch of the Turner home, looking out toward the Mississippi River. She was tired, and decided to take a break from all the dancing.

"This is the first time tonight you have not been in the arms of a soldier on the dance floor." Lieutenant Noah Campbell sauntered next to her. "I am surprised you haven't danced with that preacher you seem to be so fond of, or doesn't he approve of dancing?"

Jessica blushed at the mention of Reverend Samuel Cook. "Reverend Cook was invited and planned on coming tonight, but was called away at the last minute. He is very dedicated to his mission."

"Of course he is," Lieutenant Campbell said. "Such a pious, upstanding man."

"Yes, he is." Jessica was not sure where Lieutenant Campbell was heading with his conversation. He was usually so transparent, only thinking of himself. He had obviously been watching her all evening, and if she was honest with herself, she would have to say she had noticed him as well. He had danced with almost every woman in attendance. There weren't many, but it was still no small feat. He hadn't asked her to dance, however. Jessica didn't know why she was bothered by this fact. She didn't care what the soldier thought about her. *Or do I?*

"What brings you out here, Lieutenant Campbell? I am sure it wasn't to discuss Reverend Cook"

"I wanted to make sure you were all right. I saw you come out here by yourself."

"I needed some fresh air. I am not used to dancing quite so much." She pulled her shawl tighter around her shoulders.

"I suppose you usually have more important things to do than socialize."

"I am quite busy with lesson preparations, teaching and getting to know my students and their families. There is much more to being a teacher at a freedman school than I originally anticipated. I try hard to keep track of my new students, giving them whatever aid I can. I have been helping them to locate family or friends, assisting with care for their sick, writing letters." She smiled. "There was one woman who had me write several of the most ardent love-letters. One day, she astonished me by bringing a letter from her husband for me to read to her." She cleared her throat. "As it turns out her husband was another person. The woman seemed completely unable to comprehend that there was something improper in corresponding the way she was with another man."

Lieutenant Campbell chuckled. "That other soldier probably appreciates the kind words from her, although I do wonder what her actual husband thought about the situation."

"Yes, but it is still quite inappropriate and will only lead to trouble later on. What if that other man comes to find her and believes that she loves him and wants to marry him? The letters sure made it sound like a marriage would be in the future for the two of them, based on the context, but she is already a married woman." Jessica had been horrified when she learned that she had been a key element in the affair.

"And what did your preacher man think of this? Does he approve of your writing such ardent letters for your students?"

Jessica began to regret ever telling him the story. "I haven't told him this particular story," she admitted. "I don't believe he would approve."

"Well, don't worry about my disapproval." He looked back into the house. "As much as I would like to stay out here and continue our conversation, I do have guests inside. Hosting the party, you know."

"Of course," Jessica said, then watched him go back into the house. Lieutenant Campbell was surely an enigma.

<hr/>

"No, I will not dance with you, Lieutenant Rogers."

Victoria stopped ascending the stairs and stepped closer to the banister at the sound of Brianne's angry voice.

"Oh, not me, but just about any other man at this party you will? You cannot possibly tell me that you won't dance with me because I'm the enemy. There must be another reason."

"Yes, there is. I am not going to dance with you because I don't like you." With that, she stomped away.

Victoria watched Ezekiel turn away, dejected. She felt bad for the young man. Brianne was a bright, beautiful girl, but she was also extremely prejudiced against the Union soldiers. She may dance with them, but she would never give one the chance to even be her friend. Victoria sighed, turned around, and walked back down the steps after Brianne. She found the girl on the back stairway, head in her hands.

"Brianne Marie," Victoria spoke quietly. "The consummate belle of the ball. What are you doing sitting on these dark steps?"

"Too many Yankees stinking up the place," she scoffed. "I tried dancing with some, tried and imagine they were wearing the right uniforms, but I just couldn't do it anymore." She looked back towards the dancing. "Not like some former friends of mine."

Victoria couldn't miss the animosity in her cousin's voice. "Who would you be in reference to?"

"Alice Shirley. One of my former best friend. She hasn't had any qualms at all about getting close to the Yanks. In fact, she thought I would be excited for her when she told me that there is one Yankee in particular she has feelings for. She may even marry this Chaplain John Eaton." She spit out the last few words. "As if I can be friends with her now."

"Pray tell, why not?" Victoria asked.

"I wouldn't expect you to understand. You're still close with Mary Green, a Yankee sympathizer, which is almost as bad as a Yankee carpetbagger, and you now probably count Tabetha as one of your closest friends.

"That is something I am struggling with every day, Brianne. There are times when I want to cut off ties with everyone and anyone who doesn't completely support the Confederacy, but life is not always black and white. I am sorry you are harboring so much bitterness and I understand how difficult it can be. Believe it or not, we are all struggling with our own real and perceived problems."

"Yes, that is hard to believe." Brianne stood. "I appreciate you trying to help, Victoria, really, I do. I'm tired. I'm going to head up to bed."

"Brianne!" Rachel walked into the hallway. "Here you are. Alice is looking for you."

"Tell her I went to bed. I'm tired of all this." With that, the girl stomped upstairs.

"I tell you, that girl needs to learn forgiveness." Rachel rubbed her temple. "I know she is hurting, but she can't go on like this."

"I know," Victoria said. "They never talk of it, but I know both she and Kendall feel betrayed and abandoned by Uncle Nicholas."

"They do." Rachel shook her head. "I know their father misses their mother. I miss her too, she was my only sister and my very best friend. Nicholas was frightened of raising the girls on his own, but the distance and time away from them has made it difficult for him to come back."

"And this infernal war hasn't helped." Victoria added.

"That is true. I hope and pray every day that they forgive him if and when he comes back so they can be a family."

Victoria nodded in agreement.

"Were you heading up to bed as well?" Rachel asked.

"I was. I'm just tired." Victoria admitted.

"And likely missing Nathaniel. I recall the first conversation you had with him, it was the ball at Chatham for his sister, was it not? You told me all about it when you returned home."

"Yes, mama, and I do miss him terribly as you must miss Father." Victoria smiled sadly. "I'm sorry for leaving you to the guests."

"I understand, dear, you get some rest." Rachel hugged her daughter and Victoria headed upstairs.

Sunday, October 4, 1863
Streets of Vicksburg

"I'm not sure what to do anymore," Victoria said to Mary Green as they left Mary Graces's haberdashery. "I want to continue to write Nathaniel, but I doubt it will even be worth the cost of the postage stamp. He probably won't receive any of them"

They approached the fruit cart of Deborah Wainwright, a vocal Confederate supporter.

"I don't know what I would do either, if I were in your situation," Mary replied. "Especially when you have such important news for him."

"Exactly." Victoria stopped at the fruit stand and picked up an apple to examine it.

"At least you'll be able to give birth to your child in a house," Mary said with a smile.

"Mrs. Wainwright, I would like to purchase some apples, please." Victoria smiled at the vendor. The woman turned and gave Victoria and Mary a spiteful look.

"I can't sell to either one of you," she replied with a sneer.

"I beg your pardon?" Victoria sputtered.

"First of all, I don't sell to families that feed the Yankee trash of this town." The woman glared at Victoria. "And second, I refuse to sell to anyone that signed the oath. Traitors, the lot of you."

"How dare you say such a thing?" Victoria cried out. "My family is being forced to house and feed Federal soldiers. We have no choice, and what's more…"

"That makes no matter to me," Mrs. Wainwright yelled back. "Now, go on. I will not be selling to any Yankee sympathizers and you cannot make me. Good day."

"Well, I never…"

"I said good day."

"Come, Victoria. It does no good to argue with stupidity." Mary pulled at Victoria's sleeve.

"I cannot believe she said that. I cannot help that my family is housing Yankees, not one bit, and Tabetha cannot be considered a Yankee, she is a compassionate nurse to all men, no matter what side they are fighting for."

"You don't have to tell me that, Victoria, I know." Mary's tone caused Victoria's voice to soften.

"Why are you so calm about this? It is unacceptable behavior. It's as if you're used to this kind of treatment."

Mary looked down and shrugged.

"Does this happen to you often?" Victoria asked.

"Probably more often than it should, yes." Mary admitted. "It doesn't surprise me anymore. People take issue with Duff and the others who signed the oath. You yourself have told me that you have problems with this fact."

Victoria had no answer.

"I manage just fine, Victoria. I have friends and family who support me and understand our circumstances, including you. I can handle some hostilities."

"You're a much better person than I am in that regard," Victoria replied.

"We all have our crosses to bear," Mary replied. "This is just one of mine. Don't fret we will get through this."

Thursday, October 15, 1863
Vicksburg Headquarters of the American Missionary Association
Jessica smiled as she walked toward Reverend Cook's office. Overall, classes had been going well, but she had one student in particular, a very promising young woman named Becky, who had missed classes for over a week. Either the students truly didn't know or they didn't want to tell her where Becky was. Jessica knew which refugee camp she lived in and planned to pay her a visit. Reverend Cook would be in his office by now, she would ask him to escort her out there to check on her prized pupil.

Jessica greeted the man and walked into his office. "Reverend."

"Miss Spencer." He finished recording a note in a ledger, then closed it. "I trust everything is going well."

Jessica smiled. "Yes, it is, thank you." The reverend was always so courteous.

"What brings you here then?" He asked, linking his hands together and placing them on his desk.

"There's a particular student I have, a bright young woman, who has missed several days of school. I would like to go to her camp and check on her. I am worried."

"I wouldn't say that's something to worry about. The girl has likely moved on. Many freedmen are quite transient. I wouldn't waste my time looking for her."

Jessica's heart fell. She had been so sure that Reverend Cook would go with her. She hadn't thought of what she would do if he declined. "So you don't believe I should go and check on her? I'm sure she would have told me if she was leaving. We had formed a special relationship..."

"No, I don't believe that is wise, and besides, I don't really have the time to escort you. As I said, the girl is probably long gone. Don't worry about her."

Jessica bit her lip. What he said was likely true, but she knew deep down that Becky would have said goodbye.

She stood. "Thank you for your time, Reverend." He stood and guided her to the door of his office.

"Of course. I am always here for my missionaries. You are the reason I am able to do what I do."

"I should be thanking you, Reverend. I truly believe this is where God has called me to be." Jessica smiled as she followed him.

"Wonderful. Make sure you come to see me again with any issues. I must say, you are one of my most effective teachers."

Jessica beamed at his compliment. "Thank you, Reverend. Of course." Once she reached the street, she thought again about Becky. Perhaps if she could go and just check on her family. If Becky was still at the camp, perhaps she could get her to come back to school. Her decision made, Jessica started in the direction of one of the refugee camps along the Yazoo River.

She was just outside the camp when two men, Vicksburg citizens, stepped into her path.

"Good afternoon, ma'am." One of them said. Everything about him was thick, his body, his hair, and his Southern accent. "What's a pretty young woman like you all the way out here for?"

"I am a teacher at one of the freedmen's schools. I am simply checking on one of my students."

"You're one of them who's tryin' to teach the darkies?" The other man spit a stream of tobacco juice. He was the complete opposite of his friend in appearance. String bean slim with thin, shoulder length hair and a high-pitched voice.

"Yes, I am. I am quite proud of that fact." Jessica's heart pounded, but she strove to hide her fear from the men. She stood as tall as she could.

"Them darkies can't learn." A third man stepped over, face red with anger. "You all comin' out here, causing nothin' but trouble."

"My students have just as much right to an education as you do." Jessica hoped her voice wasn't shaking. The red-faced man grabbed her arm, bruising it in the process. He jerked her to one side and as she was about to be thrown to the ground, a shot rang out. Jessica breathed a sigh of relief when she saw Lieutenant Noah Campbell stalk over to them. It was the first time she had ever seen him angry. In fact, it was the first time she had seen him show any real emotion.

"If you know what's good for you, you'd best disappear right now." His jaw tightened.

"Yah, sir, sure thing Yankee." The thin man spoke up. "Three of us against one of you, I'll take those odds." He reached inside his coat to draw his weapon. The moment it cleared his belt, Noah fired his revolver, hitting the man's hand and causing the gun to fall to the ground. Blood oozed from his injured hand.

"Like I said, disappear." Noah's voice was low and threatening. He cocked his gun again. The red-faced man shoved Jessica to the ground and all three men scurried away. Noah holstered his pistol, dismounted, and quickly hurried to Jessica's side.

He reached down to help her up. "Miss Spencer." She drew in a deep breath and leaned on him, steadying herself as best she could. "Miss Spencer. Are you alright? What are you doing out here?"

"I'm all right. Honestly." She replied. "I was heading to the refugee camp to check on a student of mine."

"Alone?" He was incredulous. "Wherever is your preacher friend? Couldn't he escort you? Coming out here alone is dangerous. You could have been seriously hurt, or worse." He rubbed a hand through his hair. "Miss Spencer, you cannot forget that you are in enemy territory, just like the rest of us. Maybe even worse, because in reality not all Union soldiers like what you and your fellow teachers are doing here either."

"I am quite aware of that, Lieutenant Campbell. I did speak with Reverend Cook about coming out here. He told me that I shouldn't go. He said it wouldn't be worth my while. I just...I have to be sure, one of my most promising students hasn't come to school in over a week. I wanted to make sure she was all right."

"That is admirable," Noah blew out a breath. "Are you insistent on finding her?"

"Yes. I've come this far," Jessica said. "I just need to speak with her."

"All right." He walked back to his horse and picked up the reins, then sighed. "Come on."

"What do you mean?" She asked, looking down at his offered arm.

"I'm not about to let you go into a freedman's camp alone, and that's final" he replied. "There is no way I will allow that."

"You really don't have to escort me, Lieutenant Campbell."

"Actually, I do. You know that as well as I do that Mrs. Turner would skin me alive and then kick me out of the house if I let anything happen to you."

Jessica was about to protest and tell him that she would be just fine on her own, then realized she would feel more comfortable with a soldier as an escort. She trusted Lieutenant Campbell, and he was right about what Mrs. Turner would do. "That is very kind of you. I accept your offer then."

He nodded and they continued on towards the camp.

"Many of the Union soldiers reject the notion of equality for the freedmen," Jessica said, desperate to fill the silence. "I've heard they often view the blacks as a foreign population they can observe and comment upon. They rarely welcome them as equal participants in this struggle with the Confederacy. Many don't even want to welcome them as fellow soldiers. What is your opinion on the Negroes, Lieutenant?"

"I don't have much of one," Noah said. "If they want to enlist, let them enlist. Lincoln made this war about freeing slaves last year with his proclamation, it only makes sense that they should fight too."

"That's a refreshing attitude, Lieutenant." As they rounded a bend, Jessica was stunned into silence by what she saw. Decrepit hovels and in some cases, old, worn-out tents, were the only shelters the refugees had.

"Dear Lord." Jessica covered her nose at the stench. Some blacks lived in the dirty, rundown shacks and tents, and yet some looked like they had no shelter at all. Men, women and even children lay on the side of the dirt road. Jessica couldn't tell if they were alive or dead. "Oh, Noah." It didn't even occur to her that she used his given name until it was too late, but by then, she didn't care. The people she saw were spiritless, dejected, and weak from what appeared to be sickness and hunger. There were so many crowded in such a small area. She knew the refugees lived in poor conditions, but she would never have imagined these horrid circumstances.

"No one deserves to live like this," Noah said, visibly shocked as well. "Camp life can be bad, but I...this is most dreadful."

Jessica took a deep breath. "It's horrifying. I need to find Becky."

"Let's do it quickly," Noah nodded.

The two began asking around, trying to locate the young woman. It took them some time before they were able to learn which hovel she was living in. Jessica approached the small, one-room shack and took a deep breath before she went in.

Jessica believed she was prepared for what she would see in the shack, but she wasn't. There was very little light, only a single tallow candle burning, and the stench was so overwhelming that she struggled not to gag. Around two dozen sick patients, men, women and children all lay on the floor. No one even had a cot. They had no bedding, and only two had tattered, patched-up quilts.

"What 'chu two doin' here?" A bedraggled woman looked at them, curiosity in her face.

"I am a teacher at one of the freedmen's schools and Becky is one of my students. I haven't seen her in a week and was told that I could find her here."

The moment Becky's name left Jessica's mouth, she saw the woman's face fall, which caused Jessica's stomach to churn.

"I hates ta be the one ta tell ya dis, but Becky up an' died just a few hours 'go."

Jessica stumbled back, but Noah was there to hold her up.

"You must be mistaken. The Becky I am looking for is only thirteen. She can't be dead. Are you sure you're not thinking of a different Becky?"

"No, Ma'am. Dey's only one Becky who be a black gal in 'dis whole area. She done caught the pox last week and couldna' beat it. I's sorry ta be da one ta tell ya dat."

"I cannot believe it." Tears fell from Jessica's eyes. She felt herself being turned and pulled into the strong arms of Lieutenant Campbell.

"Miss Spencer, we should leave. Smallpox is nothing to fool with. You shouldn't be here." He nodded to the woman who had given them the tragic news and guided Jessica outside.

Jessica still was in shock. Becky was so young and vibrant, full of potential, the student that Jessica could always count on to assist the other students. The girl had quickly worked her way through the first and second arithmetic books and was reading an advanced primer. She had been wonderful with the children and always a bright spot in Jessica's day.

"I am so sorry for your loss," Noah said once they were out of the refugee camp.

"She was a wonderful young woman," Jessica said. "I know as teachers we aren't supposed to have a favorite student, but...well, Becky was mine."

Noah chuckled, trying to lighten the mood. "I always knew teachers had favorites, but I never was one of them."

"And you probably have no idea why that would be." She smiled through her tears, touched that Noah was trying to make her feel better.

"No, I have always wondered why that is, Miss Spencer. You know me pretty well. Tell me, wouldn't I have been one of your favorite students?"

She wiped a tear from her eye. "Of course, of course, Lieutenant Campbell. Absolutely."

The soldier sobered. "I truly am sorry. I can tell, you really care about your students."

"I do. They are so eager to learn, so hungry for knowledge, and Becky..." A fresh wave of emotions rose up. "I will miss her terribly." She brushed another tear away. "Thank you, Lieutenant Campbell. I really do appreciate everything you have done for me today. From rescuing me from those nasty men, to coming with me to the camp, then comforting me...I'm very grateful."

"You didn't mention the smile I gave you at breakfast. It started your whole day off right." He smiled again, then became serious. "I know I'm not the best person to be lecturing another about safety, but you really shouldn't have tried to go off on your own. It can be dangerous for a whole slew of reasons, some of which you did run into today."

"I know, but something inside of me needed answers and I had to find her."

"I understand, really, and I'm not saying you shouldn't follow your instincts. I'm just saying you shouldn't do it alone."

"I didn't want to go alone," she explained.

"I know, I know, but if you ever need to go somewhere again and your preacher can't accompany you, please find me, or Ezekiel or Steven. Any of us. We can make sure you get there safe."

"Thank you, Lieutenant Campbell," she said.

"You know, at one point today, you called me Noah. I must say I liked the sound of that. Perhaps you should do it more often."

"That was a mistake, I apologize. It was quite improper." Jessica realized that it would be very easy to call him by his Christian name all the time.

"If you say so," Noah said. "But if you ever change your mind, feel free to call me Noah."

"Of course." Jessica knew she wouldn't and knew that Reverend Cook would disapprove.

The two finally arrived back at the Turner home.

"Thank you again, Lieutenant," she said. "Will I see you at dinner?"

"You most certainly will," he replied.

"Well, until dinner, then."

Tuesday, October 27, 1863
Turner Dining Room

"Good morning, Miss Kendall," Jessica smiled at her housemate.

"Good morning," Kendall replied, then took a deep breath. She may not like the Yankees being here, but she could at least be cordial to the young teacher. "Are you enjoying your teaching position? How have your students been faring?"

"I enjoy it very much. Thank you," Jessica replied. "Sadly, we have lost several of the students to smallpox and some have moved on. But the ones that continue to attend, for the most part, are quick to learn and have a desire for education."

"I must confess, I find it hard to believe that any Negro would have such an aptitude for book learning." Kendall wasn't trying to be rude, only honest.

"Oh, but they do," Jessica replied. "I have students of all ages and abilities and they all come from different backgrounds. It seems the freedmen have flocked here to Vicksburg."

"Well, why wouldn't they?" Kendall asked. "Life is easy for them here. They receive food from the army, live in the homes of old plantations, they can get an education for free and they have the Yankee army to protect them."

"I assure you, Miss Larson, you have it all wrong. The lives of these refugees are anything but easy. They struggle ever so much. They have very little food, and those homes you speak of are little more than hovels. And yes, they are receiving an education, but while we may be having some success with improvements to their daily living conditions, it is a very difficult world for them. They must deal with illness, this hot, humid climate, poor, unsanitary facilities, and they also fear assault by your townspeople."

"I understand your frustration, but you're the one who chose to come down here," Kendall said. "We were just trying to live our lives and get through this war unscathed. We just wanted to be left alone."

"We just want to help those who are less fortunate." Jessica rarely argued and she was under the impression that Kendall was the same way. "Listen, Miss Larson, I am not much for quarreling. Why don't you join me at school someday? It will allow you to really see what we are trying to accomplish. Perhaps you could even donate your time and assist some of the students. Believe me, even though you're young and not a formally trained teacher, there are many things that you can do to help. I already have some of my more learned students assisting me with the younger ones. Do you remember Cicero? I believe he stayed with your family for a time."

"Of course I remember him. I miss him dearly." Kendall had enjoyed talking with the boy, and wished it was socially acceptable for her to befriend him.

"He is one of my special students." Jessica tried not to get emotional as she thought of Becky again. Class just wasn't the same without her.

Jessica looked at the clock. "I must be on my way, but please consider stopping by." She stood and smiled. "I hope to see you later."

⁓

"Esther!" Victoria smiled when she entered the kitchen. "I feel like we never talk any more, now that you're only here during the day." She picked up a potato to begin peeling it. "How are Caesar and Cicero?"

"Dem two is doin fine, jus fine. Caesar be a Union soldier still, an Cicero be enjoyin' his school."

"Yes, Miss Spencer has mentioned what a fine student he is," Victoria said as Rachel came up behind her.

"Yeh, o course. Cicero be talkin' about dat Miss Spencer all de time. She a very kind person."

"She is well-liked here," Rachel said. "How are the dinner preparations, Esther?"

"They's good, Miss Rachel." Esther nodded.

"Esther, you must give me the opportunity to talk you into moving back here," Victoria said. "I have heard of the living conditions in the refugee camps and I can't imagine you live in anything as nice as our home."

"No, Ma'am, I can't stay. I b'long wit my husband. He already bein' understandin' bout me workin here."

"Well, I am so glad that you are," Victoria said. "And you and Cicero and Caesar can come back here to live at any time, you remember that."

"Yes, I will ask again, Esther, are you sure you are in no danger of contracting smallpox?" Rachel asked. "There are so many cases in the camps, as well as other illness."

"Yes'm. De's had some people pass on 'cause o' dat dere illness," Esther said.

"I am so sorry to hear that," Victoria said. No one deserved to lose loved ones, especially children. A pang of sadness hit her when she thought of Adam. Losing him still hurt deeply, so much so that she occasionally cried herself to sleep.

Victoria placed a hand on her stomach and yet again prayed for her unborn child, her husband and all her family members away fighting. She thought of the story she heard recently from Mary Green, where a group of Federal soldiers came upon the most appalling scene. Near the Yazoo River, North of town, they found a group of cabins, more like shacks, that had been built and occupied by freed people. Their small community had been ravaged by an unknown disease and the soldiers had only found corpses. The bodies had been decomposing, and some animals had ravaged the bodies as well. It had been one of the most horrible stories that Victoria had heard.

"Yes'm," Esther said, continuing to prepare dinner.

"Well, I am glad we have you for the time being," Victoria said.

"I'm going to spend the morning with Mary Grace. They will likely be joining us for dinner." Rachel smiled.

"Al'right, I'll prepare for dat," Esther said.

Rachel excused herself, leaving Victoria with Esther.

"I truly am glad you're here," Victoria said. "There have been so many times when I just...I wished I could talk to you like we used to."

"'Ain't no reason we cain't. Fact is, I been waitin fo yu to be tellin me dat youse expecting a chil'. B'for da war, you'da tell me dat right 'way."

"I know. To be honest, I'm still getting used to the fact myself," Victoria admitted.

"Well, I's wants ta congratulate ya. It be a fine ting."

"Thank you so much. I..." Victoria had been thinking for the past few days, and one of the reasons she had come down to the kitchen that day was to have this specific conversation with Esther. "I have actually been thinking, hoping...I know you're a talented midwife. You were wonderful with Mary Grace both times, especially with the twins. I was hoping you would assist me when my time comes."

"I'd be honored by dat, Miss Victoria. I been tryin' ta think of a way ta tell you dat I'd want ta do dat fo ya."

"Thank you," Victoria said, hugging Esther in her joy. "You have put my mind at ease. I appreciate it."

"I 'preciate ya askin'." Esther smiled, and the two continued working together, talking as they used to.

Thursday, October 29, 1863
Freedman School

Kendall smiled and looked around the schoolroom. She was glad she had taken Jessica up on her offer to come and help at the school. She had learned so much today. The plight of the freedmen was worse than she was led to believe. Kendall's heartstrings had been pulled when a boy of about five years had crawled onto her lap while she was reading to some of the younger children. Part of her wanted to retch, as the boy smelled as if he hadn't bathed since the day he was born, but the other part of her longed to pull the boy into her arms and cuddle him like she used to do with Adam.

Kendall also learned that Jessica Spencer was a very good teacher. She was impressed with how the woman was able to manage the different age groups and learning levels. The students weren't always well-behaved, yet Jessica handled them well, and it was clear that her students adored her, especially Cicero.

"You looked like you enjoyed yourself today, Kendall," Jessica said. "Have you ever considered becoming a teacher yourself?"

"I have, actually, which is why I was keen on coming with you today. I wish I had accompanied you sooner." Kendall sighed. "I think that being a teacher would suit me. I have even considered heading west once I'm old enough. I believe there will be a need for teachers there and perhaps, just maybe, I can find and get to know my father."

"You really have thought about this," Jessica said, then took a good look at this young woman. Kendall was no child; she was fourteen considered to be a young lady.

"I have," Kendall replied. "Would you help me...I mean...how would one go about preparing for and taking the teacher examination?"

"Of course I would help you." Jessica smiled. "I am apprehensive only because I don't feel your family will be agreeable to the idea of you moving west, especially by yourself."

"But you did! And I don't plan on leaving right away. It's still a ways down the road," Kendall said. "Two to three years, most likely."

"You must remember, Kendall, that both of my parents are dead. I was to live with my aunt and uncle in Michigan, much like you and Brianne live with your aunt and uncle. However, because of my age, I chose to go my own way. I do like your adventurous personality." Jessica shook her head. "I am glad you came with me today. It has been delightful having you here today. You were a big help to me and if you continue coming, you will gain some valuable experience, and then we can work on that examination."

"I will enjoy that." Kendall said with a smile.

"Kendall Grace!" Victoria called out and waved to her cousin. "Where have you been today?"

"I was helping Jessica in her classroom. It was quite an illuminating experience."

"What a wonderful idea! With your love of teaching, I bet you enjoyed it immensely. I am on my way to visit Mary Green. Would you like to join me?"

"I'll go with you," Kendall said. "I have nothing pressing to do, and I always enjoy seeing little Annie and William."

The two made their way to Lakemont, but Mrs. Lake informed them that Mary was out visiting elsewhere. The use of calling cards had gone to the wayside following the siege.

"Please tell her that we stopped by and I would love to see her soon." Victoria said, disappointed.

"Of course," Mrs. Lake said. "And you tell your mother I said 'Hello'."

"I will," Victoria said, and they turned to walk home.

"Is there anyone else you would like to visit?" Kendall asked.

"Would you mind if we stopped to check on Mary Grace? She's coming for dinner tonight, but I'd like to see how things are going at the store."

"Of course that's a good idea." Kendall smiled, and the two made their way to the haberdashery. They opened the door to see business booming. Mary Grace stood at the counter, assisting several customers and several others were looking at the inventory.

Mary Grace noticed Victoria and Kendall and smiled. "Victoria! Kendall! Thank goodness you are here. I am quite busy as you can see. Could you give me a hand?"

"Certainly," Victoria said. "Where are mama and the children?"

"Mama brought them over to your house already."

"Well, let's get to work." Victoria said to Kendall as they helped Mary Grace take care of her customers.

Much later, Mary Grace went to the entrance and flipped the sign on the door to 'closed'.

"My goodness, thank you so much for your assistance. I was drowning and all after Mother left. I would never have been able to assist everyone without your help."

"That's what families are for." Kendall smiled. "You certainly are running a bang up business."

"Yes, although it can be quite a burden to be so busy." Mary Grace turned as the shop door opened, ringing the bell. "I'm so sorry, we're closed..." Her eyes widened as a haggard Confederate soldier on crutches entered the shop. She immediately noticed that his left pant was pinned up at the knee. An amputee.

"Abraham!" Mary Grace jumped up and threw herself into the arms of the soldier, tears running down her face. He kissed her hair and held her tightly. Victoria and Kendall stood, looking at Abraham in disbelief.

"Abraham, welcome home!" Victoria smiled and comfortingly rubbed his arm. Kendall gave him a quick hug, then Mary Grace stepped back into his arms.

"Oh, my Abraham, what has happened to you?"

"I don't wish to discuss the details at this time, but as you can see, I lost my leg during the Battle of Chancellorsville. I was mustered out as I can no longer fight. If that's not bad enough, I come home to find Yankees everywhere." He sighed and rubbed his temple. "Where are my children?"

Victoria's heart sank as she realized that Abraham probably didn't know about Adam, with the Confederate mail system being so unpredictable. Victoria wasn't even sure if Mary Grace had even written Abraham of Adam's death after the city fell and the mail service started up again. She pulled at Kendall's arm. "Brianne and Mama have them at our house. We'll go and get them while you two catch up."

Mary Grace gave Victoria a grateful smile and the two walked out the door.

"Do you think he will be able to run the store without a leg?" Kendall asked innocently enough, obviously referring to Abraham's amputation.

"I would think so, especially with Mary Grace at his side, but I am more concerned that the Yankees may not let him continue to run the store. They will likely force him to sign their blasted oath of allegiance."

"Oh, I didn't think about that," Kendall said. "I would like to know more details on where he's been and what exactly happened to him, as I am sure the Yankees will too."

"Indeed." Victoria ached for her sister. "My concern right now is how Mary Grace is going to tell Abraham about Adam's death." This reunion would be bittersweet. Abraham was home, but Mary Grace would have to share the tragic news of their son's death. She brushed a tear from her cheek.

"They'll be just fine, Victoria. They have each other, and Gabriel and Hope," Kendall replied.

"I know. Still."

"Not to mention all of us."

"You're right, of course." Victoria pulled Kendall into a side-hug. "And family is what's most important. When did my little cousin become such an intelligent, sensitive young lady?"

Saturday, November 14, 1863

My Dearest Nathaniel,

I continue to write you, both in my journal and in my many letters, hoping and praying that you receive at least one. I long to hear from you, about how you are getting along. To know if you are fighting or if you are waiting for me safely at your home on Stafford Heights. Have you been able to see your family? My cousins? It's been ages since I've heard from them. From anyone, really.

The best news I have to report is that Abraham is back in Vicksburg, however, he was seriously wounded, and had his right leg amputated just below the knee. Mary Grace doesn't care about that in the least. She is just glad to have him home. He has his moments of despondency, but he knows just how much Mary Grace and the children need him, which brings him out of his doldrums. He was hesitant to sign the oath of allegiance, but realized he had no choice. If he hadn't, he would have been arrested and had his business confiscated from him. That is the state of the city right now. Abraham, like so many of the men here, must support his family above all else.

I have written this every time, so perhaps you have already heard. First, the sad news that our Adam is now in Heaven. The loss pains me still, and I dread the Christmas holiday that is approaching. He loved it so much, and the hole his death has left us with is unthinkable.

The good news is that you will be a father come spring. The doctor has seen me and all is going well in regards to my health and the health of our child. Mother and Esther will be with me, of course. In a perfect situation, you would be here as well, but no need to worry, as I will be in good hands, so you need not worry about me. You just worry about yourself, your safety, and coming home to me. I miss you dearly.

In regards to our daily lives, we are truly an occupied city. I spend my days caring for the wounded and sick soldiers.

The Houghton family recently lost a newborn baby girl. They called her Lydia. Many people were affected by that loss especially Mary Green and Mary Grace. They understand what it is like to lose a child, and I know that even for me, hearing of such a loss made our loss of Adam ever so much harder to bear. The feelings of despair and heartache are endless. I must confess that I worry about the life of the child growing inside of me. I would be devastated if anything were to happen to our child.

I dream of the day when we will be together again. I pray the war leaves you unharmed and safely back into my arms. I love you with all my heart.

Victoria

Sunday, November 29, 1863
Christ Episcopal Church

"Good morning, Mrs. Balfour." Rachel Turner greeted her friend.

"Good morning, Rachel." Emma Balfour smiled and acknowledged Victoria. "I see that congratulations are in order, Mrs. Prentiss. I am so happy for you and your husband, and for you too, Rachel."

"Thank you, Mrs. Balfour." Victoria blushed, then looked around, hoping to see Mary Grace with her family. Abraham had been home for a month, yet still didn't tell the family anything specific about his injury. He had informed them that Gregory and Charles had been well when he left Virginia.

Victoria didn't see Mary Green and her family yet either. Tabetha was at St. Paul's, escorted by Major Rogers, and Jessica was attending services led by Reverend Cook with the other teachers from the Missionary group.

Victoria finally saw a red-eyed Mary Green approach her.

"My goodness, Mary, you seem distraught. Whatever has happened?" Victoria asked. Mary shook her head.

"We just received news that the Houghtons have had another devastating loss." She wiped at her cheeks. "Dear Jane has passed away. She never fully recovered from losing her sweet daughter Lydia."

"Lord in heaven!" Rachel Turner exclaimed. "That leaves the judge to raise his six remaining children alone!"

"Yes, ma'am," Mary said. "Such a tragedy."

"I will go over there right now to see how I can best help," Rachel said.

"I'll go with you," Mrs. Balfour said.

"Aunt Rachel, what about church?" Kendall asked.

"I am positive God will understand," Rachel replied. "When you three get home, I would appreciate it if you would help Esther start a stew. Make enough for our household and the Houghtons as well. If I'm not home by dinnertime, please bring the meal over to the judge's house."

"Yes, ma'am," Victoria said. "We will take care of it."

"Please let me know if there is anything I can do," Mary Green said. Rachel nodded and hastened away, with Mrs. Balfour at her heels. Just as she was out of sight, Mary Grace, Abraham and their children approached.

"Wherever is Mother going in such a hurry?" Mary Grace asked. Victoria quickly explained, and Mary Grace shook her head. "What more can go wrong for that poor family?" The church bells rang, and the Turners and Greens walked in.

Rachel didn't make it home for dinner, so after she dropped the stew off at the Houghton's house, Victoria stopped at her sister's home. Though they had seen each other at church, they hadn't had a chance to really talk.

"How are the Houghtons fairing?" Mary Grace asked after Victoria had greeted Abraham and hugged Gabriel. Father and son were working in the haberdashery.

"The younger children don't quite understand what has happened. The judge is going to need a good amount of help. Mother, Mrs. Balfour, and Mrs. Lake are coordinating the neighbors and friends to help until permanent arrangements can be made."

"Yes, they are very good at organizing whatever comes their way," Mary Grace replied. "I certainly will do whatever is necessary to help." The sisters went into the kitchen area located at the back of the haberdashery.

Victoria and Mary Grace sat down at the table. "Tell me honestly, how is Abraham? Is he adjusting sufficiently?" Victoria asked.

"He's adjusting better than I could hope for," Mary Grace replied. "He jumped right back into his duties as if he never left to fight in the war, other than the leg, of course."

"Does he speak about it? How he was wounded, that is."

Mary Grace glanced in to the storefront where Gabriel, now almost five years old, helped his father. Hope was upstairs taking a nap.

"He told me what I told you, the very basics. I don't want to pressure him to talk about it. I desperately want to know what happened to him, every detail, but I don't want to upset him. Right now he is here, he's alive, he is the man I fell in love with and I don't want to ruin anything."

"I don't blame you for that. Not one bit." Victoria wasn't sure if she would do the same if it was Nathaniel. She wondered if the lack of communication would become problematic.

"I haven't asked so far for a similar reason, but you haven't mentioned how he took the loss of Adam," Victoria said quietly.

"Shockingly well." Tears formed in Mary Grace's eyes. "You know, Victoria. Adam was always so weak, so sickly. He was never strong like his brother. It was difficult at times to see him in so much pain, yet he never complained. I think in the back of my mind, I always knew Adam wasn't going to live very long. I have come to realize that I was blessed to have him in my life, even though it was only for a short time." Mary Grace wiped a tear from her eye. "When you think about it, was he ever really mine? He is God's child, and God just allowed us to spend time with that wonderful, witty, kind-hearted little boy." Tears steadily fell down her cheeks and she pulled out a handkerchief and wiped them away. Victoria couldn't stop the tears from her own eyes. She went to her sister and pulled her into her arms, a little awkwardly because of Victoria's growing abdomen. The two held each other and cried. Victoria lost track of the time, but they were interrupted when Hope began calling out from upstairs, awake from her nap. Mary Grace pulled away.

"I am comforted in knowing that my Adam is now in Heaven with his Heavenly Father." She wiped her eyes again. "Thank you for listening to my ramblings, Victoria and for all your help and support these past few months."

"Of course," Victoria said. "I am here for you anytime."

"Thank you. I must go check on Hope. Will you be staying?"

"No, I will see Hope for a few moments, but after that, I must be on my way."

"All right, then. Let's go and get her."

Wednesday, December 2, 1863
Turner Home

"My goodness, I can't remember the last time that everyone who lived here was together at the dinner table." Rachel looked around. Victoria, Tabetha, Jessica, Brianne, Kendall, Major Rogers, Lieutenant Rogers and Lieutenant Campbell, all together for dinner.

"I don't recall this ever happening," Tabetha replied.

"I don't think it has either," Victoria added.

"And the Lord only knows when or if it ever will happen again," Major Rogers said.

"You're not leaving us anytime soon, are you Major?" Brianne asked with a glance at Ezekiel Rogers. Her look clearly told the young soldier that she wished he would be leaving soon. She wanted all of the Yankees out of the town immediately.

"Not that I know of, no," Steven replied. "However, one never knows when or if they'll be transferred."

"And the Major wants nothing more than to be somewhere where he can see more action and move further up the ranks," Lieutenant Campbell added.

"I won't deny wanting out of the monotony of constant guard duty, but it's not because I am looking for a promotion, Campbell." The Major protested.

"Yes, Noah, he can't help it if he gets promotion after promotion and you remain a lowly Lieutenant. I don't believe you even worked hard to get that ranking." Ezekiel joked. Noah laughed as if he didn't have a care in the world.

"Haven't you all figured it out? I don't care if I remain a lieutenant." He stabbed a piece of ham from the platter. "I get the privileges of being an officer with few responsibilities."

"There are opportunities to prove oneself here, I suppose." Major Rogers changed the subject. "We have yet to solve the dilemma of guerillas in the area."

The Turners all became silent.

"I suppose it is difficult for the army to control the countryside around Vicksburg," Jessica said. "They say that outside the city limits it is quite unsafe for anyone."

"Especially those who are not supportive of the Confederacy." Noah complained. "East of here, those organized Rebel units and their accomplices are frustrating our forces."

"Yes, and the community of Yazoo City and the surrounding farmers continue to supply them with whatever provisions they can scrape together." Major Rogers couldn't hide his irritation, but he almost sounded impressed at what the Confederates were able to accomplish.

"It has been quite difficult for us to reach some of the freed people because of those guerillas, as you call them," Jessica said.

"Not only that, these blasted Rebels target the traffic on the Mississippi as well. They terrorize our Federal units and abduct freedmen," Ezekiel said. "Those raiders should all be arrested and thrown into the deepest prison, if not executed for their crimes."

Victoria looked at her mother, who had become quite somber and pale. The women at the table, save Jessica, all knew who many of those raiders were, and who many of the local farmers aiding them were. Victoria feared for her brother and for Hannah's family every day. Victoria was proud of Jason for fighting with the militia, as well as her father and Gregory, all still fighting against the tyranny of the Federal government. Though the Turner family ate dinner with Union soldiers and even considered some Yankees friends, they were still the enemy.

"Yes, ladies, I must say, it is quite a relief to be able to stay in a house where we are not hated," Lieutenant Campbell said, oblivious to the ladies' solemnity.

"At least not openly," Brianne muttered, though only Victoria heard her.

Tabetha, knowing how uncomfortable the Turners must be feeling, finally joined in the conversation. "Not that I support either side, gentlemen, but can you blame the Southerners for their actions?" Tabetha asked. "I am a Northerner, but the federal government has usurped these people's way of life. You have been witnesses to what the citizens have endured these past months. They have lost so much. Of course their loved ones would continue to fight in any way possible to secure their safety. I can understand why they would stiffen their resolve to resist Federal rule. Would you not do the same if this were your hometown?"

"You can't possibly say that you believe our soldiers are the unrepentant, bloodthirsty vandals that some of the townsfolk think," Jessica said.

"I am not saying that at all," Tabetha insisted, glancing at Steven, hoping he wouldn't be angry. He didn't appear to be. "Many of these civilians you talk of have lost their livestock, their homes, personal belongings, and in some cases, the life of a loved one."

"You and I have spoken on this before, Miss Norton," The Major said. "I agree with you, to a point. Union soldiers shouldn't be able to do whatever they please just because we hold the town, but we must be diligent with our dealings in regards to the guerillas. If we allow known conspirators to continue to aid them, it will only prolong the war. We want to end this as quickly as possible and unfortunately, total war is the only way to do that."

"It doesn't make it right," Victoria found herself saying.

Tuesday, December 22, 1863
Office of Reverend Cook

"Reverend! I have some reports for you." Jessica smiled at the handsome man sitting behind the desk. "Reports on the progress of my students and the self-evaluation you wanted."

"Thank you. I'll review and file these. After the new year, I will be making rounds and evaluating all of our teachers down here."

"Wonderful." Jessica tried to muster enthusiasm for the news, but in reality, she despised being evaluated, even though she realized their necessity. She changed the subject.

"It will be quite strange to not have a snow at Christmas, don't you think?"

"Yes, I suppose. However, we must remember the true reason for this special day, the birth of Jesus Christ."

"Oh, yes, I know that. I simply love all the traditions of the Christmas season. I will miss spending it with my family." A pang of sorrow hit her, when she realized this would be the first Christmas without her father. Perhaps it was a good thing that she wasn't at home in Oberlin with all of the memories.

"Yes, but we can make the season just as special anywhere we are." The Reverend didn't even notice Jessica's distress. "The love of Jesus finds us wherever we are."

"Of course, of course." Jessica composed herself. "Do you have plans for Friday?"

"One of the couples from the American Missionary Association has invited me to dine and spend the day with them. They have a daughter they would like me to get to know better."

"Oh." Jessica tried not to show her dejection at the news. "I see. That should be enjoyable."

"I suppose," the Reverend replied. "I have met the young woman, however, and she seems to be a bit on the childish side, with a shallow heart. When I court and marry, it will be a woman willing to give her life to the Lord and assist me in fulfilling my mission."

Hope surged in Jessica's heart. Perhaps she still had time to earn the Reverend's affections.

"I trust the family you are boarding with will allow you to celebrate the holiday with them," he said.

"Yes. In fact, if you didn't already have plans, I was going to invite you."

"Thank you for thinking of me," he said. "I have been meaning to visit you at the Turner home, as I have yet to meet them. I do feel a responsibility to you, and all of my missionaries, of course. I have been told that the Turners are a good family, very well-respected in the town."

"They have been most hospitable. I am very blessed to be with them."

"We have many blessings here." Reverend Cook smiled, then looked at the clock. "As much as I have enjoyed our conversation, I have some work I must get finished."

"Of course. I am so sorry for keeping you," Jessica nodded. "Good day."

"Until next time, Miss Spencer," the Reverend replied.

As Jessica exited the building she smiled at the knowledge that she would be able to get home early today, but when she reached the street, she noticed they were more crowded than usual.

"Miss Spencer!"

Jessica turned to see Lieutenant Noah Campbell stride toward her. "Good day, Lieutenant. May I help you?"

"Are you heading back to the Turner home?" He gripped his rifle and looking around warily.

"Yes, I am. Why? What's wrong?"

"I would like to escort you. There was trouble earlier today and I want to make sure you arrive home safely."

"I'm sure I'll be perfectly fine on my own." Jessica insisted. "You needn't worry."

"That may be true, but Mrs. Turner would have my hide if anything happened to you."

"I believe we've had this conversation before, Lieutenant." Jessica appreciated the soldier's worry, but knew it was unwarranted.

"Yes, we have, and nothing's changed." Noah took her hand and tucked it into the crook of his arm. "Come." They began walking quietly and comfortably with the silence between them.

"What is the trouble that you spoke of?" Jessica finally asked.

"Some of our soldiers were a little rowdy earlier today. You might even say they were rioting."

"With your history of fighting, I'm surprised you weren't a part of it."

"Trouble usually finds me, Miss Spencer, not the other way around, and rioting solves nothing. Besides, I must start behaving better. My commanding officer, Major Rogers would have my head."

"So he has a tighter rein on you now that you both live in the same house?" She teased.

"That is true, he does, but I believe it is Mrs. Turner who is encouraging me to behave better. She lets me know that I do have potential. I'm more worried about what she thinks of me, to be honest."

"Imagine that. I believed you didn't care what anyone thought of you," Jessica replied.

"Hm." The Lieutenant gave a short shrug. "I do her. I never really knew my own Mother. She passed away when I was young. I have two older brothers and one younger one. Mixing it up was a part of growing up in my life."

"Mixing what up?" Jessica needed clarification.

"You know, just...fighting, but not really to hurt the other person. Nothin' too serious. It is something that most brothers do with one another, even the Rogers brothers."

"I see." Jessica shrugged. "I suppose there are things I never learned, being an only child."

"Musta been boring, not having brothers and sisters," Noah said.

"Perhaps. I suppose I never knew any differently at the time, but now, being a part of the Turner household, well..." She looked up at her escort. "I am starting to enjoy being a part of a big family. It was just me and my father for so long."

"Well, the Turners are a quite hospitable for the most part. I'm not sure how Mrs. Turner does it, welcoming the enemy into her home. I overheard her talking with Mrs. Prentiss about the men in their family. She has every reason to hate us, yet she treats us like her own." He shook his head. "I don't think I would be able to do it."

"I think it's difficult to know what we would do in certain situations until we are actually put into them." She pointed out. "I'm sure you could muster up compassion."

"I suppose you're right," he replied with a smile. "Thank you for thinking that of me."

"I only speak the truth." She smiled. "Mrs. Turner isn't the only one who sees good in you."

"Thank you, Miss Spencer." Lieutenant Campbell smiled back, then escorted her up the steps of the Turner home.

Friday, December 25, 1963
Christ Episcopal Church

"Merry Christmas, Mary!" Victoria embraced her friend, then gave Duff a friendly smile.

"Merry Christmas, Victoria." Mary's breath fogged the air. It was a chilly day for Mississippi. "There are quite a few Union soldiers here for services this morning."

"Yes, they continue to infiltrate every aspect of our lives." Though Victoria was making an effort to be more forgiving of the Yankees and be less judgmental toward them, she couldn't help but resent their presence. "However, I suppose it's a good thing that they're attending services. Perhaps it will lead them to be better Christians."

"We can all work on that," Mary said, then smiled as Duff took their children into the church to find a seat. "With all of these Union soldiers in attendance, I do wonder what this Reverend Fox will say in regards to our prayer for the president."

"The thought crossed my mind as well," Victoria said.

According to the *Book of Common Prayer*, the minister was supposed to offer up a prayer for the president of the country. Since the secession of Mississippi and the election of Jefferson Davis, the minister had prayed for the local politician, even after the fall of the city. However, today, many of the church attendees were the conquering soldiers. Not only that, a Union official had asked a Unionist Pastor, James A. Fox to conduct the services.

"I do miss Reverend Lord," Victoria said. The Reverend had chosen to leave with the Confederate Army when the city fell. "I wonder if Reverend Fox will have the courage to pray for Davis in the presence of Yankee troops."

"I suppose we'll see," Mary said as the two began walking into the church.

"I know members of our congregation will be very unhappy if he prays for Lincoln and may even retaliate if that happens." Victoria sighed. "Oh, Mary, I do wish I could talk to you more, but Mother and the others are saving me a seat, and it's almost time to begin. I will see you after services."

"Of course," Mary quickly found Duff and the children, then sat and took William into her arms. As the service began. Mary tried to focus on the celebration of the day, but she could feel the tension in the room, especially from the Southerners. Everyone knew Reverend Fox was about to make a critical decision. *Lord, please help him make the right decision, and please allow the people to accept that decision.* She prayed, though she wasn't even sure what the right decision should be.

Finally, the moment of the prayer arrived. Mary held her breath and looked around, meeting Victoria's concerned eyes for a brief second. Reverend Fox paused and looked around the congregation, locking his eyes on one pew in particular. Mary tried to discreetly look and see who was sitting there. The pew held five young women from the town, Kate and Ella Barnett, daughters of one of the local judges, Mrs. Moore, Laura Latham, and Ellen Martin. All five of the women seemed quite agitated. Mary didn't know any of them well, but knew they were quite vocal about their dislike of the Yankee presence. Now, in church, on Christmas Day, it appeared as if they were anticipating Reverend Fox to say the wrong thing.

Mary looked around at the soldiers. Many of them were emotionless, and some even looked bored. The minister cleared his throat and looked around. Finally, he took a deep breath and began the prayer. Mary held her breath, and she felt Duff stiffen next to her and reached to take her hand.

"Lord, our Heavenly Father, the high and mighty ruler of the universe," Reverend Fox recited. "Who dost from thy throne, behold all the dwellers upon earth, most heartedly we beseech Thee, with Thy favor to behold and bless thy servant, the president of the United States, and all others..."

His next words, 'in authority', were difficult to hear, because at the utterance of the words 'United States', the five restless young women stood up.

"Don't make a scene, please don't make a scene," Mary whispered to herself.

The five women stood tall, and with a swishing of their skirts, left the pew with their heads held high. They marched down the aisle, not even attempting to be quiet, right out the front door of the church.

Inside, the tension remained thick. Reverend Fox tried to continue with his service, but the damage was done. Union soldiers looked around angrily, almost daring other Southerners to follow suit. The townspeople glared at both Reverend Fox and the Union soldiers. Duff pulled Mary and Annie closer to him, as if he expected an altercation to take place, however, cool heads prevailed. Reverend Fox was able to finish the service without further interruptions.

As soon as the churchgoers filed out of the church, Victoria approached Mary.

"That will cause some talk about town," Mary said.

"Indeed," Victoria agreed. "I have a bad feeling. I fear the Yankees will retaliate and use those five women as an example to all of us. Obey them and their rules fully and without complaint or you will face the consequences."

"I do hope you're wrong, unfortunately, I fear you're right." Mary sighed.

Victoria shook her head in dismay. "Oh, botheration, I see my family is leaving." Victoria gave Mary a quick hug. "Esther has the day off to spend with her family, so I must help Mama with Christmas dinner for all our boarders, and Mary Grace and her family will be coming over too."

"Very well," Mary said. "I would like to get together for tea soon. It would be especially great if we could visit Hannah as well. It has been so long."

"I agree." Victoria smiled. "You have a blessed Christmas."

"You as well," Mary replied, then turned and left.

Jessica sat on the front steps of the Turner home that evening, her arms wrapped around her knees. Christmas was her favorite day of the entire year. Past years would find her with family and friends, and snow blanketing the landscape. Sleigh rides, sledding and caroling made up the day. The magical celebration of the birth of Jesus Christ. It was much different down here in Mississippi. There was no chance of snow, and while it was chilly enough to see her breath in the air today, she was quite comfortable in just her dress and a shawl.

Lieutenant Campbell's voice broke through the stillness. "You have been unusually quiet all day today." He strode to the railing and leaned against it.

"I just have a lot on my mind," She admitted. "And Christmas down here isn't at all like Christmas in Ohio."

"Nor where I am from." He replied.

"Ah, that's right. You were raised by your father and grew up with three brothers on a farm. I suppose Christmas celebrations could be difficult."

"Yes, but we usually got something small from St. Nick, although it was also practical." He pulled out a small pocket knife. "I still carry this one."

"What a thoughtful present." She smiled, then sighed. "I apologize. I should be thankful for all I do have. A place to stay, a job with a purpose, and friends who are like family. I have things I want to achieve and now have the means to do so." She glanced at him. "What ambitions do you have, Lieutenant? I know you must have some thoughts on what you want to accomplish in life."

Noah stared out into the darkness. "I want to make something of myself, make my Ma and family proud, even though my Ma is in heaven. I suppose sometimes...I don't know." Noah shook his head. "It's difficult to explain, Miss Spencer."

"You're afraid," she stated, knowing deep down she was right. "You are afraid of the responsibility. You're afraid if you truly work to the best of your abilities, you'll have to take on even more responsibilities, and for some reason, you don't want that." She had worked with students like Lieutenant Campbell before. "You mustn't be afraid to let your light shine, as the Bible says, for when you do, you will help others reach their potential."

Noah gave her a reflective look. "I never thought about that, Miss Spencer."

"Well, I want to be more than just a teacher, Lieutenant Campbell. I want to inspire people to be their very best. No matter if they're my students or not."

"I never had much formal schooling," he admitted. "Maybe I would have attended longer if I'd had a teacher like you."

Jessica blushed. "I hope my students feel that way about me. I do want to make a difference. These Negro children want to learn so badly, and their parents..." She smiled to herself. "They have a long, difficult road ahead of them, but they are so eager to better their lives. Most of them, at least." She thought of some of the freedmen she had met who believed schooling was unnecessary. "We can always use volunteers. Even if you didn't get very far in school, you could still read to the students. If you wanted to, that is."

Noah's jaw clenched. "That wouldn't work Miss Spencer."

"Why not? I know you've been talking with some of the freedmen, and I have witnessed you playing ball with some of the children. It doesn't appear as though you take issue with them like many of the soldiers do."

"It's not that, Miss Spencer." He gritted his teeth.

"Heavens, are you afraid of being short on time? Perhaps your commanding officer..."

"Not that either." He didn't want to tell her his reason, that much was clear, however, she desperately wanted to know.

"Well then, what is it, Lieutenant Campbell?"

He blew out a breath. "When I said I was never much for book learning, I really meant it. Never really learned to read well at all. Fact is, I shouldn't even be an officer. I was appointed to the position with the understanding that I could read and write, but honestly, I struggle with it. I just don't see the letters the way I am supposed to. There is no way I can advance, I have trouble enough writing the reports I do now."

"Goodness, I believed you were still a lieutenant because of your tendency to get into fisticuffs." She had assumed, based on his conversations with the Rogers brothers, that he would be promoted if he didn't get into so many scuffles. Perhaps that was just a disguise to cover the fact that he couldn't read.

"Do the Rogers brothers know this?"

"Well, yes. As a matter of fact, they do. They both help me with my reports, but they can't seem to help me with my reading." He admitted, then looked up at Jessica with concern. "Miss Spencer, you cannot tell anyone this. I cannot lose this appointment. It would disgrace my family."

"Well, Lieutenant, there are many men and women in our country who struggle with letters. It is nothing to be ashamed of. In fact, if you wanted to, I could try and teach you with a different method."

"No, Ma'am. I wouldn't want to bother you."

"It wouldn't be a bother," she assured him. Jessica could now understand why this apparently kind and vulnerable human being acted the cocky, arrogant man. It may actually be a pleasure to teach him. "Please let me help you."

He sighed, then gave her a teasing smile. "All right, I'll think about it and tell you what I decide. I suppose it can't hurt to try, and it will give me an excuse to spend time with you."

Jessica blushed. "I hope you do, though let me assure you, it will just be educational."

"Of course," Lieutenant Campbell said. "I would expect nothing else."

Sunday, December 27, 1863
Turner Home

"Well, I don't care what you or your Major General say, I think what those women did was incredibly brave."

Victoria and Tabetha entered the foyer to see Brianne, squaring off against Lieutenant Ezekiel Rogers.

"In fact," Brianne continued. "I should have walked out with them. You Yankees are so pompous and overbearing and this new order proves it."

"Not all soldiers agree with what happened to those women. They should be held accountable for disrespecting our president and disturbing the Christmas service, but I don't believe they should have been banished from town."

"It's true then?" Tabetha interrupted. "I had hoped it was just a vicious, unfounded rumor."

"Yes, Ma'am," Ezekiel said. "General Orders Number 52 was issued today. It states that anyone who disrespects the president, the Government or the US flag will be fined, banished or imprisoned. The punishment rendered for those five women is for them to leave Federal lines within 48 hours or face a penalty of imprisonment."

"They can't possibly do that." Victoria was appalled. "Just because we don't agree with a Yankee...they can't banish us for our thoughts and feelings. You cannot force us to respect your president. We have our own president."

"It does seem a bit tyrannical," Tabetha said.

Ezekiel held his hands up, palms out. "As I said, I'm not disagreeing with you ladies, but the fact remains. Those ladies made a choice and now they must suffer the consequences." He tipped his head, put his hat on, and strode out the door.

"Oh, that man! He is so infuriating!" Brianne shrieked. "All of these vile Yankees just need to disappear." She glanced at Tabetha, who looked slightly offended. "Present company excepted, of course. Miss Spencer is also growing on me, although she is almost too cheerful at times." The young woman shook her head, then walked into the parlor and sank onto a settee.

"I really thought that was all just a rumor." Victoria and Tabetha followed Brianne. "Can they really do that?" She asked Tabetha.

"Yes, they can, unfortunately. Remember, this is war. The governments don't follow common sense or have a sense of compassion. Most of the Federal soldiers are good men and want to do the right thing, but they have fears as well. They're afraid if they don't keep a tight rein and follow their commanders, they'll be court martialed and face penalties themselves. They don't want that."

"But banishing young women?" Brianne was incredulous. "I don't understand that. We have friends and relatives who are dying by the thousands from wounds and illness, fighting for independence. We have been through a horrid siege with terrible tragedies, and now, even in our homes, in our very own church...like you said, Victoria, we can't express our own thoughts and beliefs. This is not the democracy our forefathers fought for. It all seems so hopeless now."

Victoria placed a hand on Brianne's back.

"Unfortunately, many people will blame Reverend Fox for starting this whole fiasco," Victoria said. "The church was quite empty today."

"I surely don't want to go back there and have to sit alongside the enemy. You know as well as I do that those soldiers will continue to attend services. I can just see their smug Yankee expressions already." Brianne wiped a tear from her eye. "Is all lost, Victoria?"

"No, I don't believe so." Victoria placed a hand on her unborn child. She had to have hope for the world that she would bring a child into. "I cannot believe that all hope is lost, Brianne. God has a plan for us, you remember that." Victoria smiled. "I remember a time when you were about three or four. You had just come to live with us after losing your mother. Mary Grace, Gregory, Jason and I were having fun with you, asking you questions. I don't even remember the exact question or who asked it, but your answer was said with complete confidence. 'I don't know, but God does. He knows everything and we'll be fine.'"

Brianne smiled back at Victoria. "I was just a child. I didn't know what I was talking about."

"It sounds to me like you did," Tabetha replied. "Young children have such innocence and believe with all their heart. I think that was very wise for a child to say."

"You had that hope then, Brianne. Don't let this war take it from you." Victoria hugged her cousin.

"I suppose you have a good point, Victoria. I will try."

"Please remember your family is always here for you."

Brianne nodded. "I am going to visit Alice Shirley; we made plans earlier. I just hope her Yankee beau isn't hanging around. Perhaps I can talk some sense into that girl." She stood. "I will see you all for dinner."

After Brianne left, Victoria turned to Tabetha. "I wish I could do more for her. Brianne and Kendall are at such an impressionable age to be dealing with all the despair in town, as well as all the other problems this war has caused."

"They are two intelligent and kind young ladies," Tabetha stated. "Your mother has done a wonderful job raising them. I believe you said just the right thing to Brianne."

"I'm glad, and I just hope," Victoria emphasized the word 'hope'. "I can remember my own words when I need them the most."

Part 4:
1864

Sunday, January 24, 1864
Wheeler Farm

"It is so wonderful to see you all." Hannah smiled. "I have missed you."

"I am thankful for the invitation." Jessica smiled. She had been pleasantly surprised when Victoria asked her to go to dinner at the Wheelers'. After all, she was an outsider and could even be considered the enemy. This invitation made Jessica feel like she was part of the family.

"I am glad you were able to accept the invitation. It will be nice to become better acquainted with my best friend's boarder," Hannah said. She had only met the energetic teacher a few times, as they were all busy and it was still difficult to get into town sometimes.

"I feel the same way." Jessica smiled. She had enjoyed spending time with the young widow who radiated her faith as Jessica aspired to do.

The women all sat down around the table.

"Where are Ambrose and Caroline today?" Victoria asked. "I didn't see them in the yard."

"I am surprised your mother didn't mention it to you. They're currently at your house with my mother-in-law for a visit." She picked at the cloth that covered the table. "Ambrose continues to ask so many questions about Adam and his death. He asked if I thought Benjamin, my late husband," she explained to Jessica, "would adopt Adam in heaven. That way, Benjamin would feel as though he still had a son." Tears glistened in her eyes. "I must ask, how is Mary Grace? I think of her often. I cannot fathom what she is going through, losing a child, especially since Abraham was away at war. It was unbearable when I lost Benjamin. If I were to lose Ambrose..." She shook her head.

"The loss of Adam is still difficult for all of us," Victoria replied. "I believe Abraham's return has lightened our spirits and lifted Mary Grace's burdens. Some of them, at least."

"And how is Abraham?" Hannah asked. "He has had much to take in since his return."

"Actually, he is faring quite well. He won't talk about the war, or give details about how he sustained his injury, but I can understand that."

"Begging your pardon, Victoria, but I believe to discuss his war experiences, especially with his wife, would be quite beneficial," Jessica said. "I think that all the soldiers should talk about what has happened to them instead of keeping it down deep inside."

"Nathaniel rarely discussed his feelings about the war and his experiences," Victoria said. "He told me that he didn't want to expose me to the indelicate nature of war."

"I..." Tabetha choked on the word, hesitated, and then decided that it was time to share her secret past with Jessica. "I can attest to the horrors of battle and how they affect a soldier. Not only does a soldier not want to burden their loved ones with the horrible thoughts and images, but it is also difficult for them to explain the...dread, the panic, and the terror. All the emotion you encounter in battle, while at the same time, feeling excitement and anxiety. It is hard to explain unless you've actually lived through it."

Tabetha's thoughts drifted back to visions of her battle escapades. She could clearly visualize some of the men she'd shot and one she knew that died from her bullet. She could still vividly see the chaos of a charge, and then the aftermath of battles. The muddy, bloated corpses of both men and animals. Lifeless eyes. The stench of decay. The memories haunted her.

"You sound as if you have experienced this firsthand," Jessica said. Tabetha looked at her and cleared her throat.

"I have, Miss Spencer."

Jessica's eyes widened. "I don't believe I understood you correctly; you just insinuated that you have witnessed the horrors of battle firsthand."

"Then you understand correctly." Tabetha glanced around the table they were sitting at, grateful for the support of her friends.

"But Tabetha, how would you know that. You have never been married, and I don't see you as being a camp follower; you have never mentioned a father who is fighting." Jessica was confused, as those were the only reasons she could think of that would put Tabetha that close to a battle.

"Jessica, there are few people who know what I am about to tell you. The women in this room, Mrs. Turner, Brianne, Kendall and Esther." Tabetha took a breath and told her story. She finished by describing her relationship with her commanding officer.

"He became a very good friend, and unfortunately, even as my commanding officer, I found myself drawn to him."

"And now you're in love with him," Victoria stated. Tabetha blushed.

"I had hoped it wasn't that obvious."

"You are speaking of Major Rogers? He was your commander while you were in the cavalry?"

"Yes, he was." Tabetha's response was very quiet.

"And he understands why you did what you did?" Jessica asked.

Tabetha took another breath and bowed her head. "He doesn't know. Jessica, please, I ask for your discretion, please don't tell him, or Lieutenant Rogers, or Lieutenant Campbell or anyone for that matter."

"Oh, I won't." Jessica assured her. "You have my word."

"I would have thought…" Hannah started to speak, then halted, not wanting to judge.

Speculating on what Hannah was thinking, Tabetha replied. "I just haven't found the right time. It feels like there will never be a right time now." She sighed.

"It is an unfortunate situation," Victoria said. "I can see why you would hesitate to bring it up. Before, you didn't know if you could trust him with the secret."

Tabetha nodded. "Yes, and now that I know he can be trusted, he'll feel betrayed that I didn't tell him sooner."

"If you'd like to know my opinion?" Hannah asked. Tabetha nodded. "I haven't met the Major, but the way you all talk of him, he is a good man, and he cares for you. You need to tell him. He will be upset, of course, and rightly so. However, if he cares for you the way a true friend should care for another, he will forgive you."

"I hope so." Tabetha nodded, thankful for the advice.

The talk turned to other subjects, especially of how the civilians were faring since the occupation.

"This winter has been especially difficult for many families," Hannah said. "When the Federals besieged the city, we were unable to care for our crops and it was quite difficult to harvest. There were so many acres of farmland destroyed by the troops. They ride right through the fields without any concern of what may be growing there. I am hoping, we'll be able to plant in the spring and begin anew with the growing season."

"I always assumed the growing season was year-round in the south," Tabetha remarked.

"We do have a longer season than the northern states, but remember we have different crops. We may get some more vegetables later in the year, but we still must watch what we plant and when," Hannah explained.

"At least the Federals are helping out," Jessica said. "I spoke to Lieutenant Campbell on Friday and he said that on that day alone, 340 people applied for rations. Men, women, children, babies."

"That may seem like a large number, Jessica, but there are so many destitute families," Hannah stated. "In December, the Yankees allowed the sale of provisions and firewood to any civilian in need, and I must admit, I know for a fact they provided firewood for those who couldn't provide for themselves, and will likely continue to do so."

"Yes, but it is not near enough help," Victoria said. "The farmers, the refugees, they all need so much. Our family has been quite lucky to be honest. However, I believe the soldiers can be doing much more. After all, they are the cause for most of our problems." While she was trying not to be judgmental and prejudiced against the Yankees, her anger won out at times.

"Yes, but at least they are doing something," Tabetha reminded her.

"Of course, of course," Victoria replied with a forced smile.

"With the influx of refugees, both black and white, the Federal government may unfortunately have to change their policies of feeding everyone." Tabetha shook her head. "The hospitals are now overflowing, not just with injured and ill soldiers, but also sick and injured refugees. The government will not have the resources to sustain those in the army and hospital, much less the general public."

"Oh, that would be tragic," Mary said. "And I do believe you're right about the conditions of the hospital. Duff wants me to stay far away from our home, mainly because he doesn't want me to catch any of the sicknesses."

"I understand his worry," Hannah said, then rose. "Can I refill anyone's tea? I know it's not the strongest or best-tasting, but it can't be helped."

"It tastes just fine, Hannah," Victoria said, adjusting her attitude. "As with many things, it is not what we are doing but who we are with. I am glad to be spending this time with you all." She thought of the future. The war wasn't going well for the Confederates, and when it was over and when Nathaniel came back, she would be moving to Virginia. She must enjoy her time with friends while she could.

Wednesday, January 27, 1863
Turner Home

"How much longer 'til your baby comes, Aunt Victoria?" Gabriel asked.

"My best guess would be a month or two," Victoria answered with a smile. Mary Grace had come over for dinner and she and her children were now sitting with Victoria, Kendall, and Rachel in front of the fire. It was a cozy evening, and Victoria was dearly enjoying her time with her family, a nice, quiet...

"Those blasted Yankees have done it again! I tell you that Ezekiel Campbell is lucky he's not here, because I cannot be held accountable for what I may do right now." Brianne stormed into the room, more angry than Victoria had ever seen her.

"My goodness, Brianne, what in the world has happened?"

"They've done it, they have really done it now." She furiously paced back and forth.

"Brianne, dear, it may be best if you calmed down. You're frightening the children." Rachel glanced at Gabriel and Hope.

"It's all right, Gramma," Gabriel said, standing. "Come on, Hope. Let's go find Dinah, she can watch us while the grown-ups talk."

Hope followed her brother. Victoria wanted to smile at the two, but Brianne's agitation worried her.

"Brianne, what is it?" Kendall asked.

"It's Emma. Emma Kline." Brianne sat down, a bit calmer. "She's been arrested."

"What?" Victoria was stunned. "Emma Kline? Whatever for?"

Emma was the 20-year-old daughter of a local planter and a friend of Brianne.

"She's been arrested for smuggling." Brianne groaned. "The story I heard was that she and Dr. Anderson's granddaughter were attempting to smuggle contraband goods out of the city. They had medication hidden in their skirts that would eventually get to a Confederate field hospital. They were arrested and brought back into the city. This all happened yesterday. I was briefly able to see her today and she told me her whole family was being banished. Sent into Rebeldom, because they are 'acting in bad faith toward the government.'"

"Rebeldom?" Mary asked.

"That's the term people are using to describe the territory across the Big Black River." Kendall explained. "It's where all our banished people go because it's still held by Confederates."

Brianne shook her head. "There are times I wish I could be brave enough to do what Emma did."

"My goodness," Rachel shook her head. "Will they be able to bring anything with them?"

"Whatever personal property they can. The rest will be confiscated by the Yankees." Brianne practically growled. "For simply doing what she could to help her soldiers."

"If you're talking about Miss Kline," a masculine voice came from the doorway. Ezekiel Rogers stood there. "Then you must know the entire Kline family is well-known to the Union authorities. Miss Kline is a very fiery Rebel who has made it very clear where her loyalties lie."

"So you're just going to arrest anyone who isn't loyal to your precious Union?" Brianne stood slowly, her voice low. "Is that what you're saying?"

"I'm saying she broke the law," Ezekiel said. "I'm fairly certain she knew what she was risking. At least she's able to go free and be with her family."

"Oh, I see. To you, everything is fine, simply because she's not in some Yankee prison. The fact that she, all of us, really, are not free to do what we want, is unimportant to you. We are trapped under your blasted Yankee rule." She then stomped out of the room, purposely driving her shoulder into Ezekiel's chest as she passed by. Victoria's eyes widened.

Ezekiel's jaw tightened. Before Rachel could apologize for Brianne's behavior, he turned and marched away.

"Poor Patience," Rachel said, referring to Emma Klein's mother. "I hope she knows someone who will take them in."

"I'm sure they will be fine," Mary Grace assured her. "There are likely many people willing to help them. Emma may very well be considered a hero over there."

"I can't believe the whole family was banished just for Emma's actions," Victoria said.

"Well, they would have gone with her, regardless," Rachel replied. "I know I would follow any of you under the same circumstances."

"Hopefully, that will never happen," Mary Grace said.

"Yes, and hopefully, Brianne will overcome her anger," Victoria commented.

Friday, February 19, 1864
Freedman's School

"Miss Spencer!"

Jessica looked up and smiled when she saw Mary Green wave from the doorway of the schoolhouse, arms full of books.

"Good afternoon, Mrs. Green. How are you this fine day?"

"Quite well, thank you. I thought I would stop by to see how your students are progressing."

Jessica thought of her many students and their recent accomplishments. "They are doing well. Some of the boys can be a bit...active, and some are easily distracted, but it is no wonder, considering what they once used to do."

"Whatever do you mean?" Mary asked.

"They've never had to sit in a classroom before now. They are accustomed to being active and working, moving continuously. It has been quite a difficult transition."

"I hadn't thought of that," Mary said. "That must make your job more challenging."

"Yes, I suppose." Jessica looked down, avoiding Mary's eyes.

"Whatever is wrong, Miss Spencer?"

"Sometimes I wonder if I am doing any good."

"Jessica, I have heard you are a wonderful teacher," Mary said. "And if you were not doing well, I am sure you would have been replaced, yet you are still with us. I know you to be dedicated and sincere in your work, you have a positive attitude, even in these harsh conditions." Mary looked around at the bare-bones school, then seemed to remember why she had come in the first place. "On that subject, I brought these readers. I found them while browsing through the library at my Mother's house. Will you be able to find use for them?"

"Oh my, yes! Thank you so much for thinking of us." Jessica smiled greatly and took the offered items. As she moved to stack them on her desk, she knocked some papers off. With a heavy sigh, she bent to pick them up, aided by Mary.

"Thank you." Jessica took the last paper from Mary, then sighed heavily again and rubbed her temple.

"Is that bad news?" Mary asked. Jessica glanced at her friend and slid the paper towards her.

"Just my most recent teacher evaluation," Jessica explained, a bit frustrated. "Apparently having admirable zeal and a profound sense of devotion isn't quite enough."

"This doesn't sound terribly bad," Mary said. "They acknowledge many good things about you, Miss Spencer."

"I know. Unfortunately I usually focus on the criticism rather than the praise. I desperately want to be the best for my students and in memory of my father. He was a wonderful teacher, and I want to be the best for..." She caught herself before she said Reverend Cook's name, but Mary smiled knowingly.

"Your supervisor? The very handsome, quite single Reverend Cook?"

"Yes, I want to do well for him also," Jessica said. "I feel as though I am where I need to be. God placed me here for a purpose as part of his plan for me, but there are times I feel as though I am in over my head."

"I believe we all feel like that at some point in our lives," Mary said.

"Maybe," Jessica said. "Thank you so much, Mrs. Green, for the readers and your encouragement."

"My pleasure," Mary replied.

Wednesday, March 16, 1864
Turner Home

"My goodness," Mary Green stood from the chair in the Turner parlor. She had expected to visit with Victoria in her room, as she was quite close to her time. Instead, Esther had told her to wait downstairs. "Victoria Prentiss, what are you thinking? You look like you could have that baby of yours any day now. Why are you working in your condition?"

"I just cannot sit down," Victoria said. "I am so restless. Mama agrees with you, she says I should be abed. I just cannot bear the boredom."

The two women embraced, awkwardly. "I am prepared, though. Abraham and Mary Grace brought their bassinet over, with some baby clothes, and Mama and I have been sewing diapers and I even made a cute blanket. I believe everything is in place."

"And are you excited? To have a son or daughter?"

"I am. At least I won't be giving birth in a cave, like someone else I know." She smiled. "What is the news in town?"

"Well, Duff was quite offended when he heard about the corruption of some of the Union soldiers."

"Well, I could have told you that long ago. What are they doing to us now?"

"Apparently, they are using military raids as a cover for finding and stealing cotton that they send North. They say it's confiscated Confederate property."

"That doesn't surprise me. It would be quite easy for an officer to pass through the lines on a supposed raid and then make deals for buying the cotton that hardworking southerners have raised and stored."

"Yes, that's what is happening."

"And does Major General Dana plan on doing anything about this?" Major General Napoleon Jackson Tecumseh Dana was the new provost general of Vicksburg. "What a ridiculous name. They say he would rule with a firm but fair hand; what will he do now? I don't believe for a minute he will be fair for all."

"Duff said Dana is determined to put a stop to the cotton corruption. He's levied a tax on each bale brought in and is attempting to stop all trade with the Confederacy. Nothing can be brought across the lines except the personal property of refugees."

"My goodness, what will he decree next?" Victoria shook her head, then bent over in pain. "Oh, goodness," She looked at her friend. "Maybe I should be getting back to my room."

"I think you may be having that child today," Mary said, then helped her friend upstairs.

◦◦◦◦◦

Hours later, Mary, Tabetha, Jessica, Brianne and Kendall sat in the Turner parlor with Gabriel and Hope. Mary Grace, Rachel and Esther were in the room upstairs with Victoria. Mary Grace had been updating them on her progress.

"When will Aunt Victoria's baby be here?" Gabriel asked. "And will I get to hold it?"

"Of course you'll be able to hold your new cousin," Kendall said.

"Will it be a boy or a girl?" Gabriel asked.

"We will know soon enough," Brianne replied. "It won't be long now."

"Not long at all." Mary Grace entered the parlor.

"Mama!" Hope ran to give her mother a hug.

"Victoria is doing well. She has a healthy baby girl." Mary Grace smiled.

"Did she give her a name yet?" Tabetha asked.

"Yes, after very little hesitation," Mary Grace replied. "I believe she put a great deal of thought into the name beforehand." She focused on her son. "Your cousin's name is Felicity Grace. Felicity was Nathaniel's mother's name, and Grace was our grandmother's."

"Such a beautiful name," Jessica said with a smile. "It sounds absolutely perfect."

"Were there any problems?" Mary Green stood.

"No, the delivery was quite normal," Mary Grace replied. "Before you leave, Mary, Victoria would like to see you,"

"Victoria knows me well. I wouldn't leave without seeing the baby," Mary Green said, then headed upstairs. Mary Grace bent down and picked Hope up.

"So both Victoria and Felicity are safe and healthy?" Jessica asked, thinking about her own mother and newborn brother who had both died in childbirth.

"They are perfectly well. You can check on them yourselves when Mary Green comes down," Mary Grace looked at her children. "You two can meet Felicity Grace tomorrow. It is almost time for bed."

"But, Mama, I want to see her now." Gabriel said.

"You will soon, love, first thing tomorrow." She took Gabriel's hand and nodded at Jessica and Tabetha. "I will see you ladies tomorrow. Have a good evening."

Brianne looked up towards the stairs. "I don't want to bother Victoria, but I so want to hold Felicity. I love babies."

"I know," Kendall agreed. "I am quite excited to meet her."

"Well, she won't be going anywhere. She is here to stay," Tabetha said.

"Although I don't envy you, Tabetha," Kendall said, always practical. "I sure wouldn't want to share a room with a newborn."

"The boys and I were talking about that."

The women turned to see Major Rogers enter the parlor.

"We are all in agreement that Mrs. Prentiss and the baby should have their own room, and Mrs. Turner should keep her own room. We decided the three of us will stay in one room Miss Norton can stay in my old room. Miss Spencer could move in there as well, allowing Miss Brianne and Miss Kendall more space in that room."

"It's not your room, it's Jason's old room." Brianne spoke up. "The room you are currently staying in is not yours, it is my cousin's. You just took it over." The girl then pushed past Ezekiel Rogers who had entered the room. Mrs. Turner entered and sighed.

"Once again, I feel the need to apologize for my niece. In addition to all the other emotions she is feeling, she recently discovered that one of her very best friends is planning on marrying a Union officer. She feels quite betrayed by this turn of events."

"That is understandable," Major Rogers said, considerate as usual. Ezekiel looked less than understanding.

"It will be quite different with a newborn in the house," the major commented. "But this change will be good."

March 20, 1864
Lakemont

"Duff! Whatever is wrong?"

The moment her husband entered the parlor, Mary knew he was upset.

Duff fell onto the settee next to her with a huff. "I thought Major General Dana would be the answer. A man who would be firm and fair and perhaps make things easier for the civilians of this town."

"What has he done now?" Mary reached over and rubbed his shoulder.

"He's closed all businesses, fixed a ceiling on the price of items to be sold, and ordered that no one can hold onto their business unless they sign the loyalty oath."

"Oh, goodness. That may not affect us, but it will be disastrous to many others!"

"Yes. He will select former Union soldiers, carpetbaggers, scalawags and some of his personal friends to be the new merchants of the city."

"This is not good at all." Mary worried about many of her friends, those who depended on their businesses to survive. "Can they...they can at least work, correct?"

He shook his head. "Only those who signed the oath can hold a job, buy goods, or have a pass to go in and out of the city. He's trying to force loyalty on the people."

"A week or so ago, before Felicity's birth, Victoria told me Dana is trying civilians in military courts and forbade the sale of gray cloth."

"That is true." He ran a hand through his hair. "I understand why he feels the need to do this. I just hate that he thinks this is the way to keep the peace. He is making it so difficult for everyone. It is impossible for some people to even grow a garden. The army has confiscated all work animals...it's just a mess."

"Has Dana done anything good for the city?" Mary asked.

"He has done a good job of cleaning it. Repairing roads and making things more sanitary, and is apparent that crime has been reduced since he came. He is stern with the civilians, but he is also stern with his own men."

"I suppose so," Mary said.

Duff changed the subject. "Have you been able to visit Victoria today? How is she doing?"

"Very well, I'd say she is as good as she can be. Felicity is a beautiful child. I only hope that the baby will boost her spirits."

"You have mentioned before that Victoria has been melancholy," Duff said.

"Yes. Just when I believe she is her normal, happy self, it seems as though she gets into a downcast mood. I know she is worried about many things, but I don't know what to say to her."

"She has had many disappointments of late."

"Yes, she feels this military occupation is worse than the war. I don't know that she's even gone to see Adam's grave yet." Mary shook her head. "I just pray that she can recover from this. The war is taking too many things from us physically. We can't allow it to take our spirits as well."

Monday, April 4, 1864

My dearest Mother,

Things here in Vicksburg continue to go well. I know you have forgiven me, but I must say again that I am truly sorry for leaving the way I did. I wish I could come home, but travel back would be too dangerous now with troops moving and guerillas riding around the countryside.

I am still staying with a wonderful family, the Turners, yet I miss our home dearly. I missed having a white Christmas, and singing carols around the piano. I can remember Adam singing Silent Night all on his own when we were young, and how wonderful of a singer he was.

I have also found a purpose here. I spend most of my time at St. Francis Xavier's convent. It has been converted to a hospital here, helping the wounded and sick soldiers. It reminds me of when I helped the wounded at the lumber mill. There are many wonderful people down here, both Union and Confederates. It makes you realize how complex this war has become.

I cannot wait to see you. As soon as the war is over, I will make my way north.

Love,
Tabetha

St. Xavier Hospital

Tabetha turned and smiled when she saw Major Rogers walking toward her.

"Excuse me," she said to the young soldier she had been writing a letter for and stood to greet the major. She hadn't been able to visit with him in over a week, and she missed spending time with him.

"Do you have a moment to talk?" He asked.

"Of course. I am glad you're here," Tabetha said. "It's been so long."

"Yes, I have been buried in paperwork and training exercises. One of the other officers has come down with an ailment, so I have taken over his duties as well." He led her out the door and onto the street.

"I see," Tabetha said. "I understand perfectly."

"I'm hoping to have more time now that we have a new commander in the city," Steven said.

"I had heard we were getting a new district commander. What do you know of him?"

"Major General Henry Slocum is from New York, a graduate of West Point, he fought well at Gettysburg and Chancellorsville. His instructions are apparently to clean up the city and the surrounding areas."

"By taking care of the guerillas still plaguing the countryside," Tabetha interjected.

"That task is probably at the top of the list. He has a reputation of being a strict disciplinarian and he supports black troops. There is a rumor that Grant and Sherman supported him in this role for many reasons, but one of them was to remove him from a feud with Major General Hooker. Over in Tennessee, Slocum gathered refugees, both freedmen and whites coming in from the countryside and put them in camps to make them more manageable and easier to supply, so he may attempt that here."

"My goodness," Tabetha said.

"Yes. He is a definite supporter of hard war. He's rumored to have forced wealthy Confederates to help provide for the destitute and also targets guerillas and others who attack the Unionists."

Tabetha shook her head. "That will make the already angry civilians of this town feel even more oppressed."

"I agree," Steven said. "In fact, when Ezekiel heard the news, his first thoughts were of how Miss Brianne would call us tyrannical Yankees."

"She does seem to take issue with the Federals more than anyone else in the Turner household," Tabetha replied. "But she truly is a special young girl."

"Yes, I agree," Steven replied. "I hear Mrs. Prentiss and the young Miss Felicity are doing well."

"They are. Felicity is just adorable and Victoria has been getting up and around for a few days now."

"That's good. She will make a wonderful mother."

"She already is. I hope if the good Lord blesses me with many children that I will be a good mother."

"Miss Norton, I have no doubt you will be blessed with children and you will be the best of mothers. The father of those children will be extremely lucky as well."

Tabetha blushed at his words.

Major Rogers stepped closer to hold Tabetha's hands. "Miss Norton, I…"

"Major! There you are. A soldier Tabetha did not recognize approached them. "You have been summoned by Major General Slocum. They're sending a unit out to track that Rebel, Nathan Bedford Forrest, and you're to lead them. Not sure how long you'll be gone, but you're to pack for an extended assignment." The soldier spun away. Tabetha's heart beat rapidly.

"This is just what you have been waiting for, isn't it?" Her voice cracked. "A chance to get away from guard duty, a chance to fight."

"It might not be exactly what I want, but it will be better than sitting around here, filling out forms and filing paperwork." He reached up and tentatively touched her chin. "I will miss you, Miss Norton." His eyes searched hers, then he leaned down and kissed the hand he held. "I may be falling in love with you," he said, then kissed her lips.

"I will pray for your safe and speedy return." She reached up to touch his cheek.

"I appreciate that more than you know." He backed away, tipped his hat, and headed in the direction of the Major General's headquarters.

"I love you too, Steven," she said, though she knew he couldn't hear her.

Wednesday, April 13, 1864
Freedman's School

Jessica looked up at the sound of heavy footsteps on the floor of her classroom.

"Lieutenant Campbell. To what do I owe this pleasure?"

Noah Campbell was now the only soldier in the Turner house, as Lieutenant Ezekiel Rogers had gone with Major Steven Rogers's unit to chase Confederate raiders.

"I was just thinking...actually hoping..." He pulled a chair over. "Do you remember what we spoke of at Christmas? What you offered to help me with?"

"Of course," Jessica replied. "However, you never spoke of it again, so I didn't think that you were interested in my offer anymore."

"Well, I can be bullheaded, you know, but yes, if you're still willing and the offer still stands, I'd like to take you up on your generous offer. I'd appreciate if you could teach me to read better."

"Spendid! Would you like to join us in class during the day? You won't have an issue learning in a freedman's school, will you?"

"Like I mentioned before, I've no problem with the Negroes. I know there are a lot of mixed views about the blacks, especially black troops. I will say that seeing the plight of the slaves has softened many attitudes. Before I joined up, however, I was quite indifferent toward freed people. But no, it is not the school I would take issue with, it's just, well...I would like to keep this quiet. I...I don't want word to get around that I can't read that well."

"Well yes, I understand that perfectly," Jessica said. "Would it be better if we met here, in the late afternoons, when you're available?"

"That's fine with me, as long as your preacher won't have any problems with it."

"He won't." Jessica hadn't really thought about what Reverend Cook would say, but once Noah mentioned it, she wasn't quite sure if he would approve. "I am glad to hear you are more understanding of what the black men have had to endure. Not everyone is like you. Is it true that some soldiers have been violent towards black troops?"

"That is true, unfortunately. During the battle over at Milliken's Bend last year, white soldiers victimized black soldiers and terrorized their women and children. The things I heard they did...well, it would be improper to speak of those atrocities in front of a lady." He closed his eyes, trying to block out his own memories. "At least the blacks were eventually allowed to testify against the soldiers."

"Small justice, I suppose." Jessica didn't know what else to say.

"You have the views of an abolitionist, yet you don't go to the extreme. I admire you coming down and how you practice the kindness that you teach others." Noah gave her a crooked grin.

"Honestly...you shouldn't. I did grow up in Oberlin, which has long been associated with the anti-slavery movement. We actually have a college that allows blacks and women to attend. It is very progressive. In reality, though, I came down here because I didn't want to go to Michigan and live with my father's brother after he died. I wanted to do something important with my life. I wanted to make a difference, as well as have an adventure."

"I'm sure the good looks of your preacher and his persuasion didn't hurt," Noah replied.

"Reverend Cook is a very good man," Jessica said. "He will be the perfect husband for a lucky woman someday. He is kind, attentive, smart, and has a solid faith."

"All the traits I don't have." He spoke so quietly, she wasn't sure if she was supposed to hear him or not.

"Don't sell yourself short, Lieutenant Campbell. I've mentioned before, you have many good qualities."

"Maybe," Lieutenant Campbell replied. "You haven't been wandering around the countryside again, have you? Major General Slocum's efforts to clean up the city may give some people a false sense of security."

"No, I haven't."

The Major General had immediately began his attempts to clean up the city after his appointment. He had replaced the provost marshal, withdrew all the troops within the fortifications, arrested unruly soldiers and civilians, and enforced an 11:00 curfew in town.

"Good. It can still be dangerous," Noah said. Slocum's most recent efforts had included arresting a corrupt Treasury agent forcing the resignation of a dishonest assistant quartermaster. He appeared to make the city a safer place.

"I heard Slocum announced a limit for the speed of horse traffic on the streets," Jessica said. "Riders must lead their steeds at a pace no faster than a walk."

"Yes, he made that announcement after a soldier rode recklessly through town and ran over a small boy." Private Campbell leaned back in his chair casually. "Thank goodness the boy wasn't hurt too badly, just some bruises and scrapes."

"Well, I appreciate the fact that he is at least attempting to make things more tolerable here, especially for the freedmen."

"I agree." Noah glanced at the clock on the wall. "I suppose I have taken up enough of your time. We can start my lessons tomorrow. Would you like an escort home?"

"Yes, I didn't realize it was so late," she replied and stood. "Thank you for the offer. Let me just pack up some things."

"Of course," Lieutenant Campbell said, and as soon as she was ready, they were off.

Sunday, April 24, 1864
Lakemont

"Every act of pillage, and every unjustifiable encroachment upon the rights of citizens, serves only to bring disgrace upon our arms and encourages a spirit which should be unknown among brave men engaged

in a noble cause," Victoria closed the newspaper. "General Order Number 7."

"This General Slocum is really trying to tighten the reins on the soldiers and civilians here, but hopefully it will make the streets safer," Mary Green said.

"I don't believe that, Mary. There is no way we can ever forget that we are under military occupation. There must be hundreds of soldiers patrolling the city on a daily basis. Just to walk the streets today, I had to show a pass from post headquarters that Mama only obtained with the help of Lieutenant Campbell." Victoria shook her head. "The Lieutenant told Jessica that he abhors provost marshal duty. The men consider it the least desirable of assignments."

"I imagine it would be," Mary replied. "At least the streetlights are back on. That should help maintain the law and order after dark too."

"Yes, I noticed that. I heard there was an agreement with the gas works, yet there was also a tax levied on all businesses in the city and on the homes that front a street with lamps on it. We are the ones paying for the lighting."

"Don't fret, Victoria. All these changes will continue to make Vicksburg safer," Mary said.

"Yes, but how high a price must we pay for that safety? What freedoms will we lose?" Victoria shook her head again. "The other day, before Lieutenant Campbell obtained the pass for us, Mama and Kendall went out to visit Judge Houghton's family. A soldier stopped them, looking as fierce as possible with his loaded gun and bayonet fixed. He asked for their pass, and when they told him they didn't have one, he forced them home. Told them that if they tried to come out again without a pass, they would be brought to the provost marshal's office. It scared poor Kendall to death. I can't believe I am admitting this, but I am actually glad we have Lieutenant Campbell around to assist us as needed."

"Are you still finding time to volunteer at the hospital?"

"I haven't been to the hospital, no. I don't want to risk bringing an illness home." Victoria couldn't imagine life without her baby girl. "I haven't really had time to do much else anyways. I remember the days when a woman had a baby and there were slaves around to assist with all the work. I find myself doing all the daily chores of caring for a newborn. It is exhausting work. I have my family and they are willing to watch Felicity for a short while, but they have so much work to do now also."

Victoria had tried to get a wet nurse, but was unable to locate an acceptable candidate, even with Esther's help. Victoria did like the closeness she felt with Felicity while feeding her. "Brianne, Kendall, my mother, they have all been so helpful with the newest member of our family."

"And what about you, Victoria?" Mary asked. "How have you been adjusting?"

"As best as can be. Felicity wakes up to eat every few hours so that makes for some sleepless nights and I want to make sure she's near me or with someone I trust explicitly. I fear I will lose my baby as so many children die before their first year of life. I love Nathaniel with all of my heart, but I must say that my love for Felicity transcends even that. I would do anything imaginable to keep her safe. Is that normal, do you think, or is it just because of the life we are currently living?"

"It is quite normal," Mary said. "Have Hannah or Jason met her yet?"

"No. I plan on bringing Felicity out to the Wheeler farm in a few weeks, on a Sunday. Hopefully, Jason will be there." Victoria longed for at least one of the men in her life to meet her child.

"The Wheelers will love meeting Felicity. She is such a dear."

"Yes, I am anxious to get out there. Everyone says that she looks like me, but I can see much of Nathaniel in her as well." She felt tears threaten and tried to hold them back, but Mary immediately sensed a change in her friend's demeanor.

"Victoria?" She asked hesitantly.

"I hope and pray that Nathaniel has a chance to...that he is able to come back. I don't want Felicity to never know her father." Tears now fell down Victoria's cheeks as Mary moved to hug her. She wished she knew what to say to comfort her, but the words wouldn't come. Victoria's husband was hundreds of miles away, putting his life on the line for his beliefs, while her own husband was home in Vicksburg, safe and sound. She finally understood some of the animosity she experienced from the local citizens.

"At least I have comfort in knowing that I have a part of Nathaniel with me, in case the inevitable happens."

"I sincerely don't believe it will, but if it does, you know you have the love and support of your family and friends."

"I know, I know." Victoria pulled away. "I thank the Lord for my family and friends on a daily basis. I know I will never be alone."

Friday, April 29, 1864
American Missionary Association Offices

"Reverend Cook, I have my weekly reports for you." Jessica entered the office. Samuel Cook smiled at her.

"Miss Spencer! It is so good to see you, please, sit." He gestured to the chair across from his desk. "How was your week?"

"It went well. The students make so much progress every day. It is wonderful to witness their enthusiasm. They are so anxious to learn, well..." She shrugged. "Most of them, anyway. I do have one boy, an eleven-year-old, very bright, but he doesn't much care for book learning. Maximus. He is such a sweet boy, but can be quite mischievous. Hopefully I'll get through to him eventually."

"You have such a fine attitude, Miss Spencer. It is one of the things I admire most about you." He nodded. "You make it seem as if we can do anything."

"I've always believed that with the help of God, we can, Reverend. I have heard you quote St. Paul. 'I can do all things through Christ which strengthens me.'"

"Right you are." The Reverend looked at his watch. "It is time for me to leave for the day. Would you like an escort to the Turner home?"

"That would be very nice." Jessica tried to contain her excitement. He stood and took her arm, then led her out of the building. Soldiers lingered around the city, checking the passes of civilians. Most of them knew Reverend Cook, so the couple was only stopped once.

"The soldiers are being quite diligent of late," Jessica commented.

"As they should be," The Reverend agreed. "There is a rumor that a Federal treasury agent has recently made allegations that the city is full of Confederate spies."

"I suppose that's possible, though with the searches and checkpoints, it would be difficult to get much information in or out of the city."

"Yes, but spy rings can be quite clever and intricate. Legends of George Washington's spy ring credit ordinary men and even some women as being instrumental in our victory over the British, yet their names will be lost to history."

"That must be difficult, sacrificing so much for your country, yet knowing that the better you are at your mission, the less likely it is that you will get credit for it."

"Exactly," the Reverend replied. "The Bible says, we must do things because it is the right thing to do, not because we will get recognition for it."

"Of course." That was something Jessica struggled with. She liked helping people and making a difference in her community, but it also felt very good to be acknowledged for what she did, and she thrived on the praise she received.

"I heard today that some anti-Union civilians destroyed some property at the United Episcopal Church." Reverend Cook commented. "Books that had the word 'United' on them were all crossed out. Such a waste."

"The local civilians are frustrated," Jessica said. "Their world as it once was has been turned upside down, and they will continue to be under the control of the Federal government whom they see as the enemy."

"Are you spending too much time with the Rebels, Miss Spencer?" The Reverend's voice sounded slightly disapproving. "You sound like a sympathizer."

"No, Not at all, but living with a Southern family has made me more understanding of their plight. I disapprove of what they believe in, but you must remember the civilians here have loved ones fighting for the Confederacy, and the enemy in their very homes. How discouraging that must feel."

"I suppose empathy is a good trait for a missionary to have. Do you also empathize with your students and their families?"

"Absolutely," Jessica said. "It's what makes me a better teacher, I believe."

"Yes, and you are one of the best teachers I have," Reverend Cook said. Jessica inwardly beamed with pride.

"Thank you. I only strive to be the best I can be." She frowned when she saw the Turner's home come into view. Her walk with Reverend Cook was coming to an end. "I was wondering if you had plans for Sunday dinner yet. Mrs. Turner and her servant are wonderful cooks, and they usually make extras on Sunday. I am sure she wouldn't mind if you joined us."

"I would be delighted. Thank you for the invitation."

"Wonderful," she said. "I will talk with you after services and we can make our way back here."

"I look forward to it." The Reverend tipped his hat and left her on the porch steps. Jessica smiled, almost giddily, and turned to go into the house.

Friday, May 13, 1864
St. Xavier Hospital

"And then they made me their captain," The peculiar soldier that Tabetha had been caring for grinned and reached up to smooth his dirty beard. The man desperately needed a shave, but would not let anyone take a razor to him.

"That is quite the story, Captain John." The man's first name and rank was all the medical staff knew about him.

"Miss Norton, there is an officer here to see you. "An orderly placed a hand on Tabetha's shoulder to alert her. "He is in the main office."

"Thank you, Jimmy." She smiled at the young man, who couldn't be more than sixteen years old. She quickly made her way to the office, hoping for good news. She knocked once, then opened the door. The officer turned. She smiled and hurried toward him.

"Oh, Steven, I am so glad to see you." She held him tightly, then pulled back to get a good look at him. She noticed his shoulder was bloodstained with a tear and he grimaced. "What happened here?" She touched his wound.

He bent down to gently kiss her. "It is just a small injury, nothing to worry about, though I may need help changing the bandages later on."

"It's a good thing you know where to find an experienced nurse." She was impressed with herself for the flirtatious words, yet hoped she didn't seem too forward. She blushed and buried her face in his shoulder, loving how it felt to be in his arms. He tightened his hold on her.

"I missed you more than I thought possible," he murmured.

"I missed you too," she replied. "Vicksburg just isn't the same without you, Major."

"Actually." He smiled. "It's Lieutenant Colonel now."

"Steven! Congratulations." Tabetha reached up and kissed his cheek. "Another promotion! Your mission must have been a success."

"Parts of it were. Do you have time to join me?" She nodded and he pulled her out to the balcony of the office, where two crates sat against the outer wall. He sat down on one crate and patted the other, inviting her to sit.

"I can spare a few moments, especially for a hero such as yourself." She sat next to him and arranged her skirts.

"Why would you call me a hero?"

"I'm only assuming, what with you leading the mission and now being promoted, you must have done something out of the ordinary to get that recognition."

"Well, we thankfully only lose one man, and we were able to gather some intelligence, but I would not call the mission a great success." He took her hand in his. "It feels like we're chasing phantoms. I now know why they call Mosby over in Virginia the Gray Ghost. Nathan Bedford Forrest is just the same here. They attack our troops and escape into thin air. It is so disheartening."

Tabetha could hear the frustration in his voice. "I would think that Slocum's new General Orders would make it easier to find the Rebel guerrillas."

"Yes, General Orders Number Six. Slocum will extract payment or confiscate property from disloyal citizens within thirty miles of the site of any guerrilla destruction. You would think Forrest would take that into consideration.

"Perhaps he will." Tabetha said. Steven slid his hand towards hers and threaded their fingers together.

"Tell me." Steven asked. "I've often wondered how it is that you know so much of military tactics. I know you said your brother was a soldier, but you seem to know more than the average woman."

It was the perfect opening. Was this the opportunity she had been waiting for? Could she risk everything and tell him her past?

"Steven…" she turned toward him.

"Miss Norton, being away from you has made me realize just how much I care for you." His voice was just above a whisper. "I love you."

Her heart sped up. Could she really tell him now? She must. "I love you too, but Steven, there is something I have to tell you…"

"Lieutenant Colonel Rogers!" A male voice called out from inside the office. Steven sighed, stood and helped Tabetha stand.

"Out here." He called as an officer stepped onto the balcony.

"Slocom wants you to report to him posthaste," the officer said.

"I'll be right over." Steven nodded, then turned to Tabetha. "Would you join me for a walk tonight, Miss Norton?"

"I most certainly will. I would enjoy that immensely." She smiled. He looked over, saw that the other officer had already exited the room, and quickly give Tabetha a parting kiss.

"I will see you at dinner, then." He smiled, then quickly left to report to his commanding officer.

Tabetha leaned against the doorframe. There was no escaping it now. She had to tell him everything. She had been about to divulge her secret right then, when the officer had interrupted. She had to tell him tonight. She finally had the courage to say what should have been said months ago. He would be hurt, perhaps angry or betrayed, but she couldn't lie about it anymore. If she wanted a future with him, and she did, she couldn't let this farce continue any further.

That night, Tabetha sat on the front porch. Steven still hadn't come home, and it was now after dinner. Ezekiel had informed the family that his brother was filling out paperwork and reports at Slocum's office. He wasn't sure when Steven would be back. Tabetha sighed as she looked out across the Mississippi River. If he didn't arrive soon and take her on that walk, she may lose her courage.

"Waiting for your officer?" Rachel Turner said from the doorway.

Tabetha smiled. "Yes, but it doesn't appear he will make it any time soon. The streetlamps have been lit, so he may not even get back before curfew. It wouldn't matter for   him much, but we spoke of going for a walk"

"I am sure he's trying his best to finish his work," Rachel said. "He is very diligent, but my guess is that he prefers to be with you."

"The problem is, I was about to tell him earlier today, you know, about my true identity, but we were interrupted and he had to report back to the office. My plan was to tell him on our walk tonight, but now that won't happen either. The timing never seems right." She looked at the kind woman who had been like a mother to her over the past year. "Do you think he'll even forgive me?"

"He is kind and decent. He'll likely be upset at first, but that's to be expected. After all, he is a man. I believe he will understand why you were unable to tell him the truth, he will just need some time to accept the news."

Tabetha nodded. "Thank you for the encouragement. I really need it."

"Of course, Tabetha, but you really don't need me to encourage you. God will see you through anything."

"Well, thank you anyway." Tabetha looked at her watch. "I suppose I'll go up to my room. I have an early shift at the hospital tomorrow." She shook her head. "I heard earlier today that there was a fierce battle in the wilderness just west of Fredericksburg, Virginia. You have family in that area, do you not?"

"Yes, my husband's family plantation is near Fredericksburg. We haven't heard a word from them since before the siege. Oh, all the conflict they have endured this past year."

"It sounds like this last battle was devastating. Three days of bloodshed. General Grant is now in charge of the Union Army of the Potomac." Tabetha closed her eyes, thinking of what life was like during the siege. "I remember all too well how Grant gets his victories."

"I worry so for everyone over there, my husband and Gregory, Nathaniel, our family, and our many friends and neighbors. They have been in the midst of the fighting for so long. It is surely worse than what we've been through. I don't know how they can endure. I can't pray enough for all of them." Rachel took a deep breath. "Did they mention casualties for this latest battle?"

"I'm afraid so," Tabetha replied. "I heard close to 30,000 total men were killed, wounded, captured or missing."

"Dear God," Rachel placed a hand on her chest.

"They say many of the wounded were carted back to Fredericksburg. It's known as a hospital town now."

"I look around Vicksburg and what it once was compared to now. When I think of Fredericksburg, with its many confectionaries and quiet shops." Rachel shook her head. "I imagine it has changed, more so than Vicksburg has, and not for the better."

"I know I am thankful that we don't have very many new wounded coming in," Tabetha said. "I remember how tiring it was when we were under siege, receiving all the sick and wounded soldiers. It felt nonstop. The people of Fredericksburg must be overwhelmed again."

"I must confess, I am weary of all that has occurred since this conflict started, and now with all of the arrests. Just the other day, Mr. Hornish was arrested on the charge of 'using disrespectful language towards the Government'. We must be so careful, with all we say and do. I am especially fearful for Brianne with her attitude. Women are not exempt from being arrested. There is so much to worry about and I try to be strong, Tabetha, but..." She drew in a shaky breath. "Inside, my heart is crying. I have no idea if my Charles or Gregory are alive or dead. Charles is my rock, you would like him, Tabetha. I fear for my dear boys, for I know they are in constant danger. My daughters are struggling to keep themselves and their children healthy, and losing Adam..." A tear fell down her cheek. "My home is no longer my own, I must entertain the enemy. We just wanted to be left alone. We wanted to make our own decisions. Why couldn't the Federal government just leave us alone?"

Tabetha hugged Rachel, not knowing what to say. The woman was always so strong, so comforting. It was heartbreaking to see her like this, yet Tabetha knew there was nothing she could do about the situation.

Rachel finally pulled away and wiped her eyes. "Oh, my dear, I am so sorry. I didn't mean to weep all over you."

"It's all right, Mrs. Turner. It's oddly comforting to see that you have these emotions. I know you always try to be strong, and I really admire you for that, but I think it's good for us to see that you have fears and worries as well."

"That is such a nice thing to say. Thank you. Shall we pray for our friends and families and for you to muster the courage and the right words to speak with Steven?"

"I would like that very much," Tabetha said, and the two women joined hands and bent their heads.

Wednesday, May 18, 1864
Streets of Vicksburg

Mary Green looked up and down the street. It was more crowded than usual, and there was quite a commotion a few blocks down. As she scanned the crowd, she saw Jessica Spencer.

"Jessica! Miss Spencer!" Mary called out.

The teacher turned, wiped at her cheeks, and maneuvered through the crowds to get to Mary.

"What is all the commotion, Jessica?" Mary asked.

"Oh, it's just awful." Jessica gripped Mary's sleeve. "I had to let the students go home, there may be retaliation and it will not be good."

Mary pulled Jessica into the Lakemont yard. "Jessica, tell me what has happened?"

"There was an altercation over on McRaven Street. One of your local men, a Mr. Bobb, found a group of black soldiers in his garden, picking vegetables. There are mixed reports, as usual, but they say this Mr. Bobb confronted the soldiers, then became angry when they would not leave, so he threw a brick. It hit one of the soldiers. Oh, Mary, the soldiers, they...they killed Mr. Bobb. Some reports say the soldiers shot him right away, others say the soldiers left, then came back and shot him. Then there are others who say they...stabbed him with their bayonets until he died." She clutched her stomach, feeling nauseous. "It really doesn't matter how or when. This poor man is now dead and no one knows what General Slocum is going to do about it."

"Dear Lord." Mary felt sick. She knew John Bobb. He was originally from Philadelphia, a brick maker. "That's murder, there is no other way to look at it. He has the right to defend his home. Poor Selina, his wife, she must be beside herself."

"I must agree with you, the soldiers had no right to kill him, there is no denying that." Jessica said, heart pounding. "But, as I said, I fear retaliation, especially since they were black soldiers. There's no telling what the people of Vicksburg will do to the innocent freedmen in the name of revenge, just because of their skin color."

"The freedmen have a right to be worried, especially if General Slocum does nothing to the soldiers." Fear coursed through Mary. The soldiers were supposed to protect the civilians, not target them. "You don't understand, Jessica! This is what all Southerners fear most, slaves with guns. There could be other attacks from former slaves and black soldiers, perhaps even a revolt."

"We won't let that happen." A deep male voice spoke.

Both women turned to see a solemn-looking Lieutenant Campbell. Jessica wiped at the tears on her face, as the Lieutenant handed her his handkerchief.

"I gather you have heard the news, ladies. I believe, Miss Spencer, it probably would be best if you stayed home for a few days. You should not attend your freedman's school. I will go out there if you need me to get something, but you need to stay in town. As you know, there may be some retribution. When you are able to return to school, you may want an escort and you will need someone to stand guard while school is in session. I will see if I can volunteer to be assigned that duty."

"Thank you, Noah. That is kind of you to offer. I must admit I am fearful today," Jessica said.

"Slocum's already denounced the murder, although he does believe Bobb provoked the men."

Mary didn't feel that was a fair statement. To her, Mr. Bobb was just defending his home and family. She was about to interrupt, but Lieutenant Campbell continued.

"Furthermore, General Slocum maintains that anyone who victimizes a black soldier will be punished, and he says neither soldiers nor civilians should ever take the law into their own hands." He took back the handkerchief he had given Jessica. "I know you're worried, Miss Spencer…"

"For my students as much as for myself," she said.

"That is understandable." Noah smiled.

The Lieutenant turned to Mary. "Mrs. Green, you should go back inside your home. While we are trying to keep the order, there's no telling what may happen on these streets today. I will escort Miss Spencer home."

"Thank you for your concern, Lieutenant Campbell." She turned to Jessica. "Take care of yourself, Jessica."

"You as well, Mrs. Green."

"I can't believe this has happened. In town, in broad daylight." Victoria shook her head. The women of the house had gathered in the parlor, with the exception of Rachel who had gone to have dinner with Mary Grace and Abraham. The officers of the house were all out on patrol.

Brianne was flushed with anger. "The Yankee officers need to open their eyes and see what will happen when they don't watch over their men. Will the Yankee army really allow the black soldiers to take their revenge against the whites of our town?"

"No, Brianne, that is not how it is," Tabetha said. "General Slocum even issued a new general order where he denounces the act and says that the men who did this will be held accountable."

"The way I see it, Slocum is so enamored with his black troops and the significance they may have in the history of our country that he won't make them take any responsibility." Brianne retorted.

"He's already said they'll be held responsible, Brianne, haven't you been listening? What we must be aware of are the white men of this city going after any black person they can find to take revenge upon." Tabetha tried to remain calm.

"Really, do you honestly believe the Yankees will give their own soldiers a proper punishment," Victoria's snippy words were drowned out by Brianne's next outburst.

"I'd expect you to respond in that fashion. To care more for the blacks than you do for your own kind."

"Brianne, that is a bit out of line." Jessica rose to stand behind Tabetha.

"I don't think so." Kendall joined the conversation.

"I may be out of line, but it is the truth." Brianne said. "You may think you're doing an act of kindness, teaching the blacks, Miss Spencer, but to most people here in Vicksburg, you're just another Yankee invader trying to take away our way of life." She looked at Tabetha. "And you, Miss Norton, I like you a great deal and respect the fact that you care for the soldiers of both sides, but in reality, you were a Yankee soldier. There is no denying that fact."

Tabetha quickly glanced towards the doorway, sure that Steven would be there to hear Brianne's thoughtless outburst. "Brianne Marie Larson, how dare you? You know that must be kept a secret. Any one of the officers staying here could have overheard you. How careless of you?"

Victoria spoke up. "There's no need to blame Brianne. If you had the courage to tell Steven Rogers in the first place, it wouldn't matter what we said."

Tabetha shook her head. "I have tried many times to tell him, you know that. I just dread it...the moment that I do. Tabetha didn't finish her sentence and, though she rarely showed emotion, tears threatened her eyes as she looked around the room. It appeared as though she and Jessica were squaring off against the three Southern women. They were all overly emotional.

"You Yankees couldn't let things be." Brianne started the argument again. "We just wanted to be left alone. We didn't want to secede. We never wanted this war."

"And you think we did?" Tabetha yelled. "One of your rebel soldiers killed my brother. Do you think I wanted that?"

"Of course not," Victoria interjected. "But you and..."

"Ladies, ladies, what is going on in here?" Rachel Turner stood in the doorway, disappointment on her face. The five younger women immediately sobered.

"I am so sorry, Mrs. Turner." Tabetha's voice cracked. "I'm afraid my emotions got the best of me. Everything that has happened today..."

"You mean to say everything that has happened in the past few years," Victoria amended.

"I'm not the one you should be apologizing to," Mrs. Turner said firmly. "You are all ladies, I presume, and a lady does not argue in this manner." She gave a stern look to Victoria, Brianne and Kendall. "I know I raised you three to act better than this."

"Yes, ma'am."

"You're right, Aunt Rachel."

"Of course, Mama."

"I am sorry as well," Jessica sighed. "I must admit, I am terrified of absolutely everything that has happened today. We are in the midst of a civil war and the violence is about to erupt here." She shook her head. "It already has."

"Really, Jessica, you don't know what you're talking about. You should have been here during the battle and the siege afterwards." Brianne's anger was dwindling. "Tabetha at least knows what that was like."

"Yes, Brianne," Rachel said. "And we will continue to face difficult times, but if we are to survive, we must support one another. We are women, we are supposed to be peaceful, kind and loving. If we aren't, our tempers will get the best of us and explode like a bottle of champagne that has been shaken. We say things we may not really mean just to be spiteful, like what has apparently just happened."

"Yes, ma'am," all of the women answered.

"Now, let's all get to bed. It's been a long, trying day and you all need a good rest."

The women all nodded and followed orders.

Monday, June 13, 1864
Turner Parlor
My dearest Nathaniel,

I can't wait until the day you are back here in my arms, reading all of the letters I have written you in this journal. To see you holding your daughter. She longs to meet you, I know that in my heart. It is hard to believe she is already three months old. She can hold objects and it seems as if she's playing with them, but she loves the wooden otter you carved for me during the siege most of all. She loves to cuddle and still spends much of her time sleeping. She has your smile, Nathaniel, and she does smile so much.

Life in Vicksburg has steadily changed, and it seems like it is for the worst. Northerners continue to flock down here, leasing plantations that don't even belong to them. They are trying to make fortunes from our misfortunes. It is difficult to witness. Most are leasing the confiscated land from the Federal government, but some are leasing from locals. Our soldiers and guerillas target many of these operations, especially those plantations that line the pockets of these Northern carpetbaggers. They'll take whatever they can find, including livestock and supplies for their own profit.

There have been some truly horrifying events that have happened with the guerillas. Not long ago, our boys fired into a river steamer between here and Natchez. Unfortunately, a woman who was coming to teach at a school for former slaves was killed. I think of Jessica, the young woman staying with us who is a teacher at the freedman's school. The most sickening part of the whole event was that the residents of Natchez were apparently celebrating her death. They were convinced that God had directed the shot that took her life. It is horrible to see what this war has turned people into.

You know how I hate arguing with people, and I have never understood why some women seem to live for creating melodrama and intrigue among their groups of friends. Unfortunately, that seems to be happening all around me. We have truly become a town divided.

On one side are those individuals who hate the Yankees with a passion and they hate all those who are tolerant of the Yankees, and there are no exceptions. I fear that Brianne falls into this category. I sometimes feel I fall into this category except for the fact that I have to share a house with Yankees, and I know they are not truly bad people. In fact, I find they are working for what they believe in, just like most of the Confederates.

Then there are the townspeople who seem to try and get along with everyone, the families of the men who signed the loyalty oath like Duff and Mary Green, or businesses that serve the Yankees simply because they have to make a living, like Mary Grace and Abraham.

Finally, there are those who fully support the Federal cause, the soldiers, freedmen, missionaries and carpetbaggers. Most of these individuals are so sure of their cause, and believe that what they are doing is right and there is nothing else that can be said about it. I realize that my family was very lucky in terms of our boarders. The soldiers who have been placed with us are decent enough men, and they act respectfully towards us, my mother especially. I enjoy Tabetha's company for the most part, in spite of an argument we had last month, and Jessica and I are becoming friends. The young teacher is sweet, though very naive.

We continue to hear about the fierce fighting in the East, much of it in the area near your home. I hope and pray you are safe and will return to me as soon as this war is over. I love you with all of my heart,
   Victoria

"What are you in here so quiet for?" Kendall wandered into the parlor.

"Oh, I was just finishing a letter to Nathaniel. Well, writing in my journal to Nathaniel." Victoria explained, then looked down at Felicity, who was lying contentedly on the floor, chewing on the wooden otter carving from Nathaniel.

"I see. It is so sad you can't hear from him more often." Kendall shook her head, then laid on her stomach, facing Felicity and smiling at the girl. "Hey, pretty girl."

Felicity gurgled and smiled at her cousin. Victoria couldn't help but feel a tug at her heart.

"She is so beautiful, Victoria, though I think I say that every time I see her." Kendall said.

"Thank you. I think that every time I am with her." Victoria slid to the ground and sat next to the two. "How is it going at the Freedman's School?"

"Very good. Many of the students come and go, and we are never quite sure how many students we will have on a given day, but it is very rewarding work. I think I have a knack for teaching."

"I can see that," Victoria said. "I had notions of teaching once upon a time, as I dearly love to read and write, but I must admit, arithmetic always gave me difficulties."

"I love it all." Kendall braced herself on her elbow and tickled Felicity's stomach. "I think when I'm older, I may even travel west to be a teacher."

"West?" It didn't surprise Victoria. Kendall was always looking for adventure, more of a wanderer like her father, Nicholas.

"Yes," Kendall replied. "There is so much to see in our nation. I love Vicksburg and my family here, but I dream of adventures out in the great wide country."

"I believe you have mentioned that before," Victoria said.

"Oh, Victoria, here you are!" Rachel came in, with a distressed look on her face. Victoria could tell that her mother had been crying.

"Mama, what is it?" Her voice was shaky.

"I am afraid I have some upsetting news…"

"NO! Not Nathaniel, please not Nathaniel."

"No, it isn't Nathaniel." Rachel looked to Kendall. "Will you take Felicity upstairs for a little while?"

"Of course, Aunt Rachel." Kendall picked the child up. Victoria's stomach felt as if it had a mortar shell inside.

"What happened, Mama? Not Gregory or Father?"

Rachel sat down and took Victoria's hands in hers. "I just came from the home of Rose Williams."

"Oh, no, is everything okay with Magdalena, her child?"

Rachel shook her head. "It has been so long since any mail has gotten through to the city, Victoria, and now there has been a barrage of bad news for the Williams family. Magdalena died while giving birth."

"Oh, Lord, no." Victoria's heart felt heavy. She hadn't been close with Magdalena for a few years, but that didn't mean she hadn't considered the woman one of her closest friends. At one point, they had been as close as sisters.

"Poor Zachary. What about the child?" Tears flooded Victoria's eyes.

"The child was stillborn."

"No…" Victoria hunched over, unable to take the shock. "How could this have happened? Magdalena was always so strong…"

Rachel took another breath. "I hate telling you this, but Victoria, Magdalena heard the most dreadful news and the stress made the child come early."

"What dreadful news?" Victoria's heart was racing.

"The news of her husband's death. Zachary was killed in a skirmish in Tennessee." Rachel spoke softly.

"No." Victoria almost whispered. "Not, Zachary too. How could they all…how is that possible? Why would God do that?"

"We never know why God allows some things to happen, you know that," Rachel replied.

"It's times like this that I wonder if God really cares or is it just something the preachers tell us." Victoria croaked. "Why would this happen? How? Magdalena insinuated that they would come here to live after the war. We would be reunited, and I would have one of the sweetest women in the world as a friend again." Victoria didn't consider the fact that she would likely be moving to Virginia when the war was over. She was too upset to think straight. "Oh, God, why?"

Rachel was at a loss for words. She knew deep down God would make good come from this tragedy, but she just couldn't fathom how, and she had no idea how to help Victoria accept the loss. The life they were living and the war they were experiencing was taking the lives of so many people. It was difficult to wonder who would be lost next.

Thursday, June 16, 1864
Turner Home

"I can't believe that another branch of the Turner family is under siege," Brianne said. "At least, that's what everyone is talking about."

"Why would the Yankees do that again? I can understand with Vicksburg, but what is so special about Petersburg?" Kendall asked.

"Well, from what I've learned it's just south of Richmond, Kendall," Brianne explained. "If the Yankees are able to take Petersburg, they will cut off Richmond, and it's possible the war could be at an end. Which we will be defeated and our lives will never be the same."

"Our lives will never be the same regardless." Victoria looked down at her daughter, then thought of Magdalena, Zachary, Cousin James from Fredericksburg and so many others that had died. She gulped back tears.

"Our lives haven't been the same in over three years." Brianne looked out the window at the Union soldiers patrolling the streets.

Victoria rubbed her temple. "After what we experienced during our siege, I can sympathize with Aunt Susannah they are going through. I am concerned though, as we have heard nothing from Aunt Susannah or Cousin Bekah since the start of the war. For all we know, they aren't even in Petersburg. At least Nathaniel was able to give us information on Belle and her family."

"I often wonder how Susannah's sons are," Rachel said. "Jonah and Jacob were always disagreeing with each other." She shook her head. "My goodness, I recall those two boys would fight at the drop of a hat. If ever there were siblings that embodied the brother against brother aspect of this war, it is those two."

"Indeed. I remember the arguments they had when we visited." Victoria sighed at the memories. "Even Jonah's wedding wasn't off-limits to their arguments." She thought again of the town south of Richmond across the James River and their last family visit for Cousin Jonah's wedding to Miss Bethany Parker.

May 1860
Petersburg, Virginia

"Jacob Andrew Turner, you had better remember the promise you made me."

Victoria could barely hear her Aunt Susannah threaten her younger son as they were sitting down for dinner at the home of Aunt Susannah's parents.

"Of course, Mother. I understand perfectly. I just hope no one else brings up any current events."

One of the first things Victoria had been reminded of when they arrived in Petersburg was Jacob's passion for states' rights. His older brother Jonah, was fiercely loyal to the Union, like their father. The brothers had engaged in fisticuffs the afternoon before, just before Victoria and her family had arrived. It seemed war fever was sweeping through the state.

Victoria sat between her cousins Charlotte, from Pennsylvania, and Bekah, Jonah and Jacob's sister.

"That was a beautiful service," Victoria said to Bekah. "Jonah and Bethany seem very well-matched."

"They are a perfect couple," Bekah replied. "I hope to make a similar match someday."

"I believe you will, Bekah," Victoria said. "Are there any prospects?"

"Not at this time. They are either intimidated by my military father or offended by one of my brothers for their political views, and frankly, my own political views." Bekah took a sip of her claret, and glanced at

Cousin Belle, who was shamelessly flirting with a good-looking, brown-haired, blue-eyed man that Victoria had been introduced to as Jonah's new brother-in-law, Daniel.

"I was hoping Mary Grace would be able to join us, but I completely understand, what with her condition and all."

"Yes, we are all quite excited about it." Victoria smiled.

"Do you know...I mean, has Abraham mentioned hearing anything from his cousin? Mr. Reynolds?"

Victoria remembered how well Bekah and Tex had gotten along, that is, until Cousin Belle had persuaded Bekah that Tex wasn't good enough for her.

"As far as I know, he is back on his ranch in Texas," Victoria replied. "Do you ever write to him?"

"No, we didn't part on friendly terms," Bekah confessed.

"Hey, Turner!" Daniel Parker appeared to have had quite a bit to drink already. "Now that you have married my sister, will you wizen up and leave that pathetic Federal Army? A war is imminent if that ape is elected president. You can bet all our good Southern boys will be leaving the army and West Point by the hundreds, as they should."

"For goodness sake, Daniel Parker," the young woman on Bekah's other side muttered under her breath. "You insufferable boor, you need to keep your mouth shut." The woman had been introduced as Miss Juliette LaRoux, a very close friend of Bekah's. Victoria looked back at Daniel, the heir to the Parker Estate.

"You know better than to ask that, Daniel." An older gentleman, Bethany and Daniel's father, spoke up. "This is your sister's wedding dinner, young man. Don't disgrace yourself further."

Victoria looked at her Uncle Samuel, a proud Union officer. His jaw was clenched, clearly not happy with the turn in conversation.

"I apologize, Father, I just thought it was an important question. Still not understanding why you'd allow Bethany to marry a Yankee." He slurred his words.

Everyone at the table was silent.

"Daniel, that is quite enough," his mother said.

"A'right, a'right." Daniel's eyes were bloodshot. "But we all know I speak the truth. They'll likely vote for that no good Lincoln come November." The man's eyes went to Jacob. "'Ceptin' the younger Turner. Jacob is with us. He's on the right side, ain't ya, boy?"

"Of course I am, Parker, but this isn't the time or the place to have this discussion." Victoria could tell that Jacob was trying to restrain his emotions.

"Maybe so, but soon, we'll all have to choose a side." Daniel stood and threw his napkin on the table, then stumbled from the dining room.

"Good riddance," Juliette LaRoux sputtered.

"Samuel, I don't know what to say. I am truly sorry for my son's behavior. You know he is quite opinionated and he has had too much to drink." Mr. Parker didn't really look sorry. Victoria knew there were many issues between the Northern and Southern states and that the country was likely headed for trouble, but the animosity between the supporters of the Union and Southern sympathizers was much more apparent in Virginia than in Mississippi, from what she observed.

1864

"If only I knew back then how the small arguments would bring the entire country to such a distressing climax, and how much we would lose in the process." Victoria chided herself. "I was so naive."

"Did anyone really know that those arguments would get so out of control? No one could have dreamed the destruction this war would bring," Rachel said. "I remember at the beginning, the night before your father and Gregory left, Charles told me not to worry, he said the war wouldn't last but a year." A tear escaped Rachel's eyes. "But it is going on four long years now. We had no idea it would last this long or be so costly, not just monetarily, but also with the loss of lives and the destruction of property and families. I never knew it would keep my man and my boys from me for so very long." She shook her head and Kendall went directly to her aunt and gave her a hug.

"The war can't drag on much longer, Aunt Rachel. Like you always say, God will give us the strength we need to get through this."

Monday, June 27, 1864
Freedman School

Jessica clutched her books to her and looked around the classroom one more time. Kendall had left hours ago at Jessica's insistence, but she had stayed much later than she intended. The gas lights of Vicksburg would be on by the time she returned to town. She would have asked Noah to meet up with her and escort her, but he and Lieutenant Colonel Rogers had been sent on patrol.

I should have gone home with Kendall. She thought. Recently, the Yankee officers had been ordering aggressive attacks throughout the region, which meant that only select positions along the river were being garrisoned. This also meant that the Union was withdrawing protection from minor posts and exposing planters, freed people, missionaries and teachers to raids by the Confederate cavalry. Even though Noah had argued with his superiors that he or someone should watch over Jessica and the other mission teachers, he had been denied his request to stay in the city.

The moment she stepped outdoors, she noticed a small group of riders approaching. She held her breath. Was it Noah? Were the riders friendly, or would they try to harm her? As they got closer, she saw that they were not Federal soldiers and a feeling of dread began to wash over her.

"Lord, help me." She clutched her books to her. "Help me and give me courage." She stood as straight as she could.

"What can I help you gentlemen with?" She hoped they couldn't hear her heart pounding. They pulled their horses up and examined her. There were three of them, all dirty, with unkempt, shaggy hair. Not one appeared to be friendly.

"Well, now, little lady, yer too pretty to be some Yankee teacher." One of the men spit a stream of tobacco juice toward the school. It landed on the steps, not far from her shoe.

"I thank you for the compliment, though it is inappropriate. If there is nothing that I can help you with, I'll thank you to allow me to be on my way." *Drat, they know who I am.*

A second soldier pulled out a pistol and aimed it loosely at her. "You're one of them Negro teachers and this is a Negro school."

"Can them darkies even learn?' Tobacco Chewer spit again.

"I'll have you know, they can. Very well, in fact." Jessica took a deep breath, again praying for courage. Would the soldier with the gun actually shoot her? "Many of them learn better than some white students I have taught in the past."

Gun raised the pistol and pulled the trigger. She gave a short scream as the bullet hit the window next to her. Her books fell down the steps to the ground. The third man, quiet until now, dismounted and approached her. Her mind flying with what would happen next, she backed away until she met the door of the schoolhouse. Quiet One picked up one of the books.

Is he actually going to be a gentleman? Her hopes were dashed when, instead of handing her the book, he ripped it in half, threw it in the mud, and stomped on the pages with his boots.

"No! What are you doing?" Jessica cried out.

"Them darkies be slaves. They don't deserve to learn nothin', they can't anyhow."

Gun and Tobacco now dismounted and stalked toward her, while Quiet One tromped up the stairs. With terror in her heart, Jessica turned toward the door. If she could get back inside, she could lock the door, something she should have done from the very beginning. As she tried to close the door, one of the men stopped it with his boot, then pushed his way into the schoolroom.

"No!" Jessica cried out. What were they going to do to her? Would they actually go so far as to kill her? Assault her? Her stomach churned. Gun nodded to the other two men,

"Have at it, boys. No darky deserves a room this nice. You should be teaching white folks, lady."

Tobacco and Quiet One pushed further into the room and began their destruction, throwing what few books she had on the ground and tearing them apart, overturning the furniture and kicking it apart.

"No, please, don't!" Jessica tried to get them to stop, but Gun grabbed her roughly by the arm, spun, and pinned her against the wall.

"What is going on in here?" An authoritative voice from the doorway made the three men stop and turn.

"We're just following orders," Gun said. "Causing mayhem for anyone aiding the enemy."

"Attacking innocent women is not how we accomplish our task!" The new man stomped farther into the school room. "Let her go. Now." There was something familiar about this new man, as if she had seen his image somewhere. His commanding tone worked, and Gun let her go, scowling.

"We need to get out of here." The newcomer said. "A Union patrol is heading this way. Move out."

The three men stomped out of the building and mounted their horses. The new man focused on her. "Miss Spencer, I am truly sorry for how you have been treated. Please make sure from now on you are never alone here and always have an escort home. The outskirts of town are much too dangerous." He tipped his brown slouch hat and proceeded to leave. When he got to the doorway, he turned around again. "Please tell your landlady that her oldest son is well and loves her dearly."

Jessica followed him to the door and watched as he hastened down the stairs, mounted his horse and rode off.

"My landlady...oh!" Realization hit her. "That's Mr. Jason Turner." *No wonder he was such a gentleman.* As she watched him and the other Confederates ride toward the tree line, a second group of men emerged and gave them chase. Tears of relief slipped down her cheeks. She found herself hoping that those Confederate soldiers, well, at least one of them, would get away. As the Union soldiers chased after the Confederates, one member broke away from the group and rode straight toward her. She breathed a sigh of relief when she recognized the man.

"Noah," she cried in relief. He jumped from his horse before it even came to a complete stop, flew up the stairs to her and without thought, hugged her tightly.

"Miss Spencer, are you alright? What happened?" He moved after realizing what he had done and simply took her hands in his. Jessica squeezed his hands lightly.

"I'm all right, truly I am," she said, "especially now that you're here."

He pulled back and touched her cheek. "Those..." he swallowed the oath. "They bruised you." His jaw clenched, fury apparent in his voice. "I will hunt them down and beat them all to a bloody pulp." He growled, then took a step toward his horse.

"No." Jessica tightened her grip on his arms. "Please."

Noah gave Jessica a look that she couldn't quite decipher.

"I'll get you back to town first." He then noticed what had happened to the schoolroom. "Ahh, Miss Spencer, I am so sorry."

"It could have been worse," she replied. *So much worse*. She shook her head at the memory, then wiped at her cheeks. "But you're here now. Please don't leave me." She focused on keeping her voice from shaking. "I assume your mission was a success."

Noah led her down the steps after locking the door, then left her for a moment to gather the damaged books. "I feel we're fighting a battle we can't win." He confessed to her as he led her to his horse. "We send out thousands of soldiers each day to patrol and capture the renegade Confederates, but we can never quite catch them. Personally, I believe we are going about it the wrong way. We travel noisily, in groups of at least fifty men and we stick to all the main roads...I can't help but wonder how often we simply pass our enemy unknowingly. These men know this land, many of them grew up in these parts. They know all the backroads through the swamps and how and where to hide." The two reached his horse and he stowed her books in his saddlebags then helped her mount.

"It is very frustrating." He mounted the horse in front of her. "But you shouldn't have to worry about that" He nudged his horse. "Come, let's get you home."

Thursday, June 30, 1864
Lakemont

"Mary, you're looking well," Victoria entered the back porch area. Mary Green sat there, watching Annie play in the yard. William sat on the ground next to Mary, playing with some wooden blocks. "Alice told me you were back here." Alice was one of Lakemont's slaves.

"Victoria, what a pleasant surprise." Mary smiled. Annie looked up, saw Victoria and rushed up the porch steps.

"Mrs. Prentiss! Did you bring baby Felicity? I haven't seen her in ever so long."

"No, I didn't, sweetheart. My mother took Felicity over to Mrs. Corbel's to see her cousins."

"Oh, botheration." The girl looked disappointed, then raced back down the stairs to play.

"I cannot believe how fast the children are all growing," Victoria said. "It won't be long before, my Felicity is six months old, and look at William. He is one already and he looks like he wants to start walking. I can hardly believe it. And to think Nathaniel may not even know he has a daughter."

"He will be overjoyed when he sees her for the first time," Mary replied. "I still cannot believe how such a beautiful little girl can look so much like her father. The resemblance is uncanny."

"Nathaniel is a handsome man and I agree, Felicity does have his looks. I am very fortunate to have married such a fine-looking man."

"Once he comes home, I imagine you two will give Felicity many brothers and sisters," Mary said.

"I hope so." Victoria wiped a tear from her cheek.

"Oh, Victoria, I didn't mean to upset you." Mary immediately felt regret for her remark.

"No, no you didn't, Mary. These are just tears...I am so blessed, really. I have a beautiful daughter, and I see Nathaniel every time I look at Felicity."

"That is a good way to look at the situation." Mary nodded. "Speaking of beautiful daughters, some news came in about the Davis family in Richmond. Our first lady has given birth to her first daughter. They named her Varina."

"How wonderful!" Victoria exclaimed. "Mother and daughter with the same name, how interesting."

"Yes. Unfortunately, there is sad news that comes with the good. Just three weeks before the birth of Baby Varina, the Davis family lost their son Joseph. He fell from a balcony at the President's house in Richmond."

"Oh, good Heavens, no!" Victoria's hand flew to her mouth. "Not little Joseph! He was only..." She thought for a moment. "He was born the same year the twins were born, if I'm not mistaken. He couldn't have been more than five years old."

Mary shook her head. "Losing a child is the hardest thing a person can go through. I remember when she had little Joe, too. Poor Varina. To lose a child is hard enough, but when your life is as public as the Davis's, it must be very difficult to grieve when everyone is around and constantly wanting something from you."

"And to think, they didn't even want the prestige of being appointed to the presidency in the first place." Victoria shook her head and thought back to some conversations she had with the now first lady. "Varina has always been a very interesting woman to talk to."

"Better you than me," Mary said. "I was never quite intelligent enough to follow some of your discussions, or perhaps I just didn't prefer to."

"You know when I think back, much of what she predicted has come true," Victoria said. "Ahh, Varina. She was ill-suited to be First Lady of the Confederacy from the very beginning and she knew it. Her family background of Northerners that relocated to Natchez, her education in Philadelphia, her outspoken personality, and even her appearance has been attacked time and time again since her residency in Richmond." News of the first family of the Confederacy was quite popular in Vicksburg. Varina Davis was known to make cordial remarks about the North, she corresponded with her Yankee family and friends, and visited with wounded Union soldiers in the Richmond hospitals. "I would assume her sharp wit is difficult for some socialites to understand."

"I can certainly understand that being the case," Mary said. "Right now, I can only sympathize with her loss and rejoice in the birth of her baby, something I myself have had to do."

Wednesday, July 6, 1864
Freedman's School

My dearest Amanda,

I hope this letter finds you and Joseph well. I am so happy for the news I read in your last letter. You will both be such wonderful parents. I miss you so much, especially our conversations and all of the fun we used to have.

The one-year anniversary of the fall of Vicksburg has come and gone. Many of the locals frequently demonstrate their inclinations against the Federals who have taken over. At times, they do so openly and without hesitation. They hate everything northern, yet will still accept rations and other goods and services from the Federals while openly admitting their Confederate sentiments. This may sound contradictory, but hunger can be a powerful motivator.

Though it was our Independence Day, no formal ceremony was planned here in town. I imagine it was mostly because the locals don't want to remember what happened a year ago, when they were taken over by their enemy. The Federal officers ended up having an impromptu celebration, loyal business owners displayed American flags and a contingent of Federals traveled downriver to Davis Bend to mark the occasion.

The commander of the city takes disloyalty to the American flag very seriously. Southern civilians have been arrested or even exiled for being disloyal, using treasonable language or aiding the enemy. The family whose home I stay at have taught me to understand the perspective of the locals. They have friends and family risking their lives, fighting against our Federal troops. It must be very difficult for them to respect the flag and what it stands for at this time.

My students are coming along very nicely. I love what I am doing and have no regrets moving here as a missionary. I have made many new friends, including some Southerners, if you can believe that. I also feel my relationship with Reverend Cook has improved. I am happy to report that I have become a confidante of his.

I miss you dearly. I hope that once the war ends, it will be safe for me to come up for a visit, as by then, you will have a little one for me to meet.

Take care of yourself and the child you carry,
Jessica

"Miss Spencer!"

Jessica looked up from addressing the letter to Oberlin and stood when she saw Reverend Samuel Cook.

"Reverend! What a pleasure to see you."

"And you. Working hard, I see."

"Of course. I was just finishing a letter home. I was going to try to get to the post office and send it yet today."

"Wonderful. Would you like me to escort you there? I just spoke with your Federal guard and sent him home."

Jessica smiled at the knowledge that Noah had been at his post. He must have done some real convincing, because ever since the attack on her school, he had been very diligent when it came to her safety. It made her feel special. He was a good friend, much like she supposed a brother would be.

"I would appreciate that very much, Reverend." She took his offered arm and they began their walk into town. They spoke of her students and his work, and had started discussing the town by the time they made it inside city limits.

"They say there has been a rise in crime this summer," Reverend Cook said. "I am glad you are having a Federal soldier escort you from place to place. It eases my mind a great deal. You must never go anywhere alone."

"Of course," Jessica replied. She had decided not to tell the Reverend about the attack. She didn't want him to worry, and nothing had been permanently destroyed. She had been able to salvage the pages from all but the one book, and Noah Campbell had repaired the desks. He hadn't been able to replace the window that had been shot out, so they had removed all the glass and covered it with a cloth. Jessica discovered that Noah was very good at making repairs and had a knack for woodwork. While Jessica felt Reverend Cook should know about the incident, she didn't want him to think she was unable to handle her job. "It has been rather helpful, having Miss Kendall Turner with me for many of the school days. She is well-known in town, so if any Southern sympathizers should want to attempt some mischief, having her present should stymie them. When she doesn't accompany me, one of the soldiers from our house escorts me."

"It's good to know you're well taken care of. I would hate to have something happen to my most effective teacher." He beamed at her.

A soldier approached them, checked their passes, and then allowed them to continue on their way.

"I appreciate the kind words, Reverend. I just do my best to help others."

"That's one of the qualities that I admire most about you. It is a quality that the wife of a pastor should have."

Is this it? Jessica's heart raced. *Is Samuel Cook going to propose to me?*

Before he could say anything more, the two were roughly shoved into the alleyway they were passing. A man dressed in tattered civilian clothes pulled a derringer out and pointed it at them.

"I will tell you just once to empty your pockets. Now." The man looked to be a white refugee, displaced by the war.

"Now see here…" Samuel stepped toward the man. With one swing of his arm, the rebel knocked the Reverend to the ground, unconscious.

"Samuel!" Jessica cried out. The thief turned toward her, a menacing look in his eye. "Stay away from me." She backed away.

"You heard the lady."

The thief spun around to see a Federal officer standing there, a Calvary pistol pointed right at him. Jessica expected to see Lieutenant Noah Campbell, as he was usually the one sweeping in to rescue her. Instead she saw a different housemate, Lieutenant Ezekiel Rogers.

"Get out of here before I have you arrested, and don't let me see you harass anyone again." Ezekiel jerked his head and the man scrambled away. On the ground, Samuel shook his head as he started to regain focus. Jessica hastened over to help him up.

"Thank you so much for your assistance, Lieutenant." Jessica and Ezekiel both helped the Reverend to his feet.

"Yes, thank you." Samuel placed a handkerchief to the cut on his left temple. "What happened to the thief that accosted us? Am I correct in assuming that you allowed the man to get away?"

"He just wanted money," Jessica said. "He looked quite destitute."

Ezekiel nodded. "I just didn't have the heart to arrest him. I am sorry."

"I suppose I must appreciate your compassion," Samuel said. "I don't believe we've met." He stuck his hand out. "Reverend Samuel Cook, American Missionary Society."

Ezekiel took the offered hand and shook it. "Lieutenant Ezekiel Rogers, 5th Illinois Cavalry." He smiled. "I must say, it is good to finally meet Miss Spencer's pastor."

"I am surprised I haven't met you before when I have had the pleasure of dining at the Turner home."

"Will you be home for dinner tonight, Lieutenant?" Jessica asked.

"Unfortunately no, Miss Spencer, I am on patrol this evening." He tipped his kepi. "But my brother and Lieutenant Campbell will likely be there." He nodded toward Samuel. "It was good meeting you, Pastor."

"And you, Lieutenant." Samuel took Jessica's arm and they began walking again. She looked up at the wound on his head.

"You should stop at one of the hospitals and have someone patch that up," she said.

"I'll be just fine," he replied. "If it worsens, I'll have someone check it later."

"All right, then." She looked forward, wondering if she should ask him what he had been about to say before they were accosted, but quickly decided to let him bring it up again himself. If he was about to ask her what she thought, she didn't want to rush him.

"I thank you again for escorting me home, Reverend," Jessica said. "Would you like to join us for dinner?"

"I would be delighted, as long as it's no inconvenience."

"Mrs. Turner says feeding the hungry and welcoming the stranger is God's work, and God's work is never an inconvenience."

"That is a wonderful attitude," Reverend Cook said. "In that case, I accept the invitation."

Friday, July 29, 1864
Turner Home

"I am so excited that we are all here together," Mary said, smiling at her friends. A quiet evening with friends was long overdue.

"Hannah, I am especially glad you were able to get here. Did you have much trouble?" Victoria gave the woman another hug.

"Not bad. I was stopped a few times and had to show the pass I obtained, but we made it here. I have been wanting to visit with you all and I simply cannot leave without seeing that daughter of yours again, Victoria."

"I will make sure Dinah brings her down before her bedtime," Victoria said.

"Good." Hannah meant to have a private conversation with Victoria, so that would be a good excuse to stay behind.

"I keep meaning to ask, have you gotten more students?" Mary asked Jessica. "It seems the city is overflowing with refugees, black and white. They continue to enter the city. It is overwhelming."

"A few gained, a few lost," Jessica explained. "Though that isn't unusual, we've always had some transiency with my students."

"Have you heard they have created a house for refugees now," Tabetha said. "I've gone there a time or two to tend to sick patients. They're primarily women and children."

"I had heard that," Mary replied. "Duff said the Federal Army approved $1,000 from post funds to open the home."

"And a member of the Western Sanitary Commission has agreed to manage the shelter," Tabetha added.

"Imagine that," Victoria said. "The Union army devastating the countryside and displacing thousands of civilians now have found themselves providing food and shelter for the very refugees that they've displaced. I suppose that's what you'd call ironic."

"It is," Hannah agreed.

Tabetha continued. "As the many refugees come in, Lieutenant Colonel Rogers told me that Major General Canby stipulated that only loyal refugees will be permitted to remain within the lines. If a refugee is believed to be a nuisance or if their presence will disrupt the military operations here, they will be sent upriver to Cairo, in Illinois. They will give them enough provisions to reach that destination, however."

"The citizens of Vicksburg are more concerned than ever," Victoria said. "If the army is sending refugees with questionable loyalty away, how long will it be before they exile everyone who will not pledge absolute loyalty to the Union?"

"Many are afraid that they'll either be sent away or, that they may be kept prisoners in the city. Again." Mary shook her head. "That would be too much like being trapped here as we were during the siege. I will never be able to go through that again. The constant bombardment, uggg…" She shuddered at the thought. "I can still hear them in my dreams."

"Yet another siege is happening, in Virginia, and yet another branch of the Turner family is to be under siege."

"Yes, I heard that in the news. Those poor people." Hannah shook her head. "It's been seven weeks already for them, with no end in sight."

"Already more than what we had to endure." Tabetha shuddered.

"We must hope and pray that everyone stays safe," Jessica said. She still couldn't imagine the atrocities that her friends had lived through.

"They say that if Petersburg falls, there will be nothing between the Federal army and Richmond," Victoria said. "And if Richmond is taken…"

"If it is taken, then the war will be over," Tabetha said.

"Even when the war ends, I doubt anything will change," Hannah said. "The Federal troops will not leave. Life in Vicksburg will never be as it was before the war."

"I agree," Victoria said. "We will continue to be an occupied city, unless somehow a miracle happens, and we are able to win this war." She shook her head. "At least when the war ends, our Confederate soldiers will be able to return home. Nathaniel, Father, Gregory, Jason, and all of the others." She rubbed her temple. "Although I'm not sure if that…what will happen to them?" A tear rolled down her cheek. "Will they be imprisoned, executed, banished from the states? I would go to the ends of the earth to live in peace with Nathaniel and Felicity. That is, if he even comes home. If he's even alive."

Hannah moved closer and put a comforting arm around Victoria's shoulder. "He'll be fine, just as your father and brothers will be," she said. "They are strong men and I have absolute faith that they will all return."

"Thank you for saying so," Victoria said. "And thank you for all of your support, all of you." She looked around the parlor. "I am blessed that God placed you all in my life."

"I heard there was a dangerous commotion over on Levee Street the other day," Hannah said. "Was Mary Grace's store spared?"

"It was, the mob didn't make it up to Washington street." Victoria nodded. "Thankfully."

A few days prior, a mob of white Federal soldiers passed through Vicksburg and made their presence known. They had started by attacking a watermelon cart, then continued through six different stores and barrooms, robbing them and causing much damage.

"I am so sick and tired of all this uncertainty. We are under the complete control of the enemy and can do nothing when our freedoms are trampled on." Victoria sighed. "I just want this to all go away."

Hannah patted her friend on the back comfortingly.

The conversation continued, and sometime later, Mary announced that she needed to leave and Tabetha and Jessica decided to head up to bed.

"I'll have Dinah brings Felicity down," Tabetha said.

"Thank you," Hannah said, then turned to her friend.

"I'm glad you're staying the night. I didn't like the idea of you going home all by yourself."

Dinah entered, carrying Felicity and handed her to Hannah, who immediately cuddled the girl.

"I rode in, so it wouldn't have been too bad, but it is nice for you to allow me to stay. I know how crowded it is here, but I appreciate the consideration." Hannah studied her friend. "How are you, Victoria? I mean really. It's just you and me, you don't have to be brave in front of Mary Green or hold your tongue for fear of offending Tabetha or Jessica."

"Whatever do you mean?"

"I have heard some talk, not to mention the fact that I know you. Where should I start? With the fact that you actually got into an argument with your housemates? Or perhaps the moods that I have noticed you having for the past year or so, the bitterness. Or perhaps I should start with the rumor I heard about how you have not visited Adam's grave once?"

Tears fell down Victoria's face before Hannah even stopped talking.

"Oh, Hannah, I have been trying so hard to be strong like Mama, but I'm afraid I just cannot do it." Victoria collapsed back on the chair she had been sitting on. Felicity looked up at her, almost as if the child knew her mother was distraught. Hannah sat down next to her friend and placed a comforting hand on her back. "Talk to me, Victoria. Let's start with that argument I heard you had with Tabetha and Jessica a while back. You seldom argue with anyone, not like that."

"Who told you about that?" Victoria asked.

"Kendall. She was visiting Caroline and I overheard them talking. She also mentioned how you have been quite depressed and moody, and I have witnessed that myself. Kendall is concerned for you."

"Perhaps I have been depressed," Victoria admitted. "It has all just been so much. You know everything I have been through, and I am fairly sure that being pregnant with Felicity made me more emotional."

"That is normal, Victoria," Hannah assured her. "I recall being that way with Ambrose."

"Yes, but you had your husband with you at the time."

"True, but you still have the promise of seeing your husband again." Hannah didn't mean to sound harsh, but someone needed to put things into perspective for her friend.

Victoria buried her face in her hands. "Oh, Hannah, you're right. I am so sorry. I am so selfish. Why am I having such a difficult time with all of this? Everyone around me is dealing with tragedy, and they aren't moody and irritable like me."

"Faith," Hannah responded. "Victoria, I don't mean to pry, but how often are you really praying?"

"I have, Hannah, and I've been going to church whenever I can."

"Yes, but you and I both know that faith is more than that."

"I know," Victoria whispered. "I just don't know if I can right now."

"You can, you just need to let yourself," Hannah said. "And I think a good way to start is by visiting Adam at the cemetery. I know neither of us believes that he is there any more, but I believe it would help you accept his death."

"It's been over a year, Hannah. I just..."

"Trust me, Victoria. It will make you feel much better. You must come to terms with that loss."

"Do you still visit Benjamin's grave?"

"I do, and I know Mary Green visits Annie as well. It can be a very calming and peaceful experience."

"I suppose you're right," Victoria said. "I just need to find the strength."

"And you will find it. I have faith in you, and I will continue to pray for you. I suggest you bring Felicity. Tell her about her cousin, Adam and what a dear child he was."

"Thank you, Hannah, I will."

"And know that I am always here for you. Well, if the Yankees will let me back into town, of course." Hannah dropped a kiss on Felicity's head.

"And I am here for you. Really, I am." Victoria hugged both Hannah and Felicity.

"I know you are. We've all been through a lot, and our problems are far from over. We must persevere."

Saturday, July 30, 1864
Turner House

"Another blow." Victoria dropped the newspaper onto the table with a sigh. Tabetha picked it up.

"General Canby issues General Orders Number 31. This requires all able-bodied men within the district to enroll in the Yankee militia, regardless of their loyalty."

"Forcing men to enlist with them is just another way to control us." Victoria sighed and sat down next to her friend. "This may actually distress both Southerners and Northerners alike."

"You're right," Tabetha agreed. "Especially the men who came down here just to escape the Union draft. They will now have to serve. Many of the so-called carpetbaggers came down here to get rich and avoid fighting." Tabetha continued reading the article. "This newest set of General Orders also prohibits any person subject to Confederate soldiers and officers to send their families into Union lines for safety and comfort, and also mandates that all disloyal refugees who enter the department be sent to Cairo, Illinois. These Yankee generals are attempting to control every aspect of the town."

"Tightening the noose, I would say," Victoria said. "What will they do to us next?"

"Miss Norton. Mrs. Prentiss." Lieutenant Colonel Rogers entered the parlor.

"Speak of the devils. Good evening, Sir." Victoria nodded.

"Lieutenant Colonel." Tabetha smiled.

"Miss Norton, I have...I was hoping I could interest you in taking a stroll with me." He smiled. "I have some things I would like to discuss with you."

Tabetha glanced at Victoria. "Have a good time." Victoria glanced at the Lieutenant Colonel. "I trust that you don't need a chaperone?"

"I will take good care of her," he replied. Tabetha rose and took Steven's offered arm. "Would you like to head towards the river?"

"That sounds wonderful," she replied.

It wasn't long before Steven brought up the subject he most wanted to discuss.

"I've received new orders," He said. "I'll be heading out within a few days, possibly even tomorrow."

The way he said it told Tabetha that it wouldn't be a short mission. "I take it you won't be just hunting guerillas in the woods around Vicksburg?"

"No, I'll be going a bit further, and may not return for quite some time." He pulled her to a stop. "Perhaps not until after the Confederates surrender."

"I see." Tabetha tried not to show her emotions. She needed to be strong for Steven. "I must admit that I will miss you dearly. Would it be all right if I wrote to you?" She tried not to let her voice crack.

"I was going to ask if you would," He replied. "I will write to you as often as I can."

"I know you will do well in whatever your assignment may be. Will your brother be going with you?"

"No, Zee will stay here. Patrol duty is the safest thing he can do while I'm away. I can't lose him. Not when it's partially my fault that he joined the army. He wants to be just like me."

"You don't always have to worry about your brother, Steven. Ezekiel is his own man. You mustn't be scared of losing him like you lost Caleb."

Steven's face froze, confused. "How do you know about Caleb?"

"You...you once told me that he was your brother and best friend and that you felt responsible for his death..." She searched her brain. When had he told her that? Was it when she was Pistol Pete in the army or as Tabetha in Vicksburg?

"I repeat, how did you know that?" Steven asked, shock and suspicion apparent on his face. "Miss Norton, I have only shared that with one other person, I know that for a fact, because I regretted it the moment I said it."

"I...Steven, I..." Tabetha's voice shook. This was the moment that she had to tell him everything. However, judging by the look in his eyes, her chance had escaped. He had figured it out on his own.

Steven shook his head, recognition finally flashing in his eyes. "I cannot believe it." He paused, and she could tell he was thinking back, likely back to when he knew her as Pistol Pete. "You were a soldier. Peter...Kent, I believe the last name was. We just called him Pistol Pete. How can this be possible?"

"Steven, I..."

"It's true, isn't it? You cannot deny it. You have been lying to me this whole time. I thought you were dead!"

Tears formed in her eyes; she didn't know what to say. Based on the look of absolute betrayal on his face, she didn't believe she could say anything to make the situation better. She reached out to take his hand. "Steven..."

"Tell me the truth, admit it. I need to hear what you have to say, Miss Norton. You...You enlisted in the Union Army. You masqueraded as a man. It is so clear to me now. Then you vanished... you disappeared, and made us believe you were dead. I thought I had lost a good friend. But then...when we met again here in Vicksburg...why? Why did you neglect to tell me who you really were?"

"Steven, I just couldn't..."

"Don't tell me that. You cannot tell me that. There were plenty of opportunities for you to admit your past to me." Steven turned and stalked away. He wasn't more than a few steps away when he turned back and marched back to her. "I'm not sure if I...I cannot believe I didn't realize this sooner. Why did you deceive me? I...cared for you...you knew that."

"I was afraid. I didn't know what would happen to me if it was discovered that I enlisted as a man. And furthermore, I could be charged with desertion since I didn't return."

"Do the Turners know? Or are you duping them as well?"

"They know. They are the ones who found me when I was injured and saved my life."

Steven clenched his fists, trying to control his emotions. "I was told you were shot and killed."

"I was severely injured. I fell from my horse. I was feverish, I don't even know how long I wandered or was unconscious."

"You could have let me know. I mourned you! I thought that you died!" He shook his head and placed a hand on his forehead. "I should have realized...when we first met here, I knew there was something familiar about you, I felt so comfortable with you. I just thought it meant you were supposed to be in my life. I am such a fool."

"I wanted to tell you. So many times." Tears slipped down Tabetha's cheeks and she gently wiped at them.

"You should have told me. You should have trusted me enough to do so. I trusted you, I shared so much with you. I was a fool to think you were a friend." He scoffed. "With both of our acquaintances."

"Steven, please believe me…"

"I can never believe anything you say again." He shook his head. "And to think, I brought you on this stroll to…" He paused and clenched his jaw. "I must go, Miss Norton." He turned and stormed away.

"Steven!" She called, hoping that he would turn around again, listen to her, give her one last chance to explain, but what more could she say? More tears escaped her eyes as she realized she had probably lost him forever.

Sunday, July 31, 1864
Turner Home

Tabetha stared out the window of her bedroom before church, going over the conversation she had with Steven last night for what must have been the hundredth time. She ran a finger across the tintype of Steven he had given her a few weeks earlier. She took a deep breath. Perhaps he would be at church today.

Steven had left the Turners' by the time she had composed herself and returned home. Lieutenant Campbell said he was going to stay in a tent near headquarters. She had gone to bed feeling lonely and empty inside, hoping she would wake up and learn that it was all a dream. However, it wasn't to be.

"Are you all right, Tabetha?" The soft voice of Mrs. Turner caused Tabetha to turn around. The motherly woman came in and sat down on the bed. "I understand you and the Lieutenant Colonel had a bit of a falling out last night."

"More than a bit." Tabetha admitted. "You must have spoken with Steven last night."

"I did," Rachel said. "He is hurt and confused, as he should be. You cannot blame him for that."

"No, I don't. I should have told him the truth long ago."

"That would have solved a lot of heartache," Mrs. Turner said. "But at least he knows now."

"I don't believe that is a good thing anymore. He may never return to Vicksburg." Tabetha just couldn't believe that she may never see him again.

"He has many feelings to sort through. Remember, he admired you as a soldier and thought you dead only to find out he had romantic feelings for you as a different person. That is a complicated matter to comprehend. Just remember true love will survive the worse situations," Rachel said.

"I must be quite transparent in regards to my feelings for Steven. I do love him, Mrs. Turner." Tabetha blushed.

"Steven couldn't hide his feelings very well either," Rachel replied. "Now that your secret has been uncovered, he can start the healing process. With him being reassigned to a location farther away, he may find he cannot live without you. Stay busy, keep up your spirits. Don't dwell on the bad thoughts. All will turn out as God has planned."

"I know you're right, Mrs. Turner." Tabetha sighed. "You have always been so supportive of me through this experience with Steven and my injuries before that. You should hate Steven and me and all Northerners. You have no reason to be so encouraging. I don't know how you manage to be so kind to us when we actually fought as your enemy."

"We all have different feelings and beliefs, but we must still respect one another." Rachel smiled as she noticed the image of Steven. "It was good that he found a photographer to get that tintype made for you before this all happened."

"Yes, I will treasure it." She focused on the image. "It may be the only thing I have left of him."

Thursday, August 18, 1864
Turner Home

My Dearest Nathaniel,

Our daughter is now six months old. It's hard to believe she has been with us for half a year already. Still, even harder to believe is that it's been over a year since I have seen you. We missed spending our first anniversary together. Some days, I feel like it has all been a dream, but then I see our precious Felicity and realize that it wasn't. I miss you so much.

I mentioned in a previous letter that I named our dear little girl after your mother. You always spoke so highly of her. I hope you approve. Felicity seems to learn more every day, and she is growing like a weed. She can roll over, and I feel certain she understands me when I'm talking to her. She still loves to play with the carved otter you gave me more than any other toy.

As swiftly as life is changing here, many things remain the same. I spend my days with Felicity for the most part, and help Mother and Esther with the household chores. Esther, thank the Lord, continues to be a Godsend. Her devotion to Mother far exceeds most Negroes. Dinah also returned to us and is wonderful with Felicity. I do find a few hours a week to help at the hospital too.

Last week, a group of the religious Sisters of Charity returned from Atlanta, where they were tending to the sick and wounded. Unfortunately for them, their convent is now occupied by Yankees who, of course, cannot be convinced to return possession of the home to their rightful owners. Perhaps the commander Dana will see fit to find these kind women a place to call their own. I don't know that I ever told you, especially with your Catholic background, but as a child, I had a fondness for a particular nun, Sr. Mary Jean. She always treated me so kindly, and always had peppermints to give away to the children.

I love you dearly and can not wait until you are in my arms again.

Forever yours,

Victoria

Victoria set the letter she had just finished addressing on the entryway table and entered the dining room. She saw Tabetha sitting at the table. "Is there any informative news in the Vicksburg paper this morning?" Victoria asked.

"Secretary of War, Edwin Stanton was contacted on behalf of the Sisters of Charity. They were able to restore the property back to the Sisters. The building and grounds were ruined while the Federals were there, I am sorry to say. I think I will go and help the nuns clean and do repairs before they move back in.

"That is so thoughtful of you. I just wrote of the nuns' troubles in my letter to Nathaniel. I was hoping their plight would not last long."

"Yes, the nuns are overjoyed and consider it a huge blessing." Tabetha took a sip of her tea. "I don't suppose there is any news from Petersburg?" Victoria poured a cup of tea for herself.

"No, not really. The city is still under siege, but I don't know any specifics. There's not much news in terms of the war at all, with the exception of our Federal Admiral Farragut. He destroyed the Confederate fleet at a place called Mobile Bay down in Alabama. I know this isn't the news you want to hear, but it's one step closer to ending this war. Hopefully, it will all be over soon," Tabetha continued. "And that is a good thing."

"Perhaps." Victoria sighed. "I am so weary of this conflict, and it seems nothing will be resolved. All this death and destruction for nothing. I just want it over. I worry about all our loved ones and wonder what has become of them. I wish we could at least get letters through. Not knowing is the hardest." She looked at her friend. "Speaking of letters, have you ever heard from Lieutenant Colonel Rogers?"

"Not since he left." Tabetha sounded dejected. "It may be he's busy, or as you say, the mail delivery is slow, to nonexistent. More likely, he's still upset with me and he doesn't want to write. I just hope and pray that, after he has sufficient time to think over the events, that he decides to come back so I can explain it all better."

"If I may speak bluntly?" Victoria asked. Tabetha nodded. "In spite of Steven being a Northern Yankee, I have the utmost respect for him and I consider him to be a gentleman. That being said, if he can't forgive you and continues to allow this issue to divide the two of you, then he is not the man for you, nor is he the man I thought him to be. You may be a Yankee, Tabetha, but I must say, you deserve better."

"I appreciate those kind words," Tabetha sighed. "I do hope he comes back."

"We all do, Tabetha. You have become so dear to us. We want you to be happy." Victoria reached over and covered Tabetha's hand with hers. "I know we have our disagreements, you being from the North and all, but I consider you to be one of my very best friends."

"And you are the best friend I have ever had, with the exception of my brother of course. I thank God every day that He brought you and your family into my life."

Thursday, September 15, 1864
Turner Home
"You just get to back where you belong, Yankee gal. No one wants you here anyways."

"You only teach the blacks 'cause no white schools want you. You're not good enough for the white children."

"Why on earth do you think I would sell anything to a negro-lover like you? I don't sell to no carpetbagging, Yankee trash."

Jessica closed her eyes, remembering all the slurs and insults that had been hurled at her since she arrived in Vicksburg. The latest one, however, was too vulgar to even repeat in her mind. Jessica leaned her head back and gently rocked in a chair on the front porch.

"You look troubled. Not your usual, perky self."

Jessica opened her eyes and glanced at the crooked smile of Lieutenant Noah Campbell.

"I'm sorry, Lieutenant, were we supposed to have a reading lesson this evening?"

"We were, but I can tell that you are not up to more teaching today." He sat down in the chair next to her. "Instead, how about I help you for a change and just be a good listener."

"I would appreciate that, Lieutenant, but…"

"But you've already spoken to your Reverend about it." Noah sounded slightly disappointed.

"I have, as a matter of fact." *And he dismissed it. Told me to turn the other cheek.* "I just get frustrated sometimes. Here I am, miles from home trying my best to help others, and yet, what do I get? The local women show me animosity and the men throw horrid insults at me."

"What exactly do the Rebs say to insult you..." Noah shook his head. "Obviously there is a specific comment that has distressed you much. Come now, what did he say?"

"I'd really rather not repeat it." Jessica blushed.

"It was that malicious?" Noah's jaw hardened.

"I just want to forget the incident."

"Well, I won't press you, but if you ever get harassed by anyone, and I mean anyone, you need only let me know and I'll take care of it."

"I wouldn't want you to get into trouble just because you were helping me. I know your propensity towards fisticuffs." She was flattered by the defensive actions he would take on her behalf.

"I wouldn't get in trouble. I would be defending the honor of one of our young missionaries. Even Rogers would agree with that."

"I thank you for your offer, Lieutenant, but I think I can handle it myself." She closed her eyes again. *"Blessed are those who are persecuted for the sake of righteousness, for theirs is the Kingdom of Heaven."*

"That is quite poetic," Noah said. "Don't know that I've heard it before."

"It's one of the Beatitudes. From the Gospel of Matthew."

"Oh, from your Bible. I'm impressed that you have that information memorized."

"Parts of it are quite easy to remember. Don't you have a favorite verse?"

"Can't say that I've ever read the Bible straight out, only listened to the sermons. I can't recall any verses in particular that I liked."

"Good Heavens...do you not believe in God, Lieutenant Campbell?" *How has this never come up in conversation?*

"Yes, ma'am I believe in God. My ma used to take us to church before she died. I just...well, I figured that since He took my ma from me, God didn't want much to do with me. If he's not concerned with me, then I shouldn't be concerned much about Him."

"Noah, you must know that's not true. Wherever did you learn that about God?"

Noah shrugged. "It's what my Pa always said, and I never really witnessed anything that made me think different."

"God does care for you, Noah, he cares about all of us." Jessica leaned forward and grabbed the sleeve of his shirt.

"Not to be disagreeable, Miss Spencer, but like I said, I've never seen anything to contradict my point of view." He closed his eyes. "Honestly, if you had witnessed even a small amount of what I have seen over the past few years, you might question how much God really cares about any of us." His jaw tightened again. "Listen, I know that God is important to you, and I will never judge you for your beliefs, but religion...it's just not for me, not now anyways."

I imagine it could be, though. Jessica thought, then decided she would do whatever it took to convince Lieutenant Campbell of God's love. "Well, then, sir, for now we will leave it at that." *For now.*

Thursday, September 29, 1864
Turner Home

"It's a wonderful day for a wedding, is it not?" Victoria smiled at Brianne, who turned and glared at her.

"Really, Victoria, how dare you say that to me? My dear friend, Alice, a good, Confederate girl, is marrying a Yankee officer, and an old man at that! The absolute absurdity of it all. How can this ever be a wonderful day?" Brianne scoffed. Alice Shirley had fallen in love with Yankee officer, Colonel John Eaton. Today was their wedding day, and Brianne was very much against the match.

"I suppose the heart wants what it wants," Kendall said. "It's actually quite romantic. Star-crossed lovers and all that."

"Really, Kendall," Brianne shook her head, irritated. "You cannot be serious."

"Well, Kendall is right, Brianne. The general consensus of the townspeople is exactly why they had to elope up the river," Victoria said. "I am truly surprised Alice even told you, what with your attitude."

"Alice actually believed I would be happy for her." Brianne shook her head. "Why ever would she think that? I must admit, for a Yankee, he's better than most, but the fact remains. He is a Yankee, he is our sworn enemy, and he also is far too old for her."

Victoria gave her cousin a puzzled look. "She's twenty years old, Brianne, and John Eaton is only fifteen years her senior. Thirty-five is not that old. It is quite an acceptable age difference as you well know."

"Well, I can't imagine being in her situation. Why she even considered marriage to a Yankee is beyond my comprehension."

"Marriage has its benefits," Victoria looked down at Felicity, who lay sleeping peacefully in her arms.

"Come, Brianne, you can't tell me you have never entertained thoughts of marriage," Kendall said. "You were quite friendly with a few of the Confederate soldiers when they were garrisoned here, and even during the siege."

Brianne thought for a moment, as if seriously considering Kendall's question, then shook her head. Victoria wished she could see inside her cousin's mind.

"No." Brianne finally answered. "I don't believe that I have. Perhaps a brief flicker of love amidst an ocean of friendships, but never anyone that old and most certainly never a Yankee."

Victoria suspected there was more to Brianne's comments, but didn't want to press her cousin overly much.

"Well, the two of you are both wonderful young ladies who will make the perfect wives when the time comes," Victoria commented. "Just make sure you don't rush things, even if you feel you will become old spinster aunts." She smiled and kissed Felicity's baby-soft cheek. "God has a plan."

"You are a wonderful example of that, Victoria," Kendall said innocently.

"Nathaniel and Abraham have set very high standards for husbands," Brianne admitted.

"Mary Grace and I did choose well," Victoria replied.

"Has Mary Grace said anything to you about Abraham's injuries yet?" Kendall asked. "Don't you think enough time has passed for him to be able to talk about what happened?"

"From what I understand through Nathaniel and Tabetha's experiences, soldiers feel there are certain experiences they endured during battles that they'll never be ready to talk about." She sighed. "I know Tabetha still has nightmares, but she will not discuss them with me."

"Jessica told me about Tabetha's nightmares," Kendall said. "But Nathaniel...he has nightmares as well?"

"Yes, actually, he did, usually when he was in the deepest of sleeps."

"Do you think...Abraham has nightmares as well, and...even after the war, do you think the bad dreams will continue for the soldiers?" Brianne's voice was quiet.

"I hope not," Victoria said. "But I fear the battles will live on in many soldiers long after the war has ended. How can it not?"

Monday, November 23, 1864
Lakemont

"Good day, Mrs. Lake," Victoria waved at Mary Green's mother, who was in the in the front of the yard, tossing a ball back and forth. Victoria could hardly believe William was big enough to do that already. "Is Mary available for a visit?"

"Oh, gracious, Victoria, have you not heard? She went to visit Mahala Roach, that poor, dear girl."

Victoria sat down in the chair next to Mrs. Lake. "I heard that her mother was one of the five women banished yesterday, but I thought the accused were going to contest the orders."

"They were unable to do so. Elizabeth Eggleston has been deemed by General Dana as a 'general busybody with rebel interests, a rebel philanthropist, a mail receiver and a carrier of smuggled funds to prisoners in jail." Mrs. Lake twisted her handkerchief in her hands.

"General Dana has no idea what he's doing. I'll go to the Roaches as well. I will see if I can do anything to help the situation. Oh, these infernal Yankees and their blasted orders." Victoria was quickly on her way. The day before, Major General Dana had issued General Orders Number 82, which then prompted the expulsion of five more women from the Union lines for treasonous activities, including smuggling, spying, mail carrying and Confederate sympathizing. One of the women was Elizabeth Eggleston, a prominent local citizen and the mother of Victoria's friend, Mahala Roach.

Victoria was worried about this new order for many reasons, but mainly because simply carrying unauthorized mail was considered treasonous. Could she be arrested for bringing mail from her family out to the Wheelers for Jason? She had thought it was a good arrangement. She had actually received a letter from her Father and Gregory this way. Victoria didn't know what she would do if she was banished. She would probably go to Virginia, but would she be able to take Felicity?

When Victoria reached Mahala's home, she was immediately shown to the parlor. Mary Green sat with her arm around Mahala in a comforting hug.

"Oh, Victoria, thank you for coming!" Mahala rose to embrace her.

"Of course. I want to show my support."

"At this point, I am afraid that simply supporting Mother and our family could be considered treasonous." Mahala sighed. "I feel so helpless." She and Victoria sat down.

"What exactly happened? Can anything be done?" Victoria asked.

"You heard the charges, I'm sure. The cavalry came in this morning and escorted all five of the women out of Union territory. They are forbidden to return for the remainder of the war. A message was delivered for Mother from the Major General yesterday, telling her that she will be transported with her belongings out of town today. If she wasn't ready for them, she would be taken outside the picket line and then have to find her own transportation. She left an hour or so ago. The rotten Yankees, even her luggage was inspected." Mahala took a deep breath. "I just cannot believe she's gone."

"Oh, for Heaven's sake." Victoria could not believe this was happening. How could the Yankees be so heartless? Poor Mrs. Eggleston had to be in her late fifties. What did they honestly expect her to do? How was she to survive? "Can anything more be done?"

"We tried convincing the Major General of Mother's innocence right away, but it was to no avail. I have delivered separate notes to the Major General's wife and son. I pray it will work, and I vow not to give up. Young George Dana promised to speak with his father on Mother's behalf. I hope something can be done."

George Dana was a well-respected Union officer, and Victoria has knew that Mrs. Dana, the Major General's wife, was a close acquaintance of Mrs. Eggleston.

"Your family will be in our prayers, as well as those poor other banished women" Mary said. "I simply cannot imagine what I would do if I were banished."

"I don't think you need to worry about that," Victoria said. "Your husband signed the oath, remember."

"That doesn't matter anymore." Mahala said. "I thought we were on friendly terms with the Danas...I don't know what a person has to do to be safe anymore in this town."

"I don't know either," Victoria shook her head. "Mahala, please let us know if there is anything we can do. I know Kendall will want to help Nora in any way possible." Nora was Mahala's daughter, and a friend of Kendall.

There was a knock on the door and a servant brought a letter into the room for Mahala. She eagerly took it, ripped it open and read it. Her face fell.

"It's from Mrs. Dana. She insists that her husband has acted out of his sense of duty, not personal animosity." Mahala shook her head. "She assures me that the family home will be secure and that she wishes my mother's innocence can be proven." She set the letter on her lap, a stoic look on her face. "It is a certainty that General Dana will not change his mind." She shook her head. "I really believed our family had become quite friendly with the Danas during this occupation, I thought Mrs. Dana would be able to do something."

Tears threatened Victoria just thinking of what her friend was going through. The continued loss of rights through the General Orders worried her dreadfully. What would be the next Yankee order?

Friday, December 2, 1864
Turner Home

Nathaniel,

I wish I could receive a letter from you, though simply doing so could get me banished, Hannah arrested or Jason executed as a spy if we were to pass it from one person to the other. I long to send out another letter by way of Jason, but I am afraid to risk that also. Simply carrying unauthorized mail is a treasonous offense with banishment as the consequence. Mrs. Eggleston, who is not much older than my mother, was exiled. She and her daughter tried to convince the Major General to reconsider, but to no avail. It seems as though the Yankees want to make an example of her and the other four women. Major General Dana's wife even wrote a letter to Mrs. Eggleston's daughter, Mahala, begging her to keep her own daughter, Nora, 'quiet and prudent in all she may say and do. Just because the women openly support the Confederacy, they are being punished. Young Nora Roach, has admitted to carrying out letters for Confederate prisoners around town and made no effort to hide what she was doing.

This entire situation worsened when an anonymous letter to Mrs. Dana accused Mrs. Eggleston and Nora of smuggling money out of jail. It also accused them of treason. I cannot believe what is happening. I feel so helpless.

Mahala Roach did hear from her mother, Mrs. Eggleston, and the older woman is cheerful and well. I also heard that yesterday, Mrs. Dana visited Mahala and was kindly received, though I am not sure how she was able to maintain a kind demeanor with that woman. I do not believe Mahala will let this situation rest. She will do what she can to bring her mother home. I don't blame her, as I would do the same.

I fear the Yankees continue to slowly tighten the noose on Vicksburg. No one knows what will happen next. I pray for the war to end so that you, Father, Jason and Gregory can come home, yet I don't know what you will be returning home to. You may not even be allowed entry into the city. I wonder if the Yankees will allow us to be with each other once the war is over. I know that's a silly thing to believe, but at this point, nothing would surprise me.

The Yankees are such a destructive group. They have no respect for tradition or history. They are using abandoned houses and commercial buildings for their administrative space, officer's living quarters or anything else they may want. At times, they have even destroyed long standing structures, to make room for new fortifications. Tragically, one of the buildings razed was our beautiful castle, despite the fact that its owner, Armistead Burwell, is a staunch Unionist. To see such a magnificent building destroyed for more silly fortifications is truly a waste.

The Yankees have also evicted many civilians so they can make use of their homes. As you may have read in a previous letter, we were fortunate not to be evicted but we have had to give some of our rooms to Yankee officers, and we had no say in this action. Thankfully, we have been blessed with kind officers. Other Federals officers are not so well received and will only give back property when the military finishes with it, if that is the case, but they always put the needs of the military above the needs of local citizens.

I realize this entry may seem haphazard, but there are so many thoughts running through my head right now. It's times like this when I miss you, my best friend, more than ever. It would be wonderful to have you here, to be able to talk things through with you, to have you hold me and comfort me and tell me that everything will be alright. I love you with everything I have, and anxiously wait for the day I see you again.

Victoria

Victoria put her journal down, wishing she could actually send it to Nathaniel. All she really wanted was to hear from him, to know that he was safe. She laid her arms on her desk, buried her head on them, and sobbed.

Friday, December 23, 1864
Turner Home

"Mrs. Prentiss?"

Victoria looked up from feeding Felicity mashed sweet potatoes to see Lieutenant Campbell in the doorway.

"What can I help you with, Lieutenant?"

"I'd like to talk with you and your mother regarding a special surprise for Miss Spencer." He sat across from her. "Last Christmas, she was quite down because the holiday wasn't quite the same as it had been at her home. I know we can't make it snow here or make the holiday exactly as she remembered, but I would like to try and do what I can. She has done much for me this past year, and I would like to return the favor."

"What makes you think the Yankee officers in charge will allow us to even have a Christmas celebration this year?" Victoria scoffed.

Campbell gave a short laugh. "I know for a fact that the Major General has set forth an order that states locals should enjoy themselves, just not too much."

"Of course, an order with a stipulation."

"Our commanding officers are encouraging all citizens, soldiers and officers to maintain peace and good order and they are required to report any disorderly conduct to the authorities."

"So he wants us to spy on and betray our own neighbor?"

"No, it's not that," Noah said. "The brass just wants to have a nice, peaceful day for everyone. In fact, we're having a dress parade on Christmas morning, then all the soldiers will be off duty until the 27th unless absolutely necessary. We'll have that same break over the new year celebration."

"And what will happen if we choose not to be peaceful?" Victoria asked.

"Careful, Mrs. Prentiss that tone could land you in trouble." He smiled good-naturedly, almost as if he believed the orders and situations were ridiculous himself. "Any troublemakers during the holiday season will be arrested and confined until the second day of the new year."

Victoria brushed back Felicity's hair, dark like her father's. "And the good Lord knows we don't want that." It would be her daughter's first Christmas, and she wanted it to be special. "Now, I do insist that we sing Silent Night at some point during our celebration, but tell me, what else did you have in mind?"

Noah grinned, then told Victoria his ideas.

Sunday, December 25, 1864
Turner House

"Ahh, I wonder if any excitement will take place today as it did last year." Brianne joined the family in the dining room.

"I do hope that is not the case," Rachel replied. "I am looking forward to a peaceful day attending church services, a quiet family dinner, and exchanging gifts with my family."

"Perhaps a few surprises," Victoria said, thinking of Lieutenant Campbell's sweet gesture for Jessica. He had arranged a wagon ride with sleigh bells, caroling around the family piano, and he had obtained a copy of Charles Dickens' *A Christmas Carol* and was going to read it aloud. The Lieutenant had confided in Victoria that Jessica was helping him learn to read better, and he had been practicing extra so he could surprise her.

"Don't count on me for dinner, Mrs. Turner," Jessica said, a huge smile on her face. "I forgot to tell you yesterday, but I will be spending the day with Reverend Cook. He asked me to join him after Church services for dinner and other festivities. I'll be gone almost the entire day. Who knows what else may happen?"

Victoria glanced at Lieutenant Campbell, whose face fell. "My goodness, Jessica. Why didn't you mention these other plans before now?"

"He only asked me yesterday," She admitted. "I should have said something last night, but as I said, it slipped my mind."

"I'm sorry you won't be here with us, we had special plans. Are you able to spend at least some of the day with us?" Rachel asked.

"I don't believe so. I'm not sure exactly what the Reverend has planned."

Victoria was unsure of what to do. She knew how hard Lieutenant Campbell had worked to make Jessica's Christmas a special one and now it seemed his efforts were all in vain. She watched as he excused himself and walked out of the dining room.

"Pardon me, I'll be right back." She frowned and quickly followed the officer.

"Lieutenant Campbell!" She called to him as he headed up the stairs. He turned and nodded.

"Yes, Ma'am?"

"I...I know you must be terribly disappointed about this turn of events."

"No, Mrs. Prentiss, it's quite alright, really. I just have to call on a few people and tell them their services will no longer be needed. Besides, she'll have a much better day with the Reverend, I reckon." He nodded and touched the brim of his kepi. "I'll see you at dinner, Mrs. Prentiss."

My Dearest Nathaniel,

The first Christmas for our daughter, and our second since we have been married, yet we have not spent one together. It is by far my most favorite time of the year, as you well know. We had a pleasant celebration overall. Esther, Mama and I made a delicious roast beef dinner. I suppose having Yankee boarders that supply us with rations does have some benefits. Abraham, Mary Grace and their children joined us, of course. Felicity had very little concept of the holiday, but she loves being around her family. I cannot wait for you to see her, to hold her. It makes me happy when I see just how much she looks like you. Your eyes, your smile. She's beautiful, an absolute delight.

Vicksburg continues to change, and perhaps it is starting to benefit the civilians as much as the Yankees. We have dentists, attorneys, restaurants, photographs, saloons, sawmills, cotton gins, clothing stores, even a professional undertaker. Some of this, you may remember from before you left. There is also an active theater that has many performances. There are many amusements for our civilians and the soldiers, even a dancing school. However, I feel these are ways the Yankees are attempting to unionize the city; at least that is how I see it.

There is one thing you would want to be a part of. Earlier this month, they established a baseball club. I know how much you enjoy that game. I hope you have been able to play some.

Another big change for many of our citizens is a revised policy that says no more destitute white people including women and children have received rations from the army except the thirty worst cases. As always, I consider our family fortunate that Father made sure we had some gold. As mentioned above, we also continue to receive additional provisions because the Yankees staying with us are kind enough to share.

I hope you have found some peace this Christmas and that you were able to celebrate the birth of our Lord in some way. I pray that next Christmas we will be together.

With all the love I can give,
Victoria

Part 5:
1865

Monday, January 2, 1865
Wheeler Farm

The Wheeler family finished their prayer before the midday meal, then began to eat. It was a meager affair, vegetable soup and hard boiled eggs. Meat was expensive to buy in town, and Hannah still felt uneasy going out to hunt. She realized that going out alone would be a bad idea with so many strangers around. She was also uneasy about carrying a firearm with so many Federal soldiers in the area. The last thing she wanted was to be arrested over a misunderstanding. Few Southerners felt safe in or around town.

Dinner conversation mostly focused on the war, with some discussion on the farm and what the coming year would hold.

As they were finishing up, there was a knock at the door.

"I'll get it." Hannah stood, trying to remain calm. Her heart beat rapidly as it always did lately when facing the unknown. It settled down when she saw who was at the door.

"Jason! It has been ever so long! How are you?" She grinned broadly. He gave her a small smile.

"I'm all right." He nodded and pulled his hat off, then ran a hand through his hair. He looked as though he hadn't groomed or bathed in three months, which made her realize that was probably close to the last time she had seen him. She gestured him in.

"Jason, how nice to see you again." Cordelia said, coming to the door. "You are just in time for dinner."

"It looks as though you are about done," he said as Ambrose came up and gave him a big hug. He was growing so tall, he almost reached Jason's shoulder.

"Mr. Jason, I am so glad you're here."

"It is good to see you. I can't believe how tall you have grown since the last time I was here."

"Yes, he is becoming a key part of running this farm." Hannah ruffled her now eight-year-old son's hair.

"Well done, Ambrose." Jason turned to Cordelia. "I can't stay long, Mrs. Wheeler. I actually just came to drop off some venison I managed to get." He handed Cordelia the package.

"Thank you so much, Jason. We will get you some biscuits and hard-boiled eggs for you to take with you when you leave." Cordelia nodded and took the package, then she and Caroline began to clear the table.

"Mr. Jason, are you sure you can't stay?" Ambrose asked, longing apparent in his voice.

"I'm sorry, I can't." Jason put his hat back on and turned to head out the door.

"But Mr. Jason!" Just as Ambrose grabbed at Jason's arm to halt him, Caroline dropped some of the dishes on the counter. At the noise and the pressure on his arm, Jason startled, and in his surprise, he reached out and struck Ambrose in the shoulder, knocking him down to the floor.

"Jason!" Hannah cried out and went to help comfort Ambrose, who looked shocked more than hurt.

"I am so sorry, Mr. Turner." Caroline straightened the dishes.

Hannah glared at Jason, livid, but Jason looked just as shocked as anyone that he had pushed Ambrose. Hannah and her son stood as Ambrose wiped at his eyes.

"I am so sorry, Mr. Jason. I shouldn't have grabbed at you." Ambrose looked at Hannah, discouragement clear in his eyes. "I'll help with the dishes." He gave a last look at Jason, almost frightened of him.

"I'll just be going." Jason pushed open the door. Hannah stared after him for a second, then angry hastened to catch Jason. She slammed the door behind her and grabbed his arm. "You stop right there, Jason Turner. What is wrong with you?"

Jason stopped, but didn't turn around or acknowledge her. She walked around him to face him. He was stoic, showing no emotion.

"How in the world could you treat Ambrose like that? How could you treat anyone like that? And to not even apologize?" Jason's lack of reaction infuriated her even more, but it also scared her. Something was wrong with him. He simply stared out toward the tree line. Hannah tried to gentle her voice.

"Jason, you know how much Ambrose looks up to you. I know you were startled, but I can't believe that you would react that badly if I hadn't witnessed it myself." She took his hand. "Jason, what has happened?" After a brief hesitation, she reached up and touched his heavily bearded cheek, gently forcing him to look at her. He finally met her eyes.

"The war happened." He then shook her off and stepped toward his horse. She grabbed his arm again.

"No you don't, Jason Turner. You just broke my son's heart. You owe him an apology, you owe Caroline and Cordelia an apology and you owe me an explanation."

"I can't give you an explanation," he said without any emotion in his voice. "But please give my apologies to your family. I deeply regret my reaction." He moved towards his horse again.

"Jason, please!" Her heart pounded. "You are my dearest friend, you are important to me, to my family. Jason, I..." Her heart was heavy at what she was witnessing. The dear man who had become like family was not the man who was now standing in front of her. Had they lost Jason in some way, not physically, but had he died some other type of death? "Jason, please. I love you. With the exception of Ambrose, you are the most important person in my life. Please talk to me."

"Hannah, I..." He shook his head. "Hannah, I wish I could say the same thing back to you. Perhaps a year ago, I would have. But now...I don't think I have any love left to give you."

A tear slipped down Hannah's face. "Jason, I know you have been through some terrible times, but please don't shut me out."

Jason finally met her eyes, and she saw pain and confusion in them. She wished she could make whatever was haunting him go away.

"Hannah, I..." He sighed and rubbed his face. "I really do need to leave. I shouldn't have put your family in jeopardy, but I just...I had to see you. To know that there was still some...normalcy left in the world. I hate myself...the way I behaved...perhaps someday soon I can tell you. I do want to share my life with you. I just cannot do it right now. I'm not ready"

"I understand, but please know that I will always be here for you, and you will be in my prayers."

"I appreciate that, Hannah."

Then, without looking, or saying goodbye, Jason mounted his horse and rode away.

Wednesday, January 11, 1865
Wheeler Farm
"My goodness, what a sight for sore eyes! What brings you all out here?" Hannah Wheeler stood and wiped her dirty hands on her skirt and smiled at Victoria, Mary Green, Tabetha and Jessica. "Miss Spencer, Miss Norton, how did you both manage to get away during the week?"

"These three stopped by to pick me up on their way out." Jessica hopped down from the wagon.

"It has been so long since we have had a visit. I do hope we are not intruding." Victoria hugged Hannah and whispered, "I have some letters for you to pass on."

Hannah gave a quick nod, then hugged Mary and Tabetha. She only hoped that Jason would come again. They all went inside.

"I haven't heard much news from town. Is there anything of interest happening?" They all sat down at the table. "We get into town for church occasionally and sometimes for supplies, but we rarely do much more."

"We now have a 'Ladies' Refreshment Salon'." Victoria said, sarcasm evident in her voice.

"My goodness. What does one do at a Ladies' Refreshment Salon?" Hannah asked.

"I am not really sure," Victoria laughed. "None of us have had the opportunity to visit the establishment."

"I just don't have the time to go," Jessica said.

"Did you have a pleasant holiday?" Victoria asked.

"Yes, it was quiet for the most part."

"And where is the rest of your family today?" Victoria asked Hannah as she started to chuckle.

"As a matter of fact, my Cordelia took Ambrose and Caroline into town. Ambrose is growing like a weed and needs a new pair of jeans. Caroline wanted to do some visiting, I believe she wanted to see how Nora Roach was doing," Hannah shook her head. "That is such a difficult situation. Are there any updates on poor Mrs. Eggleston?"

"Mahala appealed to Brigadier General John P. Hawkins, and some family friends wanted to go so far as to petition the Federal Secretary of War and General Grant. She really wants to get General Dana to help the family, but he refuses. There is much letter writing. Mahala insists that her mother would not knowingly violate the law, and even points out the fact that one of the women who accused her mother was later banished herself. She is trying desperately to get General Dana to consider his feelings for his own mother and family and find the kindness in his heart to allow her mother to come home. I'm not sure if that will ever happen, though." Victoria shook her head. "I would be willing to bet that you have many issues out here in the country as well."

"Of course," Hannah replied. "As you all know, Northerners are coming down and leasing plantations. The widow on the next farm over had to lease her land to some brothers from New York. It ended up being quite fortuitous for her. Our Confederate raiders targeted the brothers less because they were sharing their prophets with their landlady. The brothers told many locals that they originally came from St. Louis, a Confederate city, which is false. They also make sure the locals know they oppose the more radical aims of Lincoln's administration."

"And is that true?" Mary asked.

"Generally, yes," Hannah replied.

"How do you happen to know so much about these brothers?" Victoria asked.

"The younger brother, Samuel, was quite sweet, actually, and very friendly. We had several pleasant conversations."

"You said 'was'. What happened to him and his brother?" Tabetha asked.

"Samuel died in June. Disease." Hannah looked down. "He was a kind man. His brother left town after Samuel died."

"We've lost many men," Victoria stated. "And I doubt that trend will stop any time soon."

Thursday, February 2, 1865
My Dearest Tori   *November 3, 1864*

I know we agreed to write in our journals so that we can share them when we are together again, and I have indeed been doing that, but I also continue to write letters hoping somehow they get through to you. I have now written you seven letters with this same opening statement, hopefully you will get at least one.

As you may have already read, I have made it safely back to Virginia. I just recently was able to visit my sister, however AJ has made some poor decisions of late. I don't wish to go into much detail, but it has to do with marrying the scum of the earth. A man by the name of Richard Evans. You may remember him because I know you had a situation with him at one point.

Victoria stopped reading the letter. She looked again at the date it had been written. November 3rd. It took three months for the letter to be delivered to her, but she had it. Confirmation of his safety was just what she needed. The news of AJ was a little concerning, though. Nathaniel was right about Victoria's encounter with Richard Evans. The man was a cad. Her mind wandered off as she remembered the incident.

1859
Fredericksburg, Virginia

"Well, good day, Miss Turner."

Victoria looked up and saw one of Fredericksburg's local citizens, Richard Evans, approach her. She had heard rumors that he toyed with the affections of many women, and he had paid particular attention to her cousin, Charlotte, but Victoria still found him handsome all the same. Besides, Charlotte had already left on her return trip home to Pennsylvania and she had made it well-known that she had no interest in Mr. Evans.

"How has your day been so far?" The blonde-haired, blue-eyed charmer flashed a smile that could light up a cotton barn. He walked up the steps of the Turner's back porch, where Victoria was reading.

"Quite well, Mr. Evans, thank you. What brings you to Turner's Glenn?" She placed a ribbon in the book to mark her place.

"I accompanied Mr. Samuel Gray. He wished to call on Miss Belle," he replied. Samuel Gray was a very close friend of Victoria's cousin, Belle, and he was also Richard's best friend. The man gestured to the chair next to Victoria. *"May I?"*

"Of course." Victoria smiled, pleased that the handsome young man was paying attention to her. The next hour passed pleasantly in his company, and when he left, he promised to call on her again. Just as he bent to kiss her hand, she recalled seeing a well-dressed Nathaniel Prentiss, flowers in his hand, turn and walk away, looking dejected.

1865

Victoria shook her head at the memory. She hadn't realized it at the time, but Nathaniel had been coming to call on her. However, when he saw her with Richard Evans, a man he had despised for years, he left. She hadn't seen Nathaniel for another week, when her cousins had hosted a small party for the soon-departing Vicksburg Turners. Richard had promised to be her special guest, but before the party, he had sent a servant with a message, begging forgiveness for not being able to come on account of not feeling well. That hadn't been the case, however. She had inadvertently overheard Belle talking with Samuel Gray.

1859

"What do you mean Richard simply got a better offer? He promised to escort Victoria." Belle was clearly offended, but at her words, Victoria felt completely embarrassed. She quickly went out the door and into the night, tears flooding her eyes.

"Are you alright?"

Victoria jumped at the voice. Nathaniel had followed her out the door and stepped closer to her.

"Richard Evans has that effect on people, you know. What did he do to you, Miss Turner?" His voice was soft, but she could sense an underlying tenseness.

"He didn't do anything, it was all me. My belief that a handsome, charming man like Richard Evans would be interested in a nondescript girl like me. The very idea is laughable and I should have known better." She shook her head, then gently wiped her face with a handkerchief.

"You clearly need to look at yourself better," Nathaniel said. "Richard Evans is the one who doesn't deserve you. You have a lot to offer anyone who has the pleasure of knowing you."

"Thank you," she replied, and was about to say something more when the door to the house opened. Nathaniel's youngest sister Liberty stuck her head out.

"Nathaniel, Miss Turner, there you are. Come, Mr. Turner is about to offer a toast."

The moment was broken. Victoria was secretly relieved. She wouldn't want to be spurned by two men within one day, and she was quite sure that Nathaniel was in love with Cousin Belle. Though Belle was very friendly with Samuel Gray, they didn't have an official understanding. At any rate, Nathaniel was a good man, likely too good for her.

1865

Victoria continued to read the letter from Nathaniel.

What was AJ thinking? I know they say that 'love is blind', but she is throwing her life away.

On to better news. Almost as soon as I returned to Virginia, I was officially exchanged, and so I am now able to fight with the Confederacy. Again, I am glad to be back with my unit. They had believed me to be dead, and I cannot say that I blame them. They welcomed me back with open arms and were very anxious to hear firsthand accounts from the war in the West.

I miss you terribly. I can't wait to see you again, hold you in my arms, and begin our future together. The hope and faith that I will see you again keeps me going. I look daily at the tintype you gave me and read your words on the back. "For I know the plans I have for you," plans to give you hope and a future." He will give us that future, and I cannot wait to be with you again.

Victoria smiled to herself and held the letter to her lips. She still felt Nathaniel was too good a man for her, though it was quite amusing that she now knew he felt unworthy of her. That was likely a good thing: neither would take the other for granted. However, it appeared as though Richard Evans had become a better man. Though Nathaniel felt differently, Victoria knew that AJ Prentiss wouldn't marry a man who wasn't worthy of her.

Sunday, February 19, 1865
Turner Home

"We have some news! Just came over the wire!" Noah Campbell came into the dining room where the Turner family, Jessica, Tabetha and Ezekiel were eating breakfast. "Charleston has fallen. It won't be long now. We'll have all the Rebels surrendered within a few months." He paused, as if he realized that wording was disrespectful. "My apologies if I've offended, Mrs. Turner."

"Don't worry yourself, Lieutenant Campbell," Rachel replied as she gave Brianne, Kendall, and Victoria a look telling them to not say anything negative.

"General Sherman will probably move towards Richmond now."

"Do you really believe the war will be over soon?" Tabetha asked.

"There were peace discussions earlier this month," Ezekiel said. "Lincoln, William Seward, Alexander Stephens, a man by the name of John Campbell and Confederate Senator Robert Hunter all met during the Battle of Fort Monroe."

"Yes, but I heard that conference was a complete failure," Victoria pointed out.

"True," Noah replied. "But it did still occur. Either way, once Petersburg falls, and it will, Richmond is next. After that, it won't be long at all." He looked across the table at Jessica, then Rachel. "Mrs. Turner, I was hoping that I could have the honor of escorting you and the rest of your family to church this morning." He noticed the women's surly looks, but disregarded it.

Rachel nodded. "That would be wonderful, Noah."

"All right, then." He nodded, then caught Jessica's eye again and smiled. She had noticed a slight change in his demeanor the past month or so, good changes.

"I'm happy you are attending church services, but why the change in attitude? I remember we spoke a while back and you had no interest."

"Well, to be honest, it has been living with you and the Turners." Noah looked around the table. "You all have been through so much, yet you pray and attend church every week. You all have an inner peace about you. I mentioned that peace to Ezekiel and he told me it was probably faith. I would like to…see if that kind of faith can help me and my life."

"That's wonderful news," Jessica said.

Wednesday, March 10, 1865
Freedman School

"Miss Spencer, I've come to escort you home."

Jessica looked up. She had expected young Lieutenant Rogers to come for her today, as it was not one of the days she was helping Noah with his reading. "Lieutenant Campbell? What are you doing here?"

"Ezekiel was unable to make it today, he had to take care of some other business."

"All right, then." She took his offered arm and they began walking.

"It will be so nice when, this war is finally over," Jessica said. "What will you do? Do you plan on going back home?"

"I am not really sure. My family doesn't need my help on the farm anymore, they've lasted this long without me. I was contemplating staying around here. There will be much to do to bring our country back together. I thought of perhaps staying in the army, but then I realized I would like to do something similar to what you're doing. Help the freedmen adjust to living as free people."

"That's an admirable plan."

"I hope so. There is much to admire about the work you missionaries do."

"What made you decide this might be something you wanted to do?"

"Just...some things that I have witnessed. There are many black troops here, as you know. More than white troops by a long shot. Yet they're treated differently. I do have to say that some of the black soldiers have the idea in their heads that they are now free to do as they wish without fear of punishment. What happened to that Bobb fellow a few months back is a prime example. Despite there being executions to deter them from taking the law into their own hands. I feel some black soldiers try to get back at their masters by attacking any white Southerner." He shook his head.

"Are you thinking of one execution in particular?" Jessica asked. He was silent for a moment, lost in a memory.

"A Negro was tried for...I don't even remember what for. Desertion, most likely." Noah stared ahead. Jessica pulled him over to a rock and they both sat down. "I can still see the man in my mind, when the chaplain spoke with him, the soldier was just...unemotional about the whole situation. There were other black soldiers lined up and a band even played. The man finally spoke and told his comrades that they should never do as he had done. I don't even know if he said that because he honestly wanted to warn them or if he was ordered to do so." He took a breath.

Jessica placed a comforting hand on his arm.

"The man was seated on his own coffin when the firing squad shot him." Noah sighed. "What affected me the most was a comment the man next to me said. I will never forget it." He paused. "He said 'the regiment has one less private in its ranks returning to camp.' Then he said that he was going to get some peaches to cook. The man said it so casually...we had just watched a man, a Union soldier executed, a human being died in front of us and the man beside me was thinking about dessert." He shook his head. "I don't know if he felt black soldiers were disposable or if he would have felt like that if the soldier were white. At any rate, it made me question my fellow humans."

"But you've started attending church," Jessica said. "Many times when someone witnesses a tragedy like that, they will turn away from God, not toward Him."

"That is true enough, I suppose, but there are other reasons. Because of what I have witnessed these past few years, I have begun to think about our lives here on earth. So many men I've known have died fearlessly because they knew they'd have eternal life. I spoke of this with Mrs. Turner, who, as I said a few weeks ago, has impressed me with her faith since I have met her. I've been reading the Bible as well, thanks to your help with my reading."

"I am sorry you have witnessed such tragedy, Noah, but I am happy that it has encouraged you to turn to God."

"I'm glad you feel that way." He turned and looked at Jessica. "It's a step in the right direction to become the man I want to be."

Jessica saw sweet emotions in his eyes, and her heartbeat quickened. Why hadn't she realized earlier that Noah was an honorable man, and she could actually have feelings for him? She stood, breaking the connection. She enjoyed his company, and the friendship they had developed, but she couldn't let there be more, especially when things were progressing so well with the Reverend, the man of her dreams.

"That is wonderful, Lieutenant Campbell. I am so happy for you, that you now have some direction in your life." He stood.

"I have you to thank for it, partially. Not only have you inspired me through your actions, but, you've taught me how to read and write with efficiency and that will also help me towards my goal. You're a very special friend. As a matter of fact," he beamed with pride, "I have some good news. I am now a First Lieutenant, and I have you to thank for the promotion."

"Congratulations! That is such wonderful news. I am very proud of your accomplishments." Without thinking, she gave him an excited hug, then backed away and hoped she didn't blush. "I appreciate our friendship as well," Jessica pushed a strand of hair away from her face. "As well as your protection. Thank you so much for escorting me home. Shall we be on our way?"

"Yes, of course."

Monday, April 3, 1865
Turner Home

"I love this view." Rachel Turner sat on the porch looking out at the Mississippi River. She glanced at Victoria. "Your father knew I loved the river so he bought this house with its beautiful view for us. He can be very romantic."

Victoria smiled. It was hard to imagine her father, a staunch lawyer, as romantic.

Before she could say anything in reply, they saw Lieutenant Campbell trudging up the hill. It was odd to see him so melancholy. They watched as he approached the house. He walked up the steps, then looked at them and frowned.

"Lieutenant! You look absolutely dreary. Whatever is wrong?" Rachel asked. He sat on the step, leaning over so that he faced them.

"Unfortunately...I...I don't know if I can tell you." He shook his head, and Victoria thought she saw a glimmer of tears in his eyes.

"Please tell us, Noah," Rachel said. "What has made you so sad? Is it Jessica? Is it Colonel Rogers or Ezekiel?"

"No, it's not that. It's military activity. I probably shouldn't say anything, but I am sure you'll eventually hear the story. I was patrolling on Calvary detail when we heard a disturbance. We were east of town, and the commotion was coming from the Hard Times Plantation."

"The Cook home?" Rachel asked.

"Yes. When we arrived, we found two children crying, and a women was just lying on the ground. She'd been shot."

"Oh, dear Lord, not Minerva!" Rachel's hand flew to her throat.

"Yes, Ma'am, I am sorry to say Mrs. Cook had been mortally wounded. She was lying on the ground, bleeding to death. A third child, a boy of about nine, said his father had also been shot and the oldest brother brought the father to relatives for help."

"And he just left Minerva and the other children at the house?" Victoria's heart pounded, unbelieving. "Edward and Anna are the two younger children."

"Yes, I believe that is what their names are. The boys thought Mrs. Cook was dead already, but I...we were able to talk with her before she actually expired." Noah leaned against the porch column, staring out at the evening sky as he continued. "She told us that a party of black soldiers came in and looted the home, and she and her husband were shot in the commotion." He shook his head. "Just when I think I am starting to understand God and his plan, something like this happens. It is such a waste."

Victoria didn't know how to answer him. Even though she wasn't close with the Cook family, it was still a most tragic event. The thought that anyone, especially Hannah, unprotected with her family on their farm, or maybe even her own family, were at risk troubled her. Being in town hadn't helped poor Mr. Bobb. No one was safe.

"We never understand God and his plans, Noah." Rachel's voice cracked. "We just have to trust that He can bring us through all tragedies." She took a breath to compose herself.

Victoria couldn't stop a tear from falling down her cheek and quickly wiped it away. "What about Mr. Cook? You never said if he was all right? And the oldest, Alexander?"

"Mrs. Cook was the only one who died, as far as I know. General Dana has offered a $500 reward for the men who did this. When they are caught, they will be executed and made an example of," Noah answered.

"If people truly learned from the examples of other, this wouldn't have happened," Victoria said angrily. "The men that did this didn't learn from the soldiers who murdered Mr. Bobb. If they had, then they would never have attacked the Cook home." She stood and strode to the corner of the porch, trying to control her anger. "Although, look who they are learning from. When the black soldiers see and hear what men like General Sherman are doing? How he's destroying homes, land, and just about everything he can over in Georgia. Why wouldn't any soldier think he can do the same in the name of war?"

"I agree with you, Mrs. Prentiss." Noah continued staring out at the river. The trio was quiet for several moments. The stillness was finally broken when the door opened and Felicity waddled out, followed by Kendall, who had opened the door for the toddler.

"Mama." Felicity went right to Victoria, who bent down to take her daughter in her arms.

"How's my sweetie?" Victoria held her daughter tight.

"Sorry if we're interrupting," Kendall said. "She kept asking for you, saying your name."

"She is never an interruption." Victoria placed a kiss on Felicity's cheek, then smiled at Kendall. "You're not either, you know."

The girl smiled, and Victoria was brought to the realization that her baby cousin was no longer a baby, she was now sixteen. A beautiful young woman. The same age as Alexander Cook, the young man who had just lost his mother in such a brutal way. Needlessly murdered in front of her own family.

"Why is everyone so glum?" Kendall asked hesitantly, as if she was afraid of the answer.

"I'm sorry to be the one to tell you, but Mrs. Cook was killed by black Union soldiers earlier today." Victoria spoke quietly.

"No! That cannot be!" Kendall grabbed the railing to keep from stumbling in shock. "What about Alexander, and the other children?"

"Apparently, Mr. Cook was shot as well, but I believe everyone else is okay. Is that right, Noah?"

Noah simply nodded.

Tears began falling down Kendall's cheeks as she looked at Noah, who had just stood. "What is wrong with you Yankees? How can you allow your men to do this? To kill and banish innocent people?"

Rachel stood to take her niece in her arms. "Kendall, it is hardly Lieutenant Campbell's fault. There are Northerners who do not condone these actions. There are a great many Union soldiers who would never do anything like this, just as I am sure there are Confederates with no moral compass."

Kendall shook her head. "They wouldn't burn houses, ruin crops, steal priceless heirlooms, and destroy personal property like that Sherman is doing. He is making it impossible for the southern people to survive. I cannot believe this has happened." She turned and fled into the house. Noah rubbed his head, not knowing how to respond, then headed into the house as well.

"I don't know how much more we can take, Mama." Victoria admitted. "I just don't know how much more of this we can handle."

Tuesday, April 4, 1865
Turner Home

Victoria watched Felicity sleep. It was hard to believe her daughter wasn't a baby any more. She was over a year old, yet had never even met her father. She was the most pleasant of children, loving to spend time with her cousins and anyone that would give her attention.

"Victoria, are you up here?" Mary Green called out, then poked her head into the bedroom.

"Mary!" She put a finger to her lips, shushing her and pointing to the sleeping Felicity. "What a surprise to see you here."

"I told Dinah you'd be all right with my coming up, but unfortunately, I don't come bearing good news," she said apologetically.

"There is very little good news these days." Victoria sighed. "Shall we sit on the balcony? It is a nice day out."

"I would enjoy that," Mary replied. They sat down and faced the mighty Mississippi river.

"So what is the bad news today?" Victoria asked.

"The news is all over town. Petersburg has fallen."

Victoria's heart tightened. "So we are defeated? It is over, as Lieutenant Campbell predicted. He said once Petersburg fell, it wouldn't be long before Richmond followed."

"Richmond is already in Federal hands as well," Mary said. "President Davis has fled the city, as have most of the other Confederate government leaders. General Lee is still moving, however. Duff said he'll likely try to join up with Johnston and continue the fight. Davis must still think we can win, because he brought Varina with him, along with printing plates and millions of dollars in Confederate gold and silver. They're going to continue fighting for Southern independence."

"Is there even a reason for it anymore? What do we hope to gain? I don't see any way that we can win this fight." She shook her head.

"I hate to see us just give up, we have sacrificed so much, but I have to agree with you."

"I am so scared, Mary. What will happen to our Confederate soldiers? From a Union viewpoint, our soldiers are traitors. Many people will judge them in that way. They will fail to acknowledge the fact that most men only fought for their family and their homes. They don't consider themselves traitors. In fact, many of our men compared themselves to the heroes of the American Revolution." She shook her head. "Oh, Mary, what will the Federal government do with them?"

"I wish I knew what to tell you." Mary once again was grateful that she didn't need to worry about Duff. "The uncertainty of all this must be driving you mad."

"I keep wondering if it was all worth it." Victoria spoke quietly. "Four years of fighting and destruction. Thousands of deaths. Hundreds of thousands of lives destroyed and forever altered."

"Every person in the south from the Atlantic Ocean to our own Mississippi River and beyond has somehow been affected by this war," Mary said.

"Yes," Victoria agreed. "Perhaps we'd all do well to move west. It will probably be safer there. I will be leaving Vicksburg either way. We just need to go wherever Nathaniel will be safe."

"I can understand your feeling," Mary said. "Have hope, though. Duff believes Lincoln will be generous with his terms of surrender when the time comes. I am praying that our country can become one as it was before."

"I hope you're right, though I feel it may take years before our nation is back on friendly terms with each other." She paused to think, then stood and went into her room and returned with a newspaper. "This is from last month, but…"

She turned the pages. "Here it is. You're right about Lincoln. I only hope he will follow through on his promises. When he gave his inaugural address for his second term, he discussed his hopes for after the war. He says: '*With malice toward none, with charity for all, with firmness in the right as God gives us to see the right, let us strive on to finish the work we are in, to bind up the nation's wounds, to care for him who shall have borne the battle and for his widow and his orphan, to do all which may achieve and cherish a just and lasting peace among ourselves and with all nations.*'" She closed the paper and set it on the floor next to her. "I do hope he remembers his own words when this war is over."

Sunday, April 9, 1865

My dearest Nathaniel,

We received word today that Lee and your army of Northern Virginia have surrendered. The news is everywhere. The Federals are rejoicing, knowing that the war has ended and they are the victors. Everyone knows that the Army of Tennessee and all of the other, smaller Confederate armies will soon follow.

The Southerners in town are mixed with their reactions to the news. Some are disappointed, others are angry. Some seem to be relieved and still others are wanting to continue the fight, to never give up. I personally have ambivalent feelings. I am happy that there will be no more fighting, no more death or destruction. I hope and pray that you will be paroled soon so you will make your way back to me, or send for me. I am grateful that the terms of surrender seem quite reasonable. I had some apprehension about you not being able to return to Vicksburg, or Stafford Heights. I don't know where we will decide to live the rest of our lives. I do wish we would have won this war, for now it is as though it was all for nothing.

I fear the Union Army will be a continued presence here in town, and refugees and freedmen alike will continue to arrive here. There are so many displaced people, Nathaniel. This will be the most prevalent problem in our country for years to come.

On a brighter note, your daughter is walking everywhere and is even talking in short sentences. Of course, I may be the only one who can understand her. She understands what we say and follows directions quite well. I know I say this often, if not every time I write to you, but I cannot wait for you to see her. I miss you and I love you and I hope to see you soon,

Victoria.

Wednesday, April 12, 1865
American Missionary Association Offices

"Reverend Cook, I have some reports for you." Jessica smiled as she entered the office. The Reverend nodded at her and set his pencil down.

"Miss Spencer! I am so glad you're here. I have been meaning to talk with you. Please, have a seat." He folded his hands on the desk. "Now that the war has ended, what are your plans for the future?"

Jessica was taken aback by the question. "I'm sorry, I don't understand what you mean. I had no plans other than to continue teaching here. Just because the war is over doesn't mean our work is complete. The Negroes will need an education now more than ever."

"Indeed, I don't disagree with you. The American Missionary Association will continue its work here, so there will be a position for you, if you wish to remain. However, I will be leaving."

"I'm sorry to hear that," Jessica said, and it was the truth, yet for some reason, she wasn't as distressed as she would have thought. "Where will you be going?"

"I'm heading further west. I will be ministering to the Indians out there."

"My goodness that is quite ambitious." Jessica was surprised at her lack of emotions that the Reverend was leaving. She should be heartbroken that the man she wanted to marry would soon be gone from her life, but she wasn't.

"Yes. That is what I wanted to speak with you about. I would like you to come with me."

Jessica's head was reeling as the Reverend continued. "You are exactly the type of woman that I want with me on this journey. It would just be the two of us to start, but more will join us eventually."

"Reverend...just the two of us? Would...that would be highly improper."

"Oh, you misunderstand, or perhaps I should not have assumed..." He shook his head. "We would be married first, of course. I would like you to be my wife."

"Reverend..." She smiled. This was just what she wanted, the very reason she came out here. Why wasn't she elated?

"You are everything I could ask for in a wife, Miss Spencer, and I am confident that God put you in my life for a reason. Being my wife is far more important than you being one of my teachers here in Vicksburg."

"My goodness, I...I am not sure what to say. I am honored, of course, that you would ask me, I really am. I would like to have some time to think about it, though, and to pray about it. Marriage is a big commitment and this is all so unexpected."

"Of course, of course," Reverend Cook said. "It will take a week or so for me to get my affairs in order."

"Thank you so much for the proposal. I will get back to you as soon as possible." She stood. "I should be going. Mrs. Turner will have dinner ready shortly."

"Very good. I look forward to hearing from you soon." He stood and led her to the office door. When they reached the doorway, he gently pulled her to face him and leaned forward. "May I?" He asked softly. Her heart beat steadily as she nodded. He bent down and kissed her gently. It was pleasant, and she smiled when he pulled back. "I will await your decision."

She nodded and then walked out the door. She had a lot to think about and hoped she would get the advice she needed.

⌇⌇⌇

Jessica ate dinner quietly. She hadn't had any time to discuss the events of the day and all of the decisions she had to make with Mrs. Turner, Tabetha or Victoria, and she didn't want to do so at the dinner table with the officers in attendance. Lieutenant Campbell must have noticed her distracted disposition, because the table had just been cleared when he asked her if she wanted to take a stroll. She looked toward Mrs. Turner, as she usually helped Esther with the dishes after meals.

"Go right ahead, Jessica." The older woman nodded at her. "We'll take care of the cleanup."

"Thank you," she replied.

"Don't feel as though you must go with me," Noah stated.

"No, no, of course I want to," she told him, taking his offered arm.

"Just making sure," the lieutenant said. "I wouldn't want you to do anything you didn't want to do."

"I appreciate that, Lieutenant, but trust me, I can definitely use some fresh air."

"And some good conversation." They made their way to Sky Parlor Hill.

"Was it that obvious?" She asked.

"To me, it was. I am not sure about anyone else," he replied.

"You do seem to know me better than most."

"So what's on your mind?" He asked.

She hesitated. Should she confide in this man? He was always willing to listen to her, and she did consider him a good friend.

"Please keep what I'm about to tell you in the strictest of confidence."

"Of course," he replied. "I would keep any secret for you."

"Earlier today, Reverend Cook told me he was moving west in a few weeks. He's going to establish a mission among the Indians."

"That is a noble goal for your esteemed reverend," he said nonchalantly.

"And he asked me to go with him."

"Oh." Noah hesitated in his pace, then continued. "Well, I am sure you will do well wherever you go. We will miss you here in Vicksburg, however."

"I haven't made a decision yet," she admitted. "I originally came to Vicksburg because I didn't want to be the poor, orphaned relation living with my aunt and uncle. I wanted to go somewhere and be somebody. I came here to help others."

"And you did," he said. "You have been an enormous help to the refugees of this town, and to me, of course," he admitted. "I would never have learned to read sufficiently had it not been for you."

"Thank you for saying that," she said. "I do want to go with Reverend Cook; it would be a great adventure. I just...I feel as though I have unfinished business here. I would hate to leave my students, the Turners." *You.* "All my friends. I know many things will change with the war ending, but I just...I feel as though I can't leave Vicksburg quite yet." She sighed. "Even if that means turning down the Reverend's proposal."

"Proposal?" He gave a short laugh. "You make it sound as though he asked you to be his wife, not just go west with him."

"Well." She paused. "He asked me that as well."

"Oh." The Lieutenant hesitated again, as if he wanted to say something, but then thought better of it. He continued on. "Well, you've wanted that for some time now, if I am not mistaken."

"I thought that was what I wanted, but now, with the opportunity right in front of me, I am not sure what I want."

Lieutenant Campbell thought for a moment, as if considering what to say. "Reverend Cook is a very lucky man." He stopped and smiled at her. "I am very happy for you, Miss Spencer."

"So you think I should say yes, and go with him." That wasn't what she expected to hear from him and she quickly realized that it wasn't what she wanted to hear from him.

"I think you should do what you're heart tells you to do. You are a kind, sweet, intelligent woman. You will prosper wherever you go, whether it is staying here, or going out west." He shrugged. "I'm sorry I can't tell you exactly what to do but I know you'll do the right thing."

"I hope you're right, Lieutenant. I do hope you're right."

Thursday, April 13, 1865
Duff Green Hospital

"Miss Norton!"

Tabetha stood from the soldier she was caring for who, tragically, had developed gangrene in his wound. She smiled at the young orderly who had been paying her special attention since he had arrived in Vicksburg a few months ago. He was sweet, but her heart was still with Steven Rogers. She prayed every day that he would return, though she didn't truly believe he would. She hadn't heard from him since their argument. She knew he was able to write and get letters through, as Ezekiel had received several letters from him. Tabetha shook her head, as if that would shake the memory of him.

"Mr. Lewman. What can I do for you?"

"I heard a rumor that you won't be with us much longer." He pushed his messy hair back out of his face. "I do hope that isn't true."

She gave him a bittersweet smile. "I am leaving. Within the next month or so, actually."

"I am dreadfully sorry to hear that," he said. "I had hoped that we could get to know one another better."

"I understand," Tabetha replied. "However, I am overdue for a visit home. It has been three years." She grabbed a pile of sheets that needed to be washed, rolled them into a ball and began carrying them toward the laundry room. She stopped abruptly when she saw a familiar form in the doorway.

"Steven." She couldn't believe her eyes. "Welcome back! What..." Her statement was cut short when he crossed the room, took her face in his hands and kissed her. She let the sheets fall to the floor and wrapped her arms around his neck. He may not have written, but these actions spoke loudly of his feelings for her. Out of the corner of her eyes, she saw Mr. Lewman walk away with a dejected look on his face.

"Good day, Miss Norton. My apologies for...uh…"

"You don't have to be sorry," she said softly. "I am so glad you are back and looking quite healthy."

"I was afraid you wouldn't be," he said, picking up the sheets she had dropped, then leading her to a bench in the hallway to sit down. "I was hoping you would still be here. I thought perhaps you would have already gone home. Ezekiel wrote to say you would be gone by the end of the month."

"I was planning on leaving within the next few weeks." She smiled. "I didn't believe, I mean, with the way we parted, I didn't believe you would ever come back."

"I wrote letters," he said, "but I never sent them. What I had to say, we needed to discuss in person."

"I agree. I've been...we've been watching the casualty lists, and didn't see your name, so that was encouraging."

"Thousands of men will never be identified," he said. "I fear many families will wait for a husband or father or son who will simply never make it home."

"That to me is worse than finding someone's name in the papers. Never knowing where your loved one is." Tabetha took his hand. "I am so glad you're alive and so glad that you came to see me. I didn't dare believe you would ever come back. Does this mean maybe, just maybe, you could forgive me?"

"I have forgiven you, Tabetha, and I regret how I left without saying goodbye."

"So is everything...all right between us?"

"Not quite," he replied. Tabetha's heart fell.

He continued talking. "I have forgiven you, and I still care for you, as evidenced by my...ahhh...greeting you as I did, but Tabetha, you deceived me. You lied to me so many times, and I understand why you felt you had to do it, but I trusted you with everything in me and that trust was shattered. It will take me some time before I can trust again."

"I understand. I don't blame you for being angry. I should have admitted the truth to you long ago. I regretted not telling you so many times, but, I just couldn't find the right words and the timing never felt right."

"I understand. What hurt me the most was that I had developed an affection for you." He placed his hands over hers. "I fell in love with you, yet I was betrayed."

"And I am so sorry. That was never my intention." Tabetha's heart was joyful. He had told her he loved her.

"I do want to court you, but we must start over, get reacquainted. There is much more for me to learn about you."

"And I will look forward to spending time with you."

Friday, April 14, 1865
Turner Home

"I am so happy Colonel Rogers has decided to forgive you," Victoria said. "I always knew the two of you had something special."

"Thank you, I am as well," Tabetha said with a big smile. "It feels good to get everything out in the open, nothing more to hide from him."

"Have you discussed marriage?" Mary asked with a twinkle in her eye.

"If it were up to me, we would be getting married this coming Sunday."

"On Easter?" Victoria smiled. "I'm not sure that would be the best of ideas."

"Yes, well, no matter, Steven still needs time. He has forgiven me, but he still has some issues to get through, and I understand that, but he's here and willing to give me a second chance."

"Where is he now?" Jessica asked. "I know he got home late last night and was gone again earlier this morning before breakfast."

"He is still an officer, as you know," Tabetha said. "We spoke briefly last night when he returned. He was visiting some comrades with Lieutenant Campbell. He then had to report for duty this morning."

"Yes, the Army of Tennessee hasn't surrendered yet," Victoria said. "It makes sense they would still be on alert."

"That's what he said." Tabetha smiled. "My beau."

"It must be wonderful to say that," Jessica said. She hadn't talked with anyone else about her proposal other than Noah Campbell. He had helped her make her decision, without knowing about it.

"Good afternoon, ladies." The officer Jessica was thinking of entered the parlor. He focused on her. "Miss Spencer, may I speak with you? Privately?"

"Of course," she answered, and he escorted her to the porch.

"I have decided to come right out and say what is on my mind. I spoke with Steven last night, a man who has never steered me wrong."

"Lieutenant."

"Miss Spencer, please let me say what is on my mind." He smiled nervously. He was usually so self-assured, so confident. "I care for you, Miss Spencer. You have become very important to me. I know you care for Reverend Cook, but Steven made me realize that I have as much to offer you as the Reverend does." He shook his head. "My apologies. I feel as though I can't speak or think straight..." He took a deep breath. "Miss Spencer, I want you to stay in Vicksburg. With me. I just needed to let you know that you have other options. I will understand if you leave with the Reverend, but I had to let you know my feelings."

"Lieutenant."

"I can stay here after the war and help the freedmen with you. I love you and will do everything in my power to take care of you and make you happy for the rest of your life."

"Lieutenant."

"I want you to make the best decision for yourself, though. If you really want to go west with the reverend, I won't hold you back, but..."

"Noah!" Jessica grabbed his arm and pulled him to face her. "I have already made my decision and have spoken with Reverend Cook. I have given him my answer."

"I see." Noah's face fell. "Well, then Reverend Cook is ..."

"I told him no," she interrupted. "I told him that I wanted to stay here and continue my work in Vicksburg, but to be honest, I wasn't sure how you felt about me. I was hoping if I stayed, perhaps you and I could become better acquainted. You see...I care for you as well."

He grinned widely. "Well, then...I am very happy to hear that, very happy indeed."

Saturday, April 15, 1865
Vicksburg Streets

It was noisy in the streets of Vicksburg when Victoria and Jessica left the Turner Home, yet the commotion was not a celebratory one for either the civilians or soldiers.

"Mary! Mary Green!" Victoria saw her friend with her husband Duff and waved them over. "What is the commotion all about?" They moved toward the two women. Duff appeared to be angry, and Mary had tears in her eyes and was clinging to Duff's arm.

"Lincoln was shot, assassinated," Duff said. Jessica gasped, and Victoria felt sick to her stomach. Duff continued. "He was shot last night and we just heard that he died early this morning."

"Dear God," Jessica prayed. "How did this happen?"

"He was watching a play over in Washington City. Some actor, a brother of Edwin Booth, shot the president in the back of the head and then ran like a coward." Victoria's thoughts began to race at the mention of Edwin Booth. She had heard his name before. Duff continued. "Called Lincoln a tyrant. He supposedly injured himself while trying to run, so they should be able to find the murderer quickly. He's just a coward to shoot someone in the back, just a coward." Duff shook his head.

Finally, Victoria remembered where she heard the name. "I met Edwin Booth. Before the war. In Richmond, I went to a play with my cousins from Petersburg." Victoria shook her head. "Edwin played Hamlet and his brother, John I believe his name was, played Horatio." She focused on the memory. "If I remember correctly, Cousin Belle flirted shamelessly with both brothers after the show."

"If I remember correctly, your cousin Belle flirted with most anyone," Duff replied.

"What will happen to us now, Duff?" Victoria asked, quickly moving from her memories of Lincoln's assassin to concern for her family. Would the Yankees blame all Southerners for this tragedy? Would it now be more difficult for the Confederate soldiers to get home? According to Lieutenant Campbell, the initial terms of surrender that Grant gave the Army of Northern Virginia were quite generous, and he believed Lincoln heavily influenced those terms. What if his successor didn't have the same beliefs about post-war relations?

"To be honest, Mrs. Prentiss, I don't know. Lincoln was all for making peace and healing the wounds, he even said so in his Second Inaugural Address. I believe a lot depends upon what Andrew Johnson thinks. He will take over the presidency now."

"I hadn't realized that's what would happen," Jessica said. "Although I should have."

"It's only happened twice before," Victoria stated. "John Tyler took over when William Henry Harrison died after only being in office a month, and Millard Fillmore became president after Zachary Taylor died. This is the first time a president has been assassinated, though. Killed in cold blood."

"Johnson is a Southerner, born in North Carolina and raised in Tennessee. He should be qualified to bring the country together." Duff squeezed Mary's arm.

Wednesday, April 19, 1865
Turner Home

"Felicity is finally napping," Brianne said, coming out to the porch.

"Thank you so much for helping," Victoria said.

"You know I will always take time to rock a baby to sleep." Brianne sat down and picked up her knitting. "Aunt Rachel, I was wondering if you would be okay with my staying with Alice for a few days. Mrs. Shirley is going for a visit, so if I travel with her, I would be perfectly safe."

"Of course," Rachel said. "I think that would be wonderful for you both."

"Thank you," Brianne said. "I'll only be gone for a week at the most, like I said."

"You'll have fun," Victoria said, then something down the steps caught her eye. "Goodness, is that…" she jumped out of her chair. "They're home!" She shrieked and ran to the door. Rachel, Brianne and Kendall were on her heels.

"Nathaniel!" She threw herself into her husband's arms. He was thin and looked worn and bruised, but he was here in front of her.

"Oh, Victoria." He hugged and kissed her, then hugged her again.

"You're here, you're alive," she murmured, holding him tightly, tears of joy in her eyes. After another quick kiss, she locked eyes on the other two soldiers.

"Father! Gregory!" She had to wait to embrace them, as others had surrounded them. Gregory was being especially fussed over. "I am so glad to see all of you."

She finally got a good look at Gregory.

"Gregory! My goodness! Whatever happened?"

The left side of her brother's face had the appearance of candle wax. She looked down at his hand, which was reddened and blistered. He shook his head, clearly not ready to talk.

"All in good time," Charles Turner said, his arm around his wife. "It's not a pleasant tale."

Victoria turned back into Nathaniel's arms. "How were you all able to get here so fast? And how were you able to get through all of the checkpoints?"

"We received parole papers," Charles explained. "Grant's surrender terms were quite generous. We simply had to pledge to stop fighting and deliver our arms to the Union Army. Our papers guaranteed us safe passage home."

"We had heard the terms were more than fair," Rachel said. "I'm just glad you weren't detained because of Lincoln's death."

"No, we weren't," Nathaniel said. "I had searched out your father and Gregory after the surrender and we headed west together."

Charles nodded. "Yes, congratulations, my dear. I always believed the two of you would make a fine couple."

"Well, there is one more thing you all should be congratulating Victoria for," Kendall said. "Both Nathaniel and Victoria, actually."

Victoria felt Nathaniel tense up.

"Happened about nine months after you left, Nathaniel," Brianne added.

"What are they talking about, Victoria?"

She turned to face Nathaniel, smiling widely. "You have a daughter, Nathaniel. A beautiful little girl."

"A baby?" He was shocked.

"Apparently, you didn't receive any of my letters," she said as they moved back into the house.

"None of us have received any letters from home in almost two years," Charles said. "Not since we heard Vicksburg was under siege. I tell you, I have been out of my mind with worry for my family."

"I was afraid you hadn't heard." Victoria led Nathaniel up the stairs. The others stayed down in the parlor, giving the couple some time alone. "I wrote to you so many times, hoping you would receive a letter. Although I must say, I am glad that I get to see your face." She opened the door and placed a finger on her lips. "She fell asleep just before you all arrived."

Nathaniel froze when he saw her, scrunched up on the small bed that Abraham and Mary Grace had given her.

"She's bigger than I expected, although she must be over a year old."

"Thirteen months." Victoria placed a hand on Nathaniel's shoulder. "Born March 16, 1864."

"She looks absolutely perfect." He shook his head. "But she won't even know me."

"I showed her your picture every day. She'll learn who you are fast enough."

"I can't believe this, although I should have known it was possible." He reached out and gently brushed a sweaty lock of hair from Felicity's forehead. "Is it strange for me to say that I am already in love with her?"

"Not at all," Victoria replied. "I completely understand."

Later that evening, most of the Turner family sat around the parlor. Steven and Noah had decided to take Tabetha and Jessica out for dinner at one of the local restaurants in town. Brianne had packed and left to visit Alice Eaton, and Ezekiel was on patrol duty. Mary Grace, Abraham and their children had joined the family. It had been a day of tears, laughter, and joy. Victoria couldn't remember a time when she had felt such a mixture of emotions in one day, but it was wonderful to have all of her family back with her.

"I can't believe the blasted Yankees are staying in our own house." Gregory growled. He hadn't smiled since he had been home, which greatly concerned Victoria.

"It has come in surprisingly handy from time to time," Rachel admitted. "And the men who have been staying here have been perfect gentlemen."

"Yes, we were lucky in that respect." Victoria said, looking down at her husband and daughter. Felicity had been slightly wary of Nathaniel when she woke up from her nap, but she had warmed up to him very quickly. At the moment, she was crawling all over him, and he looked as though he couldn't be happier.

Gregory shook his head and changed the subject. "I hope Jason can come home soon. "

"As do I," Rachel said. "The worst part of the Federal occupation is that he hasn't been able to come into town."

"Though he does stop at the Wheelers when he can," Victoria added.

"Yes." Gregory looked out the window and tightened his jaw as a Federal soldier passed by. "If you'd all excuse me, I'm tired. I'll be heading up to my pallet."

The return of the Confederate soldiers had made the tight living arrangements in the Turner home even more crowded. Gregory had been relegated to Esther and Caesar's old room.

"Are you sure, Gregory?" Rachel asked.

He stood. "Yes, Mama. I'll talk with you more in the morning." He hugged his mother, Kendall and Victoria, then picked Felicity up off the ground and gave her a kiss on the head.

Once he was out of the room, Rachel turned to Charles. "I have been trying to be sensitive to Gregory, but I must know, what happened to my son?"

"In short, my dear, the war happened," Charles answered. "The years dragged on but he was his usual self until the battle of the Wilderness. May of '64." He shook his head. "A day I will never forget."

"I remember hearing about that battle," Victoria said as Nathaniel sat up and leaned against the chair she was sitting in to hear the story. Felicity continued stacking wooden blocks. "Isn't that the one where the forest near Fredericksburg caught fire?"

"It is. Our battle lines went back and forth over a piece of ground I'd say was a mile or so wide. We would advance, then retreat, leaving our wounded men scattered. The strip of woods caught fire in so many places." He choked out the words. "Some wounded were unable to escape. Many suffocated or were burned to death." Charles's face was blank as he spoke. "We were falling back, away from the flames, trying to help anyone in our path. Gregory saw one of his friends, Christopher Martin, get shot in the chest. The boy was instantly killed, but Gregory, it was as if he was compelled to save him. As Gregory tried to pull Christopher out of the flames, he was hit and knocked down by some falling debris." There were tears in Charles's eyes. "I tell you, Rachel, my heart stopped when I saw our boy go down."

Victoria leaned forward and put a hand on Nathaniel's shoulder. Rachel wiped a tear from her cheek as Charles continued the story.

"I ran to him as quickly as I could and pulled him out, but not before the fire had burned him badly, burned some of his clothes right off. I don't think I took a breath until I got him out. I threw him over my shoulder and ran as fast as I could to get him to a field hospital. My God, it was worse than when Abraham was injured, if that's possible."

"Oh, Charles." Rachel hugged her husband tightly.

Nathaniel took Felicity in his arms and slid into the chair next to Victoria. Gabriel looked at his grandfather, a man he barely remembered, and crawled into his lap. Charles dropped a kiss on the boy's head.

"I love you, Grandpa," he said. Tears welled in Charles's eyes.

"I love you too, Gabriel."

That night, Nathaniel stared at his daughter as she slept.

"She is so perfect, Tori. I can hardly believe she's ours." He brushed a lock of Felicity's dark hair from her face. "I just wish I could have been here for you."

"It's all right. Besides, we'll have more children."

"I hope so. A whole houseful," he smiled.

"Were you with Father and Gregory at the Wilderness?"

"Not with them, but I fought in the battle." He slid into bed next to her. "It was the most haunting thing I have ever experienced, Tori." He pulled her close. "The smell of burnt powder, dense volumes of smoke, the wounded lying scattered among the burning trees. I don't know if I'll ever forget their wretched moans, and...they held onto their rifles, Tori, some even cocked and ready to..." he swallowed the words, unable to voice them. Victoria wiped a tear from her own face.

"That must have been dreadful...its beyond words." She kissed his cheek and brushed his hair back from his face. "But it's over."

"I wish I could agree with you, but for many soldiers, it will never be over."

Sunday, April 23, 1865
Christ Episcopal Church

"Our first church service together again." Kendall gripped Gregory's arm. "Well, except that Brianne is visiting Alice Eaton, and Jason isn't back yet, but he will be." She looked up and smiled when she saw the Wheelers approaching.

"Caroline!" She waved.

"Oh, Rachel, your boys have come home!" Cordelia smiled. "Charles, Gregory, welcome back."

"Thank you, Cordelia. It is good to see you again," Charles Turner said. "Hannah, you are looking well. Caroline, my dear, you are a fine young lady now, however..." He grinned down at Ambrose. "I do not recognize this young man at all. It cannot possibly be young Mr. Wheeler."

"Yes, sir. I am." Ambrose stood as tall as he could.

"So hard to believe all the growing you children have done while we've been away," Charles said.

"Indeed," Hannah replied. Just as they were about to walk into church, Ambrose pulled at Hannah's arm. "Mama, Mr. Jason is coming!" She looked up to see the familiar form ride down the road.

"Victoria!" Hannah smiled and gestured toward the rider. Victoria's face broke into a smile.

"Jason!" Victoria called and waved at her brother, who quickly dismounted and approached his family. He went directly to his mother and hugged her tightly, then moved to Victoria, Kendall, and finally his Father. He balked briefly when he saw Gregory's face, but pulled him into a hug in spite of it. Then he shook hands with Nathaniel and dropped a kiss on Felicity's head. He quickly pulled Ambrose into a hug, then smiled at Cordelia and Caroline.

"Ladies." As he was about to speak again, the church bells rang.

The group began walking into the church. As Hannah moved to follow everyone, Jason pulled her back to him. Without a word, he took her in his arms and kissed her.

"I love you too, Hannah I have for so long." He murmured.

She thought back to the last time they had seen each other, when she had shared her feelings with him yet he had turned away from her. Whatever had been tormenting him must have become more tolerable. She hugged him back tightly.

"Oh, Jason. I am so glad you're back," she said softly.

"I am too." He brushed a strand of hair back from her face. "And we have much to discuss. I still have some problems I need to work through, Hannah. The war…I think it did something to me, in my head. However, I believe with my family and friends, especially you, I can get through it."

"We will get through anything together, Jason. There are a lot of people like Gregory and Abraham that will need help as well as those with less visible problems, like you." She hugged him again, then walked side by side with him into church.

Thursday, April 27, 1865
Green Home

"I am so pleased to have you all here!" Mary said. "I fear our time together will be limited now that the war is ended and everyone will be getting on with their lives."

"Sadly, that is true," Victoria said. "Nathaniel, Felicity and I will head back to Virginia within the month. We have decided that living in Stafford Heights would be best for our family. It will be difficult to leave, but at least I will have cousins nearby."

"Where is Nathaniel now? Spending time with Felicity?" Mary asked.

"Yes, that is who he spends most of his time with," Victoria said with a smile. "They're fishing right now with Gregory, Jason and Ambrose Wheeler."

"I saw Jason was back Sunday. How wonderful, especially for you, Hannah!" Mary smiled.

"Yes, when Joe Johnston surrendered the Army of Tennessee, he was able to come home," Hannah said.

Victoria nudged her friend. "Yes, and I hope the two of you make something official before I have to leave for Virginia. I have waited a long time for my dear friend to marry my brother. We will finally be sisters."

Hannah blushed as Mary clapped her hands.

"Oh my goodness, that's splendid! Hannah, why didn't you tell me first thing?" She shook her head. "That must be why you and he came into church so much later than the rest of your family."

"Yes, well, there is nothing official to tell you yet, Mary. There is still much for Jason to work out within himself before we make anything official. The war somehow affected him inside."

"Gregory as well," Victoria said. "He still hasn't smiled since he's come home. He is extremely bitter. Sometimes he acts like our father did him a disservice by saving his life."

Mary nodded, "Well, at least they are all home safe, unlike those poor passengers on the *Sultana*. I trust you've heard that tragic news."

"Yes." Tabetha shook her head, explaining the story of how a wooden steamboat called the *Sultana* was traveling from New Orleans to St. Louis and had stopped in Vicksburg to pick up former Union prisoners, to bring them north to their homes. Yesterday, the ship exploded in the middle of the water, just outside Memphis. "They say more than 1,000 passengers died, many from drowning or hypothermia. Such a tragedy. Most of the prisoners were from Ohio, Michigan, Indiana, and our newest state, West Virginia."

"That is just terrible, such a tragedy," Jessica said. "We all expected the dying to stop now that the armies surrendered, and these men and their families had high hopes of being reunited, just to have it torn from them again."

"Yes, but we must continue to endure," Mary turned to Victoria.

"People like Jessica and Noah will help everyone get new starts." Tabetha smiled.

"I did hear that you will be staying in town, Jessica. I'm glad that we will have the opportunity to get to know one another better." Mary turned to Tabetha. "And what are your plans? Have you and Mr. Steven Rogers worked things out."

"We are taking things slowly," Tabetha said. "I lost the trust he once had in me, and I must restore it. It will take some time, but at least we will be together. I will be going back to Michigan soon, and he said he would like to escort me, with Ezekiel, of course. They were both honorably discharged from the Union army."

"Where has that boy been?" Victoria asked.

"Off on some mission right now." Tabetha answered. "We'll wait for him to return before we leave." She shrugged. "Perhaps by that time, Steven will be ready to marry me."

"Yes, and Mother and Mary Grace will be happy to plan any and all weddings."

"That would be wonderful," Tabetha replied.

"Gregory will undoubtedly be resentful about it. He's not happy at all that our home is host to the Yankees. As Victoria said, he is quite bitter. Jason as well. I fear both of my brothers have been spiritually affected by the war." She looked at Hannah, who nodded.

"It will be difficult for many of the returning soldiers to simply accept the Federal presence here," Mary said.

"Yes. Gregory and Jason both spend a lot of time out at the Wheeler plantation, mostly to get away from the overbearing Yankees."

"At least they have that escape," Tabetha said.

"The wounds run deep," Victoria agreed.

The women continued visiting until it was almost time for supper. Tabetha, Jessica, Hannah, and Victoria said goodbye to Mary, then headed toward the Turner's for dinner. Hannah and Ambrose were going to join them as well.

Victoria turned to Hannah, Jessica and Tabetha. "I'll meet you at home, I told Nathaniel I would stop and walk with him when we were done visiting."

It didn't take long for Victoria to find her family. Gregory, Ambrose and Jason had already left, and Nathaniel had taken his shoes and socks off, rolled up his trousers, and was wading in the river with his daughter. The two of them together made her heart melt.

Nathaniel saw her approach and waved. Felicity saw her as well, and began shakily running toward Victoria as fast as her little legs would carry her. Nathaniel gathered their belongings and walked toward them. Victoria knelt down and wrapped her daughter up in her arms.

"Mama, Dadda fishie!" She exclaimed.

"I am so glad you had a good afternoon, sweetheart." She stood, holding Felicity. Nathaniel came up to her and gave her a quick kiss.

"Time for dinner?"

"Yes, it is." She smiled. He took Felicity from her and sat her on his shoulders, straddling his neck. He held her ankles and Victoria took the basket of fishing gear and put her other arm around her husband's waist. They began walking toward the city.

"Did you have a nice visit with Mary?" Nathaniel asked.

"We did. It's hard to believe we'll be moving away soon," she replied.

"Are you sure you don't mind moving to Virginia?" He asked.

"It will be difficult to leave my family and friends here, of course," Victoria said, "but it is what's best for our family. I have a strong feeling that it is part of God's plan for us."

"I agree." Nathaniel stopped and gave Victoria a brief kiss. "It is what's best for our future."

"Indeed. All part of God's plan for our future, full of hope."

Author's Note

I have always had a love of history. To me, history isn't just famous people, events and dates. It is the stories of those who lived through these times. While researching this novel, I was able to read diaries, letters, and accounts from the individuals who lived through the Civil War. It fascinates me how they were able to get through the war.

While this novel is considered fiction, it is based on real events. Mary and Duff Green were actual historic figures who lived in Vicksburg during the war. Her firstborn son William really was born in one of the caves of Vicksburg, their house was a hospital, and Duff was harassed during the war. You can visit and stay at the Duff Green Mansion if you are ever in Vicksburg. There are no surviving images of Mary or her family, and unfortunately, neither Annie nor William lived long enough to have their own children. Many of the one-time mentioned characters were soldiers or citizens of Vicksburg as well. The Turner, Spencer, Wheeler and Norton families were all created by me. The characters of Tabetha and Jessica were inspired by two Civil War cavalry reenactors that I have been lucky to know.

Reenactors Tabetha and Jessica

There are many people who I would like to thank. First and foremost, my mother, who instilled in me a love of history and accompanied me when I visited the historic sites and helped me gather research material and information. She was also invaluable as an editor and agent, as well as moral support. This would not have happened without her. There are so many other people: family, friends, and students, who gave me support and encouragement. I would like to especially thank my nieces, Brianne and Kendall, who also accompanied me on some research trips.

A very special thanks to Harley at the Duff Green Mansion in Vicksburg, and the people of Vicksburg for their help and guidance in the early days of my research.

I would like to acknowledge the many authors who gave me information. A few of the books and diaries that helped me in my research include: *Vicksburg: 47 Days of Siege* by A.A. Hoehling, *My Cave Life in Vicksburg: With Letters of Trial and Travel* by Mary Ann Loughborough, *Under Siege!* by Andrea Warren, *Angels of Mercy: An Eyewitness Account of the Civil War and Yellow Fever* by Sr. Ignatius Sumner, *Mrs. Balfour's Civil War Diary* by Emma Harrison Balfour, *Battles in Focus: Vicksburg* by TA Heathcote, *Occupied* Vicksburg by Bradley R. Clampitt and *Vicksburg and the War* by Gordon A. Cotton and Jeff T. Giambrone.

I have truly enjoyed writing about these Vicksburg civilians. Make sure you check my website and Social Media for future books about the Turner family.

Images

Emma Balfour

Lucy McRae

Alice Shirley

John Eaton

Mary Ann Loughbough

Orion P. Howe

Dora Richard Miller

Anne Shannon

Jefferson Davis

Varina Davis

Ulysses S. Grant

John C. Pemberton

Caves dug in Vicksburg and the Shirley House

A Refugee Camp

Duff Green House

About the Author

 Erica Marie LaPres Emelander is a middle school social studies/religion teacher and lives in Grand Rapids, MI. Erica has always enjoyed reading and writing, and with her love of history and God, she has incorporated all four loves into her writing. When not working on and researching her books, Erica can be found coaching middle and high school sports, being a youth minister, and spending time with her friends and family.

Find Erica on:

Email: ericamarie84@gmail.com

Facebook: "Marie LaPres"

GoodReads: Marie LaPres

Instagram: marielapres

Blogger: authormarielapres

89803491R00250

Made in the USA
Middletown, DE
18 September 2018